READER'S DIGEST

CONDENSED BOOKS

FIRST EDITION

THE READER'S DIGEST ASSOCIATION LIMITED
25 Berkeley Square, London W1X 6AB

**THE READER'S DIGEST ASSOCIATION
SOUTH AFRICA (PTY) LTD**
Nedbank Centre, Strand Street, Cape Town

Printed in Great Britain by Petty & Sons Ltd, Leeds

Original cover design by Jeffery Matthews M.S.I.A.

For information as to ownership
of copyright in the material in this book see last page

ISBN 0 340 25270 7

Flood

A CONDENSATION OF THE BOOK BY
RICHARD MARTIN STERN

ILLUSTRATED BY ROBERT CHRONISTER

PUBLISHED BY SECKER & WARBURG

Jay Harper, a young geophysicist, comes
to Harper's Park to explore the village of
his forebears. Nestled in a valley below the
snowy peaks of New Mexico's Sangre de
Cristo Mountains, the village is submerged
beneath an artificial lake. It has not rained for
months and the lake behind the big dam is low.
As Jay, in scuba gear, swims through the
placid waters looking in the old cemetery
for family tombstones, he notices
disturbing features in the construction of
the dam. Would it hold, he wonders,
if mountain torrents set loose a flash flood?
Jay warns of the danger to the town, but the
powerful and rich do not care to listen
to anything that might threaten their
prosperity, and the poor Spanish-Americans
in the shanty town below the dam
are hardly considered. Then, high up in the
mountains, it starts to rain, and rain. . . .
Only when it becomes alarmingly clear that
the dam may not stand up to this unexpected
danger, do the inhabitants of Harper's
Park forget their differences in desperate
moves to avert catastrophe.

Reader's Digest
CONDENSED BOOKS

FLOOD
Richard Martin Stern

THE SUMMER OF THE SPANISH WOMAN
Catherine Gaskin

ALL THE GREEN YEAR
D. E. Charlwood

THE TWELFTH MILE
E. G. Perrault

COLLECTOR'S LIBRARY
EDITION

In this Volume:

Flood

by Richard Martin Stern   (p.9)

In the lake behind the huge dam in the mountains lies the drowned village of Jay Harper's ancestors. As he explores underwater, his trained mind spots telltale signs which point to flaws in the dam. As the storms build up in the mountains, threatening a flash flood, Jay warns the people of Harper's Park of the danger they are in. But in their complacency will they heed him in time to avert disaster?

The Summer of the Spanish Woman

by Catherine Gaskin   (p.141)

Uprooted from their home in Ireland, young Charlotte Drummond and her glamorous mother, Lady Pat, must adjust to life in Jerez, Spain. There, where the grapes cluster thick on the hillsides, Charlotte enters the exciting world of the sherry vintners. Staunchly she holds her ground against the powerful marquesa, the legendary Spanish woman her grandfather had loved. And in the arms of Carlos Santander she tries to forget her own faraway love, never daring to hope he might be hers again.

A compelling story of passion, violence and family intrigue.

ALL THE GREEN YEAR
by D. E. Charlwood   (p.307)

Once in a while there appears a book which magically captures for ever the spirit of a period, place and human experience. *All the Green Year* is such a book. Through these pages flow the essence of the part-terrible, part-comic dilemma of growing up: that chaotic time when life is a jumble of wonder and apprehension.

Don Charlwood grew up in Australia during the twenties and this book—vital and gay, poignant and at times frightening—tells exactly how it must have been in those not so far off tram-clanging, horse-clopping days. Critics throughout the world have hailed it as a masterpiece.

The Twelfth Mile
by E. G. Perrault   (p.399)

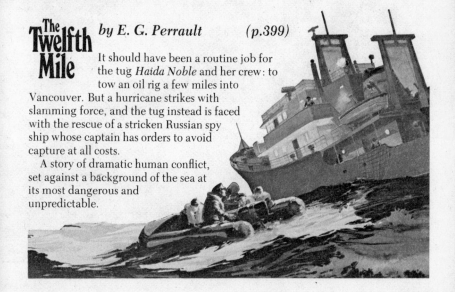

It should have been a routine job for the tug *Haida Noble* and her crew: to tow an oil rig a few miles into Vancouver. But a hurricane strikes with slamming force, and the tug instead is faced with the rescue of a stricken Russian spy ship whose captain has orders to avoid capture at all costs.

A story of dramatic human conflict, set against a background of the sea at its most dangerous and unpredictable.

1

Jay vaguely supposed that the urge to visit the place of your origins was buried deep in everybody, but, being by nature a self-contained man, he had never bothered to ask how others felt about it, nor would he have cared what their answers might be.

For him there had always been his great-grandmother's journals and their descriptions of this place and of the old man buried here, the first Jedediah Harper, whose name Jay bore. And that was enough. Jay was here to see for himself, and he was some ten years too late. Guilty thought, and he had only his own procrastination to blame.

Sitting relaxed but anticipatory now on the stern seat of the rented boat, the outboard motor switched off, he waited while the ripples on the water died and the peaceful mountain stillness returned. And then he could look down and see clearly on the bottom of the lake the stone buildings.

Once they had been a village. Now, drowned by the water backed up behind the dam built ten years ago, they were as dead as Pompeii. But at least they were still intact. With water movement, however slight, with inevitable erosion and silting, they would not last forever. He would see them now, or never.

As he looked down through the clear, cold water, Jay thought about his great-great-great-grandfather. It was here, one hundred and fifty years ago, that old Jed, one of the fabled mountain men, had made his solitary way through the towering peaks; wintered beside the stream in the now flooded valley; and, remembering, returned one day to settle down. The village which grew up around his cabin had been called Harper's Park. Old Jed's own accounts of all this were recorded in his very old age by Jay's great-grandmother, in a journal which as a boy Jay had almost memorized.

In the valley in old Jed's days; deer and elk, unafraid, came morning and evening through flowered meadows to water at the stream. Trout were his for the mere dropping of a baited hook into the pure, rushing water. Migrating waterfowl covered the surfaces of the small lakes and quiet backwaters. Bears searched out berry patches and occasionally fished the mountain stream. Sometimes in the stillness, old Jed recalled, he might catch a glimpse of a fox or a hunting marten, graceful shadows quickly gone.

Beyond the meadows in those early days the forests began— evergreen and aspen—and in their depths woodpeckers and jays, chickadees, juncos, hawks and even occasional haughty eagles went about their business as if man had never arrived. At night the great owls hunted, each surrounded by a private zone of silence, their soft broad wings absorbing more sound than their movements produced.

Above timberline—at this latitude eleven thousand feet—the snowcapped mountains rose clear and almost bare against the cloudless skies. The Spanish, seeing them reddened by the sunset glow, had named the range, Sangre de Cristo, Blood of Christ. Here and there in sheltered hollows, patches of forget-me-nots, mountain sorrel, and yellow meadow cinquefoil clung valiantly to what soil there was in this high, harsh land.

So it had been, and Harper's Park village itself had done little to change it. But two thousand feet below on the plain, wagons rolling west had reached the welcome mountain-born stream, paused beside it, and stayed. Cattle came, the railroad, industries, a highway linking East and West. Harper's Park village withered, and when the dam was built to provide the growing city on the plain with water and hydro-electric power, the mountain village was put to death by drowning.

When Jay steered the rented boat back to the dock, there was a large man in uniform waiting for him. "John Boggs," the man said. "I don't think I've seen you here before." His voice was neither friendly or truculent, merely official.

Jay got out and secured the painter to a cleat. "Should I have registered? Or maybe applied for a visa?"

10

"On the motel register," Boggs said, "you put your address"—he frowned—"Al Hoofoof. What is that, some kind of joke?"

"Al Hufuf. My last address. It's in Saudi Arabia. I don't happen to have a next address yet."

Boggs took his time for a long, appraising look at this man dressed in a heavy, hand-knitted Norwegian crew-neck sweater, jeans and sneakers. Late twenties or early thirties, Boggs thought, compact, moves well and carries himself with assurance. Chip on his shoulder.

"It's September—too late for the summer season," Boggs said, "and you weren't fishing. You just poked around the dam and looked down at the buildings on the bottom of the lake."

Jay nodded. "And tomorrow I'm going scuba diving—unless there is a law against it. I want to see the village up close."

"What do you want to see those old buildings for?" And then, face clearing with vague comprehension, "The register says your name is Harper," Boggs said. "Any kin?" He waved his hand at the lake and the buildings of Harper's Park village beneath the waters.

"Yes."

Boggs waited, but there was no more. "I guess it's all right," he said, then added, "You sure don't talk much." He watched Jay start up the hill toward the motel and called after him. "What were you doing in Saudi Arabia?"

Jay stopped and turned. "Working."

There was resignation now in Boggs' face. If you wanted answers from this one, he thought, you sure had to ask the right questions. "Okay. What do you do when you work?"

"I'm a geophysicist." Jay turned away then and walked on. The feeling of depression from the sight of that drowned village was still with him.

Jay had always found that new places—and he had seen many of them, maybe too many—yielded first an impression, then a few facts, and lastly, if you spent the time and the trouble, an understanding. And all knowledge had a way of turning out to be useful sooner or later. The trick was to ask questions and then really listen to the answers. So now, to the short-order chef in the motel coffee shop, he said, "Been here long?"

The chef was the image of a Mexican bandit, with sweeping black mustache, and information flowed from him as from a tap. His name was Pancho, and he had come from the city down on the plain. "Me, I was born there. Used to be a nice little place, nice little plaza, nice river, highway, railroad. I'm talking about right after the big war, what they call World War Two, you know?"

Jay nodded, sipped his coffee and listened.

"Too many people down there now. Up here I can fish, hunt, and there are still deer if you know where to look. Trouble is, it's been dry, dry. Lake's way down. More coffee?"

Jay pushed his cup forward. "Like California," he said. "Dry there too. The whole West. Long drought."

Pancho filled Jay's cup, and poured himself a companionable inch in a heavy mug. "Yeah. I read. And they're gonna get that big earthquake too, no?"

"One day, probably," Jay said. Almost certainly, he thought. The San Andreas Fault was a lengthy pressure line that sooner or later would succumb to the enormous forces working upon it.

"Maybe we get it here too, huh? Even this far away?"

"What makes you say that?"

Pancho shrugged. "We already had one, a little one."

Interesting. As far as Jay knew, this was a fairly stable area.

"Here?" he said. "Right here?"

Pancho nodded. "One of my cousins said they didn't hardly feel it down in the city. But up here— You know how coffee sloshes when you carry a full cup on a saucer? That's how the lake was. I watched it. Like somebody was shaking it."

A seiche, Jay thought. The entire body of water set to oscillating at its own rhythm by the seismic disturbance. The maximum movement would have been at the edges of the lake. The center, the node, would have remained almost motionless. Calculating the force of a seiche was tricky business, but fluid in motion could generate enormous power. It was something to be reckoned with.

"When was this earthquake?" Jay asked.

"Couple weeks ago. You think we get more?"

Usually, but not always, Jay reflected, earthquakes come in clusters. They were not his specialty, but he was familiar enough with the basics. "Hard to tell," he said, "but this isn't considered a particularly active earthquake area, like some places."

People, Jay had observed, tend to think of the earth as set, as if poured in concrete. Wrong, dead wrong. The earth's crust is constantly in motion, fracturing here, creeping there, rising, sinking, contorting. The huge continental masses are now con-

12

sidered to be resting on larger masses called plates, which move about on weaker underlying material in response to forces so vast that the mind cannot grasp them, let alone exert any kind of control over them. Distortion of the earth's crust is the inevitable result.

"Your first time here?" Pancho asked. He watched Jay's nod. "You got time, there's a nice walk up along the river above the lake."

And it was a pretty walk, Jay discovered, through aspens and evergreens, the aspens just beginning to turn but in some spots already brilliant yellow. With the lake left behind and only the stream and the forest around him, it was, he thought, almost as it must have been in old Jed's day. Jay felt refreshed, relaxed and at home, some but not all of the depression gone.

Squirrels chattered, scolding him. A mountain chickadee spoke his unmistakable phrase in the privacy of the woods, and somewhere a woodpecker gave his drumbeat roll. From a clearing Jay saw against the limitless sky a turkey vulture soaring on planed wings, rocking gently in the updrafts.

Man's senses were feeble things indeed, Jay mused. But man's capacity to alter what was, and sometimes, too often, to destroy it, was almost limitless. Another of those bitter thoughts flowing from his contemplation of the drowned village—part of his heritage —which had fascinated him since his first reading of his great-grandmother Julia's journals. Actually he knew little about her. Maybe one day he would go to Boston whence she had come, to try to learn something about her background, and to understand the reasons which had brought her west and finally to Harper's Park.

Julia had been an educated woman; her journals, written in a small, precise hand, demonstrated that her interests ranged widely. All of her observations about the Harper's Park area, including the tales garnered from old Jed, were impressive to a young boy, beckoning him to a village now sitting at the bottom of a lake.

It was near dusk when Jay came back to the motel. It was not much of a place, but his bed was comfortable enough. He had stayed in far worse places around the world.

When Jay walked into the lobby, the motel desk clerk waved a paper. "Phone call for you." John Boggs, the policeman from the dam, was leaning against the counter pretending not to listen.

The paper bore a name, Parks, and a telephone number in

13

Alberta, Canada. What was Cooley Parks doing up there? Jay had seen him last when they parted in Rome after leaving Al Hufuf.

"Get the number for me and put the call through to my room," Jay said to the desk clerk, and walked on. The reaction was automatic. Maybe this passion for privacy was a flaw in himself, but his thoughts were his own.

The phone was already ringing when he let himself into his room, and when he picked it up and spoke his name, the familiar voice roared, "Jay, baby!" Cooley's broad, solid presence almost filled the room.

"What are you doing up there?" Jay asked.

"Knocking myself out trying to find you. Boy, you leave faint tracks! Look, get on up here! *Pronto!* We've got oil!" Cooley's voice dropped a full octave. "But we got problems too. This is one of those fancy ones. I've told them we could ruin the whole damn field drilling without having a good look first. I know rocks. But what we need is your fancy instrument-computer technology to see that we get everything there is and not waste a drop. There isn't that much anymore."

Through the window Jay looked out at the lake, the dam and the towering mountains. He glanced at the bag in the corner which contained his scuba gear—tank, weighted belt, mask, fins and wet suit. He had not really bothered to think about it yet, but Pancho's description of the seiche caused by the recent tremor had started flags of caution flying in his mind.

When you were immersed in a fluid, as he would be down there in the lake having his close look at Harper's Park village, you were at the fluid's mercy. If it began to move, you moved with it. If another tremor hit and the lake began to oscillate again, he could take an awful beating against those stone walls.

But he was here, right on the scene after all this time, and those submerged buildings would not last forever. Once Jay set his hand to something he hated to turn away; maybe old Jed's stubborn genes had something to do with that.

"I'll only be here a day or two," he said to Cooley. "Then I'll come up."

Cooley's sigh was audible. "Okay, boy. I've learned not to argue with you. Just tell me one thing. What the devil are you doing there, anyway? You're no fisherman."

"Hunting for ghosts," Jay said.

14

IN HIS YOUNG DAYS Bill Williams had always tended to move in a straight line, usually walking with head down, hard fists punching if necessary, as confident of his strength as a fighting bull. He was now the leading construction company executive in the city, but the tendency to impatience remained, although he had tempered it, harnessed the inner drive, learned to contain it. "You broke me to the plow," he had often told Martha, "and I'll have to admit it's a lot easier going around stone walls than through them."

Martha had always smiled in her quiet way and denied responsibility. "You're your own man. That was why I married you. One of the reasons." She was dead now, and at times the world was an empty place for Bill Williams, but Martha's influence remained. Subtlety was not his style, but he had learned to be persuasive rather than demanding. As with his boyhood friend—Harry Wilson—the governor, on that afternoon nearly two years ago.

They had sat that day in the governor's big office in the state building, coats off, relaxed. "You've got the facts and figures right there, Harry," Bill Williams had said. "From your own state engineer *and* public service people. Without more power, *and* a larger assured water supply, the city can't continue to grow. We've got to enlarge the Harper's Park dam."

The governor had left his chair and walked to the windows that faced the great mountains. Harry Wilson was a slender, elegant man, neat, well-dressed. It had always been so. He turned and smiled faintly. "When we were kids growing up, Bill, I thought of you as just a pair of fists and hand-me-down jeans. Now you wear tailored four-hundred-dollar suits, but you still love a good fight."

Once, maybe, Williams had reflected, when his life capital was unlimited and he could afford to squander it. But not any longer, not for a long time. "I don't pick them anymore, Harry—unless there's a darn good reason. And this time there is."

"Money, Bill?" In the silence the governor had walked back to his desk. "Suppose we do push the project, get the funding. Then your construction outfit stands to make a lot of money, doesn't it?"

"Probably. I'll get at least a piece of the job and maybe the whole thing. Do you think that's the only reason I'm pushing?"

"No, and if I did, I wouldn't even listen to you. You're convinced this is in the city's and the state's best interest, aren't you?"

"I am."

"I believe you. A number of people call you a number of things,

15

but I know you better than they do." The governor had sighed. "All right, Bill. We'll set the wheels in motion. Do you plan to take an active part?"

"No. For the reason you just said, Harry. If I'm for something, a lot of people are automatically against it. But I'll be around if you need me."

That had been two years ago. Tonight Bill Williams sat over after-dinner coffee with Kate, his daughter, in whom there was much of Martha. And something of himself too, no denying that. "You were asking why I've stayed pretty much out of the dam-enlargement question, honey? Well, because I could lose my temper with some pipsqueak bureaucrat and ruin the whole thing."

"You're a fraud," Kate said. Her smile was fond, like her mother's. "You'll get the contract for the job. And the old Harrison land you bought up by the dam will be valuable water-front property when the lake expands and reaches it. So you didn't want to be too much out in front."

"What do you know about George Harrison's land?"

"That you bought it. Before the dam-enlargement issue even came up."

"You think that's wrong?"

"Other people will."

Ridiculous, a man having to justify himself to his own daughter. But there was a core of honesty in Bill Williams which would not be ignored, and he could not leave the matter there. "You're asking if your old man rigged the deck by buying George Harrison's land and then pushing for the dam change. Isn't that it, honey?"

Kate's eyes were clear as she faced him. "You're my father," she said. "That means I give you the benefit of the doubt. Every doubt."

There was a long silence. Through the glass wall of the big living room Williams could look out and up at the towering mountains now bathed in moonlight, their peaks almost bare after the long drought. Union Peak, Taylor, Washington, Baldy. He had climbed them all. This land was, and had always been, his home. "Honey," he said, "I built this city. Oh, not alone. But there's a piece of me in every part of this city—the dam, the transit system, the con-vention hall, the stockyards. And in doing it, I made a lot of money. Is that what sticks in your craw? Does a man have to be poor to be honest?"

16

In her own way Kate was as strong as he. "I told you," she said, "that I have to give you the benefit of the doubt. I always do."

And that, Williams told himself, was as much of an answer as he was going to get. The old fierce impatience stirred briefly. "Okay, honey. We'll leave it like that. You're going out tonight?"

Kate shook her head.

Martha would have known what to say. He did not, and was conscious of his own shortcoming. "I always thought that girls— young women—wanted dates, good times, maybe a husband."

"Are you trying to get rid of me?" Kate's smile was gentle, but amused.

"You know better than that." He could remember all too vividly the lonely time after Martha had gone and Kate was still away at college in the East. "But, honey, that doesn't mean you have to stick around looking after me. What I mean is—"

"I know what you mean, Daddy." The amusement was gone. "Now you give *me* the benefit of the doubt." She smiled again. "And don't you stay up half the night talking business with the governor. You don't have to do everything yourself."

The hell he didn't, he thought as he walked out to his car. He had in a sense begun this dam-enlargement project, and although he had since kept pretty well out of sight, he had been on top of every step of the negotiations; somebody had to, unless you wanted to see the thing mired down in details.

"Simmer down," he said softly to himself in the privacy of his car. What was that fancy medical term Jim Stark called that sudden fluttery feeling in his chest and the shortness of breath? Atrial fibrillations. Silly name. What it all meant was that the old pump, his heart, which he had never even thought about, wasn't running too smoothly any longer. Letting himself get upset over things was just what he was supposed to avoid. Fat chance. For the certain knowledge that you were not indestructible, as you had always thought yourself to be, carried with it a nameless fear.

At the first traffic light on the way to the governor's house he took out a small, silver box, opened it and popped a pill into his mouth. A tranquilizer. How far downhill he had come from the old carefree brawling days!

The governor's mansion sat by itself on a ridge. From the front it commanded a view of the city and the almost endless plain. At the rear a roof-covered porch called a *portal* faced the mountains surrounding Harper's Park valley, and on moonlit evenings like this it was here that Governor Harry Wilson preferred to relax after dinner. With coffee and cognac, he listened while chamber music played softly on the record player. Tonight it was a Mozart quartet. He answered Bill Williams' ring himself and led the way straight to the bar in his study, where he poured a double jigger of bourbon over ice and put it in his guest's hand. In silence they walked out to the *portal* and sank into deep chairs.

"I didn't want to tell you over the phone," the governor said. "These days no one knows who might be listening, and above all we want to avoid land speculation. But the word from Washington is that we'll get the appropriation and that the Army Corps of Engineers will take over and the enlargement of the dam will go ahead just as you laid it out."

Williams tasted his bourbon. It went well with the good news.

"I don't expect you'll have any trouble getting the contract," the governor continued.

"We're the only ones in the state equipped to do the work. You know that, Harry."

The governor sniffed his cognac, then set the glass down. "It's a lot of money. Are we spending it wisely, Bill? I'm thinking of that aqueduct Los Angeles built back in the 20s up into Owens Valley, supposedly to supply the city with ample water for all time. Instead, they just sucked Owens Valley dry and had to reach out to the Colorado River for more water. Are we making the same mistake?"

Williams snorted. "We knew there'd be a howl two years ago when we made the decision to go. We've already fought the penny pinchers in the legislature and the bureaucrats in Washington. Now when the final word comes out, we fight the rest, the environmentalists and the ecologists, as well as the Harper's Park property owners who'll start thinking their land is pure gold and want a million dollars an acre for it. And there'll be those who say the dam isn't safe. But the bottom line, Harry, is that we need it. We have to have it to grow."

Geologically speaking, the great mountains surrounding the Harper's Park dam and lake were young, their jagged peaks and sheer cliffs not yet eroded into the softer contours of old age.

18

The mountains had been upthrust, not all at once, but over the millennia, bit by massive bit. As the earth's crust fractured and the rock was forced upward to form the mountain chain, the moisture which fell as rain or snow upon the steep slopes began to find, and then follow, natural channels leading down to the plains. Through constant erosion these natural channels were carved into stream-beds, deepening as the mountains continued to tilt and rise.

Where the gradient was relatively shallow, the downflowing water could afford to spread, eroding a broader channel, and in time in these places mountain meadows were formed, called locally *ciénegas*, flanking the stream. But where the gradient was steep and gravity forced the water to hurry, the stream concentrated its cutting power in zones of relative weakness, producing narrow, steep-sided gorges and plunging cataracts. It was across one of these gorges, immediately below Harper's Park village, that the dam had been built and anchored solidly in the rock of the gorge walls.

Below the dam, where the stream continued after passing through the spinning turbines of the power plant, were more gorges—although none as high or as narrow as the dam gorge—and in places there were more *ciénegas* where houses had been built.

Where the river emerged from the mountains and made its final descent to the high, sloping plain, it swung in a great curve called simply the Bend, where the city's wealthier residents, Bill Williams among them, had taken advantage of the magnificent views, the high, clean air, and proximity to mountain parks and pleasures to build their homes. A concrete wall and a storm drain protected the Bend from possible spring flooding.

The city itself had grown largely without plan, beginning as a mere settlement below the Bend on the banks of the river. Here, in what was to become the *barrio*, the original church had been built and still remained. But fears of miasmic fevers from the low-land, combined with the advantage of spectacular, almost limitless views as one moved to higher ground, caused the plaza itself to be located at some distance from the river and well above; it had gradually become the center of things.

The old Governor's Palace, now a museum, filled one side of the plaza. The palace was a one-story adobe structure, fronted by a rudely columned *portal*, beneath which blanketed Indians peddled their silver and turquoise wares and their pottery to tourists. The other three sides of the plaza were now filled with commercial buildings, most dating from the turn of the century.

As the city became a terminal for east-west and later north-south traffic, it had spread outward and upward. To the north and east, on rising ground toward the mountains, were new high-rise buildings: banks, insurance companies, the expensive retail stores and apartments.

To the west, also on higher ground, were the state buildings, the federal courthouse and main post office, the general hospital.

To the south, crowding down to the river and across, was the old *barrio*, bilingual, a conglomeration of small houses of adobe, frame and cinderblock; mobile homes; tenements; bars and liquor stores; the single adobe church, the spiritual center of this almost separate community.

Before the building of the Harper's Park dam two thousand feet above, the river had regularly flooded over its banks in springtime as the winter's snowpack melted; in some years the lowest streets of the *barrio* had been awash. So it was that in the city the gap between relative wealth and poverty had come to be represented by location. High ground represented wealth; low ground near the river was for the *barrio*.

Bridges spanned the river, some of them old and suitable only for light automobile traffic; some new, like the East-West Interstate, and capable of carrying the big commercial tractor-trailer rigs that rolled day and night.

There were those who claimed that the city's population had reached the half-million count, but the last official census was eight years past, and now no one knew the figure for sure. But that there had been growth (some said too much) no one could dispute. Still, in many respects the city retained its small-town characteristics, and among these was the ease with which news circulated in knowledgeable circles.

AFTER THE GOVERNOR and Bill Williams, George Harrison, scion of one of the city's founding fathers, was the next to hear that Washington had approved the Harper's Park dam-enlargement project.

George's family had lived in the area since early territorial times. There was a Harrison Park, a Harrison Street, and, overlooking the old plaza, the now aged but still desirable Harrison Building, with its turn-of-the-century bow windows, high ceilings, and suites of law offices which had passed from father to son to grandson. In the plaza there was also a statue of the first George Harrison, last of the territorial governors.

The present George was unathletic, plump, pink and—in an area of the country where informality was the rule rather than the exception—invariably carefully dressed in tailored suits. He was also a scholarly man, widely read in the history of the region. His collection of Southwestern Americana, his pride and joy, was known to booksellers across the country.

It was already late morning in Washington, D.C., when George came into his law office punctually at nine a.m. A call was awaiting him from Bruce Haggard of the Library of Congress.

"I thought you might be interested, George. We have been offered, and we have turned down, a copy of Bernal Díaz's *The True History of the Conquest of New Spain*, the 1632 edition. You are familiar with it, I know."

George was indeed. Bernal Díaz del Castillo had accompanied Hernando Cortes in his 1519 campaign which had conquered Aztec Mexico and its vast treasures. Years later, in Guatemala, Díaz had written his personal account. First published in Madrid in 1632, it remains one of the primary historical sources of the conquest.

George blinked. A rare treasure indeed.

"It's an estate settlement thing," Bruce Haggard continued. "Here's the executor's name and address."

George wrote them down carefully, but what Bruce had to say next drove all thoughts of Bernal Díaz from his mind.

"What made me think of you," Bruce said, "was that at a cocktail party here last night your part of the world was mentioned. You have a dam at a place called Harper's Park?"

"We do."

"Well, apparently they're going to enlarge it, one of those make-the-desert-bloom-like-a-rose things."

The ignorant insularity of the East was always annoying, and George's rejoinder was automatic, even while his mind was already elsewhere. "Harper's Park," he said, "is hardly desert. Its elevation is eight thousand feet, which puts it eighteen hundred feet above the top of New Hampshire's Mount Washington, which you consider high country for skiing. But thanks for the information."

George Harrison hung up and leaned back, stunned. The Harper's Park dam was only ten years old, and he could not understand the necessity for its enlargement. Had he even dreamed that it would be considered, he would never have sold that mountain property to Bill Williams.

Step one, of course, was to verify or disprove Bruce Haggard's information. He instructed his secretary to put through a call to the governor. One of the advantages of being named Harrison was that local doors opened quickly. From the governor's office Harry Wilson's voice said, "Yes, George?"

"I have heard that the dam enlargement has been approved."

"Mind telling me where you heard that?"

"My source is not important. The question is, is it true?"

The governor sighed. "It *is* true, George."

"Bill Williams' doing," George said with conviction. "He bought property from me up there, knowing the enlargement would be approved. He is unscrupulous." George hung up angrily.

The governor sat for a short time staring at nothing. Then he had a call put through to Bill Williams. "Bill? George Harrison just telephoned. Word of the dam approval is out."

"There was no way to keep it a secret, Harry. People talk. Did George mention the property he sold me?"

"He did. With considerable vehemence."

"Okay. Thanks. See you."

Williams hung up and leaned back in his chair, looking at his office view of the mountains. With that core of honesty in him which could not be denied, he wondered: *had* he merely been making a long-term investment in buying the Harrison land, or had he already known that the dam enlargement would be his next project?

The telephone on his desk buzzed once more. It was John Boggs, the policeman at the dam. "I just thought you'd like to know, Mr. Williams, that there's a guy diving in the lake with underwater gear. Says he's a—geophysicist. I think he's harmless, but there are a couple of things about him I thought you might like to know."

"What things?"

"His name is Harper and he says old Jed was his kin. He put his last address as some place in Saudi Arabia. Yesterday he was looking at the dam. And there was a phone call for him from Alberta, Canada. Somebody wants him up there and he wouldn't tell them what he was doing here. I don't know, Mr. Williams. It just *sounds* kind of funny."

Williams nodded. "He's staying at the motel? Right. I'll take it from here. Thanks for the call, John."

Bill Williams' intercom buzzed. "Mr. George Harrison is here to see you, Mr. Williams."

Sooner or later, Bill thought. It might as well be now. "Send him in." He did not get up when the door opened. "Come in, George. Sit down."

What was between them, Bill thought, was not open, active hatred, but mutual dislike that went back to the schoolyard. George had been the plump boy from the big house on the hill, Bill the scrappy kid from the *barrio*. George, for all the privilege he had behind him, had been physically afraid of Bill, envious of his strength. And Bill, conscious of the world of difference between his background and George's, had always been ill at ease in the plump boy's presence. These antagonistic feelings were still with them. "What can I do for you, George?" Williams asked.

"The dam enlargement has been approved," George said. "I have verified it with the governor. You are responsible, Bill. I'm sure you've pulled the strings, applied the pressure. Now I suppose you have every reason to feel proud of yourself."

"You didn't come here to pat me on the back."

"Quite right. I came here with a business proposition. You have a quarter section of my land, one hundred and sixty acres."

"My land, George. I bought it over two years ago."

"I am quite aware of that. You paid five hundred dollars an acre, eighty thousand dollars."

"A fair price. You set it."

"I will give you a thirty-percent profit, one hundred and four thousand dollars. That's my top offer."

"No dice, George. Sorry."

"I dislike being bilked."

"Nobody bilked you," Bill said. "You put the land on the market. I bought it."

"With certain foreknowledge that it would become waterfront property when the dam is enlarged."

"I had no certain foreknowledge, as you call it. But even if I had, I would have gone right ahead. Do you expect me to be conscience-stricken because I got the best of a business deal?"

"No. Your kind doesn't know the meaning of the word conscience."

Williams took a deep breath, then let it out slowly. He could take just so much of George Harrison. "Okay, George. You've said what you came to say. Now get out of here before I kick you out."

AN HOUR LATER, in his office at the First National Bank, Tom Gentry heard the news. A friend in the nationwide holding company which owned Tom's bank telephoned from Los Angeles. "Our New York guy got it straight from Washington, Tom. Approval for the dam enlargement was finalized this morning. Maybe you can put the knowledge to use."

It was widely rumored that Tom Gentry, president of the First National Bank, was distantly related to John Wesley Gentry, the gunfighter. Tom's cold gray eyes gave the rumor credence. His calm was unshakable. "Maybe I can at that," he said. "Thanks, Joe."

Gentry hung up and began thinking hard. Once information such as this was known to the general public it was worthless; but before, it could usually be made to turn a profit. The only problem was finding the right handle. Quickly.

He sat motionless for a little time and then flipped the switch of the intercom. "Ask Jack Marble to step in, please."

Jack Marble, the bank's loan officer, was in his late thirties, trim and fit. He was on his way to the top, and eager to get there. Jack sat down and waited for Gentry to speak.

"Brooks Thompson," Tom Gentry said. "We turned down an extension of his loan."

"Yes, sir. I didn't want to. He's such a nice guy, but he isn't going to make that landscape business go."

"He offered us some property as further collateral?"

"Yes, sir. Way up above Harper's Park lake. Fifty acres, worth maybe four hundred, five hundred dollars an acre—if you could find a buyer for it."

"He's keeping up his loan payments?"

"Yes, sir. It's strapping him and his wife, but they're hanging on."

"Okay, Jack, thanks. The Thompsons are a nice couple. I'd like to see them make it."

"I'd like that too, sir. He and Mary have worked like dogs."

Tom Gentry waited until the door was closed again before he took the phone book out of his drawer and hunted in the Yellow

Pages under Landscaping. He asked the switchboard for an outside line and dialed the call himself. A young woman's voice
answered.

"Mrs. Thompson?"

"Speaking.."

"This is Tom Gentry at the bank, Mrs. Thompson. I called—"

"If it's about this month's loan payment, Mr. Gentry, Brooks
will be taking care of it this week for sure." She sounded hopeful
rather than assured.

Gentry's voice was as soothing as he could make it. "It isn't
about that at all, Mrs. Thompson. I just wanted to talk to your
husband about your application for a loan extension—"

"You mean you could reconsider it?"

"I'm not sure, exactly. But we like to help local businesses whenever we can. Do you suppose your husband could have lunch with
me today? The Hilton? Twelve o'clock?"

"Mr. Gentry, I'll see that he makes it. Oh, thank you!"

"Not at all." Now he had the handle. Gentry sat back to
consider exactly how he was going to go about turning it.

Eighty feet down, the water of the lake was still clear and the
visibility reasonably good. It was cold, even with the wet suit he
wore. Jay had studied topographical maps of the area, and had
noted that the stream which flowed into the lake rose in a hundred
upland valleys, ravines and steep-sided canyons. Some tributaries
were marked on the maps as intermittent, and now with the
drought were presumably dry; others drained directly from
hanging valleys and even small natural lakes, all of them snow or
glacier-fed.

Now that Jay was actually down here among the buildings of the
drowned village, what Pancho had told him of the seiche caused
by the recent tremor was very much in his mind. Close up, some
of the stones of the walls looked sharp, menacing.

He had adjusted his belt weights, and now, balanced easily a
few feet above the bottom of the lake using only his swim fins, he
glided along what had been the main street of the village. Here
was the mill. The waterwheel remained. How many thousands of
bushels of grain had been ground to flour by this sturdy, simple

and efficient mechanism erected in what had been wilderness before "progress" arrived?

He swam on. Here was the first house, built by old Jed Harper. No, Jed's first house had been of logs, Jay remembered now from Julia's journal. This stone house had come later, so positioned, he noticed, as to afford a fine view up the valley to the mountains.

On another dive, Jay told himself, he would have a better look at Jed's house. Now he clung to his original plan of a general survey of the entire village. The church was next, even its modest steeple intact except for its bell, which had been removed. Behind the church was the graveyard, row upon uneven row of headstones. He would need a light to read them, and an underwater camera to photograph anything of great interest; even on a clear day such as this, not enough sunlight reached the lake bottom to make out some of the weathered inscriptions. But the stones were there; that was the important thing, maybe old Jed's among them.

Actually strolling along the village street and through the grave-yard really would have been preferable, Jay thought. And yet, in another sense, floating among the buildings like a disembodied spirit gave him a feeling of observing from *within*, seeing through windows, doorways, even walls, himself unseen, a ghost among ghosts. And as he had yesterday in the boat, he had now that strange illusion of being at home.

He glided on, the full length of the main street. There it was, he thought, as ahead the dam wall rose sheer: journey's end at last. He swung around and headed on a long slant upward toward the light. A pilgrimage, he told himself, a silly business, really, but unaccountably he felt better for having made it.

It was not until he had pulled himself into the boat and, mouth-piece hanging loose and face mask pushed up, sat relaxed on the stern seat, that he realized how tense he had been underwater. His muscles ached, and despite the cold he was sweating. He started the outboard motor; its raucous clatter was annoying after the silence of the village.

At the hotel, there was a message from someone called Williams beneath the door of his room. It included a local telephone number. When Jay had showered and dressed, he had the desk clerk place the call.

Bill Williams introduced himself. "I haven't any real reason, Harper, but I'm curious to meet you. You seem to be interested in the dam, and I know all about it. There's no decent food up there unless you cook it yourself. Come down to my place for dinner and we'll both satisfy our curiosities."

Jay liked Williams' kind of directness. And Pancho's cooking *did* leave a lot to be desired. "Invitation accepted with pleasure," he said. "Tell me where and when."

THE CITY'S MAYOR, José-María Lopez y Baca, had been born and raised in the *barrio*. Now that he had prospered, he lived in an alien, Anglo world, and a bitter resentment fueled his determination to show that he or any Chicano could succeed. In a city in which there were two governmental chief executives, himself and the governor, clashes of authority were inevitable.

Now, over the telephone, he was saying to the governor, "You're going ahead with that Harper's Park dam enlargement, right?"

Harry Wilson would dearly have loved to know how the mayor had come by his information so soon, but he refrained from asking. "I haven't had official word yet," he said, "but that seems to be it."

"For once," the mayor said, "you and I are on the same side of the fence. We need that enlargement. But water rates will go up. The job's going to cost money, and somebody has to pay for it. A few bucks a month doesn't mean anything to a rich Anglo, or a big company. But to a poor Chicano family, it means fewer beans in the pot. The trouble is, the rate structure's upside down."

The governor thought about it. "Meaning?"

"There's a minimum charge," the mayor said. "Then as you use more water, the price per unit goes down, right? Why not raise the rates on the big users, make them pay the premium? The more they use the *more* they pay, instead of *less*. Give the little guy a break and help conserve water. How about twisting the Public Service Commission's arm?"

I should have seen this coming, the governor thought. "The Public Service Commission is autonomous," he said. "You know that, José-María."

"Hell," the mayor said, "you can make them jump through a hoop anytime you want to. You're a nice, polite fellow, Harry, but there are a lot of characters walking around carrying their heads in baskets because they didn't do what you wanted them to do. The politicians around here know it."

"You overestimate me," the governor said. "But I will give your

27

suggestion some thought when funding and amortizing the dam enlargement gets to contract time."

Later that morning the mayor had a caller at his office, Carlos García, who taught the seventh grade at the *barrio* grammar school and who also provided what sports coaching the school had. Like the mayor, Carlos was a product of the *barrio*. In fact, Carlos had once blacked the eye of the future mayor, and as sometimes happens between males who have fought and then discovered that their differences are not irreconcilable, the incident forged an enduring bond between them.

Carlos' English was not as good as the mayor's. He had never lost the Spanish lilt. "That drought in Texas is over," he said. "It's on TV. One place they got twenty-two inches of rain in twenty-four hours. A tropical storm."

"I heard, Carlito."

"We got a drought too. They got bad floods. What if we get floods too? Remember how it used to be when the snows melted? Only with rain like that this could be much worse."

"That's why we've got the dam. And they're going to enlarge it."

"I didn't know that." Carlos was silent for a few moments. "Okay," he said at last. "But just in case something goes wrong and we do get a flood. All those people in the *barrio*, on low ground. Suppose, just suppose. . . . Have we got a plan? Some idea what to do to get people out safe—just in case?"

The mayor leaned back in his chair. He said slowly in a voice filled with sudden wonder, "*Madre de Dios!* I don't think anybody ever even thought about it. How about that?"

BROOKS THOMPSON was in a thoughtful mood when he came back from lunch with banker Tom Gentry. Brooks was tall and lean, in his late twenties, with longish brown hair and plastic-framed glasses. After graduating from Princeton he had worked for a firm of investment bankers in New York. But he had decided after three years that he had had more than enough of the rat race, and had headed west with Mary. The landscaping venture had been her idea. She had always liked flowers, and knew quite a bit about them. They had discovered that that was not quite enough. They were having a hard time making ends meet; it was a struggle to pay the rent on their tiny house on the fringe of the *barrio*.

"What happened?" Mary said now. "Sit down. Tell me. Everything!" She was a tall girl with long blond hair, dressed in short-sleeved shirt, faded jeans, sneakers. "Well?"

Brooks sat down and stretched out his legs. "I don't know," he said thoughtfully. "If this were New York, I'd guess that somebody was trying to pull a fast one. Tom Gentry's what Wall Street calls a gunslinger. Or that's how I'd size him up if he were hustling a bond issue, or selling short in a bull market. Here—" Brooks shook his head slowly. "I just don't know. All of a sudden he's just a little too friendly. He wants to give us a hand until we really get started."

"Sometimes I wish you'd never worked in New York," Mary said. "You were getting so you didn't trust anybody. What does Mr. Gentry want to do?"

"Buy that property up above the lake. Where we're planning to build the cabin."

Mary was silent for a time. All their plans, she thought, dreams really. She said at last, "Did he mention price?"

"Four hundred and fifty dollars an acre. That's twenty-two thousand five hundred dollars. A fair price. More than we paid."

Mary brushed her hair back with both hands. "We certainly could use the money."

"No argument. But why does Gentry want that land?"

"Honestly, Brooks! What difference does it make?"

"I don't know." Brooks smiled helplessly.

"We could pay off that loan, and have plenty left for that small tractor and the sprayer."

"True."

"But you don't think we should sell."

"It's just a feeling. I don't have anything else."

Mary leaned against the cluttered desk. "We could ask Daddy for a loan."

"No. We agreed on that. He doesn't think we can hack it out here, and maybe he's right, but we'll give it a darn good try."

Mary's smile was less than convincing. "That was the bargain."

There was a long silence before Brooks heaved himself out of his chair. He took a deep breath. "Okay," he said, "I guess that settles it. I'll call Gentry and tell him he has a deal."

THE WILLIAMSES' house was impressive, Jay thought as he drove up. It was large, adobe-colored, and it fitted into the brown earth and scattered piñon and juniper trees as if it had grown there. A low adobe wall surrounded the considerable property, and inside the courtyard was a three-car garage connected to the main house by a covered walk.

The entire place reeked of money, and Jay was not at all sure he was glad he had come. He resented the arrogant assumption of infallibility that tended to go with wealth. He walked to the carved front door, which opened before he could lift the heavy wrought-iron knocker. A girl smiled at him and held out a cool, firm hand. "Kate Williams, Mr. Harper," she said.

Inside, the house was pleasantly cool, with whitewashed walls and weathered wooden ceiling beams. The brick floors were polished by age and care, and covered by brightly patterned Indian rugs. Jay was aware that the girl was watching him, smiling.

"Do you approve of what you see, Mr. Harper?"

Money, of course. That had been his first thought. But admit it, he told himself, there is taste as well. "Very nice," he said, and followed Kate through sliding glass doors at the rear to a flagstone *portal* with a stunning view of the mountains.

A somewhat surly young man, Kate was thinking. Ill at ease? Hard to tell. She told herself sternly to reserve judgment.

Two men sat on the *portal*, drinks at hand. "Mr. Harper, Daddy," Kate said. Bill Williams heaved himself out of his chair. He was a big man, broad and solid. His handshake was gently powerful.

"Glad you could come," Bill Williams said, and nodded toward the other, younger, larger man. "Sam Martin, my chief engineer."

When he thought about the evening later, Jay realized that he liked Williams. But the arrogance of wealth was in the man, along with a tendency to set a goal and head straight toward it at full throttle. In Jay's judgment these were flaws, sometimes dangerous.

He found that he disliked Sam Martin. The man seemed reasonably knowledgeable as an engineer. He could, and did, listen when another talked. He smiled easily, and there was no reason to think the smiles were insincere. So what was there in him to object to— except that he was a lightweight?

About Kate, Jay was not sure. She was decorative—medium height, slim and pleasingly rounded, and she moved with easy grace. She spoke little, although she did seem to listen, and she wore almost continually a small, assured smile that could have been infuriating, and somehow was not. There was about her a directness that matched her father's, a quiet forcefulness that Jay

30

found attractive. Yet he could not decide if he liked Kate or not.

Bill Williams said at once in his blunt way, "You're old Jed Harper's kin, so John Boggs tells me. There weren't any Harpers left around here when we built the dam ten years ago. Even when I was a kid, I don't remember any up in the valley."

"They moved west. California. Around 1900, I think." Julia's journal mentioned the breakup of the family only briefly. She herself had stayed behind.

"It was a pretty little place, Harper's Park village," Williams said. "But, of course, you've seen it now. How does it look when you're down there?"

"Empty. A ghost town. Just buildings."

"A movie set?" This was Sam Martin.

Jay shook his head. "Movie sets aren't real. This is. Was."

"A sense of—having been lived in?" Kate said unexpectedly.

Jay thought about it. Slowly he nodded. "Yes. You expect to find washing hanging on a line."

"I've never really looked at it," Kate said. She turned to her father. "When you build the dam higher, the lake will be deeper, won't it? Will you be able to see the buildings then?"

Jay looked from one to the other. "Are you enlarging the dam?"

Williams told himself he was sick and tired of pussyfooting. If George Harrison knew all about it, then others knew too. "Yes," he said. "Sam here has had plans for eighteen months. The Army Corps of Engineers has gone all over them, up, down and sideways. He looked straight at Jay. "You're a geophysicist, Boggs tells me. That covers just about anything you can name."

"Oil is my bag," Jay said.

"Suppose," Williams said, "there is opposition to the enlargement and we need some expert testimony. You've been down on the bottom where nobody else has been. Would you be available?"

"Afraid not. I'm off for Canada in two, three days," Jay said. "Why would you want a geophysicist, anyway?"

"I learned a long time ago," Williams said, "that when it comes to open hearings, public opinion is all on the side of the fellow with the most experts, especially experts who can talk about things nobody else understands."

Sam Martin said, "The engineering's all done, Bill, and nobody's going to argue with it."

Williams shook his head. "I count my winnings, Sam, after everybody else has thrown in his hand. Not before." His eyes on Jay were appraising. "You ever make mistakes, Harper?"

"I try not to be wrong too often."

"My feelings too."

Dinner was superb, a standing rib roast, baked potatoes with sour cream and chives, a crisp mixed green salad, California Zinfandel wine, cheese and crackers, coffee, port or cognac. Jay wondered if Kate was responsible for the menu.

As host, Williams dominated the conversation and sent it off on odd tangents without warning. "Canada in a few days," he said, looking at Jay. "You get around quite a bit, don't you?"

"Here and there."

"Such as?" Martin said. The question held a challenge.

No, Jay thought, I do not like the man. "The last stop was Saudi," he said, his voice without special inflection. "Before that Iran, and before that a rig anchored in the North Sea off Norway." He shrugged. "I go where there's work for me. My job is to try to prevent trouble—or waste. And if there are no emergencies, no heroics, then I've done my job. I like the quiet life."

Kate, watching, listening, allowed herself to wonder. Was it a quiet life on a drill rig in the North Sea?

They sat on the *portal* again after dinner. In the high, clear air the warmth of the day disappeared quickly. A maid appeared and lighted a fire in the corner fireplace, piñon logs standing on end, their burning fragrance filling the air. The warmth was welcome; and the only lighting, from candles in hurricane lamps on the table, cast a pleasant, unobtrusive glow.

Here and now, Jay thought, you can almost recapture the atmosphere old Jed must have known, the sense of loneliness and yet belonging; like an owl he had heard last night, in tune with the environment, rather than against it, an invader.

Kate broke into his thoughts. "You'll dive again tomorrow?" she asked.

"If it's clear, and it looks as if it will be. I'd like a closer look at some of the details, the graveyard in particular. It would be nice to see old Jed's grave marker, and maybe Julia's too."

Kate said on impulse, "If I came up, might I go out with you? I've never really looked at the village since the lake covered it."

She was, after all, his hostess, Jay told himself, and the good dinner did carry a certain amount of obligation. "It'll be cold just sitting out there in the boat," he said. "But if you'd like to come, yes, of course."

JAY WAS awakened from sleep that night by what sounded like distant heavy explosions, and he realized it was thunder echoing and reverberating among the high peaks of the watershed. A break in the drought? Maybe. In mountainous regions like this, a heavy thunderstorm could be either an isolated phenomenon or a signal that a front was moving in. Whichever it was, Jay was glad he was snug in bed rather than camped out in a high valley.

Thunderstorms in the mountains are awesome displays of almost incalculable power. And if you are close, there is about them a personal quality, inescapable, as if every sudden flash and every simultaneous crackling explosion is seeking you out, you alone. The lightning flashes blind you; the thunder deafens you; and on open, rocky slopes and in shallow hanging valleys there is no place to take refuge.

And the rain, which frequently turns to hail, can be unrelenting and unbelievable in its ferocity. Rivulets turn in an instant to streams which become torrents, rushing steeply downhill un- impeded, catching up loose rocks, scree, even boulders, and flinging this detritus with shrapnel effect down upon lower elevations. There, when the storm at last subsides, it lies alien and scattered to testify to the fury that has been.

Caught among the high peaks in such a storm, man rapidly becomes aware of his mortality; perhaps a good thing, Jay had often thought. Now, the bedclothes tucked snugly around him, he closed his eyes and with the ease of long practice in strange places went almost immediately off to sleep again. In the morning, out of curiosity, he would see what effects of the storm he could find.

Before breakfast at Pancho's counter he went for a walk along the shore of the lake. After about a mile he found what he was looking for, a brownish stain in the lake's clear water; it was silt, carried by the multitude of tributaries down to the main stream, proof of the force and cutting power of the down-rushing water which the thunderstorm had loosed. Where the silt-laden stream met the still waters of the lake, it would precipitate the material it had carried in suspension down from the mountain flanks.

As he walked back to the motel Jay met John Boggs. "I had

dinner at Williams' house last night," he said. "His daughter is coming up to go out in the boat with me this morning, so nobody objects to my diving in the lake."

Boggs only nodded, but some of his official wariness had disappeared at the mention of Williams.

"That storm last night," Jay said. "Have you heard any weather reports? Is there a front moving in?"

"There's rain to the west. Whether we'll get it—" Boggs shrugged.

Jay went in to breakfast. There remained that feeling of kinship with the valley and with the drowned village, a feeling he found impossible to shake.

Father Rodriguez was the priest of the *barrio*, pastor of the church of Santa Rosario. He was a small man in his late sixties who customarily dressed in rusty black and usually, because he shared the human frailty called vanity, wore a black beret to hide his baldness.

He had spent forty-five years in the *barrio*, and was content with his lot. His parishioners brought their problems to him as a matter of course. On this day Angelita Leyba, fat and fiftyish, mother of eleven, a widow, dressed as always in unrelieved black, told him her problem. It concerned Juan Cisneros.

"He says he can afford to go fishing in the lake now," Angelita said, "and with his big car and his store and all, maybe he can."

Father Rodriguez had never known Juan Cisneros to display the slightest interest in fishing.

"You know that when he came back from the big war my Inocencio—may he rest in peace—lived for a while up above Harper's Park. He built a little house. When we were younger, we would sometimes drive up there on a weekend. When Inocencio went to his reward, the lawyer told me that the property, the little house and the land—ten acres, I think—belonged to me. But what would I do with it without Inocencio? I have not even seen it for three, four years. And now Juan Cisneros wants to buy it, but all I can think is that it was Inocencio's, and I do not know what to do."

Father Rodriguez was silent, thoughtful.

"Two thousand dollars," Angelita said, "is a great deal of money.

We are poor people. With two thousand dollars—" She raised eyebrows, shoulders and hands all at once in a gesture of awe at the enormity of the sum. "Maybe a new cookstove. For Felipe, boots like the *vaqueros* wear. Luis wants a skateboard, María-Victoria new pants. What should I do, Padre?"

"There is no need for haste," the priest said. "You have waited this long. Another day or two—"

"Juan Cisneros says that when he decides to do something, he wants to do it quickly. Or not at all."

That was Juan Cisneros all right, the priest thought. "Give me a little time, Angelita. I will think about it and let you know." He watched Angelita waddle down the aisle of the church, pause and genuflect, then walk out into the sunlight.

Father Rodriguez turned his thoughts on Juan Cisneros. Like the mayor, Juan Cisneros (HONEST JOHNNY'S - TV - RADIO - APPLIANCES) had grown up in the *barrio*. To the priest, Johnny was an enigma.

Father Rodriguez had watched Juan grow up, hustling, always hustling, a businessman by the time he was eight, working the tourists in the plaza. He knew where one could get a drink on dry Sundays, bargains in silver and turquoise jewelry (that were neither silver nor turquoise), genuine Indian rugs (from machine looms in Mexico). Always on his toes, always running.

Boys like that sorely strained the good priest's faith in humanity, and yet HONEST JOHNNY'S warehouse on the riverbank and his retail store up near the plaza, right on the fringe of the high-rent district, were proof that such boys did not always turn out badly. Still, in the back of Father Rodriguez' mind was the conviction that beneath the legitimate Johnny Cisneros there still lurked the boy Juan who never did things without reason, or profit.

Angelita Leyba's dilemma wanted careful thought, the priest decided. And what if in the end his advice was wrong? He was no businessman. But he could not shirk his responsibilities.

Father Rodriguez walked from his *barrio* church to HONEST JOHNNY'S retail outlet in the area of the better shops. He stood outside for a little time admiring the shining window display of magnificent television sets and high-fidelity receivers that seemed to stare arrogantly back at him. At last he roused himself and walked into the store.

Cisneros was at his desk, a telephone at his ear. He saw Father

Rodriguez and waved him to a chair. "What I mean," he said into the phone, "if you want the business, then you perform. You said you'd ship today. Now you say maybe next week. I don't do business that way. I want those TV sets on the truck today." He hung up and swung his chair to face the priest.

"You're lucky you're in your business, Padre. Here it's nothing but hassle. What can I do for you?"

Away from his church, Father Rodriguez thought, he was at a disadvantage. Here he was dealing with the secular world, where the values were those which man, not God, had set. And here Juan Cisneros was like a jungle cat in his native habitat. For a moment the priest regretted his decision to come.

But he began. "You have offered to buy the property of Angelita Leyba, Juan." Unconsciously, as always in times of stress, he spoke in Spanish.

Nothing changed in Johnny's face, or even in his eyes. "Sure." He spoke English, totally unaccented. "Like I told her, Padre, I want a place where I can relax. You know, a little fishing, maybe a few pals up for drinks and a friendly poker game."

"That is your only reason, Juan?"

Johnny's smile was open and friendly. "What else?"

The trouble was, the priest thought, he could think of no answer to that question, although ever since Angelita's visit he had been trying to find the ulterior motive he was convinced was there.

Johnny watched the priest's face, and let his friendly smile disappear. "Padre, if the old girl wants to make such a big deal of it, probably using you to try to shake me down for more money, why, let's forget the whole thing. I just thought I'd do myself a favor, and her too, but not if it's going to be a hassle."

Juan's motives sounded plausible, Father Rodriguez thought, and all he had to set against them was unfounded suspicion, which was both uncharitable and unchristian. And the last thing he wanted was to spoil a legitimate, and for Angelita profitable, transaction. "I will tell Angelita what you have said."

Now Johnny's expression turned doubtful. "I just don't know, Padre. I don't want the old girl saying I pulled a fast one on her. Maybe I better stay clear of the whole thing."

There was a false note here, the priest thought, and he pounced upon it. "I do not recall that anything anyone ever had to say about you weighed very heavily upon your conscience, Juan."

Johnny smiled easily. "I'm a businessman now, Padre, and I got a reputation to worry about. People start saying bad things and business starts to fall off. That's why I don't want the Leyba woman unhappy. But if you say it's okay, then I'll go along. Tell her the offer holds. But I want to wrap it up this afternoon. My lawyer will bring her the papers. Okay?"

Father Rodriguez had a feeling that somehow he had failed. But there it was. "I will tell her, Juan," he said.

Johnny watched in the angled wall mirror which showed the entire store until the priest was out on the sidewalk. Then he picked up the phone and called his attorney. "All systems are go on that land purchase I told you about, Manny. First thing this afternoon get the woman's signature on the bill of sale and give her the money. Two thousand. I want the whole thing recorded and wrapped up today." Johnny started to hang up, then changed his mind. "And, Manny—that bill of sale. I want it to read, 'For one dollar and other valuable considerations.' No actual sale price."

"I know exactly what you mean," Manny's knowing voice said.

One more call to make, this one to State Senator Walt Duggan at his insurance brokerage office. "Okay, Walt," Johnny said. "We'll have the Leyba property this afternoon. You're sure about that dam-enlargement approval?"

"I told you, Johnny. It has to go through my committee, so I have the word direct. And I don't want my name in the deal."

"It won't be. Just your money By the way, there's one thing. The Leyba woman sent the priest up here. He just left."

"Why did she send him?"

"If you're a *barrio* Chicana like she is, and you got questions, you go to the church. The church fixes everything. Including the price of land. It's four hundred bucks an acre now. Four thousand dollars."

"Johnny, we agreed on two thousand! And it was my idea! My information!"

"That was before the church got into the act. Now, do you want in, or not?"

Walt Duggan said heavily, "Okay. Fifty-fifty, as we agreed."

"I'll expect your check for two thousand."

Duggan's voice was both resigned and resentful. "You'll get it as soon as I see the bill of sale."

"Fair enough, Walt."

38

Johnny hung up again and sat quiet, thinking that the smug Anglos were just as vulnerable as anybody else. Honest Johnny Cisneros was going to come out of the deal with half the Leyba property, which was going to be worth a bundle, *and* for free. Not bad, not bad. All in all, he thought, a good morning's work.

THE SKY was the incredible blue it frequently is when you see it from high elevations through thin atmosphere; against it the jagged mountains stood out sharp and clear. Only the raucous sound of the outboard disturbed the scene, Jay thought, and when he switched the motor off and let the little boat drift, the silence was a welcome relief.

Slowly the ripples died away. The surface of the lake became flat and again transparent. "There it is," he said to Kate, pointing downward. "There's the church, minus its bell. There's the mill, the smithy, houses, barns—" He looked at Kate's face and tried to probe her thoughts.

"You resent it, don't you?" Her voice was quiet.

"Not really. I just wanted to see it." That was the original idea, true, but it was a little more than that now.

First there had been Pancho's offhand mention of the tremor and the seiche; then Bill Williams' confident talk of the dam enlargement, and finally Jay's telephone calls to three widely spaced seismograph centers where he had friends. Now what both impelled him and troubled him was more than mere curiosity.

Kate watched him pull on his fins, struggle into his air-tank harness and fasten his weighted belt. There was about him this morning, she thought, a kind of intensity that had not been discernible last night. "Is something wrong?"

Jay shook his head. "Nothing." Nothing, he thought, unless another tremor hit. That last one was three-point-nine on the Richter scale, the seismograph records had shown. No major quake, but enough to set the lake water in strong motion which would fling him about like a chip in a river rapid. Okay, he had to put up with that risk if he was going to dive at all.

He put on his faceplate and started his watch to time his air supply. "Thirty minutes," he said in a hollow, nose-blocked voice, "no more, maybe less." He slipped his mouthpiece securely into place and, with an underwater light in one hand, slipped over the side of the boat.

Kate watched him begin his descent into the cold, clear water. She could remember the village only vaguely before the dam was built. Harper's Park then had been merely a place you went through on your way into the high country for picnics or camping trips. Now, watching Jay glide effortlessly among the buildings, she found herself wishing she had taken the time and effort to know the village and the people who lived in it before it was covered by the waters of the lake.

She knew of old Jed Harper, of course, the real-life mountain man. He was a local legend. She supposed she was being ridiculously romantic to attribute to someone she'd known so briefly some of old Jed's bold qualities to his three-times great-grandson, but the temptation was there, and it arose from several sources.

First and most important was her father's reaction to Jay. Last night Kate had felt in the older man a respect for Jay, something he accorded few men and then usually only after long acquaintance. Her father's reaction had been immediate, unhesitating. And Jay, she thought, had felt it too. Despite the age disparity, the two of them had hit it off. Sam Martin, on the other hand, had resented Jay, probably precisely because of her father's reaction to him. Why? Jay posed no threat; he would be gone tomorrow.

She concentrated again on the empty buildings and village streets she could see so clearly on the lake bottom. Few people had still lived there, she remembered, when the dam was planned. There had been opposition, of course, to loss of homes and property; and she remembered sympathizing privately when she thought how awful it would be if her own home were to be purposely destroyed.

Now, submerged, the village took on an importance in her mind it had not had before. She could almost feel what Jay had said last night, that you would not be surprised to find washing hanging on a line, because a sense of *living* still remained.

But against the needs of the city, the feelings of this tiny hamlet were unimportant, or so it had been decided when the dam site was chosen and approved. It occurred to her now, as she watched Jay approach the edge of the graveyard, that she was no longer sure that the greatest good to the greatest number ought always to be the basic criterion.

Meanwhile, eighty feet down on the lake floor, Jay flashed his light on a gravestone, and with a little shock of recognition,

40

stopped to read the crudely chiseled and weathered letters: "Jedediah Harper 1801–1888."

No epitaph, Jay thought, probably because old Jed had given orders to that effect. No doubt it was being now in the actual presence of the grave that started a train of memories, and the exact words the old man had spoken not long before his death and Julia had recorded in her journal, popped unbidden and with stunning force into Jay's mind:

"I've had a good life doing just what I wanted to do," Jed had said. "Not many can say the same. I've gone whichever way my stick floated, enjoyed damn near every minute of it and have no regrets. You can't ask for more than that."

No, Jay thought, you couldn't. Those words summed up a lifetime. "Whichever way my stick floated." That was the old man's creed. It was whichever way curiosity and desire and courage and conscience led. Or impelled. Big words; big thoughts. Something for a boy to remember. Something to remember now. With his free hand, Jay made a gesture of farewell to the gravestone and swam on.

Julia's stone was newer, less weathered. It read: "Julia Hopkins Harper, 1855–1930, Beloved Wife and Mother. R.I.P." She too, Jay thought, had gone where her stick floated, out of the settled East to this mountain valley, and here she had stayed.

He realized he was tense again, as he had been yesterday, one part of his mind and all his senses tuned to, even waiting for, the first movement of the water. He turned the light on his watch. Twelve minutes of air left. Decision time, he told himself.

The choice was simple: whether to take the first step toward what might become involvement, or to ignore what was actually none of his business. He had seen as much of the village as he had intended to see. He had found and paid his respects to Jed's grave and Julia's. Mission accomplished? No. Not yet.

In Jed's phrase, his stick was floating now in a different direction, through no fault of his own. True, but he had better follow it, as Jed followed his, or risk regretting for the rest of his life that he had not.

Jay turned and swam purposefully toward the right-hand shore, where the dam met the side of the gorge.

From the boat, Kate watched him disappear and wondered where he had gone, and why. In only a few minutes she caught sight of him again, a figure and a shadow on the bottom, swimming back across the dam's face toward the left-hand shore.

She did not see him again until he surfaced suddenly only a few feet from the boat, raised his face mask, took out his mouthpiece and, treading water, handed the light over the gunwale. He followed it himself with a dextrous heave, and in moments had the outboard motor started and the boat headed for the dock. Only then did he start to relax. Two dives and no trouble, he thought, no sudden water movements throwing him around helplessly. He was lucky. He would not crowd his luck again.

"Your teeth are chattering." Kate had to raise her voice above the engine's sound. "I felt the water. It's almost freezing." But there was something else, she thought, something troubled him deeply. "What's wrong? It's more than the cold."

As if in sudden decision, Jay asked, "Can you stick around? I'll buy you a cup of coffee. Meet me in twenty minutes in Pancho's."

"Of course. Will you tell me then what's wrong?"

He could still walk away, he told himself, and avoid any possible entanglement. But where, really, could be the harm in merely reporting what he now almost certainly knew? "I'll tell you part of it," he said. "But I have some work to do before I go into the whole thing."

AGAIN JACK MARBLE sat in Tom Gentry's office in the bank, this time feeling uncomfortable. "Uh, twenty-two thousand five," he said, "unsecured? I mean, you know how the comptroller's people in Washington have been clamping down on 'insider loans,' sir—" He stopped. Gentry's cold, gray eyes unnerved him.

"I am buying some property from Brooks Thompson, Jack," Tom Gentry said. "Fifty acres. Up near the Harper's Park lake. The property will secure the loan."

"Oh." In the single word there was vast relief. Jack stood up. "You'll be wanting a check?"

"Yes, Jack."

"Then I guess I'd better get right on with the paperwork."

HIS HONOR Mayor José-María Lopez y Baca sat in his office without his jacket, shirtsleeves rolled up, necktie loosened. It was hot, and there was no air conditioning in these old municipal offices. But the mayor could remember vividly how sweltering it

42

had been in late summer down in the *barrio*, where tin roofs turned shacks into bake ovens; even after the sun went down and it cooled off outside, the houses did not. So now he paid little attention to the heat, and concentrated on the matter at hand.

"What we've got here," he said in his accentless English, "is one of those damned things everybody thinks somebody else ought to be responsible for, and nobody is. Carlito here—" he nodded at Carlos García, the schoolteacher "—brought it to my attention." He looked from his chief of police to his fire chief. "What happens if we get a disaster of some kind? Have we got any emergency plans?"

The chief of police, Bud Henderson, was large and beefy, a southwestern-born-and-bred Anglo who resented having a Chicano as his official boss. He said impatiently, "What kind of disaster?"

"A big fire. The kind of floods they've been getting in Texas. Maybe a tornado. The sort of thing you can't predict but that would require evacuation of at least some part of the city. How would we cope?"

The fire chief, Rudy Smith, was also Anglo, but a quieter, more thoughtful man than Henderson, and lacking ethnic resentment. He said, "We had civil defense plans, but I don't know what happened to them. You're right, Mr. Mayor, we ought to have contingency plans at least for the *barrio*. It's a firetrap."

"I know it, Rudy," García said. "The *barrio* also goes right down to the river, and that's what started me thinking when I read about those floods in Texas. The river could be a death trap too."

"One thing, though." The police chief took his time. "You're talking about evacuating the *barrio*. Do that and you get looting." He nodded at Carlos García. "He knows. Some of those Chicano punks he tries to teach will steal anything that isn't chained down."

The mayor opened his mouth and closed it again carefully. He looked at Carlos García and waited. García said slowly, carefully, his Spanish lilt quite plain, "Unfortunately, for reasons you would not understand, Chief, what you say is only too true."

"Okay," the mayor said then, closing the door on a possible altercation. "We just take looting into consideration as one of the factors involved." His voice had hardened a trifle. "What I want from you, Rudy, and from you, Bud, are disaster plans.

Concentrate on the *barrio,* but don't forget the rest of the city."

And when the two chiefs had left, "They're hard to get along with sometimes, aren't they, Carlito?" the mayor said.

"We have our own who are just as bad," García said. "Maybe sometimes a little worse."

"Like Honest Johnny Cisneros?"

"He's a good example."

JAY GOT OUT of his car in the Williamses' courtyard. It was the evening of what had been a long, busy day, and he was tired. But he felt looser, easier in his mind than he had last night. Maybe it was because this was a business call, dealing with matters he understood, rather than a purely social engagement, at which he was never at his best. Soon he could be on his way, conscience clear.

Kate opened the door, unsmiling. "Daddy's waiting," she said, and led the way across the entrance hall to a carved door Jay had not seen before. "I didn't really know what to tell him. You didn't tell me much at Pancho's."

"You'll hear it now, if you're interested."

"I'm interested." She knocked on the door and opened it, and they walked into what was evidently Bill Williams' study.

Jay took a comfortable club chair facing Williams, who was behind a desk. Kate sat on a sofa, legs curled beneath her.

"This is your show," Williams said to Jay. He was not the affable host of last night. The change was subtle, but plain: he, too, viewed this visit as business.

"Okay," Jay said. "I don't have any charts or computer print-outs. As a matter of fact, I have little data, but what I have seems to me conclusive. I had a close look at the sides of the dam this morning, on the bottom and a little above. The rock sides of the gorge which support the dam show signs of fracturing. You had an earthquake—"

"A little one," Williams said. "We hardly felt it."

Jay nodded. "Down here, maybe. But I'm told the water in the lake sloshed the way coffee does in a cup when you carry it on a saucer. That's called a seiche, and it means there was more than a little bit of earth movement nearby. I did some telephoning to some people I know. The Richter scale reading on the seismographs was three-point-nine, and the epicenter was right in the

Harper's Park area, which is why you didn't feel the tremor as much down here. Have you noticed the others?"

"What others? There haven't been any."

"I did some more phoning after my dive this morning," Jay said. "I got some people to check back on seismograph readings for the last five years. During that time, in the area we're talking about, Harper's Park valley, there have been twenty-three measurable tremors, of which this last was the strongest."

Williams' face showed nothing. "And your conclusion?"

"That enlargement of the dam," Jay said slowly, "doesn't seem like a very good idea. The dam may not even be safe as it is. The Corps of Engineers keeps routine track of all dams of any size, and they'll have this one on their lists as 'highly hazardous'. That doesn't mean they think it's unsafe. Obviously they don't, or after their investigation they wouldn't have given you an okay for enlargement.

"What 'highly hazardous' means to them is that the dam is above a large population center, and if anything were to happen, maybe wartime and a missile strike, bombing, anything at all, why, the dam could kill a lot of people if it broke. And with 'highly hazardous' dams, I don't think you should take *any* chances."

Williams took his time. "A lot of people talked about danger when we built it. But it's still there. If you'd been here ten years ago—"

"I'd have been against building a dam," Jay said, "flooding a village and ruining a lovely valley. But I'd just have been clicking my teeth. I'm talking about something else now."

"Suppose," Williams said, "that you thought the dam was perfectly safe. How would you feel about enlarging it?"

"To get more electricity to run more hair blowers and can openers?" Jay said. "And more water for green lawns that have no business in this part of the world in the first place?" He shook his head. "I'd be against it."

Williams watched in silence, his face expressionless.

"So," Jay said, "if you're implying that my testimony is biased, then I can only say that I'm giving you my best professional advice, not advocating a personal preference. In my judgment, based on the data I have, admittedly incomplete, that dam as it stands, with no enlargement, is a potential hazard that had better be looked into very carefully."

The room was still. Williams said at last, "Let's suppose your worry is correct. What could happen? And why hasn't it happened already?"

Jay settled down to make it clear. "A few facts. The lake is close to twenty feet below normal now. Let's say, very conservatively, that the lake is ten square miles in area. That's six thousand four hundred acres. One acre-foot of water is just what it says: the amount of water it would take to cover one acre to a depth of one foot. You're with me so far?"

Nothing changed in Williams' face. "I follow you."

"Now one acre-foot of water," Jay said, "weighs a little under three million pounds. Multiply the weight of that single acre-foot of water by the number of surface acres, and multiply that by the twenty-foot depth of water that isn't there now, and you come up with just under one hundred and seventy-five million additional *tons*, not pounds, of water that the dam will have to hold back when the lake is filled to normal again. That may be why nothing has happened already: because of the drought, that additional pressure against the dam hasn't been there."

Unreal, Kate thought; and yet it was not, if the man knew what he was talking about.

"Now," Jay went on, "when the drought breaks, it may break gradually, and then again it may not. Last night's thunderstorm dumped a lot of rain somewhere in a very short time."

Williams said, "How do you know that?"

"Because the stream coming into the lake was carrying silt this morning, which meant it had been cutting, eroding, instead of flowing in its normal clear, harmless way."

Williams' accepting nod was grudging, almost imperceptible.

"But suppose," Jay continued, "the drought breaks, not gradually, with a succession of gentle rains, but all at once with four, five, six inches of rain in the mountains, the kind of break they've had in Texas. Then, instead of a slow rise of the lake level, what you get is a gully-washer banging down from those high canyons. You grew up here. You know what flash floods can do."

Again that barely perceptible nod.

"For all practical purposes," Jay said, "water, any liquid, is noncompressible. If you have a container full of water and hit it on one side with a hammer, the water doesn't give, like a sofa cushion, compressing and absorbing the shock. Instead, it transmits the force of that hammerblow in every direction without losing any of its force. If you have a weak place in the container, maybe a pane of glass on the other side, it will probably break."

Again Williams nodded. "I think I see it now."

"So," Jay said, "a flash flood of, say, a few million tons of water banging down into the head of that lake would be exactly the same as if it slammed against the dam itself. The lake water would transmit the entire impact just like the hammerblow."

Kate's eyes were fixed almost hypnotically on Jay's face.

"And if there is weakness in the supporting rock structure," Jay continued, "if the signs of fracturing I saw this morning are indicative of what I think they are, if the tremors have damaged or distorted the existing rock formations, then your dam might be unable to stand the shock of that flash flood."

Williams said tonelessly, "Go ahead."

"If the dam gives way in only one place," Jay said, "then the whole thing goes as well, because its strength is its unity. Think of Johnstown in 1889, only this would be worse, much worse, with the whole city downstream."

Kate sat motionless, her eyes turned now on her father. He had not moved in his chair and his expression had not changed. Not even his strong hands were making any of the small telltale movements that betray emotion. At that moment he was a stranger, almost a nonhuman, unaffected by the possibility of disaster. He said at last, "*If* this, and *if* that—you paint quite a picture. But as you said last night, you try not to be wrong very often."

"I could be wrong," Jay said. "I hope I am."

"But—" Kate was unable to keep silent any longer. "But you don't think you are."

Jay's face too was expressionless, and his tone betrayed nothing. "But I don't think I am." He stood up. "That's all I came to say. That, and thanks again for the dinner last night."

Williams still did not move. "What now?"

"That job in Alberta." Jay smiled gently at Kate. "I can find my way out."

"I haven't thanked you for this morning," she said, "the village, the—"

"*De nada.* It was a pleasure." He was gone.

They heard the front door close gently, and somehow Kate and her father were very much alone in an empty room.

"Still giving me the benefit of the doubt, honey?" Williams said. His smile was crooked, painful. "Let's not jump too fast." He raised one hand as Kate started to rise. "No, stick around, while I try to see where we are." He took an address book from the desk drawer, consulted it, pulled the phone close and dialed a number in Houston, Texas.

While he waited for the connection to be made, he sat quietly as before, staring through the window at the great mountains, deliberately closing his mind to the implications of the possibility Jay had suggested. There were always the doom chanters, the viewers-with-alarm, the fools who assured you the world was going to end next Tuesday at exactly half past ten.

Suddenly a quiet voice was speaking in his ear and he said, "J.G.? Bill Williams here. How are you?"

Kate sat quiet, watching her father's face.

Preliminary greetings over, Williams said at last, "A young fellow here, a geophysicist, does oil work. I wondered if you'd ever heard of him. Harper is his name, Jay Harper. He—" He stopped, and was silent, listening.

After what seemed an interminable time Williams said, "Thanks, J.G. No, it doesn't have anything to do with oil or gas. I wish to hell it did. Fly on up one of these days and I'll give you some fishing. See you." He hung up and leaned back in his chair.

"J. G. Harkness says he's one of the best, one of the new breed I don't know much about, computers and seismographs and gravity measurements, *and* the kind of mathematics you can't even read, symbols instead of numbers—" Williams stopped suddenly. "I'm babbling."

It was an admission totally unlike her father, and Kate felt a sudden pang of pity. "What are you going to do?" she said.

Her father seemed to gather himself, producing a fresh smile, almost convincing this time. "The point is, honey, you put him in an oil field with all the equipment he needs and a computer to work things out, and he's a ring-tailed whiz. But down on the bottom of a lake, just looking at rock, he's probably no better than the next guy. So I'm not going to go off half-cocked and start hollering 'Fire!' Not yet. Not by a long shot."

"You won't do—anything?"

"Of course I will, honey. I'll talk with Sam Martin, and we'll plug in the Corps of Engineers, and we'll make sure everything's all right. Maybe we'll have to patch up a little here and there. The important thing—"

"You won't—stop the project until you're sure? You'll call in other experts, geologists, people who know?"

Williams put his hands flat on the desk. "Honey," he said, "it's taken almost two years to get the enlargement plan to where it is now. You stop a project at that point, and you've killed it. Dead. Believe me, I know." He shook his head. "We'll use some caution, but we'll go ahead. It can't be as bad as Harper thinks." His smile was full-blown now. "How about the benefit of the doubt, huh? You'll see. Your old man knows what he's doing."

He watched Kate uncurl her long legs and stand up slowly, her eyes avoiding his. She said nothing as she walked out of the room, closing the door gently behind her. She does not believe my assurances, Williams told himself. And the trouble was that he didn't believe them himself.

The pikas—squirrel-sized, industrious, high-elevation cousins of the rabbit—were sunning themselves in the rocks on this fine afternoon. A vulture soared past, rocking gently in the variable updrafts, but the pikas paid no heed: no danger there; vultures were interested only in dead meat. But somewhere on the steep slope a marmot whistled, and instantly the whole slope was alert.

There was a trail of sorts, faint, in places broken away, rising in sharp switchbacks on the mountain face; and a man came up it at the slow, deliberate pace of the experienced mountain walker. He wore shorts and climbing boots over heavy socks, a khaki shirt with the sleeves rolled up, and a shapeless hat with a single vivid blue feather from the tail of a Steller's jay stuck jauntily in the band. He carried a bulging day pack and a staff, and a pair of lightweight binoculars was slung around his neck.

His name was Pete Otero. He was six inches over six feet and still held his football-playing weight of two hundred and sixty-five pounds. There was an eight-inch surgical scar on his right knee, and there were times when he wondered if the scar was in his mind as well.

He was in no hurry this fine afternoon. The Mount Union fire lookout would put him up for the night, snug and warm. Such hospitality was probably against forest service regulations, but Bernie Adams was an understanding girl, and she and Pete had long had this kind of occasional thing that worked well for both of them, something more than casual, but far less than demanding. Whose business was it but theirs, anyway?

The marmot whistled his warning again. Pete grinned at the sound, waited until the echoes had died across the high valley, and then with two fingers in his mouth blew a precisely tuned answering whistle which sent the nearby pikas skittering.

"I'm harmless, fellows," Pete said aloud. "Honest."

The trail was steep, and here at something over twelve thousand feet the air contained little oxygen, but Pete's pace was steady, his breathing deep and easy. There was nothing wrong with his wind, and the knee was as good as ever, almost. There were even times when he was tempted to turn up at a football-training camp early one fall as a free agent and give it another try. But the doctors had made it plain that one more injury of the wrong kind and Pete Otero would walk with a fused knee and a stiff leg for the rest of his life.

And so, Pete had to tell himself from time to time, you can't even dream anymore. It's too dangerous. That was the part that hurt worst of all. That was why sometimes his need for Bernie was much more than physical. Between himself and Bernie there was a kind of like-to-like attraction.

During summers Bernie deliberately chose the lonely life of a fire watcher on top of a fourteen-thousand-foot mountain, when most guys and girls her age, and his, were frolicking in weekend groups. Well, Pete, maybe because of his size, had felt that same need for withdrawal all his life. What it amounted to was that he was comfortable with Bernie just the way he was comfortable with these big mountains, the warm sun on his back, the sky that stretched from here to yonder and beyond.

It was an hour now since his last stop; time to take five. He sat on a flat-topped, sun-warmed rock and slipped off his pack. Then he unslung the binoculars and had a look around. Here, with high peaks all around, he was looking at tens of thousands of square miles of country, some of it forested, some naked rock; here and there he saw the sparkle of water, running or still; there below was the sprawl of the city's outskirts and beyond, the painted plains stretching endlessly.

Closer, he caught movement in the glasses and quickly brought into focus three mountain goats moving on a treacherous, almost nonexistent ledge as easily as if it were flat meadow. He admired their balance and agility, smiling as he thought what a running back that big fellow would make, all horns and hoofs and shifting pivots to fake a tackler right out of his socks.

He started to put the binoculars down when something else caught his attention; the sparkle of standing water where he remembered none quite so high. He studied it for a time, seeking the cause. The torrents of rain that had fallen during last night's thunderstorm, he decided, had loosened rock from the steep mountain face, and this had plunged down and across a natural bowl, what was called a hanging valley, to come to rest at the bottom and form a kind of dam behind which a small lake had formed, fed by constant seepage from rock fractures above.

There were times, Pete had often thought, when it almost seemed that the mountains arranged things to suit themselves, sometimes malevolently, as when they loosened rock slides or avalanches to trap or crush unwary humans; sometimes, as here, setting about reconstructing the landscape in whatever form and shape they chose. When you got to know the mountains, they were *alive*.

He hung the binoculars around his neck again and heaved the pack to his shoulders. When he stood up, there was stiffness in his right knee, but it no longer caused him even annoyance. Maybe, he thought as he started on up the trail again, just maybe, he was beginning to learn to live with the realization that Pete Otero was not the superman he had once thought himself to be.

MOUNTAINS, even young, jagged mountains, rarely rise to sharp, witches'-hat peaks. At 14,026 feet, Mount Union dominated the area, but its top, tilted only slightly, resembled a huge, irregular table. There was ample space for a helicopter to land with supplies for Bernie Adams in her solitary lookout post.

Pete Otero came over the rim of the table at his steady, unhurried pace, waved up at Bernie in her glassed-in eyrie, and paused, as he always did, for a brief look back. He could see now the entire course of the stream and its tributaries that flowed into Harper's Park, the lake behind the dam, and the curving gorge the river had cut below the dam—occasional wide, green meadows dotted with houses. Farther down, the silvery water curved around the Bend and entered the crowded area of the city proper.

To the west, above the setting sun, heavy clouds suspended tendrils of moisture that evaporated before it reached the ground; precipitation was a threat, but not yet an actuality. To the north the sky had darkened, and the gray cloud masses were streaked here and there with a reflected sunset glow which reddened the snowcapped Sangre de Cristo mountains.

Bernie had come out on the walk-around porch of the lookout. She wore, as usual, faded jeans, wool socks, leather moccasins and a flannel shirt. A large malamute dog appeared beside her and stood quiet, watching. Bernie was smiling. "Did you just walk up to admire the view?"

Pete nodded solemnly. "More or less."

"Then have your look and walk right back down again."

"Where am I going to cook this steak I brought? And drink the wine?"

"Under those circumstances," Bernie said, "I guess we'll have to put up with you." She snapped her fingers at the dog. "Go down and bring him up, Buddy."

Inside the lookout it was warm despite the growing chill outside. "Wonderful stuff, solar heat," Bernie said. "Sun coming through this double-paned glass—" She stopped, suddenly shy. For a few moments there was silence between them. "Well," she said, "aren't you going to take that thing off your back?"

Pete slipped off the bulging day pack and handed it to her. Even using both hands it was an effort for her to carry it to the sink shelf. She was smiling. "A burro wouldn't carry this up that trail. Neither would a mule."

"I'm not as smart as either one."

"Cut that out. You hear? How's the knee?"

"As good as it's ever going to be," Pete said, "which is good enough for anything I'll need it for."

Bernie said slowly, carefully, "I read you were in Hollywood."

His smile was crooked. "Old football players never die; they just go to tinsel town. You see a lot of old friends, Jimmy Brown, Karras, O.J., Woody Strode—I watched him when I was a kid." Pete shook his head.

"But you came back."

He nodded. "There was somebody I wanted to see."

Bernie's fingers were not quite steady as she undid the day pack. She said at last, "I'm glad. Very glad, Pete." And then quickly, "Will you open the wine?"

They sat on the sofa bed with their drinks, companionably close while they watched the last of the flaming sunset fade quickly and disappear.

"I could turn on the radio," Bernie said. She spoke a little too fast. "Up here I can get every FM station and every TV channel without any kind of outside antenna. Would you like some music?"

"Not now." Pete was watching the girl carefully. There were overtones, harmonics he did not understand. "Something's wrong, Bernie. What's bugging you?"

She shivered. "I'm scared. Have you ever been scared, Pete?"

"Hell, yes."

"I've never been scared before up here. I've been through winds and blizzards and thunderstorms—but not like last night, never like that. Hailstones—" she made a circle with her thumb and forefinger "—that big. Thunder that wasn't thunder—it was explosions. Lightning I could almost see strike. Buddy and I were right in the middle of it. He crawled into bed with me, and I- pulled the covers up over our heads and it went on and on—"

"Easy," Pete said. He laid one large hand on hers and squeezed with gentle strength. "It's all over now."

Bernie shook her head. "And then I dreamed," she said. "It was a nightmare really. All summer we've had fires. I've lost count. No rain. And then last night, that storm and the dream."

She looked up at Pete's face. "I never thought I was a hysterical female, Pete, but sooner or later droughts end. Last night was just a warning. I know it. And when this dry spell ends—"

"Go on," Pete said.

"That view you admire," Bernie said. "I admire it too. Every day. I look down on the real world and it's—beautiful. But what do you think Noah must have felt when he looked down from the top of that mountain after the rains had stopped and the water had receded? That's what the dream was. I looked down from here after it was all over and saw—nothing!"

KATE WILLIAMS drove up the Harper's Park road. It was almost dark now, and the headlights of her little sports car seemed to carve a tunnel in the gloom.

Dinner with her father had been filled with long, awkward pauses during which the sounds of silverware on china seemed overloud.

"I think you should tell the governor, Daddy," she had said at one point, not even bothering to identify the subject as the dam, since Jay's recent discourse was very much on both their minds.

"There's nothing to tell him yet, so let's forget it, honey. I told you Sam and I would look into it."

"Sam Martin," she said with scorn.

"You used to think Sam was quite a fellow. He hasn't changed."

"No," Kate said, "I did—while I was away."

Bill Williams' voice took on a defensive note. "It was your mother's idea to send you East," he said.

"I know. But it wasn't just the East that changed me. It was Mother's dying."

"That changed pretty much of everything."

"You wouldn't let me come home."

"There wasn't anything you could do, honey. There was no need to put you through all the—bad part."

There was another awkward silence until Kate said at last, "That was when I changed, Daddy. When I realized I was useless."

"You aren't useless!"

"I was." And maybe I still am, she thought now, as she drove through the gathering darkness up the winding mountain road. But at least I can do what I think is right.

HAD JAY HARPER known about those twenty-three earlier tremors, he told himself, he would not, repeat, not have made that second dive. And in that case he would not have seen the signs of fracturing in the rock sides which supported the dam. Mere suspicions would have carried no weight at all. On the other hand, what he had told Williams hadn't seemed to make much impression anyway, so it was probably all effort wasted. But he had tried, his conscience was clear, and now his stick floated toward Alberta.

He looked around the motel room to make sure he had missed nothing in his packing. To the telephone, then, to call the Alberta number. Cooley's voice filled the room almost immediately, as if he had been sitting waiting for the call. "You clear now, boy? Then make it the Palliser Hotel in Calgary. Did you find whatever the heck it was you were looking for?"

Jay smiled at the wall. Jed's gravestone and Julia's, and signs of danger no one seemed to heed—a mixed bag, Jay thought. "Yes and no," he said to Cooley, "but I had a couple of nice swims."

"There are times," Cooley said judiciously, "when I don't think you play with a full deck of cards. You—"

There was a knock at Jay's door. "Hold it," he said to Cooley. He raised his voice. "Come in!"

The door opened and Kate Williams stood quiet in the doorway. Her face was troubled. "I'm interrupting. I'm sorry. But please. It's important."

Jay hesitated only a moment. "I'll call you back," he said into the phone and hung up. He stood up to face the girl. "Come in."

She came slowly into the room and shut the door behind her. She had her father's assurance, perhaps his stubbornness as well, Jay thought. Maybe arrogance was the proper word. "Sit down," he said. "What can I do for you?"

Kate sat in the single chair. "After you left," she began, "Daddy telephoned a friend of his—J. G. Harkness—in Houston. He told Daddy you were one of the best. Do you know him?"

"I've done work for him. I don't think he'd complain. But I still don't know why you're here."

"To ask you to stay." Her eyes did not leave his face.

"Did your father send you?"

"He doesn't even know I'm here. Do you fly?"

"Sometimes, on jobs. I'm not a pilot."

"I am."

Yes, Jay thought, you would be. You probably have a number of other expensive hobbies too. "So?"

"I know how the river rises. I've seen the hundreds of tiny tributaries." She watched Jay nod. "The flash flood you described—it could happen. All these mountains drain right down into Harper's Park, just the way you said. I'm not talking about just another flash flood. I'm talking about the kind of—I hate to use the word—catastrophe that you described. If you saw it all from the air—"

Jay shrugged. "I've seen the maps. And there's nothing I can do to change it. So?"

Kate said slowly, "I am trying to like you, or at least not to dislike you, not that it makes any difference to you. But you resent me—"

"What is it you want me to do?"

"Stay over here just tonight, and then fly with me tomorrow morning."

"Tell me why."

"Because I have—faith in you," Kate said. "Sam Martin, even Daddy—they've gone too far to admit they're wrong." Her tone was bitter.

"And all you want me to do is change everybody's mind, lead them out of the wilderness." Jay shook his head angrily. "Look. In my business I do my computations, make my reports and my recommendations. I've done that here. Once over very lightly, true, but I wasn't even asked in the first place, so I think I've done more than my share."

"You've satisfied your conscience, is that it?"

Damn the woman, Jay thought. She saw too deep. "Put it that way if you want."

Kate said, "Do you remember what you said to Daddy and me: 'Think of Johnstown in 1889, only this would be worse, much worse, with the whole city downstream.'"

"You're a real Bible banger when you get started, aren't you?"

"Look, will you stay? And fly with me in the morning? You might see something that isn't on the maps, something no one else has noticed, but that might mean something to you. New evidence to convince Daddy."

"You're going to be awfully disappointed," Jay said.

"Then you'll stay?" Her smile appeared quickly.

"Okay." In the simple word there was resignation. "If only to show you there's nothing I can do."

"Thank you. Thank you very much." Her eyes were no longer unfathomable. She rose from the chair.

"Just tell me where and when to meet you in the morning," Jay said, angry with her, and with himself.

He stood in the doorway of the motel room and watched Kate walk to her car. For the first time, he thought, they were on even terms, and he could look at her now, not as the daughter of a local big wheel but as a very attractive woman.

He went back inside, closed the door and walked to the telephone to call Cooley again. He had a fleeting feeling that he was losing control of the situation, that events were gaining the upper hand. Nonsense, of course.

56

6

When Brooks Thompson came home that evening, Mary sat expressionless on the sofa. The newspaper was folded on the coffee table in front of her. "How did it go?" she asked tonelessly.

"Well, I'll say one thing," Brooks said. "Gentry does what he says he'll do. The papers were all waiting, all in order, bill of sale and a certified check." He sat down beside Mary on the sofa and put his arm around her shoulders. "I think now we can make it go."

Suddenly her shoulders were shaking, and tears were running down her face, dropping unheeded into her lap.

Brooks caught her chin with one hand and raised her head. "What's the matter?"

She pointed at the coffee table and the folded newspaper. "I—" She stopped and tried again. "I—tried to call you. But the bank switchboard—was—closed!"

Brooks released her and reached for the paper. He unfolded it slowly, and stared for long, silent moments at the banner headline: DAM ENLARGEMENT APPROVED.

He set the paper down gently. "So the property Gentry just paid twenty-two thousand five hundred for," he said quietly, "is going to be worth at least ten times that when the lake is enlarged." He put his arm around Mary again. "I was right the first time, wasn't I? He is what Wall Street calls a gunslinger. And I can think of other names for him too."

Mary's voice was unsteady. "My fault. I—pushed you."

Brooks shook his head and squeezed her shoulders. "No fault, no blame. Just damage done. To us."

BILL WILLIAMS sat behind his desk, and Sam Martin, summoned, sat in one of the leather visitor's chairs pulled up close. Sam had rolls of drawings on the table, but so far Williams had refused to look at them.

"Sam," he said, "what about the rock fracturing Harper says he saw? How strong is that dam, anyway?"

Sam was less than comfortable. Williams in this kind of mood was unpredictable. "We designed it properly," Sam said, "and we built it well—what else can I say, Bill?"

"Since then we've had not one earthquake, but according to

Harper, twenty-three of them. How do we know what damage they might have done?"

"The dam doesn't show any signs of weakness," Sam said. "I've been down below it and there's nothing to show any problems."

It was a good point. From the downstream side the entire dam structure was exposed, unlike the lake side, where you had to dive to have a look. Still, Williams pushed back his chair, got up, walked to the windows and stood looking out at the mountains, his back to the office. "We've put a lot of work into this enlargement idea, Sam," he said without turning. His voice was quiet, thoughtful.

"And money, Bill. And you stand to make it all back, and then some, if we go ahead as planned."

Williams turned to study Sam's face. "What does that mean?"

There was something in Williams' manner that made Sam even more uncomfortable. "Is it a secret, Bill? The Harrison property you bought up by the dam? I mean, if I'm not supposed to know about it, okay, it's forgotten. No business of mine."

Williams walked back to his desk, lowered himself into his chair and put his hands flat on the desk top. His movements were deliberate. His eyes had not left Sam's face. "It's no secret, Sam, but I'm just wondering where you happened to hear about it. Have you been talking to George Harrison by any chance?"

"He bought me a drink yesterday."

"And what did George have on his mind? The enlargement?"

"He wanted to know how it was going. I didn't see any harm in talking about it, Bill. Was there?"

"No harm at all. And then he happened to mention the property he sold me?"

"Well, yes, I guess he did."

"What did he want you to do, Sam?"

Sam shook his head with emphasis. "He didn't ask me to do anything. We just—talked. He asked me what I thought of the idea of making the dam bigger. Was it necessary? Was it safe?"

"And what did you tell him?"

"The same thing I've been telling you." Sam's hand went automatically to the rolled drawings as if to draw strength from the precise lines and dimensions they contained. "Just because some character we don't even know goes diving with scuba gear, Bill, we suddenly begin to sweat about all the engineering and the planning we've done. Does that make sense?"

Williams sat for a long time in silence, his eyes fixed on the far wall. He said at last, "Maybe not, Sam. Let's think about it." He raised one hand in a gesture of caution. "But let's not talk about it while we're thinking. Not to anybody. Is that clear?"

"I won't talk." Sam gathered the rolls of drawings and walked out with a feeling of relief.

FROM THE Mount Union lookout that early morning, the world consisted of islands in a sea of white mist that stretched to infinity. Above, the sky was clear, blue, directly overhead almost purple, and although the air was chill, the sun was already beginning to warm the day.

"Sometimes on mornings like this," Bernie said, "I pretend that I'm the last person on earth. But—" she smiled with sudden brilliance "—I like it better like this, with one other inhabitant, preferably large and male."

Suddenly, without warning, the radio loudspeaker came to life. A voice was speaking what sounded to Pete like gibberish, and Bernie smiled. "That's Charlie Hunt. He takes a little getting used to." She listened for a few moments. "A real low-pressure system moving one hundred and fifteen degrees—that's our direction from him—carrying a full bucket, which is Charlie's way of saying we've got some kind of precipitation coming. Now, how about breakfast?"

They sat out on the encircling porch with their cups of coffee and watched the white mist burn off and the valleys and canyons begin to appear beneath them. "I never get tired of it," Bernie said. "It's always a surprise, like the packages under the tree on Christmas morning. The air warms up, the water vapor evaporates, and there's the world again, just the way you left it last night." She glanced at Pete, smiling again. "Well, not quite the way I left it last night. This morning it looks a lot better."

"It does for me too." Pete's long legs were stretched out. His eyes went to the surgical scar on his knee, and then quickly away. He was aware that Bernie watched him, but she said nothing.

She looked at her watch. "Time for the full weather report." She got out of her chair. "Why don't you sit here and enjoy the sun?" She walked inside, and voice sounds began almost immediately on the muted speaker.

Bernie had her life pretty well together, Pete thought, which was a lot more than he could say for himself. And although he hadn't really thought about it before, it was probably vague guilt feelings about his own lack of direction, feeling as he did about Bernie, which had brought him up that long trail yesterday, to sit here looking out at the world and do some thinking. He glanced again at the scar. Eventually, of course, he would have had to face the question: what next? Decision time was suddenly now, long before he had expected it.

No fairy godmother was going to wave a wand and set Pete Otero up as a resident millionaire. It was going to be just the way it had always been: anything he got was going to be the result of his going after it. So all right, already. That was what Tim Bernstein from Flatbush, the best defensive end Pete had ever played with, used to say when he dug in and defied anybody to try to go through, around or over him. That's my thought for the day, Pete told himself, and felt suddenly, unaccountably better.

He sat quietly, relaxed in the sun. Then, looking down at the city, he watched a small, sleek red airplane taxi to the head of the municipal airport runway, make its run, and lift off gracefully, tucking its wheels into its belly and reaching for the sky. He wondered idly who was in it and where they were going.

"We've got weather coming," Bernie said at his shoulder. "Of course, that's a maybe. These last months a lot of storms have looked as if they were coming right at us and then changed their minds and swung away. But this one, coming down from the north looks serious, and if it and Charlie's little number with the full bucket collide, we could catch it." Her voice was solemn.

"Go on," Pete said. He looked up at her face. "You're saying something, aren't you?"

"I guess what I'm saying," Bernie said, "is that you'd better split now, or figure you might have to stay awhile. You don't want to be caught on the mountainside in a big one." Her hand touched his shoulder with affection. "But I don't want you to go. Not yet."

"Why, then," Pete said, and covered her hand with his, "it's settled, isn't it?" His own problems could wait a little. "Lady, I like it right here on our mountaintop."

KATE FLEW the sleek red plane with almost professional competence, Jay thought, as he was sure she did many things. It was easy to picture her riding a horse, swimming, driving a car, playing tennis or golf with effortless grace.

He settled down to study the terrain below.

Jay had seen the topographical maps, as he had told Kate, and had one open on his lap now. The contour lines crowded close on the map indicated steep slopes or even sheer cliffs; but the reality—steep rock faces dropping into darkness, bottomless canyons into which the sun would penetrate only for short hours or even minutes a day—these seemed features of another world. In north-facing crevices and hollows, last year's snow still held. Here a steep talus slope testified to exfoliation, the relentless erosion of alternating heat and cold, expansion and contraction, water seepage expanding into ice during the night hours.

"Oxygen," Kate said, and handed him a mask. She already wore her own, and her voice was muffled. "We'll be up above fifteen thousand, and it can sneak up on you."

Jay put on the mask without a word.

From this height, the dam and the lake as they passed over them looked small indeed, like toy representations of the real thing. There was the stream that fed the lake, and there were its countless tributaries, some gleaming faintly with running water, some dry now but easy enough to pick out from the way they extended upward from the main stream course like branches of a tree. On the flat top of the highest peak Jay saw a fire-lookout building. From its walkway someone waved, and he waved back.

He had warned Kate to expect nothing, Jay told himself, and yet his professional pride rebelled at the thought of returning to the ground entirely empty-handed. Where they were now, a thousand feet above the highest mountains, the view was awesome; more mountains, some snow-covered, stretched northwest as far as visibility went. It was through this unknown, tangled mass, Jay thought, that old Jed Harper and others like him had found their lonely way. Whatever else they might have been, and some of them were probably unsavory types, they were men.

Beside him Kate seemed to be waiting for some kind of signal. That sense of professional pride made Jay swing his hand in a circular motion, and speaking with difficulty around the edge of the mask, he said, "Maintain this altitude, but swing back over the lake and dam again." At once the horizon shifted as they began a wide, swinging turn.

As the ground moved slowly beneath them—illusion, of course—Jay caught the gleam of standing water near the top of a high canyon; it was the same new lake Pete Otero had noticed yesterday, created by the thunderstorm and trapped behind its natural dam. Jay searched in vain on the map for a small lake where the standing water was. Strange. He marked the spot, and resumed his study of the ground.

They were coming over the dam now, and although he had no idea what he might be looking for, he searched carefully every slope, every canyon, every steep drop-off and peak. Now the dam was behind them, and ahead was the curve of the Bend and then the city sprawling in the morning sun. Kate was watching his face, and Jay wished she would not. In sheer exasperation he repeated the circling motion with his hand. Instantly Kate obeyed, the wing dropped, and they began their return swing to the dam.

The early low sun came in slantwise, creating elongated shadows and strange, almost surrealistic effects. The curving top of the dam seemed to continue beyond the edge of the gorge, as if Sam Martin in his engineering had forgotten to stop. On the opposite side of the gorge there was a corresponding line.

A trick of the light, no more. *Or was it?*

Kate's eyes were on his face, and she said, "What do you see?"

Jay shook his head in silence. He studied the map. There was nothing there to explain the shadow that was almost a straight line. He looked at his watch and checked the time: 8:22; their altitude: 15,000 feet. He marked the data on the map.

Kate's questioning eyes had not left his face. "I don't know," Jay said. It was no time to throw out half-baked theories. "I want to think about it." They were over the dam now. "Let's make one more pass from the downstream side."

This time the shadow was gone. "Okay," Jay said. "We can pack it in now. I've seen all I'm going to see." If I've seen anything at all, he thought.

They landed, taxied to the hangar and got out. "When you make up your mind," Kate said, "perhaps you will let me know what your conclusions are. Thank you for staying and having a look, anyway." She walked to her car, her back straight, started the engine and drove away.

Jay walked slowly to his rented car. A prickly, unpredictable female, he thought, used to having her own way. He was tempted to get on the next plane to Canada. But there was that matter of professional pride, and the puzzle of that disappearing shadow;

62

it bothered him because he was not sure that he understood it.

Wrong, he told himself; he was pretty sure he did know what that disappearing illusion was. And again the feeling was strong that events were getting the upper hand. He had told himself that, in old Jed's phrase, his stick floated toward Alberta. Now he was not at all sure.

A car speeding into the airport parking lot swung in a tight curve, throwing gravel, and slid to a stop beside Jay. Sam Martin was out of the car almost before it stopped moving. Sam was still uncomfortable after the scene with Bill Williams, and now his annoyance had a new focus. "I saw Kate's plane in the air," he said, "and I met her driving away just now. Were you flying with her?" A large solid man, truculent now. "Well, were you?"

Jay tossed the topographical map into his car. Over his shoulder he said, "Why don't you ask her?" He opened the car door.

"I'm asking *you.* Answer me!" Sam caught Jay's arm just above the elbow.

After that, things happened a little too fast for immediate comprehension. Jay spun like a dancer, threw off the hand, caught Sam's wrist in mid-air and delivered a chop that paralyzed Sam's forearm. Then, standing balanced, he said quietly, "Don't ever lay a hand on me again. Is that understood?"

Sam was holding the hurt arm with his good hand in angry bewilderment. No words came to mind.

"What I do is my own business," Jay said. "Remember that." He got into his car, closed the door, started the engine and drove unhurriedly away. Sam, still holding his hurt arm, watched him go.

Jay drove back up the same road he had traveled this morning, past the curve of the Bend, with the fine houses which were almost estates, climbing steadily to Harper's Park valley. There he pulled the car to the side of the road and sat studying the dam and the sides of the rock gorge.

He could see nothing to explain the optical illusion he had seen from the air. But he knew what it was, he told himself; all he needed was corroboration. One more step, he thought, and then he'd walk away, back to his own world.

He drove on to the motel, and called Alberta. "I need help, Cooley," he said, "and you're the best rock man I know."

"Flattery isn't going to buy you a thing," Cooley said, when he had listened in silence for a time. "I don't know anything about dams, and I don't want to. All I want—"

"Maybe you didn't hear me, Cooley. I need help."

Cooley said at last, "Okay, I owe you a couple. I'll come down. You say they've got an airport there?"

"And a pretty girl to fly you in the morning for a look-see. You can sit right next to her and everything."

"Now you've fallen in love, is that it? Okay, I'll let you know when I get there. Today sometime, I suppose."

One more telephone call, this one to Kate. "Can we fly again tomorrow morning?" Jay said. "Three of us, same time?"

Kate's voice was cool. "Am I allowed to know who, and why?"

"The best rock man I know. I want him to see what I saw this morning, if it's really there."

There was silence on the line. Kate's voice said at last, "The airport. Same time." She hung up.

In the large, air-conditioned, paneled office above Pine Street, the sounds of New York traffic were muted. The intercom on the desk buzzed, and Spencer Willoughby's secretary's modulated voice said, "Mrs. Brooks Thompson is calling, Mr. Willoughby."

Willoughby picked up the phone, smiling. "Hello, dear. Are you making the desert bloom?"

"We're trying, Daddy, but I'm afraid we're not setting the world on fire yet."

"Is this a social call, or is there something I can do for you?"

Always he had been able to see right through her, Mary thought. Even two thousand miles away he had caught immediately the overtones of pain and frustration. "What do you do, Daddy, when you've been—cheated?"

"That's a hard one, dear," Willoughby said. "Do you want to tell me the story?"

He listened quietly, expressionless, and when Mary had finished he said, "Yes, I see why you and Brooks are upset."

"It's our own fault," Mary said. "I can't deny that. The trouble is, it's more my fault than Brooks'. He mistrusted Mr. Gentry's motives from the beginning, but he let me talk him into selling the land. I talked to Mr. Gentry just before I called you."

Willoughby said quietly, "And?"

"He was not very—pleasant. He said we should have stayed in the East. I guess I can't blame him."

But I can, Willoughby thought. And to Mary, "I'm sorry I have no solution to suggest, dear, but I will say one thing. It won't help much, but maybe it will give you a little consolation. Far more experienced people than you and Brooks have been cheated. Badly."

"Thanks, Daddy. I feel better just for having talked to you."

Willoughby hung up and leaned back in his desk chair. It was beautiful country to which Mary and Brooks had gone, he thought; secretly he did not blame them. Gentry's single reported remark to Mary, that she and Brooks should have stayed in the East, told volumes. The effete East, Gentry was saying, as opposed to the West, where men were men, etc, etc.

Well, sometimes we Ivy Leaguers know how to play hardball too, Willoughby thought. He leaned forward to flip the intercom switch. "I want to speak to Mr. Thomas Gentry, please. He is president of the First National Bank. . . ."

The call went through quickly. "This is Mr. Gentry."

"This is Spencer Willoughby in New York, Mr. Gentry. I am just about to telephone an old friend of mine in Los Angeles. Henry Warfield. He is president and major stockholder of the holding company which owns your bank, among numerous others."

"I know who he is." There was uncharacteristic caution in Gentry's voice.

"I am going to tell Henry a sordid little tale about one of his bank presidents. It concerns dubious use of inside information, and deliberate fleecing of one of the bank's customers. I shouldn't be surprised if it also concerns hasty arrangement of the kind of 'insider loan' which the comptroller of the currency, who is also a friend of mine, is viewing with considerable displeasure these days. I can guess at Henry Warfield's reaction. Can you?"

"Who the hell are you?"

"I told you, Mr. Gentry. My name is Spencer Willoughby. My office is on Pine Street in New York City. Mrs. Brooks Thompson is my daughter. When you are looking for a new job and seeking references, I would not suggest you ask her or her husband, but you might remember them. Good day."

Gentry hung up angrily. The idea of some Easterner threatening him was almost more than he could take. Maybe, he thought, somebody was running a bluff. That was it. Gentry had sat around poker tables himself, lots of them. In his phone book he looked up the direct number of his good friend at the holding company headquarters in Los Angeles. He dialed with a steady hand.

"Joe? Tom Gentry here. I just got a phone call from New York. Fellow calling himself Spencer Willoughby. You know the New York scene. Does the name mean anything to you?"

When Joe spoke, his voice was filled with something very much like awe. "You really are playing in the big leagues, Tom," he said. "Spencer Willoughby? I don't know him, but I sure know *of* him. You've heard of the Chase-City Bank, number two in the world and gaining ground? Well, Spencer Willoughby is their general counsel, among other things. He sits on their board and on half a dozen other little boards like GM and AT&T and IBM. Look him up in *Who's Who* if you don't believe me."

"Never mind. Thanks, Joe."

Gentry hung up. For fifty lousy mountain acres, he thought, and the profit on twenty-two thousand five hundred lousy bucks, he had walked into this mess. Damn!

His telephone buzzed and he picked it up with a jerk. "Yes?"

"Mr. George Harrison is here to see you, Mr. Gentry."

George Harrison probably had some inconsequential beef on his mind. On the other hand, George sat on the bank's board, a position he had inherited from his father, who had put up some of the original capital to form the bank. Tom Gentry was in no position to make any enemies. He might be needing every friend he could lay hands on. "Send Mr. Harrison in," he said, and hoped when he stood up from his desk that he looked as if nothing had happened to disturb him.

When George Harrison thought back upon it later, he found in his conversation with Tom Gentry that morning a strange sense of unreality. It was not quite as if he entered a tiger's cage and found a purring pussycat, but there *was* a quality of make-believe.

"The long and short of it," he confessed to Tom with some pain, "is that Bill Williams out-sniggled me in buying my land by the dam. My pride is hurt. I admit it. But I am also concerned as a matter of principle. I am outraged when someone like Bill Williams turns what amounts to inside information on the dam enlargement to his own profit. Aren't you?"

Gentry's poker face showed nothing. "Why," he said, "as a matter of fact, yes, I guess I am."

"Williams will bid on the construction," George said, "and no doubt will be successful. In such matters a construction loan is customary, is it not?"

"It is."

"Will this bank be asked for the loan?"

"I would assume so, George."

"What would it take to ensure our refusal?"

Gentry's reaction surprised Harrison. He had not expected such a mild, almost favorable response. Gentry's gray eyes widened a trifle, and he appeared to be thinking hard of something George could not even guess at. Strange.

Gentry said at last, "It would take only a majority vote of the directors, George. You have some influence, and if you are determined—"

"I am."

"Then it might turn out to be a horse race as to whether the dam enlargement goes through."

And if I could show Warfield even a close vote, Gentry thought, and convince him that I was actually trying to help the Brooks Thompsons out of their financial dilemma by buying their land instead of conning them out of it for my own benefit, it might turn out all right.

Of course, Gentry was also thinking that if the enlargement project failed to go through because Bill Williams didn't get his construction loan, then he, Tom Gentry, would be left with fifty acres of property which he needed like a hole in the head, and a twenty-two-thousand-five-hundred-dollar loan to pay off. But that would be better than being tossed out of the bank.

"Loan applications," George Harrison was saying, "don't normally go to the board of directors for decision, Tom."

"But in a matter of this importance, George," Gentry said, "where a great deal of money will be involved, it is at my discretion whether a decision is requested from the board."

"And you would bring it to the board's attention?"

"Under the circumstances, I think I might very well."

"I appreciate this, Tom," George said.

Gentry smiled. "I am considering the best interests of us all."

Strange.

BILL WILLIAMS came home for lunch, something he rarely did. His need for companionship, however, was urgent today, and he hoped Kate might be at the house. She was. They sat on the *portal* facing the great mountains, while Carmen, the maid, quietly set a table for two in the dining room. "I saw your plane in the air this morning, honey," Williams said. "Young Harper with you?"

"He was. He saw something, but I don't know what it was, and he says he isn't sure either. We're going up again tomorrow and taking along what he calls 'the best rock man I know.'"

"I'd like to know what they think," said Williams. "Tell Harper that, will you?"

Kate studied her father's face. "You're worried."

"Not really." Williams' smile belonged at a poker table, but from her mother Kate had learned that seeing through a man's pretenses was no excuse for accusing him of them.

She was silent for a few moments, staring up at the canyon where the river dropped out of the mountains. She shivered suddenly. "When I left the airport," she said, "I went to the library and took out a book on the Johnstown flood, the one in 1889, when the dam collapsed. A wall of water thirty feet high, twenty-two hundred people killed—" She turned to look at her father. "Jay Harper said this would be much worse, with the whole city downstream."

"Honey, the easiest thing in the world to start is a panic rumor. You're dreaming up a nightmare—the way you did when you were a little girl."

As they sat down to eat, Williams said, "I had a letter from Bud Wilks this morning. He's living in Honolulu now, and he says why don't I come on over and spend a few weeks. Would you like to go? I watched you the other night when Harper was talking about places he's been. You're tied down here."

"I'm tied down only by choice, Daddy. I'm right where I want to be."

"You need a man. Sam Martin wants to marry you."

"I know."

"You could do worse."

"That's a poor criterion."

"Okay," Williams said, smiling. "I never got anywhere arguing with your mother either. But at least we aren't talking about that dam."

"But we're both still thinking about it, aren't we? Do you still want to know what Jay Harper and his geologist think after we fly tomorrow morning?"

Williams nodded slowly. "I'd be a fool not to, honey. I may be pretty well over the hill, but I don't think I'm that far into senility yet."

"You," Kate said, "over the hill?" She shook her head, smiling, hiding the pain she felt at the concept. "That will be the day. Eat your lunch."

For a time Williams ate obediently, but what was in his mind would not go away. Was this why he had wanted to come home for lunch today, why he had hoped that Kate would be here?

The mind played funny tricks, no doubting that. He said slowly, "What are you going to do, honey, when I'm not here any-more?"

"Daddy!"

"Don't try to brush it off," Williams said. "I won't last forever. I want you to think about it. What'll you do?"

"Miss you. Just the way I miss Mother. But let's not talk about it now."

Williams shook his head. "Sooner or later we're going to have to talk about it. I don't want to make a big deal out of it, but when your heart begins behaving in a way that you notice it, where you never even gave it a thought before—well, then, you start getting the message that you aren't going to live forever, and you start thinking about things you've put off attending to."

Kate, suddenly close to tears, could only nod in silence.

"You're the main thing, of course." Williams said, his voice fond and gentle. "I'd like to see you married." He held his hand up quickly. "Let me finish. I'd like to see you married *and* happy about it. That's the first thing. Okay?"

Again Kate could only nod.

"Now this house," Williams said. "You call it home. That's fine, that's great. But it was *our* home, your mother's and mine. We built it and changed it around until it was the way *we* wanted it. If you want to stay here, fine. If you don't, get rid of it. If we're where we can know about it, we'll understand."

She had mastered the tears now and could trust her voice. "I'll remember. Promise."

"Good. Now I don't know what to do about the business. You'll own it, but who's going to run it? Not Sam. If you tell Sam what to do he's fine, but somebody has to tell him first. Well, I'll try to think of something." Suddenly Williams looked uncomfortable. "Now there's one more thing, and maybe it's the most important of all."

"Daddy, please. You make it sound as if—"

Williams shook his head again, stopping the protest. "I've given this a lot of thought, honey," he said, "and this is something I've been wanting to say, not just write down for you to read after I'm gone. I'm no good at writing down things I feel. Hear me out."

Her tears close again, Kate managed a single word, "Okay."

"You aren't going to be the richest girl in the West, honey, but you're going to have quite a pile. I've been stashing money away like a pack rat ever since my first paper route. And that's what I want to talk about. *Enjoy* it! Blow the bundle, if you want— although you'll have one hell of a time doing it—but *enjoy* it. After your mother died, and it was too late, I realized what a fool I'd been because I was always more interested in adding to the pile than in enjoying what was already there. Don't you make that mistake. You get some pleasure out of it. Remember that. Okay?"

Kate nodded, swallowed and managed a faint smile. Her voice was not quite steady. "Okay," she said.

COOLEY PARKS got off the plane carrying a worn canvas kit bag. In it were a geologist's pick, a spare pair of pants, a pair of light-weight, worn boots, toilet gear, a shirt, socks, his passport and a bottle of whiskey. With that bag, and the clothes he stood in, Cooley was prepared to go any place in the world.

"What kind of a wild-goose chase is this, anyway, boy?" Cooley's voice echoed in the passenger terminal.

"I hope that's all it is. Then I'll apologize, and we'll head for Canada as fast as we can go."

Cooley's eyes, pale blue in his lined, tanned face, looked long and carefully at Jay. "And if it isn't?" His voice now was quieter.

"I haven't thought that far ahead. Have you eaten?"

Cooley held a thumb and forefinger about two and a half inches apart. "What about a steak like so, nice and rare? And maybe some talk along with it?"

"You have a deal." They walked out to Jay's car.

The steaks were large and rare and good. Cooley ate, listened, and drank quantities of Danish beer. He said at last, "I always wondered where you came from. This figures. Your three-times great-granddaddy, huh?"

"California," Jay said. "That's where I come from. You know that."

"No. There had to be big mountains, like these, in your background. But let it go for now, boy. Want to tell me what you thought you saw from the plane this morning?"

"I want you to see it without any preconceptions."

"I told you, I don't know a thing about dams—except they hold back water, lots of water, and every now and again one of them comes apart at the seams. That's what's worrying you?"

"Actually," Jay said, "it's none of my business."

"No?" Cooley's smile was amused. "Look, your three-times great-granddaddy's country's got hold of you. And maybe the girl too. Is she pretty? Or maybe rich? Always pick one or the other. And bear in mind that most times money lasts longer than looks."

It was still light enough to see when they drove out of the city, around the Bend and along the course of the river into the canyon that climbed to Harper's Park.

Cooley, sitting quiet and relaxed in the passenger seat, let his eyes swing from side to side, studying rock formations, the river's course, the high, sloping canyon walls. "Igneous and metamorphic rock," he said. "Nothing sedimentary right in here. I picked up a geologic map of the area before I left Canada. I was looking at it a bit on the plane."

Which meant, Jay thought, that a detailed picture was already clear and vivid in Cooley's intuitive mind, and that he knew right now, and would know tomorrow in the plane, precisely what he was looking at, and even possibly what he was looking for.

They came around the final turn in the climbing road and there was the dam, blocking the gorge, rising high above the stream and the generating plant. Cooley whistled softly. "All I can say, boy, is that if that thing decides to let go, I want to be above it, not below it. The water is how deep, you say?"

"About eighty feet, twenty feet below normal."

"And the gradient of that stream above the lake?"

"In places it's nearly vertical," Jay said. "In fact, there are a couple of waterfalls upstream, and some of those hanging valleys and high canyons that feed down have sheer drop-offs."

"Correction," Cooley said. "If this thing decides to let go, I don't want to be above it, I want to be fifteen hundred miles away in Canada."

"Wait till you see it tomorrow from the air."

ONCE AGAIN Bill Williams sat on the governor's *portal* with the moonlight making the nearby mountains seem ghostly, unreal.

"It isn't like you to twist and squirm, Bill," the governor was saying. "You've always come right out and said what was on your mind. Now you're fancy-footing around. You've lost some of your enthusiasm for the dam enlargement?"

"I didn't say that. Not exactly."

The governor sighed. "But you're thinking it? Why?"

"I don't have any reasons. Not real ones." He shouldn't have come, Williams told himself; it was a foolish thing to have done. He sipped his drink in silence.

"Bill," the governor said, "aside from the fact that I don't like to look any more fickle or stupid than the next man, I simply cannot afford to. We have pushed this project through Washington channels pleading urgent need. We have pounded on desks and twisted arms. We have used the state's natural resources as bargaining chips. And all to get federal cooperation on this dam-enlargement project. Now before I make any change in my position, Bill, I am going to have to have some very good reasons."

Williams got out his pillbox and popped a tablet in his mouth. "A character went swimming in scuba gear," he began. "He just wanted a good look at Harper's Park village because it was named after his three-times great-granddaddy, and he'd heard about it all his life. He dove and he looked, and he found some things, he says, down at the bottom of the dam where it ties into the sides of the gorge. . . ."

The governor listened quietly, and when Williams finished, sat for a long time in silence. At last he said, "And what is your assessment, Bill?"

"I don't know, Harry, and that's the honest truth. But before we go ahead, we'd better make sure."

"You seem to be putting a considerable amount of faith in this Harper, whom you scarcely know."

"J. G. Harkness in Houston says he's one of the best, and that's good enough for me. But what's just about as important is that he hasn't any axe to grind that I know about. So why shouldn't he give us his honest opinion?"

The governor was silent. He said at last, "Opinions are what we're talking about, right, Bill? What are the facts?"

Williams shook his head again. "I'm no geologist, but I've built a lot of things in a lot of places, and I'd say that in something like this there aren't any facts, Harry. Out in California they've been waiting ever since I can remember for that big earthquake that's been predicted by all the experts, and it hasn't happened yet. Or ask J. G. how many dry holes he's drilled when the best opinions he could get said there was oil. Sometimes, until you can actually see the results, all you have is guesswork."

The governor's mind was off in another direction. "Bill, we're talking about something that could panic this city into a madhouse. I want an honest answer. The enlargement idea aside, in your opinion is there danger *now?*"

Williams had thought about it and thought about it until he felt as if he were a squirrel running inside a wheel in its cage, getting nowhere. He said, "I don't know, Harry, and that's what's beginning to scare me." He stood up. "I guess I'm glad I came, after all. At least I've got it off my back."

"And put it right on mine." The governor stood up too. "Thanks."

When Kate opened the front door in answer to heavy knocking, Sam Martin was standing there. She smiled. "Come in, Sam. Daddy isn't here, but he said he wouldn't be too late."

"I came to see you."

"I'm flattered. You—"

"You aren't flattered," Sam said. "Not really. That's what I wanted to talk to you about." He had worked himself up to this confrontation, even tried to rehearse it. Now, watching Kate's smile begin to lose its brilliance, he decided that right off the bat he wasn't doing very well.

"What's the matter with your hand?" Kate said in sudden concern. "You keep working the fingers. Did you hurt it?"

"It's all right. I just—banged my arm against something." She had always had this trick of keeping you off-balance, Sam thought. Suddenly he was in the position of supplicant rather than being, as he had hoped, in command of the scene. "Can we talk? I mean, you know, just sit and—talk?"

Her smile had reappeared in all its brilliance, and she led the way through the living room to the *portal*. When they were seated, Sam took a deep breath and began again. "Once upon a time," he said, "we had a kind of—thing going. Didn't we?"

"We did, Sam." Kate was unsmiling now, but her expression was compassionate. "A real boy-girl thing."

"I don't know you anymore, Kate, that's for sure. I thought I knew all about you. Then you went off to college. East, where I don't know the ground rules. I mean—"

"And something else happened too, Sam," Kate said. "Mother died, and Daddy wouldn't let me come home to what he called shadows and gloom. It took me a little time to realize how shattered he was. Then I saw that I was useless. Maybe that's when I started to grow up. When I came back finally, everything was changed and I was, too."

There was a long silence, broken when Sam asked, "What do you want, Kate? What are you waiting for?"

"I'm not consciously waiting for anything. At lunch Daddy gave me a talk on what to do after he dies. Ever since, I've been trying to forget that, and I can't. What do *you* want, Sam?"

"That's easy. You."

"But you don't want all of me, Sam. You may not know that, but I do. I'd make your life miserable."

"Because I've never done wonders on an oil rig in the North Sea? Because I'm just a plain ordinary engineer and not something fancy like a geophysicist? Because—" The words suddenly ran down and he sat silent, shamed by his outburst.

"Sam, stop hurting yourself." Kate's eyes had not left his face, and her expression, fond and gentle, somehow hurt worst of all. "Jay Harper means nothing to me," she said. True? False? Kate asked herself, but she allowed no indecision to show. "He flew with me over the dam this morning—"

"I know." Sam flexed the fingers of his still partially numb hand. "That's how I got this, afterward. Superman didn't like being touched. It was my fault. I lost my temper, and got put in my place. I'm not in his league, Kate. I watched you make that plain the other night at dinner. Your father made it plain this morning. So maybe you're right and I'd better play in my own ball park."

Kate's eyes closed momentarily. When they opened again they glistened with tears. "I'm sorry, Sam."

"It's okay." Sam stood up. "Now we have it all straight, don't we? You know, it's been quite a day. First Bill, then Harper, now this. Good night, Kate."

GEORGE HARRISON sat alone in his beloved library on this evening, and thought again of his talk with Tom Gentry. He could not shake the sense of unreality that Gentry's reaction had produced.

And here came one of the maids with another surprise. "Mr. Sam Martin is here, señor."

George was unused to visitors, but he hoped he did not seem off-balance. "Show him in, by all means."

Sam was both ill at ease and a little astonished to find himself here. He had driven away from the Williamses' house after his painful confrontation with Kate, seen George's gateposts, and on impulse turned in. In the long driveway he had a change of heart, but he found no convenient place to turn around until he reached the garages and the parking area. By then he feared he might already have been seen, so he let his temper have its way, shut off his engine and headlights, got out and marched up to the front door. Bill Williams wouldn't like his being here, not even a little bit, but Sam had had a bellyful of Williamses on this day, and to hell with what Bill might think.

George was all cordiality. "I'm delighted you stopped by," he said, and dispatched the maid for drinks. They sat in deep leather club chairs flanking the corner fireplace, and Sam launched at once into the only possible subject that could justify his presence here. "About the approval of the dam-enlargement project," he began. "There's maybe a hitch."

George set his glass of cognac down very carefully. "Will you explain that, please, Sam?"

"There's this superman in town," Sam said, "and he's got Bill Williams more uptight than I've ever seen him. He's afraid of shadows."

"Indeed?" Bold Bill Williams? "Why?"

Sam went through it all, and in the process drained his drink. "Maybe I shouldn't be telling you this," he said, "but—"

"Nonsense," George said, and pushed the bell beside his chair. The maid appeared immediately and George gestured at Sam's empty glass. "It concerns us all, doesn't it? We're talking about public safety, and that is not something to be kept secret."

When the maid returned with Sam's refill, he accepted it eagerly. "It isn't settled yet," he said. "I mean, it's just in the first talking stage." He took a long pull at the fresh drink.

"I understand," George said, "and I appreciate your bringing it to my attention."

"Look, Mr. Harrison—"

"My friends call me George."

"Okay. George." The temper that had brought Sam here was oozing away fast and the alcohol was not taking its place. "If Bill Williams knew I'd come here with all this, I'd end up without a job. He can be mean when he thinks he's been crossed."

The faint crackling of piñon logs in the fireplace was the only sound. George warmed his glass of cognac between his palms while he thought about the matter. "I see your dilemma," he said at last. "Nothing has been decided yet, is that right?"

Sam felt a little better. "Exactly. Bill is still talking to himself the way he does before he makes up his mind."

As if the decision were entirely Bill's to make, George thought, and felt anger stirring in his mind. Maybe this time arrogant Bill Williams had managed to get his feet tangled. "And Harper? Why does Bill place credence in what Harper tells him?"

"Bill checked him out in Houston. J. G. Harkness says Harper knows his business."

Better and better, George thought. Throughout the Southwest, Harkness was known as a man who paid top dollar and hired only the best. It was, then, a tale to be believed. George had another sip of cognac. It had rarely tasted so good. "If and when a decision is made," he said, "you'll be notified, won't you, Sam?"

"I'd better be. If we go ahead, I'll be the engineer in charge. If we don't, I'm going to have a lot of explaining to do to the Corps of Engineers people I've been selling on the project for the last eighteen months."

George nodded. "Good. So you can keep me informed, can't you, Sam?"

"I don't know about that," Sam said. "I mean, what Bill tells me—"

"But you came here tonight," George said. "It was a matter of conscience, I'm sure, and it took courage."

And, Sam told himself, it had been a stupid thing to do, because he was no longer his own man, or even just Bill Williams' man; he now served two masters. Play ball with George, and George

76

wouldn't bother to mention this talk. But refuse to keep George up-to-date, and it would take only a phone call to Bill. Sam didn't even like to think about what would happen then.

Well, that was the way it was, and Sam supposed he'd better start getting used to it. He had another deep swallow of his bourbon. Might just as well get a little drunk; he wasn't going to feel very good tomorrow anyway.

George raised his glass. "As I said, Sam, I'm delighted you dropped by. Another drink, perhaps?"

During the night, above the eight-thousand-foot level, scattered snow showers fell. Long after the city down on the plain was in near darkness, Bernie and Pete, still in sunlight on their fourteen-thousand-foot perch, had watched the changing weather approach.

"Cirrus clouds first," Bernie had pointed out. "See them? Streamers. I think of them as the outriders of the main storm body, carrying their warning flags. And see those big dark masses over there? They are the troops, carrying the muscle, all the moisture and all the winds. And if they want to, they can break out the lightning and turn it loose—" she paused, unsmiling now, shaking her head gently in awe "—with more power," she said, "than you can believe possible, more energy released."

Pete nodded. "I dig."

"Well, those big black clouds aren't static. Inside they boil and churn and enormous forces are at work—updrafts, downdrafts, sudden cooling, sudden warming, generating enough electricity to light that whole city a dozen times over."

Pete listened quietly, his eyes on the distant clouds.

"Moisture inside the clouds condenses on little specks of dust," Bernie went on, "and as it goes up in an updraft it turns to ice. Then maybe it comes down, accumulates more moisture and goes up again, forming more ice. Up and down, growing all the time. That's how you get hailstones the size of eggs." She paused.

Pete was smiling. "You've studied all this."

"I'm a fire watcher," Bernie said. "That's my main job, but I turn in weather reports too, temperatures, humidity, barometer readings, wind direction and velocity—and, well, I like to watch the weather and have some idea how it works. And Buddy likes to watch with me." Her shyness appeared and she paused to rub the malamute's head.

"So do I," Pete said. "From right here."

They watched until the sun was down and the night closed in. The air turned colder. Stars appeared and were blotted out as the clouds continued their advance.

Some of the snow showers that night were mere dustings which nevertheless held on the chilled ground and rocky ledges. In other places the passing storm dropped as much as three or four inches of dry snow, which here and there accumulated in miniature drifts.

Next morning Pete Otero looked down on this altered world, feeling the new chill that had come unheralded, along with the snow. "Still want me to stick around for a while?" he asked. "I could make it down okay now."

Her greatest fear, Bernie had long ago decided, was that she would try to cling to him after she was no longer wanted. "Do you want to stay, Pete? It could be for days if the weather really closes in. And the report says it may."

"I'm enjoying myself," Pete said. "Good food, lazy days, energetic nights." He was watching her face, and what he saw there stopped the words and turned him suddenly, uncharacteristically solemn. "I want to stay, baby. I haven't had near enough of you yet, and I'm beginning to think I never will."

"Pete. You don't have to say things like that."

"You underestimate yourself."

Bernie started to turn away to end the conversation before it got out of hand. "Let's have breakfast."

Pete caught her arm and turned her with careful gentleness to face him again. His voice was quiet, still solemn. "I know what I am, Bernie, a big lunk who once upon a time was real good at knocking people down on a football field. Now I'm going to have to find out what else I can do, and I can use some help."

"Please, Pete. Don't say it. Let's just leave it the way it is." She turned away again, pulling her arm free from his grasp, and almost ran inside the building. Pete decided to give her a measure of privacy. It was beyond him why women cried.

The low sun lighted the mountaintops, turning the new snow to clear pink, accentuating the shadows of the canyons and valleys beneath. Down at the airport, already in full sunlight, Pete saw, as he had yesterday, the red airplane lift off.

78

COOLEY PARKS sat in the right-hand front seat of the plane, Jay behind him. Kate could not have said what she had expected, but Cooley did not fit the picture. He seemed entirely too casual. Remembering Jay yesterday, she had said as they approached the plane, "No map, Mr. Parks?"

"It's Cooley, ma'am, and, no, I've already looked at a map. Nice country. It kind of stands on end, doesn't it? Like the Alps, only there's more of it."

When they were airborne, Kate said, over her shoulder to Jay, "Straight to the dam?"

Jay looked at his watch. "We've got a few minutes yet. What about a big circle to give Cooley a general look? Then let's follow the river upstream."

The city's buildings rose like a child's toy blocks, and the traffic of miniature automobiles was already heavy on the bridges and main thoroughfares. Cooley looked at it all in silence. They completed their large circle and Jay glanced again at his watch. "I think we can start upstream now."

They approached the Bend. "Quite a little swing there," Cooley said, looking down with interest now.

Jay was leaning forward, his head almost between the two front seats. "I was thinking the same yesterday."

They seemed to read each others' minds, Kate thought, and they spoke in a kind of shorthand which both impressed and annoyed her. In a way it was like hearing surgeons speak together at the hospital, where three days a week she worked as a volunteer.

"In normal years," Cooley said, "that wall at the river bend comes in handy, yes?"

"There used to be occasional flooding," Kate said. "That's why—" She stopped and suddenly found herself looking at the Bend curve of the river with wholly new eyes.

"Water," Cooley said almost offhandedly, "tends to flow down-hill in a straight line unless something makes it change course." He glanced over his shoulder at Jay. "Shouldn't wonder if there's an igneous intrusion in there that caused the bend in the first place."

"Likely," Jay said, and glanced again at his watch. "We're just about on schedule. I allowed a change of one minute from yesterday. That ought to be close enough."

Cooley glanced at Kate and smiled faintly. "He's allowing for

80

the change of sun angle in twenty-four hours," he explained. "Shouldn't wonder if we're looking for shadows."

"There it is," Jay said. Suddenly the dam stood clear and plain ahead. As it had yesterday, its top seemed to extend beyond its boundaries on both sides. Jay said, "See anything?"

"Yeah." Cooley's voice was expressionless. "I sort of figured that was what you might have in mind. You're thinking horst?"

"Could be. What do you think?"

"Take some looking. You poked around?"

"That's why I wanted you."

"Slickensides?"

"I didn't find any evidence. Again, that's why I wanted you."

Kate said suddenly, "Horst! Slickensides! What on earth are you two talking about?"

Cooley said with gentle patience, "You know about faulting, ma'am, movements of the earth's crust?"

"Of course."

"A horst," Cooley explained, "is an uplifted area bounded by two or more faults. Sometimes it's almost a straight line of higher ground. That could be what's casting those straight shadows at each end of the dam. Could be."

"Oh." Kate's voice was subdued. "And the other?"

"Slickensides? Well, when there's faulting, rocks rub together, usually under enormous pressure, and the rock faces become almost polished, as if you'd ground them with a polishing wheel."

Kate looked down at the mountains, the lake, the dam, and she shivered faintly. "What does it mean?"

"We don't know yet," Jay said. "We're just looking at the possibilities."

Cooley said, "It wouldn't be the first time a dam was built right smack on a fault where it has no business being. But if I were you, ma'am, I'd keep that possibility to myself until we know better what we're talking about."

"Let's go back now," Jay said. "We've seen all we can see."

"About time," Cooley said, "for me to get down to work."

HIS HONOR Mayor José-María Lopez y Baca considered this matter too important for the telephone, so he appeared in person at the governor's office, and was shown in at once. "When we talked about the dam enlargement and water rates," he said without preamble, "I was almost beginning to think you were human after all, Harry. Now I'm not so sure. Every time I start trusting an Anglo, I get a kick in the teeth."

"Sooner or later," the governor said, "I expect you'll let me know what you're talking about, Joe."

"You know perfectly well what I'm talking about. The dam. It's unsafe as it is, and you know it."

"Oh?" How did the mayor—

"If she breaks, Harry," the mayor continued in a quieter, even more intense voice, "you know who's going to get it. It won't be the rich Anglos in the Bend, and it won't be you in the governor's mansion up on the ridge. It'll be the poor Chicanos down along the river and in Old Town. They'll be the ones flooded out, drowned like rats in a cellar. That's what I'm talking about."

"Now, see here, Joe—"

"This isn't a political debate, Harry. This is just you and me. I've never liked you much. You know that. But I never thought you'd keep something like this bottled up and maybe get a lot of people killed just to save your reputation."

The large office was still. The governor said at last, "Is your temper tantrum over, Joe? Are you prepared to listen instead of foaming at the mouth? Then suppose I tell you that the first word I had that the dam might be questionable—*might be*—was last night. What would you say then?"

The mayor opened his hands, studied them in silence, obviously struggling for control; and closed them again—almost, but not quite, into hard brown fists. He looked up at the governor's face. His voice was quiet now. "Are you telling the truth?"

"It's the truth, Joe. Bill Williams told me."

"Bill is one Anglo I'll believe. How long has he known?"

"Night before last a man, a stranger, told him he thought—no, *suspected*—the dam may have been weakened when we had that earthquake."

"That earthquake didn't even knock the pictures crooked in my house."

"Apparently up at the dam the quake was harder," the governor said.

Again there was silence. The mayor's brown eyes searched the governor's face. "Are you leveling with me, Harry? You heard first last night and Bill first heard the night before?"

"That's it. Now what I want to know is, where did *you* hear about it, and from whom?"

"George Harrison and five or six other Anglos were talking about it over coffee this morning at the Hilton." He could not resist adding, "Nobody pays any attention to a Chicano busboy, and one of my wife's cousins heard the whole thing. I came straight over here. So what are you going to do?"

The governor leaned back in his chair and looked out the window at the mountains. "I wish I knew, Joe," he said at last. "We're waiting for more information, but when it comes, it isn't going to be definitive, I'm afraid, and in the end we're just going to have to make a judgment call." He sat up straight. "Before that happens," he said, "I'll let you know. That's a promise. That's the best I can do. Thank you for the information."

The mayor stood up. "The damage is done. If the story isn't all over town yet, it will be soon."

The governor stood too. His voice was solemn. "We don't want this to go any farther than we can help. Newspaper, radio, TV— you have influence—" He left it there, his implication plain.

The mayor nodded. "If I have to," he said, "I'll scare the day-lights out of some people to keep them quiet."

"Thanks, Joe. What are *you* going to do?"

"Try to figure out how to evacuate Old Town and the *barrio*, and wait for final word from you." Crises, like politics, produced strange bedfellows, the mayor was thinking. "This time," he said, "you and I are going to have to forget our differences, Harry."

"The same thought was in my mind, Joe."

ON THE GROUND at the airport, the sound of the red plane's engine no longer beating at them, Kate said, "Now what?"

Cooley sighed. "I start digging like a badger to see what's under the surface. It's an undignified trade I picked."

Jay looked at Kate. "Can you drive him up to the dam?"

Cooley said, "Where you going, boy?" Then comprehension dawned quickly. "Downstream, huh? Have a look-see there?" He nodded. "Good thinking. How about it, ma'am, can you give me a lift up the mountain?"

"Of course," Kate said. "My car is over here."

Driving out of the city, heading for the Bend, Kate said, "You and he—?" She left the question hanging.

"We've known each other quite a spell. Ever since he broke into the oil business as a young pup. Those of us who'd been around a long time just waited for him to make a fool of himself."

Despite herself, Kate was smiling. "And did he?"

"Nope. He made fools of the rest of us. Kept us from rushing in the way we always had, drilling holes without enough planning and maybe lousing up a good field, leaving oil and gas down in the ground beyond reach forever. That was in Indonesia."

Kate concentrated on her driving.

"Don't get me wrong," Cooley said. "He sometimes makes mistakes, just like the rest of us. But he makes damned few of them. There may be better men than he is, but I've never seen one."

"You're loyal." Kate glanced curiously at the tanned, lined face. "Why is he going downstream?"

"To see if there's evidence of previous flooding from the mountains—to get an idea of what we might be up against in case of another flood." Cooley glanced at Kate. "That's what we're all thinking about, isn't it?"

Kate shivered. "And that dam that we've been taking for granted? What can you tell? And what can you do?"

"I'm a geologist."

"But you know about these things."

"No." Cooley's voice was definite. "Nobody knows about them—until they happen. And then it's usually too late."

SAM MARTIN, again summoned to Bill Williams' office, sat in one of the leather chairs drawn up to the conference table. He had come prepared with drawings as well as piles of engineering data.

"We've got a geologist up there looking things over," Williams said, "and Harper's out on the plain looking around." Kate had telephoned him from Harper's Park with a brief report. "You know what they're thinking is a possibility? That maybe we built that dam right on a fault line."

"We couldn't have."

"Tell me why. It's been done before."

"The Army Corps of Engineers—"

"Yeah. They've been wrong before too."

"Look, Bill," Sam said, "who are these two characters, anyway, to turn into instant experts on local conditions?"

"I told you I checked Harper out. And I just finished checking out this geologist, Cooley Parks. They're top hands, both of them. Anyway, none of that matters at the moment. What does matter is the problem they've raised and what we're going to do about it *if* it turns out to be real. Can we empty that lake?"

"Sure. In three, four weeks, maybe longer." He snapped his fingers. "Wait a minute. There's the old diversion tunnel. The way the water level is now, we'd have to blast a channel to it, but—"

"If we get evidence that there is a fault," Williams said, "then we'd better be ready with answers that don't take three or four weeks to work. There's already talk. You've heard it?"

"No."

Something in the instant decisiveness of the answer caught Williams' ear. He studied Sam carefully. "You said that a little fast, Sam. You haven't been getting any calls? I have. All morning. So has the governor." Williams' voice grew slow and distinct. "You wouldn't have any idea where this talk you haven't been hearing got started?"

"No."

"You wouldn't have been talking to George Harrison again either, would you, Sam?"

"I—had a drink with him at his house last night."

"And today the rumors start." Williams nodded in sad acceptance. "In my place, Sam, what would you think?"

I can't face him down, Sam thought. I never could. "Okay," he said. It was admission, apology and appeal all at once. "I told Harrison what Harper had said, that we'd be crazy to think of enlarging the dam and that maybe it isn't even safe as it is. But I told him it was only one man's opinion and mostly guesswork—"

"That's enough, Sam." Williams' voice was suddenly weary. "Take your pictures and your papers and beat it."

As if on cue the telephone buzzed quietly. Williams reached for it, his eyes never leaving Sam's face. He listened briefly. "Okay," he said into the phone. "Send him in. We're all through here." There was finality in the words.

The door opened and Jay Harper walked in.

Sam picked up his papers and drawings from the conference table and walked out in silence, closing the door behind him. Williams waited until Jay was seated. "Kate called. She told me what you and Parks think."

"He's looking into it. If there's evidence, he'll find it."

"And you've been doing what?"

"Poking around. Did you ever notice those big rocks behind your house? The gray ones, partially sunk in the ground? Twenty or so feet across. Fifteen, twenty feet high, some of them."

"I used to play there when I was a kid. What about them?"

"They came down out of the mountains," Jay said. "There's nothing like them in the basic rock structure anywhere around. The river brought them down. In one hell of a big flood."

The large office was still. Williams said at last, "Go on, what are you getting at?"

"When the big flood I'm talking about happened, that's where it went, right where those big houses at the Bend are now. There wasn't a big concrete dam up there then, holding back all that lake water that could come down the canyon at once, so maybe now we're talking about something even bigger. That's the first thing."

"And the second?"

"There wasn't a concrete retaining wall at that curve, either. A big flood right now, or at least a part of it, might be diverted by that wall and carried right around the curve."

Williams said slowly, "Right down into the city? Old Town? That's where a flood strong enough to move those big rocks might go if we have one? Is that what you're saying?"

"That's it."

Williams closed his eyes, thinking of the implications, of stark, unrelieved catastrophe. He felt suddenly dizzy, as if the floor beneath his feet were rocking. Automatically, his eyes still closed, he got out the pillbox, popped a pill into his mouth and swallowed it dry.

He supposed that the mere act of taking the pill had some immediate psychological effect, because all at once the dizziness disappeared and the floor was again steady under his feet. He opened his eyes. Jay was watching him. "Nothing serious," Williams said as he tucked the pillbox away.

"I'm not so sure," Jay said. "Didn't you feel it?"

Williams was frowning now. "I felt dizzy, like the floor was moving. But how did you know?"

"The floor *was* moving," Jay said. "We just had another tremor. And probably, like the others, the epicenter was up closer to Harper's Park and they felt it more." He got out of his chair. "I think we'd better go up and find out."

Jay and Williams drove hurriedly to the lake and stood on the bank looking out toward the dam. Beside them Kate listened quietly while Cooley Parks, in work boots, sweating, his sleeves rolled up on his brawny forearms and the knees of his trousers dusty, described the last tremor. "Yeah, we felt it." He gestured with the fist that held his geologist's pick. "So did the water of the lake. I watched it—"

"A seiche?" Jay said.

"Just like the textbooks say. Against the face of the dam the water sloshed up maybe ten feet. Out in the middle of the lake, at the node, there was hardly any movement at all."

"You were where?" Jay said.

"Out on the right-hand shoulder."

"Find anything?"

Cooley opened his left hand. In his palm lay one large and half a dozen smaller pieces of grayish rock, their faces glinting like mirrors in the sun.

"Is that what you called slickensides?" Kate asked.

"Yeah," Cooley said. "Right where the dam is."

"Somebody bring me into the picture," Williams said.

He listened to Cooley's explanation. Then, "Okay, I'll take your word for it. What do we do about it?"

"There is one more thing I can do," Jay said. "I'll take one more dive and see if I can find any changes because of this last tremor."

"Don't be a fool, boy!" This was Cooley. "You don't know how deeply that tremor affected the rock structure. That dam may be getting ready to go right now, and if you're down there when it does—"

"Or it could last for years," Jay said. "So I'll see if I can cast any light on its condition." He turned and started for the motel.

ON THE MOUNT UNION fire-lookout tower Pete and Bernie had felt the tremor too. "Kind of scary, isn't it?" Bernie said.

"Will you report it?"

"Not really. What we usually do is get on the air and talk it around, and somebody makes a phone call to someone at the university seismograph, and then *they* pass the word around. If we see anything, like, say a rockfall, we'd report that. The forest service would want to know. We're supposed to report not just fires, but anything that might affect the environment. Along with the weather, I mean. And now it's time for the weather reports. I'll be right back."

Pete waited, arms behind his head, grinning up at the incredibly blue sky. What was keeping him here, he decided, was a girl he was beginning to care more about than he would have thought possible. He was still sitting motionless and relaxed when Bernie came back out. "That rain and snow we were supposed to get—it's coming, Pete. You'd better go while you can."

"You know," Pete said, "I never dug the vine-covered cottage bit, but I'm beginning to think there might be something to it, after all. There's a guy in Santa Monica—he's got this chain of sporting goods stores—"

"Pete, you aren't even listening to me."

"—and they're slanted toward big guys. Like me. Guys who can't find boots or golf shoes or sweaters—"

Bernie had dropped to her knees beside him. "Aren't you going to listen? This time it's coming for sure. Two fronts, converging on us."

"I don't need to listen, because I'm not going anywhere. Not without you. Not ever again. I just decided. The only question is when do we leave here—together?"

Bernie took a deep, unsteady breath. "Pete—"

"I'll be damned," Pete said. "What did I say to make you cry?"

WHEN Honest Johnny Cisneros heard the rumor that the dam was unsafe, he immediately called State Senator Walt Duggan, who had talked with the governor that morning, and had been secretly hoping to sell his half of Angelita Leyba's property to Johnny, before word got around. Now that plan went down the drain, and Duggan found himself faced with another dilemma.

"What I want to know, Walt," Johnny said, "is it true? My warehouse is down in the *barrio*, right by the river. I got a whole truckload of new TVs coming in. Once we unload them and put them in my warehouse, they belong to me, not to the distributor. And anything happens to that dam and we get a flood, right away they belong to you, you know what I mean?"

The senator knew precisely what it was that Johnny meant. He was in the insurance business, and he had written the insurance on Honest Johnny's warehouse and contents himself. "I get the message, Johnny."

"*Bueno*. Now, do I try to stop that delivery? Then what happens to my semi-annual sale? I don't like to let my customers down."

"Get that truckload stopped, Johnny." And, Duggan thought, empty that warehouse too, but he would not go so far as to say that openly.

There was a short silence. Then, "Just what do you know, Walt? You better tell me."

"I don't *know* any more than you do, Johnny. But there is a chance that that dam isn't safe. I've talked with the governor. Now that's strictly between you and me, okay? We don't want the word out that he's worried. People start hearing that right at the top of state government they're concerned and—"

"Sure, sure. I dig you, Walt. I'll try to stop that shipment. Thanks for filling me in."

The snow began in the high mountains in almost tentative fashion, but in minutes the fall became heavier and the ground began to whiten. From within the fire-lookout building the effect was magical, a swirling, shifting pattern of light, now obscuring, now revealing nearby mountain peaks and canyons, the dam and the city far below, still untouched by the coming storm.

A voice came from the radio speaker. "Hey, Bright Eyes! Come in, Bright Eyes! Snow reached you yet? Over."

"Affirmative," Bernie answered. "Just beginning."

"Batten down the hatches. We're going to catch it for good and for sure, and there's a warming trend behind it. First snow, then maybe rain, even at your elevation. You been feeling tremors?"

"Affirmative."

"Small stuff, in case you were worried, under three on the Richter scale, with the epicenters over in your area."

"Thanks, Charlie." She switched off the hand mike.

COOLEY SAT in the stern, hand on the tiller, swinging the boat in slow, patient circles around the spot where Jay had gone over the side.

Bill Williams and Kate stood on the shore of the lake watching. Kate did not look at her father. She knew what she would see and it was painful to accept. Williams had aged almost before her eyes.

He still held himself straight, but the confidence he had always exuded was no longer there.

"Maybe he'll find that everything is all right," she said. "Even if it isn't, it's not your fault."

"Wrong." For a moment the strength returned. "The guy at the top is responsible. Always. He may try to weasel and pretend he didn't know or he was let down by people he trusted. But that's my dam. I built it. And if it's in the wrong place, then it's my fault, period."

Kate tucked her arm through her father's and stood silent. There was only the lake and the spreading ripples from the circling boat, and Cooley's worried attention, and the waiting that seem to have no end.

"That's a good man down there," her father said suddenly. "They both are. You can't buy men like that. There isn't money enough."

It was true, Kate thought, and from some source she drew more sure knowledge. "You're that kind of man too, Daddy."

In the boat Cooley looked at his watch. Come on, boy, he thought. Come up out of there and let us get safe ashore.

Eighty feet down it was colder than Jay remembered it; and he told himself it was only his imagination. Or fear. He was almost touching the base of the dam. Now he swam along its face, holding his camera in one hand and with the other flashing his light on the weed-covered concrete. He expected to find no obvious flaw. Not yet. If he did, he would head for the surface as fast as he could go. Even the smallest crack would mean the dam was already crumbling.

It was at the sides, where the dam tied into the walls of the gorge, that he might find indications of possible imminent trouble, further fracturing, however minor, of the supporting rock structure. That, viewed against Cooley's broad analysis, could lead to only one conclusion: the dam was already unsafe.

He continued his sweep up the dam wall, but he found no flaws. And here was the side of the gorge, the rock rising almost sheer, apparently solid and strong. But only at first quick look. There was—yes, he was sure of it—a freshly exposed face of rock, perhaps a yard square. His memory told him it had not been there two days ago.

He swam quickly to the bottom, searched for and found some of the pieces of rock which must have come from that freshly exposed face. In the light he examined one of them. No question: this side had been exposed to the water of the lake for a long time, and the other side had been protected, hidden, a part of the rock structure itself—until it had been shaken loose by today's tremor.

He had all the indication he needed. Holding light and camera carefully, he took pictures of the freshly exposed rock face and of the pieces lying on the bottom. Okay, he thought, now we get out of here.

He started for the surface, but after only a few feet he hesitated, arguing with himself. A job half done. The shadow he and Cooley had seen from the air extended from *both* sides of the dam structure, and if that was indication of a fault line, then there probably should be some indication of damage from today's tremor on the *other* side of the gorge too. If so, that would double the evidence of clear and present danger.

He was already swimming back across the dam face. Professional pride was a dreadful force, and would not let itself be ignored. Only when he had reached the far side of the gorge did he feel the water beginning to move. Almost simultaneously he heard a deep rumbling sound as of rock in torment.

He played his light on the dam face. It seemed to be holding solid. Quickly he turned the light on the rock structure. As if in slow motion, pieces of rock dropped like falling autumn leaves to the lake bottom. A crack appeared in the rock face. Around it more rock detached itself and drifted down through the water, which was still oscillating with sluggish but irresistible force.

Jay waited for no more. He drove himself upward with desperate strokes of his fins, broke surface and shot waist-high out of the water like a performing seal. Cooley headed the boat toward him at top speed. He slowed, and reaching down with one brawny arm, helped Jay over the gunwale. "Of all the stubborn fools!" he roared. The little boat's bow lifted as he opened the throttle and they headed toward the dock.

Williams and Kate came toward them at a run.

Arms full of diving gear, Jay scrambled from the boat to the slip. Behind him Cooley switched off the engine, clambered out and dropped the painter over a cleat. He and Jay hurried on to the shore, stopped and turned to look. The dam stood apparently unscathed, and the sloshing of the lake water was beginning to die away.

Jay turned to Williams, controlling his voice with effort. "Okay," he said, "that's it. I can tell you what I saw and what I *know*—now." His knees were suddenly weak and there was a hollowness in his stomach.

FATHER RODRIGUEZ, walking through the *barrio*, passed the schoolyard, where children were at play. Some of them waved. One little girl, in a voice filled with urgency, called, "Padre! Padre!"

The priest stopped and turned. "Teresa! *Qué pasa?*"

"You have heard? It is said that the dam is not safe! That it may break! Do you know of this, Padre?"

"Heard?" the priest said wonderingly. "From whom did you hear this—this rumor, Teresa? Tell me."

From Juan, her brother, who heard it from Antonio, who drove a taxi; Antonio had heard it from a garage mechanic who had been told by one of the busboys who worked at the Hilton and overheard men at coffee talking. "Is it true, Padre? That we will all be washed away?"

"No, Teresa, we will not be washed away. And you must tell this to no one. Do you understand, Teresa? No one!"

The girl hesitated. She said at last with vague disappointment, "If you say so, Padre."

"Good girl." The priest turned and began to walk purposefully away. He would find out the truth of this rumor from the man who always knew before anyone else what was happening.

Johnny Cisneros was supervising two crews of men loading trucks with television sets, radios and record players from the warehouse on which the huge sign HONEST JOHNNY—TV—RADIO—APPLIANCES appeared. He saw Father Rodriguez approach, and he sighed. Well, sooner or later fat Angelita Leyba and those damned ten acres of land would have to be discussed. "Hi, Padre," Johnny said.

"It's a little early for your fall sale, isn't it, Johnny?" The father's voice was not unfriendly, and he spoke in English

"Yeah. Well, you know, Padre, you got to get ready."

"For what?" There was a little emphasis this time, but Father Rodriguez spoke still in English. "You don't believe in rumors, do you, Johnny?"

"Rumors, Padre? I don't know any rumors."

"You were always a skillful liar, Juan." The priest had switched to Spanish, a sure indication that a serious matter was in his mind.

"I refer to the talk about the dam at Harper's Park and the possibility that it is weak." He watched Johnny's workmen loading the trucks at a pace they would not usually maintain. "Could that be the reason for your haste?"

"Look, Padre, I'm real busy." Johnny stuck to English. "These guys cost money. You got to get as much work as you can for each buck."

Father Rodriguez said, still in Spanish, "Juan, I believe I can say with assurance that eternity in damnation awaits those who turn their backs on their fellowmen and allow them to perish when they might be saved."

"Padre, I'm not doing anything."

"Precisely." There was a subtle change in Johnny's manner. From countless hours spent listening in the confessional box, the priest recognized the signs. He was convinced now that he was on the right track. "What is it you know that is the cause of this desperate haste?"

"I told you, Padre, what you got to pay—"

"Juan! I will not be trifled with!" He was a small man, Father Rodriguez, in his shabby black suit, beret and dusty shoes, but there was dignity in his manner and force in his formal words. "I will ask you once again, Juan. What is it you know?"

Johnny's resistance collapsed. "The dam is going to go, Padre. Even the governor knows it. He just isn't talking yet."

Father Rodriguez turned away and hurried toward the church. So Teresa had been right, and now there was much to be done.

THE GOVERNOR sat behind his desk in the position of command. The mayor, Bill Williams, Cooley Parks and Jay were in chairs facing him. "The long and the short of it," Cooley finished his summation, "is that the dam sits right on a fault line."

The governor said, "All right, what does it add up to?"

Jay spread his hands. "Anybody's guess. We can tell you that the supporting rock structure is weak and that it has been affected by the tremors there've already been. I can also tell you that as far as I know, no concrete dam has ever failed just because of an earthquake."

"But," Cooley said, "there's a first time for everything."

"It is snowing in the mountains," the governor said. "The weather service is predicting up to a foot of snow, turning to rain.

93

I assume that is one more factor to be brought into the equation?"

"If we get a flash flood," Bill Williams said, looking from Jay to Cooley, "it'll be worse than one of these little earthquakes, right?"

"I can't give you a definitive answer," Jay said, "but my guess is it would. I'm talking about a real gully-washer now."

The governor looked at the mayor. "Joe?"

"We're already working on plans to evacuate the *barrio* and Old Town, just in case. But it will be one heck of a job. How much warning would we have if that dam does start to go?"

"I clocked it driving down just now," Jay said. "The road follows the river. It took us twenty-one minutes and I'd say you'd have that much time at least."

The governor was silent for long moments. He said at last, "I will be frank. What we have here is the unsupported word of one man, and he is the only person who has actually seen indications of rock failure. Is that not correct?"

"That is correct," Jay said. He smiled grimly. "I'll lend my scuba gear to anybody who cares to have a look for himself."

The governor looked at Cooley. "We have your opinion, the opinion, I am told and believe, of an expert, that the dam is actually resting on a fault line. That, too, is correct?"

"An *active* fault line, Governor," Cooley said. "I'll stake my reputation on it. But you *can* bring in a couple more rock men."

"Have we time for that?"

"I'd say no," Jay said. "I'd say you'd better start doing what you can yesterday afternoon. Or the day before that."

"And just what steps do you suggest?"

Not my field, Jay told himself, and none of my business, anyway. But he was *here—involved*; and that was an end to it. He set himself to answer the governor's question. "You'd better start draining that lake as fast as you can to relieve pressure on the dam. Divert what upstream water you can into other channels. Keep the seismograph monitored so you'll know about any further tremors. Above all, set an around-the-clock watch on the dam itself and decide what to do about anyone in those summer cottages below it, because if it goes, they won't have nearly as much warning as the city will."

The governor was making quick notes, impressed by the calculator speed of Jay's mind. "Go on," he said.

"You'll probably also want a standby warning system," Jay said, "both TV and radio. And people too, standing by to direct that evacuation you—" he nodded at the mayor "—are already planning. And there is one thing more. That flood-control wall at the big bend of the river ought to be mined. And if the worst happens, it ought to be blown. When the river is normal, its natural course is around the curve, but as you found out when you built out in the Bend, even little spring floods sometimes refuse to make the curve and slop up over the Bend property. That's why you put up that concrete flood-control wall, isn't it?"

Reluctantly Williams nodded. He said nothing.

"As I told you," Jay said, "the evidence shows that at least a good part of the big, ancient floods also refused to make the curve. We're talking about a solid wall of water thirty, forty feet high traveling down the gorges between here and the dam at maybe forty miles an hour. Destroy that wall and let *some* of the water go straight instead of around the curve, and you've at least helped the *barrio* and the city."

The governor put down his pencil. His face showed strain, but his voice was strong, steady. "Every now and again an elected public official, like Joe, like me, comes to a situation where it's up to him to earn his pay and everything else that goes with his office. This is one of those times. You've given us your best advice. Now it's up to us to make the political decisions." He looked at the mayor. "You agree?"

The mayor nodded. "That's what they pay us for."

"And so," the governor said, "if you gentlemen will wait outside, the mayor and I will try to live up to our responsibilities."

In a short while the door to the inner office opened and the governor, his hand on the doorknob, looked at Jay, Cooley Parks and Bill Williams. "Will you come in, please, gentlemen? For once the municipal and state governments are in accord."

As before, the governor sat in the position of command behind his desk, and the others faced him. "I am not going to declare an emergency," he said. "Not yet. But—" the governor was looking at Jay now "—we are thinking of following your suggestions to start draining the lake, diverting upstream water, establishing an around-the-clock dam watch and so on. There is no way we can disguise what we will be doing, but we will attract as little attention to it as possible.

"We want you to oversee the entire operation," he said to Jay.

"You're the one most familiar with the situation, and as you said, there's no time to bring in someone else."

Jay opened his mouth, and closed it again in silence.

"I am putting the resources of the state at your disposal," the governor continued. "We will get you whatever you think you need to prevent—disaster."

"I'm a geophysicist," Jay said in protest. "This isn't my field. I came here only to look at a village on the bottom of a lake, and—"

"Why don't you stop clicking your teeth?" Cooley said. He pushed back his chair and stood. "Let's get at it. The sooner we do, the sooner it'll be over. One way or the other."

"One suggestion," Bill Williams said. "Let's use my office. You don't want orders coming directly from here, Harry." He looked at Jay. "Don't worry, I'm taking orders, not giving them. You're the boss. What's first?"

Okay, Jay thought. He said to the governor, "Around-the-clock watch on the dam. National Guard. They've got the equipment and manpower—"

"By the time you get to Bill's office," the governor said, "there will be an officer reporting to you. Give him his orders. Have Bill phone me for anything else you need."

In Bill Williams' car Jay said, "Your engineer, Sam Martin. We'll want him, with his drawings and specs."

"I don't want to lay eyes on him," Williams said angrily.

"He was chief engineer on the dam, wasn't he?"

Williams nodded. "Okay. You'll get him."

A full colonel of the National Guard was waiting when they reached Bill Williams' office. He introduced himself. "Colonel Watkins. I was told to report to you, sir," he said to Williams.

Williams shook his head and pointed at Jay. "To him."

The colonel studied Jay's jeans and sneakers, but said nothing. "A twenty-four-hour watch on the dam, Colonel," Jay said. "Flood-lights at night, and constant radio communication to this building. Any indication that the dam is showing signs of weakness—"

"And rock fracturing at the sides," Cooley added.

"Sir," the colonel said, "the Army Corps of Engineers—"

"You do your job, Colonel," Jay said. "We'll take care of the consultations." He turned to Williams.

Williams reached for the telephone. "Sam Martin coming up." His eyes went to Watkins, who stood uncertainly. "If I were you,

Colonel," Williams said, "I'd start moving. You've got your orders."
And into the phone, "Find Sam Martin, honey. Get him here with
all his papers."

Cooley watched the colonel's stiff back disappearing. The door
closed with a small bang. "Suppose," Cooley said to Jay, "I find
out who runs the nearest seismograph. By now they'll have had a
fix on today's tremors and we can see where the epicenters were."

"Keep in touch," Jay said. He looked again at Williams. "Now
the weather service. I want forecasts and reports kept up-to-date
on everything this side of the watershed."

Jay rested his hip on the corner of the big desk. His mind was
already off in another direction. "You're a construction man, Bill.
How are you fixed for dynamite?"

"We've got it. What's on your mind?"

"Upstream diversions, for one. For another, and most important,
some way to drain that lake. And mine the flood-control wall. And
we may even think of getting ready to blow one of those big
bridges and drop it across the stream. It wouldn't stop a flood, but it
would slow it and disperse it a little."

Williams whistled soundlessly. "When you get started, you're a
real high roller, aren't you?"

"We're playing for lives," Jay said, "and they're the biggest
stake I know."

IN THE fire-lookout building on the mountaintop they felt
completely alone now, the rest of the world obliterated by the
swirling snow. From time to time the radio speaker crackled and
Bernie gave it her full attention.

Pete said, "I can't make out a darn thing."

"You get used to it. The weather-service people are calling each
lookout. They'll get around to us."

There was another crackling sound from the speaker, and this
time Bernie picked up the hand mike and spoke into it. "Roger.
Mount Union here. Over."

The voice went on at some length. Pete, watching Bernie, understood that this was no mere routine. As she listened her face grew
tight with emotion. When the voice ceased, Bernie spoke into her
mike, her voice not quite steady. "Roger. We will keep you posted.
Heavy snow now. Visibility zero. So far we have had an estimated
three inches. Over, and out." She put down the hand mike.

"What's doing, baby?"

"You remember that far-out dream I told you about, looking down from here and no world left?" She took a deep breath. "The Harper's Park dam. It may go. That's what they're afraid of. The weather service wants everything we can give them. Like if that warm front does come through, and this snow turns to rain—have you ever seen what a flash flood can do, Pete?"

"You're looking for trouble, baby."

Bernie shook her head. "The weather service doesn't usually get excited, Pete. I've never heard them uptight like this."

SAM MARTIN came into Bill Williams' office as if he were entering a courtroom for sentencing. His arms were filled with rolled drawings and papers, and once he had pushed the door shut, he just stood, waiting to be told what to do.

"Put them down on the table," Williams said. "Harper is in charge. You got that? And this time you keep your mouth shut about what happens in this office, is that clear?" Automatically his hand brought out the small silver pillbox.

Jay was already bending over the piles of papers. "Let's spread out this topographical map. While you were pouring the dam, where did you set your upstream diversions? Here? Here?" His pointing finger moved swiftly, without hesitation. "Maybe here?"

Sam was unaware that the door had opened and Kate had come in silently. She leaned against the desk, listening, her hand resting lightly on her father's broad shoulder.

"The outflow through the turbines in the power plant," Jay was saying. "Can you increase it?"

"Sure. But the turbines can only take so much—" Sam stopped, suddenly in the presence of another idea.

"Yeah," Jay said. "If there's no other way, we'll open that outflow wide and not worry about the turbines. How much increased flow would that give us?"

"Maybe ten percent."

Jay nodded. "Every bit will help."

The office door opened again, and Cooley Parks came through. "These two tremors today registered only two-point-eight and two-point-nine on the Richter scale," he said. "That's the more or less good news. The bad news is that we may get more little tremors. And the epicenters—guess where?"

"Probably right where we don't want them—under the dam."

"Bingo." Cooley said. "And so was the one six days ago."

"So every tremor is having its effect on the dam and its anchorage," Jay said. "Reinforced concrete doesn't give very much without fracturing."

Sam Martin took a deep breath. "You're sure about that fault?"

Cooley nodded. "We're sure."

"There was no indication. The Army Corps of Engineers—"

"Look," Jay said in a tone that commanded silence. "We're not trying to fix blame. We're trying to figure out what to do."

"And?" This was Williams. "What *do* we do?"

"First," Jay said, "those upstream diversions, to shut off the flow of water into the lake. They'll take time which maybe we don't have, but we'll have to try anyway." He looked at Sam. "You did it once when you were building the dam. You can do it again, but on a crash basis this time.

"Next, the power station." Jay looked at Sam again. "Is there a bypass? Good. We'll open it too." He turned to Williams. "Tell the power company we want all the water flow we can get. We've got to drain that lake."

Williams said to Sam, "That diversion tunnel. How about it? You said you'd have to blast a channel to it, no?"

"Diversion tunnel?" Jay said. "Near the dam?" He looked at Sam. "There has already been rock fracturing at the sides of the dam today. Would you do any blasting in the area?"

"I'd hate to," Sam said.

Cooley said, "I'll go up with him and have a look. I've set off a charge or two in my day."

"In the meantime," Jay said to Williams, "the outflow to the generator plant is our first move. That, and getting the military started mining that flood-control wall."

It was the first Kate had heard of it. "At the Bend? Oh, no! Our house! All those lovely houses!"

Williams said, "I'll see about blasting equipment." His voice was expressionless, his shoulders squared as he walked out.

A short time later a column of military vehicles was winding slowly up the Harper's Park road. Sam Martin, driving, swung into the left-hand lane, and began to pass the trucks loaded with soldiers and equipment. They passed the lead jeep, hurried on up the winding road and came around the final turn that exposed the entire dam structure and the generator station at its base. Cooley said, "Let's park above the dam and see about that tunnel."

Sam led the way, on foot, off the road. "We cleared all this out," he said, indicating the loose rock around them, "and then we diverted the stream down this way to the tunnel. It's over there."

Cooley followed the pointing hand. "I don't see it."

"It *was* there," Sam said. "Right there."

After minutes of searching, Cooley finally stopped and pointed. "Those rocks were piled there. Carefully and cleverly. It's good dry-wall construction, blocking off the tunnel."

"But who would go to all that trouble?"

"Riddles aren't my thing. Let's see about the other end?"

THE MAYOR was back in his own office again. Bud Henderson, the police chief, asked, "How much warning will we have?"

"Call it twenty minutes," the mayor said. "They're setting up radio communication with the dam now."

"But we can't clear the *barrio* in twenty minutes," said Carlos García, the schoolteacher. "Old people, sick people—they have to be moved well ahead of time."

"Okay," the mayor said. "Then we need places to put them. School buildings, the hospital, the convention center—"

"I've got room in the firehouses," Fire Chief Rudy Smith said. "We'll need cots and bedding and food—"

"Food," Carlos went on. "We can use the school kitchens, and volunteer help."

The mayor was making rapid notes. "Okay. The old people, the sick—we get them to high ground at the first sign of trouble. Now—What about transport?"

COLONEL WATKINS was back in Bill Williams' office. "We're setting up at the dam," he said to Jay, "and starting work at the flood-control wall. In a few minutes we'll have communication here. I've arranged for a direct phone line to the weather service, and they'll keep us up-to-date, but communication with that Mount Union fire lookout is bad and getting worse, and that's the best source of information of local mountain conditions. It's snowing up there, or was an hour ago."

"As long as it stays snow," Jay said, "maybe we're all right. But if it turns to rain—you'd better send a man with a walkie-talkie well upstream from the lake, Colonel. He can keep an eye on the water level, and the color of the water too. If we start getting silt, it may be serious. He can warn us."

AGAIN IT WAS Cooley, determined and indefatigable, who found the lower end of the diversion tunnel. He summoned Sam, and crouching down, pointed. "There's your explanation," he said. "Ten to one it's kids. A ready-made hidey-hole with both ends blocked."

It was a small entrance, surrounded by carefully placed rocks, hidden by transplanted brush, and blocked by a stout wooden door with a cheap combination padlock.

Sam watched, shaking his head in wonder at the amount of work that had gone into the project, while Cooley picked up a rock and hammered on the padlock until it came apart.

He removed it, and opened the door. The air that emerged was dank, musty. "A lantern and matches, right handy," he said. "Nice of them. Now, let's have a look at the other end. If we can get water to it and through it with the kind of force the weight of that lake will give us, we don't have to worry about this end. The water will blast those rocks loose without even slowing."

They reached the tunnel's upper end and Cooley held the lantern high to examine the careful rock work which had blocked the opening there. "I don't know who the kids are," Cooley said, "but I'll bet you couldn't hire them to do all this work. But when it's their idea, they'll go at it like beavers. For free. Now let's get down to cases. How do we get water here from the lake?"

Sam said doubtfully, "We blocked off the channel because we didn't think we'd ever need it again."

"Okay, now we do, so we unblock it. Obviously the water level of the lake is much higher than we are, because you were just diverting the stream which is now at the bottom of the lake, no?"

"Well, yes."

"We've got a lot of rock to move, including all this. And once it's moved, a lot of water is going to start coming through this tunnel. You've got a pocket calculator?"

Sam handed one to Cooley, wondering what he intended.

"A ten-foot tunnel," Cooley said. "Water coming through at— let's take Jay's forty-mile-an-hour figure." He punched buttons. "About two hundred and seventy-six thousand cubic feet a minute

101

coming out of the lake. That will relieve a lot of dam pressure."

"We reinforced the rock we replaced with concrete," Sam said. "It's going to take a heavy blasting."

"We'll just blow it all up at once and hope the dam stands it," Cooley said, "and that we've got our dynamite in the right places, and that the good Lord's on our side."

"You can't do that!" Sam said.

"Sonny," Cooley said, "there's only one word that upsets me. It's 'can't'. It makes me lay back my ears. We'll blast a channel down to this tunnel because there isn't a damned thing else we can do that amounts to anything. Now let's find a phone and call Jay."

George Harrison dined early, alone, and well that evening at the Territorial Club, where his family had long been honored members. Now that the dam enlargement was out of the question, he, not Bill Williams had profited from the sale of the mountain land, which had become almost worthless. George savored his victory with a snifter of special cognac and a fine cigar.

The sun was just sinking below the distant horizon when he walked out to his Mercedes. He felt comfortably relaxed as he slid behind the wheel, started the engine and drove slowly away.

There were floodlights at the Bend where the river swung in its great curve. There was also the subdued clatter of mobile compressors and the thunderous racket of air hammers driving star drills deep into the face of the concrete flood-control wall.

George stared, and then he saw Sam Martin among the National Guardsmen. He braked to a stop, got out and headed straight for him. "What in the world is going on, Sam?"

"Pretty obvious, isn't it?" Sam said. "We're drilling holes. For explosive charges. When we detonate them, they'll blow this flood-control wall to pieces."

Suddenly the euphoria of the evening was all gone. George considered the full implications of what Sam had said, and his voice turned quiet. "On whose authority?"

Sam shrugged. "Jay Harper's." He turned away, studied the nearest soldier's air hammer and the depth of the star drill it was driving, and raised his voice above the clamor. "That's deep enough! Move on to the next hole!"

George shut off the angry words that were in his mind and went back to his car. He turned the Mercedes around and headed it toward the governor's residence.

The governor was on his *portal*, a telephone at his elbow. He had just finished talking with Jay Harper at the improvised command post.

"There's a diversion tunnel," Jay had said. "It's blocked now. It has to be blasted open, and a channel blasted to it. If we can do that successfully, we can take half a million tons of pressure away from the dam every hour. We're going to go ahead and try."

Perhaps they would destroy the dam in the process, but in this crisis, what was the alternative? "Good luck," the governor had said. "I will stand behind your decision."

Now came George Harrison, and the temptation to have the man sent away was almost overpowering. Instead, out of long acquaintance and habit, the governor said, "Send him in."

"They are mining the wall at the Bend," George began. "Is the plan to destroy that wall if—?"

"If the dam fails," the governor said. "Yes, George."

"You can't do this, Harry! The—important people have their houses in the Bend! And against them you have—what? The *barrio*. Shacks! Trailer homes! Cheap hotels and little stores—"

"And thousands of people, George. Against perhaps two hundred in the bend."

"My family's house was the first in the area. I was born in it and I would live nowhere else." Until this moment George had not realized how strong were his roots. "And I will do everything I can to see that my house is protected. Do you want money, Harry?"

Nothing changed in the governor's face, but when he spoke his voice was a hoarse whisper. "I think you'd better leave now, George." He reached for the bell button on the wall.

George hesitated, then turned quickly and walked away. He drove home, and when he had parked at his house and let himself in, he went straight to his beloved library, where he closed the door and temporarily shut out the world.

Just down the hall was a room filled with memories of the past. On the walls were trophy heads of deer, elk, bighorn sheep and a single snarling cougar, all taken on the plains or in the towering mountains of the area since the first Harrison wagon had rolled into this country and stopped for good beside the river.

Now, with the sounds of the air hammers at the flood-control wall reaching even into the quiet of his library, George felt a rage such as he had never known.

Rising from his chair, he left the house, and returned to the flood-control wall to speak to Sam Martin again. Rock dust diffused the glare of the floodlights and made breathing uncomfortable. When Sam saw George approaching, he turned to the nearest soldier with a drill and shouted, "That's enough! Start setting the charges! Pass the word along!"

"Do you think," George said, "that the people who live in the Bend are going to be happy about losing their homes, Sam?"

"I can't help it," Sam said.

"There is a lot of money and influence in the Bend, Sam. And you have a great future here in the Southwest."

"What do you want me to do, quit my job?"

"No." The compressors and drills were silent now, and George lowered his voice. "You're an explosives expert, Sam. Suppose there failed to be an explosion? Or it was not sufficient to destroy the wall? There have been honest mistakes before."

"It would be my neck."

"It would also be money in the bank. I will be very plain. If the dam does collapse, and this wall remains intact protecting the Bend, there will be twenty-five thousand dollars to your account. You have my word."

ATOP MOUNT UNION, daylight had been blotted out by clouds and falling snow. Lightning flashes and crashing thunder were close to the fire-lookout building now.

At a time like this, when there was nothing to do but wait, talk passed the time, Pete thought. Besides, what was on his mind wanted to be said. "You know, I meant it." His voice was casual, interrupted occasionally by thunderclaps. "That guy I know in Santa Monica with the string of sporting goods stores—"

Bernie understood. "Would you be happy, Pete, just—selling things?" she asked.

"I once had a defensive-line coach, baby, who taught me a lot. He said to me, 'Look, Pete, nobody can do everything. What you want to do is know your strengths, and your weaknesses. Then you play to your strengths. That goes for everything.'"

Pete smiled at Bernie. "It stuck in my mind. I took a lot of time figuring out what I could and couldn't do on a football field. It worked. And I've been doing it ever since in everything. Like, I'm not the brightest guy in the world, but what I don't know about sporting goods I can learn, because sports have always been my bag. I think I could do a good job for the Santa Monica guy. And when you know you're doing a good job, it feels good, and so, yeah, I could be happy selling things. And besides, I'd have you around close, not sitting up here on the top of a mountain."

Bernie felt near to bursting with joy. She controlled it with effort. "I could work too, Pete."

"Sure—"

"Pete." Bernie's voice was quiet, but sharp. "Listen! Don't you hear it?" Suddenly she was on her feet. "That isn't snow anymore! It's *raining!* That warm front they talked about—it's moved in!"

She hurried to the radio table and switched on the speakers. Static filled the room. She picked up the hand mike, pushed the button that silenced the speakers, and spoke into it. "This is Mount Union calling. Come in, weather service! Over!"

There was no answering voice. Bernie raised the hand mike, and spoke with urgency. "This is Mount Union! We have rain, not snow! Repeat! We have rain, not snow! Acknowledge!"

Static again filled the room, and through it Pete said, "Wow! Did you see that? It—"

The sudden crack of thunder drowned the rest of his sentence, and all at once the lightning and the thunder and the sheeting rain were all around them, filling the tower with blinding light; the following darkness seemed filled with showers of sparks. In one of the flashes Pete saw Bernie put down the mike. She was sobbing, and he gathered her in and held her tight. "I can't get through, Pete! They have to know about the rain! And we can't tell them!"

A FRESH COLUMN of olive-drab trucks wound up the road toward the dam, carrying compressors and drilling equipment and men skilled in their use. Colonel Watkins rode with Cooley in the lead jeep. "I'll show you our little problem," Cooley said.

Minutes later, standing with the colonel and a captain of engineers at the head of the blocked tunnel, Cooley said, "There's going to be quite a bit of rock flying around unless your men are good and careful, but it can't be helped."

The captain said, "You actually want us to blow it all at once?"

"Stagger the blasts, if you want," Cooley said, "but we don't have time for one small charge and then a clean-up operation before the next one is set. This isn't a neat and pretty job."

"Better get to it, Captain," Colonel Watkins said.

THE LIGHTNING still flashed around them and simultaneous deafening thunder shook the lookout structure. Bernie's dog had crept to her feet and lay huddled against them, trembling. Pete said, "What could they do if they did know it was raining up here?"

"They could start evacuating people, instead of waiting until the last minute, when it might be too late."

"How about the other lookouts? Maybe they're getting through."

"It's what happens right here, at the head of the drainage system that feeds that lake, that's important, Pete. It's what *we* say that counts. And we can't warn them."

Pete was silent. In the intervals between thunder crashes he could hear the rain drumming on the roof. In a lightning flash he watched it falling, sheeting, wind-driven.

Pete now knew what he had to do. He said, "You know, Bernie, you asked me once did I know what flash floods could do. Yeah, I do. I've known these mountains since I was a kid." He stood up. "Where's the nearest phone?"

"Pete, no! What you're thinking—I won't let you! The phone's at the dam! You can't! Not in the dark! Not in this weather!"

"I've been wet before," Pete said, "and I didn't melt. I'll borrow your big flashlight, and leave my pack here. It'll be faster going down. Two hours, maybe two and a half." He put on his poncho.

Bernie, too, was standing now. "Pete, please! That trail—"

Pete's big hands caught her shoulders. "Baby, it's fun up here on your mountaintop. But we're still part of the real world. That's why you're so upset that you can't get through on the radio."

Tears stung her eyelids. "Pete, if something happens to you—"

"It's the guys who keep worrying about getting hurt that get it. If it happens, it happens. You hold the fort up here. Keep trying the radio. If you can't get through, I'll tell them what's happening. See you, baby."

The sliding door opened and the room was suddenly filled with the sound of wind, rain and fury. The door slid shut again, and it was quiet, and lonely. Bernie saw Pete's enormous ponchoed figure bend into the storm and disappear down the outside stairs.

106

ON THE THEORY that a sober man has a distinct advantage over a man who is even mildly under the influence, Tom Gentry was usually circumspect in his drinking. But on this night, after a call from Henry Warfield, president of the holding company which owned Tom's bank, he had taken more than his usual amount of alcohol, and had now reached that stage where inhibitions no longer seemed important: to have an idea was to act upon it immediately.

He appeared at the Thompsons' small house without warning and hammered on the door with his fist until Brooks Thompson appeared.

"Out here," Gentry said, "we kill our own snakes."

Brooks blinked in surprise. The last time he had seen Gentry was at the closing of the land sale at the bank, and the difference in the man now was startling. He had shucked off his air of calm as one shucks off an overcoat, and sheer fury was exposed.

"I'm not sure what that picturesque statement means," Brooks said, "but I think you've had too much to drink, Mr. Gentry."

"What it means," Gentry said, "is if you've got a bone to pick with a man, you don't go behind his back and get somebody else to do the dirty on him."

So, Brooks thought, Spencer Willoughby had reacted, as Brooks had imagined he would.

"I take it you've heard from my father-in-law?"

"That is just what I'm talking about. He got me fired!"

"I'm not sorry about that," Brooks said. "You have the profit you're going to make from that land to console you."

"Why, damn you, I don't have anything, except a twenty-two-thousand-five-hundred-dollar debt, and fifty acres of land I don't want! There's not going to be any enlargement of the dam! All they're thinking about now is how long before the dam collapses!"

Mary had appeared beside Brooks. "Oh, no!" she said.

"I'm going to take it out of your hide," Gentry said threateningly.

"You are going to do nothing of the sort," Brooks said. "And I don't want to hurt you, so you are going to get in your car and go."

Gentry threw his first punch. It was also his last.

Brooks caught the fist in a single movement and, without apparent effort, he used the captured hand and arm as a lever to spin Gentry around; the arm was now bent up behind his back in a painful hammerlock.

107

"I can dislocate your shoulder without any trouble, Mr. Gentry. Any more foolishness, and I will."

He gave Gentry a sudden, hard shove as he released the arm. Gentry stumbled a few running steps, and almost fell. Slowly he turned, his eyes wide with surprise.

"Now walk out to your car, Mr. Gentry, and go away. In your vernacular, if I have to, I'll kill my own snakes. Meaning you."

He turned, gestured Mary back inside the tiny living room and closed the door.

"I didn't want to do that," Brooks said. His tone changed. "So, no dam enlargement. And maybe the dam collapses. We'd better keep the radio on in case there's news."

ON THE MOUNTAIN TRAIL, Pete Otero was using the big flashlight sparingly, relying mostly on lightning flashes to show him the precarious way. In his playing days more than one sportswriter had likened him to a big cat for his sense of balance and his ability to shift his weight with almost unbelievable speed and accuracy. Here among these high peaks the storm winds swirled in all directions, now blasting at him head-on, now attacking from the flank or the rear, threatening to throw him off the narrow trail and down the mountainside. It took all his agility and strength to maintain his balance and forward momentum.

The rain was a torrent, and Pete's poncho, far from being a protection, was instead a menace, catching the gusts and filling like a sail, threatening to send him over the edge. He got the poncho off and let it go flying into the darkness.

The buffeting wind and driving rain, the lightning and the crashing thunder played rough. All right, he told himself. There was a trail, wasn't there? It was downhill, and all he had to do was stay on it, and keep himself more or less upright. Eventually the punishment would cease.

His first fall was not too bad. A rock slipped beneath his foot, and when he felt himself going down, he shoulder-rolled toward the mountainside, away from the drop-off. Okay, he thought as he picked himself up, I've got a few scratches and some bruises. Small damage.

The second fall was different. Without warning, a sudden shower of wet dirt and rocks from the mountainside hammered him to his knees, leaving him blinded, bloody, bruised and choking

108

on mud that had filled his eyes and mouth. He struggled free and by the light of the flash found a solid rock face to lean against. Raising his face skyward, he let the rain wash off some of the debris. How long he leaned there he did not know, but at last he pushed himself away and started off into the storm once more.

It was the third fall that almost finished him. It was sudden and vicious. He felt himself fall, away from the mountainside this time, as part of the trail gave way, and neither his agility nor his sense of balance could keep him from going over the edge backward.

He felt his head hit rock, and then his shoulder and ribs, as he cartwheeled. His head hit again, and his flailing, reaching hands found only loose rocks until his bad knee slammed with agonizing force against something unyielding. His head hit again, face down this time, and at last he stopped.

For a few stunned moments he lay motionless. Then, purely by reflex, he gingerly moved his neck, his hands and his feet. Everything worked. He was lying on a steep slant, head downhill. Clumsily he got his good knee beneath him and began clawing, crawling upward toward the trail, dragging the bad leg.

He came at last over the edge to more or less level ground again, moving entirely by feel now because he had lost the flashlight. He stopped to rest before he struggled to his feet, afraid to try the bad knee. But miraculously, when he put weight on it, the knee held and, although painful, it would even flex a little.

It hurt to breathe, so a couple of ribs were probably cracked. Despite the driving rain he tasted blood running down his face; that meant his scalp must be torn. And his right shoulder felt as if it needed attention. But the important thing was that he still functioned.

The wind still howled and tore at him relentlessly, driving rain droplets at him like tiny clubs. He had no clear idea where he was, but he was still on the trail downhill, which was all that counted. He started forward again, limping badly now.

A sudden lightning flash illuminated the entire scene and seemed to endure and endure, almost like one of those magnesium flares that used to light up night-time targets so pitilessly in Vietnam. And there, yes, there was that small lake he had noticed on the way up. But my Lord! It was a big lake now, and getting bigger by the moment. Water was spilling through the rocks that dammed it, and more water was pouring down from above. Sooner or later

110

the loose dam of rocks would give way, starting a flash flood roaring down from the mountains with unchecked fury. Okay, Pete told himself, all I can do is carry the message down the mountain. He limped painfully on into the howling darkness.

The first to see him was a soldier stationed well upstream from the dam with a walkie-talkie and a large lantern. In the lantern light Pete's enormous, bloody shape came limping toward him like something out of a horror movie.

The soldier raised the walkie-talkie and spoke into it in a voice that was not quite steady. "Somebody coming down the trail. He looks like he's hurt. Bad. Over."

"Coming from where?" asked a disembodied voice on the walkie-talkie. "Over."

Pete overheard. "Mount Union lookout," he said, still moving forward, trying not to break the painful rhythm he had established.

The soldier, backing up to stay with him, repeated over the walkie-talkie what Pete had said.

"Can he make it here by himself? Over."

"Can you?" the soldier said.

"If you get out of my way," Pete said, limping on.

He heard the roar of compressors and drills before he caught sight of the floodlighted scene, crowded with men in uniform. A civilian with obvious authority caught his upper arm in a powerful supporting grip and helped him to sit on a nearby rock.

"What's it doing up there?" asked Cooley Parks.

"Raining like hell. Lightning. And I saw a lake . . ."

Parks listened only briefly and then gestured to Colonel Watkins. "Get on the horn. Tell Jay we're coming down. We'll want to locate that lake on the map." And to Pete again, "Can you make it? Can the hospital wait?"

Pete lifted his bloody head. "Sure. Give me a hand up, is all."

"Good man," Cooley said, and with a strong grip almost lifted Pete to his feet for all his bulk, and helped him to a jeep.

The colonel drove. "We better make tracks," Pete said. "I only came out of the rain maybe a mile, two miles back. If it's a flash flood you're afraid of, you've got all the makings."

Kate, Jay and the governor were waiting in the office when Pete limped in, one hand resting heavily on Cooley's solid shoulder. His injuries all hurt like the devil now that the cold and the shock had worn off. But he and pain were old acquaintances.

111

Jay said, "It's raining hard, right? Was there much runoff?"

A little guy, Pete thought, but he seemed to know what he was about. "When I started out, the runoff was normal for a heavy rain-storm. But I was in it maybe two hours, and streams that hadn't been there the other day were beginning to form, some of them good-sized."

Jay was at the topographical map. "That lake you told Cooley about." He put his finger where he had seen water from the plane that first day flying with Kate. "About here?"

"I know north from south by a compass, but picking out a spot on one of those contour maps—"

Cooley said, "Here's your trail." His finger traced its course. "You'd be seeing the water off to your left, across a canyon and fifty feet lower than you were. The drop-off below the trail where you were standing is steep. On either side of the spot where we think the lake may be, there's a ridge, and the whole thing comes out on a kind of shelf. Does that ring bells?"

Pete closed his eyes. Slowly he nodded. "Yeah. You've got it. I was maybe a third of the way down." He opened his eyes again. "When I first saw the lake, on the way up, it was maybe a quarter full. Now it's almost overflowing." Pete could close his eyes and see the picture the lightning flash had revealed, water pouring down into the lake, water leaking through the rocks at the lake's foot and falling into empty space.

Both Jay and Cooley were looking at the map now. "Oh, brother!" Cooley said. "Look at the drop when those rocks give way."

"I am looking," Jay said. He was counting contour lines so close they were almost on top of one another. "Eight hundred, a thousand feet, and then a downhill run with the main stream."

Kate said, "Are you finished with him now? If you are, I'll drive him to the hospital and see that he's taken care of." Compassion, concern and admiration were in her voice.

Pete showed his crooked grin. His job was done. Never mind the pain. He felt good. "You know, lady," he said, "that's the best offer I've had today."

After they had left, the governor, the colonel, Jay and Cooley stood close around the table, where the map was spread. "Spell it out for me," the governor said. "What does it mean?"

Cooley said slowly, "An almost certain flash flood when that

112

natural rock dam goes, which will happen when the water reaches a certain weight."

The door opened and Bill Williams came in. He seemed younger, Jay thought, more as he had seemed that first night. Responsibility agreed with him. Williams said, "Dynamite, caps, wire and detonators are on their way both to the dam and the flood-control wall." He stopped and looked from one to another. "Trouble?"

"Perhaps." The governor's voice was calm. He looked at Jay, at Cooley. "You cannot predict when this—break may occur?"

"Not even if we stood there watching." This was Cooley. "And by the time we started to speak, it would be all over."

"If you can open that diversion tunnel," the governor said, "and start draining water through it before that rock dam collapses, the main dam might be able to withstand the shock of the flash flood when, and if, it comes?"

He paused. "On the other hand," he said, "I think we had better take certain precautions." He dialed the mayor's office. "This is Governor Wilson. May I speak to Mr. Lopez?"

"Right here, Harry," the mayor's voice said.

"I think we've gone as far as we can without issuing a broad warning, Joe," the governor said.

There was a brief pause. "Something's happened?"

"No one thing. A combination—" He left the sentence hanging.

"I'll take your word for it," the mayor said. His voice was brisk. "We'll start moving the old and the sick and the handicapped to schools, churches and firehouses on higher ground. The TV and radio guys'll give me time on all channels and frequencies. We'll need National Guard troops to help us in the *barrio*—"

"You'll have them."

"They'll blow that flood wall at the Bend if the dam does go?"

"They will," the governor said.

"Okay, Harry. Wish us luck."

The governor hung up and looked at Colonel Watkins. "The municipal authorities will require National Guard assistance to start evacuating people, Colonel. Will you see to it, please? As for the rest—" The governor looked at Jay.

"We push both projects," Jay said. "Cooley can ramrod the blasting at the dam." He looked at Williams. "And if you will—"

"Make sure that we're ready to destroy my home?" Williams asked with a bitter smile. He nodded. "Will do."

113

"I *am* sorry, Bill," the governor said. "If there were any other way—"

"Let it go, Harry. See you." Williams walked out.

COOLEY braked the borrowed jeep to a skidding stop alongside the trucks parked above the dam. He jumped out and looked around. Here, in the glare of floodlights, men swarmed among the rocks, heaving their pneumatic drills from spot to spot, sending clouds of dust shimmering in the air and making the night hideous with noise. Above it all, rising from the power station below the dam, came the painful scream of turbines spinning out of control as the outflow of water was increased.

The captain of engineers came toward Cooley. "Sir," he said, "I know something about explosives, and if we set off what it's going to take to open a channel to that tunnel and open the tunnel itself all at once—well, that kind of explosion may collapse the dam all by itself."

"You're absolutely right," Cooley said. "But there's a hanging valley upstream, and a lake that's going to come down on us all at once. . . ."

"Okay, sir," the captain said. "You're calling the shots."

"Correct. How long before we can clear the area and blow it?"

"Maybe by daylight."

Cooley shook his head. "Not good enough. Two hours at the most."

A SOLDIER sent downstream to warn anyone who might be in the summer cottages below the dam turned in from the main road past five mailboxes. A single house showed light, and he went up to knock on the front door.

The porch light went on, the door opened and a man in pajamas said, "What's going on?"

"Mister," the soldier said, "the word is that the dam might give way. We're setting charges to open that old diversion tunnel, and they're mining that flood-control wall down at the Bend to blow it if they have to—"

"My Lord! The Bend? Well, what am I supposed to do?"

"Mister, if it was me, I'd climb that hill yonder and spend the rest of the night there. Just in case." The soldier indicated the other houses." Anybody else here?"

"There wasn't anybody else last night. I came up to get some early morning fishing, me and my wife. Look, soldier, this is for real?"

"Mister," the soldier said, "I'm telling you what they told me when they sent me out. They think the dam's unsafe."

KATE WILLIAMS walked slowly down the hospital corridor with the staff surgeon. "It looks to me," the doctor said, "as if Otero's knee will have to be fused. I don't think there's enough left there to work with. For the rest, we're stitching him up here and there, and strapping that shoulder. He's taken punishment before. He'll shake it off."

"He didn't have to do it," Kate said. "He could have stayed safe on the mountain with his girl."

"Sure." The doctor smiled briefly, without humor. "Even in war-time there's usually some way to play it safe. Rumors are flying around that they're afraid of the dam. I guess Otero's taking all that trouble to come down the mountain confirms them, doesn't it?"

"Yes."

The doctor whistled softly. "Then this hospital should go on alert." He glanced at Kate. "Flood, earthquake, hurricane—you can't predict which way any of them will spread. But there's one thing you do know: hospitals always get busy when a disaster happens."

It was Angelita Leyba's son Luis, his precious new skateboard under his arm, who brought her the news. "Hey! Guess what? You know that dam up at Harper's Park? Well, it's going to bust!"

Angelita's eyes grew large and round, and she shook her head in silent disbelief.

"Everybody's talking about it!" Luis said. "*Todo el mundo!* Maybe there's something on the tube." Luis trotted across the small room to turn on the television set.

The picture came into focus and Luis turned up the sound. José-María Lopez, the mayor, was speaking gravely. "We are merely taking precautions," he said, speaking each sentence slowly in English and repeating it in Spanish to be certain he'd be under-stood. "We are asking all those in the *barrio* who are ill, or

115

handicapped, unable to move quickly, to leave their homes now. There are soldiers in the streets who will tell them where to go and who will arrange transportation if that is necessary. There is no cause for panic. I repeat, this is merely a precaution. . . ."

THAT REALLY blew it, Johnny Cisneros thought as he watched the mayor's image on TV and listened to his careful warning. Soldiers in the streets and old people milling around, leaving their homes unprotected, probably not even locked! This could be the start of looting.

Johnny had seen to it that his warehouse was emptied and those TVs and stereos hauled off to higher ground. The building where they were now stored was safe from flooding, and couldn't be broken into very easily. His retail store was something else. Given man's avarice—which who knew better than Johnny?—there was always the possibility of people breaking in.

So, okay, he was insured. Walt Duggan might have to take a bath after all, but that was Walt's worry. Except—wait a minute! Two thousand dollars in cash was sitting right there in the store! Just in case Walt had gotten suspicious and asked his pal Tom Gentry about it, Johnny had drawn four thousand from his own bank account so it would look like that whole sum had changed hands, instead of the two thousand Angelita Leyba had actually received. There was no insurance on that two thousand dollars in cash. There was nothing else to do but to go down to the store and take the money out before some thief broke in and found it.

BROOKS AND MARY THOMPSON heard the mayor's warning on the radio and when he finished speaking, Brooks said, "Gentry was right. The dam's probably going to go."

"We have the car," Mary said. "We can go where we want."

"Your grandmother's silver? The china? Your clothes?"

Mary drew a deep, unsteady breath. "We can lock the silver in the trunk of the car and park the car on high ground. As for the rest—Grandmother told me once: " 'Things aren't important, child. People are. Remember that.' "

Mary was silent for a few moments. "I have Red Cross training," she said. "Maybe they can use me at the hospital."

Brooks' smile was fond. "I'll see if I can make myself useful too. Maybe City Hall can find something for me to do."

116

IT WAS NOW three thirty in the morning, but Bill Williams' office, the official command post, was a flurry of activity. The governor was just hanging up the phone in the outer office when Jay came through the door. To the soldier manning the radio equipment Colonel Watkins had had installed, Jay said, "See if you can raise Cooley Parks, up above the dam." He stood waiting beside the table. Lord, he was tired! But, then, so was everyone else. When Cooley's voice came on, Jay asked him, "How we doing?"

"We'll be ready to blow in about a half hour. It'll be a fine big bang, boy. You'll hear it way down there."

"Any discoloration in the stream yet?"

"A little. Not much. We've still got a chance."

"Hang in there," Jay said. "Call me if there's any change."

AT THE BEND'S flood-control wall, Bill Williams, legs widespread, shoulders hunched, stood facing Sam Martin in the white glare of the carbon lights. "You're dragging your feet, Sam. Why?"

"I want it to go right, is all."

There was something not quite right in Sam's manner, Williams thought. He didn't like it. "You have the powder, caps, wire and detonator. Why aren't you ready to blow?"

"It means your house if we blow this wall, Bill."

"Don't you think I know that, dammit? Now get those charges wired and ready!" Williams watched Sam turn away reluctantly, and added further impetus. "And make sure you do it right!"

He walked back to his car and got in, reaching automatically for the silver pillbox. His pulse was erratic and overly strong; he could feel it pounding in his throat. He picked up the car telephone and called the familiar number of his own office. Jay answered.

"I've got them moving here," Williams told him. "Maybe forty-five minutes and we'll be all set. I'll stay and keep an eye on things. Anything else?"

"A couple of things," Jay said. "Cooley says he'll be ready to blow within a half hour. When he gets that tunnel open, you'll have quite a bit more water coming at you. Don't mistake that for the real thing. There'll be radio warning if the whole dam goes, and you'll have plenty of time to set off your charges."

"Got it. What's the other thing?"

"Kate called. She wanted me to tell you she's staying at the hospital. Says she can be useful there."

"Thanks." Williams hung up and sat quiet, his hands resting on the steering wheel. He thought about Kate. And about Martha, who was never far from his thoughts.

The familiar fluttery feeling began without warning in his chest. He had the strange feeling that maybe one day soon he might be seeing Martha again. He hoped so, and smiled in contemplation. He would be sorry about leaving Kate, of course, but she had her own life to live. He had had his time, he and Martha together. Now it was Kate's turn.

His eyes automatically watching the soldiers at work under Sam's direction, and his mind satisfied now with their efforts, he picked up the car telephone again and called the hospital. Kate was found. "Hi, honey. Just checking in. How's it going?"

"Daddy, these poor people! They're bringing them from the *barrio*. They've left everything! Everything! I could cry! But you— you don't sound very good. Are you all right?"

"I'm fine. I'm watching Sam do the work." Williams hesitated. No interference, he told himself. But maybe, just maybe, there wouldn't be another chance to say what had been growing in his mind. "I said it before," he said, "but I'll say it again: that's a good man sitting up there in my office making the decisions for us."

"Jay?"

"That's right, honey. You could go a long, long way and not do nearly as well. Just remember your old man said that. 'By now." He hung up quickly before Kate could answer.

She put the telephone down slowly, puzzled. The conversation had not been like her father. And that last bit, almost pushing her at Jay Harper, whom she scarcely knew and was not even sure she liked, was totally out of character. Unless—dreadful thought—it actually *was* the last thing he intended to do, his last gift; unless out of affection he was throwing away all restraint. He—

"Another busload coming in," a voice behind her said. It was Mary Thompson, a stranger, who had merely walked into the hospital and started making herself useful. Tall, composed, Mary was now saying, "I don't know any Spanish. So you're needed, not I."

Wrong, Kate thought. We're both needed. Mary was the one to whom the old, ill or handicapped people from the *barrio* seemed instinctively to turn for guidance, reassurance. "Let's both go meet the bus," she said.

Its passengers came out slowly, hesitantly, strangers in a strange

118

land. "There are sandwiches and soup and coffee inside," Kate said in Spanish. "You will be comfortable here, and safe." But she was close to tears as she saw the bewilderment and fear on almost every face. Mary spoke to them too, in English. Her tone and her smile clearly conveyed comfort, but not all were reassured.

"They did not tell me it was the hospital we were going to," one man said in Spanish. He stopped at the bottom of the bus steps, rested both hands on the head of his cane and looked at the two young women defiantly. "Hospitals are for dying."

Kate shook her head. "This hospital is for living, señor. You must believe that."

The man studied her in silence. "Do I know you, señorita?"

"My name is Williams. My father—"

"Señor Bill?"

"Sí."

The man nodded gravely. "Then I will believe you, señorita." He straightened and walked slowly toward the doorway.

Mary said, "I understand enough of that. Your father is obviously well known."

"He is." I want to go to him right now and find out what that telephone call meant, Kate thought, but I cannot leave here. To the bus passengers, in Spanish again: "Inside there are sandwiches and soup and coffee. Do not be afraid. You will be safe here."

THE MAYOR'S office was busy. Brooks Thompson stood against the wall sizing up the situation. The mayor could be seen at his desk in the inside office, taking telephone call after telephone call.

A man was in the outer office, winnowing out visitors who came in from the hallway, allowing some to penetrate the inner office, dealing with some himself. It was Carlos García, the schoolteacher, and there was resistance in his face when he saw Brooks.

"What do you want?"

"To make myself useful, if I can. Run errands, whatever."

"Do you speak Spanish?"

"Unfortunately, no."

"Then what—?" Carlos stopped. "There is a problem," he said. It had been bothering him for some time. He knew of no one to send, because a man of Spanish descent would have to be a brave man indeed to challenge the authority in his own church. But an Anglo—"Do you know the church in the *barrio*?"

119

"Yes."

"The priest?"

Brooks had seen him many times, small, frail, old, carrying himself with careful dignity. "Yes."

"He is in his church and he won't leave it. He ought to be in a safe place with the other older people."

Brooks nodded. "Consider it done."

IT WAS funny how few people there were in the streets, Johnny Cisneros thought as he hurried toward his store. A jeep with two soldiers passed him, driving slowly. The soldier next to the driver held an automatic weapon of some kind, its butt on his thigh. He looked at Johnny, then spoke to the driver. The jeep stopped and the soldier with the automatic weapon got out and approached warily, his rifle at the ready.

"You got business in this part of town, Mac?" the soldier said.

When Johnny was a kid he had avoided authority like the plague, running and hiding when it appeared. But he wasn't a kid any longer, and he could buy and sell these punks in uniform in carload lots. "Get back in your kiddie car, soldier," he said. "I live here."

The jeep's radio crackled briefly, and the driver called, "Leave him, Gus! We got looting down at Sears!"

The soldier with the weapon hesitated, then trotted back to the jeep and jumped in. The jeep roared off.

Looting, Johnny thought, just like he'd expected. And the sound of the jeep's radio had started another train of thought, too. He should have brought along a transistor radio himself. How the hell was he going to know if and when the dam collapsed? A bad oversight, but the store was full of radios. On the way back he'd be able to keep abreast of developments.

COOLEY stood with the captain of engineers, and with a jerk of his head indicated the nearby communications man surrounded by equipment. "The soldier upstream is reporting more discoloration," Cooley said. "And it's raining on him now too, which means the entire watershed is getting it. Your time has run out, Captain. Clear the area. Then blow it."

Cooley walked over to the communications center. "Get me the downtown building." He stood quiet while he waited, watching the orderly bustle as soldiers hauled their equipment away from where the channel to the blocked tunnel would be blown.

"They're on the horn, sir," the communications man said, and handed Cooley the handset.

"Go ahead." It was Jay's voice.

"We're clearing the area and we're going to blow. Hold it a minute!" He turned to face the interruption. "Yes?"

The lieutenant in charge of the dam-watching detail was at Cooley's elbow. "You want us to pack up too?"

Cooley shook his head. "Definitely not. You're our eyes. Take what cover you can, but keep your floodlights on that dam. If it shows any signs of weakening, we want to know it fast."

Cooley raised the handset again. "That's all I've got at the moment, boy. I'll stay on the line and keep you posted."

UPSTREAM it had suddenly happened. All at once, the natural dam containing the lake in the hanging valley was strained beyond its strength, and it collapsed. As Cooley had predicted, the actual collapse took less time than would have been required to describe it. The loosened rock simply toppled over the edge of the hanging valley, and the thousands of tons of water it had restrained followed, dropping, as Jay had calculated, eight hundred to a thousand feet into the gorge below, there to add its crashing energy to that of the already swollen and down-cutting stream fed by a thousand mountainside rivulets. The flash flood had begun, and from the moment of inception it was a thundering monster.

It gathered more force and speed as it rushed downstream, now broadening and slowing momentarily as its head entered a wide place in the streambed or a *ciénega*, now narrowing and picking up more speed and strength as it entered the next gorge. All the while it was fed by tributaries and normally dry channels, down which water was pouring from the torrents of rain above.

The flood tore rocks from their beds and ripped all support from beneath trees, and rising six or eight feet above its normal level, it demolished a wooden footbridge in its path as if the sturdy timbers had been matchsticks.

It reached the soldier sent upstream to report the first discoloration. First he heard a deep-throated roar approaching. Then in the cone of his flashlight he saw the ragged wall of dirty water sweep into view and past him; for a moment, stunned, he was unable to speak. Then he raised his walkie-talkie and managed to say, "Good Lord! Here it comes! Watch out! It's a wall of dirty water! It's tossing heavy timbers like twigs, so it has to have taken out that footbridge, and the bridge is six, eight feet above the normal water level! Or was! I never saw such a thing!"

The captain of engineers was standing near Cooley and heard that first hysterical message. He looked immediately to Cooley for decision.

"Blow it!" Cooley said. "Set the damned thing off!" He raised the handset. "We've got our flash flood, boy," he said to Jay. "And it's a good one."

"Okay," Jay said. "You're going to blow that tunnel open?"

"There she goes!" Only Cooley's roaring voice could have carried the message over the sound of the first great explosion, which in the confines of the dammed valley was storm, war, apocalypse, deafening the ears and threatening the soul with its fury.

Rock and rock dust filled the air. The ground shook. In the glare of the floodlights the surface of the lake rippled and stirred, set in motion by shudders deep in the earth. Fragments of rock splashed into the water. Echoes of the first explosion reverberated among the mountain peaks and grew to a rolling thunder as each fresh explosion from the staggered charges added its force.

Explosion by explosion the channel grew, beginning at the lake's edge, gouging great scars into the earth and rock, moving inexorably toward the blocked tunnel.

Cooley was crouching, his hands over his head for partial protection. His eyes had not left the exposed dam face rising above the water of the lake.

It was holding! No crack, no faintest blemish appeared!

And as he watched, water began to fill the channel the explosions had blasted free. Only a little water at first, moving sluggishly, impeded by loose rock. But the quantity grew, a trickle, a stream, a small river, and then all at once—driven by gravity and speeded by the weight of lake water behind and above—it was a flood tossing aside rocks in its path.

The final explosion opened the tunnel, and where the boys' careful dry wall had hidden it, the entrance suddenly appeared, a black hole quickly filled by downrushing water from the channel.

Still the dam held intact, and the captain of engineers, his young face grimy from the dust of the explosions, shouted to

Cooley in triumph, "You were right, sir! You were right!"

Cooley was looking the other way now, and listening. In the ringing silence that followed the last explosion they could all hear it now, even above the painful shriek of the power-plant turbines: the deep-throated roar of the flash flood, led by its ragged wall of water and debris, slamming out of the last gorge upstream and approaching the edge of the lake.

Cooley shook his head. Into the handset he said quietly, "We'll know the whole story in just a couple of minutes, boy."

Jay said immediately to Colonel Watkins, who was at his shoulder, "Get on to Bill Williams at the flood-control wall. Tell him what's happened and tell him to stand by."

Jay nodded then to the governor. "The mayor. He'd better know too. He's the one to push the panic button."

The governor walked into the inner office, seated himself and dialed the city offices. Into the phone he said, "Joe? Harry. This is the situation. . . ."

COOLEY PARKS, handset hanging at his side, awaited the appearance of the roaring monster he could plainly hear upstream. For a moment nothing moved; the world seemed to hold its breath.

And then all at once, it came.

Wall of water was not the proper description. The flash flood was led by an upstanding *face* of dirty water and foam, a vertical cliff, a battering ram, slamming into the lake.

Instantly there arose a wave such as one would expect to see only on an ocean shore in a great storm. Later accounts of its height varied from ten feet to thirty, but all agreed that it seemed to pause as if gathering strength and fury before it began its terrifying rush across the lake toward the upstream face of the dam.

Of all who watched, probably only Cooley and the captain of engineers gave thought to the unspectacular but far more dangerous underwater shock of hydraulic pressure transmitted almost instantaneously against the dam through the lake water.

The surface wave slammed against the dam with a crash like that of a gigantic automobile collision. The wall of the dam seemed to flinch with the impact and then somehow regain its shape. Water and spray flew high into the dawn air.

Guardsmen manning the floodlights on high, safe ground above the exposed downstream side of the dam saw, as if by magic, a crack appear in the concave face. Instantly every eye went to it.

The soldier manning the radio line to the command-post office downtown gave his report in a voice that was not quite steady. "There's a crack in the dam wall! It's maybe ten feet long! It's twenty, thirty feet from the top and it runs diagonal-like from upper right to lower left."

"Is the crack enlarging?" Jay asked.

"It doesn't seem to be."

"Is there any sign of leakage?"

"There's a little water coming through. You know how a sidewalk turns dark in a rain? That's how it is."

"Stand by, over and out."

Above the dam, on the lake side, Cooley raised his handset. "I heard, and I guess that's it, boy. I can't see anything from here, but if that fracture has gone all the way through, and it has to if there's leakage, then it's all over. We gave it our best shot. It just wasn't our day for miracles."

"Right." Jay's voice was expressionless. Then, speaking to someone at his end, he said, "All whistles and sirens, everything we have."

Over the handset Jay now said to Cooley, "The soldiers in the *barrio* have orders to get everybody out when the sirens and bells go. They also have orders to shoot looters on sight. Can you think of anything else?"

The speaker, tuned to the communication center below the dam, suddenly came alive again with the soldier's voice, hollow and high-pitched now with excitement. "That crack's growing, and water's beginning to spurt through! It's like—like a hundred fire hoses all at once! Oh, my Lord! It's like in the movies, like stop-action on TV!"

"I can see it!" Cooley said over the handset. "He's right. There's an illusion of slow motion. There's—"

The speaker voice drowned out all else. "There she goes, a-roarin' and a-snortin'. She's just busted loose and filled that whole gorge from side to side and top to bottom with water. A wall of water forty-, fifty-foot high, bangin' downstream like a runaway freight train! God help them down below!"

Cooley's steady voice said, "Luck, boy."

Jay looked at the governor and the colonel. His face was expressionless. "Twenty minutes," he said.

124

TO THE EAST the sky was beginning to lighten, and here in the sloping meadow below the dam site, where earlier the warning jeep had stopped and the soldier had roused a man in the cottage, some details of terrain were already distinguishable.

After the jeep had driven away, the man, whose name was Carley, had stomped back into the cottage and told his wife about the dam.

Dressed now, he came out on the front porch to have a look. Faintly, distantly, he heard the sounds of sirens, and then his wife's voice from the kitchen.

"Joe! Joe! On the radio! Listen!" She came out, breathless, waving a small transistor radio wildly.

"The Harper's Park dam is collapsing!" the announcer's voice said. "This is not a test! I repeat, this is not a test! The dam at Harper's Park is collapsing, and all people are urged to—"

Joe switched the radio off. "Let's go! Up that hill as fast as we can!" He grabbed his wife's hand and they began to run toward the hillside. Scrambling, stumbling, they reached a high, rocky, outcropping. "Maybe this is high enough!" Carley said. "We're almost even with the top of that gorge up there, and—will you look at that!"

The gorge, visible upstream, was suddenly filled with churning water and debris, trees, pieces of metal, raw earth and tumbling rock. The sound of the flood was a roar that blotted out everything else. Beneath them the ground shook.

His wife covered her face with her hands. Carley stared as the flood reached the meadow, spread, tore trees from the ground and boulders from their resting places, flung a single mailbox high into the air, and gouged great chunks of dirt and rock from the hillside.

Carley saw his station wagon tossed like a toy on the dirty yellowish crest. Then his house, like others around it, was lifted bodily from its foundation. For a few moments it retained its form and structure; then it simply dissolved into a mass of unconnected boards and doors, a panel of windows for the moment miraculously intact, a bobbing refrigerator, and there the stove, all finally disappearing into the irresistible turbulence.

Carley scrambled a few more feet up the hillside, and from there he could see the gorge below the meadow as the flood reached it, and suddenly confined once more, rose unbelievably to fill the narrow opening to its upper limits and beyond, spreading on the high plateau before it began its steeper plunge beyond the gorge.

His wife had uncovered her eyes. "Joe!" she screamed. "Where are you?"

Carley rubbed his forehead with the back of his hand in a gesture of weary helplessness. "Up here," he said. "I'm watching the end of the world."

BILL WILLIAMS walked from his car to the face of the flood-control wall, where Sam Martin stood. "Finish up and get the men away," Bill said. "In ten minutes we're going to blow it."

"Look, Bill—"

"I'm not going to argue. Hear those sirens? Do you think I like it any better than you do? Get moving!"

He was tired, Williams realized, bone-tired, and he wanted nothing so much as to find some place to rest. But only after he had done what he had to do here.

The telephone in his car was ringing. He hurried to it and leaned in to answer. "Williams."

"It's gone," the colonel's voice said, overly calm against rising excitement. "The dam just went. Harper says—"

"Tell him we're blowing in nine minutes," Williams said.

THE PRIEST was pulling on his bell rope and praying, his lips moving visibly, when Brooks walked into the church. From the steeple, the sound the *barrio* had heeded for almost a hundred years was added to the newer, louder sounds of sirens and horns throughout the city.

"Time to go, Padre," Brooks said. "They sent me from the mayor's office to get you to safety."

A young Anglo, the priest thought. He had seen him on the street, but never in the church. "This is my church," he said, "my post. I cannot leave."

"Right," Brooks said. It was merely an acknowledgement of the situation. He had expected resistance, and had already decided how to deal with it. "Sorry, Padre," he said, and without visible effort he picked the priest up on his shoulder in a fireman's carry, and holding him fast, headed at a trot for the door, the street and high ground. As he ran, it occurred to him irreverently that the priest could continue to pray just as well upside down as he could while pulling on a bell rope.

126

JOHNNY CISNEROS was listening to the shiny new transistor radio he carried as he came out of the store and carefully closed the door behind him. In his concentration, he did not hear the jeep coming around the corner in his direction.

"Hey, you!" It was the same Anglo soldier who had challenged Johnny before. "Stop where you are!"

Johnny, reacting instinctively, tucked away the envelope containing the two thousand dollars.

"What's that you just hid?" The soldier was already out of the jeep and advancing on foot, his automatic weapon at the ready.

Over the radio the announcer's voice was saying, "It is estimated that floodwater will be at least forty feet above normal river level when it reaches Old Town!"

"You heard the man," Johnny said. "We'd better get out of here. This is my store, and I'm going home."

"Sure," the soldier said. He held out his hand. "I want to see what's in that envelope you hid. And I want to know where you got that radio. You didn't have it when we saw you before."

"To hell with you!" Johnny said. He turned and began to walk quickly toward the high ground of his apartment house.

Just around the corner, Brooks Thompson, still carrying the slight priest over his broad shoulder, heard the sudden rattle of automatic-weapon fire. Brooks stopped instantly and lowered the priest to the sidewalk. "Stay here, Padre. I'll have a look."

The priest nodded slowly and stood motionless as he watched the young Anglo approach the building at the corner and peer around it. He drew back immediately, and then said, "Padre, you'd better come. I think you may be needed."

Johnny Cisneros lay face down where he had stumbled and fallen. The shiny new transistor radio lay a few feet away, still turned on but no longer finely tuned, and the announcer's voice was muffled.

The jeep was at the curb, its engine running, and the driver was standing beside the soldier who had fired the shots, staring incredulously at the money from the envelope Johnny had hastily tucked away. Both soldiers turned quickly as Brooks and the priest hurried toward them.

"A looter," the first soldier said, holding out the money. "Look at this! And the radio!"

The priest knelt, his hand touching Johnny's cheek. Blood

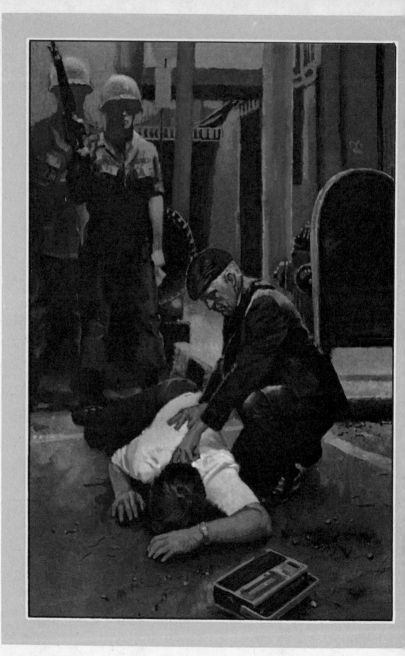

Flood

stained the sidewalk. The priest prayed quietly, and Johnny's eyes indicated comprehension. It seemed only a short time before the priest's voice stopped and he made the sign of the cross. The sirens and the whistles sounded on, but their noise seemed to have receded and here it was quiet now.

Johnny's mouth opened. Blood ran down his chin as his lips moved. His words were scarcely audible. "Thanks, Padre," he said, as his eyes closed for the last time.

Slowly the priest got to his feet. He looked at the soldiers.

"A looter," the first soldier said again. He was aghast at what he had done. He held out the money. "See?"

GEORGE HARRISON was in his library, a balloon glass of cognac at his elbow. He had not turned on either radio or television, and although he could hear the sirens and understood their message, he ignored them.

His offer of money to Sam Martin at the wall had been a considered act, and he was prepared to keep his promise. What he did not know, of course, was Sam's decision, and everything depended on that.

George reached for the glass of cognac, held it cupped for a little time in the palm of his hand to warm it, sniffed the bouquet appreciatively and took a sip.

George knew perfectly well what Bill's reaction would be if he learned of George's offer to Sam Martin, but George doubted that Sam would tell him, and Sam *was* the explosives expert. So in the end it all came down to what Sam decided. And whatever Sam Martin decided, and regardless of Bill Williams, George Harrison was not going to desert his home.

TWO THOUSAND FEET the flood had to drop before it reached the Bend. Cooley, marooned at the dam site, stood quietly watching the water level of the lake diminish as if by magic, and hearing the trailing roar of the torrent as it poured through the gorge below.

The floodlights, brighter by far than the early dawn, still illuminated the scene, casting black shadows into what had been water and was now an expanding area of shiny mud. He could hear the bellowing thunder of the water as it tore through the gap where the dam had been, and where only a few remnants of concrete and reinforcing steel were left.

As more of the lake bottom emerged, Cooley's attention was fixed not on what was but on what was not. The stone buildings he had seen on the bottom of the lake while Jay was diving had disappeared, wiped away as if they had never been. Harper's Park village was no longer merely submerged; it had ceased to exist.

"I guess it was like this after the Flood," the captain of engineers said.

Cooley nodded. "Something like."

"And what's happening downstream—" The captain shook his head.

"This," Cooley said, "is just a preview. Down below at the Bend they'll be seeing the main feature in a few minutes."

THE LAST of the National Guard trucks, loaded with soldiers, and towing compressors, generators and floodlights, pulled away from the flood-control wall. Bill Williams drove his car close to the wall and got out. "Okay, Sam," he said. "Time's up. Beat it. I'll blow it." He spoke with determined calm, trying not to think of the house he and Martha together had planned and built.

"It's a makeshift job, Bill," Sam said. There was that evasive quality in his voice again. "We had to hurry too much. And we didn't have as much wire as I'd like."

"You're dragging your feet again, Sam," Bill said. "Why?"

"Bill, it isn't going to do any good to blow it!" There, it was out! The twenty-five thousand dollars George Harrison had offered was a lot of money, Sam was thinking, and he had almost convinced himself that the destruction of the wall was of questionable efficacy. He doubted if much of the flood would be diverted from the lower city even if the wall were destroyed.

Bill controlled himself with effort. "That's how you think, Sam. You're overruled. Now beat it."

I could stop him, Sam thought. I'm young enough and big enough and strong enough. And twenty-five thousand dollars is waiting. Why am I holding back?

Bill Williams watched him quietly, almost as if he could see the struggle in Sam's mind—and knew already how it would come out.

I'm holding back, Sam thought, because I'm kidding myself that I could do otherwise. I'd have to kill him to stop him. That had always been the fact you faced in Bill Williams: total commitment once the chips were down.

Sam's resistance crumbled. "Okay, Bill." There was a sense of shame underlying the words. He turned and walked quickly away to the jeep that had been left for him. He did not look back, and he drove as fast as the jeep would go. He was a half mile away when he saw in the mirror, then heard and felt the explosion.

Inside the thick adobe walls of his house George Harrison heard and felt it too. He finished his cognac, put the glass down carefully and went outside. The last stars were gone, and the sun was almost rising. In the direction of Harper's Park there were still clouds, but down here the sky was clear. It was going to be a fine day.

George hesitated. He was determined not to desert his house. On the other hand, he had to know whether Sam Martin had rigged the explosion, or whether the wall had indeed been destroyed. By George's watch there still remained a few minutes of the twenty predicted following the first sirens and horns. He began to walk quickly, skirting cactus, piñons and juniper.

He reached water where there should not have been water. And then he saw the debris of the wall, and for a moment the rage he had felt before rose in his chest. Damn Sam Martin! Damn Jay Harper! Above all, damn Bill Williams! If it had not been for him—

It was then that he saw Bill's car—lying on its side, windows shattered, side panels dented as from massive hammerblows. And pinned beneath it in the rock and the rubble, in the dirt now turning to mud, something moved feebly. George advanced slowly, his shoes making squishing sounds. He bent forward. He could not believe his eyes. It was Bill Williams, scarcely recognizable from the explosion!

George put his hands against the heavy car and pushed. Nothing happened except that his feet sank deeper into the dampening ground. He tried again.

"Cut it out, George." It seemed impossible that Bill could speak, but his eyes were open, and his voice was audible. "You can't move it. Beat it, man! It's coming. Can't you hear it?"

George *could* hear it, a distant sound that shook the earth.

"Head for that high ground!" Bill said. "You may still have time."

But George's mind was made up. "I've run and I've hidden all my life," he said slowly. "This time—" unconsciously he quoted a line of old western verse "—I'll die before I'll run."

"That's just plain stupid!" Bill's eyes closed. The roaring flood was closer now, louder, and the earth was trembling. Bill opened his eyes again. "No," he said, "maybe it isn't at that. Sometimes a man has to make his choice." He closed his eyes again. Martha seemed very close.

THE GOVERNOR, Colonel Watkins and Jay had watched the explosion at the flood-control wall from the windows of Bill Williams' high office. It was too far away, and the sounds of the sirens and horns were too loud, for them to hear the actual blast, but they saw rocks and dirt blown high into the air and a huge cloud of dust that began to settle slowly.

Jay looked at his watch. "Maybe ten minutes now," he said. He glanced at the colonel. "Are you ready?"

"Yes, sir."

The governor looked from one man to the other. "What does that mean?"

"If it's necessary," Jay said, "we have one more shot to fire. We've mined the railroad bridge."

"Why wasn't I told? Have you any idea what cutting that will do in terms of the economy of this entire section of the country?"

"I was sure you would react like this," Jay said, "and maybe issue countermanding orders. But if we drop one of those big bridges into the river, it might help disperse and slow the flood. How do you measure lives against the economy, Governor?"

A silence grew. Time seemed to stand still. The colonel, at the window, broke it at last. "Will you look at that!"

Jay and the governor arrived at the window at the same time and all three men stared in silence, awed. The flood had broken free from its final upstream confinement. Now, its yellowish white crest lifted high in the early-morning light, it swept down upon the Bend, tossing great rocks and boulders aside as if they were pebbles, gouging a fresh and wider channel, raging at the earth.

Seeming at this distance to move in slow motion, the cliff face of the torrent reached the Bend. A single dark object, Bill Williams' car, was picked up and thrown high, bounced for a few brief moments as a ball is bounced on a breaking ocean wave, and was then overwhelmed.

Two far smaller objects, not even visible from the distant windows, were picked up too, then engulfed in the raging waters.

There at the Bend, where the flood-control wall had been, the torrent forked. One part swept toward the great houses the wall

132

had protected and swallowed them up. The other part followed the river channel, rising high within its confines, too high, tearing at the earth and partially straightening the curve. Then, seemingly undiminished despite the division, the flood bore down upon the city and the spanning bridges.

Jay said with soft urgency, "Blow it, Colonel! Now!" He glanced at the governor, and waited.

The governor closed his eyes, opened them again, and nodded.

The colonel hurried to the outer office and the radio.

THEY HAD worked all night, and the job was done at last. The lieutenant in charge of the detail which had mined the railroad bridge sat wearily on a bench high above the river smoking a cigarette. The detonator was on the ground beside him. The yet unseen torrent approached with the hollow, rushing sound of a subway train slamming into the confined space of a station, but amplified as in an echo chamber.

"You're wanted on the horn, Lieutenant!" The sergeant raised his voice above the growing thunder.

The lieutenant seized the mike. "Colonel Watkins here, Lieutenant. Blow it! Right now! Acknowledge!"

"Yes, sir! We're blowing it!" He waved one hand at his sergeant, who raised the plunger of the detonator and bore down hard upon it. "There she goes!" the lieutenant said.

The great railroad bridge shuddered, its superstructure shimmering as it vibrated in the sun's first light. The explosion was a roll of gigantic timpani as the sounds of the nearest charges reached them first and the farther sounds followed. The bridge, in one piece, began slowly to lean, as planned, in an upstream direction. As it fell farther from the vertical its speed increased, its riveted steel structure still holding intact. Whatever sounds it made were drowned out by the thunder of the approaching torrent.

The bridge fell at last into the river with a mighty splash, filling the channel from bank to bank, a barrier against the flood which now appeared, sweeping and tearing around a curve.

The bellowing roar of the flood drowned out all other sound. The irresistible force of the water met the immovable object of the steel bridge, jammed by its own weight between the banks of the river. The sturdy truss was twisted and bent by the impact; supporting members failed; the steel rails were contorted and the entire structure was compressed into an unrecognizable twisted mass. But what remained of the bridge held, and the water in all its raging power was forced to find ways through and over and around the obstruction.

Like an army regrouping its forces after surmounting a physical obstacle, the rampaging waters gathered once more into a coherent force below the smashed bridge and bore down upon the *barrio*. Much of the flood's force had been lost. But not all.

A mere shoulder of the flood caught Brooks and Mary Thompson's house, ripped it from its foundation and tore it to bits. The water demolished the church, scattered the pews, tore down the steeple. It smashed Angelita Leyba's house into lumps of adobe, and for a time bore a television set from Honest Johnny's store like an oversize eye on its yellowish crest.

It caught the unwary, the unheeding, the careless, and drowned them mercilessly. From the high ground, *barrio* residents watched the destruction, some crying aloud, some weeping quietly, some kneeling in prayer, some stunned and silent in grief.

It was as if *Dios* himself had decreed absolute devastation. Automobiles and mobile homes, smashed beyond belief, were carried along on the flood until the water reached the broad plains below the city where they could spread, dissipate their fury, drop the burdens they carried and sink at last into the thirsty ground. They left the area strewn like a wrecker's yard with sheet-metal carcasses.

How long the process of destruction lasted, no one watching would ever know for sure. Gradually the bellowing roar diminished. The water level dropped, exposing the devastation it had caused. At the twisted bridge the sound of the rushing water fell in volume until it became no more than a gurgle.

The comparative quiet was almost deafening.

The sergeant said in a hushed voice, "Lieutenant, if we had not dropped that bridge, it would have been a lot worse, don't you think?"

"It sure would. They ought to give the guy who thought of it a medal."

NOW BEGAN the clean-up, the assessment of loss and damage, the fresh cries of anguish and grief. On the telephone the governor said to the mayor, "Keep me posted, please, Joe. I have a call in

134

to Washington to see what help they can give us. Can you give me some assessment now?"

"It's bad," the mayor said. "It's very, very bad! We did our best, and it wasn't enough. We got most of the *barrio* people out. How many we didn't get out, I don't know yet. Maybe a hundred. Maybe five times that. Upstream there is nothing left, nothing!"

"We need an overall look," the governor said slowly. "I'll arrange a Guard helicopter. Will you come with me?"

"Yeah," the mayor said. "Maybe between us we can figure out how we go about starting over. We can't give up."

"No," the governor said. "That's the one sure thing: we can't give up."

12

When he looked back upon that day, Jay Harper found in his memory mostly isolated and unconnected incidents and episodes.

In the *barrio* there were minutes when Jay was frantically digging with his bare hands through the rubble of a shattered house toward vague human sounds, and presently there was someone working beside him, helping to lift heavy timbers. His helper was a tall, lean type, wearing glasses and cursing softly in an eastern seaboard accent, when they reached the trapped man at last and made him lie still where he was. There was unmistakable authority in the voice of the man in glasses when he shouted, "Medic! Here! On the double!" In that brief encounter, a man to remember.

There was Cooley, solid and tireless as ever, saying, "Hi, boy. I hitched a ride down in a chopper. We didn't do so good, did we?" Nothing less than perfection would ever satisfy Cooley.

There was Father Rodriguez, a little old fellow in a black beret, tirelessly comforting, bearing sadness for what was, and exuding hope for what would be. Once Jay saw him and the tall, lean man in glasses passing one another. Their smiles seemed to have a special significance, and Jay wondered why.

And then, without warning—later he could not even remember from whom—he had word of Bill Williams' death, and all at once that brought into sharp focus what had been confused.

Driven by a compulsion against which there was no defense, he left the *barrio* and made his way to the hospital. "Kate is very busy," a tall Anglo girl told him. "But if it's important—"

"It is. It concerns her father."

Kate knew, he thought, the moment she saw him. She seemed to falter; then she gathered herself and came toward him. Jay took her arm and urged her out into the sunshine, where for a time they walked slowly in silence. Finally Kate said, "How?"

"He blew the flood-control wall. I have that from Sam Martin. Your father didn't get away in time. We don't know why. I'm sorry."

"Why didn't Sam—blow it?"

"I think your father—"

"Yes." Kate nodded gravely. "He would do it. His home." At last tears were very close. "Thank you for coming to tell me."

There were strange thoughts in Jay's mind. He had been unaware that they had been forming, but now that they had surfaced he found them somehow inevitable, and without the pain he would have expected. "I wanted to tell you something else too."

Kate watched him in silence.

"I—failed. I am sorry."

"No. You didn't fail." Somehow at the moment reassuring the living was more important than grieving for the dead. "You—succeeded." It was strange that suddenly she was thinking of the stone buildings on the bottom of the lake. They were gone now, she had heard, all gone. "You came here—searching. For home."

"Maybe that was it. I never wanted a home," Jay said. "Before."

They had stopped, and now they stood facing one another in the sunlight. "And now," Kate said, "you are staying?"

"No," Jay said. "I—made a commitment."

"And you keep your commitments." As Daddy always had, Kate thought, and again found tears very close. Had Mother had to compete with commitments too? Or had she learned to live with them?

"I keep my commitments, yes. I'll keep this one." Jay hesitated, because what he was about to say was in fact another commitment, not to be made lightly. But it was a good commitment, and right, and it took no effort to make. "But I'll be back," he said.

Richard Martin Stern

"There are times when I think I carry this business of research too far," says Richard Martin Stern. "Between drafts of *Flood* I managed to take a rather spectacular backward cartwheel fall down an Alaskan talus slope, necessitating a floatplane flight to the hospital a hundred miles away. Afterwards, I rewrote from actual experience Pete Otero's fall from the mountain trail."

Stern does combine research and personal experience to give his fiction its realistic immediacy. The setting for *Flood*, for example, is one with which he is thoroughly familiar. A fourth-generation Californian, he grew up in the West. Now, with his wife, Dorothy, he lives near the mountains in Santa Fe, New Mexico.

"In the West," he writes, "flash floods coming down from mountain canyons are far from rare." Stern remembers one particular day in 1968 when "in less than twenty minutes, the Santa Fe River in the centre of town rose to fourteen feet over the walls of its channel to flood the streets hub deep." This awesome memory has been transformed into an exciting scene in *Flood*. He adds, "Small tremors in this geologically young area are not unknown, and we *have* had recent dry summers. Put them all together with an imaginary dam, and . . ."

Flood is the author's twenty-first book, and the fourth to be a Condensed Books selection; earlier novels include *Snowbound Six*, *Power*, and *The Tower*. On the last of these was based the hugely successful film, *The Towering Inferno*.

DOROTHY STERN

The Summer of the Spanish Woman

A condensation of the book by
CATHERINE GASKIN
ILLUSTRATED BY BEN WOHLBERG
Published by Collins

With the sudden death of her grandfather,
Charlotte Drummond must leave Ireland and
all she holds dear—the beautiful estate,
Clonmara, and her secret love, Lord Blodmore.
Charlotte, with her spirited mother, begins a
new life in the famous sherry-making area of
Spain, but she soon finds herself dominated by
the wealthy, powerful Marquesa de Pontevedra
and her autocratic husband, Don Paulo. Even
Charlotte's impulsive marriage to Carlos, Don
Paulo's natural son, does not free her from their
mysterious hold. Then, as they are all drawn
into the vortex of the Spanish Civil War, she is
confronted once more with her lost love and
compelled to make a fateful choice.

I Irish Morning: 1907
CHAPTER ONE

The Irish Sea crashed in breakers on the sand, as the man and the horse came thundering towards me. I knew at once who he was, and I had been prepared to dislike him, even to hate him. But I saw now the man and the stallion almost as one being, and I coveted them both.

He drew in the stallion, needing all his strength to do it; the horse had to be a full seventeen and a half hands, I judged. It was milk white, with mane and tail tinged with cream. A dream of a horse. A quiver ran through the mare I rode, as blood and beauty seemed to recognize each other. At the same time I looked at the man, and my own body quivered. He returned the stare. Then slowly he raised his hat. "Miss Charlotte?"

I patted the neck of the mare, in a vain attempt to calm us both. "And you are Richard Selwin—Lord Blodmore."

He was unsmiling, and seemed at that moment as handsome as the horse he rode. He had the Blodmore features, the Blodmore eyes. He had more than a passing resemblance to my grandfather, who had once been called the handsomest man in Ireland. It was

141

hard to hate him. But because of him we had to leave Clonmara.

All these months we had been waiting for the new Lord Blodmore, because my mother had not had the good sense to have been born a boy. We had been waiting since the day my grandfather had put his famous hunter, Wicklow Lad, at a bank which had proved too much even for that great heart and strength. Wicklow Lad had broken a leg, and my grandfather had broken his neck. So the earldom of Blodmore and its entailed estate had passed to this second cousin whom no one at Clonmara had ever seen before.

Now I saw him, and some new, strange feeling stirred; the half-veiled suggestions of Nanny, and my mother's broader innuendos of the last months, became a faint hope in my own heart. My mind flashed back to that morning of last January when the frost was still white on the north side of the hedgerows and I had seen my grandfather killed. Everything had seemed to die with him; I had loved my grandfather. I was never sure, at that time, whether I actually loved my mother, Lady Pat. Of course I admired her, as many people did, admired her spirit, her charm, her way with people. But there were many things I found hard to forgive her. There was that disastrous marriage, which had lasted only long enough for one child to be conceived—myself, a girl, who couldn't inherit Clonmara. I had been born here; Clonmara was the only world I had ever known, and now there was no uncle, no brother, to inherit it. Fondly, and sometimes a little sadly, my grandfather had called me Charlie, as he had called his daughter Pat. It was a poor world, I thought, in which to have been born a woman.

My mother had gone back to hunting that same winter, restless and unable to maintain the formalities of mourning, beyond the black band on her sleeve and her heavily black-draped top hat. She had ridden, and flirted, more recklessly than ever before. But I, halfway between the schoolroom and womanhood, hadn't been able to face the rather wild camaraderie of the Irish hunting field without the stabilizing influence of my grandfather. So I had taken to riding alone—something my grandfather would have forbidden, but which my mother didn't seem to notice. I had, in spite of the fear and anger of the head groom, Andy, dared to mount Half Moon, that mare of beauty and still uncertain temperament who had already given us the best foal, my mother said, ever bred at Clonmara. The mare, under-exercised, and feeling the lightness of the creature on her back, had at once thrown me. I had mounted

142

her again, and had again been thrown. I mounted her once more.

"Is it wanting to kill yourself you are, then?" Andy had demanded furiously. "And what will I be telling Her Ladyship?"

I didn't answer him, because Half Moon had headed down the long avenue that led to the break in the dunes, where the sea glittered distantly. There was no choice for me: at that time I went where Half Moon took me.

I persevered in my efforts to win the mare, to steady her and to banish my own fears. But an awful uncertainty hung over us at Clonmara, mostly unvoiced.

One person who always spoke of it was Nanny. She had been a young nurserymaid when my mother was growing up, and had still been at Clonmara when I was born. "Well, child," she would moan softly to me, "it's the end for all of us. What can we do but go out to that place in Galway that the earl settled on Lady Pat? And it with the roof falling in on it, and the mice in possession of everything." Then she would usually rattle the poker briskly against the irons of the grate. "Unless . . . unless, Miss Charlotte, you would bestir yourself to be a little pleasant to himself, the new heir. It wouldn't hurt, now, to comb your hair once in a while and put on a decent dress. You're not half bad-looking, though not the beauty Lady Pat was at your age." Then she would shake her head and add with bitterness, "It isn't as if any of the gentlemen around here would have you—you without a penny to your name—and even that name your mother has made a scandal of."

"*You* don't have to go to Galway, Nanny," I answered. I was wearied of all this talk of money. "The new Lord Blodmore will need servants at Clonmara."

Nanny at this point would draw herself up stiffly. "If you think for a moment, Miss Charlotte, that I'd abandon you and your poor mother . . ."

My mother had put the matter of the new heir more bluntly, but still without much hope. "He's busy in London, they say, and somewhere down in the south of Spain, where, it seems, he had some business connections. He's been mixing in commerce all his life, I hear. Heaven only knows when he'll turn up here and turn us out. Oh, I tell you, Charlie, it's not fair. He's probably some miserable little inky-fingered clerk, but he's to get it all. Those laws they have. . . . Women don't have a chance."

She was referring, of course, to the laws of primogeniture and entail, which prohibited any but the male closest in line from inheriting the title and estate. "Just a second-odd cousin who left Ireland as soon as he could, got some schooling in England, then went out to Spain and worked there for a while. I sometimes wonder if he wasn't trying to make Father give him some introductions there. Father must have known a lot of people from the time he spent in Spain; but that was quite a long time ago, when he was chasing after that woman who was here that summer. Oh, if only he'd married *her!* They used to say she was richer than the King of Spain." Then she would shrug. "Well, never mind that. If he'd only married *someone* and had a son, then surely *we* wouldn't have to be turned out of Clonmara. He would have let us stay, somehow." Always, at about this point, she would reach for the brandy decanter which stood ready at her hand.

"I'll tell you, though, Charlie—inky-fingered little clerk or not—if I weren't still tied to that wretched husband of mine, I'd have a try for him myself." And then her tone would grow more hopeful. "But there's you, Charlie. *You're* not tied to anyone. And he's only about thirty, not too old for you."

She would purse her lips and look hard at me. "Perhaps we should go to Dublin and get you some new clothes." Then she would sigh and shrug again. "But who'd make them? I owe money to every dressmaker in town. Perhaps we could try Miss Doyle in Wicklow Town. They say she is quite clever."

However, she forgot about it, as she forgot about most things of a practical nature, and the arrival of the heir to Clonmara became only a distant threat.

The winter was over, the hunting ended, and Half Moon was mine—or as much mine as any animal of her pride would ever belong to another. My mother, without the long days in the hunting field to tire her, grew more restless. I never seemed to pass through the hall without seeing the hats and riding crops of her gentlemen visitors. The laughter and the talk went on late at night—sometimes I heard stifled voices in the passage outside my bedroom.

My mother was the affectionately-tolerated scandal of the society in which she now mixed, and she was the coldly-talked-of scandal of the society which would no longer receive her. An earl's daughter she might be, but she was now a married woman living apart from her husband. At eighteen she had had a brilliant season in London; she had been presented at Queen Victoria's court, and then hustled back to Ireland because she had caught the eye of the Prince of Wales. She had then run away with a quick-talking, seemingly charming rogue, the son of a poor Scottish farmer who had managed to squeeze out the money to buy him a commission in an unfashionable regiment that was stationed in Ireland. His name was Thomas Drummond, and I had never seen him. My grandfather's lips were sealed about my father. He had welcomed his daughter back when she returned to Clonmara, a short time later, and no one had ever heard him reproach her. My father went on to serve in India and remained there, stubbornly refusing either to divorce his wife or to die conveniently of some tropical disease. He sent no money to support us. My mother told me he had written to the earl, "They will have my support when they come to live with me in the regiment."

And so I saw my grandfather, in the years when I was old enough to observe such things, struggling futilely to make some kind of fortune for us against the day when he would die and we would have to leave Clonmara. I knew he moved desperately from one venture to another, and when he died on the hunting field he had been old beyond his years.

Since his death we had lived in a kind of limbo—my mother making the most of every day left to her at Clonmara, refusing to face the inevitable future; I spending my days as I pleased, riding Half Moon.

NOW THE WAITING was over. This day had brought with it the man and the horse, and a sharp new hunger in my heart for both of them. This was no inky-fingered clerk. He was like some phantom of my adolescent dreams, a man rich in looks and authority.

The wide acres of Clonmara lay between the sea and the gentle slope to the Wicklow hills. It was good land that gave grazing to Clonmara's famous horses and sleek cattle, arable land which yielded plentiful harvests of wheat and barley, potatoes, turnips, beets—a fair and beautiful inheritance—and now this man had come to claim it. Through the turmoil of what I felt for him, a shaft of jealousy and pain stabbed me.

I could stand it no longer. I dug my heels suddenly into Half Moon's flanks, and she shot away with a swift motion which was half indignation, half delight, at the chance of an all-out gallop. The mare was supremely suited to the soft going of the wet sand;

145

we moved easily, almost flying along the shore. Clonmara wasn't quite lost while there was even a single moment like this left.

The thunder of the hooves increased. Glancing back, I saw that the man and the stallion were coming after me. Half Moon was lighter, swifter, more used to the terrain: we held our lead. I heard myself laugh aloud with the triumph of it. But the stallion slowly gained. I urged the mare on, but I knew that soon she must be spent, and not for any race nor for any man would I ruin a horse. So gently I began to rein her in. The man had waited only until he was a clear length ahead of me before he, too, began to rein in. We fell into stride together, the horses moving smoothly side by side. At last we halted, and I slid from Half Moon's back, contrite when I saw the lather of dark sweat on her silken coat.

The man did the same thing. We turned back towards the road to Clonmara, each leading a horse. Then suddenly he took the reins of both animals in his hand and, with his free arm, gathered me to him. The first kiss of passion I had ever received was hard and warm and searching. It surprised me, but, being my mother's daughter, it did not shock me that not just my lips but my whole body responded.

For half a minute we were still, I clinging to the new, wondrous creature who had come into my life. A wave of happiness caught me up. It was, then, I thought, possible to love in an instant, and to know it would last a lifetime. It was absurd—and true. I drew back, laughing, happy.

"I can hardly believe it. I never thought it could happen. You're Richard Selwin, and I love you."

He still held the two horses. Now his free hand went to sweep the tangled hair back from my face. "Hush, child. I shouldn't have done it. I should never have done it."

I remember laughing, so confident I felt. "But why undo it? We have this, and we have so much else—" I gestured widely "—this place, the horses, and . . . we were made for each other. They all said it might happen. Grandfather would have been so happy."

Afterwards, for all the years afterwards, I would remember how ingenuous I must have sounded—a child, foolishly seizing on love like some new toy.

He touched my hair again, traced his finger along the line of my cheek. "Red hair you have, and eyes that are no particular colour, like the sea. And I should never have kissed you."

146

"Have you to ask, then, to wait until we know more than each other's names? Do we have to sit and talk in the drawing room before we may kiss again?"

"I may never kiss you. I have no right. It's too late."

"Too late?" I echoed, and already the first disillusionment of love was upon me.

He gave me back Half Moon's reins and started to walk towards the break in the dunes where the road began.

"Wait!" I called. "Tell me why it's too late. *Why?*"

He looked back at me. The resemblance to my grandfather came and went every time he turned his head. He had the high cheekbones of the Blodmores, the strangely greenish eyes. But he was darker than any of us, darker of skin and hair, and his body had a springing, lithe power as he walked on the soft sand. He was so strange to me, and yet I did know him, and I loved him.

"Why? Better to have asked your grandfather why he would never let me come to Clonmara. Ask me why I hadn't the sense to come as soon as he died. I was trying, against my own inclinations, to be kind, to give you all time to get used to it. I didn't hurry because I wanted to be the gentleman he never thought I could be. If I had once seen you . . . *That* was the error. A mistake I will pay for. If I had only known what was waiting here . . ."

"It's all here," I said, but a cold fear was growing in me. "It's all here. I'm here—"

He cut off my words with a jerk to the stallion's reins. "We'll walk the horses until they've cooled. Then we'll go back to the house, and I will introduce you to my wife—my bride, whom I married in Spain three weeks ago."

THE NEW LORD BLODMORE'S arrival, unannounced, had thrown Clonmara into confusion. We met it first in the stableyard, where grooms were rubbing down four perfectly matched carriage horses and a little mare almost as beautiful as Half Moon, tossing clean hay into the stalls and, I guessed, congratulating themselves on the tone and style the new earl set. A look of reverence was on Andy's face as he took the reins of the white stallion, and it tore into my heart. So quickly were allegiances changed. I turned my back and started to walk to the house.

Richard was at my side as we came around the rhododendron-lined path to the south front of the house. While Clonmara wasn't as big as the largest of them, it was said to be one of the finest houses of its kind in Ireland. Built in the early eighteenth century, it was pure and spare in line and style, belonging to the great Palladian age of Irish building. It was an almost square, balanced house of pale grey stone, with curving colonnades which had been added at a later date, each ending in an elaborate pavilion, some of whose windows now were broken and whose walls were threaded with the devouring ivy. It was beautiful, and for the first time I was acutely aware that it looked to be decaying. Involuntarily we both paused, as if Richard Blodmore were looking clearly for the first time at his inheritance, and I were seeing it for the last time.

"Clonmara," I said quietly. "So much better a name in Irish—it means meadow by the sea."

Inside the house my mother seemed to have gone into a mild state of shock at the unexpected arrival of two coaches, a string of horses, the earl's bride, her personal maid, a valet, and two female servants. I learned later that of them all only Lady Blodmore spoke careful, correct English. She sat now on a sofa in the little sitting room, and her eyes seemed to miss nothing. The room was dusty and strewn with magazines and newspapers, a few half-chewed bones left by dogs, three of my grandfather's gundogs themselves, and two gentlemen friends of my mother's who had chanced to call that afternoon and stayed on to see the fun.

It was obvious that my mother had had a little too much wine. She seized on our entrance with a kind of relief. "Ah—so you found her, then. That's a marvellous horse of yours, Lord Blodmore. Comes from the Hispano-Arab breed, Lady Blodmore tells me. He looked so fresh, you'd never imagine you'd just ridden him down from Dublin."

"We stopped overnight on the way, Lady Patricia. But I thought I said that in the telegram."

"Telegram? I didn't receive a telegram." My mother was now feverishly searching the piles of papers and unanswered letters spread on the table. Her face grew long as she discovered the telegram form and read it. "Oh—how stupid of me! I—I don't bother much with the post any more. It's mostly bills. Farrell must have forgotten to tell me there was a telegram." She gestured at the confusion of the room, and then her voice cracked in a laugh of desperation. "But if you'd given us two weeks' notice instead

148

of two days', we still wouldn't have been ready for you. Charlie will tell you how hopeless I am. Isn't that so, Charlie?"

I never admired her quite so much as at that moment—her life in total disarray, but still laughing, putting a good face on it all.

"Can you forgive me, then?" my mother asked. "Oh, and I've made things worse, not even introducing my daughter. This is Charlie, Lady Blodmore."

"Charlie?" she repeated with a small frown. "Is it not a boy's name?"

"Charlotte," Richard Blodmore said quickly. "Her name is Charlotte. Charlie is a . . . a . . ." He didn't know how to finish.

"A pet name," my mother said.

It might have helped, I thought, if Lady Blodmore had been plain or plump or insipid. Or if she had had the dark Mediterranean looks one might have expected in a Spaniard. But she was golden-haired, with vivid blue eyes strikingly outlined with brown lashes; she had delicately modelled features and small hands, soft in my own as I took one of them and stumbled out some words of welcome. She had tiny feet in soft leather boots, and she wore an elegant dark blue travelling costume. I was miserably conscious of my own breeches and shirt, my uncombed hair, the salt spray that had dried on my face.

The countess was young, hardly older than myself, but she had a far greater sophistication. Her lips faintly twitched in a smile that revealed perfect little teeth, but it was a smile of judgment, not of friendliness. I guessed at once that she thought she had been dropped suddenly into a land of barbarians, people with titles but no manners. I was cruelly aware of how graceless I must appear. And I was never, for a second of that terrible hour that followed—an hour in which my mother and her friends switched from tea back to their brandy and their laughter grew louder, an hour in which both tea and brandy were spilled and a stack of newspapers knocked off the table, taking the sandwiches and fruitcake along—never was I unaware of Blodmore's eyes on me and the awful echo of his words, "Too late."

SOMEHOW we managed to put together what passed for a formal meal that evening. My mother prevailed on her friends, Lord Oakes and George Penrose, to stay and dine with us. Everyone was pressed into service in the next hours to do what they could;

Nanny was summoned to help Farrell clean the silver. The maids scurried about, carrying hot water and linen, more anxious to catch a glimpse of the new earl and his bride than to see to their comfort. As my mother was about to show Richard Blodmore and his wife to the principal guest room, I abruptly checked her.

"Mother, don't you think . . . well, shouldn't Lord and Lady Blodmore have Grandfather's room? After all—" The anguish on my mother's face halted me.

"Of course! How stupid of me." She turned and hurried across the passage. The room had not been used since my grandfather had died. She rushed to the bureau and swept my grandfather's things together, his brushes, his tray of studs and cuff links. "Here, Charlie, take these. I must get the drawers emptied. I'll send hot water."

Richard Blodmore bent and helped me pick up the small, spilled mementos of my grandfather's life as my mother hurried from the room. I followed as quickly as possible, desperate to be out of there. As the door closed behind me, a torrent of Spanish broke from Lady Blodmore, answered and cut short, also in Spanish, by her husband. I stood, clutching my grandfather's belongings, and watched my mother go downstairs. But instead of going to the kitchen to give the necessary orders, she headed at once to the sitting room where her friends waited. At the door she paused, and I saw her brush her eyes with her hand. Then she lifted her head and entered, and a moment later there was the sound of laughter once more.

I put my grandfather's things in my own room; then I went to the kitchen, where I found there had already been an altercation between the Spanish maids and the Clonmara servants. Since none of them understood what the other lot shouted, it was a stand-off, with neither side willing to give way.

Nanny stood in the middle of the big flagstoned room, her face grim. "Miss Charlotte, it is not *my* place to give orders, but someone must do *something*, if we're not to be disgraced entirely."

And so I, for the first time, and unwillingly, began to give orders.

I HAD JUST TIME to scramble into the old green velvet dress, too tight now across my breasts, I noticed, before Farrell sounded the gong for dinner.

My mother looked beautiful, if somewhat disarrayed, in pale

green satin, her famous dark red hair drawn up in an enchantingly precarious mass. Lady Blodmore wore blue again, a light blue which gave her the appearance of fragile china. In deference to the hacking jackets which our two guests still wore, Blodmore had not changed into a formal dinner jacket but wore a dark suit. It made him seem older, more sombre. In the tight green velvet, I flushed as I felt his eyes on me again. Didn't he know how dangerous it was to look at me like that?

Farrell had brought the best wine from the cellar, but apart from that the meal was a disaster. We ate a soufflé which had degenerated into something like scrambled eggs. There were potatoes roasted black and hard, and chicken, tough and underdone. I could not remember a dinner quite so bad at Clonmara.

Lord Oakes and George Penrose evidently thought it was time they could decently ask a few questions. After all, the Blodmores were going to be neighbours.

"And what part of Spain, may I ask, Lady Blodmore, are you from?" Oakes smiled hazily at her across the table. "Where was this chap, Blodmore, lucky enough to find you?"

She answered quite coolly. "I was mainly brought up in Madrid, Lord Oakes. But during the holidays from the convent I usually went to whatever part of Spain my aunt was in. Galicia, Cádiz, Valencia . . ."

"Elena," Blodmore put in, "was orphaned very young. Her aunt is her only close relative."

"Your aunt is not married?" George Penrose asked. "She has no family?"

"My aunt is married to the Marqués de Santander. She has no family," Lady Blodmore confirmed quietly.

Blodmore gave up sawing at the chicken and said, "Elena's aunt once visited Clonmara—many years ago. She was then the Marquesa de Pontevedra."

Oakes's mouth dropped open. "Good Lord! *I remember her!* The Spanish woman! Just imagine that! You remember her, Lady Pat? You would have been about . . . about . . ."

My mother was staring at Elena. Her voice was dry and flat. "I must have been about ten years old."

"About twenty-five years ago," Oakes said. "The Spanish woman—" then he corrected himself "—oh, I say, I do beg your pardon, Lady Blodmore. Terribly rude of me to call her that. But y'see,

151

I didn't remember her title. Everyone expected Blodmore and she would be married. He followed her to Spain and came back unmarried. Must have broken his heart. And now you're here as . . . as Lady Blodmore. Romantic, what? Very romantic, eh, Lady Pat?"

"Yes," my mother said. She tapped her glass, and Farrell rushed to refill it. "Very romantic."

"Well, then." Penrose lifted his own glass. "Well, then, Lady Blodmore. Permit me a toast. To the return of the Spanish wo—lady," he corrected himself. I hardly dared look at my mother's face at that moment.

"Remember the magnificent horses she brought with her?" Oakes went on.

The years that had passed lent a kind of enchantment to their memories of the Spanish woman. I could almost have recited the story myself. Twenty-five years ago a Spanish lady whom my grandfather had met in London had come to visit Clonmara. She had been a great horsewoman, and she was also, it seemed, a very important lady. The viceroy had given a reception for her in Dublin Castle, and people talked of her carriage, her horses, her clothes, her jewels. No one had ever said she was beautiful, but they had never forgotten her presence. And when in the autumn she had set off again for Spain, my grandfather had followed her. He had stayed a long time in Spain, but he had come back alone. It was then he had begun to plunge recklessly with whatever money he could squeeze from the estate. It was then the rot had begun.

George Penrose returned to his first subject. "Tell us, Blodmore, how you were fortunate enough to meet Lady Blodmore." There was just the faintest tinge of envy in his voice.

Elena Blodmore answered for Richard. "My aunt and her husband—Don Paulo, the Marqués de Santander—have sherry vineyards and a *bodega* in Jerez. My husband and I met some years ago, at various social functions in Jerez, and then—"

"And then," Richard said, "I went back again early this year." He sipped his wine gravely. "I was employed for some years in a very humble position in the bodega of Díaz O'Neale. They sent me to work in their London office, and Don Paulo was kind enough to invite me back to Jerez for a visit." He straightened and spoke with determination. "No, I was invited back to Jerez when it became known that I had inherited the earldom of Blodmore." He refused, it seemed, to put a polite face on it. "So, I had the good

fortune to meet Elena again, and she consented to be my wife."
It sounded so cold, so formal an arrangement.

"Well, then—" Lord Oakes strove to cover the silence. "That must be an interesting part of the world. This town . . . what did you call it, Blodmore?"

"It's pronounced Hereth—which is simply the Spanish name for what we call sherry. It's the centre of a unique wine-growing region which produces the grape that becomes sherry."

My mother broke in, her voice still flat and too calm. "Is Hereth spelled J-e-r-e-z?" Richard Blodmore nodded and she continued. "That was the place my father went to in Spain—"

She passed her hands across her forehead, as if striving to pull together her thoughts. "He never talked about it. The solicitors told me after he was killed. There's some sort of property there. A house, and a small vineyard which seems to be no longer in production. There's been no income from it all these years, or at least none that came here to Ireland. There are also some shares in a sherry company." She turned to Blodmore. "Is there a company called Thompson?"

"Fernández, Thompson is the sherry firm headed by the Marqués de Santander."

"Yes, that's the name. Father's solicitor, Siddons, wanted to see what the property in Spain could be sold for. It can't be worth much, but Siddons thought it might be enough to set us up in the place in Galway. Heaven help me, I'd as soon be in Spain as that place out in the bogs." She shuddered, then switched the subject abruptly. "And are all your horses from that part of Spain, Lord Blodmore?"

He nodded. "They claim, and with justice, that the finest horses in the world are bred in Andalusia, and in Jerez the conditions for breeding are perfect. The Andalusian horse was bred by the Carthusian monks there, and it was this strain which first supplied the Spanish Riding School of Vienna."

My mother was all attention now, as the talk turned to the technicalities of horse breeding.

"Tell me," I said, breaking into the sacred subject of horses, "about this place—Jerez."

Lord Blodmore considered for a moment. "It's very pleasant. Very ancient. And surprisingly, until you know its history, very British. England has traditionally been Jerez's best customer for

153

sherry. The trade brought the English there, and it was a haven for the Catholics who fled these islands. Catholic Spain welcomed them, but they have evolved to this day into a close-knit little group, all of whom, I'd say, have some English, Irish, or Scottish blood. Most of them speak English like their own language, and it's a custom to send boys to school in England and for the girls to have English governesses."

"I say, Lady Pat, it sounds nice," Oakes said. "How big a place is it, Blodmore?"

"It *looks* big because of the many bodegas—the places where they store the sherry. It has, however, the manners and preoccupations of a small town. It has a strain of old Spanish nobility there, because it was once a border town between the Christian and Moorish kingdoms—hence its full name, which is Jerez de la Frontera. The monarchs demanded that certain nobles settle there to give the place some sense of permanence. They built great fortresses and walls to hold out the Moors."

"Do you know anything about my grandfather's vineyard?" I asked Blodmore.

He shook his head. "No. But then, as one sees the miles of vineyards outside the town, it is impossible to say who owns what."

Lady Blodmore turned to my mother. "Perhaps you should investigate Jerez yourself, Lady Patricia."

At these words my mother jerked herself out of her dreaming state. Her voice was terse. "Oh, don't worry. We'll be taking ourselves off. But not to Spain." She turned to Richard Blodmore. "Do you remember that old saying they used to have when all the Catholic landowners in Ireland were supposed to become Protestant or give up their land and go west of the Shannon? They used to say, 'To hell or Connacht'. Well, it's Connacht for Charlie and me, I suppose, and it surely will be hell."

I was belatedly conscious of how little I was ready for this life which was to be thrust upon me. Why did they—the men—continue to leave girls in such ignorance, always with the thought that some man would come along, marry them, and take charge? But as my mother's eyes grew more misty over her wine, as her speech grew slurred, I began to realize that it was I who would have to take charge. The thought made me gulp down my wine in sudden fright. I coughed and spluttered, and they all turned to look at me. Tears of humiliation stood out in my eyes.

154

And that cool little beauty, the well-endowed niece of the Spanish woman, barely concealed her smile. She would be making plans for the changes that would come when we were gone. It was all hers, I thought; she had all the time in the world, and all the money, too. And she had Richard Blodmore.

CHAPTER TWO

Sleep came reluctantly for me. My nerves thrummed with a kind of exhaustion I had never known before. I woke finally from my few hours of sleep to escape my dreams of Richard Blodmore, but with my waking he seemed to be more urgently present. The first twitters of the birds had begun about the house. I got up and went to the window. Yesterday's fresh wind had gone, and there was the dewy fragrance of early summer on the air.

I went downstairs to the library, a room seldom used since my grandfather had died. The painful knowledge that I would have to go out and fashion a life for myself and my mother pressed upon me still harder. What had I been taught? Almost nothing except how to read and write and sit a horse. I didn't even have the traditional skills of a woman: I couldn't sew, I knew nothing about cooking or menus. And not only lack of money made me ineligible for, in Nanny's words, "any of the young gentlemen around here". I was also the wrong religion.

My grandfather had explained that in penal times in Ireland, most of the native Catholic families had been driven off their lands by the ruling English and herded west of the Shannon. Catholics were seldom now found among the landowning classes. The Blodmores were Protestant, and my grandfather had defied tradition when he married the daughter of a small shipping merchant from Waterford. Her beauty and a true love of her could have been the only reasons, I thought, because she had had no fortune of her own and she had been a Catholic. My grandfather had honoured his promise and the Catholic Church's demand, and had permitted his daughter, Patricia, to be brought up in her mother's faith. And so, in my turn, had I followed her.

I looked around the still shadowed walls of my grandfather's favourite room, and thought of that strange revelation last night that he had property in a Spanish town called Jerez. In those first frighteningly lonely weeks after his death my mother had thrust my grandfather's keys into my hands. "We must clear out his papers, darling. There are probably old letters and things." The task was beyond my mother. So during the winter afternoons I had come here and unlocked the drawers and the cupboards. The litter of a lifetime seemed to pour out, including the jumbled accounts of the place in the Galway bogs.

Along with them, in a desk drawer, I found a set of papers tied with faded pink legal tape. They went back more than twenty years, and each separate sheet was dated the first day of the year. Each was headed "Jerez", and each was signed with the name Santander. They each repeated the same words, "*Ella está viva.*"

Now the words Jerez and Santander had taken on a troubling familiarity, two words my grandfather had never spoken to me, which yet were somehow part of his life. I shuffled through the ribbon-tied sheaf of notes. "*Ella está viva.*" I sat staring at the words, and then I felt a draught as the door opened.

He didn't hesitate but came directly to me. "I'm sorry, Charlie." Richard Blodmore was close to me, leaning across the desk, his eyes fixing mine so that I could not look away. "I can't be sorry that I love you. But I'm sorry I let you know it."

The warm blood mounted in my face; I was both angry and hurt. "You really think I'm such a child? I'd have known if you'd never touched me, never spoken to me. The way you look at me—no one has to be very wise or old to understand *that*. Do you suppose the others didn't see it? You have a beautiful wife, but you don't love her. She's everything I'm not. She despises me because I'm poor and badly dressed and I don't cut much of a figure in the drawing room. But she knows now that you'd rather have had me. *Me*—a nobody!"

"Charlie, I never asked myself if I loved her. I never believed in love before. I just *wanted* Elena. I'm an opportunist, Charlie. I have been all my life. Elena is a glittering prize. She's rich and she's beautiful. And my prospects were nothing until Lord Blodmore died. He could still have married and had a son. . . ."

"Yes . . . yes. We knew that. My mother used to urge him, and it was the only time he seemed to get angry and upset with her."

"So, you see how it was. He had sent me to school in England and paid for it, probably because he didn't want Clonmara inherited by an ignorant buffoon. But I had to make my own way after that. I knew he had some connection with the sherry trade.

156

So I hunted around in London, using his name, until I found a position as a clerk with the London office of Díaz O'Neale. When I was sent out to Jerez to learn the shipping side of the business, I introduced myself to Don Paulo, the Marqués de Santander, because it was in his bodega that Blodmore had an interest. Quite obviously Santander wanted nothing to do with me. I was nothing but a clerk working for a sherry shipper. The fact that I was possibly Blodmore's heir made no impression. So I was stuck there in Jerez, writing out bills of lading and living on next to nothing. Of course, no one took me as being eligible for any of their precious, guarded daughters—"

"Richard, I don't *care* what happened before."

He put his hand on mine, to quiet me. "Be patient, Charlie. I want you to know how it happened."

I nodded, but my attention was on the warmth of his hand on my own.

"I met Elena once or twice in Jerez, but she was still a child, a young girl. Her aunt has an estate at Sanlúcar de Barrameda, where she usually stays, rather than with Don Paulo in Jerez. She's a strange woman—very independent, with the freedom that her wealth and position give her. She outranks her husband, and she is known by her own title, the Marquesa de Pontevedra. Sometimes I wonder if she even remembers she once married Don Paulo. The town still nods its head over that, believe me, because Don Paulo, although he's good-looking and of a noble family, was very hard pressed for money. He'd been married before—had a young daughter, sixteen or so, who died. His sherry business was floundering—which was probably why he permitted your grandfather to buy into it. Now he's rich in his own right. It was a lucky day for Don Paulo when the marquesa threw over Blodmore and chose him instead."

"But Elena—"

"I'm coming to Elena. After a few years I was sent back to the London office. It was supposed to be a promotion, but London was a dreary place for me. I missed the climate, the horses, even the little bit of society I had in Jerez. And then your grandfather was killed, and everything changed."

"It changed here," I said.

"Almost at once I was visited by Don Paulo—commanded, you might say—to visit Jerez. So I found myself staying at Don Paulo's house—which I'd only been in once before—with the marquesa and her niece, Elena, in residence. It was clear, almost from the first day, that the marquesa intended Elena and me to marry. Why, I'll never exactly understand. Elena could have had her pick in Spain. But I took what was offered and asked no questions. I had a fair idea of Clonmara's finances, and Elena's huge dowry weighed heavily there. I told you I was an opportunist, Charlie. I thought Elena and I were well-enough suited. The question of love didn't occur to me, since I didn't really believe in it."

I nodded. The facts of his life would seem to have made his actions inevitable. But I couldn't stop myself saying, "If only—"

He knew at once what I had started to say. "Yes, if only Blodmore had even once invited me here. I, as his heir, and you, as his only grandchild . . . if we'd married, it would have been the perfect solution."

"Perhaps that was why. Because it would have been too perfect. He loved me, Richard. He would have wanted me to marry whomever I wanted: he wouldn't have wanted any pressure on me."

"Then he made a terrible mistake, Charlie. If he'd given us half a chance . . . if I'd ever come here just once—"

I laid my hand across his lips. "Let's not talk about it any more. There are too many ifs and whys—and no answers." I got up and took his hand. "I want to show you my grandmother's rose garden. My grandfather had it made as a sort of wedding present for her."

Together we crossed to one of the long windows that led to a flagstoned terrace. The cool, morning-scented air met us as I opened it. The flagstones were still wet with the night's dew. At the end of the terrace, steps led down to an elaborate wrought-iron gate bearing the crest of the Blodmores. In contrast to the general state of the house, the gate gleamed with new paint, and it opened easily at my touch.

It was the only place at Clonmara which had never lacked care. The formal garden had high walls of mellow brick, on which climbing roses were trained. Here the cultivation of roses had reached a high art, and now the earliest ones, those along the warm, south-facing wall, were beginning to bloom. "My grandfather," I told him, "brought an expert from England to lay out the garden and to teach the gardeners about roses. A sort of legend grew up around it. They called it the countess's garden—a garden made for love of my grandmother—and they seem to think it will bring bad luck on the family if anything dies here. So they look after it very carefully." We walked between the budding roses to the farther gate and stopped.

Then we were in each other's arms. Too late I thought that it had been a mistake to bring him here. But I had so craved his touch, to feel his mouth once more on mine. In a future that looked so bleakly empty, I had to have some memories.

"This is our own place, Richard," I said. "I will always think of you here. And you will never open the gate of this garden without thinking of me. That way we will always have some part of each other."

"Some day I'll be with you, Charlie," he said.

I shook my head in some newly acquired wisdom. "Let's make no promises for the future, Richard."

I took his arm and we walked back along the grassy path, conscious that sounds were coming from the stables; the hounds had begun their early-morning keening cry. At the gate we embraced once more and kissed, not caring that each time it was more painful and that the bond grew stronger. We went up the steps together, our hands touching only lightly. The hems of my thin gown and robe were wet and bedraggled. I looked along the length of the house, the grey stone warmed now by the touch of the sun. Directly above us I caught a movement, as if a lace curtain had fallen closed behind a window. A breeze, perhaps? But the morning was windless. I said nothing to Richard.

It had been one of the windows of my grandfather's room, the room now occupied by Richard and Elena.

WE WENT BACK through the open window of the library, my joy at being with Richard giving place to a sadness I knew I must not let him see.

"Richard, you speak Spanish, don't you?" I said, going to the desk and picking up the ribbon-tied notes.

"Of course."

"What does this mean? It *is* Spanish, isn't it?"

His face tightened as he looked at the heading, "Jerez", and the signature. His fingers flipped swiftly through the pages as he counted the dates.

"*Ella está viva.* It means, simply—She lives, or, she is alive."

"She lives," I repeated. "She lives."

"What does it mean, Charlie? *Who* is alive? Surely Don Paulo can't have written all these years to taunt Blodmore about the marquesa. It wouldn't be like him."

I shook my head. "My grandfather's dead now. Whatever it means, it probably doesn't matter any more." I locked the papers again in the drawer.

"HE HAS OFFERED ME the *back gate lodge!*" My mother whispered it to me as if she were in some sort of agony. "The gate lodge of my own home! Charlie, have you ever really noticed the size of that place? Have you ever been inside it? It's like a dog kennel. Well, the man's no gentleman. I always knew it!"

"Did he offer anything else with it, Mother?"

"A pittance. A tiny annuity. Use of the horses and stables. A girl to come from the house to do some cleaning and cooking."

"It's not nothing." Already the tug of unreason was there, the hopeful thought that I would see him sometimes, we might meet on the shore, in the rose garden. . . . I tried to hide my misery.

My mother looked at me sharply. "No, don't look away! *Look* at me, Charlie. It's he, isn't it? It's Richard Blodmore you want. And he wants you. All these things he's suddenly offering me. They're to keep you here. Isn't that what it is?"

I didn't answer. All at once her arms were about me, rocking me like a child. "Oh, my poor little Charlie. Here I've been feeling sorry for myself and not noticing that my little girl had grown up and fallen in love. It's no good, you know. He's married, and she'll never let him go. Has he said anything to you, Charlie?" she asked, and got no answer.

"Oh, Charlie, you *want* to stay, don't you? Darling, you can't imagine the hell it would be. Trying to cover up, trying to hide it. You're not made for scheming and conniving, and I'll not have your heart broken, if I can help it. You'll give all your young life to loving him, and one day you'll find it's all gone into a stale, sour routine. Love doesn't stay the way it begins, you know. I've been down that road. And look at me now, a foolish woman with no husband and no future, who takes a drop too much. I'm thirty-six, Charlie, and I've got nothing. Nothing except you. Oh, Charlie, dear, I've been so careless and neglectful."

"What shall we do?" I said dully.

"We must go," she said. "We must leave at once."

"You mean, go out to Galway?"

She shook her head. "No, not to Galway. There's no future for us in Galway, and we'd be forever thinking of coming back here. No, we'll gamble on the next throw, the way Father always played it. We'll go to that place he left me in Spain. We'll go to Jerez."

IT WAS ALL DONE more quickly, it seemed to me, than anything had ever been done at Clonmara. My mother summoned the solicitors from Dublin, and they came, with a slightly reproving air. Siddons said to me, "Concerning your grandfather's properties, there had been a small income from his shares in the sherry business of Fernández, Thompson over the years, all paid into a bank in Jerez. We are at a loss to understand—"

"Then that's settled," my mother said. "There is an income, a house, the annuity Lord Blodmore has suggested to me. It will suffice. We will be very economical, Charlie and I."

So the decision was announced. It was greeted with ill-disguised approval and relief by Elena and with silence by Richard Blodmore. My mother then set out on a round of farewell visits to her friends, leaving Nanny and me vague orders for packing. She would return slightly tipsy for dinners at Clonmara that each day grew better, as Elena started to come to grips with the cook and Farrell.

Nanny refused to be left behind. "Lady Blodmore tells me that in Spain every young lady like Miss Charlotte has someone to be with her all the time. A du . . . a duenna, it's called. I'll be that. I'm still useful for something. Besides, hasn't himself, Lord Blodmore, paid me five years' wages and the price of some new clothes?"

"To be rid of you, no doubt," I snapped. I was feeling the strain of the worry and uncertainty of what we were about to undertake. I did the packing and made arrangements for the passage to Gibraltar while my mother played her farewell scenes to the hilt.

"Let's get the heartbreak over and done with," she would say to friends who came to call. It couldn't have been easy for Elena Blodmore to listen to such talk, but my mother didn't seem to care.

In the stables the new Spanish horses were still a wonder to all the lads, especially to Andy. There was a source of pride also in the fact that Lord Blodmore was a skilful rider. He would be a worthy successor to the dead earl as master of hounds. So it was a shock when Andy came to me and asked if he might go with us.

"It'll be strange for you and Lady Pat without a man around, Miss Charlie. To tell you the truth, I've had a notion to travel this long time now, and indeed I was thinking of America. But with the horses they have in this Spanish place, it seems I might do just as well there."

I looked at him for a long time. "Andy, you no more want to go than we do—especially not now, when there's a bit of money at Clonmara and you'll have good horses to look after. *He's* done this, hasn't he? Lord Blodmore?"

I got it out of him. Andy was very fond of me and my mother, and it would be a pleasure to accompany us and see us settled in. He had Lord Blodmore's promise that once that settling in had been accomplished, he could return to Clonmara if he wished. His wages, meanwhile, would be paid for as long as he was with us. I knew that Richard had selected Andy with great care, and possibly at a sacrifice to himself, because Andy was the best there was at Clonmara. Another bond was forged between Richard and me in the gift of Andy's patience, endurance and devotion.

I went and sought out Richard Blodmore. "You give us Andy! And what have I got to give you?"

He replied, "If I had money, you'd have had a good deal more. I've managed the few arrangements I've been able to make—your mother's bit of money, Andy, the rest—by going over the estate books very carefully and seeing where we can be more economical. I've borrowed to do what's been arranged so far. The money to be spent on improvements at Clonmara is, of course, Elena's. There are strings attached to it. The marquesa saw to a very scrupulously-worked-out marriage contract. So you see, Charlie, while Elena is rich and Clonmara will benefit, I'm still a poor man—and will be until the estate begins to throw off good profits again. I have to see you and your mother go like beggars, and I can do nothing about it."

"You've done more than you know."

So it was Andy who was saddled up and waiting behind the Blodmore coach on the morning we left. We were to get the mail boat from Kingstown, and at Liverpool connect with the P & O steamer to Gibraltar. It had all happened in barely more than two weeks, and now that the moment had come I felt a fear clutching at me. My mother and Nanny were already helplessly in tears.

Elena had risen early to say goodbye, a difficult thing for a

Spaniard who liked staying up late. There was no sign of Richard.

"He has gone riding, I believe," Elena said. She could not quite keep a trace of satisfaction out of her voice. I guessed what she might be thinking. Her husband was not present to bid goodbye to this unruly little hoyden he had appeared to admire, and the keys of Clonmara were firmly in her hands at last.

I heard myself murmur stiff words to Elena. I even tried to thank her, for what I didn't know. A great coldness had come on me; not only was I leaving Clonmara, but there was no word of farewell from Richard to ease the going. The carriage started; the oaks and beeches planted almost two centuries before to line the avenue of Clonmara slid by. For ever in my memory I would name and count every one of them.

He was waiting by the gate lodge, astride the great white stallion, Balthasar. On a leading rein was Half Moon. He murmured some words to Andy and slid from the stallion's back. Andy climbed into the saddle and took Half Moon's rein. The three of us in the carriage were dumb as Richard thrust his head in the window.

"I have telegraphed ahead for the mail boat and the steamer to accommodate the horses," he said. "You will need good horses." Then he went to the lodge wall and brought to us a canvas bag containing my grandfather's best guns, including the ones made especially for my mother. "They all say you're a great shot, Lady Pat, and you'll surely be invited to Doñana for the hunting."

Then he half bowed over my mother's hand, and raised it nearly to his lips in a gesture I came to know as typically Spanish. He barely glanced at me, but his words were for me. "If you need me, send word. I'll come."

Dimly, as the high green hedges of Ireland slid by, as my mother leaned further and further out of the window to catch the last glimpse of him standing there in the road with his hat off, I heard her say in a choked tone, "The horses, Charlie—the horses! Only a gentleman would have given us the horses."

CHAPTER THREE

*I*t was almost three o'clock in the morning, and still a fierce heat lay on the land. From the few dim lights we had seen clustered as we had topped the last rise after leaving Puerto de Santa María, we knew we must be very close to Jerez, but not even that knowledge could cause any of us in the stuffy carriage to straighten our backs or attempt to brush the white dust from our clothes.

"Mother of God, do you think there'd ever be a cup of tea at the end of it?" Nanny demanded. My mother and I had given up trying to answer the same querulous demand ever since we had left the steamer in Gibraltar.

A carriage and driver had been hired, and for two days we had followed the coast road that skirted the formidable mountains, the Sierra Blanquilla, and then the road that plunged through two mountain ranges, and bypassed Cádiz to turn inland to Jerez. The very countryside, I thought, had a formidable presence—the high bare crags of the sierra, the herds of goats cropping almost bare ground, the olive groves of silver grey—all had an austere beauty which nothing in Ireland had prepared me for. The bones of the country seemed to show through, presenting a lean but aristocratic face.

The carriage and the driver were both old, and the man spoke not a word of English. We had spent one miserable, sleepless night in an inn along the road and had hoped to make Jerez by the second evening. Even Andy, riding Balthasar abreast of the carriage and leading Half Moon, was finding the day in the saddle under the sun more than enough. We urged the driver on, but it was not until early the next morning that the first paved road of Jerez came under the wheels.

"And now," my mother said, "we have to find the house—and not a word of Spanish among us." We had passed through an arch which appeared to signal the beginning of the town proper, and almost immediately there were shouts from two young boys who rushed at the carriage waving lanterns. I heard the words "Plaza de Asturias", which was where the house was. The sudden shouts and the lights upset Balthasar, who swerved violently. For a sickening half minute I thought Andy was going to be thrown. The two boys eyed the big white horse fearfully as they gave their message in Spanish to the driver. He leaned around from the box to give us his toothless grin; then he slapped the reins on the backs of the listless horses and began to follow the lamps of the two boys.

The town was dark, and mostly shuttered, though lights shone in one or two cantinas. We passed through broad streets and narrow alleys, through plazas where oleanders scented the night air and palms rustled above our heads. The sculptured outlines of tall elegant houses could be seen against the warm night sky.

164

The boys, barefoot and wearing ragged clothes, led the carriage into a small square which was silent and deserted. A fountain and the outline of a church were its only grace notes. They stopped before the tall façade of a house, where a pair of ancient iron-studded doors barred our way. One of the boys knocked with his stick, and the sound seemed to reverberate endlessly within. Then there was silence again.

"Can there be anyone there?" my mother said. "No lights, nothing." Balthasar pawed the ground. He wanted a stable, his oats and water.

At last there was the drawing of stiff bolts, and a man and a woman, shabbily clothed and of indeterminate age, emerged and came close to the carriage. They stared up at the three dust-streaked faces, clearly unsure which they should address themselves to. The woman bowed; the man took off his cap, twisting it in nervous hands.

"You are welcome, Doña Patricia. You are welcome to the home of your father." It was all said in Spanish, but the meaning was plain enough. My mother fell back against the old leather cushions. "Thank God, at last we're here." Then she leaned forward again. "*Gracias . . . muchas gracias.*"

There were smiles now, but another delay while the man and the woman, assisted by the boys, struggled to open up both sides of the big doors. They moved grudgingly on hinges that had long been without oil. The carriage rolled forward through the portal and into a courtyard. There was an impatient whinny from Balthasar; Andy climbed stiffly from the saddle. The man opened the carriage door and helped my mother alight with all the flourish of a great gentleman on a great occasion. He had clearly decided which of us was Doña Patricia.

"This is my daughter, Miss Charlotte," my mother said with great distinctness.

"Char . . . Char . . ." He shook his head.

"Doña Carlota," the woman hissed, digging him with a sharp elbow. Comprehension broke on the man's face. "Ah! Doña Carlota! *Bienvenida!*"

For the first time in my life I liked the sound of my own name. "Doña Carlota, indeed!" said Nanny as she scrambled out of the carriage.

"This is Nanny," my mother said to the manservant.

The two smiled, but briefly. Then, astoundingly, the man said, "Ah, *sí*, English nanny."

"*Irish!*" was Nanny's retort.

When the bags were unloaded, Andy, the driver and the horses were escorted to the stables. I stood looking around me for a moment. Even in the dim light a feeling of decay hung on this strikingly handsome house. A series of arches formed a cloister on three sides of this inner courtyard, broken by the entry to the stable area. But there was rot in the wooden shutters which barred the windows; the finely decorated stonework of the arches had crumbled in places; weeds grew rampantly between the stones of the courtyard and on the cracked marble basin of the central fountain. It was beautiful and sad.

"Charlie! Are you dreaming, Charlie?" My mother's voice. We followed the woman's flickering lamp into a long, wide passage beyond a broad flight of shallow marble stairs. The floor was black and white marble squares, cracked in places, dulled with a film of dirt. Little piles of leaves and curls of dust lay in the corners.

"I'm thinking there might be a ghost or two in this place," Nanny whispered.

Now the woman paused before a set of elaborately carved doors. With an attempt at a grand gesture, she flung one of them open.

"*Las señoras*, Don Paulo!" She bobbed a curtsy and hurried forward to light candles which were placed on a long table.

In the dark room only one window was unshuttered, and I caught a glimpse of stars in a dark blue night sky, heard the rustle of palms. The embers of a fire still glowed in a great carved stone hearth. From a high-backed chair a figure rose slowly, as if he had been dozing there. As the light of the candles reached him, I saw a man dressed in a suit of fine black linen, a white linen shirt, and a black tie. His iron-grey hair sprang back thickly from a lean face that was darkly olive in complexion. He had hooked black brows over eyes whose thick lids gave them a hooded, secretive appearance. Except for those hooded lids, he would have been strikingly handsome. He wore his manner of command and position with ease, like his clothes.

He bowed and came slowly towards us. Beside the chair an enormous hound had risen, stretching as if she also had been sleeping. She was brindle-coloured, with a square skull, black muzzle, ears and nose. Her appearance of grandeur was only slightly

166

diminished by an air of great good nature. With a flick of his finger the man commanded her to sit. He then approached my mother, took her gloved hand, which was grey with dust, and lifted it near to his lips in the gesture Richard Blodmore had used.

"Lady Patricia, allow me to present myself. I am Paulo Fernández Medina. On behalf of my family I welcome you to Jerez."

"*Enchantée*—no, that's French. Forgive me, señor. You will find us sadly lacking in Spanish. May I present my daughter, Charlotte."

My hand was also taken and raised, as he bowed. "Miss Charlotte, my pleasure." His English was very nearly accentless.

My mother was confused. "Your name again, sir?"

"Paulo Fernández. Husband of Lady Blodmore's aunt, the Marquesa de Pontevedra. Forgive this poor reception, Lady Patricia. There was very little time to prepare. Richard Blodmore's letter did not reach us until yesterday. I have given orders that rooms be prepared, but you must expect deficiencies. The house has been unused for many years."

My mother shook her head. "But you—you don't live here?"

A wintry smile touched his lips. "No, Lady Patricia. This house belonged to your father. I have my own house."

My mother looked at him in astonishment. "But you are here to . . . to receive us. It is after three o'clock in the morning! You have waited so long. . . ."

He bowed slightly, as if to dismiss any idea of discomfort. "It is my duty—no, my pleasure, as head of my house, to receive you and welcome you to Jerez. The hour does not matter. Doña Elena has also written, telling us of your . . . your kindness to her. I hope you will not find us lacking in gratitude or manners."

The import of the words finally sank into my mother. "You are . . . you are, then, the Marqués de Santander."

"To you, Lady Patricia, and the whole of Jerez, I am Don Paulo. We are simple people here. We much look forward to visits of strangers. I hope you will have a most pleasant stay among us." He turned towards the table, where glasses and a decanter were set. "Do sit down. A meal has been ready since ten o'clock, but still there will be a wait. May I offer you a glass of sherry, a 'copita' as we say here. This wine is among the best my bodega produces."

He poured four glasses, gravely handing one to my mother and one to me, and then, after only a fractional hesitation, he brought one to Nanny, who had remained silent and in the background.

167

"Oh, no, sir. I never touch it."

He shook his head. "You will find that all of us here touch it. It is our life. Sherry is the wine of Jerez."

The big hound went to sniff at my mother, then came to me. I put my hand on the silken ears; she rasped it with her rough tongue. "Pepita, mind your manners!" Don Paulo said. As if ashamed, she slumped down, and her head went between her enormous paws.

"What breed is she? I don't think I've ever seen such a dog before. So beautiful, so gentle."

"She is a Spanish mastiff. Hardly more than a puppy yet. Doesn't know her manners. One of my sons gave her to me. You think she is beautiful, do you, Miss Charlotte?"

"She *is* beautiful."

"Then you shall have her. You can take her back to Ireland with you. She is yours. A remembrance of Jerez."

A frown came to my mother's brow, but then she smiled and held her glass forward to be refilled. "This *is* a marvellous wine. Somehow the sherry at home never tasted quite like this."

"Only in Jerez does the wine taste like this, Lady Patricia. You must enjoy it in its home while you may."

My mother laughed. "Then I shall be enjoying a great deal of it. You do understand that we have not come on a visit? We have come to stay."

Don Paulo's lips curved upwards in the semblance of a smile. "A visit may be any length you choose, Lady Patricia. It may last a short time—it may last a lifetime. In Spain, there is always time. But we are sorry to see our guests depart."

WE HASTILY WASHED OFF some of the dust, and Don Paulo came with us to the dining room when we were summoned. The room, like the one we had left, was sparsely furnished in the same heavy dark oak. We were served in a flustered, clumsy fashion by the manservant, Paco, while his wife, Serafina, brought dishes from the kitchen. Don Paulo refused food, just sipped his wine, and as hungry as we were, it was difficult to eat under the gaze of those hooded, secretive eyes.

When the door to the kitchen opened we could hear the ceaseless talk of the driver and Serafina, the chatter of the two boys who had met us. Everyone was obviously eating with gusto, and Andy was at the table with them. I realized then that Andy would be the first of us to learn Spanish.

There was fish, then chicken, and beautiful fat shrimps, and delicious vegetables we had never tasted before.

At last it was all cleared away, and Don Paulo rose. "I will bid you good night, Lady Patricia."

A sense of panic seemed to penetrate my mother's fatigue. She half rose from her chair. "But when . . . when are we to see you again, Don Paulo? There are affairs to discuss."

Don Paulo bowed with finality, cutting the conversation short. "I am to be found at the bodega most days, Lady Patricia. If not there . . . someone always knows where I am."

He started towards the door, and Pepita, the mastiff, who had lain at his feet during the meal, rose also and went with him. Don Paulo turned. "Pepita, I have bidden you stay with Doña Carlota. Stay! *Quédate!*" He stared at the dog and pointed to my feet. The expression on the dog's face was as unbelieving as my own must have been.

"Oh, no!" I said. "I couldn't take such a wonderful dog from you, Don Paulo. She is obviously devoted to you."

"Then she will show her devotion by doing as she is commanded. *Pepita!*" He pointed once again at me. Finally, with only the faintest whine of protest, the mastiff turned and lay down beside my chair.

Don Paulo said, "You will have to learn English, Pepita." Then he was gone. Paco went ahead to light his way through the passages.

Pepita got to her feet and whined once more. "How could he?" I said. "The poor dog is brokenhearted. How could he give her away just like that! Pepita!" She gazed at me with huge dark eyes which pleaded for some understanding of this separation from her master. I stroked the silken head, feeling the contact with the animal as a sop to my desperate homesickness. I thought that if I stopped talking to the dog I might weep instead, and for my mother's sake I could not do that.

"It's my opinion," Nanny said, "that *that* man would give away anything, if it pleased him. He wanted to upset you, Miss Charlie. Pity it's such an ugly brute, isn't it?"

"Pepita is a beautiful dog," my mother said. "And we don't need your opinion of Don Paulo, Nanny." She poured herself more

170

sherry. "But obviously we are not exactly welcome. All this talk about a *visit*. This is our house, isn't it? And don't we own part of his bodega? And isn't there a vineyard? Come to welcome us, did he? He came to scare us off!"

I looked around the room. It was very large, and the walls were bare, showing patches of mildew.

"I wish . . . I only wish it weren't so big. We'll need so many things . . . servants—"

"Listen to them." My mother jerked her head towards the kitchen. "We *have* servants."

"We have very little money."

"We'll manage." She drank deeply. "There has to be good wine in the cellar. That Paco man didn't get *this* in a cantina."

WE WERE SHOWN upstairs to rooms with big brass bedsteads. The beds were made up with linen sheets which bore yellow marks along all the creases, as if they had lain in the cupboard, waiting, for a very long time.

Our rooms opened on yet another courtyard. I said despairingly, "Why did Grandfather have such a huge house? I hate the thought of opening all those doors."

My mother spoke with unexpected clarity. "We'll open each door as we come to it, my darling. We've come to the land of sunshine and oranges and wine. And jasmine. Oh, Charlie, do you smell the jasmine?"

In my room I sat down on the bed and stroked the mastiff's head. "We'd better go to bed, Pepita. It will all seem very different tomorrow—today. Jasmine and oranges and wine. There will have to be a bit more than that. How I wish I were back at Clon—" I stopped the words, even though there was only the dog to hear them. I must never say them.

I woke to the harsh bars of sunlight falling across my face through the wooden louvred shutters. I had dreamed of a man on a distant shore, a gate to a rose garden.

"Richard . . .?"

I sprang up and threw open the shutters, letting the full blast of the Andalusian sun fall on my face. It was strong and alien, far from that soft and misty shore. The dog touched my hand then. I looked down at her beautiful, sad, square face. She was real, and so was the sun. I had to stop dreaming.

WE OPENED only a few doors that first day. Some rooms were empty, some only partially furnished. We had given Serafina a little money, and she produced two cousins who helped her with the immense task of sweeping and washing the marble floors. But we could not afford to keep them on full-time. We selected a few rooms we would try to make presentable. For the rest, the doors must remain closed.

"There's stabling for twenty horses," Andy told us. "But it'll take more than a coat of whitewash to make the place fit again. There's repairs needed."

"You'll have to manage with whitewash, Andy," I said. "There's simply no money for anything else."

My mother sighed. "Charlie, go and ask Paco for the keys to the wine cellar."

With gestures and patience I made Paco understand what I wanted. He grinned and produced the keys with pride. He lighted a candle and beckoned to us all, Andy as well, to follow him. We descended by a circular stair, narrow and dangerous, with moss on the walls and treads. We reached the bottom at last, and in the gloom of an enormous room, rack upon rack of wine was revealed, dust-covered. The labels were black with mould and mildew.

My mother was trying to read some of the labels on the bottles. "You know, I think Father has left us a small fortune in wine. Perhaps we could sell it . . . but for lunch, since this is the first day, we'll just have this Bordeaux, and perhaps this Chambertin for dinner." She gave a small laugh of pleasure. "What luck! He always had such great taste in wine."

I sighed. The wine would never be sold.

CHAPTER FOUR

*I*t was not yet eleven o'clock on the morning of our second day in Jerez, but the sun already beat like hammer strokes as we rode, a rather improbable three, I thought, led by Serafina's nephew Pepe, and followed by Pepita. I was riding Half Moon, and my mother had claimed Balthasar; Andy had a tired mare hired from a livery stable. We'll have to find him a decent horse, I thought. Have to get a trap and a carriage horse so we can go about more easily. The thoughts ran on. Have to . . . Always the second thought following—How are we to find the money?

"Have you ever seen such a blue sky, Charlie?" My mother sounded gay, excited. She had forgotten the difficulties. We were going on a visit and that was enough to make her happy.

"There had better not be any rain," Andy said, "or it could ruin the harvest. The grapes don't like rain at this stage."

"Andy, how do you know such things?"

"Oh—" He glanced back at me, his expression sheepish. "Oh, I listen, Miss Charlie. The old woman speaks a few words of English."

"That's another thing," I said. "We have to have someone regularly to give us lessons in Spanish."

"Oh, Charlie, dear, my learning days are over," my mother answered. "Besides, there are enough people who speak English. Enough to keep me going, at any rate."

Some of the streets through which we passed were lined on both sides with bodegas. I had always thought of wine cellars as being deep in the ground, but these were long, high buildings, built above the ground. Their high, grilled windows were open, and the air seemed saturated with the warm scent of the sherry as it lay in its casks. Whole streets of bodegas stretched through the town, their walls painted with the famous names of the trade—Williams and Humbert; Domecq; Duff Gordon; González Byass; Osborne— and Fernández, Thompson. No doubt half of them were owned by families who now mixed their English, Irish, and Scottish names with the Spanish.

At the main offices of Fernández, Thompson, we passed through a handsome gate into a paved courtyard, with cultivated areas of flowers and bright pots of geraniums. In the passages between the bodegas, grapevines grew on gnarled old stems.

A man came to help us dismount. He seemed to know who we were; it was almost unnecessary to ask for Don Paulo. With many bows he ushered us to a building deeply shaded by a colonnade. Its heavy, ornate doors were open. After the aching glare of the sun, the dimness inside was like cool water. We were led past a row of offices whose half-glassed walls gave us a view of many men at work at desks. One or two lifted their heads and then frankly stared. My mother was something to stare at. She was at the height of her almost outrageous beauty, with creamy skin and silken, dark red hair that escaped entrancingly in little tendrils to touch her cheeks. We passed from this corridor into the quiet of a reception area. Here there were big carved velvet-covered chairs set on a silken carpet.

"*Momentito, por favor.*" The man knocked at a door and stepped inside, and almost at once Don Paulo came out to meet us. He had the air of one to whom courtesy to visitors was more important than any work. At the sight of him Pepita flung herself forward with delight, and was sternly rebuked by her former master.

"Miss Charlotte, you will have to be more severe with Pepita."

Don Paulo formally took my mother's hand, and then mine, and waved us into his richly furnished office. Already, as if some silent message had been passed, a manservant in white coat and white gloves was setting out small, inward-curving sherry glasses; three bottles were placed on a silver tray. A second silver tray bore small pieces of bread spread with pâté, and tarts filled with shrimp and melted cheese. There were silver bowls of olives and nuts.

"You will take a copita, ladies?" Don Paulo was pouring, our agreement taken for granted. "Will you try our local custom of drinking the sweet—the cream sherry—before the dry, the fino? It would be a pity if you left Jerez without knowing how we drink our sherry."

"I like Jerez," my mother said. "I'm sure I shall stay."

He behaved as if she had not spoken. "We say here that the cream sherry, the oloroso, cradles the stomach, and we take it as our first copita of the day. From that, one goes to the amontillado, which comes in the middle. After that, the fino, which we then stay with for the rest of the day. For us it is the greatest wine, dry, pale, delicate on the tongue." He raised his glass. "I salute your health, ladies."

Gravely we tasted the warm, sweet wine, dark and rich in colour. Don Paulo held the glass beneath his nose for a moment, swirled it slightly, drew in the bouquet, then drained it almost in one mouthful. Already he was pouring the next wine, which was lighter in colour, less heavy. That also went quickly. My mother seemed to have no trouble keeping up with Don Paulo, but I found my third glass filled with the fino before the first was empty.

Don Paulo now held out the silver dish with its spread of small delicacies. "Do have some, Lady Patricia. We call them *tapas. Tapa* is—" he gestured with one of the tiny tarts "—our word for lid or cover." He held the tart so that it neatly topped the rim of the glass. "To cover the glass. We seldom drink without eating."

174

I didn't want to eat, but under the spell of Don Paulo's compelling voice I both ate and drank. I cautioned myself that if it continued much longer we would be leaving with our business unstated.

Finally I said, "Don Paulo, if you don't mind, we must discuss the matter of my grandfather's interests in this bodega. We understand there is a bank here which received payments from this firm but did not remit them to Ireland. We also heard of a vineyard. My grandfather's affairs seemed to be in some . . . some disorder when he died."

"I'm not entirely surprised to hear it."

My mother's voice rose in protest. "Oh, but my father was the dearest, kindest man. . . ." Her voice broke.

Don Paulo was filling her glass again. "Your love and faith do you credit, Lady Patricia. Not all children are so respectful." He raised his head and nodded towards the door. "Now, here is one—" I was aware of the change which had come over his face: those hooded dark eyes widened with pleasure "—here is one, a rascal who shows little respect for his elders. May I present my son, Carlos? Lady Patricia Drummond. Miss Charlotte Drummond. I might have known he would find his way here. Beautiful ladies draw him unerringly."

I saw a tall, slender young man. He had dark, curling hair. His cream linen suit and embroidered silk waistcoat gave him the air of a dandy, but he was perhaps the most powerfully masculine creature I had yet encountered. He bent over my mother's hand, then turned to take mine. As he executed the gesture of kissing it, his eyes, dark as his father's, ran over me in a practised, knowing fashion. Then he smiled, and it was possible to believe he thought me the only female in the world. He had an oval face with regular, beautifully defined features. I thought he was the most beautiful young man I had ever seen.

"What pleasure for our little town to gain at one time two ladies of such beauty." He took a copita with us. As he drank he talked about Ireland and questioned us about Clonmara, "the new home of my father's . . ." For a time we all fumbled as to how to describe the relationship of Don Paulo and Elena. Finally Carlos found it: "My father's niece by marriage." Then he talked of England. "I had the good fortune to go to school there, but Father dragged me back to scrape a living out of the sherry business."

175

I could see that my mother was enchanted with the young man.

He looked at Don Paulo. "Father, you can't deny me the pleasure of showing our guests through the bodega."

Don Paulo nodded. "You may, Carlos. Who am I to stand in the way of a young man's legitimate pleasure? Especially since, Lady Patricia, he will tell the story of our sherry as well as it can be done. I trained him myself." He rose, and so did my mother.

"I should be delighted to be shown through the bodega," she said. "I'm very ignorant, though. I don't know anything except a little about horses."

"Ah, horses," Carlos echoed. They were off in pursuit of my mother's favourite subject, and his enthusiasm seemed to match hers. They had reached the door before Carlos was aware that I had not stood up. He looked back at me. "Are you not coming, Doña Carlota?"

I hesitated, then I turned back to Don Paulo. "You must allow me to stay a little longer. A few questions only. . . ."

Carlos bowed. "Then I shall have the pleasure of taking you through the bodega at some later time." He closed the door quietly.

I looked at Don Paulo and I was frightened. His expression was wintry, without encouragement. What had made me think I could handle a man like this? I felt I had run headlong into a combination of Spanish pride and austerity, and a streak of cruelty. I delayed a long time, lest my voice should tremble.

At last Don Paulo's impatience broke through. "Come, say what you must. You will not leave here without answers, I can see. You are not like your mother."

I put my glass on the table and took a deep breath. "Don Paulo, we wondered if my grandfather's investment in the bodega was substantial or trivial. All we know is that the moneys paid by your bodega remained here in Jerez."

He shrugged. "The dividends due under that investment were paid each year into the Banco de Jerez. What happened to them after that is no concern of mine."

I almost blurted out a question about the note that had come each year with its cryptic message, "She lives." But a newly found sense of caution stopped me. And I said nothing about the fact that Don Paulo had married the woman my grandfather had been expected to marry. One did not say such things. Not yet.

He took up the thread again. "A number of times, Doña Carlota,

176

I offered to buy back your grandfather's interest in the bodega. He did not respond. Now you are here asking questions. I can only tell you that the bodega has known the good times and the bad times of the sherry trade. When we had the scourge of the phylloxera—the plant lice—years ago, in 1896, our vineyards were destroyed and no one had any profits. Those were lean years in Jerez, and we are just beginning to emerge from them now. However, you will find every dividend scrupulously accounted for. The state of your grandfather's bank account will be communicated to you by Don Ramón García, who is head of the Banco de Jerez. I myself will send a messenger to him."

He leaned back, and his words were slow. "And now, Doña Carlota, I would like to renew my offer to buy back those shares. I will make a handsome offer—well above their market price. Enough to make the return to Ireland much easier. I will even take that monstrous ruin of a house off your hands. The ground it stands on has some value."

"And the vineyard?" I murmured.

His lips stretched thinly. "You are greedy, Doña Carlota. The vineyard your grandfather bought is worth nothing but the value of its *albariza* soil—the soil which produces the sherry grape. It was never replanted after the phylloxera scourge. There is plenty of my own *albariza* land which is not yet planted in vines." Then he waved a hand as if granting a sweet to a child. "But if you insist, I will buy the vineyard."

I shook my head then and smiled. For some reason he wished us gone, and the knowledge gave me a sense of power. "But that is not, of course, for me to agree to, Don Paulo. It is my mother who owns these things."

He gestured as if dismissing me. "You think I am a fool? It is you, Doña Carlota, who will make the decisions."

"My mother appears to like Jerez. She says she will stay."

He nodded, and his eyes almost closed. "Very well, then. Play your game if you must. My offer stands. My bodega is for me—for me and for my family. We want no outsiders."

I rose. "Then may I, Don Paulo, see the bodega? I am anxious to see where my—my mother's interests lie."

He considered for a moment, staring at me silently. He rose. "Come—*I* will show you the bodega, Doña Carlota. You will have the best guide in Jerez."

WE WALKED through a passageway laced with overhanging vines, and the heat smote us. Don Paulo led me to one of the big open doors of the nearest bodega. In the dim light I became aware gradually of the huge space about me, and the quiet. It was a vast building, vaulted in arches, which rested on thick pillars, almost like a church. There was a damp smell of wood and wine. We walked on a cobbled pathway between rows of dark butts piled on stout wooden beams.

Don Paulo had taken a stick with him and he pointed at the intersecting rows of butts. "The smell is our wine as it soaks through the oak casks. It breathes through the wood itself, and through the bunghole, which is only lightly stoppered. We never completely fill a butt, so a large part of the wine within it is exposed to air."

His speech had become slower, the tone almost ruminative. The antagonism that had bristled between us in his office seemed left behind. Now he was talking as a man talks of something he loves. His face and eyes had assumed almost the same expression they wore when Carlos had entered his office. I sensed that this man who could appear so coldly reserved was capable of great, perhaps terrible, passions. His wine was one of his passions.

He pointed to the butts stacked about us, reaching high over our heads. "The solera system makes sherry different from other wines. We have no vintage years in sherry. Instead, we strive to achieve a uniform wine, one which does not vary in quality or character. What we do is move and blend our wine in a sort of perpetual cycle.

"A solera consists of a number of casks stacked in tiers. Here—" pointing with his stick from one side of the aisle to the other, where the casks were stacked three-high "—is an example of a solera of six tiers, or as we say here, scales. This bottom one, the first scale, contains wine ready to be sold. This is the real solera—the other scales we call *criaderas*—nurseries. The cask above the solera contains wine about a year younger, and the one above has wine a year younger still. Over here are the fourth, fifth and sixth scales. The sixth cask holds wine which is about five years younger than the wine in the first scale.

"When we draw off wine to sell from the bottom, we refill the first scale with an equal amount of wine drawn from the second scale. This amount is then made up with wine from the third scale, and so on, right through the fourth, fifth and sixth scales. We call this running the scales. In this way we refresh and rejuvenate the older wine by blending it with the younger."

He paused, his eyes moving over the dark butts with their white markings. When he spoke again, his tone was musing. "I have often thought, Doña Carlota, how wonderful it would be if we could apply the solera system to ourselves. Think, if we could draw on the young for refreshment and invigoration as we aged."

"Surely," I ventured, "the young have a callowness you'd hardly want to mix with your own maturity, Don Paulo."

"Age without youth dies," he answered. "Perhaps you will still be here in September when we harvest our grapes, and press them, and bring in the liquid from the pressing to the bodegas. We call this liquid *mosto*—must. It is not then wine. Even as it is brought to the bodega it goes into a state of violent fermentation. It froths and bubbles—and this to me is the excitement, the strength and the enthusiasm of youth. Some people describe the smell it has then as nasty, and it is certainly undrinkable. So youth has its bad qualities, but we older ones observe and classify, trying to eliminate what is undesirable and to encourage that which we think will make great wine.

"The must quietens down in about a week, as youth settles down a little. It is during this second, quieter fermentation that it begins to develop the characteristics which will distinguish it in later life. Then, when winter comes to Jerez in December or January, the fermentation stops. The must, which up to then has been a turbid and yellowish liquid, becomes clear. This is when we say, 'The wine falls bright'.

"And so, Doña Carlota, youth has turned the corner. The young wine begins to indicate whether it will be fino or oloroso."

He clapped his hands together and called out an order in Spanish. Almost at once a man brought something Don Paulo called a *venencia*, an object which looked to me like a candlesnuffer. It was a small cylindrical cup made of silver, on a black flexible whalebone rod. The man also carried stemmed sherry glasses, perhaps ten of them, between his fingers.

Don Paulo indicated one particular butt, and the man hastened to remove its wooden bung. With a swift movement Don Paulo plunged the silver up through the hole. He took a copa from the attending man. Holding the *venencia* high, he poured the liquid in

179

a long steady stream, which fell, miraculously, it seemed to me, into the narrow neck of the sherry glass. It was a gesture of great flamboyance and skill. "Only the smallest sip," he said, handing it to me. "You will not like it. It is last year's vintage." The wine was slightly cloudy, thin and acid to the taste.

He took me in this way through the scales of a solera of finos, rinsing with water and then plunging the long *venencia*, taking a fresh glass each time, and each time pouring with that marvellous accuracy. Year by year the wine grew better, until finally we reached the oldest scale of the solera, where it had attained the delicate, topaz perfection of the fino we had drunk in Don Paulo's office.

We moved across to another bodega. Pepita had followed, moving between us, not seeming to know which of us she should look to for her commands. Don Paulo studiously ignored her.

"The cellar instinct," Don Paulo said, "is almost as important to the sherry shipper as his nose for his wine, or his decisions about where to plant his vineyards. Wine here in Jerez develops better when stored in bodegas on the south or southwest of the town—possibly because of the moisture and aeration of the breeze blowing from the sea, but that is scientifically unproven."

There was a feeling of quiet in the bodega, and as I walked at Don Paulo's side I felt strangely at peace.

"Sherry," he said, as we crossed yet another of those vine-threaded passageways between the bodega buildings, "is the special gift of God. Everything here in Jerez is exactly right for it—soil, climate, ferments, and fruit. But the special gift is the *flor*. The flor is the flower of the wine, the spores of the yeast which rise spontaneously to the surface of the wine twice a year and reproduce, then fall to the bottom of the butt again. A sherry wine will produce this flor for about six to eight years. If the older wine is not blended with the new, younger wine, the flor will die, and so will the wine. Renewed with other wines, it keeps on breeding indefinitely . . . and so I think about the family. How good if we could keep on being renewed in this way."

We had entered another bodega. A few casks were stacked apart from the others, differently marked. Once again Don Paulo called for the *venencia* and the glasses. "We use the little *venencia* so that it does not stir up any sediment in the butt. These butts should not be here. Their true home is Sanlúcar de Barrameda, where the

180

grapes are grown and where they mature best. I keep them for my own observation, to see the difference in the way the wine will develop. What does it taste like, do you think?"

It was the palest of the sherries I had seen. I sipped and hesitated. "It tastes—it seems to taste a bit salty."

I couldn't tell whether he was pleased by the guess or not. "You are right," he said. "It is slightly salty. It is called a manzanilla sherry. The grapes that produce it are grown quite close to the sea."

The many small copas I had had in the heat of the day were beginning to take their effect. I had forgotten how frightened I had been earlier of this man. "It's all one family of wines," I said slowly, trying to express the impression that the bodegas had had on me. "The grapes growing out there in the vineyards are like the unborn babies of the family. Here you teach and train them by blending and mixing them with their elders. The strength is in the family. . . ." I trailed off, embarrassed.

He looked at me for quite a long time before replying. "The family is everything. And yet your family and mine, Doña Carlota, have not been blessed with many members."

He took my arm lightly and led me down the aisle between the tiers of butts. Outside, silhouetted against the blinding light, were two figures, my mother and Carlos. The light behind them seemed to give them an aura of enchantment. Each held a copa, and, unable to see clearly into the dimness of the bodega, they appeared unaware of our approach.

Don Paulo's words came as a soft whisper; I wasn't even sure I was intended to hear them. "And there is my hope for this family. He was born of a woman to whom I was not married. He does not even rightfully bear my name. And yet he is all my hope."

We walked towards them. Pepita then seemed to decide where she belonged. She fell in beside me and stayed with me.

A WOMAN WAS SEATED in the drawing room when we returned, and Serafina had served her a copita, which she had not touched. She was thin and wiry, and dressed in black. "I am María Luisa Romero Fernández Gordon. I have come to offer my services."

I stared at her in fascination. She was outstandingly ugly, with snapping black eyes that brightened her sharp, sallow face. Pepita came to sniff her, and she put her hand on the dog's big head. "I see you have Don Paulo's dog. Carlos will not like that."

"Services?" I said, to bring her back to the point.

"Exactly. You will need someone like me if you are to stay in Jerez. You don't know how things are done in Spain. You don't know who anyone is. To survive, you must be shown the way. I can do it. I'm related to more than half the families in Jerez, and I know the facts and scandals attached to all the others. I am poor, unmarried, and ugly. I get shifted from family to family, moved around when someone needs something—a duenna, a nurse, a housekeeper. I am everyone's poor relation. Now I offer my services to you."

I blinked at the rapid delivery of the words in perfect English. "Services? We can pay for nothing."

"I didn't mention payment. I know you can pay for nothing. I need a roof over my head, food. A dress now and then. In return I will teach you Spanish. I will give orders to the servants and see that you are not cheated of the little you have. In a day or two Jerez society will start calling, swarming around, seeing what you are like. You will need someone like me or you will make many and probably fatal mistakes."

My mother said in a tone of gentle amusement, "You seem remarkably sure of yourself, señorita."

María Luisa nodded. "I am. It is the only way I survive. I'm the last of six daughters, all of the others pretty and married."

My mother leaned back in her chair, eyes closed. "I really don't know what to say. Talk to Charlie about it. You will learn that Charlie is much more practical than I."

"That I know already." Our eyes met, and I experienced not a feeling of pity, but a sense of relief.

Only one doubt came to my mind. "Tell me truthfully," I said. "Has Don Paulo sent you?"

A smile twisted the thin lips. "So you have his measure, have you? No, he did not send me. I have performed many thankless tasks in my life, but I have never been a paid spy."

"But surely to come to us for nothing—for the little you say you need—that isn't much better than thankless."

"You must let me be the judge of that. I was born a lady, and here I can be one, even if I run the kitchen. And besides, I *am* being paid. A little."

"Paid?" I started forward, and my mother opened her eyes.

"You have a friend. I knew him when he was here. A shrewd and clever man who never made the mistake of ignoring me. His name

182

then was Richard Selwin—now Lord Blodmore. He wrote to me
as soon as he knew you were coming, and made his proposition. I
think he hopes you will not stay, but if you do, you will need help.
Do you agree?"

I could not answer. Suddenly Richard's presence was in the
room, reaching out to me. Those brief minutes on the shore might
have faded from memory, I might have lost the early summer scent
of the rose garden, except that the tangible results were here with
me—the annuity to my mother, Andy's presence among us, and
now this strange, dynamic woman in our midst.

I gestured to my mother. She smiled, relieved, happy. "I think
you will be a *great* help to us, María Luisa. Now, you will stay for
luncheon with us, won't you?"

MARÍA LUISA barely touched her wine during lunch, which in
the Spanish fashion was served to us about three o'clock. She also
ate abstemiously, I noticed. When Paco had cleared the dishes,
and the port had been placed by my mother's hand, María Luisa
drew her chair closer to the table.

"I should tell you about Don Paulo," she said. "The man is very
powerful in Jerez, and he is now related to you, however loosely,
by marriage." The story spun out into the hours of the siesta. "The
Fernández family have been nobles since before the time of
Isabella and Ferdinand, but in the last hundred or so years they've
fallen on hard times. Don Paulo followed his heart when he married the first time, and the girl had little money. They had one son,
who died as an infant, and one daughter. His wife died at the birth
of the daughter, and Don Paulo went on, putting as good a face
on things as he could—Spaniards would rather do anything than
admit they are poor. His treasure was in his vineyards, his nose
for sherry, and his daughter, Mariana. I remember—she was just a
few years older than I, but even to me she looked like something
from a fairy tale. She was uncommonly beautiful and accomplished. A good musician, a rider, and she spoke several languages.
Oh, Don Paulo guessed early what her value would be, and he
squeezed out money for her education, grooming her for a high
place that could only come through marriage. *She* would not be
permitted to give her heart away, as he had done. When she was
sixteen she was betrothed to the eldest son of the Duque de
Burgos—a grandee of Spain, with money to match his titles.

183

"And then the Marquesa de Pontevedra came to her estate at Sanlúcar, which is just across the river from the great preserve of Doñana. They say she came to please her English lover, who wanted to visit Córdoba and to hunt at Doñana. He was, of course, Lord Blodmore."

My mother set down her wineglass. "We called her the Spanish woman, and my father was counted the luckiest man in Ireland because it seemed she would marry him. She was *rich*."

"You well may say it, Lady Patricia. The Pontevedra family have the right of descent through the female line, so she had it all. Estates in Catalonia and industries in Barcelona. She owns whole avenues in Madrid and a palace there. Her estate in Galicia is said to be the size of a small kingdom."

"She was not beautiful," my mother said musingly. "Handsome is a better word. Tall, very regal. I remember being a little bit afraid of her when she was at Clonmara that summer."

María Luisa took up the telling. "So Lord Blodmore came with her to Sanlúcar. It was through her that he invested money with Don Paulo. But Blodmore seemed to hold back from her just a little. He was used to *his* way, too. They quarrelled fiercely—and then made it up again. But still, they seemed to enjoy each other's company so much, we thought they would marry."

María Luisa paused to sip her wine. "Then—very suddenly—Blodmore left the Pontevedra estate at Sanlúcar. The next thing we knew he had bought this house and moved into it, all within a day or two. He went nowhere, saw no one. He seemed to us like a man gone mad, fallen into melancholy. The gossip was that the marquesa had finally decided not to marry him, had cast him out as a lover.

"Then Don Paulo announced that he and the marquesa had married. It caused a sensation. No one had any notion that the marquesa paid any special attention to Don Paulo. It seemed possible that he had caught her in the aftermath of a quarrel with Blodmore. But Don Paulo had little time to rejoice in his good fortune. The word came that the marquesa had contracted smallpox. Don Paulo and his daughter, Mariana, were there at Sanlúcar. No one can imagine why he did not send her away immediately—why he risked having her exposed to the infection. But she stayed, and the news came that she had contracted the pox, and then very shortly afterwards that she had died. There were many confusing

184

stories at the time—she was alive, she was dead. . . ." María Luisa shrugged. "The triumph of Don Paulo was in ashes. His only child was dead, his beloved child—and no one could say with certainty that he loved the marquesa. The marquesa recovered, unmarked by the pox. She went to her castle at Arcos with Don Paulo, and no one saw them for some time."

"And my grandfather?"

"Still in Jerez. Shut up in this place like a recluse. It was as if he had had an illness or a terrible shock and could not shake it off. But time passed, and one day he was gone. The house just settled down to its dust and spiders. To tell you the truth, we thought Blodmore just a little mad."

My mother sighed and reached for the port again. "You would not be the first to suggest that. Oh, well, what does it matter? My father missed his chance, and Don Paulo took the prize."

"*She* took Don Paulo," María Luisa corrected. "We have never considered it much of a marriage. There have been no children. When they see each other it is like a formal engagement. She generally stays at her palacio at Sanlúcar, while Don Paulo remains here at his house, Las Fuentes, in Jerez. When it is required, he will go to Madrid to be with her. For the rest of the time she lives a life of complete freedom. But Don Paulo has profited mightily." She tapped the table with a long finger. "From the marquesa came the money with which he expanded his vineyards and his bodegas until he became the greatest of the sherry growers and shippers. With money borrowed from her he began to experiment with new strains of cattle. He grows wheat, olives, sugar beet."

"The marquesa *lent* him money—or gave it?" my mother asked. "I thought a dowry was the husband's to spend."

María Luisa gave a dry laugh. "Soon after their marriage Don Paulo accepted as his partner in the bodega a distant cousin of the marquesa's—Don Luis de Villa Thompson. She imposed the partnership on Don Paulo to protect her own interests. And I would judge that every peseta borrowed from her has been repaid with interest. She is lavish with her money, but no fool."

I remembered the strangely yearning love Don Paulo had evidenced that morning for his son. "Carlos?" I said. "Don Paulo himself told me he is illegitimate."

"All the world knows that. Not only Carlos, but his two half-brothers, Ignacio and Pedro. Don Paulo has acknowledged his

185

sons, given them his name, and the marquesa has countenanced it. Perhaps because their mothers are unknown. There is even the story that the mother of Carlos was a gipsy. It is evident that he is the favourite. Between them, Don Paulo and the marquesa will arrange a good marriage for Carlos."

"Don Paulo has so much," I said, "and yet he still wants the small piece of the bodega my grandfather owned."

"To a man like Don Paulo, the fact that an outsider such as Blodmore should own even a tiny fraction of his business must be like a burr under the saddle. I think perhaps he would like to wipe out his memory altogether."

"But he will not succeed," I said. "The marquesa has married her niece to Richard Blodmore."

My mother drained her glass. "Are *we* burrs under the saddle to him, do you think? Then the longer we stay, the higher the price he will pay. We might come out of it well, Charlie."

But I was thinking of the enmity that had been revived each year between the two men by the words, "*Ella está viva*". There were some things even María Luisa could not explain.

CHAPTER FIVE

It is possible that we would have managed, somehow, without María Luisa, but not nearly so well. She had skills born of age and experience, and if there was anything she didn't know, she made it her business to find out. She would spend her siesta time juggling strings of figures, making lists of things to do. It was from María Luisa that I began to feel that I might learn to do more than ride a horse.

First of all we made the dining room and the sitting room where we had first met Don Paulo immaculate. "Leave the others until we need them," María Luisa counselled, as she waxed the furniture with her own hands. "We must have somewhere to receive." The bedrooms were stripped of their small pieces of china so that they might make a show for visitors downstairs. A crystal chandelier was moved from the principal bedroom—where my mother slept— washed with great care, and hung in the drawing room.

Daily there were Spanish lessons, but even María Luisa's determination faltered in the face of my mother's good-natured sloth. She finally shrugged and said, "Oh, well, what does it matter?

A woman as beautiful as that . . . the men will all practise their English on her, and she will pick up a little Spanish. She soon enough learned how to ask Paco to bring the wine." Then she pointed her sharp finger at me. "But you, Carlota, *you* must learn. You are young. You don't have a bad mind."

So I struggled with the language and with the impossible conundrums of Spanish names. "It is simple," María Luisa said. "First the father's name, and then the mother's name, and then the father's mother's name—"

"For heaven's sake! That means you have to *know* who everyone's mother was and who the father's mother was, and who the mother's father was—"

"In good society," she said, "one *does* know."

From somewhere she produced a little seamstress who toiled to create dresses for me, simple dresses that cost little money but, with María Luisa's eye for line and detail, were surprisingly effective. I was startled by the new being that emerged in the mirror, someone older, with an unfamiliar touch of style. María Luisa clung to her own eternal black. "I did not come to spend your money," she said. "People stopped looking at me a long time ago. But for *you*—this is your time to be looked at!" So she sent to Seville for muslins and dimities and taffetas, and beautiful green cloth for a new riding habit.

"Lord, Miss Charlie!" Andy exclaimed. "I hardly knew you! A fine lady you've become!"

My mother was pleased. "Why, darling, you're going to be a beauty!" Then María Luisa produced an ancient landau, hired cheaply from a livery stable, and two horses. Andy turned his nose up at all three, but he set to work to brush and groom and trim, to paint, and tack back the frayed upholstery.

For all of us, the sight of the carriage horses of Jerez was a daily treat. They pulled every imaginable sort of vehicle, in beautifully matched teams, two or four in harness, and in a style which we had never seen before: five-in-hand, three horses leading, two behind. The drivers knew the magnificent sight they made with their short jackets, round hats, and high tasselled boots, and they enjoyed it. The harnesses for the carriage horses were often embellished with silver, and there was the delightful custom of adding small clusters of colourful woollen balls, which bobbed with the horses' movements. They gave an effect of gaiety and charm.

ONE OF THE FIRST THINGS María Luisa did was to arrange our visit to the bank. Don Ramón García greeted us with grave courtesy and evident appreciation of my mother's beauty. We drank copitas and talked about anything but money for more than half an hour, but María Luisa brought Don Ramón to the point. "The money situation, if you please, señor. Lady Patricia must know exactly how much she may spend."

For a banker, Don Ramón gave a marvellous impersonation of a man who has an aristocratic disdain for money. He could hardly bear to mention it. But he ordered the ledgers brought in, beautiful books bound in fine red Spanish leather and tooled in gold. Don Ramón opened them for our scrutiny. "See, Doña Patricia, here is where Don Paulo makes his first payment of a percentage of the profits. Lord Blodmore was very fortunate he made that investment. It has not given him a great return, but it has been consistent and steady—growing a little each year—except for the time of the phylloxera.

"However—" and here his face creased "—Don Paulo might have needed money then, but he was, as ever, no fool. He gave your father a percentage of the bodega, and the produce of certain vineyards which he *then* owned. If Lord Blodmore had been able to gain a percentage of the total, he might have made a good deal of money. After Don Paulo's marriage, with the loan of money from the marquesa, he began an enormous programme of planting vineyards and building bodegas. Lord Blodmore remained forever outside the great expansion." His finger traced once more the columns of figures. "Lord Blodmore made no withdrawals from this account in all these years, except to authorize payments to the people who took care of his house here and the one at the vineyard. And, of course, each year we added the interest on the capital sum."

My mother gestured impatiently. "Don Ramón, please show the figures to Doña María Luisa. She has our complete confidence."

The ledger was turned towards her. The black eyes studied the figures for a few minutes while we waited in total silence. Finally she raised her head and looked at my mother.

"Can we live on it, María Luisa?"

An almost imperceptible nod. "With prudence—touching the capital sum hardly at all, since it is one of your few assets, Lady Patricia—we may live off the profits paid in annually."

My mother rose to her feet, and Don Ramón sprang to his. "Don Ramón, you have kept my father's trust faithfully. For that my daughter and I thank you."

While he was bowing my mother through the bank's outer offices, I glanced at María Luisa's thoughtful face. "It depends, of course," she said in a low tone to me, "on how well the money continues to come from Fernández, Thompson. We had better start lighting a few candles for good vintages."

WE ATTENDED MASS at the Collegiate Church across the plaza. María Luisa bowed to everyone, and the bows were returned, along with stares. Among the "old aunts" of María Luisa's acquaintanceship, and among some of the elderly gentlemen, the name of Blodmore was murmured, and old memories revived.

They came to call, the old aunts and the elderly gentlemen, some young matrons and the young girls they chaperoned. There were eager questions about Clonmara, and among the young ones there were questions about Richard Blodmore. The answers to these questions came painfully and stiffly to my lips.

In our turn we repaid the calls. Some of the houses could be described as "palacios"; others were smaller. Some were richly maintained, with great, wonderful gardens; others showed the kind of neglect and lack of money which our own house betrayed.

Wherever we went, Pepita was always at my side. She slept by my bed, listened to my whispered longings for times that were past and things that were gone. She gave me something on which to focus my love.

WE GREW USED to the rhythm of life—the strangely late mealtimes, the siesta. As the days passed, the younger men began to present themselves, either singly or in pairs, escorting a sister or a cousin who had already visited us. "I don't know whether they come for you or your mother," María Luisa said to me, "but neither of you is eligible. Lady Patricia is married, and you have no money. A young man in Spain may fall in love, but he rarely marries for love only. The families see to that."

Protestingly, María Luisa took us to visit the house at the vineyard. "The vineyard houses are for the foremen. Oh, yes, there are rooms for the owner when he visits, but no one *lives* there. And in the case of the Blodmore place . . ." She shrugged. "Paco has had a cousin living there for these past twenty years. Merely to keep the gipsies out. There are no vines."

But we went. Andy drove the landau, with María Luisa and Nanny in it; my mother rode Balthasar, and I Half Moon. Word had been sent ahead, but we carried food and wine with us. "A picnic in the country," María Luisa said. "Better to treat it that way, and you will not embarrass Paco's cousin and his wife."

I was growing used to the countryside around Jerez—the low, sweeping Andalusian plain that rose in gentle slopes covered with long straight rows of vines. Where the soil was not suitable for grapes there were olive groves, and sometimes cork trees, red where their bark had been stripped. The unrelenting sun seemed to cast a spell over me, so that it was a sort of dream landscape, at once gentle and fierce. The tinkle of the goat bells rose on the air; the goatherd would lift the ragged brim of a wide hat to us. And out of the dust a fine carriage would appear, with liveried driver and footman; polite hands would be waved to us, a few words called to María Luisa.

I reacted to the vineyard house with a passion that surprised me. It sat on the top of a rise, land undulating about it, looking to other rises crowned with their own white houses, against which purple bougainvillaea flamed. A light breeze fanned the sweat on my forehead, and in the sky pushed puffy clouds before it, so that the shadows ran across the vines—light and dark, dark and light— like the swell of a sea.

A smiling youngish woman, the wife of Antonio, cousin to Paco, showed us through the house. Her name was Concepción; she was dark-eyed and had once been beautiful. The child she carried on her hip and the young ones about her skirts had wearied her beyond her years. But she was proud of the simple things she did to keep the vineyard house presentable. The tiled floors were polished, the whitewashed rooms were clean. There were a few pieces of lovely dark oak furniture, also polished. Great sweeping chimney breasts gave the rooms character. There was a marvellous simplicity in that place—bare, austere, with clean, uncluttered lines, truly Spanish in character.

"It's beautiful," I breathed. "I should like to live here."

"You are mad," said María Luisa quite simply. "I have told you no one lives in a vineyard house. It is a plaything—a place for picnics. You would have no company here . . . no society."

"I wouldn't care," I muttered, and went on to walk the dim shaded rooms, to re-emerge into the aching glare of the courtyard with its stone-faced well and rows of clay pots brilliant with scarlet geraniums. The children played here, and they trooped about me as I went to look out over the vineyards. It was easy to see where my grandfather's land began and ended. It was overgrown with scrubby brush. But beyond, where the land was tended, there was orderly beauty. I stared at it a long time. Then in my hand I gathered up some of the soil that nourished the grapes from which the wine was sprung. It was strangely greyish-white in colour, this *albariza* soil, and seemed full of small, sharp stones. It was at this moment that I was first aware of the desire to see the straggling brush give way to the ordered vines, to see the pale grapes grown on this, our own land. I let the soil dribble back from my hand and went to join the others for lunch.

A snowy, darned cloth was spread on the table in the main room, and clay bowls of the delicious cold soup called gazpacho were ready. Hard-boiled eggs were set on coarse platters decorated with grape leaves; dishes of olives were at hand, and a board of cheese, and slices of hard, dark ham. It was Concepción's contribution to our picnic. We had a full, leisurely lunch.

Concepción came to clear away the dishes, and through María Luisa she indicated that there were beds enough if we wished to take a siesta. We did.

A bluish dusk was creeping over the landscape as we rode back to Jerez; there was the first hint of dew in the air, the nightly soaking the grapes needed. I felt a pang of regret as we descended the track, my grandfather's ragged acres on one side, the rows of patiently tended vines on the other.

DON PAULO did not visit our home again, and we were not invited to his. Sometimes in the salons of acquaintances we came across Carlos. He was deliciously charming, and his gaze flickered over me with more than a little interest. He introduced us to his two half-brothers, Pedro and Ignacio. They were all markedly different, Pedro having something of his father's broad, impressive build; Ignacio was lean and dark of face, with clever, intense eyes. "Ignacio keeps his nose in the company books," Carlos said disparagingly.

"And you don't?"

He laughed. "It is far more important to keep in my father's good graces. Other people can keep the books."

"And Pedro? What does he do to keep your father's favour?"

"My brother Pedro cultivates his nose!" He laughed at the expression on my face. "I mean he spends his days in the *cuarto de muestras*—the sample room—where we keep samples of all wines we export or sell in Spain. My father has the most famous nose for sherry in all Jerez."

"And have you a nose?"

He laughed with charming arrogance. "Dear Carlota, I have everything. At least I make my father *think* I have everything. That's what's important."

It was a rather frightening cynicism in so young a man; but behind the bragging arrogance Carlos had betrayed the lack of security that his birth had given him. Illegitimate, they all must fight to be first in the eyes of their father. And did they also seek, through their father, the favour of that unseen woman, the marquesa?

MARÍA LUISA was excited when the dance invitation came. "It is from Don Luis de Villa Thompson—the distant cousin of the Marquesa de Pontevedra who was put into the Fernández bodega to look after her interests. He also has money and vineyards of his own."

A dress was made for me of pale green silk. My mother had an old emerald silk gown refurbished, and María Luisa wore black lace to mark the occasion.

I suppose it was because it would be the first and, in a way, the last ball for me that I remember it so well. Don Luis greeted us. He had the long, thin face one sees in some Spaniards; he was not handsome, but his dark brown eyes were alert and kindly. There were deep lines in his sensitive face; he was no longer young. He greeted us with an expression of gentle pleasure and presented us to his wife, Amelia, a much younger woman, hardly more than a girl, wearing an over-elaborate dress and diamonds. She was too thin, and her face was peaked with fatigue. María Luisa had said to us on our way to the party, "So sad for Luis. This is his second wife, and not a child between the two of them. Of course they say it is the fault of Luis. He is not *macho*."

It was a wonderful party, and I was happy because my dance

card was filled almost at once. Carlos came to my side and claimed the supper dance.

"Be careful," María Luisa whispered to me once. "Don Paulo is watching."

"Let him watch. Carlos can make his own choice."

"Carlos is Don Paulo's son. That is more to the point."

What point, I didn't quite see. After supper I walked with Carlos to the artificial lake, where a fountain played, the whisper of water welcome on that warm night. "The Moors loved the sound of water," Carlos said. "We have it wherever we can."

Swans glided like wraiths on the other side of the lake. They and their progeny had inhabited the lake so long that the house was known as Los Cisnes—The Swans. Carlos kissed me, as I had known he would. I found myself liking it. In time we drew apart gently and walked on without speaking.

After a circle of the lake we came back to the house. Two great sweeping arms of staircase curved down to the garden. At the landing I was aware of a waiting, almost brooding figure. It was Don Paulo, wonderfully impressive in evening dress, a ribbon of some order across his chest. He bowed. Without thinking, I dropped a half curtsy, as if it were his due. Carlos inclined his head to his father, and in total silence we passed on. From that moment, for me, the party was over.

I ENCOUNTERED CARLOS several times in the next few weeks. He was polite, charming, and slightly distant. He did not come to call at our house. I found myself looking for him among our visitors, and feeling disappointed when I did not see him.

"I heard about him—" María Luisa started to say when my mother mentioned his absence, and then she checked herself.

"What did you hear?" I demanded.

She kept her eyes on her sewing. "I heard Don Paulo was displeased by the attention he paid you at Don Luis's party. I even heard that he had been ordered to stay away from you."

Carlos sat with us, though, for a few minutes one day as we watched the polo at the club on the outskirts of the town. I had never seen it played before. "It was brought back to England by officers who had served in India in 1871, I think," he said. "One of the González family, the Marqués de Torresoto, saw it played in London, and brought some polo sticks back to Jerez."

"One needs a lot of ponies to play it," my mother observed, as she watched the players changing from one pony to the next.

"Yes. And fortunately my father doesn't mind providing them." Carlos laughed without self-consciousness. "I could never do it out of my salary. You must excuse me now, Lady Patricia. It's my turn to play." He played well, and his side won easily.

After the match he went off, and we didn't see him again. The weather grew hotter. The days seemed almost unbearable and the nights airless. I grew bored with the round of visits, the small talk. María Luisa said, "When the vintage comes there will be parties and the *corrida*—the bullfight."

AT NIGHT sleep seemed to have deserted me; I lay awake and thought too much of Richard Blodmore. Then I walked the corridors of the big house to try to escape the thoughts. Sometimes I went and visited the horses. For these secret visits I saved sugar for them, with the biggest helping always going to Balthasar.

Then came the night when I discovered that I was not the only one who came to feed sugar to Balthasar. The moon was sliding towards the horizon and dawn. I heard the low words, the Spanish words I could not understand. And then from the shadow of Balthasar's box the figure of a man emerged. He gave a final, lingering caress along Balthasar's neck and prepared to close the bottom half of the door. "Andy?" It was not Andy.

"Carlota!"

Carlos. As I had never seen him before. He wore plain black trousers and an open-necked white shirt. He could have been the gipsy they said his mother was.

"What—"

"What am I doing here?" he said for me. "I come quite often to visit Balthasar."

"But why?"

"Because Balthasar was once my horse. The finest horse in Jerez. A gift from my father. And given—no, *taken* from me by my father to pay a debt to Richard Blodmore. Exchanged at the chess table. If Blodmore had lost, the forfeit was to have been the finest Irish hunter in his stables. My father actually would have preferred to have had the horse that killed your grandfather, but we heard that he also was killed. So my father took from me one of the few creatures I have truly loved."

194

My heart was twisting with misery. "I don't think Richard knew Balthasar was yours, Carlos. He wouldn't—"

He shrugged. "It makes no difference. It is the sort of gesture my father makes. The way he gave you Pepita. I had given *him* Pepita. As it was with Elena. At one time there was the possibility that Elena would be my wife. Not that we loved each other. But still . . . I would have liked the marriage. Then the Marquesa de Pontevedra, my father's wife, appeared in Jerez, and Elena was handed over to Richard Blodmore. That is the way my father is. If it serves his purpose, or the purpose of the woman he is married to . . ." He drew in a deep breath and laid his head against the neck of the great horse.

Suddenly I longed to be free of all this—this house, whatever enmity had bound my grandfather and Don Paulo, my vain longing for Richard Blodmore. All of it seemed to find expression in the sight of the dark head of this young man laid against the neck of the white horse.

"Carlos, will you ride Balthasar again? Shall we ride out—out beyond the town, while it is still cool? Before the sun is up?"

His head came around sharply, a look of incredulity on his face. "Carlota—would you? Would you do that with me?"

"Saddle up Balthasar and Half Moon. I'll get dressed. We must be very quiet."

THE HORSES' HOOVES made a great clatter in the courtyard, but no one appeared. I had put on the skirt of my riding habit and an old cotton shirt left over from the Clonmara days. My hair hung freely down my back. I felt lighthearted, almost like a child again, the last grains of good sense running like sand from an hourglass. We set out on a road I had never been on before, away from the vineyards. "The road to Arcos," Carlos said.

Suddenly the restlessness I had fought these last few days demanded release. I urged Half Moon into a full gallop. Carlos held Balthasar a little longer. Then he let the stallion have his head. Very soon he was level, and then past us. Was I, for a few instants of time, back at Clonmara? Was it Richard who passed me on the great white horse? I kicked Half Moon to greater effort. But Balthasar was far ahead before Carlos began to slow him.

Balthasar was standing still, sweat on his white coat, when I finally reached them. Wordlessly, Carlos helped me dismount, and there were no questions to ask as we drew aside from the road and entered an unfenced grove of eucalyptus trees. Carlos tied both horses, and then he took me in his arms.

LATER, before Carlos untied the horses, he took from his belt a thin, leather-sheathed knife. "Look, Carlota." He was carving something on one of the trees. "With the finest Toledo blade I sign our names. Two Cs intertwined. Whoever owned this land does not know that now it belongs to us. Our brand is here as long as this tree stands."

ANDY WAS WAITING for us by the open doors when we returned, his face sharp with concern. Typically, Carlos didn't attempt any explanations. He slipped off Balthasar's back and handed Andy the reins. He kissed my hand. "A miraculous morning, Carlota." And then he walked off across the plaza.

"Miss Charlie," Andy began. There was a tremor in his voice which could have been anger.

"It's all right, Andy. We were very careful with the horses."

"I'm wondering if it's very careful with yourself you've been, Miss Charlie. Lord Blodmore charged me to take care of you."

I flung myself down from the saddle and threw the reins to him. "Oh, damn Lord Blodmore!" The tears slid down my cheeks as I sped to my room. Had it been Richard Blodmore, and not Carlos, I had pursued as I had urged Half Moon to catch up with the white stallion?

CHAPTER SIX

*T*he rain held off through those next weeks. "Any day now they will begin to harvest," María Luisa said when September arrived. Preparations were being made for the celebration at the church. A *lagar*—a shallow, square, wooden winepress—was set up on the steps outside for the ceremonial treading of the grapes and the blessing of the must which ran from the *lagar*. I was there with my mother and María Luisa when the four solemn, burly men, called *pisadores*, wearing very short trousers and their special nail-studded leather boots, the *zapatos de pisar*, trod the first grapes. The nails of the boots trapped the pips and stalks of the grapes so that they would not break. Unbroken, they could not release their tannin, which could give the wine a harsh flavour.

All of Jerez seemed to be there. For the first time in more than a month I saw Carlos in the crowd which eddied in the plaza before the church. Since that morning ride there had been no word from him. It was like a blow to see his face turned deliberately, steadily, away from mine. For him, I told myself, I had been a girl to enjoy for only one mad moment in the dawn. I did not love Carlos—how could I when I loved Richard Blodmore? But I desperately needed the reassurance of a sign from him, a gesture.

It was Sunday, and we went that afternoon to the corrida, my mother and I protesting, and María Luisa insisting, "You *must* appear." The whole bullring was wild with the mood of the *feria*. We witnessed the full ceremonial of the occasion, the march of the toreros, their suits flashing in the sun. From the height of the box it was colourful and romantic, and one did not think of the bull.

I managed to stay in my seat all through the time when the bull and the mounted horsemen, the picadors, fought it out. But then I saw the wicked horns pierce the padded blankets which covered the horse's side. There was too much blood; I had seen enough. I pushed past the chairs of those around me. Out in the deserted corridor behind the boxes, I listened to the waves of sound that came. "Olé . . . ! Olé . . . ! Olé!" And then the waves of nausea could be held back no longer.

It was María Luisa who came. I felt her arm about my shoulder. "It is too much for you? I would not have thought you so weak-stomached." She fanned my face. Then she stopped. "What is it, *querida*? You are too pale. It is not just the bullfight, is it? *Is it?*" she insisted gently.

All her years of watching young girls, young women, were in that question.

"Perhaps not, María Luisa."

For only a moment she leaned back against the wall and closed her eyes. Then they snapped open, black, resolute. "We have a saying here in Jerez, 'The girls and the vines are difficult to guard.' I have been remiss. However, we will say, for the moment, that it is the bullfight. We must think. We must make sure."

THE NEXT DAY Andy drove us to the office of Dr. Miguel Ramírez. "Do not be afraid," María Luisa said. "He is an old friend. He will be discreet."

She remained in the room while Dr. Ramírez made his examination, and she was silent most of the way home. "Now you must tell me, querida. Who is it?"

I could not lie to her. I had no defences. "Carlos," I said. "It was not his fault. I did not resist him."

"Do not speak of fault, querida. So, it is Carlos." She sighed. "Child, you do not make things easy for me. You might have chosen other than the best-loved son of Don Paulo." She let out a sharp, harsh little laugh. "Well, now I must really set out to earn that money Lord Blodmore sends to me. We must have you married."

"But I cannot *force* him," I said. "I could not endure that kind of marriage."

"A marriage there must be, querida. And to Carlos, if it kills me. Say nothing to your mother. She would not blame you—but she might not be . . . discreet. Yes, I must make arrangements."

IT TOOK SEVERAL DAYS and several meetings with Carlos. "He resists . . . yet he is willing to be persuaded," María Luisa reported. "The harvest has fully begun, and they work long hours at the bodegas. I had to wait two hours today before seeing him."

"Do not see him again," I said. I had been ill each morning, and trying to keep it from my mother. "I *won't* be foisted on him. I'll leave—I'll go back to Ireland."

"To take your child back to Lord Blodmore?" María Luisa said sharply. "Carlos's child? No, be patient. I'm certain he cares for you, but there is Don Paulo. . . ."

"Yes," I said, "there is always Don Paulo. Even though Carlos is illegitimate, he is the favourite son. He is expected to make a better marriage than *me!*"

"You will do him honour," she answered fiercely. "Whomever his other sons marry, you will bring the most credit to his house."

She came next day, her face grey with exhaustion, her body sagging with weariness. "It is done. He has agreed, and the arrangements are made."

ANDY HAD THE LANDAU, its hood up, waiting at five o'clock the next morning. Balthasar and Half Moon were hitched to the back, and Pepita lay across one seat. We drove to the tiny church of Santa Catalina, hidden away in the old part of Jerez. An old priest came to greet us, his faded eyes gazing at me with interest. "This marriage will be blessed by God," he said in careful English.

Carlos was late, but at last he came. I could see the relief in María Luisa's face. We were married before the bells of the Angelus sounded, and went to the sacristy to sign the register.

"A small matter of interest, Don Carlos," the priest said, as we rose from the table after signing. "A long time ago . . . I remember a marriage also celebrated very early in the morning." He took an old leather-bound book from a tall cupboard, turned the stiff pages until he came to what he sought.

"Your illustrious father, on a momentous occasion . . . A happy coincidence you have chosen the same church, and that I should be the one to sanctify the marriages of both father and son."

He pointed to the page, blank except for two names. I saw the signature I remembered—*Santander*. And then, scrawled slantingly upwards across the page, as if the writer had been impatient to be done with the business, a single name—*Pontevedra*. The Spanish woman.

OUTSIDE THE CHURCH Carlos went at once, automatically, to rub Balthasar's nose. I went to his side. "I have brought him for you," I said. "It was the only wedding gift I could make." I did not add that I was not entirely sure that Balthasar was mine to give. But my mother would forgive me.

Carlos smiled down at me. "Carlota, you do me great honour. Both by this marriage and by your gift."

We were going to the vineyard house. I was grateful for the refuge. I did not want, at this moment, to return to the house in the Plaza de Asturias, nor could we go to Don Paulo's house. Later, Carlos said, he would return to the bodega to confront his father. "But first I will eat my wedding breakfast with you, querida."

I wanted to ride Half Moon, but Carlos insisted that we both ride in the landau. "I will not risk my child by having you ride, Carlota." I had thought very little of the child. I suppose it was from that moment I began to love it.

MARÍA LUISA had sent a message to the vineyard house to expect me and to prepare accommodation. But a look of astonishment swept across the faces of Antonio and Concepción as Carlos sprang down from the landau. It was evident that they thought their little

199

Irish Miss had brought off a great coup. They did not know, of course, that the marriage did not have Don Paulo's approval, and that this tumbledown vineyard house, in the midst of the fields of brush, was all that Carlos and I had between us.

María Luisa had packed a basket with our wedding breakfast, and after we had eaten, Carlos was quite unselfconscious about his intention of taking me to bed at once. Thrusting the glasses and plates aside, he led me to the bedroom Concepción had prepared. Then he made love to me, and every lingering thought of Richard Blodmore was driven from my mind. Later he dressed and kissed me goodbye.

"I must attend to the day's work at the bodega," he said. "And I must see my father." Searching his face, I saw not the least sign of apprehension.

I slept peacefully all the rest of the morning. But when I awoke the thought came, like a rain cloud over the vineyards, that now I was irrevocably committed to Carlos, to Jerez, to a life in Spain. There would be no return to Ireland for me. I must not even dream about Clonmara.

CARLOS returned quite late that night, his clothes dusty from the ride. Concepción had cooked one of her precious chickens. She put it on the table, then left us alone.

He drank some wine, talking of the vintage. It would be a prosperous year for Jerez. At last I had to ask him.

"Your father . . . you told him?"

"I told him, Carlota."

"And?"

Carlos was thoughtful as he sipped his wine. "My father seldom shows his anger. But one knows it is there, all the same. I am his beloved son, but I have made a mismatch—" The blood of shame rushed to my face, and gently he reached out his hand to cover my mouth so that I should not interrupt. "I told him truly that I had made no mismatch. No man, not even my father, may say such things and expect me not to strike back."

"But how can you strike back at Don Paulo?" I felt helpless and afraid.

"Through the only weapon I have. His love of me. That old man sees his future in me, and already one can sense his longing for the child. I threatened to take you, and his grandchild, away."

200

Carlos smiled at me, but his face was weary. "We made a formal arrangement. I am to stay on at the bodega. I shall receive my salary and nothing more. It means a little time of waiting. A man like that lives to pass on his vineyards to his grandsons. You will give him his first grandson. And one day he will die, and then perhaps *I* shall be rich!"

"Carlos, how can you talk like that? He is your father!"

His features twisted and he no longer smiled. "I talk like that, Carlota, because all my life that man has told me what to do, what to think, how to act. Today I have married my woman, without asking him. I shall have *my* son, and he shall not be just the grandson of Don Paulo, Marqués de Santander."

In that one day we had both grown in experience. I was a young girl no longer, and Carlos had paid for his freedom. The interview between father and son must have been painful and bitter. We slept that night clasped in each other's arms, as much for comfort and reassurance as for love.

THE CARRIAGE arrived early the next morning, after Carlos had left for the bodega, almost as if the coachman had waited to see him go. Its doors bore the crest of Santander. A liveried footman handed me a note signed by Don Paulo.

> I trust you will favour me with an interview. It would be best if you came in my coach, as we have some further travelling to do.

I dressed quickly, but with care. Of course, as yet my condition did not show, so I wore one of the gowns María Luisa had had made for me, a pale green muslin.

We drove to Jerez—to Las Fuentes, the mansion of Don Paulo, which was grander even than the mansion of Don Luis. The house sat on a slight rise, and it got its name, Las Fuentes, from the four fountains, each set at a different level, which sent water spuming into the air and cascading down to the lowest pool. All of this Carlos had left for the poverty of the vineyard house. No wonder he had hesitated. I had already forgiven that hesitation. Now I understood it.

Don Paulo came to the carriage and took a seat opposite me. Immediately the carriage started to move again.

"Where are we going?"

"We are going, Doña Carlota, to Arcos, to Arcos de la Frontera—where my wife, the Marquesa de Pontevedra, has a castle."

"But why?"

"That, in due course, you will discover."

Then the hooded eyes seemed to close, as if he were some kind of lizard, waiting patiently for the unsuspecting insect to come within range.

AFTER what seemed a long drive, the twin hills of Arcos rose spectacularly from the gentle swell of the country we had been travelling. On one side of the town sheer cliffs fell to the river, the Guadalete, and the plain below. Through the heat haze I saw the square towers and crenellated walls of the castle brooding over the plain. The sun was blinding, harsh, brutal. At last the carriage reached a plaza and stopped.

"Here we must walk. The coach can go no further."

Don Paulo helped me down and I walked beside him silently, up steep twisting lanes between buildings, before we gained the garden courtyard of the castle. The place itself was built of lovely yellow stone and seemed very ancient.

Don Paulo could continue his silence no longer. "It is Moorish—parts built in the seventh century. We drove the Moors from it, and held it for the Christians. At Granada we finished the Moorish conquest and Spain was restored forever to Holy Mother Church."

From anyone else, in any other place, it would have sounded absurd. Here, it was perfectly suited.

WE WERE TAKEN to a long vaulted room whose windows overlooked the river. A servant brought copitas, but I asked for water. We waited, the intense silence unnerving.

The marquesa came at last. She was very tall and slender; it might have been a young woman who came towards us, but as she came into the light from one of the windows, I saw that her hair was not golden but silver-gilt; her face had begun to show the marks of age. I had the impression of bright, cold blue eyes. She wore black, a gown almost mediaeval in its fashion. She seemed to wear no adornment until she raised her hand to Don Paulo, and then the fire of emeralds and rubies and diamonds flashed.

Don Paulo took her hand, but his lips did not quite touch it. "You are well, Marquesa. I see that."

"Very well, Santander." It was a greeting between people who have known each other a long time but are still strangers.

"I have brought Doña Carlota—now my son's wife—as you requested," said Don Paulo.

"As I requested, yes. Now you may leave us, Santander."

He looked outraged, then stifled his reply.

I waited in agony until he closed the door and I was alone with the Spanish woman of Clonmara legend.

She gestured for me to be seated. "So . . . you are Blodmore's granddaughter." As I did not reply, she was forced to go on. "And you took away Don Paulo's beloved son, Carlos. How he must hate you—as he hated your grandfather!" Suddenly a laugh, an almost wild but mirthless laugh broke from her lips. "After all these years yet another Blodmore comes to break his heart."

"I didn't know. . . ." My lips trembled; I felt ill. "I *don't* know." Then I straightened my back. "It wasn't planned, you know. Carlos and I just happened to become lovers."

"Just happened." Did that harsh, commanding voice soften just a trifle? "How fortunate for you. Many men have said they loved me. I never knew. Who would not say they loved the fortune and position Isabel de Pontevedra had to bestow? And none of my lovers gave me a child!" It was a primitive cry of anguish and anger. "I might have had Blodmore's child—but I didn't. And you —in a few weeks you are with child and you have married Carlos. How quick you Irish are, when it suits you."

"They still talk, at Clonmara, of the time you were there. They call it the summer of the Spanish woman. They expected my grandfather would marry you, but you married Don Paulo."

She half turned from me; her hands went to her face in a gesture of rage or pain. "You Blodmores! I loved him, and I didn't trust him! I knew the difference between passion and love, and I held off. I held off, and I lost him!"

I thought she had not meant to say so much. Was I really so like my grandfather that I had unnerved her?

"*You* lost him, Marquesa? You could have had him at any time, I am told. You need never have left Ireland."

"His precious Clonmara! I had to show him what was *mine!* I took him on a tour of all my estates in Spain. I played a cat-and-mouse game with him, but too long. I lost him."

"How could you have lost him? Don Paulo married you, won

you. How could my grandfather have broken Don Paulo's heart?"

"Because," she said, "Blodmore took the thing that was dearest to Santander's heart, something dearer to him than Carlos, more precious—more precious, even, I think, than his beloved vineyards."

She was silent for a time, studying me. With an abrupt gesture she turned. "Come! It is time you knew. You will live here among us, and you will know. But you will never, *never* speak of what you have seen this day. You will know how Blodmore betrayed me, betrayed Santander and ruined his own life."

She was hurrying away from me, down the long room. I went after her quickly. I sensed that something in me had thrown her off guard. The moment might never come again.

We crossed the courtyard to a separate wing. She had to pause and knock at a door and wait there until a small window in it was opened and her identity established. Then the door swung open, and the woman on the other side curtsied deeply. The marquesa swept past without even a glance at her. "Where is she?"

"At the loom, Marquesa."

I followed her to a room that was almost equal in size to the one we had left. Close to one of the great window alcoves a girl sat at a large loom, her hand skilfully throwing the shuttle while her feet worked the pedals. Her hair, the colour of straw bleached by the sun but as silken as the threads she handled, lay on her shoulders in soft curls. She was slightly built, and her hands were very pretty. She was dressed in white, the fashion of many years ago.

"Mariana?" The marquesa's voice now was soft. The movements at the loom stopped. The head turned slowly.

It was no young girl I looked at. Her hair was not straw-coloured but white. She had remarkably deep blue eyes, the colour of wild violets, but they were strangely expressionless, and her face was scarred and pitted. If she had ever had beauty, all that was left were the violet eyes.

She looked from the marquesa to me, and for an instant some sort of recognition seemed to come to those blank eyes. Then the glazed look returned.

"Mariana, will you not show us your children?"

Obediently, like a puppet, the woman rose and walked to the farthest end of the long room. We followed.

Six cradles stood there, their flounces of lawn and lace falling

204

to the floor, their hoods decorated with gay Moorish patterns and hanging silken balls. But if there were infants lying in them, they were strangely, uncannily, silent. I peered into the nearest, and a wax face, a perfect angel's face, looked back at me, pink-cheeked, its glass eyes as expressionless as those of the woman. In the corner, on a silken Oriental rug, three wax dolls sat upright. They seemed to smile sightlessly at each other. All were dressed in exquisite linens and laces. They were a perfect example of the waxworker's art, and they struck me as coldly as a sigh from the grave.

The marquesa moved among them, touching them. When she spoke her voice was gentle. "You care for them well, Mariana. Your children flourish."

The blank, ravaged features turned towards her, the lips twisted, but the woman did not speak. Gently she touched a cradle and set it rocking, adjusted a sheet about the shoulders of the sleeping infant.

Unable to bear it any longer, I turned and ran the length of that room, opened the door, and slammed it behind me. In the heat I shivered violently, as if I had come from a place of horror.

CHAPTER SEVEN

We sat in the courtyard, in the deep shade of a tree that must have struggled for centuries to grow in that rocky place. I seemed hardly to remember how I got there. The marquesa was bathing my face with a damp cloth. "You are better? Drink some wine!" I was both ordered to drink the wine and to feel better. The marquesa would have little patience with those who grew faint.

She said, "Your grandfather married that poor demented woman who believes her dolls are children. That woman is Lady Blodmore. She is also the daughter of Santander."

I sucked in the dry air and brought the wineglass once more to my lips. The words didn't make sense.

"You don't believe it? Neither did I, for a time. Neither did Santander. That woman—she was betrothed to the eldest son of the Duque de Burgos. She was to make the greatest marriage in Spain, bring great honour to Santander. He guarded her well, but he also trusted her well. He brought her to stay at my palacio at Sanlúcar, so that we could go over to Doñana for the autumn hunting. And I had brought Blodmore. The two came together. They became lovers under our eyes, and we did not see it. She was seventeen, he was thirty-three. They were married secretly, and the girl, Mariana, was with child. Except for that, Santander could have moved swiftly to have the marriage annulled."

"And you?" The words came out weakly.

She shrugged. "I was a woman scorned. This little chit had taken the man I wanted. From my own house they had stolen away to be married. By a Carmelite friar—who was sent to an order in the far north of Spain. The marriage record was removed from the register at Sanlúcar. Such things we were able to do, Santander and I. The rest—the rest was the hand of God."

I was coming to life again, strength returning. "Was it the hand of God which caused you to marry Don Paulo?"

She looked at me, anger now evident in that pale, thin face. "I married Santander because I chose to do so." She had no need to say she had done so in a passion of rage and jealousy.

"We separated them at once, of course. Blodmore, poor fool, took himself to Jerez and bought that place as a home for Mariana. A hopeless gesture. . . . He should have known I would not let him have things so easily."

"But María Luisa told us that Don Paulo's daughter died of smallpox—"

"Mariana contracted it. She was very ill. It would have solved a lot of problems if she had died. But she lived. Every day Blodmore came, begging admission, and every day he was sent away—for his own protection, he was told. When she recovered we brought her here in a closed carriage, and no one ever saw her leave Sanlúcar or enter this house. Her child came at barely seven months. It lived for two days, then died. She wept and screamed for it, until in desperation someone snatched a doll from one of the servants' children and put it in her arms. Then she was quiet and comforted. Since that time she has appeared to want nothing else."

"But my grandfather—you *cannot* have kept him away when the baby was born."

"When the child was born, we admitted him. It was his child. A son. His heir. We allowed him to see Mariana, too. The smallpox had taken her beauty, and it must have been a terrible shock to him, but he never faltered. He began to make plans to take her and the baby back to Ireland. Then the child died, and her reason went with it. For months Blodmore waited in that house in Jerez.

Mariana regressed to her childhood. She knew her father, she knew me because I was as familiar as her attendants. She knew her dolls. She did not know Blodmore. His time in her life was obliterated."

The harsh laugh broke through again. "Oh, I have to admit that he behaved well—he behaved well *then*, when the damage was done. But Mariana cried for her father and her child, and wanted no part of him. In the end he recognized that it would have been the greater cruelty to take her from here.

"So he returned to Ireland and never came again. Each year the profits from Blodmore's share of the bodega were deposited with the bank to be used for Mariana's needs. Santander, of course, has refused them."

I thought of the sheets of paper, one for each year, bearing Santander's signature and *"Ella está viva"*—She lives. Only death had released my grandfather from his marriage vows.

"He greatly wronged us." The marquesa was speaking quite softly now. "He died without an heir, and his beloved Clonmara went to Richard Selwin. *I* brought Richard Selwin back here and offered him Elena and a large dowry. In the end my family will inherit Clonmara. And now *you* have come, and the Blodmore strain is back with us once more."

I knew now the agony my grandfather must have endured during that year of exile.

"You separated Mariana and my grandfather," I said. "All to satisfy your own jealousy. And is it for more revenge you've brought me here? It's useless, you know. You can't reach into the grave. My grandfather is buried where his heart lies. *That* you can't touch!"

"So . . . the mouse stirs and squeaks and pretends to be a lion. Believe me, girl, you will know what you have done! And you will say nothing to anyone. Not to that drunken fool, your mother. Not to your husband, that charming weakling. You are a Blodmore. Twice in his life you Blodmores have struck to the heart of Santander! How he hates you! Live with the knowledge that you have no rights in this family. You have married Carlos and you must be the perfect wife. You will measure up to *our* standards. You will do as *we* say."

I rose. "I will do what I believe is right, Marquesa. I think I had better leave. It is a very long way home."

I strode down the steep slope to where the carriage waited, refusing Don Paulo's arm. On the drive back to Jerez I sat erect, as if a rod of iron had been thrust into my back. For my grandfather's sake I would have to find the strength to be all the things they did not expect me to be.

MY MOTHER INSISTED that the baby be born in the house in the Plaza de Asturias, although I had longed for the peace of the vineyard house. It had become my beloved refuge, but the journey was too long for Carlos to make each day. He had had nowhere convenient to return for the long late lunch and the siesta, and during the rainy months of the winter the track up to the house had become dangerously slippery.

As much as the vineyard house itself, I missed the daily inspection of the small venture I had persuaded Carlos and my mother to let me undertake. My dream of seeing the land cleared and orderly rows of vines planted had its small beginning. Antonio had hired some labourers to clear the first few hectares. Then, in October, the land had been ploughed—too late, everyone said—but I could not wait until next August, when the *agosto*—the first deep tilling of a vineyard—should properly be done. As winter ended and I grew heavy with the child, the land was levelled and marked out in what they called the *marco real* system, based on the square, the distance between each plant kept at a strict one and a half metres. It was my neighbour, Don Paulo's partner in the bodega, who advised me in all this.

I had found, to my delight and comfort, that the adjoining land with its immaculate vineyards belonged to Don Luis de Villa Thompson. Carlos showed little interest in my infant project, so I took it on myself to visit Don Luis. His seamed, sensitive face lit up when I told him what I was trying to do.

"It is essential that you do it properly from the beginning. You shall have the advice of my foreman, Mateo. A badly planted vineyard will cause nothing but regret. When it is ready for production in five years' time, you may, if you're lucky, see twenty-five years of excellent vintages from it."

So it was under Don Luis's eyes that the first vines were planted, with about twelve kilos of fertilizer for each hole dug. By the time I had paid for that, I knew I could not pay for the plant stock also. It was then Don Luis offered me my first loan.

"I'm sure Carlos would not permit it," I said.

"Carlos need not know. Carlos is a . . ." He hesitated, just perceptibly. "Carlos is an intelligent young man, but very easy-going; he will not look for problems. If he asks, say I managed to give the plants to you at a very favourable price, since I was buying many for myself."

"And for security? I have nothing to offer you."

"You have the best security—your future harvests."

So I signed a paper for Don Luis which was so obscurely written that I doubt any lawyer would have given it a second glance. But it was enough for Don Luis and me.

"You will have something to give your son, Doña Carlota," he observed one day when we drove out to the vineyard to watch the progress of the planting. "As he grows, so will the vines. By the time he is a young man, the vines will cover all of your hillsides and reach right around to join my land again."

I turned then and looked at his beautifully tended land, the mature vines pruned almost down to the ground, as was the custom here in Jerez. I couldn't say anything, but he seemed to know my thoughts. "Yes, it is a pity I have no son—no child for whom I grow my vines. Well—" he shrugged "—my poor Amelia is not well. I brought specialists from Seville and Madrid. They cannot understand it." He turned to me almost pleadingly. "Would you come and take tea with her today? She would like your company."

From my faint recollection of the languid young woman at the splendid party they had given, I doubted that she wanted the company of someone as socially muddied as I was. And yet, to my surprise, Amelia showed pleasure when she saw me.

"And how does the vineyard go? It is the talk of Jerez, you know. Just imagine, you have been here only a few months, and you are already married, planting a vineyard, and . . ." Primly she tried to avoid gazing at my swollen body. "And you will have a baby also. Truly, you are blessed."

Along with her envy of my pregnancy, there was a gladness—for my sake, I thought—and still a forlorn hope that soon she would share my state. There was more sadness in the face of Don Luis and no hope at all. I remembered what María Luisa had said of him: "He is not *macho*."

I found myself going frequently to visit Amelia at Los Cisnes. It was a strange friendship we formed, with so little in common. She surprised me one day by saying, "I shall be going to Vienna soon with Luis. There is some man called Roentgen who has found a way of taking pictures of one's inside, and perhaps finding out what is wrong." She reached out suddenly and took my hand. "I'm so frightened. Will you pray for me, Carlota?"

I was not religious, and she must have known it. But I nodded. "I will light a candle for you every day."

She smiled, satisfied. "I will not be here when your son is born. You must have this. Something to remember me by."

I gasped. From her dress she unpinned a brooch of diamonds and rubies. It had been the gift of Don Luis, and uniquely belonged to Jerez, since it was a tiny replica of the traditional *venencia*. "You cannot. It is from your husband," I said.

"Luis would let you have anything I wished you to have. He likes us to be friends. He keeps saying he is too old for me, and that *you* need all the friends you can find. Is that true, Carlota? Do you really need me? No one else does."

"Luis does and I do." I took her cold thin hands in mine. "You will come back well, and you will be godmother to my child." Suddenly, here amid the riches of this house, I was aware of the wealth I possessed. I was healthy, and I carried a child.

I showed the little jewelled *venencia* to Carlos that night, but he seemed to take no pleasure in it. "Are you sure it was Amelia who gave it to you? Or was it Luis?"

"Jealous?" I said. "You think any man wants me the way I am?" I indicated the swollen bulk of my figure.

Carlos rose, thrusting back his chair angrily. "Jewels are *all* Don Luis can give a woman. He hasn't got anything else!" Then he left the house, not saying where he was going.

As I was getting near to term we attended the wedding of Don Paulo's son Ignacio. It was not a good day for Carlos. All of fashionable Jerez was there, resplendent in their finest clothes, showing off their best horses and carriages. The bride came from one of the richest families in the sherry trade. She was pretty, splendidly dressed, and displayed the security that only a fat dowry can give.

Carlos had been receiving his salary from the bodega, but not even María Luisa had suggested that he contribute to our household expenses. So Carlos kept his money and spent it as he pleased. He still played polo, but he nagged that he was obliged to play on borrowed ponies, and he was openly envious of the fortune that Ignacio would now control through his bride.

MY SON WAS BORN beautiful and healthy, and so big that no one could have believed he was premature. All of Carlos's good humour and hope had returned. He waltzed the baby around the room in his arms, pausing to kiss me on the forehead. My mother watched proudly. "He is wonderful! Beautiful! Oh, Charlie, he has the eyes of the Blodmores."

"Better for all of us, Lady Pat, if he looked exactly like my father." But Carlos still smiled, happy and satisfied. Then we heard the sound of a carriage in the outer courtyard. I held my son proudly in my arms.

María Luisa entered, two unusual patches of red staining her sallow cheeks. "The . . . the Marquesa de Pontevedra," she stammered, "and the Marqués de Santander."

Carlos was bowing low over the hand of the marquesa. She took little notice of him, as if she already knew all there was to be known about him. She was dressed, as before, in black, and with jewels only on her hands. She swept towards the bed, bending low over my son, carefully examining the tiny, creased features. "He is all right?" she said. "There is no . . . no weakness?" Her tone was sharp, peremptory.

I held the baby closer. "He is perfect. He is as strong as any baby less than a day old can be expected to be." The infant's eyes were already trying to focus on the flashes of light which sprang from the marquesa's hands. His own tiny hand attempted to reach them.

"He is greedy, the little one," the marquesa said. "Already he wants the best." She was suddenly good-humoured, almost gay.

"He shall have it." Carlos was beside me, protective of us both in a way that amazed me. "He is as strong as a lion."

"And he has the eyes of a cat," Don Paulo said. "He has the Blodmore eyes." He looked at me, then at my mother. In this feature we both resembled my grandfather.

"What will he be called?"

"Paulo," Carlos answered promptly.

Through the long day I had listened to Carlos's insistence that this should be the first Christian name of our son. I had been inclined to give way to him, but now my resistance stiffened.

"He shall be called John after my grandfather."

A cry of pleasure broke from my mother. "Oh, Charlie, how wonderful. How proud he would have been!"

"John . . . Juan." The name sounded tenuous on the marquesa's lips. "Juan—that is what I used to call him. Yes—the child's name shall be Juan." It was decided, not because I had decided it but because the marquesa had given her approval.

"I shall be his godmother," she announced.

"I have already asked Amelia," I said coldly.

"Doña Amelia," the marquesa said briskly, as if it were a matter of no consequence, "will not live to fulfil her duties as a godmother. A godmother, you know, has a very special place in a child's life."

At that moment, despite the springtime warmth of the May day on which my son had been born, in spite of the blankets and shawls, I was cold. I felt depleted, as if all my strength had gone to my son. He would need every part of it if he were to fight this woman who had declared herself his godmother—and yet, if he were to fight the world, wasn't she a powerful ally to have with him? I could not refuse him that alliance.

"It shall be," I said. "Doña Amelia will be represented by proxy. You could not refuse her that?"

Through a haze of weariness I heard her voice again. "I, too, am to be a godmother by proxy. We have had news from Ireland. Richard Blodmore's first child has been born. A son . . . an heir for Clonmara."

II Noon: 1910-1920
CHAPTER EIGHT

*J*uan was only a little more than a year old when his first brother was born. We named him Martín. When my next son arrived, born after almost the same frighteningly short period, he was called Francisco. Each time, the marquesa appeared and assumed her self-appointed role as godmother. Each time, there were expensive christening presents, and on their name days elaborate presents, which were of little interest to the children. "She might try, for a change," Carlos remarked, "giving some shares in her Barcelona concerns or her mines. *That* would make more sense."

A little dressmaker was made a permanent fixture in our house, busy making up the lengths of cloth which the marquesa ordered from Seville and Madrid. "I must have my godchildren present-able," she said.

"The seamstress will have to be paid," María Luisa insisted during one of the marquesa's visits—she had a habit of descending on the household unannounced. The marquesa agreed to a small salary for the seamstress and an assistant. A laundress was engaged full-time so that the children's clothes should always be immaculate. María Luisa was jubilant. She even got a small additional stipend for Nanny.

On our tiny budget, we were always in debt against the yearly dividend from the Fernández, Thompson bodega when it was paid into Don Ramón's bank. I think it was only the knowledge that the marquesa had stood godmother to our children that made people willing to lend us money at good interest rates. Jerez was betting on the chances of my children being remembered handsomely in her will, especially the oldest, Juan, who was clearly the favourite. Those with long memories even declared that Juan bore a remarkable resemblance to my grandfather.

Jerez was forgetting the scandal of my hasty marriage to Carlos. The godchildren of the Marquesa de Pontevedra could not be ignored, so I must be accepted along with them. We were invited to many parties, and a few times a year we in our turn gave little parties. María Luisa pared the cost down to the last peseta. "I thank the Lord for the cellar Lord Blodmore laid down."

But my grandfather's cellar was causing problems for my mother. She had access to it whenever she wished, and at siesta time she often went off to her bedroom with the deliberate, upright walk of one who has drunk too much and knows it. She seemed to hark back to the past more often, memories of her one London season—the balls, the triumphs she had had, the attentions of Edward VII, who had been the Prince of Wales.

She was, as María Luisa said, a trial. But she was a loving grandmother to my children, playing with them, helping Nanny bathe and dress them, singing to them, and never with a single word of Spanish.

And yet, for all that her little "habit"—as it was politely termed in Jerez—was known, she was still invited about. She was still beautiful and she sat a horse in a way that wrung admiration from even the most demanding Andalusian horseman. The men ad-mitted, though reluctantly, that in the exercises of the high school

213

of equitation she was very nearly the match of any man among them. As soon as they were able to, my children demanded to be taken to watch Granny work her horses.

During those years Half Moon was bred to Balthasar. Her colt was a lovely graceful creature, who showed Balthasar's strain of stamina and nobility. We called him Rodrigo.

Carlos was always carelessly good-humoured, loving with his children, absent-mindedly affectionate with me—and always, from the first, unfaithful. He meant no personal insult to me by it. It was just the way he was made. My heart was not wrenched by his infidelities, for my capacity to love had been given to Richard Blodmore. So there was almost an unspoken pact between Carlos and myself. The heart of neither one would break for the other.

There was an open conflict, though, over the ownership of Balthasar. Carlos bitterly resented my mother's taking over the stallion to practise equitation and her riding him in exhibitions. So he bought himself a handsome little mare and simply handed me the bill. I saw María Luisa's lips go white as she saw the figure.

Amelia had returned from Vienna no better—and no worse. "They don't know what it is." She shrugged. "They murmur about too many white cells in my blood, and they can do nothing." But her journey away from Jerez had altered her subtly. She dismissed her, role as an invalid. "I will do what I can. I will live every minute there is." Coming to call on the day I had had the bill for the mare from Carlos, she got the story from me and insisted on advancing the money. "Please, Carlota, let it be just between us. I've never had a friend to help before."

I felt tears of shame and relief running down my cheeks. "How did you ever get mixed up with such a terrible family as this? We have brought you and Luis nothing but problems."

"You have brought me a family, Carlota. *That* I cannot buy."

I had, in my own fashion, marked the birth of my sons. Before I became pregnant with Martín I had consulted with Don Luis and had borrowed more money from him, with his encouragement. The next section of fallow land was ploughed at its proper time in August. Don Luis had wanted me to take more money, so that more land could be put into production, but I dared not. Only María Luisa knew the size of my present debt to him. For Carlos we kept up an elaborate pretence that the money was squeezed somehow from María Luisa's budget.

214

Carlos took just enough interest in his work at the bodega to satisfy his father. He was always a good representative for the firm, ready to drink with those who came to buy, ready always to make the enjoyable journey to London to sell. Before visitors Carlos would joke about "my little businesswoman" when the talk came around to my vineyard project.

Along with the births of my children, I marked the seasons and the years by the work done in the vineyards. The tasks and demands they made seemed endless.

I came to the vineyards for the planting, the tilling and weeding, and in August for the vitally important grafting, the *injerto*. It was then that the buds of the native vines were grafted onto the American root stock. Antonio was now almost as fanatical as I about the work of the vineyards, for one day he would be the true foreman of whole hillsides of vines belonging to Doña Carlota. He was as impatient for that day as I.

I did not dare talk about the vineyards in Carlos's presence—better to let him think of them as some harmless hobby. It was Amelia who was my confidante. She approved of Luis's financing a large part of the project.

The third year, in August, she insisted on watching the grafting. We were driven up to the house in the cool morning hours, and Concepción gave us breakfast. Amelia walked through the bare rooms, surveyed the courtyard bright with bougainvillaea and geraniums, and drank Antonio's own rather crude wine. She smiled. "I should come more often. It is quiet—and yet everything is growing and full of life. It gives you something, doesn't it, Carlota? Something besides Carlos and your family."

"I name each section for my children," I said. "Next year's planting will be named for you, Amelia."

"Luis also loves the vines. He puts them in place of what he cannot have. I wish before I die I could give him a child."

"You will not die, Amelia. Not for a long time. And as for a child, you are still very young. There is plenty of time."

"There isn't plenty of time. This thing in my blood cannot be resisted forever. Still, as weak as I am, I might bear a child if only Luis could give me one." She walked to the table and drank swiftly of the raw wine. "Since we have married, Carlota, there has been no possibility of a child." Her hand trembled so that the wine spilled. "Carlota—I am still a virgin!"

The intensity of her despair was in her voice. Pepita, who loved Amelia, lumbered across the room to her. I watched, heartbroken for her, as she sank down on her knees and put her face on the shoulder of the big dog and wept.

WE PAID LITTLE ATTENTION to the first talk of the possibility of a world war. Those who travelled to London for the sherry business brought back tales of the new German army. There was some nostalgia for King Edward, who had been able to keep his German nephew, the Kaiser, from being too insufferable. We listened, and tended our vines in our untroubled corner of the world. And so it came to the peaceful autumn of 1913, the last year before war turned Europe upside down. We were invited to visit the marquesa at Sanlúcar and to join the party that would cross the Guadalquivir River each day for the culling of the deer herds in the Doñana preserve.

Carlos was anxious to go. He saw it as a mark of favour. My mother was excited, as always, by the prospect of a party. She got out all her dresses, and cleaned the guns that Richard Blodmore had given her. Despite her drinking, she still possessed an uncannily true aim.

I thought there was more than a touch of malice in the marquesa's invitation. It wasn't possible that she knew of my feeling for Richard Blodmore. However, she must have known that Carlos had once thought of marrying Elena. So she had blended her wine with bitter grapes when she informed us that the gathering at Sanlúcar would mark the visit of Elena and Richard and their two young sons.

For once I was not pregnant. Francisco had been born two years before, and I had been mercifully free since then. I looked at my face in the mirror and wondered how I would appear to Richard Blodmore. And would he look as settled into domesticity as I did? Would it all seem a useless, foolish dream—the image of a man and a girl on a shore and in a rose garden? I told myself I must expect no more. But still I agreed when María Luisa stated that I must have some new dresses. "Nothing but babies for three years . . . you need something to brighten you up." She deferred paying some bills for a while so that my mother and I would not be a disgrace to our house.

I both longed for, and dreaded, the first breath of coolness in

216

the air after the heat of the summer. October would bring the tremendous migration of birds from northern Europe to winter in Doñana's marshes. I would see, Don Luis told me, if I were lucky, the beautiful Spanish lynx, the imperial eagle, the wild boar, the herds of red and fallow deer. There were vipers, too, he said. These were the beauties and dangers of Doñana.

Only my mother knew the other danger to me. While I helped her pack she touched my hand. "It won't matter seeing him again, will it, Charlie? I mean, it's all over now, isn't it?"

"Yes. It's all over."

So IT WAS among many other people that I saw Richard Blodmore again. We were gathered in the grand salon of the marquesa's palacio at Sanlúcar. There was talk, noise, laughter, the sound of glasses clinking, the sound of a guitar in an alcove. I looked across the room and saw Richard Blodmore, and everything else faded out of focus.

He saw me at the same time, as if he had been compelled to turn in my direction. He moved towards me. "Charlie!" And I knew I had been wrong. It was not all over.

"How . . . how is it at Clonmara?" I managed to say.

"Clonmara misses you. The roses flourish, but they seem to have no scent. *I* miss you, Charlie."

Wildly dangerous words to say in the midst of this gathering, but they told me that for him it was not all over, either.

DOÑANA is a wilderness on the edge of the Atlantic; it is desert and forest; it is marsh and dune and sea. Romance was woven into its being, and none of us was immune to its spell. Even the sadness which seemed to overhang the marshes was part of the legend of the woman, Doña Ana, wife of the seventh Duque de Medina Sidonia, who had given her name to this silent wilderness. She was said to have spent her whole life in prayer for the soul of her scandalous mother, the Princess of Eboli. It is the place next to Clonmara and my vineyards that I love best; it is the place where I knew finally that I could truly love no other man than Richard Blodmore.

We spent ten days there, crossing the river from the marquesa's palacio each morning to hunt. The autumn rains had filled the marshes, and the landscape now had a dreamlike quality. Sometimes the sky seemed stained pink with the colour of flamingos in flight. There was the tranquil beauty of navigating the marshes in a *cajón*—a flat-bottomed skiff—drawn by a muscular marsh horse who traversed the shallow water with ease.

And for those few precious days there was the sight of Richard Blodmore. We had little time in each other's company; and yet, whether the men shot birds in the marshes, or deer and boar in the dry sandy areas among the pines and the cork oaks, we seemed never for an instant to be able to forget each other's presence. Most days we lunched at the Palacio de Doñana, where protocol was imposed by the presence of King Alfonso, whose custom it was to join the hunting party for a few days. Wherever I was in the gathering, I would find Richard at my elbow, a glass of wine in his hand for me, a murmured greeting. At times the tension grew almost unbearable.

Once, when the party stopped for the English afternoon tea the marquesa provided, we walked alone in the area of the sand dunes. From the Guadalquivir, Columbus had set out on his third voyage to the New World; I shivered a little at the thought.

"You're cold," Richard said.

"Yes," I agreed. "I seem always to be cold when you're near me. Part of me aches so much, like an old wound when the damp crawls in. Why does it have to hurt so?"

"When it ceases to hurt, you don't feel anything."

"I'll be numb then—or dead. Oh, Richard, I can't imagine life just going on this way. I love my children; I'm fond of Carlos. But he isn't essential to me. You are . . . and you can never be part of my life."

He put his arm about me and turned me to face him. The waves crashed against the shore with a hollow boom. But this was not the feeling we had had on the shore at Clonmara. What might have been a quick, swiftly fading infatuation had matured. "I will always be part of your life, Charlie." He held back my hair which the wind whipped into my eyes. "I have no rights to you—except that I love you. And to think I didn't believe it was possible to fall in love. I will go away, and you will stay. We'll each bring up our families, and we'll always think that our children might have been ours together. I think of you every day. And I've grown almost to hate the scent of roses."

We turned and walked back towards the steep height of the

218

dunes. A woman was standing there, the wind holding her skirt close to her body. Even from a distance we knew it was Elena.

"She knows," I said. "She knows we love each other."

"Yes. She's known since the first day at Clonmara. For me, there are ghosts of you in every corner of the house, and she knows it. She is a good wife, a good mother, a good housekeeper. She is also beautiful, but she knows that for me she hardly exists. Many women could fill her function. But none can fill yours. It doesn't seem fair, does it, Charlie? But I can do nothing about it."

The woman on the dune gestured to summon us. Then she turned and disappeared down the steep slope towards the pines.

THE DAYS AT SANLÚCAR seemed endless. At night Carlos snored contentedly beside me, filled with the marquesa's superb food and wine. He was good-humoured, pleased to be among that company, and not once did any flashes of ill temper mar his charm. He was gentle with me and even paid me compliments. "A real beauty you've become, Carlota. Having children suits you. Your mother will have a rival soon."

I was aware of the extraordinary effort my mother made during those days. She counted her copitas as carefully as María Luisa counted our money. She still drew a small crowd of admiring men about her, but she was quieter than I had ever known her. Perhaps my mother, like all the party, felt the dominating presence of the marquesa.

The marquesa hunted and rode like a man; her slender, athletic body seemed that of a woman much younger. She commanded and was obeyed, and even the strength of Don Paulo's personality seemed to pale in her presence. I found myself avoiding her gaze whenever I was in the company of Richard, lest she, of all people, should guess the tumult of my soul. I wondered if the marquesa had brought us here particularly to see Lord Blodmore and his wife and their healthy sons, so that we would know all the more surely how completely lost Clonmara was to us. Richard Blodmore's elder son, Edward, would inherit the title of Pontevedra as well as the earldom of Blodmore. He would have the inheritance which would have gone to any son born to the marquesa and my grandfather. After thirty years the marquesa appeared to have settled the score.

Don Luis and Amelia were among the guests. Amelia was not

strong enough to hunt with us during the day, but she was present at all the evening entertainments. On the last night at Sanlúcar we sat alone for a few minutes before the others came down to dinner. She said in a quiet, calm voice, "You did not tell me, Carlota, that Lord Blodmore was in love with you."

I turned away from the fire and looked at her directly. "Does it show? Has anyone else noticed?"

She shook her head. "Sick people often see things healthy people are too busy to notice. And you love him also. What will you do?"

"Nothing. He will go back to Ireland. I will stay here."

She nodded. "I thought it would be that way. You are not wild, like your mother, Carlota. But be careful of the marquesa. She has sharp eyes."

I WENT BACK to my vines and to my children. In them I found some relief from the aching sense of loss that Richard's presence had renewed.

It was not the same with Carlos after that. I grew impatient with him because he was not Richard, and he, realizing that I was no longer the pliant girl who had been grateful for the fact of marriage, grew sullen for the first time. Then he withdrew from me with savage abruptness. I could not blame him. He sensed the emptiness within me and reacted as most men would, with anger and frustration. And I no longer had the simplicity or the guile to charm him back. I let him go.

THE MONTHS WENT BY, marked for me by the traditional tasks of the vineyard, and by August I could hardly sleep at night for worrying that rain would come and ruin the crop. I bored everyone with talk of the harvest.

"For pity's sake, Carlota, stop it!" Carlos said. "I hear that at the bodega all day. Do you think I want to hear the same thing at home? For centuries we have done this work. We've had good vintages and bad vintages. We have thousands of acres in cultivation from here to Sanlúcar—you have a toy vineyard!" He slammed his glass down and left the house.

It was very late and he was very drunk when he returned that night. As he stumbled to the bed he fell across Pepita, who, as always, lay at its foot. There was a stream of curses in Spanish. Then, perhaps because he had drunkenly aimed a blow at her, a

220

low, warning growl followed. The sound frightened me. "Pepita, quiet!" I called.

"He thought he married a lapdog and now he finds a terrier," María Luisa observed the next morning. "Be careful, querida."

While I worried about my vines and thought only about how I could find enough workers for the harvest I expected in September, the events of the world passed me by. I only dimly heard the reports of the assassination of the Archduke Ferdinand, heir to the Austro-Hungarian empire. At the end of July, Austria-Hungary declared war on tiny Serbia, a country I didn't know existed, and then in August, Germany declared war on Russia and France. On 4th August, when I returned from an inspection of the vineyards with Don Luis, he said as he handed me down from the carriage, "Be prepared for bad news."

I didn't understand him. I ran inside. My mother and María Luisa were in the drawing room, looking at a newspaper. My mother raised her brandy glass to me. "England, my darling, is about to declare war on Germany—so that means Ireland, too."

"What will happen?"

"For us, Charlie, probably very little. But all the men we knew, all the boys you hunted with, will probably go off to war."

I poured myself a brandy from the decanter and took a long gulp before I asked, "Do you think Richard . . . do you think Richard Blodmore will go?"

"Very likely. It would be expected of him."

Now María Luisa broke in. "But your husband, Lady Pat, is already a soldier, isn't he?"

I swung around to look at my mother. "My father?"

"Yes, darling—your father. Funny—I hadn't thought of him. He's with the Eighty-seventh Regiment, King's Own Artillery." She sipped her brandy and said little the rest of the evening.

Next day we learned that England had declared war. However, we were safe and quiet in our little corner of Europe. Spain had no obligation to anyone, and so long as ships could ply from Cádiz, we could sell our sherry.

"In any case," Carlos said, "it will be over by Christmas."

THE HARVEST BEGAN early in September. It is agonizing for the vineyard owner to decide when to cut the grapes. If he starts too early, there will be less sugar and therefore less alcohol; if he

221

waits, he risks damage from rain. I waited until Don Luis began his own harvesting.

The grapes were cut and placed in baskets of woven olive branches. Each basket held about twenty-five pounds of grapes, and sixty basketfuls were needed to make one butt of must. The grapes were carried to the vineyard house and laid out on grass mats to dry. They stayed there from twelve to twenty-four hours, covered at night with other grass mats for protection from the dew. Then they were carried to the *lagar* to be pressed.

Four men—the *pisadores*—were required to tread the grapes. They began their work about midnight, and continued on until midday the next day, so as to rest through the hottest hours of the afternoon. They worked steadily, solemnly, working one side of the *lagar* at a time.

The second pressing was obtained by piling the pulp of the grapes into a cylinder around a seven-foot screw fixed permanently in the centre of the *lagar*. The *pisadores* worked with their wooden shovels piling it up. Almost everything that touched the grapes was wood, lest the taint of metal contaminate the must. When the great screw was turned, the juice of the second pressing squeezed through an opening into the tub.

The must from the treading—the first pressing—went into butts. This would go to the bodega and eventually become wine. The must from the second pressing would produce lower-strength wines, which would eventually be distilled.

WE WERE PRESSING our last few basketfuls of grapes. I had seen little of Don Luis during this time, but his faithful foreman, Mateo, had been overseeing the operation for me, hurrying between his vineyard and mine. We were nearing the end of the pressing when Carlos arrived. He looked weary. During the harvest the men of the bodegas worked long hours. Every cartload of must had to be examined, the price decided, and the butts stored.

Carlos found me in the courtyard of the house, watching as the must ran from the *lagar*. He had slipped off his horse and was beside me before I knew it.

"So, Carlota. And how has the vintage gone?"

I was deceived. I took it as a natural greeting.

"Well enough. We have all worked hard—"

I stopped. His face had contorted in anger. "For four nights you haven't been at home! You look like a scarecrow. You are a disgrace . . . a disgrace to any man!''

I looked down at my dress, stained from the pulp of the grapes. I put my hand self-consciously to my hair; it was rough and straggled over my eyes.

Carlos continued. "Do you suppose I enjoy the laughter at the bodega when another of your carts comes in with the must? The laughter about the madwoman who leaves her children and labours like a man over her few little grapes—who leaves her husband to look after his own needs."

Perhaps it was the sun, the work, the worry. I said what I had never wanted to say to him. "You haven't missed a *woman* during these days. You have plenty of women. It's only a wife who isn't at home—and that hurts your pride. Well, let it hurt—''

We had spoken in English, so the words were not understood by Mateo and the labourers, but they were all motionless and staring when Carlos lashed out and struck me across the face. I found myself sprawled on the hot flagstones, the breath knocked out of me. Then I sat up and put my hand to my lip; it came away smeared with blood, and I could taste blood on my tongue. I spat out the blood with all the gusto of a peasant woman. Through lips that were already swelling I said, "Go back to your women, Carlos. Your scarecrow of a wife will return when her work is done.''

Carlos remounted, jerked angrily at the horse's mouth, and as he clattered through the archway he nearly ran down Don Luis, who stood within its shadow.

"Back to work!" Don Luis shouted to the gaping men as he came forward and helped me into the house. Concepción brought brandy and glasses, and Don Luis poured for us both. My hand trembled as I accepted a glass from him.

"If I were half a man," he said, "I would have pulled him from his horse. I am dishonoured, as well as you.''

I stretched my dusty hand across the table to take his. "There can be no dishonour where none is admitted, Don Luis. I admit no such thing. You are the finest man I know.''

For a moment he covered his face with his hand.

I STAYED with Don Luis and Amelia until the swelling and bruising had gone. I knew that all Jerez must be talking of the quarrel, and possibly enjoying it. Amelia's maid massaged oil into my hair to counteract the dryness and dust of the vineyards, washed it and brushed it until it shone. I had scented oil in my baths and scented cream on my hands.

Amelia produced two lengths of lawn, and her seamstress made them up for me. Amelia was very thin and pale and languid in those hot September days; she lay on her chaise most of the day and made only a small effort to walk in the garden at dusk with me and Pepita. There seemed to be a special communication between her and the dog. As they walked, Pepita kept thrusting her nose under Amelia's hand, then running around to her other side as if to give her support.

WHEN I RECEIVED MY PAYMENT for the must from the bodega, it seemed a pitifully small reward for that enormous effort, and all of it was owed to Luis. I studied my accounts anxiously, putting aside sums for an extra gift to Mateo and Antonio, putting aside what would be needed for the planting of a new slope.

"Perhaps," I said to Luis, "I should stop. Wait until the rest of the vines have come into production before I plant further. I have almost no money left to repay you." But I knew if I stopped I would have wasted the money I had spent in August on the deep tilling of new slopes.

"If you are so cautious, you will never make your fortune, Carlota. And as for collateral—your vineyards are the best I can have."

So I signed yet another note and returned to the Plaza de Asturias. My children came to greet me as if I had been gone only for the day. But María Luisa looked at me with her little sharp sideways glance. "You look well, querida."

"I have rested," I said.

"And Carlos has waited," she answered. "He has waited with a patience I did not expect of him."

Carlos returned from the bodega that evening, and he smiled at me as if there were nothing to forgive on either side. "Your visit to Amelia has done you good."

I was wearing one of my new dresses. My hands were smooth, my hair was shining. "There is a little supper party at the Garveys' tonight," he added. "We will go, perhaps."

He had decided to laugh away any tales about the scene at the vineyard house. A wife had been unruly, and he had handled it in the only way a real man could. It was all over.

224

CHAPTER NINE

We planted the new slopes in January. The weather had been dry, and Amelia was able to drive out to watch the work. She sat for an hour in the warmth of the winter sun against the south wall of the vineyard house. Her eyes were not on the working men but on the vineyard which I had named for her. Now it was nothing more than straight rows of dark, leafless roots.

Suddenly she said, "Be very kind to Luis, Charlie. He will be lonely. You, the children, the new vineyards—they give him interest. He is fond of young Juan, I know. You must take Juan to the bodega to visit him."

"He will not be lonely, Amelia. . . ." Then the words faded; it was hypocritical to protest that she would be there to keep him from being lonely. She stared at the black stumps of the vines, and we both knew that she would never see the green shoots of spring.

TWO DAYS LATER, at six in the morning, Luis sent a message that she was dead. I went to Los Cisnes and found her, with lighted candles about the bed, looking so peaceful, so beautiful, that all the ravages of her illness were wiped away. Luis sat quietly watching her. "See how lovely she looks," he said.

I dropped to my knees beside her and touched her smooth, cold hands. Then I placed my hand on Luis's. "Shall we pray for her?"

He smiled a little and shook his head. "The praying is over, as her life is over, Carlota. No, do not weep. You have always been strong. She lived longer because she drew strength from you. You give your strength to many people. Give me a little of it now."

He rose and led me from the room. In the dining room he ordered the servants to open the shutters to the morning sunlight, and he ordered coffee to be brought. I wondered what would be said in the town about us sitting here while his wife lay dead in a room upstairs. But it was what Amelia had foreseen, had wanted. In his loneliness he needed the small comfort of my presence.

AMELIA had left me what seemed a large sum of money, part of her own inheritance, and she also left me the pieces of jewellery which Luis had given her and which did not belong by descent in his family. I was stunned.

María Luisa shook her head. "They will say you were her friend for what you could get from her. I know it was not so, querida, but that is what they will say."

There was also a very old oak chest which Luis said Amelia had wanted me to have, with its contents. We went through it together, a painful and sad task. It contained an odd assortment of things—a collection of lovely fans, a few elaborately bound books of Spanish poetry, a tiny, beautifully wrought pistol with its own silver bullets, and some porcelain models of the white horses of Vienna—the Lippizaners. "All little pieces of Amelia's life, Carlota." He closed the lid; he could not continue.

I had the chest taken to the vineyard house. I knew that was where Amelia had meant her little personal treasures to be. I was aware that I had never had a friend of my own age before Amelia, and there could be none to take her place.

I wondered if I had ever properly told her what she meant to me. I had named a part of a vineyard for her, the only gift I had to give.

THE QUARREL WITH CARLOS started when he learned of the money Amelia had left me. He seemed to assume that I would give him some of it for his own use. "I must save something for the children," I protested.

He shrugged. "The children don't need it *now*. I have a few gambling debts—and that tiresome tailor in London has been dunning me for money."

"There are *my* debts," I said. "What I owe to Don Luis. For the stock, labour—oh, a number of things."

He looked at me darkly. "And how much do you owe Don Luis?"

I didn't dare reveal to him the extent of my debt. So I named half the sum.

"Well, pay him back! No man should be allowed to say that my wife is in debt to him! It is a humiliation for me!"

He left, and I did not see him for two days. Then he returned full of good humour, riding a wonderful mare, almost black in colour. "She is beautiful, is she not, Carlota?" he called to me. "Her name is Carmen. I got her from Domecq."

I gasped. This was the talked-of Carmen, the fabled mare that everyone said Don Jaime would never part with. The animal could not have changed hands for a small price.

"Now I give you back Balthasar—formally. Carmen is your real wedding present to me. And I have acquired four polo ponies. I

226

knew you would agree that I shouldn't have to beg a mount from other men."

He had taken most of Amelia's legacy. Whatever feelings Carlos might have had about my owing money to Luis had been swept away in a fit of self-indulgence. Or perhaps he wanted to force me to give up the vineyard—my little base of independence—to settle my debts. My feeling of rage was so great that I trembled. I had to go inside, away from the sight of him and the mare. Never, I thought, would I let Carlos take the vineyard from me.

THE SAME WEEK, by letter from Ireland, came the news that Richard Blodmore had joined the British army at the outbreak of war, had been commissioned, and was already stationed in France. The news came from one of our neighbours at Clonmara. "Spiteful old goose," my mother said of Lady Sybil Wareham. "She thinks we're all too safe here in Spain. Wants to shake us up a bit. Write back to her, Charlie. Find out what other news there is."

So I took to writing to Lady Sybil. It was the beginning of a long and terrible sequence of letters telling us the course of the war and the particular devastation it caused among those we knew. Never once did I directly inquire about Richard Blodmore, but I always hoped there would be some spin-off of gossip which would carry his name. In those days I grieved for Amelia, and I prayed for Richard.

ANDY HAD STAYED on with us, and that summer he married Manuela, a niece of Serafina's. I had been a little taken aback when he announced his intention, and then I stifled my exclamation of surprise and made it one of pleasure. "I'm so glad, Andy. I'm so glad you won't be . . . be alone any more."

He shrugged and smiled shyly. "Might as well make up my mind to it, Miss Charlie. There's no going back any more, is there? I mean—we'll never go home again, will we?"

I shook my head. "I doubt it, Andy." And my heart was breaking. This seemed the final severance of the link with Clonmara, the admission that none of us would ever go back.

THE DEAD HEAT of the summer months came upon us, the somnolence of the long hot afternoons. This was my second year of harvesting the vineyards; more workers were needed, more money to pay them. Luis gently offered loans and suggestions as to what needed doing in the vineyard. I hoped that after the harvest I might be able to repay him in part.

Luis often came to the vineyard house, and he would sit and talk with me very quietly. I saw him at ease in those plain white rooms and I thought of him alone in the splendour of his own house empty without Amelia. María Luisa shook her head over his visits. "People talk."

"Then let them! I promised Amelia."

"Promises like that are easy to give and a problem to keep."

As we moved towards the autumn of 1915 I continued to write to Lady Sybil and to wait with dread for the answers. Some of the men we knew were dead, many were wounded. She wrote, "We'll hardly have any hunting this winter. People have given up their horses, except just what's essential." She wrote nothing of the rumble of discontent under the patriotic surface. The Irish continued to join the British army in all ranks and no one thought it strange. The war had indefinitely postponed Home Rule. My mother read over the letters many times, speaking the names aloud, remembering. "Oh, Johnny was a beautiful dancer. I can remember . . ."

Then one day as she read I heard her give a little choking cry. "Charlie, it's Thomas's regiment! It's been stationed somewhere near Rheims."

"Thomas who?"

She looked across at me. "My darling, I'm talking about your father. Do you suppose he's still riding horses, or have they switched to lorries?"

My father meant nothing to me. He was far less real than any of the other names mentioned in Lady Sybil's letters. I spoke of this, however, to Luis the next time we met at the vineyard.

"Poor Carlota—you've not had much love from men, have you?"

"My grandfather—"

He shook his head. "Too distant, and gone too soon."

"But Carlos . . ." I protested. And then I also shook my head. "We don't have to pretend about Carlos, do we, Luis? Carlos doesn't love me, except in bed. Perhaps he's not capable of loving a woman any other way." Then I flushed, because I was too close to Luis's most sensitive point, the feeble virility on which so many doubts and aspersions had been cast in the society of Jerez. To cover

228

any unintentional hurt, I told him then of the man I truly did love.

"So I *do* have a love, Luis. And I have your friendship. I have my children, and I have my vineyards. I am richer than anyone knows, except you."

He nodded. His seamed face was serious as he studied the wine in his glass, holding it forward slightly so that the sun caught its rich colour. "I would have wished more for you, Carlota. A woman like you should not have to love at a distance."

"Life is what it is." I shrugged and poured more wine for him. I had told him about Richard, and it was sweet relief to have done so. But I could not tell him that the marquesa had brought Richard back to Jerez expressly to marry Elena. And I could not tell even Luis about the woman who lived with her wax dolls in the castle of Arcos.

THE HARVEST WAS OVER, a good vintage for me. I paid Luis the interest on the loan, and when I tried to pay back some of the principal, he gently reminded me that not all my land was yet under cultivation. I protested, but I agreed. I had fallen into the error of thinking of it as my land, and I loved it. And I made the mistake of letting Carlos see that I loved it. He simply presented me once again with fresh gambling debts and the stabling bills for his polo ponies. It was the price I must pay for peace between us. I looked at the sum, choked back my rage, and paid.

With the cool weather my mother began once again to exercise Balthasar. Half Moon was in foal, and Luis insisted that she be given the freedom of the *campos*—the fields—at his hacienda. Andy was slightly put out by this arrangement and rode out each day to see how she did. "When her time is near I will be there," he vowed. Perhaps he was so vehement about it because his own Manuela was pregnant. He was immensely proud and happy at the thought of a child. "Boy or girl, Miss Charlie, it'll be called Charlie."

THE INTERFERENCE of the marquesa continued in our lives, insistent, pervasive, and impossible to reject. She now quite often appeared at Don Paulo's house, Las Fuentes. She came to be near our children. Sanlúcar was too far for casual visits. With infuriating high-handedness she would send around her carriage with orders that the children were to join her for the *comida*—for dinner. I was never invited.

For the marquesa, there were no rules of manners or tact. The first news I had of a tutor for Juan came through Carlos. Don Paulo told him at the bodega that the marquesa had secured the services of one of the young Fletcher cousins—the Fletchers were a long-established sherry family in Jerez—who had been invalided out of the army after being gassed. He had, Carlos reported, a double first from Cambridge in history and economics.

I went to see the marquesa. "I haven't even met this man," I protested. "He may be totally unsuitable."

She laughed at me. "I think, Doña Carlota, that I am a better judge of that than you. You are young, inexperienced. Your children are good children, intelligent, but they lack polish. This young man speaks no Spanish, so Juan must learn everything in English, and his accent will be corrected. Now he speaks with an Irish accent. I have arranged for Edwin Fletcher to tutor Juan for four hours each morning, and if it does not inconvenience you, he will lunch with you. It will do young Martín and Francisco good to hear his conversation."

"The children normally eat lunch with Nanny."

"Then it is no wonder their manners require correction. I suggest you make the arrangement that all should eat together. Your kitchen can surely stretch to that."

As I climbed into the landau I held my head high for Andy's sake, but I acknowledged defeat. I was as hungry for the good of my children as I was for the good of my land and vines.

SO THE YOUNG MAN called Edwin Fletcher entered our household. I was prepared to dislike him and was terribly conscious of the deficiencies in my own education. He was thin and tall, with a pronounced stoop and a drooping moustache. Sometimes he went into terrible spasms of coughing and seemed to struggle for air. At such times he was embarrassed and profoundly apologetic. Carlos dismissed him with a shrug. "An academic milksop!"

"One, however, who has served his country," my mother said.

Edwin Fletcher was grateful to be in Spain instead of languishing in England. He tried to cope with Juan's short span of concentration and his insistence on breaking into Spanish. Gradually the two drew together, Juan's efforts to interest Edwin Fletcher in horsemanship equalling Edwin's efforts to interest Juan in English grammar. They seemed to come out roughly even. But one thing above all others made me see Edwin Fletcher as a friend—his open and unaffected admiration for my mother. "What a perfectly splendid lady!" he said of her once. "So beautiful. Such great spirit. And I hear all round Jerez that no one is her equal on a horse."

IT WAS EDWIN FLETCHER, with myself and Juan, who witnessed what happened that sharp, frosty morning in December 1915 when my mother's life was almost ended.

Edwin had looked exhausted when he arrived for Juan's lessons that day, so I suggested that we take a walk to the stables to watch my mother working with Balthasar. The morning sun would warm him, I thought. Juan was delighted at the prospect of a half hour's freedom from lessons. He adored his grandmother, and he was proud of her accomplishments as a horsewoman.

As we walked through the first courtyard we talked of the war. I had become reliant on Edwin to interpret the news which reached us. "It's a stalemate," he said. "The whole British-French offensive has failed, and the British have used gas for the first time." He paused by the old cracked fountain, holding his face up to the sun. "I can hardly believe it's December. Thank God I'm not in England. I don't think I could cope with the fogs."

I tugged at his arm and pointed to the archway leading to the stableyard. Juan, who had been jumping about in the crisp morning air, had stopped, and seemed frozen. Then he turned, his voice thin and shrill with fear. "Mama! Mama!"

I ran, leaving Edwin behind. I could hear my mother's voice calling, pleading; I could hear Balthasar's deep whinny. And I could hear Carlos shouting angry commands—his voice held a note of fear I had never heard before.

It was never possible to find out exactly what had taken place before our arrival. I am certain only of what I saw. Carlos was in Balthasar's saddle, but the stirrups had been looped up for the equestrian exercises my mother performed. I didn't know whether she had permitted him to mount, or whether he had demanded it, but it was certain that Balthasar was determined to be rid of him.

The great stallion was rearing on his mighty hind legs, lunging, pounding down with the terrifying forefeet. With no stirrups, Carlos had only the grip of his knees and thighs, and he was using his whip in a way that was intended not to control but to punish. Balthasar's white flanks were streaming with blood where Carlos's spurs had sunk. It couldn't last. The horse was stronger than Carlos, and he was in a sweat of fury. One great last lunge and Carlos came off, over the stallion's head, landing with a heavy thud. Those mighty, slashing forefeet came down again. I heard the awful impact as one foot struck Carlos's arm. Then the stallion reared again, and Carlos lay directly beneath him. The cries from my mother, the whinnies of rage from Balthasar, had brought the stableboys, Pepe and José, but they, like us all, seemed frozen.

As the stallion reared again, my mother did the only thing she could do. She leaped for the bridle and managed to loop both her hands through it. Her weight jerking Balthasar's head around was just sufficient to deflect the aim of the stallion's forefeet. He barely missed coming down on Carlos's chest.

My mother had given Carlos just enough time to recover; he rolled over, got staggeringly onto his feet, and backed away, seeking the safety of the wall. Still Balthasar followed. By now I was beside my mother, had grasped the reins as her strength gave way. The last toss of the stallion's head threw her in a heap against the wall where Carlos cowered.

José and Pepe had taken courage at last, and tugged on the other side of the halter. Edwin was there, his fragile strength added to the others to try to hold the horse. Gradually exhaustion took us all, even Balthasar. One of the boys moved to open the door of Balthasar's box, and with great caution and gentleness we led him to it. With the half door finally secured, I ran to my mother. Juan knelt beside her, and now he wept with terror. Edwin was bent over her; he could say nothing. His body was racked with spasms of coughing. Carlos was holding his arm and he was deathly pale. Slowly he came to join the group about my mother.

The side of her head had struck the wall, and blood ran from it as she lay there unconscious. I knelt down and loosened her stock. Juan's wild shrieks had turned to sobbing pleas. "Granny—oh, Granny! Mama, is she dead? Why won't she answer?" He put out a hand, as if to try to shake her into life.

"Juan, no! Don't touch her! Granny's not dead!" But I was feeling for a pulse. The blood had already stained her blouse and jacket. I looked up for help. "Pepe—bring towels, anything to wrap around her head. And blankets." I said to José, "Run for Dr. Ramírez at once. If he's not at his house, see if you can find Dr. Gordon."

At last, as we waited, I looked up at Carlos. Obviously his arm

was broken, and he bit his lips against the pain. He stared at my mother, then into my own face. I saw pain and shock; as his eyes moved from my face to my mother's, I thought I read not concern but hatred. Then he spoke. "The animal shall be destroyed."

I got to my feet. I walked away from the little group and drew Carlos with me. "If you do that," I said, "I shall take the gun you use on Balthasar and I will kill you. I swear it!"

MY MOTHER REMAINED unconscious for a long time. Dr. Ramírez cleaned and stitched the wound. Much of the famous red hair had to be cut away. Dr. Gordon arrived, and Dr. Ramírez welcomed a consultation with the older man, who had a special interest in neurology. "Quiet, rest, and patience," was what he told me. "It's a bad blow, and one never quite knows how severe the injury may be. There may be a hairline fracture."

We had three nurses, but either María Luisa or I was with my mother all the time. She slept a great deal, but when she was awake her speech was rambling and unclear. Then there would be brief flashes of lucidity, when she demanded to know about Balthasar. "Tell Andy to exercise him every day, won't you, Charlie?"

Dr. Ramírez had set Carlos's arm, and it was mending well.

When he pronounced my mother out of danger, I received a visit from Don Paulo. "Is it true," he said directly, "that she saved my son's life? There are all kinds of stories, and I can get nothing from Carlos except that the animal threw him."

"It is true that Balthasar threw Carlos. It is also true that if my mother had not hung onto the bridle, Balthasar was ready to trample Carlos and could have killed him. Carlos does not say why he mounted Balthasar, and my mother cannot say."

"She will, however, be quite well in time? I mean—there is no permanent damage?"

"Ask the doctors, Don Paulo. Wait and see, they tell me."

Against all the traditions of Spanish courtesy, I terminated the visit. There was just the faintest trace of humility in his formal raising of my hand towards his lips. "You will indicate to your mother my profound gratitude. I could not easily have borne the death of my son." He bowed and left. Don Paulo still walked with all the outward pride and arrogance of before, but it occurred to me that for the first time in many years he was a man with a debt, and the debt was owed to a Blodmore.

SHE RECOVERED; that is, she grew strong again and was able to move about just as before. But she was not the same. The hair they had had to cut away grew back, but in a great swathe of startling white. Every one of the characteristics she had displayed before was still there, but in an exaggerated degree. When she talked, she talked far too much. And in between, the spells of silence grew longer. Her span of concentration was short.

Her drinking also increased, and yet we did not know how, out of compassion, to stop it. Sometimes she complained of bad headaches and lay in her darkened room for several days. Dr. Ramírez called to see her from time to time, as did Dr. Gordon.

"There has been some permanent damage, but not to the nerves which control the movements," Dr. Gordon said. "I don't like these fits of absent-mindedness, though. Nor the headaches."

Carlos observed her sullenly one night as she sat in the drawing room, a decanter of wine by her side, staring into the fire. It was one of the few nights he had spent with the family since the accident. He did not even like to sit at the table with my mother.

"Look at her!" he said. "She's crazy. Sits there like a drunken old fool, spilling her wine, and doesn't hear a word that's said to her. She should be put away. She should be in Nuestra Señora de Mercedes."

I rose and went over to him, speaking very softly so that she would not hear. "Be quiet! No one in this house will ever say such a thing again." I straightened, looking down on him, which he didn't like. "You were the cause—"

He cut me short, his voice rising angrily. "Enough! It happened because your mother is a stupid, interfering old woman. After all, Balthasar *is* my horse. Don't tell me he doesn't know who is his master."

"Try riding him again, Carlos. You will find out who is master. If I do not kill you for your vile insults to my mother, Balthasar will surely do it for me."

He cursed me in Spanish and left the room. I moved to the fire and stood staring at it. Any pretence of affection was over between Carlos and me. Since my mother's accident I had been sleeping in her room on a cot bed, and on nights when María Luisa took over I slept in an adjoining room. We spoke only in the presence of the children and when it was strictly necessary.

I turned and looked at my mother. Silent tears streamed down

235

the beautiful face that now looked so much older. I went and knelt beside her. "Mother . . . Mother . . ."

"He said I would have to go to that . . . that place." I knew what she meant. We had once visited Nuestra Señora de Mercedes together, with our small annual donation. I could remember the frightened silence which had descended on my mother when the mother superior had insisted on showing us about the institution. When we were back in the landau I had seen that my mother was trembling violently. "That place . . . that terrible place," she had murmured.

Now she repeated the words. "He wants to shut me up in that terrible place." She grasped my arm with astonishing strength. "Promise me, Charlie—*promise* me that you'll never let me be sent to that place. Promise me. Swear it, Charlie! Do you swear it?"

I brushed the tears from her anguished face. "I swear it, Mother. Never—*never*." I remained kneeling beside her, rocking her like one of my children.

THAT NIGHT, after I had seen my mother to bed and María Luisa had arranged the cot to her liking, I went to the room next door, the room that had become my own.

There, at what hour in the morning I do not know, Carlos appeared. Pepita's low growl told me of his presence. Automatically I silenced her, thinking of my mother sleeping so near and of María Luisa. He was drunk. And then he forced himself upon me.

CHAPTER TEN

*T*he spring of 1916 came, as it does in Andalusia, with a blanket of wild flowers along the roads and in the fields. Jasmine scented the night air.

"It is heaven," Edwin Fletcher said. We had moved a table into the courtyard, where the sun would be warm. In the half hour before lunch we sat and drank our copitas, and Edwin talked with the children. Martín, too, had now become his pupil for a few hours each day.

Spring brought another advance in my mother's condition. Balthasar, after the accident, had been sent to stay permanently on Luis's hacienda. My mother went one day to visit Half Moon's newest foal, which promised to be even better than the first. Her

236

delight in the sight of her beloved horses imbued me with hope. She had a short canter through Luis's spring-greened pastures, and when she returned, her face wore the sort of radiance which belonged to the old days. After that, Luis sent his trap every morning to collect her from the Plaza de Asturias, and she had a ride on Balthasar, Andy at her side. Never again did she attempt difficult equestrian exercises. She lacked the concentration and the ambition they required.

That spring Andy's first son was born. And that spring I became certain that I was going to have another child, the fruit of the night Carlos had forced himself upon me. To forget about the child, whose coming I would disguise as long as possible, I turned my attention once more to the vineyards.

DURING THE WINTER the last of my grandfather's land had been planted out in vines. It was now May, the time of the third tilling, and I went to the vineyard house, planning to spend some days there with only Pepita for company. I was received with affection by Concepción and Antonio. The silence and sweet air of the vineyard was all about me. I had my dinner of stewed chicken, sat by the fire with Pepita, then went to bed. I lay in the big brass bed which had been my marriage bed and tried to give my thoughts to my baby, the child whose coming I did not want, but for whom I must somehow find love.

The next day was one of pure pleasure. The sun was warm; the vines looked healthy. I ate lunch at a table in the courtyard. Concepción's children played fearlessly with Pepita, and she took their pats and the occasional tug at her ears with good-natured tolerance.

After the siesta I brought out the books I had meant to study during these few days at the vineyard, the account books that told my story of debt and solvency. Then I realized that instead I had brought María Luisa's household books. The vineyard books were back at the Plaza de Asturias.

I smiled and called to Concepción to bring me some tea. It would be a holiday away from the dreaded books, away from the cares of my family.

Along with tea, Luis appeared. I asked Concepción to bring our best fino. Then I took my friend's hand. "My dear Luis, please don't think us unaware or ungrateful. My mother rides Balthasar each day out of your goodness. He and Half Moon are on your land, and so are Half Moon's foals. We had planned to sell them, but since my mother's injury she seems to need them."

"Sell them! You are mad, Carlota! They are the beginning, possibly, of a great bloodline. After all, Balthasar is descended from our great Andalusian horse, Tabal. Half Moon comes from the finest Irish strain. So don't sell your stud before it is begun."

"But I owe you—"

He gestured me into silence. "Owe! What is it to owe a friend?"

I listened as he talked seriously about my leasing land from him for a stud. "Think of what interest and occupation it would give your mother, with her eye for a horse and its temperament."

Don Luis stayed for dinner, and we talked about the war. When the meal was finished Concepción left brandy and port, built up the fire, and asked if there was anything else we required. "Leave a lantern for me, Concepción, if you please," Luis said. "I must make my way back to my own house."

"Antonio has it ready for you, Don Luis." She withdrew.

I was feeling rested and at peace, much more ready to accept the expected child and to love it. As I had once told Luis of my love for Richard Blodmore, so now I found myself telling him what no one else knew. "Luis, in the autumn I will have another child."

He turned his face fully to me. "Fruitful always, Carlota. A blessing, this child."

I shook my head. "I have not been feeling so. Only since I came here have I been able to think of it calmly. A child must be loved, Luis. But so far . . ." I did not say that this child had been forced on me, and that my door was now locked against Carlos.

"You will love your child, Carlota. It is not in you to deny love—not to the helpless—"

Luis did not finish. From where she lay at my side, Pepita rose and gave a low growl. She had heard the noise that suddenly erupted in the courtyard, the clatter of a horse's hooves, Carlos's loud, impatient voice.

We heard the hard ring of boots on the tiled floor. The door of the sitting room opened and crashed back to hit the wall. Carlos stood there and looked at us in silence for a moment. I recognized the signs of too much drink and the dreaded temper aroused. He carried a heavily loaded saddlebag, which he dropped to the floor.

"Well . . . well, our good and true friend, Luis," he said. "How convenient to find you here with Carlota. It saves me another journey." He strode to the dresser and poured himself a brandy. "I'm happy to see the best brandy is being served. After all, one does honour to one's true friends with the best one has."

"Have you come all the way here to say just this, Carlos?"

He turned and came to stand before us; he raised his glass with elaborate ceremony to both of us and then drank deeply. "I'm a good deal more interested in what *you* have been saying."

I shrugged, trying not to let my growing fear show. "The usual things. The war . . . the vines . . . the horses."

"Ah, yes. The vines and the horses. The same stimulating conversation that goes on at every meal in our house. At least I used to have a bed companion, but even *that* is now denied me. I might as well go and live with the Carthusians."

"Go any time you please," I said, and instantly regretted it. One did not talk like that to Carlos in this mood.

His face darkened. "Oh, so you're independent of me now, are you? I was all right to marry when you had gotten yourself with a brat, but now that I've served my purpose, I may be dismissed. After all, you've a plentiful supply of money. What do you need a *man* for?"

"Carlos, this is not something to discuss before Luis—before anyone."

Luis got to his feet. "I think Carlos is not quite himself. No doubt he wishes to see you alone, Carlota, but I think I will stay just a little longer." The mild-mannered man was gone. His tone was cold and unshaken.

"Stay!" Carlos shouted. "Stay as long as you please. After all, don't you *own* this place?" He put down his glass and overturned it. Then he went to pick up the saddlebag. I had already guessed what was in that bag, and I felt sick at the thought. The account books, those familiar volumes bound in red morocco, tumbled out as he upended the bag.

"So unlucky for you that I ventured to inquire into my wife's affairs! And what do I find? My wife is in debt to Don Luis for thousands of pesetas. No, not thousands—hundreds of thousands!"

"*You* speak about debts," I said. "What of the debts I have paid for you?" My fear was lessening as my anger grew.

"My debts? And why not? Didn't Amelia's will cover my trifling debts and give you a large surplus? And what of the jewellery she

239

left to you? *That* could have paid your debts. Or did . . . ?" Now he looked at Luis again, and a slow, insinuating smile grew on his lips. "Or did you demand that your wife make such a will, Don Luis? It would have been a convenient way to give Carlota more money. Are there any other arrangements you two have made? There must be some return for debts like these. No—that couldn't be the way of it. Everyone knows about Don Luis—"

Now Luis moved close to him. He said in Spanish, "Insults to myself I can bear. Coming from such as you, they are nothing. But insults to Carlota are something different. You are a corrupt and ignorant fool!"

Luis hit him with great force across the face. Carlos had not been expecting the blow. His head snapped back and he staggered against the table. Beside me, Pepita was on her feet, tense, her body quivering.

Carlos recovered himself quickly. "No man strikes me and ever forgets it." He started towards Luis, but Luis went to meet him and hit him again. Carlos's face was flushed. He had obviously expected no such skill in Luis, and his drunken rage made him nearly incoherent.

"All right, old man—so you wish a fight of it. You'll have it. I shall carve you up a little, so that when you shave every morning you will remember me." It was then he produced the knife, the Toledo blade with which he had carved our intertwined initials on a tree an age ago.

To my horror Luis actually laughed. "So you really are born of a gipsy! You fight with a knife."

With a cry of rage Carlos flung himself towards Luis. Luis sidestepped, but the point of the knife slashed across his cheek. The blood poured out.

I screamed and flung myself towards Carlos, grasping the hand that held the knife. "Carlos—you are mad!"

He paused just momentarily. Rage and jealousy had gone too far. With his left hand he slapped me across the face, and then, as my hands dropped from his arm, I felt the sharp bite of the knife in the flesh of my shoulder.

I must have screamed again. With a terrible low growl Pepita flung herself at Carlos. Her size and strength were formidable, and she put the full weight of her body into the spring. Carlos fell, and in an instant her teeth were at his throat.

240

Unearthly sounds came from Pepita, the low, awful rumble of an animal going for the kill. Carlos slashed at her with the knife, and her body received terrible wounds. But still she didn't give up. In seconds Carlos's collar and shirtfront were soaked with blood.

"Carlota! Call her off!" Luis cried.

I tried. I think I tried. But did I hesitate just that few seconds too long? At last, though, Pepita responded to my tugs at her collar and let go. She slumped down, her gaze still fixed on Carlos.

Carlos had let the knife fall, and Luis knelt over him. Shakily I brought the candle to his side.

It was then that Antonio and Concepción arrived. They stood rooted by the door for a moment; then Concepción went swiftly to Carlos. "Mother of God!" She looked from me to Luis, and then finally at Pepita. She bent over Carlos again. "He dies!"

His throat and face were a fearful sight. Antonio had run and brought towels. I could feel the tears of shock and anger burning on my face. I could feel the warmth of my own blood as it ran down my sleeve. Then I began to feel cold and deathly tired. Luis held a towel to his face.

Concepción looked up at me. "If he does not have a doctor to sew him up, he will die. I cannot stop the blood."

"I will go," Antonio said.

I thought wearily of the time it would take the doctor to get here. It was a useless gesture, but one that must be performed.

"Tell him also to bring Don Paulo." I sat and waited while Concepción and Luis did what they could. Pepita was as terrible a sight as Carlos, with her broad chest scored and slashed a dozen times. Carlos had fought hard for his life and made her pay. The seconds of their lives ticked off.

At last Luis said, "I think he is dead."

I knelt again by Carlos, trying to find a pulse. The bleeding had stopped, and Concepción had closed his eyes.

I got to my feet with difficulty, Luis helping me. I don't think it was the bleeding from my wound that weakened me but the thought of death, the ending of life, in violence. I touched Concepción's arm. "Try to make him clean before his father sees him." She nodded, understanding.

Then I spoke softly to Pepita, and she made a heroic effort to get to her feet. She followed me to the bedroom and lay down on the rug while I ran to get our best brandy.

241

I covered Pepita with a blanket against the chill which shook her. Opening her mouth, I forced a good measure of brandy down her throat. She took it trustingly.

After a moment I went and got Amelia's tiny pistol. It was more than a lady's toy; it was well made and designed for use.

I sat for a while on the rug beside Pepita, waiting for the brandy to take effect. The time was passing, and I did not dare to wait longer; I could give into the hands of no one else what must be done; the act should not be carried out in the spirit of vengeance. The brandy was working. Her eyes drooped. I bent and kissed the top of her silken head.

"Pepita—dear, good friend . . ." With great effort she raised her head to look up at me, and that deep trusting look almost unnerved me. For me she had given the most she could give. I met that sad, afflicted gaze, and then I killed her.

THE FACE OF DON PAULO was terrible to see as he looked at his dead son. He knelt, as we all had done, beside that still form, and for a moment I thought I saw his shoulders heave. It was over quickly. He rose to his feet stiffly and looked at me. "The dog will be destroyed."

"It has been done."

Even as I said the words a new pain began. Don Paulo seemed to waver before my eyes, and I must have lost consciousness standing on my feet. I did not feel myself hit the floor.

Dr. Ramírez stayed with me all night, but he was not able to stop the haemorrhaging, not able to prevent my miscarriage of the child, Carlos's last child.

I WAS TOO WEAK to attend Carlos's burial. The doctor would not even permit me to leave the vineyard house, so María Luisa divided her time between it and the Plaza de Asturias. I guessed from the agitation in her manner that some strange tales had been told of what happened the night Carlos died.

I had been sleeping through the afternoon, made drowsy by the drugs Dr. Ramírez had given me. The curtains and shutters had been closed against the strong light. When I awoke I did not see my visitor in the dimness of the room. Then a small movement of her hand brought the familiar glitter of the jewels.

"You sleep peacefully, Doña Carlota."

242

"Marquesa . . . ?"

"I have come, of course, because Don Paulo, in his grief, might make some move to destroy you and Luis. At the moment he sees no further than the loss of his son. He is not yet able to consider the position of his grandchildren, my godchildren."

She rose from her chair and came to stand at the end of the bed, gazing down at me. "Luis and I arranged the story for the police. The dog went berserk, attacked Carlos, who tried to defend himself with his knife. You and Luis intervened to help Carlos, and in the struggle, both were wounded."

"That is not what happened."

"But that is the official story. Don Paulo does not dispute it, and the police will accept it. Concepción and Antonio will say that Carlos arrived here to spend the night. They went to bed, were awakened by the noise. They found Carlos dying, and later you yourself shot the dog."

"How do you know that is all they will say?"

"Because that is what they have agreed to. They listened very carefully to my suggestions. They have dreams for their children, that they will be educated, have their chance to make their way in life. If I choose to be generous in aiding their advancement, that is entirely my business.

"One further matter. The honour of Don Paulo demands that your debts to Luis should be paid in full. This has been done. It means, of course, that this vineyard now belongs to Don Paulo."

"That is not possible. It belongs to my mother. It cannot be taken over without her consent."

"That consent has been given. Your mother is a sick woman, but she listens to reason."

I lay quiet. They had managed to wrest my beloved vineyard from me. It was mine no more.

"So I advise you to behave as you should," that calm voice went on. "You will observe a year's strict mourning. You may receive discreet callers, but you may not appear at any entertainment. You will wear black. Don Paulo will exercise a grandfather's control over anything that touches your children. You and María Luisa between you will attempt to control your mother's unfortunate habits. Otherwise we must insist that she have stronger discipline."

What did she mean? I thought of my mother's fear of Nuestra Señora de Mercedes.

Weakness swamped me, and I could make no reply. Between them, the marquesa and Don Paulo had taken everything from me—my children, my vineyard, everything that gave me hope. I was helpless except to do their bidding, trapped by events which had begun long before I was born.

WHEN I WAS WELL ENOUGH to return to the Plaza de Asturias, all our acquaintances called to offer condolences. The marquesa made her appearance the first day I was there, presiding over a beautiful Georgian silver tea service she had sent over. I realized that not only was she presenting a picture of family solidarity but, seated beside me on the sofa, she was also shielding me from any unwanted questions.

The weeks wore slowly on while the summer heat gathered force. The marquesa, satisfied that it was safe to leave us, departed for her estates in Galicia, in the cool, green, northwest region of Spain. But she took my three sons with her, saying that the Andalusian summer was too fierce for them. They went, accompanied by a flustered Nanny and Edwin Fletcher. My mother, María Luisa, and I were alone, three women wearing black, in a dim, shuttered house.

To give myself some activity I rode with my mother each morning to Luis's hacienda to see Balthasar and Half Moon. But the marquesa had warned me, "You will be most circumspect in your meetings with Don Luis. You must never see him alone." So I had lost my friend, as well as all the rest.

During those months when the heat held Andalusia in its grip and the grapes ripened, the battle of the Somme raged in France. It wasn't until November that the battle petered out in rain and mud, and by then the Allies had advanced only seven miles along their front.

The beginning of October had brought the children back to me, and they were full of tales of the marvellous times they had had in Galicia with the marquesa, whom they called Tía Isabel. "Miss Charlie," Nanny said, "they are spoiled entirely. They never listened to me a minute. They would just say, 'Tía Isabel said we could,' and now they'll turn up their noses at everything here."

Later, Edwin Fletcher and I talked in the courtyard over copitas, speculating about the extent of the marquesa's wealth. "It isn't just the estates. Her factories in Barcelona are booming, and she also owns coal mines in Asturias." He had had a summer to observe her, and he seemed to respect her abilities.

I wondered if my children were glad to be back. Once Juan said, "*We* were the ones taken to stay with Tía Isabel. She didn't invite the children of Tío Ignacio or Tío Pedro." Those were the courtesy titles he gave to Carlos's two half-brothers. "*We* are the favourites. And I am the oldest son."

I felt sick. He was so young, and yet he already knew the significance of the favour of the Marquesa de Pontevedra.

CHAPTER ELEVEN

*I*n the early months of 1917 my mother and I were invited to join a sewing circle with the ladies of Jerez. We had little informal meetings in each other's houses, where we rolled bandages, and knitted scarves and helmet-like things called balaclavas.

Every batch of newspapers that reached Jerez brought a new nightmare until I had read every name in every casualty list. I told myself that somehow I would know if Richard Blodmore were dead. But still I read the lists with fear and hope. And then, in April 1917, the United States declared war on Germany.

In an uncharacteristic rush of enthusiasm, Edwin Fletcher asked my mother if he might borrow the drawing room for a small evening reception. Where he found the champagne, I never knew. But more than a few of his friends and acquaintances turned up to drink it. We all exchanged toasts and said the war would soon be over now, and we would sell more sherry than ever to England. Then an extraordinary thing happened.

Don Paulo appeared in the doorway. He stood there only momentarily; then he went to my mother. "Lady Patricia, I am happy to see you looking so well." He turned, caught sight of Juan, who had been permitted to stay up, and bent to receive his grandson's embrace. With his hand in Juan's, he came to me. It was the first time we had seen each other since Carlos's death. He raised his glass. "I hope we may soon have a true celebration of peace."

"To peace," I said, also raising my glass.

He drained his drink, embraced Juan once more, and left. I looked at Edwin Fletcher in puzzlement. "I left a note for him at the bodega," he said, "but I never imagined he'd come."

"Peace," I said slowly. "Perhaps one day there truly will be peace." I looked at Juan and thought of the power that rested in my children.

A YEAR HAD PASSED since Carlos's death, and it was now permissible for me to accept invitations. Almost shyly I made my appearance at a few parties and found that my status had changed. I was still young, but I was the widow of Don Paulo's son. So young men would take my hand, bow over it, and pass on. It was as if Don Paulo and the marquesa had wrought some sort of screen between us and other families. I toyed with the thought of returning to Ireland when the war was over, but I knew the marquesa and Don Paulo would do anything to prevent it. Wherever I looked I could see only the need for money, and our growing dependence on the marquesa.

The agony in Europe did not end quickly, as we had hoped it would, but it was not in the casualty lists that I found Richard's name; the news came first in a letter from Lady Sybil.

> Poor Lord Blodmore has been wounded—Elena has gone to England to be with him. They say he's lucky to be alive—a shrapnel wound to the face, I heard. He could have been blinded. It was at Passchendaele.

Then we heard that he had returned to Ireland. A long leave for convalescence. Perhaps discharge. I rolled bandages and thought of Richard, and lighted candles with the prayer that by some miracle the war would end before he was sent back into service. I never thought about his shattered face. He was alive; that was all I cared about.

IN THE SPRING OF 1918 telegrams began arriving. "I don't understand," my mother said. I snatched the first from her, fearing it was news of Richard.

> DEEPEST SYMPATHY IN YOUR LOSS, BUT HOW PROUD YOU MUST BE OF HIS HEROIC DEEDS. LOVE, SYBIL WAREHAM.

"Who?" I said. "Who does she mean?"
The official telegram came only after a dozen others from

246

people we had known at Clonmara. It had been sent to Clonmara and redirected to Jerez.

> THE WAR OFFICE DEEPLY REGRETS TO INFORM YOU OF THE
> DEATH IN ACTION OF LIEUTENANT-COLONEL THOMAS DRUM-
> MOND. THIS OFFICER DIED IN THE PERFORMANCE OF DUTY IN
> CIRCUMSTANCES OF EXTREME GALLANTRY.

My mother let the telegram flutter soundlessly to the floor. "Thomas is dead! Your father is dead, Charlie."

I picked up the telegram and read it. "I didn't know my father had become a lieutenant-colonel."

"Neither did I," my mother said faintly. "Extreme gallantry . . . I wonder—" For a moment she pressed her hands against her temples; then she went to the sideboard and poured herself some brandy.

"I think I'll go and lie down for a while," she said. I could hear her muttering as she closed the door, "Extreme gallantry . . . Doesn't sound like Thomas at all."

I wondered if she wept a little, wept for the memories of a romance gone cold, for the waste of youth. She couldn't weep for whatever my father had become, because she had never known that man. Nor had I.

IT WAS IRONIC to learn from the War Office that my mother would now receive a war widow's pension. My father's estate consisted of a few hundred pounds in cash, and some shares in South African gold-mining companies and the De Beers diamond company. These he had left to me.

Don Ramón at the bank considered them carefully. "They don't represent a fortune, of course, but they should yield a small income. Always useful."

As the silence of more than twenty years had been unbroken by a single letter, so it remained to the end. Apart from his will, there was no shred of evidence that he had ever thought about us. But because of him, because of the war widow's pension, because of the small income that the gold-mining and diamond-mining shares would bring, my mother and I might be able to take some small step towards independence from the marquesa. He had restored a little pride to us, and that was the greatest gift of all.

ALL JEREZ CAME to offer congratulations when it became known that my father would be awarded the Victoria Cross. The newspapers containing accounts of his last heroic hour had by now reached the town. I was the child of an authentic hero, and my children shared in the reflected glory. My mother was utterly bewildered by it, and more often than not refused to discuss it with visitors. "How can I," she said to me, "when I know nothing about him? How old are you, Charlie? I keep forgetting."

"Twenty-nine."

"Twenty-nine, are you? Then it's more than twenty-nine years since I've seen him. How can I talk about him?"

Soon after the Armistice was signed, a letter came from my father's colonel requesting that my mother make the journey to England to receive personally the posthumous award of the Victoria Cross from His Majesty.

She was at once in a panic. "Oh, Charlie, I'm not up to that any more. You understand, don't you, Charlie?"

Since her injury she had been physically unable to undertake any such task. I had seen her shake with nerves at small social gatherings, terrified that she might do something wrong. The ordeal of appearing at Buckingham Palace, of curtsying to the King, of attending the regimental dinner in her honour, would have been too much, even if there were not the added misery of having to do without her daily intake of alcohol. She could not stand before the King of England smelling of brandy, but without it she could not stand there at all.

"Charlie, you must go. Darling, do it for me! Do it for the children. Think how thrilled they'll be to be able to say that you went and received your father's medal."

I agreed; I had to go. Juan, Martín, and Francisco would never have forgiven me if I had refused. The necessary letter was drafted and sent off. From Colonel Saunders came an enthusiastic response. The regiment would be honoured. Their headquarters were near Winchester, and I would be their guest, staying at the colonel's house. The presentation at Buckingham Palace was arranged for April, and it was even suggested that if I should like a few days to visit London afterwards, I could either stay at the London home of the colonel's sister or at a hotel, whichever I preferred. All expenses would be borne by the regiment.

The excitement in the town was intense. While cousins and

second cousins had won military honours during the war, none had achieved the Victoria Cross. My itinerary and wardrobe were openly discussed. For that short time I represented Jerez and its pride in its English connection; it was also possible that I might sell some sherry, in a backhanded sort of way, or at least get it talked about.

And then the marquesa appeared. "You have no jewellery to wear," she said peremptorily. "You represent Jerez there in England. You must represent us well."

I was furious at her for coming unannounced, as always, and for constantly assuming that her decisions would be accepted without question. "I cannot wear jewellery to the Palace," I pointed out. "It is a very simple morning ceremony, and others will have medals presented. Many of them will be enlisted men."

"The regiment will give a dinner for you, and there will be other invitations. I have written to our Spanish ambassador in London. You must have a tiara and a necklace. I have chosen these for you."

"I cannot accept such things."

"It is not a matter of acceptance. It is merely a loan." She placed a velvet-lined box on the table and withdrew a delicately made tiara of emeralds and diamonds. The necklace matched it.

I saw the hunger in my mother's eyes as she gazed at them. "How lovely you will look in them, Charlie. You must have a photograph taken in London wearing them. Do it for me, darling."

And so I went, dressed as never before in my life, carrying the marquesa's jewels—fully insured, she told me. I was to take a P & O steamer from Gibraltar. It seemed a lifetime since we had disembarked there on that hot day more than ten years ago.

Edwin Fletcher was travelling back to England with me. He was taking up a post as research assistant in an economics study being set up in Cambridge. My children surrounded us as the boxes were strapped on the carriage the marquesa had lent for the journey.

And then, just as we were about to leave, Luis came. He drew me aside, away from the others. "Will you wear this for Amelia? If she had been alive she would have been more delighted than any of us." It was a large solitaire diamond ring which must certainly have come from the collection of his family's jewels. "Gems seem to fade when there is no woman to wear them."

I could not refuse him, though the ring was more than I ever wanted to wear.

"I will see to your mother while you're gone. María Luisa knows she can call on me. Try to enjoy yourself, Carlota. Forget for a while our Spanish sombreness and the things you leave behind here. It is time to fling open the windows."

EDWIN FLETCHER AND I parted at Southampton in the presence of Captain Carton, who had been sent from the regimental headquarters, near Winchester, with a staff car, to meet me. It was the first automobile I had ever ridden in, and the first time I had seen England, except for those few hours when we had transshipped in Liverpool so long ago. I had almost forgotten how tender were the greens of the northern spring, how muted the skies.

The car came to a halt before a large Georgian house which had a slight air of *nouveau riche*. Even the ivy seemed new and washed. I sensed that more men with money now joined the regiment than had done so in my father's early times with it. What they could not buy was tradition, and that was why my father's Victoria Cross was so important.

Colonel Saunders, the regimental commander, was a lean, spare man, red-faced, unsmiling; his wife was plump and soft, wearing clothes that were frilled and lacy. I was welcomed effusively.

We walked into the polished, shining marble hall. "I'm sure you'll be glad," Colonel Saunders said, "that you aren't quite among strangers. Your cousin, Lord Blodmore, has kindly agreed to come over."

Richard stood with his back to a long window that gave a view of a vivid green lawn behind the house. I couldn't see his face clearly, but the outline of his body seemed thinner and slightly stooped. I hardly heard the noise around me, the fluttering talk of Mrs. Saunders, the barking of her many small dogs. He began to walk towards me, and I to him. I saw then that the cheekbone where the shrapnel had hit was smashed; an attempt to repair it had not been successful. One side of his mouth was pulled upwards. The handsome man of my memory was gone. It didn't matter. Richard Blodmore remained, and I still loved him.

He held out his hand formally. "Hello, Charlie."

THERE WAS a kind of agony in being so close to Richard and yet not alone with him. We managed to pace the colonel's rose garden between tea and the time to go upstairs to dress. "Elena didn't want to come," he said. "No, I don't think it was because of your being here. It hasn't been much of a marriage, as you know. At first she was jealous and possessive, and then she stopped caring. Now she can hardly bear to be in the same room with me. The very sight of me sickens her, I suppose."

I looked him fully in the face. "I love you, Richard. For however long I live, it's never going to change."

His shattered features twisted still further. "Charlie, it's never going to work for us, you know. There's no possibility of a divorce. Elena is Catholic, and she's determined to remain my wife."

"Richard, don't you think I know all this? The marquesa wishes you to remain married, and Elena will not oppose her." The buds were forming on the roses in the colonel's tidy garden. "Tell me about Clonmara."

Elena's money had restored the house, he told me. For ten years he had worked on bringing back the land. "I till and sow my acres, and I think of you, who should be there."

"And the rose garden?" I said.

"Just as you left it. I take care of it myself. They still call it the countess's garden, but for me it's Charlotte's garden."

A gong sounded in the house, and we turned obediently to answer its summons. To watching eyes from the house we were just very distant cousins, admiring the colonel's perfect turf and his budding roses, and catching up on family gossip.

WE DINED WITH THE COLONEL and his closest staff members that evening. The following night they gave a splendid dinner in the officers' mess, with dancing afterwards.

I had asked for Edwin Fletcher to be invited, and was startled to see him present in his officer's dress uniform. I had never thought of him as a soldier. And Richard wore his uniform and a medal. Their uniforms seemed as little a part of their personalities as the emerald and diamond tiara and necklace were part of me. Amelia's ring glittered in the candlelight, and I knew that many of the women guests wondered where the jewellery had come from. It was generally known that my mother and I were not well off. I tried to remember each of the distinguished strangers about the table, every detail of uniform and dress, so that I could describe them for the eager ears in Jerez. I was startled to realize that I was desperately homesick, and it was for Jerez, not Clonmara.

I listened to the speech Colonel Saunders gave, welcoming me, mentioning Richard as though he had been a close relative of my father's, honouring my father's valour. But to me my father seemed only a name on the regimental roll of honour.

I danced every dance, the partners changing all the time. I danced with Richard and with Edwin Fletcher.

"You look very beautiful, Doña Carlota," Edwin said, teasingly speaking in Spanish.

When I danced with Richard we didn't talk at all.

IT WAS, after all, very simple. I went to the Palace, escorted by Colonel Saunders and Richard, and we stood in a long line of those who were to be honoured with various orders and decorations. The citation was read; I received the box containing the Victoria Cross from the King's hand; I heard him say something and could never remember afterwards just what words he had used, so I had to invent them to tell my children. I curtsied, walked a few steps backwards, and it was the turn of the next person in the line. There were no feelings of celebration: the whole occasion was touched with sadness.

We drank champagne with Colonel and Mrs. Saunders at lunch. There was a sense of relief that it was all over. The regiment now had its VC, and a small piece of tradition called Drummond had been grafted to its pedigree. We stayed at Brown's Hotel, and that night Colonel and Mrs. Saunders were to join me at a small reception and dinner given by the Spanish ambassador. Richard was also attending, as were representatives of the sherry trade in London.

Many invitations had come from the London representatives of the sherry shippers. Mrs. Saunders beamed at me. "My dear, you could make a regular season of it. Are you *sure* you wouldn't prefer to stay a little longer—with the colonel's sister? She would be delighted to have you stay. No trouble, I do assure you."

"Everyone is most kind," I said. "But there is a lot to attend to in Jerez. I shall stay just a few days, so I think it is best if I stay here at the hotel."

"And I shall make sure Charlotte sees something of London," Richard said. "How can she go home and confess to her children that she hasn't seen the Tower or the Changing of the Guard? There are presents to buy for her sons."

That was the first time I knew that Richard intended to stay on

252

with me after the Saunderses had gone. I smiled over the champagne, and my heart was alight with the thought that I would be with Richard—even if just for a few days.

I WORE the marquesa's jewels again that evening to the Spanish embassy. I greeted the guests in Spanish, giving them their correct titles. The ambassador seemed pleased, and the reports of me would be favourable, I knew.

The hours of that splendid evening passed with aching slowness. I felt Richard's eyes upon me and remembered that he had loved me without emeralds and diamonds. And I knew that I would wait no longer to give him that love that we both hungered for. However many hours more we must wait, after more than ten years of loving we would finally give ourselves to each other.

A WEEK LATER RICHARD saw me off on the P & O liner from Southampton. It had been a week on which I must feed for the rest of my life.

I had gone sightseeing in London because Richard had insisted on my having something to tell my children; I had bought presents for everyone. I had had the photograph taken for my mother. I had accepted the most important of the invitations from the sherry families. Richard was my escort everywhere.

I counted over our times together as the ship ploughed on through rough seas to Gibraltar. Pitifully little I had to remember, and yet a bond had been welded. We had been one flesh. Now we had to go on alone. As the Rock of Gibraltar thrust itself up I shut the memory of Richard into that separate compartment it had occupied for so many years.

The presence of the marquesa awaited me on the dock as we berthed. She had sent her very latest acquisition, a Bentley motorcar, and an English chauffeur, to collect me.

CHAPTER TWELVE

The hurt grew less as I saw and embraced my children. I knew from the way they clung to me that my absence had been real to them. I saw the look that lighted my mother's face as she emerged into the courtyard to greet me. María Luisa pressed me to her bony chest. "We have missed you, querida."

253

Half the town seemed to file through our house in the next few weeks. I had to tell the story of Buckingham Palace, the regimental ball, the London sightseeing, over and over.

I drove with Andy to Sanlúcar to return the marquesa's jewels. She received me at once and ordered tea to be brought.

"You have done well," she said. "I have excellent reports from our ambassador."

"Then there is no need to tell you more. You already know everything that has happened."

She turned her face, and her lips twisted into a thin smile. "There are a few details I am not acquainted with. It matters that we were well represented. You should, however, have been more discreet with Richard Blodmore. I do not care for my godchildren to be associated with any scandal."

"There is no scandal to be associated with," I said. I wondered how far her influence went. It would not have been beyond her to have arranged to pay the servants at Brown's Hotel to report to her. "It was pleasant to have Richard's company. Otherwise I was completely among strangers."

"Quite so." She poured China tea and handed the cup to me.

I placed the jewel case on a table. "I have brought back the jewels. They were much admired."

"So I heard. And Don Luis gave you a ring that belonged to Amelia."

"No. It was a loan, to be worn as I wore your tiara. I did not like to refuse him. Amelia and I were close."

"Do not get too close to Don Luis. He is not the man for you. It is possible, in time, that I may find the man for you."

I got to my feet. "*Find* the man for me! You are mistaken, Marquesa. If I ever marry again, I will marry the man *I* choose."

She nodded. "Well for you that you can afford to be so independent. Do not count on my support, however. Think of your household, your demented mother, your children, that miserable old maid, María Luisa. Think well before you reject my help."

I started to walk down the long room. Her voice arrested me. "Oh, and you may take the jewels. You have worn them well and with credit. Take them!"

I walked back the length of the room. I thought of all that the sale of them might have given us, of all the things we needed. I swept the jewel case off the table, and as it spilled open the sun caught the bright lights of the tiara and necklace. "I am alone. I alone will make my decisions. Jewels do not buy me."

I walked out. Travelling back to Jerez with Andy, I wondered what I was to do. I had spurned a powerful ally. I was truly alone. And by now I was absolutely certain that I was pregnant.

I WAITED until after the bodega closed before going to see Don Luis at Los Cisnes. There had been no opportunity to return Amelia's ring, and I wanted to tell him the things about my journey to England that could be told to no one else.

Luis greeted me warmly. "Come to my study. It's about the only room I spend time in now." Here his desk had papers spread across it, and a small pile of books. There was a smell of cigar smoke in the air. Without ringing for a servant, Luis himself brought a sherry decanter and glasses from a side table.

"I . . . I think I would like some brandy," I said.

His eyebrows raised a trifle, but he brought another decanter. "Now tell me," he invited. "It was good of you to come especially to see me."

"To you of all people." I raised my glass to him and then drank. "You used not to be so formal."

He smiled. "I used to see you more often."

"Yes," I admitted. "So much changed so quickly." I brought out the ring from my purse. "I thought of Amelia when I wore it. It wasn't like wearing the marquesa's jewels. You probably heard about the jewels?"

He nodded. "There is little that's not talked about in this town." He touched the ring slowly, but left it where I had placed it on the desk. "So, Carlota, you went to England. It has changed you. You are older."

I found myself talking about the events of those days as they really had been. And then, after I had had my second brandy, I told him about Richard Blodmore, and finally about my angry interview with the marquesa. "I came to return Amelia's ring, but I also needed to see you because it is the first step in making my own life. My children may suffer for my independence, but I hope I'll be able to make it up to them in some fashion. I cannot live any longer in the shadow of the marquesa and Don Paulo."

Once again he touched the ring. "But you are alone."

I smiled faintly. "If you call the household I have about me being

255

alone. . . . And ever less alone, Luis. I am going to have Richard Blodmore's child."

I watched his face, tried to read its expression through the haze of smoke. For a time he didn't look at me directly—his long fingers played with the ring, as if he were fascinated by the refraction of light thrown out from its heart.

He spoke very slowly. "Will you go away? Will you go to England until the child is born? Does Blodmore know?"

I shook my head. "None of those things. If I were to go away, it would be to keep the birth a secret. My child would be given to someone else to bring up. I could never allow that. No, I—and the family—will have to face it out here." Now my voice trembled a little. "Brave talk, Luis. Don Paulo and the marquesa might be able to take my sons from me, because I will be judged an immoral woman. Can the courts do that in Spain? Can the Church? Before I let that happen I will take us all out of here, though we have nowhere to go. But I have time to think about it all; there are some months yet before others will know. You are the only person I have burdened with the knowledge."

He leaned back, and his face was almost beyond the range of the light thrown by the lamp on the desk. "If it is your decision not to go to Richard, I have something I can offer you, Carlota."

I held up my hand in dismissal. "No, Luis. I have not come for money. I came to talk, because I cannot yet lay this burden on María Luisa, and certainly not on my mother."

He leaned forward, and his face wore a look of infinite sadness, a look of pain. "I can offer you and your child my name—and therefore my protection. No court in the land can take your children from you if I stand beside you—as your husband."

I shook my head. "Did you think I was hoping for that? I would not insult you, Luis. You are my friend."

He shrugged. "Perhaps you see it as an insult to you. You, a beautiful, passionate young woman married to someone like me. I cannot be your lover, Carlota. You probably know that, as half the town seems to know or guess it. All I can do for you is to stand at the head of your household and offer you the protection which that gives."

"Luis, you do me the greatest honour. . . ."

"But you do not accept." A bitter smile, a shrug that sought to cover the hurt. "Well, it was an idea."

256

I sat and looked at him for a long time. Then I stretched out my hand and put on the ring. "I accept. Many people knew you gave me the ring. They will say we were lovers before I left. Who can prove different? Let them assume that the child is yours, Luis. Perhaps you had bad luck with two wives who were barren, but not with me. The child will be *yours*, Luis!"

A strange, dawning light was in his face. "And Blodmore? What of Blodmore?"

"Richard shall never know. Let him hate me, if he must, for rushing to the arms of another man. It is *your* child, Luis. I will swear it, before him or anyone else. No one but you shall have a claim on it."

I moved around the desk and went to him. "Let there be gossip, but you will have my fidelity, a true wife."

He cradled my face between his hands. "I fear I may shut you in a prison."

"Can there be a prison built of love and tenderness? We can make a marriage for sharing."

"Carlota, you do my house honour." I felt the press of his lips on my forehead. Then suddenly he was tugging at my hand, pulling eagerly like a young man. "Come, we'll go at once to tell your mother! And María Luisa! Through her the rest of the town will know very soon. Tomorrow I will inform Don Paulo that you have done me the honour of agreeing to become my wife." It was a cry of happiness from him that almost broke my heart.

WE WERE MARRIED five days later, and it seemed half of Jerez turned out for our nuptial mass. The two principal witnesses were Don Paulo and the marquesa.

Afterwards the carriages rolled up to Los Cisnes, which was now my home. The marquesa stood near us, greeting guests, but whenever she looked at me there was a kind of controlled rage behind her impassiveness. I had taken more than a small step beyond her control, and I think she feared that my sons might slip from her influence. So she sought to exert it once more by seeming to have not only condoned this marriage but actively encouraged it.

The occasion had a charming informality about it. While Luis was being congratulated by someone, he accidentally spilled wine on my blue dress. I shrugged. "Never mind. I was feeling rather hot." Then we laughed helplessly together, like old friends or new lovers. The town looked on, and the rumours that had gone around at the time of Carlos's death were revived. I had, they would think, waited a decent length of time since being widowed, and then married the man I had wanted all along. I would do this and much more to make everyone believe that this was truly Luis's child. If we could not be lovers, at least it would be known only to ourselves. The scorn and contempt Luis had suffered would be gone. This would be my gift to him.

IT WAS an almost unbelievable joy to learn that there was something else I could give. I undressed that night in the room Amelia had used, which adjoined Luis's. I felt comfortable there, not a usurper. Without awkwardness I went then to Luis's room. He was already in bed, with a book in his hands. "Carlota?" He half sat up. "Is there something wrong?"

"What should be wrong?" I kicked off my slippers and perched on the bed. "I just felt like gossiping. What a good party it was! Jerez never went to a wedding quite like it before."

"Never," he agreed. "It was the most muddled party I ever saw, and the best."

I took the book from his hands. "Don't go to the bodega tomorrow, Luis. Let's take a picnic to the vineyards."

I slipped beneath the sheets, placing my head against his shoulder. I felt his body go rigid. "Oh, Luis, just hold me like a child. I feel safe with you. You will take care of me. We have been such friends, and now we need never be parted."

"Querida . . . querida . . ." His body relaxed against mine; one arm slipped beneath me, while the other stroked my hair. "We will go anywhere you want. A real journey, perhaps. You have had so few treats in your life, Carlota. Let me spoil you a little, as if you were my child—my dearest companion."

"Your wife, Luis." I placed his hand against my breast.

What he had thought impossible was happening. We clasped each other, but not like children. We became lovers. The marriage was a real one.

IT WAS A FACT that Luis, in his happiness, could not help proclaiming—in the way he bore himself—the ease of our new relationship. When he talked of the coming child, no one could have doubted that it was his own child he looked forward to.

258

María Luisa smiled and shook her head. "You have used some magic and transformed Don Luis, Charlie. For the first time he struts like a man."

I smiled. "That is good. That is very good."

We did not make the wedding journey Luis had suggested. I wanted to savour the first utterly peaceful period I had ever known in Jerez. My children had settled down happily with Luis and me at Los Cisnes. My mother and María Luisa stayed on at the Plaza de Asturias. My mother glowed in a kind of reflected happiness.

OUR SON was born in January. The child had the light green eyes of the Blodmores, as the other three did, and the Blodmore cast of feature. My mother smiled over the cradle. "He looks like my father. Will you call him Luis?"

"No," Luis said. "I think he should be called after Carlota's father. We shall call him Tomás."

When she was alone with me María Luisa adjusted her glasses and examined him closely. "All Blodmore," she pronounced. "And the town is saying that you snared Luis by being able to give him a child. They do not believe this is a premature baby, any more than they were deceived by Juan. They remember the ring Luis gave you before you went to England. They forget nothing, these people."

"Let them remember; it can do no harm." I said it thankfully; let them think anything, so long as they did not think that Richard Blodmore was Tomás's father.

The marquesa came, having for once announced her arrival, and, quite humbly for her, suggested that she should again be godmother. I felt myself stiffen, but then I realized that it would look better if this child did not seem different from the others. If the marquesa had suspicions about Richard Blodmore, let them remain just that—suspicions.

I nodded towards the marquesa. "I will agree to whatever Luis wishes."

She looked at me sharply. Never in the years of marriage to Carlos had I played the role of the submissive wife.

Luis agreed, and once again the Marquesa de Pontevedra stood at the baptismal font in the church, an ageing woman, but still erect and formidable, and swore, in the name of my son Tomás, to renounce the devil and all his works.

THAT SPRING Luis took me to the fair in Seville. It was the first time I had ever been to that legendary event. My three older boys rode their beautiful ponies, gifts of the marquesa. They wore Andalusian dress. Their saddles and their soft boots were decorated with silver. Juan was eleven, Martín ten, Francisco nine; they were babies no longer, and would soon be young men. I was complimented on their good looks, their horsemanship, their manners. Luis talked of the day when little Tomás would be old enough to join his brothers.

The fair at Seville each spring seemed to serve no real purpose except as a great social gathering which included every sort of person, from grandees of Spain to the lowliest gipsies. There was a grand mix of music and lights, horses, gaily dressed men and women, wine and food. I was bewildered and delighted, and also strangely tired.

When I told Luis I was not feeling well, his face instantly clouded with concern. "What is it, querida?" Memories of Amelia's illness must have flashed through his mind. "I shall bring a doctor at once."

We were breakfasting in our hotel sitting room, which overlooked one of the beautiful wide avenues of the city. I slipped my hand over to touch Luis's.

"I consulted one yesterday when you thought I was shopping. Luis, we are to have a child."

The expression on his face was almost painful to watch, the quick succession of joy, of fear, and then of doubt.

"Do not doubt me, Luis. I gave my promise. It is truly your child." He buried his face in his hands and wept.

DURING THAT PREGNANCY I was guarded and cosseted, as if I might break in two. At times I grew weary of Luis's concern, but so much of his belief in himself as a man rested in this child that I could not deny him.

My mother and María Luisa often came after the siesta, and at Luis's urging sometimes stayed for the evening meal. They would sit with me as I lay in the bed in what had been Amelia's room, María Luisa usually with a piece of needlework, my mother fluttering restlessly about.

I had introduced only a few new pieces of furniture into the room since Amelia had used it. Luis had bought me a beautiful

Louis XIV corner cabinet. Here Amelia's exquisite porcelain models of the white horses of Vienna found their showcase. They were a special delight to my mother, and she often opened the case and handled them. I was always nervous when she did this after she had had wine with lunch but she was very careful, as gentle as with a live horse or a child.

The bottom shelf of the cabinet also displayed the beautiful little gun in its marquetry box, surrounded by its silver bullets. I had never touched it since the night I had killed Pepita with it. My mother clucked her tongue in disapproval when she saw the gun. "It's not been cleaned, Charlie." So next time she visited she brought oil and cloths and cleaned it thoroughly. "Such a pretty thing," she said admiringly.

On a stormy night late in November, a month before the baby was due, I went into labour. This was not the intense but brief labour that had characterized the other births; it was slow, protracted, exhausting. At last I heard it, the cry of a newborn child. A feeble, pitiful cry, like the mewing of a kitten. But a living cry.

Luis's daughter was tiny and fragile and beautiful. When she was washed, Luis himself came and laid her in my arms. Her eyes were very dark, like Luis's. She was the only one of my children not born with the light green eyes of the Blodmores.

FOR A TIME she hovered on the edge of life. She was difficult to feed, and yet she seemed hungry. It was torture to see how Luis hung over her cradle. Only reluctantly would he leave her in charge of the nurse to try to get some sleep at night. He grew haggard; the scar was very white against the grey of his skin.

Then one morning I awakened to see the nurse bending over the cradle, where the tiny arms were beating the air as if in anger. The baby's cry was sharp and demanding. When the nurse brought her, she sucked greedily at my breast.

"Go to Don Luis," I said softly. "Tell him she is well."

Still, it was a fragile, light form, beautiful in her white lace robe, which the marquesa held in her arms for the baptism. She received the water, and all her names, without a sound: Luisa, Isabel, Patricia, Angela, Milagro—which means miracle. She was, in truth, the miracle of Luis's life. She was the angel-child. He possessed nothing more precious. And for me, Dr. Ramírez told me that she would be my last child.

III Spanish Twilight: 1921-1936
CHAPTER THIRTEEN

*O*ur lives settled into a quiet rhythm. At times it seemed almost too serene. I kept expecting some storm to sweep down on us; I found myself looking over my shoulder watching for the thundercloud, listening for the distant rumble.

Edwin Fletcher had written and asked if he could return to tutor the children; he longed for the sun and missed all of us. So he came, and he kept Juan, Martín, and Francisco at lessons full-time. Juan was maturing quickly; he was by turn charming, boisterous, assertive, confident. His younger brothers looked to him as a natural leader. Tomás, who was just as assertive, was as yet too young to challenge Juan.

Edwin Fletcher studied them with interest. "Those two are born to scrap, I think. Be a good thing for Juan if Tomás were able to give him a run for his money. . . ."

Perhaps he used the phrase unconsciously. A run for money might be what it all turned into. Juan, as Carlos's son, had no money of his own, nor did Martín or Francisco. All they had was a natural hold on their grandfather's affections and the special standing they had with the marquesa.

Juan by now knew that he ranked first among all of Don Paulo's grandchildren. But little Tomás and tiny Luisa were the children of his stepfather and must, for that reason, be favoured by him. I noticed that Juan was very careful in his manner towards Luis—polite, respectful, as he was to Don Paulo and the marquesa. He had learned very young how to use the charm and good looks he had inherited from Carlos. It was rather frightening in someone of his age.

I had feared at first that our family would split in two parts, because of the gap in age between Carlos's children and the younger two, and the knowledge that the older boys were Luis's stepchildren. But Luis took care to spend time with the boys, talked with them, rode with them, spoke always of "my sons".

While he could speak lovingly of his sons, he worshipped Luisa. Each day on his return from the bodega he would go to the nursery to see her, as if to reassure himself that she really existed. Her beautiful little face would light up at the sight of him. She was a grave little girl, but for him she would laugh. Watching them together, I was afraid of what might happen to Luis if something should happen to her.

For all the advice we took from doctors, Luisa remained delicate. She seemed to go through the illnesses of childhood with alarming rapidity, and with each of them she took a long time to recover.

Still, our grave, sober little girl reached her second and third birthdays. She was a princess in her little kingdom, but she never took advantage of this, as Juan did. The usual faults and tempers of childhood seemed missing in her. She didn't even soil the tiny white dresses she wore.

"More like an angel than a child," Nanny would say.

DURING THESE YEARS there was the time and the money to travel. Luis took me to Paris and Rome, Vienna and London. We never discussed the possibility of visiting Ireland. I was always, in the end, happy to return to Jerez.

Though the world close about us remained calm, I was aware of the uproar throughout the rest of the country as the incompetence and corruption within the ruling structure were made clear. There was a clamour for strong, effective rule, and in 1923 Primo de Rivera, the military governor of Barcelona, "pronounced" against the government. The coup succeeded. Spain had a dictator, and King Alfonso XIII welcomed him. We didn't know then, though Edwin predicted it, that these coming years would be the last gasp of constitutional monarchy in Spain.

That year Juan came home one day with his head bloodied after a fracas in front of the church.

"You wouldn't believe what they are saying, Mother," he told me. "This Communist stuff. They're going to overthrow everything—and the Church is first. They're going to take the land from us. Every peasant will have land, they say. Every man will be his own master—so long as he does what the state tells him. They can't do it, can they? The army would never let them."

"I don't think they can do it, Juan. But perhaps there's a case for some of the things they say."

"They didn't think it could done in Russia, either," Edwin said with a certain laconic detachment.

THESE WERE RIPPLES on the surface of our seemingly placid world, but in Ireland there had been revolt and now civil war.

Richard and Elena Blodmore and their sons, Edward and Paul, came to Jerez after spending a summer at the Galicia estate with the marquesa. With Elena as the next holder of the title of Pontevedra, and the elder son, Edward, to inherit after her, it was natural that the marquesa wanted her great-nephew trained in the language and customs of Spain. There was no way of avoiding our duty to entertain them. For a time they were the focus of every party, the ones who brought the freshest news, and people were avid to hear it, even though it frightened them.

On the last afternoon of the Blodmores' visit we sat together in the garden and I thought, except for our clothes, we might have posed for one of those Edwardian family photographs, with the table laid formally for English tea, a butler and a footman in attendance. The Edwardian atmosphere was made stronger by the presence of the marquesa, who still wore her long black dresses and, outdoors, a large, black, tulle-draped hat. All the rest of us, except María Luisa, were dressed in white.

Richard and Elena were there with their sons. My mother had come with María Luisa. María Luisa's dress, like the marquesa's, was unchanging. My mother's skirts were a little shorter, but she still clung to the old styles, although her slim body would easily have carried off the loose, shapeless form that fashion now favoured. Elena wore her skirts shorter than anyone in Jerez had dared think of, and her still-golden hair was bobbed. She wore lipstick, had long painted nails, and smoked cigarettes in a holder. She crossed and recrossed her legs restlessly as we sat in the late-summer garden, obviously bored with the obligations of this family gathering.

Luis had come, and I thought that for him the departure of the Blodmores would bring relief. Richard's presence must have been almost as hard on him as it had been on me. Yet he had never once asked me about my feelings for Richard.

All our children were there. Juan was to go with the Blodmores as far as London, and in a week's time would enter an English school. He put a good face on it, but I could sense a shade of apprehension in him. It must have given both joy and pain to Don Paulo to see Juan's extraordinary resemblance to Carlos. Tomorrow's parting would hurt the old man perhaps even more than one could guess.

The Blodmores had been with the marquesa in Galicia for two months. She said now, "I hope it has been a peaceful time for you. Things have been very bad in Ireland."

Elena shrugged. "Oh, we haven't come through it at all badly. Richard is such a stick-in-the-mud. He just gets on with his farming and lets politics alone. He should have been elected—"

Suddenly Don Paulo raised his voice. "There is nothing wrong with a man tending his land and minding his own business. And since when could a member of the British House of Lords be elected to anything?"

"A member of the House of Lords doesn't even have a vote," my mother said. Everyone turned to look at her. It was one of her lucid days. "And women can vote now, can't they?" she added. "Perhaps one day we'll have the vote here. But poor Ireland—it must be hard to see the state of the people."

"The state of the people is no worse than it was. And no better," Elena retorted. "What good have they done themselves with all this strife? Oh, yes, we have an Irish Free State now, but what we have paid for it! There's been nothing but bloodshed since the Easter Rising. Estates going to ruin. The best people leaving—"

"*We* have not left, Elena," Richard said. "Nor will we. These are not times when you leave an estate to be managed by an agent."

The marquesa was nodding her head. She rose. "Come, children. We will feed the swans."

My four sons and the sons of Richard and Elena crowded about her. We watched as she spread her hands. "Come, Luisa. Come Tomás. Take Tía Isabel's hands."

The solitary black figure in the midst of the summer-white children made a striking composition.

"Damn!" Elena said.

"Is there something wrong?" I asked.

"Nothing," she snapped. "Just a run in my stocking." But it wasn't that which troubled her. She knew she had expressed the wrong sentiments when she had talked about Ireland. To people like the marquesa and Don Paulo, land was sacred, something to be guarded and cared for. Like children.

We watched them walking across the lawn. Young and beautiful they all were, but Juan and small Tomás seemed somehow set apart, as if something burned in them which the others had missed. I turned and caught the gaze of Richard. He stared at me for a

266

moment, and then looked back at Tomás. He must often, through that summer, have stared at the typically Blodmore face, have counted the weeks between that April in London and Tomás's birth. He was wondering. And I promised myself again, as I had once vowed to Luis, that he would never know.

ALMOST IMPERCEPTIBLY, after Juan left for school in England, Don Paulo and I grew closer together. Perhaps our closeness grew because not only the vineyards but the bodega itself had become one of the strong influences of my life. Almost daily now I went to fetch Luis home for our late lunch, and almost daily I found time for a walk through the bodega, where the dim light, the smell of the dampness, and the smell of the wine had a strangely calming effect on me.

Often I encountered Don Paulo. Because he knew my interest, sometimes he would call for the *venencia*, and the old expertise of hand and eye and nose would be displayed. Whereas before I had known only the growing and tending of the vines, now from Don Paulo I began to learn of the wine itself. Don Paulo was one of a number of men at the bodega with the title *catador*—taster. These were the men who classified the wine for its place in the solera. After examining the young wine for appearance, bouquet, and— sometimes—taste, they would mark the casks with chalk. One oblique stroke, /—*una raya*—meant the wine had a clean nose and the required body; two strokes, //—*dos rayas*—was a wine not altogether clean on the nose, or with some minor defect; three strokes, ///—*tres rayas*—was a wine that was not clean, or slightly acid, or very thin, and so was marked for distillation. Later came the classification for type— the finos and the olorosos—and eventually the different types of sherries which fell within these two broad types. But in the end it was the feel for the wine, the recognition of its taste, colour, and bouquet, which was vital for the continuance of its quality.

After one such session Don Paulo and I sat at the little table in the *sala de degustación*. I said, "Do you remember the talk we had the first day—about the members of the family all contributing, each his own character, as the different wines do to the solera?"

"I remember."

"Well, I've noticed that sometimes a certain wine will develop qualities that are not expected—sometimes strength and body, sometimes lightness—and you blend these to produce the wine you need. But a family can't work quite that way, can it?" I shook my head, feeling for words. "We cannot say, 'Take a little of Carlos and add the sympathetic nature of Martín.' Nor can I blend Francisco's shyness with Juan's confidence. But if a family stands together, it can still represent the strength of the solera system."

Don Paulo sipped his wine thoughtfully. "I had little hope for you when I first knew you. I marked you a *tres rayas*. At times, to this day, you have a taste on the tongue which I find acidic. And yet sometimes you seem to come through as a *palma*." I knew that this was the classification given to finos of the highest quality. I bowed my head a little. I had never expected to hear such words from Don Paulo. "Think of the wine, Doña Carlota, whenever you make decisions that will affect our family. What you add, what you take away, will determine how the wine will grow."

WHEN JUAN RETURNED from school that summer he went daily to the bodega where Don Paulo was sampling the wine. The old man's knowledge could not be imparted in a few weeks, but I saw hope in his eyes each time they held a glass up to the light.

The heat gripped the land, and the boys, with Edwin Fletcher, went to visit the marquesa in Galicia. At harvest time I heard the first rumour, and it sent me at once to Don Paulo. I found him at one of the bodegas, the frantic activity of the harvest all about him. "There is talk of typhoid at Arcos," I said.

"Probably just a few people with bad stomachs." But his face grew pinched. "In any case, they have their own wells in the marquesa's castle. They need have no contact with the rest of the town."

"It is carried on food, remember."

"I will inquire."

The story of typhoid at Arcos was confirmed. Luis was in a panic about Luisa, should the fever spread to Jerez. "We could send her north—to Galicia. You can go with her, Carlota."

"But the boys are about to come back here. They leave for school in a week." This time all three would go.

Luis thought for a while. "We will get passages for you and Luisa, too. You will stay in England until the danger has passed."

"That surely is a little extreme, Luis."

He wiped the sweat from his forehead with his handkerchief.

"If I should lose Luisa through negligence, it would kill me also. I have to send her away, Carlota. You must understand that."

I nodded. "Yes, I understand. And I will go. I will have everything ready."

A DAY LATER we were all booked on a sherry ship which would leave Cádiz at the end of the week. I had waited for hours for a telephone connection to Galicia. The marquesa had offered no resistance to the new plans. "Sensible," she had said. The boys and Edwin Fletcher would start the long train journey south from Galicia the next day. And then she asked cautiously, "And what do you hear of the situation at Arcos?"

"Don Paulo said he would see to it." We were careful what we said on the telephone, with the operators no doubt listening all along the line.

"Only a few more days and Luisa will be out of here." Luis sighed. "In the meantime, Nanny will prepare her food on the alcohol stove in the nursery. Thank God there are no reports of anyone being ill here, but I have asked the doctors to let me know at once if there should be any signs of it."

That afternoon I had a telephone message from María Luisa. "Can you come over here, Carlota? Something rather strange . . . no, I'll tell you when you come."

In the heat of the afternoon I went to the Plaza de Asturias. A quiet lay on the old courtyard with its broken fountain. María Luisa greeted me quickly, and kept me away from my mother's room, where she was resting. "I didn't want to disturb you, but a very strange thing has happened."

"What is it?"

She sighed. "Rather one should ask, 'Who is it?' Some workers found a woman walking on the road some miles outside the town. She would say nothing to them except 'Plaza de Asturias', and one of them heard her say 'Blodmore'. So they brought her here. They wouldn't have taken such trouble about an odd woman wandering on the road, I'm sure, but, you see, she is very well dressed—or was. Her clothes are now in a terrible state, but it's plain to see she's no peasant."

She led me upstairs to a room that was seldom used. We entered quietly, and María Luisa gently pushed back one of the shutters. Light streamed in. Sitting in the basket chair was

269

Mariana, with her straggling white hair tied in blue bows, wearing a dusty white dress made in the style of many years ago. In her arms she cradled a wax doll. She looked at me blankly with those violet eyes, and her cracked, parched lips moved.

I had to bend to hear the whisper. Only one word. "Blodmore." So close to her, I could see she burned with fever, and yet her teeth chattered.

I straightened and looked at María Luisa. "I know who she is. And she has come from Arcos. There is typhoid in Arcos."

BECAUSE she was who she was, we could not send her to the hospital or to be nursed by the nuns. We sent for Dr. Ramírez, who confirmed that it was typhoid. "I had better send a nurse."

I was afraid of what she might say in her delirium, and so I refused. "María Luisa and I will take care of her."

"But you are going to England."

"I can't return home now. I've been in contact with her. I might carry the infection to the household—to Luisa."

"Typhoid is rarely carried directly. Go and bathe. Have them send clean clothes from the house. Burn the ones you have on."

"I dare not," I said. "I could never forgive myself if Luisa should become ill."

He shrugged. "You are taking unnecessary risks staying here. And for a stranger! Someone you don't know. . . ." He began packing his bag. He knew a lot of our secrets, this man, and he had kept them all. He would ask no more about the identity of the unknown lady.

I had to play out the same charade with María Luisa, but she was more blunt. "You said you know who she is, but you choose not to name her." She looked at me closely. "After all these years you can't trust me, querida?"

"I gave a promise long ago. I must keep it. I know she is from Arcos. I can't tell you any more. Forgive me, María Luisa."

She shook her head. "Strange . . . strange." Then she shrugged and said, "Now, let us get to work."

After María Luisa had gone to start her preparations, I stood looking down for a while at the pathetic figure in the bed. She had been my grandfather's wife, had borne him a son. Even in her delirium she clutched the doll.

Then I went downstairs and wrote a note to Don Paulo.

HE CAME AT ONCE, his face a mask of fear and worry. "We have searched for her night and day. There is typhoid at the castle, and all three of her personal attendants are ill. Why did she come *here?* Has she forgotten her father?"

He gazed down at the figure of his daughter in the bed, but she didn't see him. Restlessly she turned from side to side on the pillow, and I wrung out a cloth and wiped the perspiration from her face and neck.

"I think the fever has made her remember the time when she was ill and was kept from my grandfather. She has remembered his name, and the name of his house here. The doll she brought with her was his child. I am sorry, Don Paulo, but I don't think the years between exist for her."

He went and stood by the window, staring down into the dusty patio. "I was mistaken," he said finally. "They had so little time together I thought it could all be wiped out. But it has endured to this day. I should not have interfered with what happened. *You* came here as a direct result of that year when Blodmore was denied his wife. And then you and Carlos . . ."

I accompanied him to the big doors that opened on the plaza. "You have been exposed to the infection," he said. "You cannot return to your home now."

"Not until the incubation period is over," I said. "Not until she is better."

"Or dead," he said. He walked across the plaza, a bent figure in his white summer suit and a wide-brimmed panama hat.

DR. RAMÍREZ injected us with the precious anti-typhoid vaccine. "Your children have gone," he said. "Don Luis didn't give them an hour in the town. Their ship leaves Cádiz this evening."

It was only when the children were safely away that Luis himself came to the Plaza de Asturias. I made him stay outside and talked to him through the iron grille on the window of one of the rooms that looked out into the plaza.

"Carlota, this is madness! Why do you stay to look after this . . . this woman?" Don Paulo had been to see him to explain. "You could get it. You could . . . you could die, Carlota." He was pained and frightened and anxious.

"I stayed because of the children. Surely Dr. Ramírez has explained that to you! Now I must wait until the incubation period is

271

over. She will be better soon. Then we will go to join the childre
in England. Together . . . as soon as the harvest is over." I was try
ing to tell Luis that I did not wish to meet Richard Blodmore alone
I was saying that I needed his help, and he looked at me wit
grateful eyes.

"Yes, querida, that is what we will do. We will make a holida
of it. Take Tomás and Luisa about—show them everything. To
gether." He saluted me briefly through the grille, blowing a kis
from his fingertips. "How absurd this all is. Anyone would thin
I was a young man courting his sweetheart." He was laughing
"I will come each day, querida. I will bring flowers. Too bad I n
longer play the guitar . . . what a suitor!"

The next morning I sent for the priest from Santa María de l
Asunción across the plaza. We knelt as Mariana was anointe
and received the Sacrament.

NO ONE COULD SAY afterwards quite how it had started or why
The Plaza de Asturias was bounded by a district where some o
the poor of Jerez lived in crumbling buildings. There was neve
enough work except at harvest time, and then, they said, th
wages were too low. At night the cantinas sounded to the rumbl
of discontent. There was much talk of the landowners, of which i
was said the Church was the greatest. It may have started with
piece of rhetoric over a glass of wine. It ended, and that was all w
knew, with a march whose target was the church across the plaz
from my mother's house.

From the back rooms of the house we heard the low murmur
that frightening sound of a mob. Andy appeared at once to repor
to us. "People are throwing stones at the church, Miss Charlie
They'd like to burn it."

"Dear God," María Luisa said. "Has it come *here*?" Fresh i
our minds were the stories of convent burnings all over Spain b
a people who thought the Church oppressive.

"The doors are closed, Andy? And the shutters?"

He nodded. "Yes, Miss Charlie. But just say your prayers tha
they don't turn around and charge this way. Those old doors woul
give if a fly pushed them, and so would the shutters."

"Andy, you can get out through the gate at the back of th
stables. Take everyone—my mother, Manuela, the children, Sera
fina, Paco. Make them all go to Los Cisnes. Don't wait to pack

If you go one at a time, you'll mix with the crowd. They won't notice."

"And leave you here, Miss Charlie? I'll not do that!" Then he shrugged as he read the expression on my face. "I can see you won't leave *her*—" he jerked his head in the direction of the room where the sick woman lay. "Well, I'll get everyone else off and wedge a few braces against the front doors."

María Luisa said, "If they start pushing their way in here, just shout one word, *tifoidea*—typhoid! That will clear them quicker than cannons."

I went to one of the rooms that overlooked the square and opened one shutter a little. A few hundred people, some with torchlights burning, had gathered in the plaza. I understood Andy's worry when I realized that in size the façade of our house almost equalled that of the church. If the mob turned away from the sacrilege of burning the church, the house was the next natural target. I looked at those torches and fear gripped me.

It was over quite soon. The Civil Guard had been called. They came in lorries and on horseback. A few shots were fired. Some people fell; others fled down the side streets that led to the *barrio*. There were shouts, orders, screams. The flaring torchlights were suddenly gone. I saw four dark, crumpled shapes lying there below me, shapes indistinguishable as men or women in the dim light. The Civil Guard made no attempt to pursue the people who ran away. They would stay just long enough to prevent their reassembling, to give a show of guarding the church.

I had glimpsed hate and need, had heard the cry of anger. I shivered in the warm night air, closed the shutter, and fumbled my way back through the dark corridors of the house.

We had been expecting the commander of the guard to come to the house, so I told Andy to open up when we heard the bell clanging in the courtyard. But when he slowly opened the big door it was not just the commander who stood there. Four of his men were grouped behind him, and between them they bore the limp form of a man.

The commander recognized me as I moved out into the light. "Doña Carlota . . . a terrible misfortune . . ."

They shuffled forward. "He must have been caught here when the disturbance began. One of the anarchists, the Antichrists, must have recognized him. They are like that—animals!"

The commander was admitting nothing. It could as easily have been a blow from one of his own men's truncheons as from one of the crowd's. Whichever it was, it had been a blow of tremendous power. Luis's skull had cracked under it, and he must have died very quickly.

The men moved into the courtyard and laid him on the stone bench surrounding the fountain. They straightened his dusty clothes. Then one of them awkwardly proffered a mangled bunch of flowers. "I found these by his side. My sympathy, señora. He was a much-respected gentleman."

I took the bruised blossoms Luis had come to the Plaza de Asturias to give me.

I stayed beside him and held his cold hand in mine, stunned, unbelieving. When María Luisa tried to take away the flowers I held, I resisted her. "Leave them. They were his last gift."

Later, I sat in the room where he lay. The false dawn had come, that silent time before even the first cock of the *barrio* begins to crow, when María Luisa came to tell me that the lady, the stranger, had died.

CHAPTER FOURTEEN

I went through all the motions of mourning, but there was a great hollow at the centre of my life. Almost the worst hurt was realizing that I had probably not managed to make Luis understand how important he had been to me. I must have loved him, I said to myself. I wonder if he ever knew.

I went to the bodega often. I found there some of the peace that had deserted me with Luis's death. Very often Don Paulo fell into step with me. In his office we would drink a copita together, talk about the children or the prospects for the harvest.

The terms of Luis's will had been precise. One third of his estate went to me, one third to Tomás, and one third to Luisa. This gave me voting rights at board meetings of the sherry company of Fernández, Thompson. I would exercise their rights also for Tomás and Luisa until they came of age. My mother had signed a proxy which also gave me voting control of my grandfather's shares. Don Paulo had nodded over all this speculatively. "You have become a small power among us, Doña Carlota. Be very careful how you use it."

I knew that Juan had been shaken by his exclusion from Luis's will. He and his brothers, Martín and Francisco, must now look to Don Paulo and the marquesa if they were to have more than an ordinary position at the bodega. Giving Tomás so much, singling him out from his half-brothers, was Luis's way, after his death, of proclaiming to the world that Tomás was his son. No one could doubt it now. Luisa's place, of course, was secure.

Luisa was too young to know or care about any of this. Her whole world had turned upside down with her father's death. She had returned from England and shrieked in anguish at the reality of finding him gone. Nothing we could do for her seemed to comfort her for his absence. I began to take her with me to the bodega. She would solemnly sip a tiny copita with Don Paulo, looking alarmingly like one of those beautiful wax dolls in the castle at Arcos. She added something to the life of Don Paulo. He had granddaughters—five of them—the daughters of Ignacio and Pedro. But I thought they seemed dull little girls beside Luisa. Now she began to charm Don Paulo, as she had charmed Luis. A smile on her grave little face brought a look of delight to his face which I had never seen before.

Luisa needed the male influence in her life. We were now a household of women. After the scene I had witnessed from the window in the Plaza de Asturias, I felt it no longer safe to leave my mother there. So she and María Luisa, and Andy and his family, moved to Los Cisnes to be with me.

All three older boys were now at school in England, and visited Clonmara each Easter. They enjoyed Ireland and had made friends with the Blodmore boys, Edward and Paul. Their bond was the love of horses, and they even spent a Christmas there, to get a taste of Irish hunting. These visits were encouraged by the marquesa.

But after Luis's death Juan became more interested in spending his holidays in Jerez. Perhaps he saw his position threatened by Tomás and by the sons of Ignacio and Pedro. So that summer of 1927 Juan began working regular hours at the bodega, doing whatever tasks were required of him and learning what he could pick up along the way. In some mysterious fashion he always seemed to know the days when Don Paulo and I met in the bodega and would contrive to join us. He listened respectfully to whatever Don Paulo had to say and waited hopefully for the invitation to join us for a copita.

It was by now quite proper for me to appear in the *sala de degustación*, among the customers and visitors to the bodega. It seemed to me that Juan began to eye any man who came near our table with hostility, especially if he was unmarried.

"When you marry again, you must choose very carefully," he said to me.

"You expect me to marry again?"

"Well, of course. You're still pretty. You're well off. You could do the family a lot of good by the right marriage."

I ached to slap that handsome, worldly-wise face. "Mind your own business, Juan."

A little coolness grew up between us after that. I was glad when it was time for him to go back to school in England.

I ATTENDED the board meetings at the bodega, tending to follow Don Paulo's lead in everything, but determined that I must, in time, gain some independent opinions, against the day when he would not be there and I would have to face Ignacio and Pedro and whoever else might then be on the board. The bodega was a complex and sometimes precarious business. Labour costs were increasing continually, and sales abroad had to keep pace. We carried the burden of the bad seasons and scrambled to make up in the good ones. I began to realize that most of the rich sherry shippers had other interests as well. And so I understood more fully Luis's concern with the breeding of his bulls, the careful experimentation with his cattle, the growing of sugar beets, the tending of his olive groves, the stocks in other businesses.

Edwin Fletcher now lived in a small house he had built near Los Cisnes, and I asked him to help me with the accounts of the bodega. I also opened the books of the other concerns to him.

When Juan returned at Christmas he resented this. "You might have waited for me, Mother. I have only another half year at school; then I shall be here all the time to help."

"I thought you were going to Cambridge. You know Luis wished that."

"That was when he was alive. You need a *man* here now."

He rode out with me when we went to inspect the bulls and the cattle, often giving advice where it wasn't wanted. But I had to admit that he had an eye for the bulls and rode among them fearlessly. He had developed as a splendid horseman and had

277

been admitted to the company of the *garrochistas*, those who tested young bulls from horseback to mark their qualities of courage.

By now Balthasar was very old; he moved stiffly. And yet when he heard my mother's voice call him, he would come at a trot across the paddock, his head lifted in eagerness, with a whinny of affection to greet her. Half Moon was gone, but their progeny were sold all over Spain, in England—even in Ireland.

That winter Don Paulo was confined to bed with a chill that held on stubbornly. He did not appear at the bodega for many weeks. I went frequently to visit him. He was thinner and rather feeble, but his head came up like a snapping turtle's when anyone suggested he take his time about coming back to the bodega.

The marquesa came from Sanlúcar to stay with him during his illness. This was so contrary to her custom that I wondered if he were not sicker than anyone else knew. But one day when the first warm sun of April was touching the bodega's walls he appeared there again, only slightly slower in his walk. At Easter, Juan returned home unexpectedly, and Don Paulo took him for several sessions alone in the *cuarto de muestras*. Here the samples of must were brought at vintage time so that the bodega could decide on the quality and make offers to the vineyard owners. When they joined me later in the *sala de degustación* Juan's eyes were alive with excitement and pleasure.

"Grandfather says that if the harvest comes early in September and I've not already left for England, I can try to grade the samples of must myself."

"You *are* going back to England in September, then, to Cambridge?" I wanted to be sure that was what he meant.

He lowered those green Blodmore eyes, looking unnaturally diffident. "Grandfather has persuaded me that it is the best thing to do. I'm doing it for him."

Politician, I thought—but glancing over at Don Paulo and seeing his dark eyes as sceptical as ever, I knew that Juan had a long way to go before he could match his grandfather in this game.

"Well, let's drink to it, then," the old man said. The servant came forward and poured the fino. We all held our glasses to the light, as we had grown used to doing, the colour and purity of the wine as much a pleasure as its taste. "*La penúltima*," Don Paulo said. In Jerez we never thought of drinking our last glass of

278

sherry, it was always the last but one—and we called it *la penúltima*. It was a going-away salute to Juan.

We sipped and tasted the wine against our tongues. It was a good thing to sit here in the spring sun in peace with the old man and the young man, and feel that I was the instrument of life that bound them.

"Grandfather!"

I looked at Don Paulo. For an instant he had seemed to smile, but Juan's instinct was quicker than mine. He sprang to his feet and leaned over the old man. The thin lips twisted now, upward, as if he held them set against the pain. Then he whispered, "*La penúltima. . . .*"

He died there in that sturdy oak chair only moments later. He had placed his glass carefully upon the table, and the wine was not even spilled.

The shock of his death was carried on to the will. He had left one third of his estate to the marquesa, one third was divided between his sons, Ignacio and Pedro, and Carlos's sons, Juan, Martín, and Francisco, and one third was left to me. The one portion of his estate which was singled out from that total was the vineyard house, which he also bequeathed to me.

A soft gasp went around the room when this was read out. I felt all eyes turned on me, most with hostility, some with outright anger. Only the marquesa remained unmoved. It was probable she had already known.

We made the barest formality of drinking a token copita together, for the appearance of family solidarity. I said goodbye to the marquesa. "Will you be going now to Sanlúcar?"

"I do not think I shall go back now," she said. "It is too far to come in here to Jerez every day. I shall be attending the bodega regularly. Don Paulo always expected people to take their responsibilities seriously." Her words had carried through the room. The knowledge that she would involve herself in the affairs of the bodega made everyone uneasy.

Juan kept his outrage to himself until we were alone. "How *could* Grandfather do that? I am the eldest grandchild. He could have trusted me. That third should have been divided between me and Martín and Francisco, with the biggest share going to me."

He didn't seem to care how he was revealing himself. "He meant you to wait, Juan."

"Wait until that old woman dies? Wait until Granny dies. Wait until *you* die. I have only *women* in my world, and now I have to dance attendance on all of them!"

I recoiled from him. "Perhaps," I said, "your grandfather intended patience to temper greed."

He did not rise to the insult. I think he hardly heard it.

WORLD EVENTS were shaping our lives, events which were totally out of our hands. In 1929, the year of the Wall Street stock-market collapse, our exports of sherry were good, but the marquesa's factories in Barcelona were hit with falling orders, and many workers lost their jobs. There were smaller dividends, not only from the bodega, but from the other shares Luis had left me. "Those with land need fear nothing," the marquesa said. "The land has always held its value."

That was also the year that the universities in Spain were closed because of student agitation, and so Juan agreed to stay on another year at Cambridge. Martín joined him there. He had never been as good a student as Juan, since nothing interested him as much as his guitar.

The bodega, on the insistence of the marquesa and myself, bought more *albariza* land that year, and the next January we started planting big new vineyards, despite the objections of Ignacio and Pedro. Yet the future seemed uncertain when Spain's dictator, Primo de Rivera, resigned. His assembly was dissolved and local government restored. All over Spain there were demands for a republic, and when the censorship of the press was removed I read denunciations of the landowners and the wealthy and realized, with a sense of shock, that they were talking about me and my family, among the rest.

"Fools!" The marquesa flung the newspaper across the desk at the bodega. "Don't they know they're going to cut their own throats?" Her holdings in Barcelona were threatened by the demand for Catalan autonomy, and in the north her estates and mines seemed threatened by the Basque separatist agitation.

She and I pushed through the decision to start our own cooperage works to make the oak butts for the sherry, and to increase our distillation of brandy. Ignacio shuddered. "You will bankrupt us yet." But when the marquesa and I voted together, we held the balance of power.

In December came news of the mutiny of the garrison at Jaca. The mutiny was suppressed with difficulty, and we were depressed, anxious, confused. The marquesa reacted characteristically by declaring that all the family should come to Sanlúcar to spend Christmas, and have some shooting at Doñana.

We gathered reluctantly, I thought. Only the authority of the marquesa now held us together. Ignacio was tense, as he always was in his dealings with her; Pedro had not forgiven me for taking such a large part of Don Paulo's estate. Our children all mixed together, much of an age, the oldest of them young men and women now, looking at each other with speculative eyes. The only carefree ones were Tomás and Luisa, the youngest. A summons from the marquesa had also gone to the Blodmores, and Elena and Richard appeared with their sons.

The young people seemed to perform an elaborate *paseo* before us, and the marquesa watched them, her expression revealing nothing of her thoughts. She was over seventy now and arthritic, but the rings blazed on her age-spotted hands, as always, and with her gold-topped stick she appeared more formidable than ever. Each evening she would summon one or another of the young ones to her side, and they would endure a sort of trial by questioning. "Say what you like," the marquesa once muttered to me, "Luisa has the most *style* of any of them. She knows who she is. She respects authority, but she will have her way."

Luisa no longer cried for her father, but she often talked of him. The early promise of beauty was every year more fulfilled; she had a lovely, grave, delicate face which would suddenly break into a radiant smile; she had the complexion which had once been my mother's but was made more translucent by contrast with her dark eyes.

"If the monarchy isn't stupid enough to run itself out of the country, she could be a wife for a prince," the marquesa declared. I dreaded the thought of the marquesa manipulating Tomás's and Luisa's lives.

Tomás, though, hardly needed to be taught how to assert his independence. He was almost eleven years old, but unlike Martín and Francisco, he refused to follow where Juan led. I often noticed the marquesa's eyes upon him broodingly. "That is how Blodmore would have looked at his age," she would say, as her stick beat an agitated little rap on the floor.

I remembered the stories at Clonmara of the long-ago summer of the Spanish woman, her style which had dazzled everyone, her wilful pride which had caused her to lead the man she loved on a chase half across Europe. I wondered if the old memories still hurt. When she called Tomás to her side she was particularly sharp with him, testing his humour and his good sense. But, like Luisa, he was not in awe of her.

Again Richard Blodmore's presence at Sanlúcar was painful to me. He still had the power to stir me. I tried to avoid him without being obvious, but one morning before breakfast he found me walking on the terrace above the river.

"Why are you out in the cold? Have you had coffee?"

"No, I thought I'd get some air. I . . . I didn't sleep well."

He was blunt. "You slept well with me—once."

I turned on him in a kind of fury of frustration and love. "Richard—don't! It's past. We can do nothing about it. Why can I never have peace from you?"

"While we're apart there'll be no peace, Charlie. Everywhere I look at Clonmara I see you. I wish I had peace. But I just keep on. I love you. It's a terrible wanting. I still wait for the day you send me a message to come to you."

"That won't ever come, Richard. Each year there is more I must do for my children. By the time they no longer need me, you and I will have outgrown the wanting. It will be a memory."

"You deceive yourself about them needing you. Children grow up. Outgrow *you* . . . leave you behind."

"But now the young ones need me."

"And one of them is *my* son, Charlie. Did you suppose I didn't know that?"

I denied it without hesitation. I had given my promise to Luis. Not even for Richard would I break it. "Tomás is Luis's son."

"I'll never believe that, Charlie. Never."

"Believe what you like!"

I turned from him and walked swiftly along the terrace. As I fumbled with the handle of the door he called after me, "I'll wait, Charlie. I'll wait till hell freezes over."

I DIDN'T GO TO DOÑANA to hunt that day. "I'm tired," I said to Juan. "Women get tired now and again and, unlike men, we're privileged to say so."

Elena was sitting alone by the fire in the great salon when I entered. She nodded in a detached fashion as I came nearer. "I'll be glad when I'm out of here," she said unexpectedly. Then she laughed. "Oh, don't look so shocked. For a Blodmore, you're so deadly *earnest!* Sometimes I can hardly believe it when I hear you going on about your vineyards and your bodega. It bores me to death—this family pretending to be so united, when we're all waiting for the old one to die to see how it gets carved up."

I sat down opposite her. "Has it occurred to you that perhaps I *like* the vineyards—*like* the bodega?"

She shrugged. "Oh, don't let's get too intense about this. Sometimes you're more Spanish than the Spanish. The real matriarch. Your only care is your children. That's what you'd like everyone to think. But you're still in love with Richard, aren't you?"

"I prefer not to discuss Richard."

"You *prefer!* Well, talk about it or not, as you like. If you could just be honest. It's Richard you want, but you also want everything that's here and anything the marquesa cares to give your children. So you must wait for one before you can take the other." She leaned forward. "Well, let me tell you something. You will never have Richard. I will stay married to him as long as I live. And as for the marquesa . . . in the end, blood is thicker than water. She always meant to have Clonmara, and she liked to dominate the Blodmores. Through me she can do both. Oh, you'll have the bodega, but who cares about that? I will have the title of Pontevedra and the estates, and Edward will have it after me. The rest . . . all the rest of it will be mine. If you're honest, you have to admit it—"

"What must Carlota admit?" The door at the far end of the long salon had opened soundlessly. The marquesa stood there, leaning heavily on her cane.

Elena turned smoothly, apparently not in the least perturbed, though neither of us knew how long the marquesa had been there or how keen her hearing was.

"Bullfighting, Tía Isabel. Carlota and I were talking about the bulls she sells for the corrida, and still she will not admit she hates bullfighting."

IN MANY WAYS that was the last ingathering of the family. We would be together at other times, but never again would we enjoy the sense that our little world was tight and immutable. Never again did we have the old certainty that this generation and the next would inherit the Spain of their fathers. All that was changed.

The new year, 1931, brought the king's announcement of the restoration of the constitution, and in the April elections there was an overwhelming victory for the Republicans. King Alfonso left Spain, and in November he was declared guilty of high treason and forbidden to return.

We awoke one morning in December to read that we were a democracy. Everyone would vote to determine the make-up of the single-chamber parliament, the Cortes, which would sit for four years. The Church was no longer to run the schools, and its property was to be nationalized. We were told that the government would have the power to take over private property and to nationalize large estates.

The marquesa, of course, had more to lose than any of us. How many of Barcelona's factories did she own, or partly own? And what of the estates in Galicia? Would they be taken away from her? How much of the output of her mines in Asturias would she be allowed to keep?

Juan had completed his studies at Cambridge, and had put in a year in the London office of Fernández, Thompson. He had now taken his place at the bodega, and he exercised his right to vote the shares which Don Paulo had left him.

Martín, with the backing of the marquesa, had gone to Paris, enrolled at the Sorbonne, and found himself a teacher of the guitar. He seemed to have emerged from Juan's shadow and had become his own man. Francisco had followed Juan to Cambridge and then into the London office.

It was Tomás who gave the heartache, and perhaps the most promise. In September he had been sent off to school in England. He had returned eagerly for the Christmas holidays and had persuaded the marquesa to open up Sanlúcar again so that he could go each day to Doñana. But he didn't go to hunt; he stayed alone with a guide, his binoculars on every living thing that moved, bird and beast. He had saved his money and bought himself a camera and had taught himself how to develop film. A record of Doñana began to emerge.

But Tomás also knew his way about the bodega; when there, he left off his formal manners and joined the workers at whatever they were doing.

"You should keep him more in check, Mother," Juan said. "I see him eating with the workers, and sometimes talking like a peasant. It makes things more difficult for the rest of us."

"Times are changing, Juan. Perhaps Tomás is wise to learn how a peasant thinks."

But Juan shook his head, refusing to believe that Republican ideals could triumph. "It would be the ruin of Spain," he said simply. "We cannot let that happen."

The marquesa had now moved permanently to Las Fuentes in Jerez. Less and less did she travel to Sanlúcar, though a retinue of servants was kept there. That summer, for the first time since I had been in Spain, she made no plans to travel to the estates in Galicia. I wondered if even such formidable courage as hers might not be daunted by the Republican sentiments which would await her there.

But she still enjoyed the privileges of her position. She had taken to visiting the bodega regularly, where Don Paulo's empty office awaited her. She would walk the aisles with me at her side. "I wonder, can it survive?" she asked once. "The anarchists would blow it all up, and then say the aristocracy was depriving them of their wine!"

IT WAS THE SPRING OF 1932, just when the vines were putting out their new shoots, that we had the message from Tomás's school that he was missing. The school had also telephoned Clonmara. Richard, in response, was on the first boat to England. He called me the next day. "Charlie, I'm trying everything. The London office . . . the routes to Ireland. Tomás doesn't know England that well."

"He's tough, Richard. He knows the land very well. He could last a long time on a little money."

It was Edwin Fletcher who said, "Have them try the sherry shippers in Bristol. Most of them go directly to Cádiz."

I sat up all night trying to contact Richard by telephone. At about four o'clock in the morning I reached him. "Try Bristol," I cried into the phone. "Try every sherry firm that ships into Bristol. Please, Richard, *find* him!"

I thought he answered, "I'll find my son," but the words were blurred, and then the line went dead. I was left weeping.

Richard went to Bristol, and then to London, and none of the sherry shippers knew anything about Tomás. Ten days later, when we were sitting down to a supper none of us could eat, Tomás arrived at Los Cisnes. He had stowed away on a ship bound for Cádiz with a load of machine parts.

He was lean, dirty, and cheerful. "I'm sorry, Mama. I just couldn't stick it. England isn't for me."

The marquesa devised a punishment for him, which turned out to be no punishment at all. "I have asked permission for him to spend the summer at Doñana, living with one of the guides. Let him work the way they do, in the heat there, and eat what they eat. Afterwards we will see about school. There are some rather strict ones, they tell me, in Seville."

That summer hardened and toughened Tomás as nothing else could have. He learned what it was like to be a Spanish peasant, and that was more of an education than his brothers had had.

"You may finally have succeeded in making a Republican of him," María Luisa said.

The idea of school in Seville was abandoned in August, when General Sanjurjo seized Seville for the rightist movement. So Edwin Fletcher returned to Los Cisnes. He looked at the lean, sunburned youth, the powerful shoulders, the hardened hands. "Well, you've become a man while my back was turned, Tomás."

A wide grin split Tomás's face as he grasped Edwin's hand in a grip that made Edwin flinch slightly. "You'll take me back, then, Mr. Fletcher. And you'll be teaching Luisa, too, won't you? She'll be glad to get rid of her English governess."

THE POLITICAL UPHEAVALS in Spain in the next years brought Elena Blodmore to Jerez a number of times, her object always that of persuading the marquesa to leave the country and go to Clonmara. The marquesa was contemptuous of her niece's suggestions. "I am not the sort to go into exile just because a few anarchists say they will take away my property."

Elena was forced to withdraw. "Well, if you're murdered in your bed . . ."

María Luisa smiled when I reported one such interview to her. "She wants the old woman at Clonmara because there she'll be completely under her influence. Of course, when Elena tries next time, she may succeed. The marquesa is of the aristocracy, and that can be dangerous in these days."

286

The marquesa learned that fact on the night a mob burned Las Fuentes. The Civil Guard cleared a path through the riotous crowd for the fire-fighting engines, but the roof of the house was already well ablaze, and in the morning only the blackened walls were left. The marquesa had been led away through the fields at the back of the house when the first of the mob appeared. She came to Los Cisnes reluctantly, I thought. It galled her to be driven out, and perhaps even more it galled her to accept my hospitality.

She was weary, dusty, but almost unshaken as she received a report later from the head of the Civil Guard. María Luisa offered coffee, and the marquesa poured with a steady hand.

"The furniture, the pictures, the tapestries—all gone. Those barbarians! And my man Alvaro dead. He was a good man. He did his duty. And for that he gets death."

The man listening to her nodded gravely. "We will find his killers. But the times are troubled, Marquesa."

"What times have not been troubled? We must resist."

So finally she came under my roof, and against all expectations, there she remained. She settled down among us, but she was not used to a household of which she was not automatically the head. She had brought her own servants with her, and there were clashes with ours.

The marquesa read the newspapers thoroughly each day and enjoyed debating their contents with Juan and Edwin Fletcher at lunch. Tomás didn't usually join the arguments. He grew grave and silent in those years in which we watched a series of coalition ministries come and go, all more or less helpless and unpopular. He worked hard at the lessons Edwin Fletcher set him, and each day he joined in the target-shooting practice which the marquesa had established for her large staff of armed guards, hired to protect the house. My mother joined sometimes, happy that she could still shoot accurately. She was meticulous about returning the guns to the locked room where they were stored, whose keys were held by María Luisa.

Then one morning, as we walked to the target area, we found that Luis's peach trees, which he had grown in a beautifully espaliered fashion along the wall of the vegetable garden, had been decimated. The empty space on the wall had been daubed with huge black letters. *Muerte*—Death.

287

ALMOST THE WORST heartbreak of those troubled years was the day Martín reappeared at Los Cisnes in the uniform of an army subaltern. We had thought him still in Paris, and I had written chiding letters, complaining of his long silence.

"I've been in Morocco, Mother, doing my training."

"*You*, Martín! You are the last one I'd expect to go into the army. You were made for . . . for music, for study. . . ."

"I think if one would have the freedom for such things as music and books, one is going to have to fight for it. The army is the only organized force. I will not have the Communists telling me how my life is to go. I prefer to choose."

He spent his short leave in Jerez, and the night before he was to return I made a show of family solidarity by inviting Ignacio and Pedro and their wives and children to dinner at Los Cisnes. We drank toasts to Spain, and there were tears in the eyes of many of the women as we drank to Martín.

Afterwards, in the drawing room, when coffee and brandy were served, Martín brought out his guitar. It was as if he wanted to offer his own farewell salute to us. He sat on a chair, wearing his uniform, his foot on a stool. Luisa sat near him, her eyes never leaving him. What we heard then was what the years in between had made him. He played only Spanish music, ranging from the tunes of the troubadours to the music of the masters of our century. All the brilliant, exotic, grand, turbulent, troubled history of Spain was there in his fingers, and it held us silent, spellbound. When he finished there was no applause; we were still silent, awed. He rose and walked over to me, holding out the guitar. "Take care of it for me, Mother, until it's all over."

CHAPTER FIFTEEN

We had several more ministries in quick succession the next year, none of them achieving anything.

At this time I felt compelled to offer Nanny a chance to return to Ireland. She was now nearing eighty, but she looked at me with her old sharpness when I spoke of leaving.

"Well, I know I'm past my usefulness, Miss Charlie, but is that a good reason for packing me off?"

"But you're always talking of going back—back to Clonmara."

"Oh, Miss Charlie," she said, "I only talk about Clonmara to be humouring your poor mother. I'd be dead in a month if I went back. These old bones would miss the warmth."

By Christmas of 1935 Francisco had appeared in army uniform and was posted to the Canary Islands. A month later Juan joined the army and married Leonor, niece of a prominent general, whom he had courted for a year. At the wedding they were surrounded by the military. It was the final brand we had set upon us. No one could now doubt where this family stood.

As the wine circulated after the ceremony, I realized that María Luisa was absent, and so was Tomás. As soon as I decently could I went to look for María Luisa. I found her at last in the little room we used as a kind of household office. She lay full length on a sofa. Tomás was with her and he turned to me with relief. "I saw Tía María Luisa was swaying a bit at the ceremony. When I got her here, she fainted."

She struggled to rise, but I thrust her back against the pillows. "I'm calling Dr. Ramírez."

She waved a hand, which I suddenly saw had become clawlike in its thinness. "Oh, don't disturb him at a time like this. I've been to see him. He gave me a tonic. But he says I can't expect to be skipping around."

"Why didn't you tell me? I'm ashamed—I haven't noticed."

She gave a dry cackle. "It's charitable of you not to notice, Carlota. We old crows don't like people noticing such things. So just continue not to notice, and I'll continue to pretend I'm indispensable to you."

"You know you are." I fussed about her. "Here, drink a little brandy, will you? And promise me not to go near the kitchen or back among the guests. Tomás, you'll stay with her?"

"I'll stay, gladly. All those generals with big bellies make me a bit sick." I hadn't time then to dwell much on his remark.

María Luisa went on as before, taking her tonic, assuring me she was quite well. "Well enough for my time of life, querida." Her appetite was poor. I noticed that Tomás was often at her side, tempting her to eat. He was gentle with her, yet irritable with the rest of us. He sat silently through meals, not joining in any of the conversation. He listened to radio broadcasts about the political situation, read the newspapers avidly, yet said nothing. Each day he put in time at target practice.

But when any of Juan's fellow officers called—he was stationed at Cádiz—Tomás absented himself. "Jealous of their uniforms," the marquesa said, "because he's too young to get one himself. Just watch him, Carlota. He'll be the next to go."

LATER WE WERE to know the sequence of events, but at the time it was a secret known only to the officers who planned the rising.

It began in Melilla, in Morocco, when the army officers declared a state of war. There was violent fighting in the lower-class districts, but the workers were taken by surprise and they had few arms. The officers telephoned their fellow conspirators elsewhere in Morocco, and also General Franco, who was in Las Palmas in the Canaries, and in the early evening telegrams were sent to the garrisons on the mainland of Spain giving the simple and long awaited password, *Sin novedad*—As usual.

At a quarter past five on the morning of 18th July 1936, Franco issued his manifesto, and Spain was gripped in the mortal coils of civil war.

We knew that all over Spain, Republicans would fight. From Madrid, the woman known as La Pasionaria broadcast, demanding resistance to the insurgent army and their sympathizers. Later our watchman came to tell us that half the guards hired by the marquesa had deserted, with their weapons. A chill wind seemed to blow through the corridors of Los Cisnes that hot July night.

DESPITE THE CONFUSION, despite the tight controls which the army had placed on the province, Elena and Richard Blodmore somehow made their way to Jerez and to us at Los Cisnes.

"We have come," Elena said to the marquesa, "to take you out of the country."

The marquesa rapped her stick on the floor. "Never!"

"This is only the beginning," Richard argued. "Germany and Italy will go for the right. Russia, of course, will try to intervene for the left. This is going to be much longer and bigger than you may suppose at this moment."

The argument raged for days. Richard was explosive in his frustration. "Look at you here! A houseful of women! Do you expect me to go away and leave you?"

The marquesa laughed unpleasantly. "You could stay and defend us. Or do you side with the Communists, who choose to call themselves Republicans?"

290

"I side with no one. I just want to know you're all out of here safely." Finally Richard turned to me. "*You*, Charlie! Surely you must see the sense of leaving. You owe it to your family."

I couldn't meet his eyes. "Richard, I don't know!" Then I forced myself to look at him directly. "Shall I leave the bodega and the vineyards? Don Paulo and Luis trusted me to take care of them."

"I can answer only that if things go wrong here, there may be no bodega. There may be no vineyards. You may destroy yourself, your children, your mother, for the sake of possessions. Have you thought that you may be killed?"

My mother had by now completely lost track of the events of those years. She drank more, and we did not try to stop her. But a few of the things we spoke of got through to her baffled, confused mind. "Clonmara?" she questioned, after Elena had spoken to the marquesa of going there. "Are we going back to Clonmara? Oh, won't that be wonderful! I'll ride again, and walk by the sea and in my mother's rose garden—"

Elena had risen and advanced towards her. "I don't know where you're going, Lady Patricia, but it isn't to Clonmara. If Richard wishes to take you out of here, he must make arrangements for you. But they won't include Clonmara. Clonmara isn't yours any more." Elena stopped to place a cigarette in her holder and light it. "You should know, since it seems to obsess you, that there isn't any rose garden any more. I had it dug up and replaced by herbaceous borders."

My mother got to her feet, her lips quivering. "You dug up my mother's rose garden! It was famous. How could you have dug it up? Who gave you leave?"

"I didn't need permission, Lady Patricia. Clonmara is mine."

Richard looked at me, his face flushed with what seemed to be anger and shame. "Charlie, I didn't—"

Elena seemed perfectly aware of the anguish she had caused. "Richard was on business in London," she said. "It was a surprise for him when he came back." She laughed dryly. "It was such a surprise that he went into a sulk for weeks. I even had a row with Edward over it. He's become, I'm sorry to say, as much a stick-in-the-mud as Richard. He *likes* farming." She turned and looked at the marquesa. "When it is Edward's turn to inherit Pontevedra he'll be an excellent estate manager."

"I'm glad there are some who take their inheritance seriously," the marquesa snapped. "But don't put me in my grave too soon, Elena. Don't . . ." She fell silent and looked beyond her niece.

My mother had drawn close. She was carrying her wineglass, and her movements were slow but quite deliberate as she tossed its contents into Elena's face. "You touch nothing at Clonmara, do you hear? It never belonged to you. Never."

Elena took her handkerchief and wiped the wine from her face. "Lady Patricia, you are quite demented. As I've said before, you should be locked up." Then she turned and left the room.

My mother stood looking at us for a moment longer, her face twisted in her anguish. "I've disgraced us again, Charlie? But she didn't have any right to dig up my mother's rose garden. She can't have me locked up for saying that, can she?" I took her upstairs.

After a week we had argued ourselves into exhaustion. I refused to go, but I said Luisa must. Elena argued with the marquesa. She offered no sanctuary at Clonmara to us.

This lasted until the night when Tomás failed to appear for dinner. Even the marquesa was disturbed. "Doesn't he know it isn't safe to be roaming out at night? He's only a boy, but people shoot these days and ask who you are afterwards."

In the drawing room later, we sat almost silent over coffee. It was then María Luisa entered, agitation making her step swifter. "I found this in my room, Carlota. I don't know why he left it there. It's for you." I took the envelope and ripped it open.

Dear Mother,

Forgive me. I can't stay here, and I can't leave Spain. I intend to fight with the Republicans. I know it will take you a long time to understand why, but I hope you will. Please do not inform the Civil Guard. I have taken guns and ammunition, and if they come after me and find me, they will probably shoot me. I have friends to go to. I will be safe with them, and they need the arms. I love you. Kiss Luisa and Granny and María Luisa for me. Tell the marquesa I fight for Spain.

Tomás

Weak with fear, I handed the note to Richard. I said to María Luisa, "He left the note in your room because he had to get your keys to open the gun room."

We went and looked. Five guns were missing from the rack, the most modern, the easiest to supply with ammunition.

ALL THE NEXT DAY a new argument raged. "The authorities *must* be told," Elena insisted. "It's criminal. He is going to give guns to the Republicans."

"The Republicans are still the elected government of this country, Elena."

"The Republicans are Communist scum, and so is he."

The marquesa pounded the floor with her stick. "Be quiet! We do not need an informer. The boy is criminally mistaken, but we can do nothing about that now. We must give him time to reach his friends, whoever they are."

I could hardly bear to look at Richard's face. I thought that if he had been left to himself he might have wept in his agony. He said only one thing to me, alone, after he had read the note. "Shall I go to search for him?"

"Where would you search without rousing suspicion?"

He bent his head. "I should have taken better care of him. I should have known what was in his mind, and stopped him."

"I think his mind was made up years ago. I'm certain he knows what he's heading into. This is not a boy's bid for adventure. He knows that he will be fighting on the opposite side from his brothers. He knows that *that* is what civil war is. He is older than any of us knew."

We got through the day and into the night. Dinner was over; we were again seated in the drawing room; coffee had been served, and I had dismissed the servants. Luisa bade us good night. She lingered as she kissed my mother, stroking her cheek for a moment. "Don't be sad, Granny. He'll be back soon. I know he will."

My mother roused herself for a moment, smiling. "Yes, child . . . dear child. . . ."

When Luisa left us, Elena burst out, "How long is this going to go on? Do you realize you are putting us all in jeopardy by failing to inform the military that he is missing?"

"Elena, that is enough!" Richard said. "Leave Charlie in peace."

Elena turned on him. "Charlie! She's all you care about, she and her wretched, traitorous son. *I* don't want to be shut up in a Spanish prison because of Tomás. You know they'd lock us up with the Republican scum, don't you? This town is ruled by the military. It is your duty to go to them. At least then we would be protected. We would have disowned him."

I hadn't realized how great her fear was. I had been so frightened for Tomás that I had forgotten the danger to the rest of us. I looked now at the marquesa. She had not wavered throughout the day. Tomás must be given his chance to get away. Because she loved him, cared more for his safety than her own. There lay the difference between Elena and her. And the marquesa was not afraid. For the first time, along with my respect for her, I began to feel an unfamiliar stirring of love. Now, when it was almost too late, I perceived what a relationship with this formidable old woman might have been, might yet become. She had been cruel in the past, but she had protected those she cared about. Perhaps she was declaring in this action a love she had been unable to declare in any other way.

"We will not disown him," the marquesa answered Elena. "We will inform no one."

The long wait was broken by Andy. He came to the drawing room himself that night, something he had never done before. "Miss Charlie, there's news."

I sprang to my feet. "What news?"

He was looking around, now a little uncertain if he should have spoken. The marquesa thumped her stick. "What news?"

"It was brought to me. I . . . I won't say how. Tomás crossed the river at Sanlúcar. His friends took him through Doñana. Now he's at a place near El Rocío. Shall I go and fetch him, Miss Charlie?"

I thought for a while. "Fetch him? He's not a child, Andy. He can't be dragged back if he doesn't want to come."

"I could go," Richard said. "Perhaps Tomás would listen to me, Charlie. It's not too late yet."

Elena rose and went over to Richard. "If you try to go, I'll find some way to stop you. I will *not* have our safety, our standing with the military, put in jeopardy for this boy. Think about it, Richard." She left the room quietly. As we talked, planned, argued, I didn't notice that my mother had left also.

It was perhaps half an hour later that a car pulled up outside. It was enough to alarm us. I went to the door of the drawing room and opened it. There had been no sound of a bell at the front door, but Elena was already there. We heard her voice in the hall and that of a man.

It was Colonel Rodriguez, the officer commanding the troops now quartered in Jerez. He had been a guest at Juan's wedding.

He addressed Elena. "I came as soon as the orderly gave me

294

your telephone message, Lady Blodmore." I understood then why he had been passed by the guards at the gate. No one interfered with the movements of the military these days.

"It was good of you to come—at such short notice." Elena gestured him towards the drawing room. "It is a rather delicate family matter, Colonel."

He smiled affably. I guessed that he rather enjoyed being asked to help with a family matter when the family was important. "Good evening, Doña Carlota," he said. Then he advanced to the marquesa. "I trust I find you well, Marquesa. And you, Lord Blodmore. These are troubled times, are they not? But we have it well in control. Ah, thank you, Lady Blodmore."

He accepted brandy and a cigarette, and we all sat down. I looked at Richard and saw that the scars flamed on his cheek. There had to be some way to stop Elena, and yet there seemed none. The colonel was here and he would want to know why he had been summoned.

"There is something—" Elena began.

"No!" my mother cried as she entered the room. "You have no business bringing the military here."

"I must do as I think best," Elena said. "Carlota, can you not control your mother? Pray excuse this, Colonel. Lady Patricia is often not quite well."

"Of course, of course," the colonel said soothingly. He rose to his feet. "There is no need for alarm, Lady Patricia. The army is only here to preserve the peace and order of this country."

I saw it before anyone, because I recognized it. She had kept it in the fold of her long, old-fashioned skirt. I sprang towards her. "Mother! *No!*"

But she had reached Elena before I could stop her. Amelia's little gun was in her hand. The gun with which I had ended the life of my beloved Pepita once again fired its silver bullet. Elena slumped in her chair. The shot had been fired at point-blank range, and it appeared to have entered her heart. I think she died almost at once. There was very little blood on the pale silk of her dress.

My mother looked down at Elena for a moment. Then she turned to the colonel. "She was going to have me shut up, you know. She'd even dug up my mother's rose garden."

He stared at her, incredulity making his face vacant. Then he put down his brandy and cigarette and bent over Elena. Richard

295

held her upright in the chair while the colonel tried to find a heartbeat. He straightened slowly. His expression was still incredulous. "Lady Patricia, are you aware of what you have done?"

My mother's face twisted in a terrible parody of a smile. "She's dead, isn't she? All my life I've been a crack shot, and she was so close." Then she laid down the little pistol on the table beside the colonel's brandy and cigarette. With the kind of dignity a drunken person can assume, she walked from the room. Immediately María Luisa followed her.

"Lady Patricia," the colonel called after her. "Lady Patricia, I must insist—"

The marquesa spoke. "Let her go, Colonel, please. She will be confined, I promise you that." Very stiffly she got to her feet. "Colonel, will you come with me to another room? I cannot—" she looked at Elena in the chair, Richard still bent over her "—I cannot talk here. Carlota, will you come?"

It was an order, not a request, and the colonel reacted to it as people had been reacting to the marquesa all her life. I followed them and closed the door on Richard and Elena.

We went to the dining room. "Carlota, another brandy for the colonel. I will also have a little. My nerves . . ." The marquesa had never displayed nerves, but she permitted her hand to tremble a little as she raised the glass. "This is a most terrible thing."

"*Terrible*," the colonel repeated. He took a large gulp of brandy. "Being a military man, I have seen many things in my lifetime but nothing quite so bizarre as this. Two *ladies*—that little gun. How could Lady Patricia have come by the weapon? In her state it is most dangerous. Do you leave guns available to whoever wants to take them?"

The marquesa raised her hand. "No, no, Colonel. The guns are carefully locked away. But who would have thought of this? It is, of course, a museum piece, always kept in a display case. That Lady Patricia would use it never occurred to any of us."

"But *why* did she use it?"

The marquesa shook her head slowly. "How can we know exactly what was in her poor sick mind? Never before, I swear, has she shown any inclination towards violence. It is a—" Her voice broke. She pressed a handkerchief to her eyelids. "Forgive me, Colonel. It is a most terrible tragedy."

The colonel looked in bewilderment from one to the other of us.

"Lady Patricia said Lady Blodmore was threatening to have her shut up. Was *that* why Lady Blodmore telephoned me? To come here to take Lady Patricia away? It is, of course, entirely outside my sphere of duty."

"None of us had any idea Elena had telephoned you, Colonel. It's true, she's been heard to say many times that she believed Lady Patricia should be confined. Unhappily, Lady Patricia must have taken her words far more seriously than we thought."

The colonel threw out his hands in exasperation. "But why call on *me*? She said it was a family matter."

I grew cold as I watched the marquesa's face. Tomás's immediate safety now depended on her. With amazement I saw tears appear in her eyes, where I had never seen tears before. "I'm terribly afraid, Colonel, that I may have been the unwitting reason for the tragedy. It is my belief that Elena asked you to come here to speak to me about leaving the country. I told her I had perfect confidence in the army. If people like me, Colonel, flee the country, what sort of example is that to others? I consider it my patriotic duty to stay and support you in this struggle."

He coughed. "Your sentiments do you credit, Marquesa. In the long term I see no possible outcome to the struggle but victory for the forces of law and order, but it is true that we need every sort of support."

She nodded. "Quite so, Colonel. But this has been a week of severe strain on all of us. And for poor Lady Patricia, I'm afraid it has tipped her delicate mental balance. Listening to our talk all week, Lady Patricia must have confused Elena's arguments with her repeated statements that Lady Patricia should be confined, and when she saw that Elena had brought you here she thought you had come to take her away. It is my opinion that if we question her she will be able to give no rational reason why she committed this terrible act."

The colonel was uncomfortable. "This is no matter for me, Marquesa. It is really no business of the military *why* this act was committed. It is obviously a matter for the doctors. But a crime *has* been committed."

"Exactly so, Colonel. It is a terrible problem. There can be no question of a trial, of course. Everyone knows she has these . . . these spells. You cannot put a madwoman on trial."

The colonel looked helpless. "What am I to do, then? I cannot put her in jail. And as for the usual places such unfortunates are sent . . . well, they no longer exist. The nuns have been driven from all their institutions."

"With your permission, of course, Colonel, after the doctors have given their testimony, I could pledge you that she would be put in a safe place, where she can hurt no one. I have a castle—a fortress, really—at Arcos. We, the family, would be responsible for her there until such time as conditions return to normal."

The old cracked voice went on, making the plans, smoothing the way. The colonel was nodding, eager to rid himself of this awkward problem. I slipped out, knowing the colonel would agree to whatever the marquesa said, and Tomás's name would not be mentioned. But my mother . . . As I climbed the stairs I heard again and again the terrible words of sentence for her crime. "I have a castle at Arcos. . . ." My mother would take the place of the woman who had inhabited it before her.

I found her in bed, María Luisa seated beside her. She was propped up on her pillows, wearing a white lawn nightgown edged with lace. Her hair had been brushed and lay smoothly on her shoulders. It was now completely silver. In the soft light she looked beautiful again, and perfectly serene. She smiled at me. A glass with a little brandy left in it was on the table beside her. She stretched out her hand and took mine.

"There you are, darling. I've been waiting for you. Everything's going to be all right now, isn't it? She's gone; she can't interfere any more. Only you won't let them shut me up, will you, Charlie? You always promised me that. I'd rather die than be shut up." I sat there, holding her hand. In an agony of love and sorrow I thought of the promise I had given so often. Gradually the pressure of her hand in mine relaxed. Her eyes were closed and she was breathing deeply.

María Luisa touched my shoulder. "Leave her now, querida. She is sleeping."

Outside in the passage I told María Luisa what the marquesa proposed to do with my mother. "It's the same as putting her in prison. And I promised her, María Luisa. *Why* did she do it? She really must be . . . mad."

"I believe myself, querida, that she never had a saner moment. She meant to keep Elena from telling the colonel about Tomás, and she achieved that."

"But does she think there will be no punishment? She hasn't just stopped Elena from talking about Tomás. She has *killed* her."

María Luisa shook her head. "You know how quickly she changes. One moment able to understand everything perfectly, the next she is back in her fog. But she trusts and loves us, querida. And she counted on your promise."

"Which I cannot keep."

"It is kept, querida. I have seen to that."

"What have you done?"

"I gave her the medicine Ramírez gave me. All of it—in the brandy. She will not wake."

"That—that *tonic?*"

"Morphine is a very powerful tonic, querida. There is nothing Ramírez or any other doctor could do for me, except to give me morphine against the pain. Along with the brandy, the dose I gave her is lethal. Your mother will never be shut up, querida. The promise is kept."

"The pain . . . María Luisa, what are you saying?"

She held up her hand, as if to dismiss the question. "I have only a few more weeks, at most. Ramírez said I should go into the hospital. But I am too old to let them start cutting me up. What difference would it have made for just a little extra time? So I took his tonic and forbade him to speak of it to you. But I am happy that, in the end, I have been able to serve you. I have kept your promise for you, querida."

I clasped her to me. She was so frail and thin; I could feel the fluttering beat of her heart, like that of a frightened bird. The tears were hot on my cheeks. "How am I to lose you both?"

She gently disengaged herself. "Where there is love, querida, nothing is lost forever. I will go now and sit with her and pray. God should understand, shouldn't He, the things it is sometimes necessary to do out of love? I do not fear His judgment."

I stayed with the marquesa when Dr. Ramírez came and examined Elena. The colonel, she said, had taken the little pistol. Ramírez came into the dining room and signed the death certificate.

"A most unfortunate business," he said. "And Lady Patricia?" he added. "May I do anything for her?"

"She is asleep," I answered.

He closed his bag. "I will see her in the morning." I thought he looked at me very closely, as if he discerned something in my quiet words. But he said nothing more. He had always kept secrets for this family. When he left I told the marquesa and Richard what María Luisa had done.

After a long silence the marquesa nodded her head. "It took great courage to perform such an act but she has done all she could for this family. She has done well."

I SAT WITH MY MOTHER as long as she breathed. It was peaceful; there was no struggle. As María Luisa had said, she simply did not wake.

Then, in the dawn, I went down and found Richard and the marquesa together. They were drinking coffee. The cigarette butts in the ashtray indicated how the night had gone. Richard looked tired and old. He was a man well on in his fifties. We were young lovers on the shore no more.

"I have told the marquesa," he said, "that we will marry as soon as possible. I will take you and Luisa to Clonmara—"

I shook my head. "Marriage will come, Richard. And you will take Luisa to safety—to Clonmara. But you know that I cannot go."

"What, in God's name, will keep you here now?"

"I have sons, Richard, who fight on opposite sides of this war. Perhaps some of them will die. But while they fight, on whatever side, I must be here. I am their mother. I will be here to hold their inheritance for them, to keep something of the good they remember, to try to keep alive what each of them believes he is fighting for."

The marquesa turned to Richard. "That is what I told you she would say."

He put his elbows on the table, his face in his hands. At last he looked up at me.

"I will take Luisa to Clonmara and give her into Edward's care. And then I will come back here. My instinct tells me to go now to look for Tomás, but the marquesa has convinced me that *your* instincts are right. He cannot be dragged back against his will, and if I should find him, I might only lead others to him. I cannot bear the thought that I may never see my son again, but neither can I put him into more danger. Oh, Charlie—help me!"

Before the marquesa's gaze he put his hand out and reached for mine across the table. And from her expression I knew that she had never doubted that Tomás was Richard's son.

RICHARD WAITED only to see Elena buried, and my mother, and this was done with little ceremony. I watched the coffins lowered into the Spanish earth, and thought of how much of me now was buried here. My past was buried in the earth with Carlos; with Mariana, my grandfather's wife; with Luis, whom I had loved; with Don Paulo, and now with my mother.

The future was with my sons and with Luisa. And, at last, with Richard. I prayed silently that I would see none of them lowered into the Spanish earth.

Very early on the morning after the burials Luisa stood before the marquesa. The old woman looked at the young one; both wore black.

"You are a very special child," the old woman said. "Much is carried in you. You bear the old Spain, and the new Spain, however that shall form itself. Go with courage and with strength, like your mother. Here, child, take these. . . ." She stripped off the famous rings that for as long as I had known her she had worn. "I cannot give you the title of Pontevedra. That belongs to Edward Blodmore. Your mother will be the heir to whatever remains after our country has settled its disputes. She has learned to tend her vines. If my husband, the Marqués de Santander, Don Paulo, were here, he would say it was the most sacred trust."

So Luisa and Richard departed, and we sat and waited, three women in black. María Luisa waited for death. The marquesa waited for I knew not what. I waited for the return of Richard and the return of my sons. I waited for the violent fermentation of a country in civil war to end. I waited for the wine to fall bright.

Catherine Gaskin

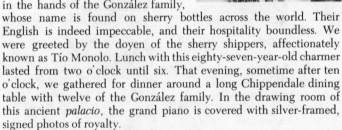

From her home in County Wicklow, Ireland, Catherine Gaskin writes: "If one has any sense of humanity, one does not go into a foreign environment confident that one can 'catch' it, and put it down on paper. So I confess that I approached Jerez, in Spain, with some misgivings. The ancient town is known for a special way of life that belongs to the sherry dons. My husband and I packed our formal clothes, and hoped that the English of these aristocratic families was as impeccable as we had heard it was.

"When we arrived we were placed in the hands of the González family, whose name is found on sherry bottles across the world. Their English is indeed impeccable, and their hospitality boundless. We were greeted by the doyen of the sherry shippers, affectionately known as Tío Monolo. Lunch with this eighty-seven-year-old charmer lasted from two o'clock until six. That evening, sometime after ten o'clock, we gathered for dinner around a long Chippendale dining table with twelve of the González family. In the drawing room of this ancient *palacio*, the grand piano is covered with silver-framed, signed photos of royalty.

"It was September, the time of the *feria* that celebrates the harvest. We toured Jerez in a carriage pulled by a five-in-hand team of matched horses. We visited the *bodegas* and the vineyard houses. We were taken everywhere; shown everything. In Jerez nothing starts on time; no one cares. We were exhausted and exhilarated, yet our hosts were attentive and unwearying.

"We visited Jerez again in April, when all of Andalusia was in flower—with poppies, irises, and the flaming Judas tree against the clear blue sky. It is when the vines send out the first green shoots of spring. We walked through the now quiet *bodegas*. The town had become familiar, a loved place; we were, we felt, among friends."

Kananook
Public School
·8TH GRADE·
1929

ALL THE GREEN YEAR

A condensation of the book by
D. E. Charlwood

Illustrated by Phillip Belbin

Published by Angus and Robertson

It was a green year indeed. . . .

The year when fourteen-year-old
Charlie and his family went to live with
eccentric Grandfather MacDonald in
his house on the cliffs. . . .

The year of the astonishing camel-
ride to school. . . .

The year Charlie and his friend
Johnno discovered that girls were
exciting and different. . . .

The year of the terrible fight with
Big Simmons. . . .

The year that included so much
pain and terror, as well as joy. . . .

After it, life would never be quite
the same again.

In this touching and hilarious story
Don Charlwood recaptures the essence
of what it is like to be a boy on the
edge of manhood.

ONE

The year I remember best from those days is 1929. This was the year I turned fourteen and went into the eighth grade. It has stayed in my memory for various reasons but chiefly, I suppose, for our final disgrace at the end.

My main Christmas present in 1928 had been a pair of long trousers. My father said he hoped now that I was dressing as a man I would behave as a man. A forlorn hope this proved to be. But both at home and at school at this time we boys felt ourselves badly misunderstood, and looking back I realize how serious everything seemed; only in retrospect do I see the humour in that year.

After five grades together this was my last year with Fred Johnston, a tall, melancholy boy of extraordinary physique, the son of a widower who ran a shop called Navy Bike Repairs. Though "Johnno", as we called him, looked awkward when he tried to fit into a desk or when he marched into school, head and shoulders above everyone else, as a swimmer and boxer hardly anyone in the town could touch him. He had learned boxing from his father, a shortish ex-chief petty officer with eyes like agates, who had been a Royal Australian Navy welter-weight champion.

Though Johnno had practically no physical fear, he was always afraid of his father and of old Moloney, who had been headmaster of our school about ten years. His fear of both men went back, I suppose, to the fourth grade. He had lost his mother in third grade, and about a year later Moloney, in a temper, had hit Johnno across the face with a strap. Johnno had told his father, who had given him a note to bring to school. But the note only told Moloney to give him more for not taking his punishment like a man.

Moloney was a little thin-lipped bachelor of about fifty. His skull showed through greying hair and he wore fairly thick-lensed spectacles. He had made a butt of Johnno for as long as I could remember—for instance, when we had begun to learn carpentry he had forced Johnno, naturally left-handed, to use his tools as a right-hander, then had ridiculed his attempts to make anything.

In school Johnno was often afflicted by what he called "seizing up". If Moloney stood near him during a test, he became incapable of reasoning. During mental arithmetic, when Moloney called, "Stand by your desks. Hands on your heads," Johnno was beaten before the question was written on the blackboard. When Moloney finally shouted "Write!" Johnno would sometimes remain with his hands fixed to his head, moving only when Moloney said, "I perceive you don't intend cooperating today, Johnston."

For both of us 1929 was critical, since at the end of the year we were to sit for our Merit. We had been assured by Moloney that without it we would not be admitted to the imposing Kananook and District High School just being built on the edge of the town.

In these days I was not even ordinarily adventurous or undisciplined; in fact Moloney's report to my parents described me as "inattentive and addicted to daydreaming". Johnno, on the other hand, he called "unconforming and a generally disruptive influence", this written so savagely that the nib had punched right through the paper.

My report was true, but Johnno's was ridiculous. Still, my father believed the reports. Even when a boy called Birdwood Peters was named "Most Improved Pupil for 1928" my father believed it and wished I would cultivate his friendship. At school no one doubted that Birdie Peters—whom we called Squid—had won this prize because his mother, a widow, had been president of the Mothers' Club for five years; indeed, there were people who said that Moloney had designs on her. We were fated to have Squid as a neighbour in 1929: one of a series of events that started the year badly.

Our move next to the Peters's place came about because my grandmother had died, leaving my grandfather alone in his old wooden house on the cliffs. It was just before Christmas 1928 that

Grandfather became peculiar—though Grandfather McDonald, with his beard and stern expression, had seemed a little peculiar for as long as I could remember, "sailing" the veranda like a ship, and brooding and muttering to himself about evolution and Darwin.

Anyway, when he became even more peculiar my mother had to go back and forth to "Thermopylae", as he called his place, to clean and cook him an occasional meal. He usually muttered and growled at her while she worked, or else sat out on the veranda to watch for passing ships—he had been an old Port Phillip pilot and before that a master in sail.

He had resurrected the wheel of the *Arabella*, a schooner wrecked years before off the Victorian coast, and had fixed it to the veranda rail. Standing there, he would steer the house towards the Heads, cursing and glaring at the horizon. No one minded when he next fitted the veranda with navigation lights and a binnacle from his collection of nautical odds and ends. But complaints from neighbours began when he found a megaphone and used it to roar and blaspheme at ships out in the channel.

After a few months of this my mother said wearily, "We can't watch him from here any longer—either we'll have to go there, or he will have to come here to us."

From behind his newspaper my father muttered, "I'd sooner bring a grizzly bear to live here." When my mother didn't answer, he sighed and said, "Very well—we'll go, I suppose. I like the pater well enough, but I know nothing about ships or what's wrong with Darwinism." He lapsed into moody silence.

After some time my mother said in a voice not intended for our ears, "It may be possible to put him in a home. Some people are doing this nowadays."

My father threw down his paper. "Stop talking nonsense, girl! Did your father put you in a home when you were a squalling brat and he had to put up with you?" My mother supposed not. "No, he did what any decent human being should do—he looked after you. And now it's our turn to do the same for him. Anyhow, he'd tear a home apart."

My father was a rate collector with the council. He studied for accountancy examinations, hoping to become shire secretary, but his studying suffered frequently from family interruptions, and in the fateful year of 1929 I interrupted him most of all. When a new shire secretary was appointed my father was not selected.

He went on all his life working as a rate collector and alway
felt he had failed. I realize now that he didn't fail at all in the
things that mattered.

His own father had been a printer and bookseller in London
and he referred to England as "home". I always associated England
with the cosy house in East Melbourne where my father had been
born and where his mother, who reminded me of Queen Victoria
still lived. Within the house's old thick walls, street noises were
reduced to rumblings, and you felt it was not Melbourne but
London that rumbled outside.

Grandfather McDonald on the other hand was a Scot, though
he had come to Australia as a child. His Thermopylae was over
sixty years old, high off the ground at the front and low against a
hillside at the back. The sloping cliffs below it were covered with
thick vegetation, all bent inland. Down through the twisted trees
a few tunnel-like tracks zigzagged to the sand, and near the top of
the cliffs the house perched like an aged seabird. All around the
house ran a wooden veranda, many of the boards now loose. Inside
was a large central living room, lined with tongued-and-grooved
pine, with pictures of sailing ships and their bearded captains on
every wall and with the other rooms opening off it. The house had
little in the way of conveniences, though it was no worse than most
houses in the town. We had only a chip bath heater and a chip
copper and no septic sewerage. Bath night was Saturdays, but I
was supposed to follow my father's example of a daily cold shower
even when the shower had to be thawed with a candle. The only
way to escape this in winter was to put no more than a leg under
and make gasping noises.

Thermopylae creaked in high winds and was draughty even in a
breeze, for even indoors Grandfather McDonald liked to feel he
was on the open deck. Outside he had a flagpole from which he
flew a flag on the King's birthday, Anzac Day and other com-
memorative occasions.

This was the house then that we were to live in during 1929.

WE LEFT our own house partly furnished, and since Thermopylae
was already furnished there was not a great deal to move. We
loaded the few things we needed on a lorry, while the family
walked.

My father and mother walked in front, my father carefully rais-

310

ing his hat to everyone we met; then I came with our Gyp on a lead; then came my younger brother, Ian, walking in the gutter, or breathing on shop windows so that he could write his "minitials" Kananook was by no means a large town and pretty well everyone knew us.

Since the blocks along the cliffs were large and the Peters's place was separated from Grandfather McDonald's by a barrier of tea-tree and banksias, we could hardly see the Peters's house at all as we approached Thermopylae.

In a fork of a large banksia Squid had made a platform where he sometimes sat, Buddha-like, surveying the world. Unlike Buddha he was far from fat; in fact at thirteen there was nothing much of him but freckles and tow hair and a wary but ingratiating expression.

Squid's father had been killed in the war. This was, of course, sad, but nevertheless Squid didn't fail to capitalize on it. On Anzac Day he always laid a wreath the size of a lifebelt and wore more medals than George V. His most graphic story was of his father's rearguard action with the Turks while the rest of his battalion were being evacuated from Gallipoli. It was ten years before it struck me that if this were true, Mr. Peters must have left home at least eighteen months before Squid was born.

Squid's full name was Birdwood Monash Peters; adults called him Bird. The family had come from South Australia—"A state with somethink rather genteel about it," Mrs. Peters said. She was a pianist with a genius for mood music, which she played by ear for the pictures at the Palais. When Tom Mix or Buck Jones galloped across the prairies, she galloped up and down the keyboard without taking her eyes off the screen.

When we arrived at Thermopylae, I saw Squid sitting on his platform trying to screen himself behind leaves while he studied our possessions. When anything special came in, like the ice chest, he would glance down and whisper loudly to his mother, out of sight below, "A big ice chest", or "A crystal wireless". These were about the total of our luxuries.

I wandered over to him when we had finished, mainly to let him know we had seen him there.

Before I could speak he said seriously, "Just as well you've come, I reckon. Somethink wrong with your grandfather all right." He tapped his head sadly.

"He's just old," I said irritably.

311

"Must be a bit barmy too, don't you reckon? No feller who wasn't barmy would shout at ships the way he does."

"He was a pilot down at the Heads—"

"I know; I know every ship he was ever on. He yells it all out." He said this dolefully, as if genuinely perturbed.

Grandfather had come onto the house veranda now, and in a moment there was a fearful shout. "Ahoy, ye bluidy fool! Y' nearly on the bank."

Beard blowing in the breeze, eyes blazing, he strode up and down. "Wear off, y' maniac!"

"There, what did I tell you?" said Squid in an awed voice.

I said defensively, "He's deaf and doesn't know he's shouting so loudly. Anyhow, the ships worry him—"

"There's not a ship in sight, not a rowing boat—nothink," said Squid mournfully.

I felt a wave of humiliation sweep over me. Then Grandfather spied Squid on his platform. "You aloft there! On deck, or by God I'll flog the life out o' ye!"

An expression of shock passed over Squid's face, but with presence of mind he cried, "Ay, ay, sir!" He backed hurriedly off his platform and let himself down by a rope into the tea-tree.

Grandfather came to the rail, ready to direct another blast at him, but my mother came out and he allowed himself to be led inside. When the door closed I turned round and saw Squid's strained face looking out of the bushes.

"He's got my mum scared stiff," Squid said.

"You too." Every freckle on his face stood out clearly.

Squid's freckles were usually part of his stock-in-trade. According to his mother they were the cause of his sensitiveness and my own mother had warned me not to mention them to him—which was nonsense, for he charged a penny for an inspection of the freckles on his back and twopence to inspect his stomach.

I could see that he was trying to think of something now to restore his dignity: he was a past master at turning defeat into victory. Presently he looked at me from under lowered lids.

"I been learning hypnotism."

"Baloney," I said.

He looked at me in a hurt way. "It's true. I got it out of a book loaned me by an Indian bloke like Gandhi."

"Try it on me, then," I said.

312

He shook his head. "Too risky. You got blue eyes and the book says it could bring on brain fever for anyone with blue eyes."

"Try it on Gyp, then." Before he could answer I whistled Gyp, who came and looked at us with interest. He was a cross between a Labrador and a Kelpie—a large black dog who spent most of his days chasing seagulls or retrieving sticks. On Guy Fawkes night, he attacked crackers.

"Here, Gyp." He slobbered over me and sat down attentively. "Squid's going to hypnotize you." He grinned and hung out his tongue.

"No," Squid said gravely. "No, it could make him go mad. If he bit someone, then *they'd* go mad. It goes on and on."

Looking disappointed, Gyp lay down and closed his eyes.

"There's one thing I can do—there's our chooks. If y' very good at it, y' can hypnotize chooks."

"All right," I said. "When do you start?"

He peered through the tangle of branches into his backyard. "Mum's down the street, I think." He threw a pebble on the iron roof and when this brought no protest, he invited me through the gap in the fence into a quiet jungle of tea-trees. In a fowl yard, a dozen Plymouth Rocks scratched half-heartedly.

"Better get going," I said tauntingly.

Squid looked hurt at my disbelief. I squatted outside the yard while he went in. The hens hardly bothered getting out of his way. He scooped one up. It squawked feebly, but stopped as soon as he held it before his eyes and began murmuring some sort of gibberish, his voice rising and falling. I was beginning to regard the performance scornfully when he lowered the hen and swung it back and forth, back and forth, while his muttering rose till it sounded like a wail from a long way off. All at once he turned the hen on its back and laid it on the ground. It stayed there, its feet pointing at the sky, the stiffest hen I'd ever seen.

Squid scooped up another, stared into its eyes, muttering the gibberish again, then began the swinging motion and in a minute a second hen lay beside the first.

By the time he had put three in a row, all their feet stupidly in the air, he whispered, "I better stop It fair takes the power outer me."

He waved his hands over the recumbent hens, fingers extended, then came out of the yard, his face haggard. The first hen presently

313

recovered, got to its feet, wobbled a bit and began pecking again.

"How do you do it?" I asked quietly.

"Some people has it, some hasn't."

The second hen struggled up and looked about glassily.

"Can I read the Indian book?"

"I had t' give it back."

I looked into his freckled face, trying to tell whether he was making all this up, but he looked serious, even a bit afraid of his own power; besides, the last hen still lay on its back as evidence. He clapped his hands and after a second it lurched to its feet.

"Well," he said, "I better chop the wood."

He left me with the air of a man to whom miracles were nothing, and I never learned his secret.

TWO

My mother was the busiest and calmest one of us at Thermopylae, and everything revolved around her. Yet she was a shy woman and inclined to depression. She felt concerned always for the family's reputation: even to receive an account-rendered from one of the local shopkeepers was to her like being accused of theft. That year she had only one hat and one handbag—this was at the beginning of the depression, of course, when most people we knew had to manage on little; and although my father's collars were always starched and shining, the patching of some of his shirts would not have allowed him to take off his coat even had he thought this proper.

Ian, who was nine then, had a soprano voice of such purity that anyone not knowing him would have thought him a paragon of holiness. When he sang something like "Oh, For the Wings of a Dove" he even convinced me; but then I would hear him singing it around the house while he tied Gyp and the cat together or tried, between breaths, to throw my marbles from the veranda into the sea.

In his day my grandfather had been a great debater and liked to argue ferociously about such things as Darwinism, or the truths revealed in the Book of Revelations. I remember him best at the table, his mouth and beard moving, as he growled a Gaelic grace to himself. He had left Scotland as a boy but he spoke as bitterly

314

about Culloden Moor and "the Royal Butcher" as if he had been at the battle himself. His jaw was larger on one side than the other as he had been kicked in the face by a horse years before. His jaw had been set by Grandmother, since he didn't believe in doctors. My father always claimed that the horse had broken its leg—which could well enough have been true.

An old debating companion, Theo Matthias, a bearded man who was said to be a Bolshevik, sometimes came to see him. Matthias was given this label after a flare-up one day in church. For years he had gone to the vestry after Sunday morning service to argue about the sermon with the vicar, and as he got older his arguments became more and more testy. At last one morning, during the prayer for the King, he stood up as Mr. Timms reached, ". . . thy chosen servant George our King—" and declared, "Chosen poppycock!" and walked out. From then on he was established as a Bolshevik, an accusation that drove Grandfather to fury. In the earlier twenties Matthias and Grandfather had gone fishing together each Saturday, and it was said that when they were a mile out in the channel you could hear their voices from Thermopylae's veranda.

Grandfather's boat was now only a relic of those days. It slept in a decrepit shed at the foot of the cliffs. Occasionally I was allowed to take it out, but I knew hardly anything of seamanship, though I had lived by the Bay all my life.

It was decided that I would sleep under Grandfather's window on the north veranda. This was the side of the house least exposed to the weather, but though thick tea-trees protected the veranda, there were nights when its canvas blinds flapped wildly and the roar of waves sounded so close that I would dream we were out at sea. These were the nights Grandfather was likely to get up and take the helm. Once or twice on windy moonlit nights I saw him, beard and hair blowing, pyjamas clinging about him, the ghost of a captain on a ghostly ship. The only way to handle him then was for my father to run outside crying, "Ready to take over, sir." Then Grandfather would relinquish the wheel and my mother could lead him back to bed.

But usually the Bay was calm and from my bed I could hear the lapping of waves on the beach. Sometimes on these still nights I could hear Grandfather through the thin wall, debating Darwinism with himself, taking first one side and then the other. Darwin

315

always lost. Earlier, at the dinner table, he would brood and then, in the middle of our conversation roar out, "He tol' men they were monkeys, an' by God they've been behaving like monkeys ever since."

Out on the veranda the sun would wake me early. The sea then was usually so calm that the cape beyond Thermopylae would lie reflected on its surface. The only sound at that hour was the whirring of Squid's pigeons. He kept these more for profit than pleasure; double profit often, as some always came back to him after he had sold them.

From the kitchen I would hear Grandfather's mantel clock rapidly striking the hour. It was an old Ansonia with cherubs on its glass and a hurrying silver pendulum. All that year it marked out hours, the frustrated hours of my father, the worried hours of my mother, the final hours of Grandfather McDonald.

THE LAST DAY of the holidays in February my mother told me it would be nice if I were to walk to school next morning with Birdie Peters. "He's such a nervous boy. He worries terribly over his poor freckled face."

I suppose I looked unhappy at the idea, because my father said sharply, "You don't seem to appreciate decent companions." He put his book of accountancy down. "This year is your last chance. If you don't do well, you'll have no hope of getting a job; you'll be out swinging a pick with your friend Johnston. There will be hundreds begging for jobs."

Poor old Johnno, I thought. He tried hard enough, but everyone was against him. I pictured him swinging his pick while Squid drove by in a car. Squid planned to become an estate agent or a stockbroker. There was no doubt he would do well. Someone else would do the work while he got the money. What a life he already had! Pictures free while his mother played the piano; favouritism from Moloney; a new bike for Christmas.

My father's voice droned on and it occurred to me that the worst of parents was the misery they caused by worrying about your future. Why did they have families if it was all worry?

My father's nose was suddenly an inch from mine, his eyes blazing. He roared, "Why don't you answer me? Here I'm trying to help you while you stare into space. What was I saying?"

"About money—"

316

He gave an exasperated snort, leaped to his feet and stamped into the kitchen. I heard him there shouting to my mother, then he slammed the door and strode outside. My mother came in to me, wiping her hands slowly on her apron, her face concerned.

"You heard that? What are you going to do about it?"

"I don't know," I burst out. "I'm sick of life. No one except Johnno understands what it's like. I never have any time to do what I want to do—"

"What is it you want to do? Swim and go out with Fred Johnston?"

I replied hotly, "That would be better than working for old Moloney, anyhow."

"Listen," she said quietly, "your father sees the mistakes he has made and he wants to save you some of them."

I said, "It'd be better fun making my own mistakes."

My mother sighed and went back into the kitchen and I went to bed. I fell asleep making elaborate plans to run away. At least I escaped walking with Squid in the morning as he had decided to ride his new bike.

All that year I seldom had more than ten minutes to cover the mile to school, so instead of going by the park, I usually had to go the short way, through the bush to the bottom of the school grounds. When I was late, the grounds would be accusingly empty and an industrious hum would rise from the classrooms. If it was a Monday I might hear the Declaration being chanted: "I love God and my country; I honour the flag, I serve the King and cheerfully obey my parents, teachers and the law." Cheerfully obey old Moloney!

There he was on that first hot morning squinting through his glasses: nose screwed up; moustache cut short; butterfly collar making marks on his neck; wooden-handled strap in pocket. A blast on his whistle and Squid began to beat the drum importantly while we marched in.

"Ah, Reeve, you have come back?"

"Yes, sir."

"You intend working this year, I trust?"

"Yes, sir."

"I think we shall sit you at the front where I can ensure you are awake and not merely pretending."

"Yes, sir."

"Well, stop 'yes-sirring' and sit down."

I sat at the ink-stained desk which had been carved and scratched

317

for fifty years or more. On the blackboard in big letters was MERRY CHRISTMAS, left from six weeks earlier as if to mock us. Dead flowers were still in a vase, and over the blackboard there was a dusty picture of Sappho, Sappho being, we understood, a goddess of Roman times.

Moloney set about making up the roll. He had already reached the Rs when Johnno appeared. There had been a crisis at his place because a coat someone had passed on to him was short in the sleeves. His sister Eileen had let the sleeves down, but the effect was worse, for the uncovered material contrasted with the rest of the coat. He stood at the door with his large hands protruding from the sleeves, his huge chest heaving and the usual strand of ginger hair falling over his right eye. At fifteen he looked too old for the eighth grade—in fact too old for school at all. He had deep-set distant eyes with a look of patience in them, but not of much hope. Moloney left him standing there while he finished the roll and began checking everyone's supply of new books.

After several minutes Johnno said, "Please sir—"

Moloney, pretending he had not seen him till then, faced round quickly. "What do you mean—'please sir'?"

"Please, sir, I'm late," said Johnno.

"Well, well, it struck me that the rest of us might have been early." Some of the girls tittered. "You have a note?"

"There wasn't time, sir. My sister had to do something for me."

"A big man to make his sister an excuse. A big man," he repeated, half turning to the class.

Johnno flushed and moved his feet uneasily. No one had been told more often than he that he was no good. There was no boy more unsure of himself in school.

Moloney rubbed his chin. "I think, Johnston, that since you need a woman's tender care, we shall sit you for today by Janet Baker."

Janet was so short-sighted that she had difficulty in seeing if anyone was next to her at all, but on principle she moved to the far side of the desk while Johnno struggled to get his knees under it and sit down.

Moloney stared at us with a mirthless smile. "This year you will be sitting for the Merit Certificate and I intend having no failures. You hear that, Reeve and Johnston?"

"Yes, sir," we said.

"I can't imagine how you're going to reach this standard, but

reach it you shall. Now I propose that we have a test every Monday morning. Mental arithmetic, dictation, grammar—" The list went on alarmingly. "You will correct each other's work; but twice a month I shall take up the papers and check your marking. I shall certainly not tell you when this is to be—'Ye will know neither the day nor the hour'."

A tremor passed over the class. It was hard to believe you could go so quickly from freedom to slavery.

I glanced around and saw the same faces as last year. There was "Fat" Benson who each month grew heavier—probably because he lived behind Fry's sweet shop by the Palais; "Stinger" Wray who was always self-important, possibly to make up for his mother's yelling at him; "Windy" Gale, whose mother and father hadn't spoken to each other for years—he had to carry notes from one to the other. Near the back was "Pommy" Ellison—not a pommy really; it was just that his parents spoke "correctly", as my father put it, and Pommy had brought this unfortunate habit to school. And of course there was Squid, basking in Moloney's favour.

The girls were a blur of dresses, giggles and self-possession. It struck me that they looked better than the previous year. Perhaps it was the way hair was caught behind ears, and arms emerged from short sleeves and a new plumpness was exhibited.

The silence roused me. I heard Moloney's level voice saying, "I repeat, Reeve: do you fancy yourself as a Don Juan?" I faced him quickly.

"What was I discussing?" he demanded.

"I'm—not sure, sir."

"Not sure! Reeve, for as long as I've known you you've never remained attentive long enough to make sure of anything."

He took out the wooden-handled strap. "Come out here."

A year of this, I thought. A year of cheerfully obeying!

AT LUNCHTIME in those days Johnno and I would climb the post-and-rail fence at the bottom of the school grounds and wander across a sandy road into the bush. There was a grassy clearing a hundred yards in, and this was where we ate lunch and in winter had boxing practice.

After the glare and heat that first day the clearing was cool. We lay at full length on the grass and unwrapped the newspaper from around our sandwiches. "What've you got?" I asked.

"Two dripping and one sugar," he said. Eileen was not an imaginative maker of sandwiches.

"I'll swap you a tomato for a dripping."

We ate lying on our sides. When we had finished Johnno said, "What about boxing practice? I've changed my style a bit—more like Billy Grimes." He stood up and flexed his arms.

"Too hot," I said. "Let's walk across to Lone Pine."

"OK, then."

Lone Pine had been named by Squid after a tree from which his father, he said, had sniped during the war. The track to it from the clearing went steeply downhill, the bush about it growing thicker as it neared a small creek. We drank at a dark pool which Squid said was bottomless. From there the track climbed steeply to the hilltop where Lone Pine, planted by some forgotten settler, stood dark against the sky.

Johnno and I began climbing without a word, putting our hands and feet in familiar places. Near the top the whole country opened, from Point Nepean to Donna Buang. We sat on a board seat we had nailed there, feeling the trunk sway gently. I could see the narrow gap of the Heads and the beginning of the ocean and the pale, small lighthouse at Point Lonsdale. The sun was shining on the beaches, but no sound reached us from the people who were distant specks there.

"The public-school kids are still on holidays," said Johnno aggrievedly. There seemed no justice in life.

Inland, all the secrets of streets and yards were open to us: lines of washing; a cable tram which was Mrs. Kelly's sleepout; old Charlie Rolls's tent that his wife made him sleep in. A cab moved slowly down Bay Street and someone chased after it and leaped on the back step. If Dan Weekly was the driver, he would lash round with his whip and yell abuse. But in those cabs if no one called "Whip behind!" and the driver didn't see you, you could climb in and lie on the mat on the floor, feel the sway of the cab and hear the sound of hooves and the running of the wheels on the road.

"If I fail in the Merit I'll run away," said Johnno darkly.

"You said that last year."

"Last year I had one more chance." He was staring unhappily towards the sea. After a bit he said, "In arithmetic, Charlie, my answers even look crazy, but I reckon I can write decent compositions, can't I?" He looked at me anxiously round the trunk.

"I reckon you can," I said—and this was true. In fact composi- tions were all either of us liked. But even when we thought we had done these well, Moloney would take half our marks for split infinitives or sentences ending with prepositions.

The faint sound of the first bell drifted up to us, so far off that it seemed nothing to take notice of. We could hear only occasional separate shouts or girls squealing. The clusters at the cricket pitch or playing stick fly looked like a prison camp of microbes from which we had escaped. I cast a glance down on the distant town; there was a sort of mystery about it, some sort of apartness, as if now that the holidays were over it was closed to us.

Once on the ground we began to run. "Where would you go anyhow, if you ran away?" I asked.

"England. Or maybe row across the bay to the Otways. There are forests there where a man could hide."

We had started up the school hill. "I wouldn't mind going with you," I said, though I knew that if it came to the point I would probably back out. I did not realize Johnno would remem- ber what I said.

THREE

When the first term was about half over, there were two happenings on one day that I'll never forget.

It was mid-April and the nights were still and cold when I said at the dinner table, "Tomorrow Johnno and I are going for our Bronze Medallions."

My mother glanced at me quickly. "It's very late to swim."

"Well, we did the land drill and the duck-diving last month," I said, "but then the examiner was called away and he hasn't been able to come back till now."

My father said, "If you paid as much attention to your work as you do to swimming— What did Mr. Moloney say about the prob- lems you did last night?"

What he had actually said wouldn't have borne repeating. "He said I used the wrong method," I answered.

"In what way?"

"Does it matter just now?" asked my mother uneasily.

"It matters a great deal. I know, and Mr. Moloney knows, that

322

Charlie can do the work. Why must he concentrate on medallions instead of keeping up with his class?"

"But I promised I'd be Johnno's patient and he's to be mine."

"Johnno! That's about the only name we hear. What do you suppose Fred Johnston will be doing next year? He'll be digging drains or assisting the nightman, I'll warrant."

"He's going to run away," I said challengingly.

My father put down the carving knife. "Going to run away?" He leaned over the table. "And I suppose you're going with him?"

My mother said quickly, "Look, this is all very silly. What do you think it's like for me to prepare a meal and then—"

"Are you?" asked my father, looking at me.

Grandfather, staring angrily down at his hands, exclaimed suddenly, "In six days the Lor-rd made heaven and earth—six *days*. And this upstart declares that man made himself out o' monkeys—"

"Evolved, Father," said my mother loudly.

"Evolved? Very well then—*who made the first monkey?*" He glared challengingly at my mother.

"I don't know," said my mother hopelessly. "But if we don't settle to our dinner like human beings, I'm going to leave this table."

My father took up the carving knife grumpily and Grandfather muttered, ". . . products of a-theism—" I remained silent for the rest of the meal. Life was becoming intolerable.

DURING that night a strong wind arose. When I got out of bed next morning I saw the waves running up the beach at an angle under a gloomy sky.

Grandfather tapped the glass and growled that we'd be lucky if the roof stayed on the house that night.

The examiner arrived early in the afternoon. There were no other candidates, so Johnno and I drove alone with him to the beach. The sea was louder now and spray blew occasionally across the L of the pier. "You're both strong swimmers?" the examiner asked.

When Johnno didn't answer I said, "He's the best in the town."

The examiner looked at me bleakly. "But you, you still want to go on with it in this weather?"

"Yes," I said. I had a good reason. Johnno was the perfect patient for when he filled his lungs with air he floated like an inflated beach toy. If he left school I might never get the opportunity of having him again.

"Very well, Get undressed as quickly as you can."

The dressing shed was deserted and had a winter look. It smelt of salt and the tea-tree creaked depressingly outside, but Johnno was so at home in the sea and so glad to be out of school that a cyclone would have meant nothing to him. We put our sweaters on and went to the beach, our legs stinging in the blowing sand. The examiner was striding up and down the pier. We walked beside him to the end, our eyes watering in the wind, the water making sucking sounds under our feet.

"It's a very poor day. Sure you want to go on with it?"

"Yes, sir," we said.

"All right. You know the twenty-yard mark—the third bollard on the L. You, Reeve, will swim to a point opposite it, then Johnston will carry out the first method of release followed by the first method of rescue."

"Yes, sir." We handed him our sweaters and climbed down onto the landing. Waves made rushing, slapping sounds round the piles as Johnno dived in and began swimming parallel to the L, his feet fluttering rhythmically. I glanced inland at the town as a man might glance if seeing it for the last time, then dived after him. The water felt cold enough to stop my heart.

"First method of release," cried Johnno.

I lifted my arms in fair imitation of a drowning man and felt them grasped and twisted outward. He turned me on my back, put his hands over my ears and presently I was riding with my head on his chest, looking up at a grey sky, its clouds racing.

As we came to the landing the examiner shouted, "First method of release and first method of rescue, Reeve."

We swam back into the oncoming sea and faced each other twenty yards out. Johnno held up his arms and I turned him onto his back. He was unsinkable; even if waves washed continually over his face, he said nothing. But one thing he couldn't do was control our direction. We ended our run ten feet from the landing.

"All right," shouted the examiner. "Swim from where you are. Johnston—second method of release, second method of rescue."

Each time Johnno's turn came he attempted to correct my drift, but even so we moved slowly down the pier. Gradually fatigue crept over me and I began carrying out each movement auto-

324

matically. Drifting as we were, we were beginning to lose the protection of the L, but from the corner of my eye I could see the waves coming and at the last moment lift Johnno's head and submerge my own.

"Johnston—fourth method of rescue." With his mouth near my ear, Johnno shouted, "You OK?"

I heard my voice answer, "OK."

"Reeve—fourth method of rescue."

On the last lap I had illusions of relief. The idea came to me that I was not in the water, but lying in bed, dreaming. From a long way off, I heard the examiner say, "Good work. Back to the landing and get dressed."

The landing was no more than fifty yards away, but it seemed beyond reach. Johnno struck across the lines of waves and I started after him, but found myself drifting rapidly towards the pier. I thought I would rest awhile, holding onto one of the piles, and I was letting myself drift towards them when I was picked up by a wave and saw I would strike one hard. I dived under the crest but in a second my head struck. As I surfaced, the swirl held me to the pile, and the next wave drove me against it with a turning motion. I felt mussel shells cut the insides of my arms and legs. In the same instant the pier lifebelt dangled beside me. I lunged at it, pushing my shoulders through and the two above hauled me onto the rough planking of the pier.

"I thought you were just behind me," Johnno said.

"Why didn't you call for help?" said the instructor.

I sat up and saw a myriad of small cuts on my arms and legs, done as if with razor blades. On my forehead a lump was rising.

"We'd better go. Do you feel equal to walking?"

"Yes," I said uncertainly. I began to walk between Johnno and the examiner, my body feeling strangely light. In the southwest the sky was black. We were halfway down the pier when the wind suddenly dropped and the air was still. Then the wind came roaring from the southwest, low cloud flying before it. Inland we saw trees bend together and branches go flying through the air. The beach was hidden under swirling sand.

"We're for it!" shouted the examiner. "Johnston, run and get the clothes and come to my car."

We found his Baby Austin with its hood torn off, but managed to reach our place as the rain began. The house was shaking as if it would fall to pieces and Gyp was hiding under Grandfather's bed.

My mother swabbed my legs with iodine, fanning them with a piece of cardboard to ease the stinging. It was impossible for me to go to bed on the veranda. Rain washed its full length, blew under the front door and dripped in several places through the ceiling.

All night the house shook and creaked as if trying to uproot itself from the cliff. Once there was a tremendous crash as Squid's look-out tree fell into our garden.

I was sleeping on a couch inside the door to the veranda, and it seemed to me that every time I opened my eyes my father or mother was going to Ian's bedroom to assure him that he was safe.

Towards dawn I was sleeping fitfully when a gust of cold air and a splashing of rain woke me. I heard, even above the storm, a bellow from Grandfather, "Ship ahoy! All hands on deck!" Then a testy cry from my father to my mother, "Isn't it enough to be perched on a cliff-top on a night like this without having to curb a maniac?"

"Lower away!" yelled Grandfather. Even the gale could not overcome his voice. "Strike away, men! Watch for survivors!"

My father tripped over something, cursed luridly, switched on the veranda light and flung open the door. Out there I saw Grandfather in a deluge of rain, his hair and beard blowing, his pyjamas almost torn off. Rain and wind swept into the room and the light went out. "Ready to take over, sir!" yelled my father. Then I heard him cry, "My God, there *is* a vessel!"

Forgetting my hurts I leaped off the couch and ran outside. In the first grey light, lying on her side on what we called "the second sandbank", was a yacht, the waves rolling her horribly.

My father took Grandfather's arm. "Here, you must get inside."

"I don't desert the bridge!" shouted Grandfather.

"Charlie, go and get Sergeant Gouvane."

I left the two of them struggling beside the binnacle and ran in my pyjamas to the police station, my legs stinging. Twigs and leaves were flying through the empty streets, the rain horizontal in the street lights. I pounded on Sergeant Gouvane's front door and his light went on immediately. When he came, he stood glowering at me, a great slab of a man looking somehow the more threatening in his pyjamas. "What is it?"

"A wreck opposite Thermopylae."

"Is this some dream of the old man's?"

"No," I said. "I saw it myself—a big yacht."

"I'll be there in five minutes."

He turned inside and I began running again down to the bike-shop. I knocked on the wall of Johnno's room beside his bed and after a bit he came tumbling out of the house. I gave him the story and we started back, Johnno running ahead since the cuts on my legs were raw from my wet pyjamas. As I went through the main street I could hear the firebell pealing weirdly in the wind. It was nearly full day, a day like midwinter rather than April.

Down on the beach the sea was heaving and sickly. The waves were breaking right over the ship now. Gouvane and my father and a couple of other men were attempting to launch a boat to see if anyone was trapped aboard, but each time they pushed it out, the boat broached to.

Johnno shouted in my ear, "We could get the reel." The door of the lifesaving club was never locked, so we went in and came back with the reel. Johnno said to Gouvane; "I could swim out."

Gouvane looked at my father. "What do you say?"

"Hardly possible," said my father, frowning.

"We're not doing any good with the boat and we can't just stand here. There could easily be someone still aboard," Gouvane said.

At this Johnno stripped off his pyjamas and stood while I fastened the belt round him. From the sandbank we heard a loud crash as if something had broken loose inside the hull. The yacht heaved onto her side and lay with her bottom turned to the beach.

Johnno ran to the water's edge, the line trailing behind him. He bounded in a few yards but was thrown off his feet. I saw him on a wave top; then he disappeared again. The sea was running in short, vicious waves, their directions constantly changing. I saw Johnno again, about twenty yards out, moving slowly. The line ran through Gouvane's hands.

"I'm not sure we should have done this!" shouted my father.

Gouvane ignored him. About a hundred yards of line had run out when we next saw Johnno. He rose up on a high wave just abeam of the yacht, his arms still going tirelessly, turned and struck behind the wreck. We stood waiting on the beach in the pelting rain and Dr. Stuart joined us, an army greatcoat over his pyjamas.

"Who is it out there?" he shouted to my father.

"Young Fred Johnston."

"He'll be damn' lucky if he gets back."

Then Grandfather McDonald was on the beach, having got away from my mother. His pyjamas clung to his lank frame and his beard was like wet seaweed. My father and Dr. Stuart at once led the old man to the doctor's car, and I heard later that Grandfather cursed the doctor for his interference all the way home.

Now wreckage was beginning to come in: a smashed chair, a lifebelt, a saturated book of signals. Johnno got back to the beach about half an hour after he had started, and went onto his hands and knees on the sand, his chest heaving. Gouvane shouted to him, "Was there a sign of anyone?"

He shook his head. "There were two broken mooring ropes."

"Could you see her registration?"

"No, but her name was *Isis*."

By afternoon the beach was strewn for a mile with wreckage, and rumours began spreading about Johnno's swim and two people he was supposed to have rescued. For the rest of the day he kept saying in an embarrassed voice, "No, it's not true; no, no one." I kept wishing for him that the rumours had been true.

FOUR

After that, Johnno came in for a good deal of admiration—not, of course, from Moloney, though even my father praised him. "But the world demands application and perseverance as well as courage," he added.

At home the wreck had serious repercussions. Grandfather had become so wet and cold and so worn out by his climb down the cliff that the next day my mother had to call Dr. Stuart. I heard Grandfather bawl out, "Who gave you permission to set foot in my door? No Bones touches me while I've breath in my body."

The doctor was a man with flaming hair and a flaming temper. He shouted back, "I won't have long to wait, then! G'day to you."

Grandfather, panting a good deal, called to my mother, "Show him the door and bolt it behind him."

But Dr. Stuart had to come back next day, Grandfather and he growling at each other during the examination. There were whispers of pneumonia, and Grandfather had to lie propped up in bed. The trouble was trying to keep him there. My mother and father

329

divided the night between them, and before long they were tired and irritable.

My task was to sit with him in the evenings after school. Winter was coming on and evening crept into the high-ceilinged bedroom very early. From where he lay Grandfather could see only thick tea-trees and each evening he would ask me how the sea was running, the direction of the wind and state of the tide, and ask me to read the barometer. Sometimes when I turned back to him I would see him staring, his eyes defiant but hopeless. In the kitchen his old clock would strike out the hour as if hurrying him away.

On some nights I was relieved by Theo Matthias, Grandfather's old friend. After these visits Grandfather was usually over-excited and unable to sleep. Despite his shortness of breath he would try to discuss the origin of man and whether T. H. Huxley was a Christian. Mr. Matthias would stride out well satisfied, stick in hand, beard pointing aggressively from one side to the other as he walked.

One Monday morning I left later than usual for school. As I began running towards the short cut, I heard Squid yell, "I'll give y' a dink." He drew up with me on his new bike and I jumped on the bar.

"That'll save you being late," he said into my ear.

But we were scarcely a hundred yards down the road when he got a puncture. He left the bike at the nearest house and came back.

"We'd better run," I said. But it was no good; Squid never hurried to school—his mother claimed it gave him constipation.

"We're going t' be a bit late anyhow," he said composedly.

"It's Monday—a test morning," I reminded him.

"Yeah," he replied, staring straight ahead, "Yeah. We'll get something on the produc's of France, I bet."

I looked at him quickly, but his face was innocent. He knew that I hadn't known the products of France last exam.

"Square root is what gets me," Squid went on, with a touch of anxiety. "How d' y' do it again?"

"Listen," I answered quickly, "we'd better walk faster."

We were only entering the bush when the sound of the school bell drifted to us. "There it goes," I exclaimed, breaking into a run. Then I realized that it was better to come in ten minutes late with Squid than five minutes late without him. I dropped back.

Squid said casually, "Mr. Moloney's giving the strap like a threshing machine these days, don't you reckon?"

"You don't get it much," I retorted. "I daresay your mother's told him about your freckles."

He looked hurt. "No; I just think things out carefully."

"You'd better start thinking now," I burst out.

He was silent for some time. Then he said, "My stomach feels crook. I reckon I might double up with pain an' you might have t' help me back home. My mother would give you a note: 'Dear Mr. Moloney, my son Birdwood was took bad an' Charlie Reeve had t' help him back home. I'm sure you will excuse Charlie for his thoughtful—'"

I could see no other course. "You'd better double up."

Instead he sat down. "I don't see why we got t' hurry."

I stood undecidedly. Then I noticed that strung out in Donnelly's paddock were the coloured vans of Perry's circus. Squid saw me staring and got quickly to his feet. He gave a despairing cry. "That's Perry Brothers. Look, y' can see their elephant—the one that turned a hundred an' two last time they was here. I can't hardly believe it. They weren't due till next month. I *can't* be took sick today. We better start running." We started half-heartedly.

"You could fall over," I said. "I could help you to school."

Even at this stage we might have been spared. Instead, fate came along in the form of a camel. It stood beside a she-oak, feeding on the branches. I caught Squid's arm and he stopped.

"It's Perry Brothers' dromedary, and it's got a saddle on." He reached a Napoleonic decision. "We'll take it t' Perry Brothers' an' Perry Brothers will see old Moloney—"

"You can if you want to."

"What'll you do?"

I could find no answer to this. I stood undecidedly while he strode towards the camel.

"I'll come, then," I said.

We reached the she-oak where the moth-eaten camel stood dribbling greenly, surveying us with contemptuous eyes.

Squid picked up its nose-line. "Now we get it to lie down. I saw how to do it at last year's circus. Hooshta!" he cried with authority. "That's telling it to lie down in Arab."

The camel roared at us, its neck striking like a snake.

"We'd better leave it."

331

"They always grizzle. The circus man said they're never happy not even when you're feeding them. Hooshta!"

It darted its head at us, baring yellow teeth.

"Listen, let's go home."

"Hooshta!" The camel dropped reluctantly to its knees and Squid's face shone triumphantly as he climbed into the double saddle. "See you at school," he said carelessly.

I leaped up behind him, and was held in the saddle by a kind of paralysis. Squid was full of wild cries. He put his school cap on backwards, with a dirty handkerchief caught under the peak of it as a desert neck-cloth. Sometimes he clapped his hand up to shield his eyes and stared into the distance. There wasn't much doubt about what lay there, for the camel was heading for the town. After we had been swinging like a pair of metronomes for ten minutes I said faintly, "It's going to take us through the main street! What are we going to do?"

"I dunno," said Squid in a hollow voice. "I don't feel well." He tried to lean on the neck of the camel, but it was too far off to be of comfort to him. "I feel crook in the stummick. Don't talk."

At that point the Presbyterian minister, Reverend Mr. Wetherby, appeared in his buggy. The horse stopped and shivered all over then, emitting a sound I'd never heard from a horse, it wheeled round and was gone. Behind it the buggy scarcely touched the ground and Mr. Wetherby scarcely touched the seat.

I prodded Squid. "We've killed Mr. Wetherby! You've got to do something."

"I'm going to jump off," he wailed.

In the paddock by the local dairy I caught sight of cows performing an unmatronly dance, and at that moment Squid half fell, half jumped off. Scarcely pausing in its stride the camel kicked him into the roadside grass. Any idea I had of following him was cut short when I heard him scream, "I'm dead!"

Alone I looked ahead down the main street. Already horses there were rearing and men trying to quieten them. I huddled miserably behind the neck of the camel. Ahead of me, lining the centre of the road, were loaves of bread. The baker's cart, its door open, was travelling fast about a furlong in front of me, while my camel advanced relentlessly, only pausing at a greengrocer's to eat most of a display of Jonathans.

Now the camel, by some fearful instinct, headed towards the

school—in fact, its last act was to eat the top off Mr. Moloney's favourite liquidambar. This brought everyone tumbling out of the school. There were cries of, "Mr. Moloney, Charlie Reeve has come to school on a camel!"

Moloney burst out of his office and strode through the ranks, his face unbelievable. "So you ride to school on a camel, Reeve? By Heavens, when I've finished with you, you will stand in the stirrups for a week! Get off that animal immediately!"

My voice came from a long way off. "It kicks, sir."

"So shall I. Get off."

I slid miserably to the ground just as, having heard the news, my father arrived from his office. "What's the meaning of this?" he said.

I waved my hand in the direction of the camel in a way intended to be explanatory.

My father said coldly, "Mr. Moloney, I leave him to you. I shall see him myself tonight."

With that he strode away and I was frog-marched into school, Mr. Moloney breathing viciously in my ear. But Squid had a week off from school after "a most unfortunate fall, which has quite upset him."

My belief in justice was dead.

FIVE

For days after the camel business no one at home spoke to me; I was ordered to chop enough wood for weeks ahead; I was not allowed over to Johnno's, even though Johnno had had nothing to do with the affair. It was of no use trying to shift blame onto Squid. I had "misled him" and that was that. At school old Moloney did all he could to embarrass me. We were studying Arabia so he made a point of asking me for authoritative opinions on the use of camels and the life of Bedouins.

It was Grandfather who eventually had me reinstated at home. One afternoon when I came in from school he was feeling slightly better and asked for someone to read to him. "You had better go in and make yourself useful," said my mother coldly.

I stepped into the dim room, nearly tripping over Gyp who had crept in and was studying Grandfather mournfully. Grandfather's beard and hands were on the turned-down sheet, his hands fidgeting impatiently. He muttered truculently, eyeing his medicine bottles, "Slow poison. Does your mother suppose I'm just goin' t' lie here till the breath has gone out o' me?"

"Of course not," I said quickly.

"I'm damn' sure that's what she's aboot." He pinned me with his eye. "Let non' of ye imagine that when God calls me I'll be lyin' in bed."

I did not know what to answer as he held me at the rapier point of his eye. Finally, I asked, "What could I read?"

He began another muttering tirade but after a few minutes he ordered, "Read to me from the scrapbook." This was a book of newspaper clippings covering the wrecks that had occurred during his years in the pilot service.

I was spoken to favourably that night. It was a Monday and not only had I read to Grandfather, I had also passed Moloney's test for the first time. We ate when Grandfather was settled, but in the middle of the meal there was a shout from him. My parents hurried to his room. He declared he was sailing through the Rip and could make no progress; the ship was drifting towards the Corsair Rock. They quietened him and came back to the table. My mother said tiredly, "There's nothing more we can do."

A few days later, Grandfather took a turn for the worse and all-night watches began again. At six in the morning I would be called in and while dawn crawled to the windows I would sit listening to his quick breathing, feeling alone. On one of these mornings I became aware in the half light that he was watching me. "And what d' they teach ye at school aboot evolution?" he demanded.

"That we had the same ancestors as the apes—" I began.

"Moloney teaches ye this?"

"Not that we are *descended* from apes, but we had the same—"

He took no notice of this. "What could ye expect from a man whose father was a bog-struttin' Irish peasant . . . ." The sentence ended in mutterings and heavy breathing, and loneliness returned to me. Then an hour later, I heard my mother get up and begin breaking sticks for the fire and filling kettles. There would be warmth in the kitchen and I could sit at the stove holding the toasting fork.

My mother came in with a cup of tea. She said quietly, "That was a great help. You had better get ready for school."

AFTER THE CAMEL affair I had avoided Squid. He sometimes glanced at me with an expression of hurt guilt, but we hardly exchanged a word. Then one Saturday afternoon his mother asked if I could go to the pictures with him. Poor dear Birdie was upset for I had misunderstood him in some way. It would be a happy reconciliation if I cared to use an extra ticket and come there afterwards for tea. On the whole my father disapproved of the pictures. He claimed that they had put an end to things like the local brass band and family songs around the piano. But this picture was the famous *The Gold Rush*, so he gave his permission. For my part a reconciliation with Squid seemed almost worthwhile.

Mr. Glossop, the manager of the Palais, used to send a cab for Mrs. Peters, usually a horse cab but sometimes a new Overland or Whippet. It rather spoiled things for Squid on the day of *The Gold Rush* when only a horse cab turned up with Dan Weekly driving. While the cab waited, the horse tossed its nosebag and Dan sat up in front looking gloomily into steady rain.

Mrs. Peters came out at last under an umbrella. If it was possible for a woman of forty to make herself look like an actress of twenty-two, that woman was Mrs. Peters. She was a mass of beads and rouge and marcel waves; there was even a change in her manner. Stepping up at the back she said, "Very well, Dan, you may go. Let down the flap, boys."

We undid the straps and let it down, shutting ourselves in half darkness with the smell of leather seats and kerosene from the lamp. The cab began swaying and the wheels made their running sound over the road. Through the little window by Dan's head I saw the park go by, then the Mechanics' Hall and the Church of England. We drew up outside the Palais where the stalls queue was waiting at the ticket box, the boys leaning against the window of Fry's sweet shop and hoardings showing Charlie Chaplin with his cane and baggy trousers.

"Birdie," said Mrs. Peters, "pay the driver, please—and tip him."

We stepped stylishly over a flowing gutter, causing a few jeers from the loungers. Mrs. Peters swept on grandly.

"You boys go to the dress circle," she said loudly. "I must study the music."

Only the most important people sat in the dress circle: the doctor's, the bank manager's and the solicitor's families—people who bought whole boxes of chocolates before the lights went out.

In the foyer was Johnno, reading the advertisement for *The Gold Rush*.

"G' day," said Squid. "Me and Charlie 're going t' the flicks."

"Listen," said Johnno anxiously, "I've got ninepence, but my money's for a haircut. I was just going to the barber's when I saw this—" He waved his hand at the advertisement.

"I've got threepence," I said. "You can have that."

Squid hesitated at the foot of the stairs. "I can cut hair. You come t' our place after the flicks and I'll cut your hair down in the Den for nothink."

Johnno rubbed his hand over his head. "My old man might notice."

"All right, then," said Squid indifferently. He started upstairs, adding over his shoulder, "We got clippers, too."

Johnno said suddenly, "All right then. I'll do it." I passed him my threepence and he bought an upstairs ticket. I doubt that this had been Squid's intention; I think he had expected Johnno to sit in the stalls. We had scarcely sat down when the lights went out and the advertisements started: Rogers the ironmonger; Wilcox the saddler; Hayes the blacksmith. Rain was loud on the iron roof, but when Mrs. Peters came in the noise was defeated by a charge up and down the keyboard as she settled to "The Entrance of the Gladiators" and "Colonel Bogey". Then there was the news, followed by the serial. A man and a girl were struggling on a cliff. Squid whispered, "He's one of Fu Manchu's blokes an' she knows he's got the opium. The other bloke's crashed over the cliff." "Help! Help! Will no one help me?" begged the caption. Mrs. Peters's arms were going like Jack Dempsey's. "Robert! *Robert!* Where are you?" Robert galloped on from somewhere and leaped out of the saddle, gun in hand.

"He's the goody," said Squid. "Watch him lay inter the crook."

Mrs. Peters whacked a few electrifying chords and Robert threw himself forward. At this the film broke. Downstairs whistling and stamping started and shouts of "Put a penny in." The only light was the little one over the piano. We listened to "Nola" before the screen lit up again. But something was still wrong. Robert ran backwards from the cliffs, rose in the air and landed in the saddle. The horse disappeared backwards off the screen. At half-time Johnno said he didn't know if coming to the pictures had been a good idea. He wasn't expected in till six, but the haircut was a terrible risk. Squid said carelessly, "My mother learned me how to cut hair. There's nothink to it."

The bell went to go inside and we watched the Coming Attractions, Johnno and I knowing very well we wouldn't see them. Then came the main feature. I doubt whether Johnno enjoyed *The Gold Rush* much. I could feel him fidgeting beside me unhappily as the picture neared its end.

The Gold Rush, too, suffered an interruption—not a break in the film, but the noise of a struggle on the fire-escape steps. "It's Sergeant Gouvane an' Big Simmons's mob," whispered Squid. Sure enough the door burst open and there in unreal daylight was Gouvane manhandling three of the town's larrikins. "They try to look in at the flicks," said Squid dispassionately, as for a few seconds the sounds of the struggle prevailed against Mrs. Peters's music. Then the door slammed and we were back in Alaska.

When we went outside, Gouvane had the three men by Fry's sweet shop and was taking notes. All wore old Oxford bags and sweaters. Big Simmons's nose had been bleeding, but he had his hands on his hips and every so often he spat beside Gouvane's feet. There was something about him that frightened me—perhaps the animal expression in the glance he turned on passers-by. He was called "Big" to distinguish him from "Little", his brother, who was no better than he was.

We had passed the group when I heard him shout, "Stop that one, copper!"

The punch must have missed. By the time we turned, Gouvane had his arm twisted up his back and Big was yelling, "You bloody copper bastard!" almost in a scream.

"We better get home," said Squid. "Charlie's coming in for tea, but we'll have time f' the haircut before mum comes in. She gets played out after the flicks—Mr. Glossop'll give her a cuppa tea."

The rain had stopped and the air was very still and cold: it nipped our ears. The prospect of the haircut was beginning to weigh heavily even on me. When we reached the house Squid led us underneath it into the Den and we waited there while he got the clippers. The Den had a sand floor and bag walls. A bullock's head painted green was in one corner; in another was a drum marked POISEN. On a nail hung an Australian Infantry Forces hat complete with authentic bullet holes. Squid came back with the clippers and a towel.

"What style d' y' want it done?" he asked.

"Do it the same way it's always done," Johnno said.

Squid pulled a decrepit chair under the light, waved Johnno into it and tucked in a towel. "Been wet, don't you reckon, sir?"

"Oh, hurry!" begged Johnno, his head bowed. Squid ploughed an experimental furrow, flourishing the clippers. "Nothink to it," he murmured. But when he went over the furrow a second time, my heart faltered. It was so deep there could be no way of fixing it. I sank into a chair and looked at the ground between my feet, hardly able to bear what was happening.

I don't think Squid realized what he had done till three or four furrows lay side by side and a heap of ginger hair was scattered on the ground. "Trouble is," Squid said, standing back, "you've had it the wrong style before."

"Just leave it the way it was," said Johnno distractedly.

But it was too late. Johnno was beginning to look like a parrot with a large crest. Squid said a little uneasily, "I reckon a bit off the front will about fix it."

He took out the scissors and clicked them a few times in the air. I turned away and when I looked back I could hardly believe it was Johnno's head. Squid had fixed it all right. In fact he himself was standing back with his mouth open.

"Is it finished?" said Johnno.

"Well," said Squid, "it needs a sort of—smoothing over."

Johnno ran his hand over it, then turned to me desperately. "Charlie, it's hacked about, isn't it?"

I felt half sick for him. "A bit," I admitted.

"Will my old man notice it? Will he?"

I was casting about for an answer when we heard Mrs. Peters come in. Squid said urgently, "You better go, Johnno."

"I'm clearing out all right," said Johnno.

Upstairs Mrs. Peters cried, "Bird-ie."

"Just getting the wood," yelled Squid.

Outside it was dusk and fog was rising over the sea.

"I'll be late home, too," said Johnno hoarsely. "Well, so long."

"So long," I said. Squid said nothing.

"WELL, it's a pleasure to have you," said Mrs. Peters when we had gone inside. "And how is poor old Captain McDonald?"

"The doctor says he's a lot better."

"A dear old man. They don't make them like that any more. My old father was the same. Kept his interlect till the end."

Squid was concentrating on the contents of various paper bags his mother had brought home. "What are we having for tea?"

"Toasted crumpets," said Mrs. Peters.

"They give me indergestion," said Squid frowning. "Can I have that cold pie from last night?"

"Of course, dear."

We sat down under the large portrait of Lance-Corporal Peters, who stared down with a mournful expression on the small gathering. "I suppose, Charlie, you'll remain at Thermopylae while the Captain holds to life?" With my mouth full of crumpet I supposed we would.

"Of course, one is lucky to get a tenant in one's own home during such an emergency period, isn't one?" I agreed that one was. Mrs. Peters sighed over the whole situation and lowered her mascara'd eyelashes. "Old age is so sad. That at least *he* was spared." She raised her eyes to the Lance-Corporal.

"Any more pie?" asked Squid.

"Dear boy, no. I'm sorry, but I have a special treat for you if you can wait till Charlie and I have finished our crumpets."

Squid supposed aggrievedly that he could wait.

"Such a poor eater," said Mrs. Peters. She returned quickly to the subject of our house. "The Harrises have your place, I know. Of course, folk in a position such as theirs could pay comparatively little, one would suppose, in rent?" I supposed not.

"When do we get the surprise?" asked Squid.

"Patience is a virtue—" began Mrs. Peters. But she was interrupted by a knocking on the front door. "Do excuse me boys. It might be Mr. Glossop come to consult me on tonight's music."

But it was my mother, a scarf round her head and her face white. "Charlie," she said, looking past Mrs. Peters, "Grandfather got out of bed and we don't know where he is. Dad is looking in the garden. I fell asleep. Oh dear, I fell asleep!"

In a moment we were both outside under the dripping trees. The garden was submerged in fog but the house stood above it, looking like the ship Grandfather imagined it to be.

My father called from somewhere ahead, "It's getting worse. Get Charlie to go for Gouvane, we need men with torches. He mustn't be out long in this sort of weather."

I thought suddenly of Gyp. I called him and began whistling. Presently we heard a scrambling up the cliff path and Gyp appeared. I shouted, "The boatshed! He may be in the boatshed." I started down between the wet tea-trees, my father ahead of me, Gyp disappearing again before both of us. Suddenly my father called, "The door's open. He's been trying to pull the boat out."

He was silent then and I could hear only the lapping of the water. Then I heard him exclaim, "Good God!" I stopped walking. "Call Gyp."

I whistled to him and when he came I held him, glad to have him near me.

"Get your mother. Then go for Dr. Stuart."

I knew then the way it was. "Yes," I said. So I climbed up the cliff path and helped my mother down, then went along the beach towards the town.

IAN WAS sent away till Grandfather's funeral was over. Then an oppressive silence fell over the old house and everywhere I went I was conscious that Grandfather lay at the centre of it, lifeless yet still dominating. A succession of people came to "see him" and some of the women came out of the bedroom dabbing their eyes. Mrs. Peters said, "Ah, what dignity, Mrs. Reeve! Reminds one of the epistles of old. Has Charlie seen him?"

My mother said no, she didn't think it necessary. But I began to feel I was being protected from something a man should face. When an opportunity came I went in alone.

The experience shocked me. Everyone had said how peaceful Grandfather looked, but to me his body looked like something discarded. It wasn't him any more. I went down to the beach and sat by the boatshed for a long time before I went back inside.

We all packed into the lounge while Reverend Mr. Wetherby conducted the service. The heavy scent of flowers drifted from Grandfather's bedroom but through the open door the sun shone reassuringly on a calm sea.

Mr. Wetherby was a colourless man. He read, "I am the resurrection and the life;" he read, "Man that is born of woman hath but a short time to live;" he read that Grandfather had been twenty years a ships' master and twenty years in the pilot services; to my mother he read "words of comfort", all in a monotone. Behind him I could see old Mr. Matthias fidgeting. Finally, when Mr. Wetherby had uttered his last amen, Matthias said in a low, resonant voice, "True; but not enough. Here was a noble man, a noble and courageous man. He can be numbered among the generation of pioneers who now, alas, are falling from among us."

Mr. Wetherby looked in a surprised way over the top of his glasses. My father's eyes were cast down and he was biting his lower lip. Most people must have thought the address pre-arranged, for they listened intently. Mr. Matthias's beard protruded aggressively as he went on. "He was a man unafraid to express his opinions even when these were contrary to the opinions of those who happened to be in authority over him." There was an uneasy shuffling—after all, Matthias was supposed to be a Bolshevik. "And now his voice is stilled. No more shall we see him looking seaward from this old home or hear him in debate. But it is your hope and it is my hope—as a Christian it is my hope—that this is not the end."

At this moment the rapid striking of Grandfather's old clock interrupted him. My father hastily said "Amen," the people muttered "Amen," and the service was over.

SIX

When I went back to school even old Moloney regarded me as a person apart. "A sad loss," he said, then avoided speaking to me for the rest of the day.

My own attention was taken away from the past few days by the sight of Johnno. He sat alone and his head was clipped as close as a criminal's. At lunchtime, in the bush, I said to him, looking at his head, "Was that because of the haircut?"

He felt it gingerly. "Yes—the old man did it." He looked at me accusingly. "You shouldn't have let Squid do it. The old man was all for half killing me, but Eileen got between us and calmed him down. Then he borrowed some clippers and did this." He felt it again. "Old Moloney said he didn't want a convict sitting with the rest, so he put me alone. I was going to take it out on Squid, but he hardly moved away from the classroom all day." We ate our sand-wiches moodily. "There's something else," said Johnno, frowning. "It's Eileen. She was pretty good to me. Afterwards she asked if I'd take her to a dance two weeks from now. She reckons my hair will grow well enough by then. Charlie, it was partly your fault that I got into trouble with the old man. Wouldn't you—?"

"We've had a death. I couldn't ask to go to a dance now."

He tugged absently at a tuft of grass. "OK then," he murmured despondently. "OK."

So he went alone with his sister to the dance, and it turned out that this made a big difference to us. At lunchtime next day I said, "Well, what was it like?"

"I did the foxtrot with Eileen to start her off." He paused, as if there were more to mention.

"You didn't dance with anyone but Eileen, did you?"

"No," he said loudly, "of course I didn't. Listen, if we don't start now it won't be worth having a practice."

Boxing practice had been going on ever since the cold weather had begun. I looked at him closely. He couldn't lie successfully there was something he was ashamed to admit. "All right," I said carelessly, "you have first go."

He took a cord from his pocket and tied my wrists behind my back. "Right?"

"Right," I said indifferently.

He began punching at me, quickly but with pulled punches, while I dodged and ducked. He could have killed me, but his blows seldom hurt. We changed over and I bound his wrists. He stepped lightly, as if the ground were hot, and while I punched he rolled and bobbed so well that I scarcely landed a blow. "You want to get in," he said. "You're fair enough at defence, but you've got to punch as if you were punching old Moloney."

"About the dance—" I began afterwards.

But the second bell saved him from my question.

It was not long after this that Johnno began cleaning his shoes and wearing a tie. Even worse, he began using hair oil on his newly grown hair. My suspicions were aroused again and I was even more suspicious when I went to his place one Saturday afternoon. Old man Johnston was working at his tool-bench amongst a mess of bicycle parts. I avoided him and knocked at the back door. Eileen came out, smartly dressed and smelling sickly sweet.

"Why, it's Charlie!" she said, twirling her strands of beads.

I ignored this. "Is Fred home?"

"I thought he was going to your place," she said, opening her eyes wide. "If he's not there, I don't know where he could be."

"You know where he is, all right!" I said. "He hasn't been the same since he went to that dance with you."

She laughed. "Run along, Charlie boy, and have a look." I glared at her, but she walked inside, singing "Charmaine" and swinging her hips. I went home in a temper. At the side of the house Ian was climbing a pepper-tree.

"You never take me anywhere," he said in a whining voice.

"Shut up," I said. "Have you seen Fred Johnston?"

"I'm not going to tell you."

"If you don't I'll pull you out of that tree."

He climbed higher. "If you try, I'll spit on you."

I ran over to the tree and, leaping up, grabbed his foot. He came down on top of me, knocking me to the ground. "Charlie's broken me back," he screamed, writhing realistically.

My father rushed to the veranda, one of his study books in his hand. "What in the name of heaven have you done now?"

"Charlie pulled me by my foot." Ian struggled to his feet, his hand on his back.

"Shut up and I'll take you yabbying," I hissed.

"What was that?" demanded my father.

"I told him I was sorry."

"And so you should be. Now clear out—I don't care where—just clear out!"

As I WALKED away into town it came into my mind to do something without Johnno, something he would be sorry to miss, but I still had no idea what it could be when I reached the Mechanics' Hall. A number of people were passing in and out while others stood in groups outside. I remembered then that it was polling day.

Polling days were interesting. All the peculiar people we didn't see for months came out like insects from under lifted stones. There were the Misses Ferguson, for instance, who never stopped chewing aspirin when they were with other people and always spoke from behind a handkerchief soaked in eucalyptus. And there was Mrs. Rolls, a proud woman who hardly ever went out because she was so ashamed of her husband's drinking. She had made him live in a tent in their own backyard for this past ten years. She had once been a strong temperance worker and had married Charlie Rolls, so I had heard my father say, with the idea of reforming him.

At the Mechanics' door Mr. Turnbull was handing out How-to-

Vote cards for the party which I knew stood for authority, respectability and other proper things. Stinger Wray's father was handing out cards for the working man and "social justice". Mr. Turnbull wore an overcoat and a bowler hat, cleared his throat a lot and looked down importantly from a great height. Mr. Wray was hatless and wore a reversible raincoat. From his face you could tell that he believed life had done him great wrongs. The two men seemed on disappointingly friendly terms.

I had been there for about ten minutes when I saw Mr. Matthias, rucksack on his back, beard thrust out, book under one arm, mackintosh tightly buttoned, steel-rimmed glasses through which he didn't see well. He was walking quickly, muttering to himself, slashing at the roadside grass with his heavy stick.

I hadn't seen him since Grandfather's funeral. The idea that he was a Bolshevik had spread still further since he had got into a political argument in the main street with Mr. Glossop. Glossop had called him an anarchist, and soon after his landlady turned him out, telling my mother that she refused to share her roof with an Antichrist. My mother tried to protect him, and we might have taken him into Grandfather's old room; but overnight he disappeared. It was said he was living in a hut in the bush east of the town. Someone—Squid, I think—had spread the story that Bolsheviks had been seen carrying a big wireless transmitter there and that Mr. Matthias had daily conversations with Russia.

As he came to the hall the two men at the door held cards out to him. He took them, tore them to pieces and threw them to the wind. "Do you know what I think of compulsory voting?" he shouted. "All I intend doing is rendering my card invalid."

"Think of your responsibilities," cried Mr. Wray.

"All *you* think of is grievances," bellowed Mr. Matthias.

Mr. Wray turned his back angrily, but Mr. Turnbull laid his hand on the old man's arm. "Now, Matthias—"

"*Mr.* Matthias."

"Very well." Mr. Turnbull drew himself up, raising his chin so that he looked down on Mr. Matthias. "I can tell you I'm proud of my right to vote; proud to be a citizen of the Empire—"

"Bosh!" declared Mr. Matthias, striding into the hall. There was the sound of raised voices and presently Matthias came out with his stick over his shoulder as if he had demolished the place. He walked quickly down the road, his stick cutting at the grass again.

I knew then what I would do: I would follow him. I don't know what induced me to do it. Perhaps it was the talk about the transmitter, and, of course, the opportunity to do something independently of Johnno. Just the same, I should not have done it.

Across the school grounds Matthias went, then over the fence and into the bush, taking the track to the Lone Pine. I hesitated—it was late afternoon and the bush looked oddly forbidding—but then I went on quickly.

The light was weak, and underfoot the sand made no sound. My skin was tingling for no reason at all. Not till I was near the Lone Pine did I see him, fifty yards on, stick still swinging and back bent. Beyond this point he put his stick over his shoulder, as if he had left the country of his enemies behind, and began walking slowly through thicker growth. The track climbed to a high, open ridge. Stooped there, I looked back and saw the Lone Pine two miles or more away; and well ahead the water of Western Port.

Now Mr. Matthias walked faster, going downhill. The afternoon was all but over and I began to see I would be late home. After about a mile, Matthias reached his hut, a rough erection of boards and corrugated iron in a clearing. He unlatched the door and disappeared inside.

I felt sorry for him, and foolish; after all, he was my grandfather's friend. But I walked round the clearing, just inside the cover of trees. There was a small spring and the beginnings of a vegetable garden. While I stood there, smoke began to rise from the corrugated iron chimney. The daylight was going quickly now; I would have to run most of the way home. I was moving away carefully when suddenly the earth snatched at me and I felt as if an axe had cut off my foot. I yelled and saw that my foot was in a rabbit trap. At the same time there was a shout from inside the hut. I stamped on the spring of the trap, jumped clear and began running. Behind me Mr. Matthias yelled, "I know who you are. Get back to your police station!"

His shouting slowly died behind me as I pounded through undergrowth in semi-darkness, my foot feeling like a piece of meat. I ran until I could scarcely breathe and it was dark. Now and then I saw stars through the trees, but on the ground I could see nothing. I stumbled through a creek and realized I was off the track. But then the ground rose steadily, and when I went on I could make out Lone Pine against the sky. The panic that had made me run had gone and I hobbled slowly towards the lights of the town, my foot throbbing. It took me an hour to get to Thermopylae. Once there, I leaned against the wall, holding my foot.

My father laid down his accountancy book. "What is it *this* time?" he said wearily.

AS IT TURNED OUT, I was kept home for a week with doctor's orders to stay in bed. Squid brought me every book from my desk and a few notes I had wanted no one to see.

"What's up with you?" he asked, looking concerned.

"Caught my foot in a rabbit trap," I said.

He nodded seriously. "Toes gawn?"

"No," I said. "Cuts and bruises, that's all."

"Been injected?"

"No," I said.

He looked glum at this. "Trouble is lockjaw. Didn't no one tell you? Starts in y' face. Y' teeth jam shut; after a bit y' head bends back till y' end up practically in a circle. Bloke mum knew in Adelaide got buried in a round coffin after lockjaw."

"Not me," I said uneasily, but I began unwinding the bandage. The foot looked impressive—black round the toes with a row of scabs across it, the whole thing shading off to blues and greens, and on top of all this the iodine. I saw Squid's face going the same green as my ankle. His eyes rolled and he crashed to the floor.

My mother came in quickly. "Whatever have you done?"

"I only showed him my foot."

At this, she sat him up gently and put his head between his knees. "Ian, bring the smelling salts—quickly."

Squid was making noises like a puppy, and when Ian came in Gyp was close behind him, eager to join the game on the floor.

"Get that dog out!" But Gyp was licking Squid's face and bringing him round.

"It's me stummick," he said.

My mother half lifted him outside. "The air will help you."

That was the last I saw of Squid for some time, though he was good enough to send in a message that anyone not knowing how to do simultaneous equations by the following Monday was "in for it".

Johnno came next day. My mother said afterwards how nice it was to see him beginning to take pride in his appearance. "His trousers pressed and his boots cleaned. What did he do to his hair though?" All the time he was in the house he avoided my eyes and spoke only of school. "We've got a new teacher—Miss Beckenstall. She's good."

"Old?"

"About twenty-three, they reckon. Moloney doesn't take us for anything now; he's with the sixth grade."

A feeling of peace came over me.

"She's given me two 'excellents' for compositions, and she's a wake-up to Squid, too—keeps him in if he's late."

Perhaps after all there was going to be a reign of justice.

I didn't see Johnno again till the next Saturday evening. I limped to Mayfield's to get the *Sporting Globe*, and there was Johnno outside the shop, behaving very queerly. Once or twice he nearly went in, but at the last minute he changed his mind and instead studied the posters outside. Then he walked away, but changed his mind and came back again, travelling sideways like a crab.

As I crossed the street he saw me and tried to behave naturally, but when he realized I was going into the shop, he was hardly able to speak. He followed me in, walking close behind me. I saw then that Noreen Logan was serving behind the counter. She had left school at the end of the past year and now was all curves and lipstick and looked about twenty.

Johnno followed me to the counter, picked up a paper and began to read it as if his life depended on it. Mr. Mayfield, who was an elder in the Presbyterian church, said, "Lad, I don't like to see young fellows reading *Beckett's Budget*."

Johnno dropped it quickly. I doubt that it could have harmed him—he had been holding it upside down.

Noreen arched her eyebrows. "Yes, please?" she said to Johnno.

Johnno motioned towards me. "*Globe*," I said, deliberately omitting "please". I wanted to show the way I imagined girls should be managed. When she brought it, I said carelessly, "Can you change ten bob?"

She frowned—probably because she couldn't work out the change. Johnno said quickly, "I've got threepence. I owe it to you anyhow for that time at the pictures." He held it out to Noreen, looking like a dog that has brought back a stick.

"Thank you, Freddie," she said softly. Freddie!

Johnno's eyes hardly left her. She leaned her elbows on the newspapers and said, "Cold, don't you think?"

347

"Yes." He would have said it to "hot" or "windy". Another customer came in, but Noreen still leaned there while Johnno gazed at her.

Mr. Mayfield looked over at us disapprovingly. "Noreen, a lady is waiting. Time to leave, boys."

"Yes," said Johnno, not attempting to move. I caught hold of his arm and led him out of the shop.

I said, "I guessed it must be something like this; something low and sissy."

He didn't even hear me. He punched me joyfully in the ribs, prancing along like a racehorse. "Don't you reckon she's beaut?"

"She's a drip. She was a drip even in the first grade."

"—and the dress she had on," said Johnno, staring straight ahead. "Reminds me of Norma Talmadge—"

"You're mad, Johnno," I said. I left him abruptly, but I don't think he even noticed me go. He was still prancing along.

SEVEN

School had improved remarkably. While Moloney thrashed the sixth grade, Miss Beckenstall had us read *David Copperfield* in a way that brought the book to life. We had been about halfway through it and until then it had been dull stuff, read without pause or explanation. Miss Beckenstall gave us each a part: David for me, Mr. Micawber for Squid, Steerforth for Johnno, and so on.

"I don't like being Steerforth," said Johnno. "Look what he's done to Little Emily."

I wasn't sure what he had done to Little Emily; in any case Little Emily was being read by Janet Baker, who had nothing to recommend her.

"A chap's really bad if he's tough on women," said Johnno, gazing into the distance. He looked sillier every day.

I tried to be serious. "It depends who the woman is."

He hadn't heard me. "I'd drop Steerforth cold." He punched the air absent-mindedly. But there was no need to drop Steerforth— he was drowned next day. "He must have been a hell of a bad swimmer," said Johnno.

Miss Beckenstall taught simultaneous equations so well that I believed I had discovered the art for myself. One day she called

Johnno and me in while she was alone eating her lunch, and I looked at her carefully for the first time. Her hair was fair and smooth, drawn back the way Sappho wore it in the picture over the blackboard. Her eyes were grey, and quick to change expression. It struck me all at once that she was beautiful. Before that, a woman's beauty had meant nothing to me. I gazed at her warmly and she smiled faintly. I felt my face get hot.

Miss Beckenstall said in a friendly voice, "You know, I had heard that you boys didn't work well, but I am very pleased indeed with both of you. I want you to promise me that if you want help you will come to me. You both have quite a gift for self-expression: I want to encourage you to express yourselves as freely as possible. I'm sure we can catch up any lost ground in mathematics. You only need to believe in yourselves."

When we went outside Johnno said, "She's terrific. She looks a bit like Noreen—"

"No," I interrupted. "No!"

He looked puzzled. "You're queer about girls, all right."

After lunch Miss Beckenstall took poetry. With Moloney we had recited together while he stood in front like a conductor: "The camping grounds were crow-ded with cara-vansa teams—"

But Miss Beckenstall told us she would read us a poem in blank verse called "Ulysses". Here was old Ulysses, home after his travels, and longing to make one more journey. At first it sounded strange, but later I began to see it all:

> "The lights begin to twinkle from the rocks:
> The long day wanes: the slow moon climbs: the deep
> Moans round with many voices. Come, my friends,
> 'Tis not too late to seek a newer world.
> Push off, and sitting well in order smite
> The sounding furrows; for my purpose holds
> To sail beyond the sunset, and the baths
> Of all the western stars, until I die."

I saw the boat launched at evening below Thermopylae and Johnno bending with me at the oars. In the bows, looking towards the setting sun, stood Miss Beckenstall....

"That poetry was pretty good," said Johnno afterwards. "That part 'To strive, to seek, to find; but'—something or other."

349

As we walked home we looked across to the faint coast on the other side of the bay. Over there somewhere were the Otways, one of the places where Johnno had said he would find a hiding place when he ran away. He hadn't mentioned running away for some weeks.

Next day we walked to Lone Pine and climbed to the board seat at the top. As we settled there, with the country sunny to the horizon, Johnno pulled a piece of paper out of his pocket. He said, "Last night I wrote something. You'd better read it, but not out loud."

I leaned round the trunk and took it. Through a lot of crossing out I read:

"*We stood alone beside the sea.*
The girl with honey hair and me
And no one else at all to see
And wind and sea all blowing free—"

It went on like this till they "came home for tea."

"I got stuck on 'ee'," he said, "and couldn't stop."

I said, "It's pretty good. But 'honey hair' sounds messy."

"Well," he said, looking a long way off, "that's what it's like— you know, like sun shining through honey."

"You're mad if you think that dumb Logan girl's got honey hair.'

"If you weren't my mate I'd dump you fair out of the tree!"

"Mate!" I repeated bitterly. "I only see you at school."

"Well," he said, sighing, "it's hard to talk about."

"Did you meet her at the dance?"

"Yes," he admitted from behind the trunk. "In a tap dance I tapped her and no one tapped me, so we had the whole dance."

I peered round the trunk at him. He looked ridiculous with his carefully brushed hair and his pimples with the tops shaved off and his huge hands.

"I'm sorry for you," I said.

"I don't want to talk about it," he replied.

During the rest of the week Johnno must have been thinking things over. On the Friday he said brightly, "What about walking to Coles Bay tomorrow morning? We could take something to cook for lunch." The suggestion reminded me of old times.

"OK," I said. "OK!"

350

A TRACK, shut in most of the way by dense tea-trees, wound along the cliff-top to Coles Bay. Through gaps you could look down on the sea, on clear days right to the bottom.

Once we had swum there, exploring outcrops of rock under the water in a silent world with the sea around like curtains. Near the bottom we had seen something move. The sand had begun to rise like slow smoke and we had shot up together.

It was September, the month we usually started swimming again, and the day was the first really warm one we had had. We took sausages with us, and grilled them over a tea-tree fire, growing hotter and hotter. "I'm going for a swim," I said.

"You should wait an hour after a meal—probably an hour and a half after a meal like this."

I looked at him. "You used to go in any time. When we raided Collins's orchard, you ate quinces with water up to your neck."

"But not long after that I saw a girl dragged out. They tried resuscitation, but she didn't come round and they said it was because she had gone in after a meal."

I found this hard to accept from Johnno, but when we lay on a sloping, grassy spot I felt too drowsy to care. Even without sitting up we could see gulls skimming above the water. Their cries came up to us mixed with the lapping sounds. Spring was coming all around us. I was dozing, dreaming that Miss Beckenstall was reading to me, when Johnno said, "We'd better go!"

"You woke me up," I said irritably. "Anyhow, let's stay here."

"All right," he said, looking around uneasily. I slipped back to dreaming. Presently Miss Beckenstall took up her position in the bows and the brown sailors hoisted the sail. Sitting with the sun behind her, she began reading above the sound of the sea:

> *"It little profits that an idle king,*
> *By this still hearth, among these barren crags . . ."*

"What'd you know!" cried a voice. "Fancy meeting you here!"

Miss Beckenstall disappeared into the sea and beside us stood Noreen Logan and Kitty Bailey, a dumb willowy blonde who had left school to work the cash register at the Continental café. The two of them stood in their summer frocks swaying their hips, swinging their beads and making sure their jazz garters were in view. I felt strangled. I looked at Johnno, but he avoided my eye.

351

"We were just out strolling—such a div-ine day," said Noreen. "And what are you men doing?"

"We've just had lunch," said Johnno hoarsely. "Sausages."

"Yum, yum! We should of come sooner, Kit."

I burst out to Johnno, "I thought no one came here."

"Well—" He waved his hand helplessly.

"*Some* people," said Noreen, "think they own the town and everyone in it. Kitty, lend me a cigarette, there's a dear."

Kitty produced a packet of Magpies and a box of matches and the two of them began puffing expertly, hand on hips. "May we sit down? Gentlemen usually ask ladies to sit down, you know."

"Yes, yes," said Johnno quickly.

They held their skirts delicately and sank beside us. Johnno and Noreen began talking in low voices; I remained silent, my face hot.

"The view here is simply gor-geous, don't you think?" Kitty looked at me over the tip of her cigarette.

"I suppose so," I said. I smelt the sea, her perfume and the coming of spring. It was pleasantly disturbing.

"Have you been for a swim?"

"No," I answered.

"I saw you swimming last year—you're terrifically fast."

"Not as fast as Johnno."

"Oh, Freddie's fast, isn't he? Just ask Noreen!"

I couldn't find an answer to this subtlety. I stared down at the ashes of our fire and Kitty looked sadly out to sea.

"You don't like girls, do you?"

"They're all right, I suppose."

She turned towards me so that her bobbed hair blew over her face. "Freddie does," she said. "He likes Noreen." She butted her cigarette, took out a compact and began operating on her lips.

"Kitty, pet," said Noreen, interrupting, "me and Fred think we might walk a little way. We want a tat-a-tat, don't we, Freddie?" Freddie made an embarrassed sound in his throat. "Do you and Charlie want to sit here, or will you toddle, too?"

"Oh, we might sit a while, don't you think, Charlie? Perhaps we'll follow—but not too close, eh?" She smothered a giggle.

Noreen stood up and brushed her frock and turned to see if it had crushed. "Oh, I've left my handbag on the ground."

Freddie picked it up like Gyp picking up the morning paper and

352

as they went off together I saw Fred take her hand, the worst mark of a sissy.

"He's rather a pet, isn't he? So fond of Noreen." Casting down her lashes, she added, "And you're a bit nice, too."

I was out of my depth now, but I said determinedly, "When did Johnno work it out to come here?"

"Oh, I suppose Wednesday when he walked home with Nor."

"Walked home?" A secret underworld was opening around me and Johnno was part of it.

"Nor was working back Wednesday night."

Kitty sat with her arms round her knees, gazing out to sea. "Do you like Ruth Chatterton? You know, the fillum star?"

From her handbag, she produced a folded page from a magazine, blew powder off it and opened it carefully. A blonde girl stared out at me with a smouldering expression. There was something about her hair-style and her shadowed eyelids . . . "She reminds me of someone," I said.

"Oh?" She was regarding me from under darkened eyelashes, her lips curved. "Who could it be, now?"

"She reminds me—of you."

"Oh, Charlie, you do say the sweetest things! You don't go round paying compliments to *every* girl you meet, do you?"

It struck me all at once that I must have known a great deal about girls without realizing it. I leaned over and took her scented, manicured little hand as I had seen Johnno take Noreen's.

"Oh, Charlie," she murmured. She leaned towards me, her hair brushing my cheek. I saw her curved lips waiting. Then somewhere beyond her, intruding alarmingly, I saw a pair of male shoes half-hidden by dirty Oxford bags.

I shot to my feet and found myself facing Big Simmons. He stood with half-closed eyes, hands on hips, breathing quickly.

"Ron," breathed Kitty. "Oh, Ron!"

"Shut up!" cried Big. "A bloke oughta belt you, telling a feller all that dope. Who's this runt?"

"He doesn't mean a thing to me. We just happened to meet—"

"You were getting on pretty good—holding bloody hands."

"He made me."

"He did? Clear out while me and him have a little talk."

Kitty scrambled up and made off in the direction opposite to Johnno. A fearful silence fell. The waves stopped lapping on the

rocks, the trees became still, the seagulls disappeared. Big spat at my feet. "Who said y' could take my sheila out?"

"I didn't take her—"

"My bloody oath you took her!" I watched him with horrible fascination—his coppery stubble and sideboards, his narrow eyes. "By hell, y'll pay for this!"

When I saw no hope of reprieve, stubbornness swam up through my fears. He was standing above me on the slope, a position of advantage. I watched him take his hands unhurriedly off his hips. He was "Big" Simmons; he had no need to hurry. I didn't wait for him to punch, but dived and caught him below the knees with my shoulder. I felt him shoot over me and crash into the grass. But then I only scrambled to the level ground and hesitated as if it had been a practice with Johnno. Big picked himself up and charged up the slope, arms out from sides and face twisted. I ducked under a straight right that would have taken my head. He came quickly again, swinging. Most of the blows missed; the rest I took on my arms and back glancingly. He pressed in closer, and I swayed right as he came in. I saw his face unguarded, punched his nose with all my strength and saw blood gush over his lip and chin. He let out a bellow and drove his knee into my groin. As I doubled up he jumped in, wrapped an arm round my head and began punching my face with his other hand, grunting with each blow. I reached blindly for his ankle and wrenched his foot off the ground but his fingers went deeply into my eyes. There was a white light and someone screamed. I felt myself rolling through darkness. Then my head came hard against something and I lost consciousness.

THE GIRL'S voice said again, "Leave him; you've got to leave him or we'll really be in for it."

Johnno's voice answered. "You can if you like."

"If you don't come I'll never speak to you again."

"You don't have to," he said. "You can clear out."

She shouted something and that was all I heard of her.

I tried to open my eyes, but gasped with pain. I heard Johnno say, "Charlie—are you OK, Charlie?"

"I can't see," I said. "Big Simmons got his fingers in my eyes."

I heard an intake of breath. "It's all my fault," he said. "Can you walk?"

"I think so," I said. But when I stood up I found it harder than I had expected. It was three miles back to the town. Even with Johnno guiding me I travelled slowly, stumbling and swaying along the track, my eyes scalding. Every few minutes Johnno asked in a worried voice, "Can you see yet?"

I could hardly answer for the pain. "They may be better in a while," I said. I tried to open my eyes again but it was useless.

After a long time we began descending towards the town. I wondered then what my father would say, but the pain drove any real anxiety out of me. Johnno said, "I better take you to Dr. Stuart's." We were somewhere in the main street when he gripped me so hard that I stopped. I heard my father's voice exclaim, "Good God, what's happened?"

"A fight," I said, my voice all at once uncontrollable. "Ron Simmons."

"It was my fault," I heard Johnno say.

My father didn't answer him. I heard him catch his breath. "What has he done to your eyes? Can you see?"

"A bit," I said.

"Did you see it happen, Fred?"

"No—no," stammered Johnno.

"He found me," I said. My voice was too unsteady to say more.

"We'll go to the doctor's. Fred, run to our place and tell Mrs Reeve we'll be late for dinner. Better tell her what's happened—but try not to make it too worrying for her."

"No, sir," said Johnno. I had never heard him call my father sir before.

I heard him go away as I went on with my father, walking slowly. "It might hurt having the eyes examined," he warned.

We came to the doctor's gate, crunched slowly up the gravel path and rang the doorbell.

I heard the doctor's sour old mother come to the door and exclaim, "Now look, Mr. Reeve, doctor's at dinner. He has to eat like other people, you know."

"My boy's in a good deal of pain," said my father. "Just show me to the waiting room and get the doctor."

Before she could reply I heard Dr. Stuart push back his chair in the dining room and call out, "Is that you, Mr. Reeve?"

"It is," said my father. "Sorry to disturb you."

"A fight with the elder Simmons larrikin, eh?"

"How did you hear?" demanded my father.

"He came in with a broken nose," said the doctor. My father began to exclaim but the doctor interrupted, "Splendid blow— about time someone did it. Now what's the damage here . . . ? Good Lord! How did this happen?"

"Dug his fingers into them," said my father.

"Pretty nasty kind of fight, eh?" The doctor took my arm. "Come into the surgery and we'll see what's to be done." He pressed me into a chair and tilted my head back. "This may hurt." He tried to open my right eye and I felt my head spin. I slid off the chair into unconsciousness . . . .

When I came round I was on the surgery table, a tremendous burning in my eyes. From behind a light the doctor was saying, "That's my advice, anyhow. I can give him something to ease the pain on the journey up. They'll probably keep him for a bit—unless there's somewhere nearby where he could stay?"

"My mother's in East Melbourne. I'll telephone her."

I put my hand over my eyes.

"Hurting, eh? We're sending you to the Eye and Ear Hospital so that they can have a look at you. Just a precaution." He began bandaging my eyes firmly.

So we went up to Melbourne by hire car. It took half my father's wages for the week.

EIGHT

To go into the cosy world of my grandmother's house was to go to another country; a country protected from Australian heat and lack of respectability by old thick walls and by my British grandmother herself. There were shelves of books bought in London and walls hung with family portraits; there were marble mantels with glass-domed clocks, and hanging lustres that split the light into rainbows. There was coal in the grates and in one corner rested a musical box. My grandmother lived there alone now, having outlived a couple of spinster daughters and a bachelor son. Sitting at the head of the table at family gatherings, body erect, hair parted at the centre, she dominated the room.

I was glad I could not see her sharp eyes this night when we came from the hospital. She made a "tch-tch" sound as we stood at the door, but instead of shaking hands as she normally did she kissed me lightly above the bandage, a rare concession. I was led upstairs to the small bedroom over the Parade, undressed, felt my way to the bed and got in. The throbbing had eased, but my eyes were bandaged firmly. I lay back listening to the Chinese market-carts, the far sad cry of paperboys and the sound of the gripman throwing the lever to coast a tram downhill. Outside, I thought, has to be London; and downstairs is Queen Victoria. Her voice came faintly to me from below, "You fought, too, when you were a boy. It's a phase. A phase."

"It's the type of lout he fought with," said my father.

"Well, the standards in a young country, you know."

I heard my father come softly upstairs. "You awake still, son?" he said quietly. "I must go home in a few minutes." He sat on the end of the bed. "You were fortunate that no permanent damage was done. Now, just what happened?" I was silent: since I couldn't see his expression it was not so difficult to remain silent. He went on. "I'm going to see Sergeant Gouvane when I get back. Whatever the cause was, I'm not going to stand for a lout trying to blind you. Now what can I say at the police station? What caused the argument in the first place?"

"You don't have to do anything to start a fight with the Simmons," I said uneasily.

"No, I grant you that. Was Fred Johnston with you?"

"No. He came afterwards, after Ron Simmons had gone . . ." I hesitated. "My eyes are beginning to hurt," I said.

"Gouvane will go to Simmons," my father persisted. "What story is he likely to hear there?"

I had convinced myself that I was in pain again. "My eyes . . ."

"Look, son, something has to be decided about this before I go home and I don't want to find you've told me only half the story. Did you say anything to annoy Simmons?"

He got up and began walking up and down.

"No," I said. But even to my own ears my voice sounded uncertain.

"So he simply walked up and hit you? Was anyone else there?" I felt my face redden. "One of the Simmons girls?" I left this unanswered too long, and he asked, "Some other girl?"

"Kitty Bailey," I heard myself say. "He thought I was—out with her."

He stopped walking. "And were you?"

"No—not exactly. I was going for a walk and I just happened to meet her."

He sat on the bed again. "What sort of a girl is she?"

"Stupid," I said. An awkward silence fell over us.

"I haven't spoken much to you about girls, when I come to think of it." He cleared his throat. "Just what happened with this girl?"

"Nothing. We just talked about Ruth Chatterton, the film actress."

"Nothing else happened? I mean . . ." I waited to see what he meant, but he didn't say.

"Perhaps you don't know that girls of her type are dangerous?" I couldn't think of anything to say. "I don't blame you for being—interested. After all, you are reaching an age when—uh—" His voice wavered. "What happened then?"

"Big Simmons came along and got mad."

"Hm." He was silent, as if thinking of things he should tell me. My grandmother called up, "George, time you were leaving."

"When you get home we must have a talk." He sounded more cheerful. "I'm glad you've told me about it, anyway. What do you think now?" he asked frankly. "Will it help to see Gouvane?"

"It might get me into worse trouble with Simmons," I said.

"It might do that, but I don't want to see him get away with it. Well, my boy, I must be off. Don't worry about things."

The bandage remained on for three days and I learned all the outside noises, from the soft footfalls of the Chinese vegetable man trotting with his pole over his shoulder, to the trundle of brewery wagons down Victoria Parade. Each day my grandmother took me by tram to the hospital.

When the bandage came off I went to a mirror. My eyes were black and the eyeballs were red; my hair had been combed forward in a peculiar Edwardian sort of way by my grandmother. Even though my reflection was blurred I saw, too, that I should commence shaving. Either I had forgotten how advanced my beard was or it had appeared in a matter of days. While I looked at myself, my grandmother came into the room as if reading my thoughts, and handed me a cut-throat razor. "It was your grandfather's," she said.

Two evenings later I was allowed to go alone into the city. I walked past St. Pat's, past cobblers and barbers, hotels and chemists, past horses tossing nosebags while lorries were loaded, in and out of lighted arcades where there were tea-rooms and book-stalls. I had turned into an arcade when I saw a man and a woman looking into a jeweller's window at trays of engagement rings. The woman held the man's arm and their heads were close together as they talked. As I passed, the woman turned to the man, exclaiming "But really, darling—"

It was Miss Beckenstall. I paused, then walked on, my heart bumping. I hadn't seen the man's face, but I hated him and I hated Miss Beckenstall for having deceived me. I glanced back and saw them coming my way, noticing nothing but each other. They crossed the road, then stepped into a tram. I saw her for a moment in the golden interior. The gripman threw the lever and she was gone. Underground the cable hummed sadly to itself.

Before I went home a letter came from Eileen Johnston. "Dear Charlie, how all this happened I don't know and Fred won't tell me, but he went to Simmons's place on his own on Sunday and came back with his clothes torn and his cheek cut. I tried to clean him up before Dad saw him, but I hadn't got finished when the police came. There was a fearful row with Dad and Sergeant Gouvane and Fred, all locked in Dad's room. I'm sorry about your eyes, but why did Fred have to pick a fight? Dad says he must start work next week at Digger Hayes." Digger Hayes was the black-smith.

On my first day back at school I saw that Johnno looked older and more than usually troubled. There were dark stitches on his cheekbone. Miss Beckenstall began to write on the board, and when she took up the duster in her other hand I saw that she was wearing an engagement ring. I knew then that all women were full of deceit.

Johnno said at lunchtime, "Miss Beckenstall saw the old man. He's let me come back to school, but I'm working on Saturday mornings until the end of the year."

Almost without thinking we climbed towards Lone Pine; it seemed an old friend who had never let us down. "How are your eyes?" Johnno said.

"Just about right," I said. "They go blurry sometimes, but the doctor says they'll get better."

Johnno smiled. "You made a mess of Big Simmons's nose."

I felt pleased. "It was the only time I hit him. Why did you go to his place?"

But he wouldn't explain his motives. "I hung about near the house," he said, "and when Big came out I called him over. His nose was all taped up. He called to Little Simmons and Little yelled, 'I'll hold him and you give it to him!' But with his nose the way it was, Big wasn't game to come close till his brother could grab me, so I knocked him down to make sure I wasn't grabbed. Gouvane came just after that, while Big was coming at me with a picket."

We had reached the tree and our hands went to the usual branches as we climbed up, and all the coast opened below us, with the Dandenongs far to the north. When we sat down on the board Johnno said, "I'm done with girls. I'll never get married."

"Neither will I," I said.

MISS BECKENSTALL had already made great changes in Johnno. She often passed books on to him, or asked him to write "brief descriptions" which she would discuss with him. Although she was equally encouraging to me, she pushed Johnno ahead both because he was older and because she wanted to convince his father of his worth.

After Johnno was sent to work at the blacksmith's, the weekends were often dreary. When Digger Hayes closed down at noon on Saturdays, Johnno had to start work at home, chopping wood or even scrubbing floors. I kept away from Navy Bike Repairs in case I caused him further trouble but a few of us would go to the smithy on Saturday mornings; some to commiserate with Johnno, others because they liked an excuse to be there. It was a long, dark cave of a place where three men at a time worked on horses, stooping over their hooves, cursing them, pulling out old nails and hammering in new ones. Half-finished spring-carts and jinkers stood at one end, and about the whole place was a smell of singed hooves and horse dung and the coke fire.

One Saturday morning late in October I dropped in to see Johnno at about ten o'clock. He was swinging a sledge-hammer, beating a length of red-hot iron while Digger Hayes held it this way and that and came in himself with a smaller hammer, using quick, short strokes, ringing his hammer on the anvil.

"All right, young Reeve, onto the bloody bellows."

Digger was a man to obey. As I pulled the bellows I saw Windy Gale come in, and Fat Benson and one or two others.

361

"Right, Windy-bloody-Gale, pick up a few horseshoes."

Then Squid came, but he remained far enough back to avoid work. I changed with Fat and went over to where Squid leaned at the door. He looked at me from the corner of his eye and I knew that he had some idea in mind. Finally, he said, "Seen a good flick last night—about a bullfight." I showed no interest, but he pressed on. "It gave me an idea. I reckon we could have our own bullfight."

"I can tell you one feller who won't be there."

"Windy would," said Squid. "So would a couple of others. And we got a bull, too. Up in the pound. Donnelly's big Hereford."

I'd seen the man from the pound pick the bull up on the road. He must have broke through Donnelly's fence. "That bull is older than Donnelly himself," I said.

"It'd be good to practise with, anyhow. I'm the pixador, on a horse. I reckoned you might want to be matador—not to kill the bull. If you just touch him on the neck you win."

"What if he wins?"

"Anyone could get away from Donnelly's bull; but OK, I'll find another mat'dor."

We left it at that and I went back into the smithy and helped paint a spring-cart.

That afternoon I began thinking almost involuntarily of the bull-fight and by three o'clock I found my legs moving towards the pound. It was on the eastern edge of the town past the main shops, the timber-yards, and a house belonging to old Charlie Rolls. Charlie Rolls lived on some sort of pension and spent most of his time drinking at the Pier Hotel. He was a sorry-looking man—turned-down walrus moustache, turned-down old hat, mournful eyes; and his wife was a grim-looking woman. As I have said, she made him live in a tent in the backyard, on the edge of some unfenced bush.

The pound was in a hollow a few hundred yards beyond the patch of bush, a pleasant green paddock with a tea-tree hedge on three sides and a high four-bar fence on the fourth. Usually a horse or two was inside, or a cow. I had never seen a bull there.

I cut through Rolls's bush and came up to the pound behind one of the hedges. I could hear voices. The bottom of the hedge was very thick, but hollowed in places where boys had made hiding holes. I pushed into one of these and saw, only a few feet away, Donnelly's bull. It had its head down and was munching grass, snorting peacefully. It was an ugly bull with reddish-looking eyes, a white face and matted, curly hair round its head. Outside the post-and-rail fence, Squid sat on an old horse with a drooping head; whose it was I had no idea. No saddle was on it, but from somewhere Squid had borrowed a bridle. He sat like Napoleon directing his troops.

"Right now, the banderliras get first go. Got y' darts?"

They had made swamp tea-tree darts about eighteen inches long. Now the two banderilleros, Windy and Fat, looked doubtfully at the rear of the bull. Windy said to Squid, "When d' *you* go in?"

"Me? Well, this horse here belongs t' someone else an' I promised not t' get it excited. I reckon it'd be best if I stuck my spear in from here."

"If outside's good enough f' the pixador, it ought t' be good enough f' the banderliras," said Fat's mournful voice.

"I'll go in," said Windy contemptuously. "I reckoned I'd fight a bull, an' that's what I'll do!"

He swaggered up to the fence and as he climbed onto it, it moved under him a little with age. The unsuspecting bull still munched and snorted contentedly, releasing an odour of chewed grass. Windy waved a piece of red flannelette. The bull looked over its shoulder, but returned to the grass.

"In the flick," said Squid, "the banderliras pranced round where the bull could see 'em. Course, it'd take a bit o' guts with the savage bulls they got over there."

Windy apparently thought his reputation was at stake. He slid silently to the bull's side of the fence, then hitched up his pants and advanced cautiously. The bull, having finished a patch of cape-weed, turned and faced his challenger. Windy took a few steps back and the bull went back to eating.

Outside, Squid said, "This bull ain't hardly worth fighting. Even a Spanish bloke couldn't get him in'rested."

Windy accepted this as a further challenge. He walked boldly towards the bull, drew back his arm and flung the dart. It passed over the bull's back and speared into the hedge just over my head. Now Windy was becoming braver every moment. "I'll stir the old coot up," he said. "Watch this now."

The dart flashed from his hand, and all at once the whole scene changed. Instead of a peaceful bull there was a bellowing monster with a dart in its neck charging the first thing it could see. The first thing was Windy. With the greatest ease Windy jumped the fence, but the bull's charge took it straight into the rails, which broke off rottenly. For a second I saw four bullfighters in mid-air, their faces horrified, and the bull running head down after Squid's horse. Then the horse came to life with a bound, galloping away from underneath Squid and for a moment I had the illusion that while he sat there the bull passed under him, roaring horribly. The horse headed for the bush with the bull about fifty feet behind it.

Then voices yelled and I crawled out and began running towards Charlie Rolls's place. As I scrambled through a fence, the horse and bull were crashing about in the bush. Well behind me I could still hear shouting.

I was skirting Rolls's place when I saw, a long way ahead, the galloping horse. The bull was nowhere in sight and I was beginning to relax when I heard a fearful bellowing and saw Charlie Rolls's tent lift off the ground with a crashing of bottles and snapping of ropes. It lurched about the yard in a weird dance. Mrs. Rolls appeared at her back door, but one look at the dancing tent sent her scurrying inside. The tent went scudding over Charlie's yard and collided with the front fence. There it rolled over a couple of times, then collapsed with a baffled roar. The bull was wrapped up like a parcel.

Half the men and boys in the town were now approaching with shouts of "What is it?" and "Keep the women back!" but no one went near the tent. Mrs. Rolls appeared with a pot-stick in her hand, her expression furious. "Disgusting!" she cried. "How can he do it?" She evidently had some idea that Charlie's DTs had materialized.

At that point Charlie himself emerged from the outdoor lavatory, shaking to the tips of his moustache. "Never again!" he cried. "I swear, never again." A fresh outburst of bellowing sent the crowd scattering back.

"It's Donnelly's bull!" shouted someone, sighting a leg. "Where's Bill Donnelly?"

There was another outburst of bellowing, then a ripping sound, and the bull's head appeared through the tent, the whites of its eyes showing. "Shoot it!" shouted someone. But then Sergeant Gouvane appeared, a coil of rope in his hand. He fastened it around the bull's legs, then stood up. "How did this animal get out of the pound?"

364

"Please, sir," Squid was squeezing through the onlookers, the other bullfighters hovering nearby. Every freckle stood out on Squid's face. "Please sir, I—we seen it get out. We was out for a horse ride near the poun'. I was having my go when we heard a fearful beller." He hesitated, casting his eyes wildly about the crowd. "We looks round an' there she is, charging out through the fence." The crowd was silent. The bull was now lying motionless, emitting moaning sounds.

"I swung round me horse an' tried t' head her orf from me mates . . ." He hesitated. "I'm not much of a rider an' got pitched off. The bull chased the horse—an' that's about all . . ."

His voice trailed away. He looked close to collapse. There was a murmur of admiration from the crowd.

"Did you see what frightened the bull in the first place?" demanded Gouvane. Squid shook his head. "How is it," persisted Gouvane, "that for no apparent reason the bull . . ."

"Easy on him, Sergeant," exclaimed someone. "The kid's pretty shocked. He's done damn' well if you ask me."

"I'm not asking you," said Gouvane coldly, but after a further question or two he relented and let Squid go.

On Monday the *Kananook Courier* came out with:

LOCAL BOY'S COURAGEOUS ACTION: FACES CHARGING BULL TO DEFEND MATES.

Australia need not fear that the lofty spirit of Anzac is dead! The tradition of mateship was seen at its best when, on Saturday last, Birdwood Monash Peters . . .

The story went on to note that the bull had been maddened when, breaking through the pound fence, a sizeable sliver had penetrated the neck of the beast . . .

At school, after we had saluted the flag and said we loved God and our country, old Moloney called Squid up beside him and read the *Courier* clipping aloud while Squid looked modestly at the ground. "Three cheers for Birdie Peters. Hip, hip . . ."

The cheers stuck in my throat. Afterwards I said to Squid, "Pity the fence broke when the bull chased Windy."

He shrugged. "If you make somethink up, who'll believe you?"

I knew the answer—no one.

NINE

"I hope you congratulated Birdie on his courage," my father said. When I didn't answer he looked over the top of the *Courier*: "Well, did you?"

"No," I admitted.

My mother said, "For such a nervous lad Birdie is to be admired, and you'll have to be nice to him tonight, even if you do feel ungracious. We're invited over to Mrs. Peters."

"Why do we have to go there?" I asked.

"This is our sixteenth wedding anniversary," said my mother coldly. "Mrs. Peters has invited us in for a cup of tea and a few songs round the piano. For my part, I think it very nice of her."

That evening, my father sang "Oh, Promise Me" to my mother and my mother sang "Because" to my father, and they sang "Until" together, while Mrs. Peters trilled away at the piano. The only alternative to listening was to escape with Squid to the Den. I could see he wanted to be pleasant to me, no doubt reasoning that I might still tell my version of the bull incident. He kept talking to me about coming attractions we could see together at the Palais, but every few sentences I interrupted him, calling him "Mighty Picador" and "Moloney's pet". This latter really troubled him. There was something about Moloney beginning to worry him, but I didn't then know what it was.

When the singing ended we were called upstairs for tea and cakes. My mother and father stood hand in hand as if they were about eighteen. "A night round the piano is really lovely," my mother was saying. "Young people nowadays only want to sit with the headphones on listening to the wrestling."

"Remember Melba when we were young?" my father put in. "That *was* singing. There's a record of her with Caruso, but gramophones are too expensive for us."

"Funny you should say that, Mr. Reeve. Only this morning I heard of one likely to go cheap. Belongs to Nettie McQueen. Poor soul; their place is getting auctioned."

Next morning my father remarked that they might be able to go to a pound for the gramophone if he went without a new hat, and at this, my mother said to me, "Do you think you could bid at an auction sale?" I supposed I could.

Johnno came with me to the McQueens' auction and it turned
out to be Johnno who was more concerned in the result than I was,
for it led eventually to his final clash with his father and old
Moloney.

We walked through the bush to the McQueens'. It was a hottish
day and very clear, with the bush scents rising about us.

"I suppose," said Johnno, "that after the sale the McQueens will
go away somewhere."

I hadn't thought of this; I had only thought of the gramophone.
I knew "Shadder" McQueen at school, but he seldom had much to
do with me. The reason might have been that my mother sometimes passed my much-worn clothes on to him: a city cousin of
mine wore them first.

Mr. McQueen had an orchard, but according to my father it was
losing money. He also had a rabbit round; in fact, meals at the
McQueens' were said to be mostly rabbit and fruit. He had been
gassed in the war and two or three times had collapsed in his cart
during his round. When my mother heard this she bought rabbits
every week till even Gyp was sick of them.

As if continuing my thoughts, Johnno said, "My old man says
they owe money to the council and Harrison's store and to the
bank."

At last we reached McQueen's house, a small, single-gabled
place with a red SALE flag by the front window.

People were tramping through the house looking for damp,
seeing that the doors opened properly. They talked loudly about
the old bath-heater, the worn linoleum and the leak in the back
veranda roof.

By the time the gramophone was put up for auction Johnno was
scowling and I was beginning to feel as unhappy as he was, for the
sight of Shadder watching from a distance or helping his mother
prepare cups of tea made me feel guilty.

"What's next, Harold?" Mr. Bolter the auctioneer, his face red
from shouting, was standing on the back of a spring-cart, watching
the crowd shrewdly.

"Number one two four one of His Master's Voice graphaphones
and assortment of recuds," answered Harold. He held the "grapha-
phone", a shining table model, over his head. "Good as noo,
Mr. Bolter." Johnno moved away from me.

"You're right, Harold, good as new. Lift it up here now, and let the ladies and gents hear a record. Something bright, eh, Harold?"

"'When I Was Twenty-One', sung by Harry Lauder." Harry Lauder's voice rose thinly over the crowd:

> "*Oh, when I was twenty-one, when I was twenty-one,*
> *I never ha' lots o' monie, but I'd always lots o' fun . . . .*"

"All right, Harold, shut it off now. What am I offered, ladies and gents? I should ask a tenner for this beautiful talking machine but I'll make it only a fiver."

My heart sank. Johnno caught my eye from several paces away. "We won't be guilty of taking it, anyway," said his glance.

"Who'll offer me a fiver for this good-as-new HMV table gramophone—twelve-inch plush-covered turntable, gooseneck tone arm and a dozen records thrown in?" No one spoke. "Four poun' ten? Four quid am I bid? Just four quid?"

Some of the crowd began to drift away. They were after furniture or implements; a gramophone was a luxury. Mr. Bolter lowered his hammer slowly. "Ladies and gents, I beg you now, be serious, think what you'd be getting here." No one spoke. "Where's your culture, ladies and gents?" he asked despairingly.

In the doorway behind him I saw Mrs. McQueen and Shadder, Mrs. McQueen holding her apron between her hands.

Mr. Bolter leaned forward and said, "Am I bid five bob, then?"

"Yes," I said.

"Five bob from young Charlie Reeve, a boy who knows his culture. Any advance on five bob? Who'll offer me seven and six?" He was speaking rapidly, his left arm raised. "Five bob it is, five bob . . . seven and six—thank you, madam." I glanced to where he was looking but no woman was there. "Seven and six, seven and six for the musical glories of Beethoven and Mo-zart, seven and six . . ."

"Ten shillings," I said.

"Young Reeve again and the offer is ten bob; just a half-note for this de luxe model gramophone, ten bob from young Reeve . . ."

Beyond him Mrs. McQueen and Shadder were both watching closely. It must have seemed impossible to them that their one luxury was to go for ten shillings. Johnno was kicking the turf with his toe, looking down at the ground unhappily. "A pound," I said.

Mr. Bolter stopped short. "Now just a minute, young feller! Yours was the ten bob bid. You understand that?"

I heard some laughs in the crowd. "Yes," I said.

He drew himself up. "Have you *got* a pound?" I went to take it from my pocket, forgetting it was pinned there with a safety pin. The crowd laughed again while I undid the pin and held the note up. "A quid it is, by God. Very well, I'll make it a pound. One pound, ladies and gentlemen, any advance . . ."

"Twenty-five bob," said Johnno, coming over to me.

Mr. Bolter hesitated. Johnno said to me, "I bid for you. Here." He thrust five shillings into my hand.

"Twenty-five bob," I said.

"Twenty-five bob it is." Mr. Bolter narrowed his eyes. "Twenty-five bob and it's going, twenty-five bob. Going, going . . ." He crashed the hammer down, then pointed the handle towards me. "Twenty-five bob to get from young Reeve there, Harold."

I handed Harold the twenty-five shillings and took the gramophone while Johnno picked up the records.

"And now, ladies and gents, the poultry and contents of one shed situate at rear of residence . . ."

The crowd moved away, leaving Johnno and me standing there. A few people grinned as they passed. When they had gone I said, "What did you do that for? I don't know when we can pay you back."

"It doesn't matter," he said. "I got it for overtime from Mr. Hayes."

Mrs. McQueen and Shadder had gone inside. I said, "Let's go."

For weeks after the sale we had boys dropping in after school to listen to records.

Squid became envious. One afternoon while I was out he asked if he could play a few records on his own, and next day "Gundagai" stuck on ". . . once more". Peter Dawson would come up to the words at full gallop, *"And the pals of my childhood once more— once more, once more . . ."*

"He dug it with a pocket knife!" claimed Ian accusingly.

"Nonsense!" cried my mother. Squid could do no wrong at our place.

WE WERE to sit for the Merit at the end of the month. Every time Moloney passed he glanced at me as if I had already failed, and my father kept me studying each night—geography, geometry, grammar. Most evenings ended the same way: "Why don't you

369

pay attention, boy? How do you expect to get a job if you dream? I tell you, we're coming into the hardest time we've known."

Only Miss Beckenstall was encouraging. "Only concentrate and you'll do it," she said.

I was sleeping on the veranda again and after these homework sessions it was always a relief to go out there and hear the sea washing on the beach and see the red light flashing at the end of the pier. Life as pictured by adults was hell.

On Saturday afternoons, however, Johnno and I were now allowed to take Grandfather McDonald's boat about a mile out to the reef, to catch flathead. The boatshed was deserted and lonely, and smelt of oil and salt and dried bait. Gyp usually came fishing with us, taking up a position in the bows like a figurehead. Usually we came back late in the afternoon and anchored over the wreck of the *Isis*. She was dark-looking and dead; sand had already covered part of the bows, and whitebait darted in shoals from the cabin.

Armistice Day came. This year the star of the occasion was a tall, gangling man with a thatch of grey hair and a boyish face. "I want to say," he said, "how proud I am to be in the land of those who so bravely supported us in the world war of 1917-18."

But actually he had said, "Ah wanna say . . ."

When Fat Benson leaned over and whispered, "He's American," a shock of disappointment hit me. Probably even Tom Mix spoke this way!

As "One bereaved by the war" and who had "the courage of his father", Squid was able to meet the American, who was, he reported, installing "a mighty Wurlitzer organ" at a picture theatre in the city.

Squid was riding high these days. Only Miss Beckenstall doubted him. She might well have doubted him—as I happened to find out.

A couple of days before the exams, I left my geography book at school. When I went back to get it, our room seemed deserted. I was walking to the back when I heard a voice above me say, "G'day." I swung round. Squid was looking down from the top of a ladder which was leaning against the blackboard beside the picture of Sappho.

"Getting me pen," he explained. It had been stuck in the ceiling for weeks, not far above Sappho's head.

"Thought you'd bought another."

"Did, but in the exams a feller might need an extra one." He reached up and pulled it out.

"Reckon you might give us a lift with the ladder?"

We carried it out and put it back behind the shelter-shed. There was something queer about Squid as we walked back; something more than usually secretive.

"I've got to get my geography book," I said. "I'll catch up."

He didn't answer, but walked towards the gate, studying his pen concernedly. In the empty room I picked up my book and looked up again at Sappho. Something was written in the dust on her glass. I moved my head this way and that till I saw: Area O π R2; Circum. O π D. I sat in Squid's desk. It was all clear from there:

$$\text{Int.} = \frac{\text{PRT}}{100}; \text{ annulus } \pi (R + r) \ (R - r) \text{ and so on}$$

—line after line of it.

Squid was away next day. Mrs. Peters said it was his old stomach trouble. "Been working so hard at algebra and all that . . ." He thought things out well, did Squid, as became apparent later. It was no good just having a plan; you also had to have a second plan in case the first failed.

The fearful day came. There was bravado from a few of the boys, but Johnno and I hardly spoke. Squid said he'd got out of bed for the exam and really shouldn't have come. His breakfast was repeating on him and he had spots in front of his eyes.

Miss Beckenstall was just saying good morning when Moloney came in and whispered something to her, his cropped moustache against her ear.

"Boys and girls," she said, "we are to change rooms at once with grade six, as Mr. Moloney wishes to write their geography examination on their blackboard."

I looked at Squid. His face was waxen.

Moloney took over. "Bring pens, pencils and rulers only." There was the sound of these items being gathered up. Squid was motionless, staring into space.

"Birdwood Peters," said Miss Beckenstall sharply.

He came to himself and gathered his belongings, staring at Sappho as if to memorize every formula on her face. We were going through the door when I saw him clutch his stomach with his free hand, spin on his feet like a shot Indian and collapse on the floor amid shrieks from the girls.

"Give him air!" shouted Moloney. "Everyone sit down. Miss Beckenstall—water!"

Squid started moaning quietly, his mouth open, his freckles clear on his pale face. When Miss Beckenstall returned with water, Moloney, who was supporting Squid's head, held out his hand for the cup. Somehow their hands collided and Squid got the lot in the face. He jerked to life, but sank back again, muttering feebly. Miss Beckenstall smiled grimly. While we did our first examination, Moloney took Squid home in a cab.

Squid came back a couple of days later to do the exam, though Mrs. Peters said he was still suffering from heartburn and dizzy spells. He did the exam alone in our room, but by that time, with Johnno's help, I had run a broom over Sappho's face. I dare say Squid had managed to find out all about the paper by then for he passed. In fact, he passed everything.

To the surprise of everyone but Miss Beckenstall, Johnno and I both got through our Merit. Our fathers gave us sixpence each to go to the pictures, and altogether life at home changed for us.

At the end of the year, when there was a holiday feeling in the air, Miss Beckenstall set us a composition subject: "An Occasion I Shall Always Remember". We finished it before lunch. Then Johnno and I went off to climb Lone Pine, though the old tree already seemed like something belonging to the past. We were, after all, almost third-form high-school students, and climbing trees was slightly beneath us. Sitting on the other side of the trunk Johnno said, "I called my composition 'The Auction'. It's about the McQueens, but I didn't give any name." I couldn't see his face, only his hand holding the trunk. "I wrote just the way it hit me: you know, the blossom and the people and Mrs. McQueen looking sad. Miss Beckenstall has been saying to let myself go, so that's what I did."

But Miss Beckenstall was away that afternoon and Moloney decided to correct the compositions himself. He sat at the table making red ink comments on each page. Every now and then he'd say something like "Good work, Birdie" or " 'Try to', Wray. 'Try and' is a contradiction in terms."

When he came to Johnno's he said after a bit, "What might this be, Johnston?" He made several jabs at it with his pen.

I glanced at Johnno. He flushed slightly. "It was a sort of experiment, sir," he said slowly.

Moloney made a snorting sound. "Really, your attempts to portray this house and these people are peculiar, to say the least. Whoever heard of a 'blossomed tree'?"

"No, sir," said Johnno faintly.

"What d'you mean 'no sir'?"

"I—don't know," admitted Johnno.

"Think before you speak," said Moloney, "and before you write, too." He went on correcting with frequent grunts and jabs. Finally he stood up holding the composition in his hands. "I believe I should read this extraordinary effusion."

He was standing beside my desk with it.

"No, sir," gasped Johnno.

"I beg your pardon?"

Johnno simply shook his head while everyone looked at him.

"You add insolence to incompetence, Johnston."

In a ridiculing voice, Moloney began: " 'I can see it still: the auctioneer on the spring-cart shouting to the crowd, all the private things: the beds and saucepans and chairs on the grass. The crowd laughing. The two alone at the door'—No verbs, you'll observe. Our friend Johnston needs no verbs, or sense either. 'It seemed wrong that the sun was shining on the blossomed trees.'" Johnno's face was white. There were titters from the girls and even a few laughs from the boys, but Johnno's friends looked down at their desks, saying nothing. When Moloney read about the woman holding her apron between her hands Johnno rose slowly to his feet, staring at the book in Moloney's hands. "*Please*, sir!"

But Moloney read on remorselessly and all at once Johnno leaned down, plucked out his inkwell and flung it. It hit Moloney's chest with such force that he doubled up, jerking his glasses to the floor.

At first there wasn't a sound. There stood Johnno, white as a sheet, and Moloney holding his chest, the ink soaking into his shirt, the composition still in his hand.

"Stamp on his glasses," hissed Stinger.

I reached out my foot and heard the glass crunch under my heel.

"I—I'm sorry, sir," I heard Johnno say.

Moloney raised his head slowly. In a hoarse voice he said, "Out! Out with you both. The police will hear about this! Your parents, Reeve, will pay for my spectacles—every penny. Get out!"

The class was speechless, everyone staring as unbelievingly as if the ink had been blood. Johnno remained in his place, his mouth half open. My heart was booming in my ears. "Out!"

We clattered from the classroom together and out into the empty grounds. Without a word we climbed the fence and entered the bush, then stopped and looked at each other. "I didn't know anyone but Miss Beckenstall would read it," said Johnno in a strained voice. I couldn't answer. In my ears was the crunching of Moloney's glasses, a sound I can hear yet. To think of it and of the next twenty-four hours is to be a boy again.

"He'll go to my old man," said Johnno flatly. "I'm done for." He looked at me hopelessly. "What do we do?"

I had no idea. We tried to talk about it; perhaps, after all, Moloney would say nothing. All we could do was go home and if we heard him coming, we could clear out.

"Where?" I said.

"Anywhere. Otways, Queensland—anywhere."

So we went home.

TEN

That evening I could hardly speak a word at tea.

"What's the matter with you?" asked my father.

"I feel sick," I said—which was true.

"You'd better get to bed early, then."

As soon as it was dark I went out on the veranda and lay down without undressing. The light winked at the end of the pier and everything was the same—lights, stars, house, sea; everything except me. I listened for Moloney, but there was no sound of him.

I must have been lying there half an hour when a pebble landed on the veranda. Dropping over its edge, I went into the shadow and a girl's voice whispered, "Charlie!"

It was Eileen, the moonlight blanching her face. "Fred's gone," she said, and began crying. I led her away from the house. "Mr. Moloney came and told us, and dad lost his temper and hit Fred in front of him." The words came tumbling out. "If only he hadn't hit back! He only hit once, but when he did dad punched him terribly and he didn't try to protect himself."

I felt sick. "Where is he?"

"I followed him to the Island, but I lost him."

The Island was a strip of coast between the beach and the creek, only wide enough for a road and a row of houses. Except at holiday time, the houses were empty. I remembered that Johnno had said once that if a chap was turned out of his home, he could find shelter there.

"I might be able to find him," I said.

"I brought food for him," said Eileen. "He's had nothing."

We saw a horse and jinker pull up at our gate. Old Moloney got out. He was bare-headed, his scalp shining in the moonlight. When he had gone to our front door, out of our sight, I said, "We can go down the cliffs to the beach."

"I'll go home," said Eileen. "It will make things worse if I stay. The whole thing has upset dad terribly. He's been sitting with his head in his hands ever since."

I took the food from her, my mind on Moloney and my father.

I ran towards the path down the cliffs just as the veranda door opened. I heard my father striding round to my bed. "Charlie!" he said. "Why didn't you tell us about this?"

I hesitated at the top of the path. "Charlie, you had better come in at once!" I almost turned back, but inside, through the open door, I could see the light shining on Moloney's head and my mother holding Ian by the hand. "*Charlie!*"

I went softly down the path. I would go to the spot where Eileen had last seen him, and then look for him at each house. I came on to the beach, crossed the bridge at the mouth of the creek and went on along the Island. Ahead lay a calm sea, white beach stretching almost as clear as day and thick tea-trees on the dunes, black and somehow sad-looking. Tracks came over the dunes from the beach and led to the flimsy houses—"Warrawee" and "This'll Do" and "Wy Wurrie". I went uneasily to the fenceline of the houses and looked at them hunched under their trees, the branches touching their sides. There was no light anywhere.

I went to the first house and called Johnno's name, my voice sounding so loud that I moved back into the shadows. "Johnno!"

I listened but could hear nothing. He would go farther, I thought; this was too close to the town. But I continued to go into each house, calling and listening. "Johnno!"

I heard only my own heart. It had been booming ever since we had left the school. A cat came miaowing out of the shadows, stiff-tailed and friendly. For a while I hung on to it, listening to it purring, wishing the whole thing had never happened.

I said more loudly, "Johnno!"

The cat struggled down and ran into the darkness. The track in front of the houses smelt of salt and rust and of the dusty bark of the tea-tree. I stopped and peered into the window of "This'll Do", and as I looked I heard a voice behind me.

I swung about. Johnno stood very still, the moon shining on his face, which was all bruised and cut, his lips so swollen that they changed his voice. He said softly, "I'm clearing out. I hit my dad."

"Yes," I said.

"So Eileen told you." He kicked at the sand. "She was mad too?"

"No, just worried. She gave me some food for you."

He shook his head. "I don't feel hungry." He stood thinking for a bit. "Could you, do you think, do something for me?"

"Anything you like," I said.

"Could you—could you, d'you reckon, row me across the bay?"

"To Queenscliff?" The idea frightened me. But then what was I to do myself? I breathed deeply. Johnny was waiting for me to answer.

"All right," I said. "I'll take you."

AT THE BRIDGE we watched awhile, but no one was near it. We crossed over and walked quickly towards the pier. Along that part of the beach the fishermen were hauling in their nets, stepping towards each other along the beach. We could see the moving water where the fish were trapped and hear the men's low voices.

Under the pier we stopped and looked towards our boatshed and Thermopylae. Every light was on, but there was no one about the beach. We edged round the cliff towards the boatshed and hid in the tea-tree. There was no sound from Thermopylae but presently we heard the Peters's wireless squeal and a voice say, "We now take you to . . ."

"Can we get the shed door open?" Johnno asked.

I said, "I'll try." I crept slowly behind the shed, drew the door latch, and lifted the sagging doors. Inside lay the sleeping boat, moonlight touching its bows. Johnno appeared without a sound and we began hauling together, pulling the boat with strong tugs out of the shed onto the sand. We hid then, watching from the shadows. No one. We hauled the boat quickly down to the water.

376

I ran back and brought down oars and rowlocks while Johnno began trampling our footmarks. Finally he came backwards down the beach, scattering sand from a bailing tin.

"Get in," he whispered. "I'll push her out."

But a single excited bark struck us motionless. Gyp came running onto the beach, making pleased, gurgling sounds in his throat, and I said, "If we don't take him he'll howl."

I lifted him over the stern, then got in myself. He took up his figurehead position, pointing his nose across the bay. Johnno stripped off his clothes and pushed us till the water was up to his chest. Then he scrambled in.

We sat listening. No sound from the shore now, and the Peters's lights went out, which meant it was half past nine. Johnno wrapped his singlet round the blade of one oar and his underpants round the other, then wet the leathers where they passed through the rowlocks to keep them from squeaking. I began rowing quietly, lying back hard. Phosphorous spun brightly in the water.

A voice came from the veranda. *"Charlie!"*

I stopped rowing. Gyp looked round, sensing something wrong.

"If you like," whispered Johnno, "you could give it up."

"No," I said. "No." The words came from me almost involuntarily. I began rowing strongly, keeping Johnno's head lined up with our house lights.

"Charlie . . !" Already my father's voice was less distinct. I kept pulling hard. Slowly the house lights drew away, but behind us our wake glittered in the moonlight. They have only to look this way, I thought, and we're done.

The pier light fell behind on my left, while the house lights were still directly behind. Johnno sat in the stern bathing his face with his handkerchief. His eyes were black and swollen and the corner of his mouth was bleeding still.

The house lights and the pier light drew together and fell lower on the horizon. Now and then Gyp's tail swished against my back. He was making impatient sounds in his throat, as if anxious to get to wherever we were going. "The tide's on the turn," Johnno said. "If you like I'll row a bit." I changed over with him. "If you keep me lined up with the channel light it should be about right," he said.

I sat in the stern with my head in my hands. I had been a fool to run away. I could have apologized and put up with a hiding and worked somewhere to pay for Moloney's glasses. But then there was Johnno. He had been thrashed at home and at school for as long as I had known him—and as far as I could see, he had seldom deserved it. Now he had hit back. It was the end for him.

I said, "Eileen told me that after you had gone your dad sat with his head in his hands, wishing he had never done it."

Johnno paused with the oars raised, looking beyond me. He said presently, "He's belted me dozens of times."

"He's had plenty to worry about," I said, repeating remarks of my father's.

"I dare say," Johnno admitted. Then he suddenly struck hard with the oars and I saw there was no hope of going back. I looked back over my shoulder. The house lights and even the pier lights had gone. But beyond Johnno's head the channel light was flashing brightly and westward I could see lights far off on the other side of the bay. Funny; we were still closer to the east side but we could see nothing of it.

"Anyhow," said Johnno, "he'd never let me go to high school after what happened. I'd probably have to work full-time at Digger Hayes's."

"My father says he was keen for you to have a good education."

"He always *said* he was keen, but he bashed me so much when I didn't know things that I couldn't think—that's true, Charlie, *I couldn't think*. It was the same with old Moloney. Only Miss Beckenstall was any good."

Johnno had paused again with the oars raised. He said all at once, "Why can't we see the pier lights? Some of the stars have gone, too."

A slight breeze passed us, then dropped off, then came again, blowing off the land very gently. I turned round. The stars low in the sky were blotted out, but higher up they were bright.

"That's fog," Johnno said. "But it's a long way off."

He began rowing hard while I waved him port or starboard, keeping him on the channel light. I looked back again. I could see car lights coming down Chapman's Hill. All at once they vanished. "It's fog all right," I said.

Johnno said, between breaths, "So long as we can see the other side we're right."

I looked unhappily ahead. Gyp was still in the bows, ears flapping and nose raised, evidently expecting to go for a row, then come back and go to his bed under the house. A few hundred yards

378

beyond him was the channel light and many miles beyond that, the few lights of the other side.

"Pull left." I said. My voice sounded unreal. "You're nearly at the channel." I glanced back over my shoulder. The fog, pale grey in the moonlight, didn't look any nearer.

The channel light on top of the piles lit the boat now with a reddish glare. "That's three miles we've done," said Johnno as we came up to it. "How long has it taken?"

"I don't know. About an hour, I suppose."

"We could make the other side before sunrise."

"There's the fog," I said. We both looked at it. "It's nearer, I think." He agreed reluctantly, and I went on, "And what's that sound? Not that foghorn. A sound like a creek running." It was a faint but somehow threatening sound.

He peered around us, listening carefully. "It's the tide running out between the piles under the light."

"Maybe we should tie up here till we see what the fog does."

"In the morning, we'd be picked up in people's binoculars," he said. "Then the motorboats would come out." To me, by now, this didn't seem such a terrible prospect. "If we need to tie up," he went on, "we can make for one of the lights in the channel on the other side." He began rowing again.

"We'd better angle a bit to allow for the current," I suggested. I lined him up on a light on the other side of the bay.

He rowed solidly for half a mile or more, then I said, "I'll give you a rest."

He was breathing hard, but he shook his head. "Both of us had better row."

I sat next to him and we took an oar each. The red channel light astern had a misty look about it. We tried to keep it at an angle to the right, but we would swing around gradually and have to correct ourselves. Then the light disappeared altogether.

"Maybe if you sit in the stern and guide me—"

"I'll have a go at the rowing," I said.

He went back reluctantly and put me on course, then bathed his face again. Blood still trickled from the corner of his mouth and his eyes were ghastly to look at.

Now the fog crept on us unawares. We could see the western lights and the stars above us, then in less than a minute a white void closed in so that I even saw Johnno shrouded in mist.

Overhead we could still see the moon. If we kept it at an angle to our left we could keep going. I began rowing again, but I had little faith that we'd reach the other side. The fog deepened and the moon became less distinct. Far off, we still heard the foghorn.

Gyp gave an impatient whimper. "Shut up!" I said. He pushed against me as if apologizing. His fur was wet with mist. "Sit!" He sighed and curled himself behind me.

In the stern Johnno was hunched miserably. Somehow the fog made his face look terrible—as if he were looking through a parted curtain at something that horrified him.

"It's no good," I said at last. "Now I can't see the moon."

Johnno looked up. Then let his glance fall dismally to the bottom of the boat. He said like a small boy, "I don't want to go back." The foghorn answered him dolefully. "Give me a go," he said.

"You can if you like—but which way?"

It didn't seem to matter to him; mainly he needed something to do. Once the mists broke overhead. The moon was on our left, which meant we were rowing towards home. "I'm sorry," Johnno said. He lined up quickly, but then the moon was gone again.

"What's that sound?" asked Johnno.

We listened. There was a deep, slow, drumming sound in the water itself; then the foghorn sounded, a good deal closer. "It's a ship!" said Johnno.

ELEVEN

I ought to have known the sound of a ship's engines anywhere. Johnno and I had heard them often through the water when we were in swimming.

"She's travelling slowly," Johnno said. "She might pick us up and take us—"

"She'd hand us to the pilot who would hand us to the police."

Johnno said wearily, "I dare say."

The drumming was clearer and the foghorn much louder, but it was hard to tell from which side the sounds came. In the bows Gyp was listening with his ears cocked, making small worried sounds in his throat. He whined suddenly.

"Lie down," said Johnno. "You're right, Charlie, they might give us to the police. And I can't go back. I'd rather swim for it."

We sat undecidedly while Gyp moved about in his small space. "It might run us down," I said.

Johnno didn't care. His face was strained, his eyes like black caverns. "We're done for all right; done cold."

Then the sound was all round us—the drumming like monstrous heartbeats. When the foghorn came we were deafened. Gyp whined loudly, and suddenly the fog was cut apart and there, high as a cliff, rose the bows of a liner. We stood up together.

"She's got us!" I cried.

"Sit down!" Johnno grabbed the oars and as the stem passed, pushed us away. Rows of portholes passed like moons over our heads. Somewhere an orchestra was pounding, all out of time with the *drum, drum* of the engines. The foghorn blasted violently.

Johnno tried to push again, but the oars slipped. He went on his back in the bottom of the boat and we bumped the liner's side. Now I myself pushed, feeling rounded rivet heads on my palms. The next minute she was past and we were swirling and bobbing in her wake. I looked up and saw *Maloja—Belfast* on her stern. Then the fog swallowed her and the drumming and hooting retreated. Johnno regained his seat and we sat, paralysed with fright. All at once he sprang up. "The oars—we've lost them!"

We looked about the small area of the surface we could see in the fog, but there was nothing. "I'm going over to look," said Johnno stripping off his trousers.

"No," I said in a shaky voice. "We'd get separated."

He put his face close to mine. "You know what'll happen if we don't get them? We'll get washed through the Heads clean out to sea. The tide's been going out for hours."

"If we were near the Heads we'd hear the surf."

We listened, but all we could hear was the retreating *drum, drum* of the ship and the blasting of its foghorn.

"There's a second foghorn," said Johnno suddenly. "Do they have one at the Heads?"

"I don't know," I said huskily.

"We've got to find the oars," he said.

"There's a rope in the locker—I could hang onto you."

I took out the twenty-foot rope. He tied it round his waist and went over the stern. I played the line out and watched him disappear in the fog. Distinctly now I heard two foghorns.

"Charlie! I see an oar. Give us more rope."

"You've got it all." Jammed against Gyp, I leaned over the bows.

"I touched it. No, it's gone. I'm coming back."

I began pulling the rope and it was like pulling dead weight. "Johnno—you OK, Johnno?" He panted something I couldn't hear. I drew harder and he appeared out of the fog, swimming strongly. He caught hold of the stern, and hung there panting.

"Charlie, we're in a hell of a current."

He had hardly said it when a puff of wind came and all at once we were under stars with shore lights winking off to the left. A wall of shallow fog lay astern and the moon stood far down to the west. Ahead of us, about two miles off, was the *Maloja*, standing between two lights, one high and flashing white and red, the other steady white. It's the Rip, I thought.

"We'd stand a chance swimming," began Johnno suddenly. "That place a bit behind us would be Portsea. We could angle across to allow for the current . . ."

"We'd never make it."

"We could give it a go." He stood up. "Otherwise we'll get washed clean out to sea." Whatever happened in the water, Johnno was always sure he could get out of it by swimming.

"We'd have to go through the Rip anyhow. If we stick with the boat—"

"What do we row with? No, we've *got* to swim, Charlie. I'll go in again and see what it's like swimming across the current."

He waited no longer, but dived in and struck towards the shore, heading for the Portsea lights. Ten yards out he turned and trod water. Straight beyond his head a light was flashing white and green on the shore. His head and the light were lined up, but in a second the light was moving left and Johnno's head right.

"It's no good," I shouted. "You're drifting too fast."

He began swimming back. I helped him over the stern again, his white barrel of a chest heaving in the moonlight.

"We've got to ride it out," he agreed hopelessly. The boat was rocking under us now with turning motions, the water hissing along the sides. "We're turning in a circle," he said.

I looked. Slowly we swung away from the lights to the left, till we faced Point Lonsdale, then round farther till we faced the retreating fog, then right back round to Portsea. Then we began again.

"We're going to miss Point Nepean," I said.

"We could yell for help."

We yelled "Help" a couple of times, then, bad as things were, felt ashamed. "I'd rather drown," said Johnno bitterly.

And now there was another sound, a sound like thunder a long way off. It was broken regularly by the blaring of the Lonsdale foghorn. "I'm not scared of the surf," said Johnno, half to himself. "It's getting through the Rip."

We were turning more swiftly now. The moon shone on great whirls of water to either side of us. Gyp came and licked my face, but I pushed him away irritably.

Lonsdale swung past and the lights of Queenscliff; then we completed an even quicker circle. The water was almost silent except for the far noise of surf. Round again—Lonsdale, Queenscliff—

"Can a rowing boat get through the Rip?" asked Johnno.

I tried to answer, but suddenly I was vomiting. I hung over the side unable to move, aware of peaks of water rising and subsiding around us, hissing in the moonlight, and then of surf breaking on the very tip of Nepean.

I gave up hope at that. As I clung to the side of the boat water burst over me, sending me sprawling backwards and at the same instant the boat rose on its beam ends.

"This is it, Charlie! Hang on to her!"

We seemed to be suspended in air, there was a tremendous jolt and water rushed in. The hissing of the waves was much louder.

"Bale, Charlie!" Then, as I was scrabbling for the tin, he shouted, "Gyp's in!"

I forgot our danger as I struggled to my knees and saw Gyp swimming, being twisted this way and that. I picked up the rope and flung an end to him, but it was too short. He had his eyes on us, his head up high.

"Johnno, he'll drown! I'm going in."

"You can't," shouted Johnno. "You wouldn't have a hope."

I stood up. "It's getting better. We're nearly through."

But at that I found myself on my back in the bottom of the boat in sloshing water. Johnno was standing over me, panting, "Charlie, you couldn't live in it. We've got to bale!"

He picked up the tin and started at it frantically, but I struggled to my knees and looked back. "He's still there." He had his head up, but we were separating fast. "We'll never get him!"

"He'll swim to the beach."

I could see him only faintly now, then not at all. "He's gone, Johnno."

A faint bark followed my words, then nothing. I lay in the bottom of the boat with Johnno baling beside me and I vomited and cried and vomited and cried again.

THE STARS had grown faint and there was no moon. A sick light was in the east. The Rip was far behind to the northwest, with Point Lonsdale lighthouse winking palely.

"We had him from a pup," I said.

Johnno sat in the stern, naked still. "I'm sorry. Hell, I'm sorry. I should've gone in myself, but—Charlie, it was no go."

The light was growing slowly, and the sea was very dark blue. We were about half a mile offshore, moving steadily down the coast towards Cape Schanck.

"He *might* swim it," said Johnno. "He was part Labrador."

"Here," I said. "You've got to wear something." I took off my trousers and handed him my underpants.

"Thanks." He put them on but they covered hardly any of him. "We're drifting that way," he said, pointing towards Cape Schanck, and other nearer headlands. The waves were slowly climbing the cliffs, the spray hanging, then falling back. "If the boat gets against those waves we'll smash on the rocks."

The sun came up, glaring on the water, and the sea took on a different shade of blue. I could see we were drifting fast towards the first headland but also getting nearer a beach.

Johnno looked at me seriously. "Charlie, we've *got* to swim this time. Swimming, we could be moving towards the beach; in the boat we aren't."

I looked unhappily at the beach. It was clear to me that we would be pitched onto the first headland, where the kelp and undertow would get us. But he was right. There was nothing for it but to swim.

"You go first," said Johnno. "Make a line for the big dune, then you'll wash only about halfway to the rocks."

We didn't speak another word. I took off my shoes, went in over the stern and struck with long, slow strokes towards the dune. I could feel the ocean rise and fall under me and the steady side-drag of the current.

When I glanced back from the top of a wave, I saw Johnno still

384

standing in the boat. Next time I looked he had gone. He's going between me and the rocks, I thought. I faced the dune and quickened my stroke, throwing all my strength into it, and when I was scarcely a hundred yards off the headland I angled sharply away from it; but as I turned the current halted me completely, then began to bear me in its own direction. The water was boiling on the rocks, then drawing back over kelp.

I angled again towards the shore. Then between me and the rocks, only a few yards off, I saw Johnno stroking confidently, turning his head sometimes my way, sometimes towards the rocks. Just ahead the waves were rising and turning over for their run to the beach. I saw Johnno pick one up and bodysurf over the last fifty yards. I tried and missed, then tried again and found myself soaring easily towards the beach ahead.

Before the next wave came I crawled to dry sand, and Johnno ran to me. He sat beside me, breathing easily, saying nothing. The coast was wild and empty.

I stood up, thinking to look for Gyp, but my legs crumpled and the sky fell in on me . . . .

I WAS LYING in speckled sunlight under tea-trees, Johnno sitting beside me looking worried.

"I passed out," I said bitterly. Then I stood up, but the horizon tilted horribly. I dropped to my hands and knees and began vomiting again.

"I'd better go and see about Gyp and the boat." Johnno said. When I didn't answer, he went away over the dunes.

Out of the wind the sun was warm. I lay down again and fell asleep. When I woke, Johnno was studying a stick he had put upright on a bit of flattened sand. I started to speak to him, but my throat was so dry that I only raised a croaking. He said, "The shadows are getting longer. It's past midday."

"Find Gyp?"

He shook his head and looked away from me. "Charlie, the boat's jammed in the rocks. She'll be smashed to bits—"

I said indifferently, "I don't care. All I want is water."

He reached behind him in the shade and handed me a half-full beach bucket. "It's got wrigglers in it—it came from a tank at a house inland."

I drank greedily. "Did you see anyone?"

"No one." I looked at him—cut cheek, black eyes, bruises where his father had hit him about the ribs, nothing more on than my underpants. "Just as well," I said. But we were alive and the sun was warm. I could almost have been happy had we had Gyp. "No tracks near the boat?" I asked.

Johnno shook his head dismally. "No tracks at all."

"We could look over the other way."

I stood up stiffly and we started over the dunes. Up the beach I could see the boat jammed on the headland, but the other way there was nothing, not even a footprint. We walked slowly for half a mile looking for pad marks and now and then stopping and whistling.

We were turning back when I saw something that looked like a heap of seaweed darker than the rest. When I hurried towards it, Johnny said, "Maybe we should go back."

But I didn't answer. Gyp was lying on his side, as he always lay by the fire. When I reached him I saw that there wasn't a mark on him. I touched his ear, but it was cold.

I jumped up and cried, "Curse your bloody running away."

Johnno stood with his arms hanging by his side as I dragged Gyp up into the dunes and scooped sand over him. When I stood up I said, "I shouldn't have said that. It could have been me drowned."

Johnno turned away. "I wish it had been me," he said.

TWELVE

It was twenty-four hours since the inkwell incident and it didn't seem to me that we were any better off.

"They'll think we're dead," said Johnno. We were walking back to our place in the tea-tree. "I didn't mean to upset my old man and Eileen as badly as that."

"Perhaps it's better that way. When they hear we're alive they'll be so pleased that nothing will be done to us. If we wait till morning, then find a telephone—"

Johnno stopped walking and looked at me. "Charlie, if I went back it'd be a reformatory this time. There's no going back for me. You *want* to go back?"

He looked so alarmed that I decided to talk no more about phoning. "I don't know what I want," I said. "Anyhow, what we've got to do is find food. If I went and asked somewhere—"

"You can't," Johnno interrupted. "Charlie, you look terrible! People would ask what had happened."

"But we've got to eat and you've got to get some clothes."

"There's the house where I got the water—looks as if no one's been there for months. But I don't want to break in, and besides, everything there belongs to someone else."

"What can we do, then? Walk up Point Nepean Road barefooted —you in my underpants?"

"I don't know. Fair dinkum, it's not the way I expected."

"Let's *look* at the house, anyhow."

He stood up reluctantly, his stomach gurgling with hunger.

The house was in scrub not far behind the beach; a small, sad, squarish place with tea-tree branches hanging over it. On a rack under the tank-stand were three long bamboo fishing-rods. Except for Johnno's earlier footprints and a few rabbit tracks there wasn't a mark to be seen. We tried the front door but it was locked, so we went round the house, running our fingers over various ledges. Finally Johnno found the key on a hook under the tank-stand. He tried the back door and it opened unwillingly.

When the door closed behind us the sea sounded farther off. I felt the house listening and watching, just as we were listening and watching. We stood in a long room—a kitchen, living room and dining room all in one.

"I don't like being here," said Johnno in a low voice.

I didn't answer, but walked quietly round the rest of the house. There was a small bathroom, and two bedrooms with blankets stacked in a wardrobe. I came back to Johnno.

"Look." He pointed to a map of the Peninsula pinned to a wall. On the beach behind Rye someone had pencilled a cross and marked OUR PLACE.

"We'd better find food," I said.

Johnno looked at me as if I had suggested a murder. "*I'm* going to eat, anyhow," I said.

He followed me unhappily while I opened cupboards. The only thing in the house was a pound of rolled oats. Johnno stared at it hungrily and I searched for matches but there were none in the house.

"You can eat it as it is," said Johnno, nibbling a bit.

"My mother soaks it overnight in cold water." I took out a saucepan and tipped some into it. "It's got worms in it."

"They'll only taste like oatmeal," said Johnno indifferently. He turned on a tap and rusty water flowed out, then cleared. We mixed the oatmeal and water with a spoon, then I sat back and looked at it. "You go first," I said.

He scooped at it, ate a spoonful, worms and wrigglers and oatmeal. "It's good."

I scooped at it with my eyes closed. It was bearable if I didn't think about it. We ate spoonful for spoonful till we had finished. Then Johnno washed the saucepan and spoon and put them away and we sat at the table trying to pretend that the situation wasn't bad at all. Every now and then Johnno got up and studied the map, but each time he shook his head despondently. The light was fading and the wind was springing up, setting twigs and branches scraping the walls. The sea was louder and more threatening.

"It'll smash the boat," said Johnno.

He fell into a mournful silence, staring at the floor. Suddenly he flung his head up. "That was a shot."

"I didn't hear anything."

He looked less certain. "Maybe not. The police wouldn't have guns anyhow."

"They probably don't even know about us."

The sun was behind the tea-tree by this time and the room was becoming gloomier and full of sea sounds. "It'd be better on the veranda," I said. "These rooms give me the creeps."

We stood up slowly, as if someone were watching us.

"Better wrap a blanket round yourself," I told him.

"Well, the blankets really belong to someone else—"

"We'll have to borrow them tonight anyhow."

Johnno frowned. "I'm not cold."

"It's the way you look that I'm thinking of—those underpants hardly cover your backside."

"No one's going to see us, are they?"

I supposed not, so we went outside. Out there the sea was much louder, its cries more threatening.

The veranda was boarded in at waist height; we leaned on the rail, staring at the clumps of tea-tree and blackwood and the spaces between. "There are rabbits here, anyhow," said Johnno.

"We can run them down and eat them raw," I said.

He looked at me from the corner of his eye. "Fair dinkum, Charlie, I didn't mean to get you into this."

From somewhere behind the tea-tree came the crack of a rifle. At the same instant Johnno fell to the floor, face down. Before I could hide myself a girl appeared about fifty yards off with a repeating rifle in her hand.

I leaned down quickly. "Johnno, are you hurt?" He didn't move. I bent closer in a panic, grasping his arm. "Fred—"

"Get down or you'll be seen," he hissed.

At that I wanted to kick him. "It's only a girl."

He groaned quietly, his face to the floor.

It was useless to move away, I thought; better to be casual. But I had never been casual with girls, not even in school.

She was standing less than twenty yards off, the rifle under her arm. She looked about fourteen, a fairish girl with one sun-bleached plait, bare-footed and wearing a faded cotton dress. She looked at me with a puzzled expression. "Hullo," she said. "Are you on holidays here?"

"Sort of," I said. "Only a day or two."

"You must be a friend of the Edwards's?"

"My mother is," I said uncomfortably. We stared awhile at each other. She had wide-open disconcerting eyes.

"Are your mother and father down?"

"Don't tell her anything," whispered Johnno.

"They're coming tonight."

"How did you get down then?"

I waved my hand vaguely. "We got a ride—"

"You have friends with you, then?"

"My brother's down," I said, quickly, "but he's in swimming."

At my feet Johnno hissed desperately, "Stop talking."

"Who was that?" asked the girl suddenly.

"No one," I answered. "I didn't hear anything."

I noticed her expression change as if realization had hit her. She said slowly, "Are you one of the boys? The boys who ran away and took a boat? It came over the wireless. What's your name?"

"Smith," whispered Johnno.

"Smith," I faltered.

She looked grave. "That's what everyone says when they don't want to give their real name. What *is* your name?"

"I've told you," I said unsteadily.

389

"Well, I don't believe you. Anyhow, I wouldn't tell anyone even if I did know. I think running away would be terrific."

We stared at each other again, while she swung the rifle carelessly from side to side. On the floor Johnno said hoarsely, "Has she gone?"

The girl had come farther forward. "That's the other boy!" she exclaimed triumphantly. I stepped quickly off the veranda to try to divert her.

"Now you'll make up some story to the police—" I began.

"Of course I won't. Where are you running away to?"

I started to say I wasn't running away but just then the colour left her face and following her gaze I saw Johnno looking over the veranda rail, only his head showing, a head so knocked about that it looked like something guillotined a few days before.

The girl came over and stood close to me. "Who is it?"

"Johnno," I said wearily. "We were washed through the Rip, and we haven't any food."

"How did he get so hurt?"

"On the rocks," croaked Johnno.

She came closer and peered. "Terrific," she murmured.

"He needs clothes," I said.

"I'll come back with some," she answered firmly. "Stand up while I see how big you are."

The head shook determinedly. "He's six feet two," I told her. We waited uneasily for her decision.

"I'll come back after tea. I'll knock at the door. We must decide on a password."

"We'll be out. We'd be safer in the bush than here. But we'll come back after dark. Leave the things under the tank-stand."

She looked disappointed. "Then I wouldn't see you."

"But the police might follow you."

After a bit she said reluctantly, "Oh, all right then."

We stood watching her go away the way she had come. She turned and waved once. When she had disappeared Johnno sat on the veranda steps, his head in his hands. "That's done it."

"Well, what would *you* have said?"

"I don't know," he admitted. "You just can't trust them, though. We'd better clear out, or she'll get some mad idea like wanting to come with us."

I went inside and took four blankets and we walked into the

390

scrub on the side of the dunes. From there we could see part of the house and the tank-stand and anyone approaching. We wrapped ourselves up and lay on our stomachs watching the house carefully. Lying that way seemed to ease our hunger.

The moon was already up when we saw the girl coming back carrying a bundle. She came slowly towards the tank-stand, stopped there, then straightened up and gazed around.

"Her old man'll come," whispered Johnno. "Sure to. If it was Eileen, my old man would be moving in now with a bike chain."

But no one came. The girl turned round and began walking back. Before long she disappeared into the shadows.

"A pretty good kid, after all," I said, standing up.

"Sit down," whispered Johnno. "It's a trap."

We watched for about an hour before we went singly to the house, keeping in the shadows. In the bundle were scones, a leg of mutton only half finished, some roast potatoes, still warm, and a jar of milk. They were wrapped in a pair of trousers and a sweater.

"There's a note in it."

We held the piece of paper to the moon. "Can't read it." Johnno tilted it this way and that. He handed it to me, but I could do no better. "Might be a warning," said Johnno.

"Keep it till morning," I said.

We went back into the scrub and ate like jungle animals at a carcass. Then Johnno dressed himself. He looked reasonably civilized except for his hair and his face and the fact that he had nothing on his feet. "We can't walk far without boots!" I said. "People would notice us—"

"At night they wouldn't."

I hadn't thought of walking at night.

"By tomorrow morning we could cover about twenty miles."

All I wanted was sleep. "Where would twenty miles put us, anyway? It would only take us nearer home."

"We could go towards the Western Port side and make for the railway."

Against this I had no real argument. "All right, then, you lead the way—but I bet you don't even know which way to head."

I was wrong. He had studied the map at the house more fully than I had known. He said, "We go along the beach to the next point, then inland by a road. That takes us to another road that goes to Shoreham."

391

We walked over the top of the dunes into a fresh wind and the roar of the waves. The sea glittered and moved in the moonlight, but sometimes clouds darkened it and all the expanse of beach too. Then the clouds would race away again as if hurrying to report our whereabouts.

Johnno said, "It'll be better walking near the water."

Down there the roar was so loud that we seemed back again in the battle of the past night. "We should walk fast," urged Johnno above the noise.

"I am walking fast," I said irritably. I wanted to lie down. Just then a cloud passed over the moon and the brightness drained out of the night. I shivered and took longer strides to keep up with Johnno. He was still a pace or two in front of me when I saw him stop.

"There are lights ahead, coming over the dunes!"

We stood close together watching them. Then we scrambled up the beach and lay on the crest of a dune. We could see five or six lights bobbing in single file and behind them the lights of a car.

"They're at the end of the road we have to take," said Johnno.

"Someone has found the boat, then."

"The girl probably told her father about us."

"No," I said. "She'd only have got herself into trouble."

We began pushing through the tea-tree, to see if we could pass behind the searchers and go on up the road. The moon came out again, brightening the whole beach and on it a group of men at the water's edge. They stood there looking, then turned and went back to their cars. They began unloading a dinghy from a trailer. The wind blew from them to us, but their voices reached us only indistinctly.

"They're going to row to where the boat hit," I said.

We moved through heavy shadows till we were scarcely twenty yards from them, then dropped on our hands and knees and crawled, finally worming towards them on our stomachs as they began carrying the dinghy to the beach. In front of them a man and woman carried hurricane lamps.

I caught Johnno's arm. "That's Eileen and your dad." Old man Johnston was bowed and shrunken-looking; he shambled along in a hopeless sort of way.

Johnno looked away. "I can't do this to him. Could we shout that we're OK, then run for it?"

"I dare say," I said unhappily.

392

"Fair dinkum, I didn't mean it to work out this way!"

The group was down at the water now. I heard a car door slam on the road and there, standing together, were my mother and father, my father half holding my mother up.

Johnno hung on to my arm, but I said, "It's no good, I've got to speak to them."

"Give me just two minutes, Charlie."

"No—you've got to come with me."

"I can't go back," he said. "Tell my old man I left you. Tell him —tell him—" He got to his knees.

"It's no good," I said again. "You've nowhere to go."

But he turned round and began to crawl away through the tea-tree.

At the water's edge there was the sound of a shot and the sudden brilliant light of a flare. The silhouettes of the men showed up against a bright sea. Out farther were the rocks with waves running over them, and there, still held fast, the smashed boat. I looked back quickly and saw my mother still leaning against my father.

"Johnno, I'm going out," I said.

I looked into the bush after him, but now it was black and I could catch no sound of him. I felt courage run out of me but I stood up slowly and walked out of the bush as if it had all been a dream.

I was close to them before my mother and father saw me. We stared at each other. I said, "We're all right."

My father lifted his hand, then let it fall again.

"Fred?" asked my mother.

"He's safe," I said.

At that she collapsed. I stood fixed to the spot while my father helped her into the car. In a voice unlike his own he said, "Tell Mr. Johnston."

I ran to the water's edge, shouting. "He's safe!"

Old man Johnston scarcely seemed to have heard me: he had the same shrunken, distant look. But Eileen grasped me by both arms. "Where is he?"

"He left me a few minutes ago," I said, forgetting all our caution.

"We must tell the police," said Eileen quickly.

"No," said her father, arousing himself. "He's alive and that's all that matters. He'll come back if he wants to come back."

That was the end of it all. On the drive home no one talked about it; in fact, no one talked about anything. I looked at first into the roadside scrub thinking I might see Johnno, but before long we were well beyond his range and by ten o'clock we were home, not believing it had happened.

AND SO 1929 ended. In January 1930, we were to move out of Thermopylae, which I would always link with the death of Grandfather McDonald and with Johnno. With Johnno gone and Gyp dead and a cloud of disgrace over me, the holidays were not worth having; but one happening brightened them.

One night I was sitting on the pier, dangling my legs over the edge. It was warm and the sea was calm, and I was just thinking how good it would be if Johnno could turn up when someone dropped down beside me and said, "Ah there, Charlie."

It was Squid. "I was thinking of Johnno," I said disappointedly.

He didn't answer, and looking at him I could have sworn he'd been crying. "What's up?" I asked.

He lay on his back looking at the stars, still not answering.

"I don't see what *you've* got to be gloomy about," I said. "You won the Most Improved Pupil again; old Moloney loves you—"

"*Don't say that!*" he exclaimed, his voice quavery. He turned on his side and looked away from me. "They've just told me. Him and my mother—they're getting married."

"They're *what?*"

"Before Christmas. We're all living together."

It was too much; I burst out laughing. I hadn't laughed for a long time and I couldn't stop. I lay on my back laughing while he blubbered beside me.

Afterwards, I felt ashamed; even Squid didn't deserve Moloney for a father, and a fortnight after this they were married. I wanted to write about it to Johnno, but no one knew where he was.

Somehow I hardly had Johnno out of my mind in those last days of the year. On New Year's Eve I decided to walk across the school grounds to Lone Pine. But the school looked shrunken and wasn't important any more; even Lone Pine wasn't the same. Perhaps if Johnno had come back it might have been the way it was before; without him it was nothing.

D. E. Charlwood

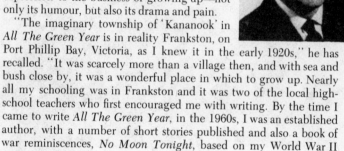

The idea for *All The Green Year* came to Don Charlwood when his elder children (he has three daughters and a son) were teenagers. The inevitable clash of wills kept reminding him of similar clashes with his own parents. He felt the urge to give some form of expression to the business of growing up—not only its humour, but also its drama and pain.

"The imaginary township of 'Kananook' in *All The Green Year* is in reality Frankston, on Port Phillip Bay, Victoria, as I knew it in the early 1920s," he has recalled. "It was scarcely more than a village then, and with sea and bush close by, it was a wonderful place in which to grow up. Nearly all my schooling was in Frankston and it was two of the local high-school teachers who first encouraged me with writing. By the time I came to write *All The Green Year*, in the 1960s, I was an established author, with a number of short stories published and also a book of war reminiscences, *No Moon Tonight*, based on my World War II experiences as a navigator in Britain's Bomber Command.

"Indeed, I had settled into my peacetime career in Air Traffic Control, in the Australian Department of Civil Aviation, work that took me around Australia, and abroad. It was an exacting job that left little time for creative effort. *All The Green Year* was written in aeroplanes and hotel bedrooms. My wife Nell, a former Canadian schoolteacher whom I had married on my way home from the war, patiently retrieved the bits of pencilled manuscript from my luggage each time I landed back home and typed them off. But I constantly felt the urge to revise: after each trip away the neatly-typed pages would come back to Nell covered with alterations.

"I was away in England when the third type-off of the manuscript arrived by mail for me, accompanied by a wifely ultimatum: 'I believe this is ready for a publisher.' She was right, for the reading public and the reviewers have been very kind about this book."

Don Charlwood has continued to write and publish short stories and in 1971 he brought out an historical work, *The Wreck of the Loch Ard*. Three years after that, he resigned from Air Traffic Control, for health reasons, which has given him the time he has always wanted for his writing. His latest book is a collection of short stories under the title *Flight and Time*. He is currently completing a book based on selections from diaries kept by immigrants during the long sea voyages to Australia by sailing ship.

The Twelfth Mile

A CONDENSATION OF THE BOOK BY
E. G. PERRAULT

ILLUSTRATED BY ALAN DANIEL

PUBLISHED BY COLLINS

The boundary of Canada's territorial waters was once the Twelve Mile limit. It is from that boundary that this thrilling story of brave men at sea takes its title.

All the elements of high adventure are here: human drama and conflict played out against a background of colossal natural catastrophe. The tugboat *Haida Noble* is caught in a fearsome combination of hurricane and tidal wave, and as skipper Christy Westholme and his crew race against time to save a threatened oil rig, they become involved in a bid to rescue a storm-tossed Russian spy ship. The Russian captain fights desperately to stop his vessel being towed into territorial waters, and his actions have tragic consequences.

A vividly told story which combines sea adventure with espionage in scenes of breathtaking excitement.

Chapter 1

The tug *Trident* shouldered its way through Active Pass, its bow wave splashing through a flat ribbon of mist that spread from Galiano to Mayne Island. Behind it, riding light and empty on the end of a 1500-foot cable, the 12,000-ton limestone barge slid solidly through the light chop of the slack tide.

The big Vancouver ferry had passed by minutes before, its rail lined with clusters of early autumn tourists, some focusing cameras on the unfamiliar sight of a barge larger than a football field making its way behind a tug less than one quarter its size.

Christy Westholme kept his right hand on the wheel while he leaned over to glance at the radar screen for reassurance. Except for a scattering of blips along the Galiano side where trollers were trying for coho and spring salmon, there was nothing to worry about. Ten minutes and they'd be out of the pass and into the broad sweep of the Strait of Georgia. He could take a break now.

The mate, long familiar with Westholme's method of doing things, appeared at the wheelhouse door almost as though summoned. Westholme glanced over his shoulder. "How'd you like to take over here, Larry?"

These two worked well together. In fact Westholme got along well with most of the company crew members. Four war years on Canadian corvettes, mostly in the North Atlantic, and twenty-five years on tugs, graduating to the big, ocean-going salvage jobs, had made him a good man to crew under. On this far Pacific edge of Canada with its 14-knot tide rips, its sudden gales and hurricanes, its murderous outcroppings of hidden reefs, and the ever-present danger of fog, Westholme had the unquestioning confidence of

his crews. The dispatcher's voice filled the wheelhouse. "*Trident*, we've got you coming out of Active Pass. Confirm your position."

Westholme pressed the microphone button. "*Trident* here. Three minutes and we're into the Strait. ETA to port . . ." He glanced at the chronometer. "1745, give a little, take a little. Give my wife a call, will you, Alex? Larry's wife too."

Westholme was feeling pretty good. All summer, things had gone right for him. After a tough six-month stint on salvage operations and dangerous transoceanic tows, this limestone run had been a break. It was pure routine; three days down the coast to the mouth of the Columbia with a loaded barge, then a two-day return to Vancouver with an empty one. Five days at sea gave him better than seven days' leave ashore.

"You going to break down and take your shore leave this time?" the mate asked. "You must have almost a month coming."

"I'd better take it if I want to stay in good with Lee," Westholme said, and he meant it.

She was beginning to show the wear and tear of too much solitude, he knew that. With both boys away at McGill, she lived for his homecomings—and they didn't happen often enough. Nowadays, when he did come home after a week or two at sea, there would be little arguments, differences of opinion.

It was time, Westholme decided, for the company to pull him in to a desk job.

"I took a chance on building up thirty days," he told Larry. "It'll give me the opportunity to spend some real time with Lee. Maybe take a trip to Vegas; get to know one another again."

"That's good thinking," Larry said. "In this business the best girl in the world can turn a little strange after a while."

There were other reasons for Westholme's thirty days, of course; house trim to be painted, a fence for the backyard, the pool table he was going to build. . . . They withdrew into a relaxed silence, while on deck the hands hustled to stow gear and get the tug shipshape

400

for arrival. *Trident* dropped the barge at anchor shortly after 1700 hours, and at 1741 Westholme brought the tug alongside the company wharf. Fifteen minutes later he was in his car proceeding home.

LEE MUST HAVE gone somewhere, for twilight had crept into the house along with the chill of a September evening. Westholme felt a sudden irritation. She knew that when he got home, he liked to find the lights on, the coffee hot, a wood fire crackling. It wasn't too much to ask after two or three weeks at sea.

He stowed his suitcase in the bedroom closet, turned up the thermostat in the living room, and lit paper and kindling in the fireplace. Crouched there above the small flame, he heard the key turn in the front door. Deliberately he remained crouched, his silence significant. Then he stood up and turned around.

"Alex told you I was coming in."

"That's right, he did," she said flatly. He had remained unsmiling and she made no effort to warm him.

"Run out of food or something?" He wanted the impasse broken now. The point had been made.

"No, I didn't." She removed her heavy cardigan and shook her thick, dark hair loose in a gesture that was almost defiant. For all her thirty-eight years, Lee was a spectacular woman. She had Irish in her, a bit of Scots and a smattering of Scandinavian. She had inherited the best qualities of all three, in his opinion.

There was no one like her; it was as simple as that. His marriage with Lee was a comfortable, unshakable way of life. It had been that way with his parents, which explained why Westholme was not surprised at his own good fortune.

"Something troubling you, Merilee?" He grinned now to break the tension. He used her full name only when he was teasing.

Her face was expressionless. "I'll put some supper on," she said in a voice that rejected his grin, and went into the kitchen.

Westholme felt worry growing in him as he went through a deliberate ritual of arranging wood on the fire. His pride was hurting. He didn't deserve to be treated like this. Finally he went into the kitchen. She was whipping eggs, and had bacon sizzling in the frying pan, but the kitchen seemed cheerless. He put his arms around her waist. "Have I done something, Lee?"

"Nothing, Chris. Nothing at all." Like a flat, bitter reproach. She transferred the bacon to a plate and put the eggs in the pan.

"I love you, Lee," he said.

"I don't know what you mean by that, and I don't think you do either." When the omelette was cooked she turned and confronted him squarely. "Christy, something has happened. I don't feel anything where you're concerned. Nothing. Love might come back again, but I wouldn't know how to bring it alive."

Anger flashed through him. "What the hell is this, Lee? Is there someone else?"

"'Someone else' would be an easy answer. This isn't easy . . . and there's no one else."

Anger boiling in him, he went to a cupboard and found half a bottle of rye. "Have one, Lee?"

"No thanks."

He poured himself a heavy shot, added ice and water and swallowed hard. "All right, Lee. Let's sort this thing out. We've got thirty days together, and I'd like it to be as usual."

"As usual!" she flared. "You mean you want me to be your housekeeper, jump through the usual hoops, then pack your bags and kiss you back onto the boat. I can't do that any more, Chris."

"You're bored, Lee. That's all that's happening here. The boys are on their own now, and you think your usefulness is over."

She turned away. "I'm not hungry. I'm going to bed . . ." She walked out of the kitchen as though she were walking out of his life.

After eating, Westholme put on a coat and left the house, but the cold September air with its faint smell of burning leaves did not soothe him. He felt the loss of something beyond recall. It was ridiculous to believe that all the good years could be written off in one evening. She had brooded about it, built up a case in her own mind, and her mood had rubbed off on him. All that was needed was to bring the thing into proper perspective.

Half an hour later, considerably calmer, he returned to the house, took a shower and put on clean pyjamas. In their bedroom, he slipped under the covers and moved in close, his hand reaching out to touch her. But he stopped. She was lying on her back, flat and unresponsive, her entire body rejecting him.

402

He lay there as rigid and tortured as she, and in the end he rose and went into the living room. This mustn't get out of control. Give him a crisis with a barge gone berserk in a high wind and a following sea, and he would know what to do. But this was different.

He went over and poked up the fire; and at that moment the telephone rang. The night dispatcher spoke apologetically.

"I shouldn't be calling you, Christy, but Hargreaves has gone into the hospital with a rupture or something. He was supposed to take *Haida Noble* out tonight. The drill-rig job. You can say no if you want."

Westholme didn't hesitate. "What's the departure time?"

"0100 hours."

"OK, I'll be there. What's the weather look like?"

"Nothing to worry about this side of the Island. There's a gale warning outside. Nothing to write home about."

Westholme hung up. He dressed in the hallway, then entered the bedroom and pulled his suitcase from the closet. In the darkness he turned to Lee. "I'm going out on a run. West coast of the Island and back in about five days. When I get back . . . maybe things will be a little better."

She said nothing.

"I love you, Lee. You may not know what I mean by that. But I know, and there's nothing more important to me." He walked out of the bedroom, down the hall and out the front door.

Chapter 2

By 12:15 a.m. Westholme had checked in with the dispatcher. His orders were clear enough, and in any event he was familiar with the job. He had skippered *Haida Noble* when the giant rig, BUTCO 17, was first towed to a drilling position outside Clayoquot Sound, and he had gone out six weeks later to move it to its next position.

"Any more on the weather?" Westholme said as he checked the crew roster.

"They're expecting a new five-day report from the US side sometime tonight. The local scene hasn't changed."

Westholme picked up his bag and left the office. Outside, he squinted into the fog rolling in off the inlet. Above him was the big arch with the company's name: OCEANLINK PACIFIC LIMITED.

With eighty-three tugs in its fleet, Oceanlink was probably the largest company of its kind in the world. Its masters, crews, and shore staff got along well, and pride in the company had much to do with it. Oceanlink had made world headlines in its time, and when people talked about towing and salvage operations in the North Pacific, Oceanlink was the name that came to mind.

Christy Westholme was convinced that Oceanlink's success was wrapped up in *Haida Noble*, a superlatively designed and equipped tug. She had become something of a legend in the Pacific. Her 4000-mile salvage of the stricken *Hellas* in 1962 had earned her news headlines. A fire on the freighter was extinguished at the height of a gale; then for thirty-seven days, *Haida Noble* towed *Hellas* through worsening weather. On the thirty-seventh day, when *Haida Noble* came through the Lions' Gate with the listing *Hellas* on shortened line astern, the city of Vancouver stood on the beaches and cheered.

And there she was now, deck lights ablaze, her bow, sharp as a chisel, angling almost thirty feet up into the wall of fog.

Westholme had shown Lee over *Haida Noble* on a night like this, when illuminated mist and sea sounds from the darkness had invested the great tug with a mythical quality. His dedication to a good ship was absolute, bordering on a religion. Halfway through the tour, Lee had said in exasperation: "It's absolutely great, Christy! But it's not a cathedral. I have a feeling you genuflect every time you walk onto the bridge."

Lee had a woman's attitude, Westholme thought. She couldn't be expected to be impressed with *Haida Noble*'s twin GM EMD diesels, twenty cylinders each, turning out a total of 10,000 horsepower, to give the tug a top speed of 18 knots. He didn't bother to show her the salvage equipment lockers, or the machine shop where practically any ship's part could be repaired or duplicated.

That was six years ago. He had logged thousands of miles since then, towing scores of ships to safety—in large part, because of Lee, because thinking of her made the job easier. A man didn't do things just for himself. "Damn it to hell!" he said, and went aboard.

THERE WERE a couple of crew members at the top of the gangplank as he went up. One of them he hadn't worked with before, a man in his late twenties, heavy-set, dark hair spilling onto the collar of his wetback. Westholme sized him up squarely.

"My name's Westholme, Chris Westholme. I'm taking her out tonight. Have you ever worked *Haida Noble* before?"

"Twice this summer; second engineer. Both times out to the rig. Name's Read . . . Stan."

The other man was a deckhand whose broad, freckled face Westholme was pleased to see. "Galbraith," he said, "you should be ashore. I thought the plan was to get another year of university?"

Galbraith grinned, "I spent all my money this summer."

"Try saving some for a change."

Westholme proceeded up to the bridge, where Lindstrom was tinkering with the radar. The tall man was a good mate, with a deep-water master's ticket. He had worked with Westholme on several *Haida Noble* assignments. Though he was painfully thin, the strength of his skeletal arms had made him a small fortune Indian wrestling. Lindstrom also had a resonant voice and a sense of humor.

"Who's aboard?" Westholme asked him now.

"The cook's aboard. That's all that matters."

"Come on!" Westholme complained.

"First officer; that's me," Lindstrom said. "Second Officer Fenton is down trying the cook's coffee. Chief engineer's aboard and he's a good one."

"Willie Thomson?"

"Yes, sir, the Scotsman is with us, complete with list of complaints. What's the plan?"

"We're moving BUTCO out," Westholme said. "The trick is to get her into shelter before the first of the big winter storms."

"Where is she?"

"Eight miles southwest of Amphitrite Point. We've got to take her into Ucluelet for winter layover." Westholme pulled out two charts from under the navigation desk and tacked them into place one beneath the other. "Why don't you go down and check the others on board," he said to Lindstrom. "Tell them to hustle. I want to catch that tide."

Lindstrom departed, brandishing his thin arms like an ape. A little too much of a clown, Westholme thought sourly. He surveyed the bridge—a great set-up with two of everything spread across its full 33-foot width: two engine-room telegraphs, plus a remote-control system; two gyro and magnetic compasses; two radar systems; two independent intercom systems; all backed up by the latest echo sounders, rudder-angle indicators, automatic pilots and other navigational aids. And a new closed-circuit television had been installed since he last commanded. It gave the bridge a view of the vessel's main quarters, as well as fore and aft maneuvering positions.

Beside the nearest radarscope was the ship-to-shore telephone. At this moment its importance grew to immense proportions. He could telephone Lee, tell her he was coming home and walk off the *Haida Noble* right now. It would take something like that to tear down the wall she had erected in her mind. But when Lindstrom reported that the crew was aboard, he said only, "Prepare to cast off."

NORMALLY, Westholme would have bunked down as soon as the tug was under way, but he didn't feel much like sleeping. "I'll hang around for a while," he told Lindstrom.

The big, half-open windows, port and starboard on the bridge, let in the sounds of the Narrows... the hoarse fog-horns and clanging bell buoys marking the passage of *Haida Noble*. From time to time Lindstrom checked the radar, but the fog had slowed traffic and they cleared the port without having to alter course.

Now the wind freshened, a brisk southerly tearing the thick fog to shreds. Midway across the Strait of Georgia visibility was good enough to increase speed to 10 knots. Lindstrom made an entry in the logbook. The chronometer showed 0237 hours.

"Damn!" he said in sudden irritation. "I meant to tell the wife to take the car in for a brake reline."

"Get on to Alex," Westholme said. "He'll be glad to hear a voice this time of night."

Lindstrom put the call through to the dispatcher and gave the instructions on the brake job. "Anything you want to say, Christy?" Lindstrom asked.

Here was a chance to leave a casual message for Lee, to let her know he wasn't bothered by what had happened tonight. Instead, "What's he got on the weather?" he said. It was running away from the thing he wanted to say.

"There's some kind of system moving up from the southwest—gale-force winds—but the betting is it'll dissipate," the dispatcher's tinny voice told them. "And you can expect more fog in Swanson Channel and beyond."

"Great!" Lindstrom said in disgust.

"I'm not the weatherman," the dispatcher said. "Have you got a camera on board? US Coast Guard reports a fleet of thirty to forty Russian fishing boats moving north along the Twelve Mile limit. They should be in your neighborhood tomorrow."

"What do you want . . . a snapshot of a bucket of borsch?"

"They say some of the big trawlers have girls in the crew. Bring me back a pin-up."

"You disgust me," Lindstrom said, and hung up.

"More fog," he repeated to Westholme.

"I heard." He gave the wheel back to Lindstrom. "I think I'll turn in. Make sure they shake me loose for the 0800 watch."

Chapter 3

The chairman of the Committee on the Peaceful Uses of the Sea Bed and the Ocean Floor worked late that night. As the United Nations year moved into its final months, many of the committee chairmen were putting in longer hours. For the Sea Bed Committee, as with many other General Assembly projects, time was in danger of running out.

How far had the Sea Bed Committee come in all these years? Not nearly far enough. Tomorrow the chairman's report to the committee would try to impress on them their desperately slow progress toward a set of principles governing the exploration and the exploitation of the deep sea bed.

Rain began to slant across the broad glass of his office window and the chairman walked over to stare vacantly at the wet shimmer of the New York streets. He was tired and depressed. The Sea Bed Committee was dealing with the world's last and perhaps greatest source of food and raw materials—or with a potential battlefield where navies could stalk one another and where fortresses and rocket emplacements could lie hidden in a hundred fathoms or more.

"We're not moving fast enough," he told his reflection in the rain-dappled window. "There's never enough time these days."

Chapter 4

One hundred and thirty navigational miles from *Haida Noble*, west and slightly south of Amphitrite Point, BUTCO 17, the biggest semi-submersible drill rig in existence, straddled an infinity of whitecaps like a gigantic crab mutation. Its three 155-foot legs supported a carapace of steel 130 feet above the surface of the sea. Bright eyes glittered along the edges and top, illuminating the antennae-like tracery of cranes and the drill mast itself, rearing another 140 feet above the shell of the beast.

British United Traction—BUTCO—had fourteen drill rigs working the continental shelves of the world, but this was the newest and most advanced of them all, able to drill to a depth of 25,000 feet. She was 12,000 tons of steel and drilling equipment, a floating equilateral triangle, each side 400 feet long, supported on three massive caissons, each resting on a pontoon.

BUTCO 17 had been drilling off the west coast of Vancouver Island since March, and had already weathered a spring hurricane with winds of more than 100 mph. Six drill holes with promising core samples and gas traces had led her toward the Amphitrite shelf. Each time she moved, *Haida Noble* towed her to the next site.

She waited now for the great tug, her caissons pumped almost clear of water ballast so that she floated high. Early that afternoon the last of the drill pipes had been pulled up after the hole had been capped. The continental shelf lay 20 fathoms below, with the drill rig's massive anchors biting deep into the sand. It was an unaccustomed position for BUTCO 17. She was designed for far deeper water.

MICHAEL VOLKOFF awoke in the small hours of the morning, feeling the slight movement of the rig, alert to changing sea conditions. The hours surrounding the repositioning of BUTCO 17 were always critical, but she became more vulnerable when she rode light in pounding seas and relatively shallow water.

Volkoff climbed into cork-soled boots, trousers, and insulated windbreaker. Dark-complexioned and tall, he had the athletic build of a swimmer. In high school he had made straight A's and made the state swimming and track teams at the same time. He had first seen the ocean at the age of ten, and had known in that instant that the sea would become his life. When he entered UCLA on a swimming scholarship, oceanography was his elected field.

His Russian father, a Colorado miner who understood mining and very little else, had complained. "What can you do with a thing like that? Go fishing? Sell seawater?"

Mike didn't take him too seriously, but he made one significant concession and chose mining engineering as his option when he entered the School of Oceanography. He had three great summers with the Scripps Institute, then a year with the Smithsonian after he got his doctorate. He then attended the International Oceanographic Congress in Moscow in 1966.

After several years on various contracts, the real breakthrough in Volkoff's career came with his job in British United. "It's a roving commission," British United's man said. "You'll be our idea man in the field. Whenever we put a rig into action, you'll go with it for as long as you feel necessary. Watch the machinery, how the rig works. We want to hear the bad things, not the good things about these rigs. We want you to come up with your own ideas and to supervise the application of our research and development." He lowered his voice slightly. "There is one other thing. I won't go into it now, but you'll meet with me and some government people tomorrow afternoon. We'll have to have your acceptance of our offer before we can hold that meeting."

Minutes later Volkoff signed the agreement. As for the meeting the following afternoon, the government agency was the CIA . . . and their people required him to file a report, whenever the occasion arose, on a number of specific subjects. It had concerned him at the time, but no longer bothered him.

He had stopped off at home on the way back to the West Coast. It was good to sit at the dinner table with his parents again, after months of being away, to tell them about the job.

His father said, "Looks as though I was wrong about making money out of seawater." But his mother limited her observations to the only thing that really concerned her.

"It's nice you got a good job, Mike," she said, the Russian sounds rolling richly from her tongue. "But all this traveling! Thirty-one years and no sign of a wife and family."

"Time enough for that," he assured her.

Volkoff had spent two of the twelve months since then off the coast of New Guinea, three off the coast of Labrador, four on a jinxed rig in the Caribbean, and the rest on BUTCO 17, with a few weeks off for head-office briefings and holiday time. Recently, he had begun to feel the grind. He needed time off, bright lights, good food, entertainment, and girls. Not girls, he decided. *One* girl if she was the right one.

It was the end of the season for BUTCO 17, ideal time for a four-week leave. He decided to put in for it, as he pushed the door open into the face of the wind.

The southwesterly wasn't doing more than 20 knots, but there hadn't been any wind at all when he turned in at midnight. Worse, the sea was pushing a heavy swell against the rig from the same direction. He squinted into a slanting curtain of rain and headed for the communications shack, passing the recreation mess building where some of the graveyard shift were watching a movie, the flicker of the closed-circuit TV tube playing across the insulated window like cold fire.

On the helicopter pad, several roughnecks were tying down the six-passenger Sikorsky S55 against the possibility of increasing wind. In the morning it would begin ferrying BUTCO's crew to the small fishing town of Ucluelet—an easy, nine- or ten-mile hop—on the first leg of their journey back to the mainland.

"Expecting trouble?" Volkoff called up to the pilot.

"Nicked a blade tip coming in tonight. I want to steady things up for a repair job in the morning."

"Serious?"

The pilot shook his head. "They can fix it with a Band-Aid."

Volkoff finished his walk to the communications shack, feeling the shifting of the massive deck beneath his feet. Inside were the graveyard foreman with the rig supervising engineer and the night-shift first-aid man. The radio operator had passed coffee around and they were all sitting back enjoying a bull session.

Volkoff poured himself a mug. "Nice to have some peace and quiet, Charlie," he said. "After a couple of months you get the notion the drill hole's going through your head."

"Son, you don't know music when you hear it." Charlie Knight, the rig's head man, was a square-set Texan with thirteen years of roughnecking behind him. "When I don't hear drill steel turning, I get a mournful feeling."

"You're up late, Charlie," Volkoff said.

The engineer nodded. "So are you. Something we ate?"

"We're getting more movement than I expected," Volkoff explained. "That's quite a swell shaping up."

"Coast guard weather report says we don't have to worry too much," Charlie said. "They caught a system a thousand miles or so west of Sacramento. Gale-force winds pushing this way. They think it'll wear itself out before it gets here."

"It's here now," Volkoff said. "That swell had to start somewhere. How old is the report?"

"It came in at 0215," the radio operator told him. "Probably three or four hours old. Just a routine forecast."

"Stick around, Mike," the first-aid man invited. "We're waiting for the late, late television special." He indicated the bank of radar screens.

Charlie Knight drained his coffee cup. "US Coast Guard says there's thirty or forty Russian boats coming north along the Twelve Mile line. They should be showing on the screen any time."

That was a lot in one flotilla, though while Canadian vessels seldom fished in groups of more than two or three—more often by themselves—the Russians fished as a team: seiners, trawlers, a cannery ship, and quite often a tanker all moving together. God help the Canadian fishermen with gear down in the path of big Russian trawlers! The trawlers moved inexorably, no matter what lay ahead, often wrecking the light gear of the Canadians. Volkoff stared closely at the radar screen. The land mass and islets revealed by the sweeping green band of light was Amphitrite Point. The jagged edge of Vancouver Island filled the right-hand portion of the screen; on the left the nothingness of open sea was disturbed only by three small blips almost dead center.

411

"Gill-netters," the operator told him. "Canadian. They're working half a mile inside the Twelve Mile, and that's where they'll stay until that fleet passes by."

Volkoff didn't join the general laughter. Canadian fishermen had had one of the worst summers yet for harassment by big Russian trawlers just inside the limit. He turned to other problems.

"Charlie, what if that wind reaches us before the tug does . . . or if we're on the line behind the tug?"

"Give me a choice and I'd like to see that wind before we go on the line. The last two rigs to get into trouble caught it while they were at the end of tow lines. I'd rather put the legs down to the bottom and sit it out."

"We should have gone into shelter two weeks ago," Volkoff said. "Doesn't BUTCO read our reports?"

"This last hole was important," Charlie said. Only Charlie, Volkoff and the rig geologist knew what the final cores from the last hole had revealed. BUTCO 17 would come back there next spring. In three days they'd be through into oil.

The radio operator was staring hard at the radar screen. "I think the show is starting," he said.

At first Volkoff saw just a little blur of light. Then, at 0349, the first blip appeared and disappeared, appeared again along with another. Big and little stabs of light, luminous teardrops weeping across the radar field. By 0517 they had counted thirty-seven vessels, several of larger than normal size. At 0527 Volkoff said, "They've stopped. We've got company."

"By God, you're right," Charlie said. "Just four miles off."

Chapter 5

Far north and west of *Haida Noble*, on the Pacific's northern edge, the chemistry of a cataclysm moved to its conclusion. Deeply confined in a vast retort of basalt and granite, its ingredients bubbled and fumed, building up a mountain-smashing pressure.

At 0630 hours, the duty seismologist at the Klyuchi Vulcanological Station on Russia's Kamchatka Peninsula, making a routine check of the seismograph tapes, noticed renewed action in the region of Bogoslof Island.

In the rogues' gallery of the Aleutian Islands, Bogoslof Island was a juvenile delinquent: most Aleutian volcanoes have million-year histories; but Bogoslof hadn't exploded into sight until the year 1796. Then, in a matter of days, a complete flame-belching island had emerged from the sea. In due course it ceased to grow, and became silent, but in 1906, 1910, 1923 and 1927, further eruptions occurred. Bogoslof had established itself as troublesome but not really significant.

Still, when the duty seismologist at Klyuchi drew attention to the island's new mutterings, more than one seismologist began to suspect that Bogoslof would bear watching.

Chapter 6

At 0730 hours, Westholme slid from the bunk, stripped off shirt and underwear top and went into the lavatory he shared with the first officer. There he turned on the cold water and stared at the alien face in the mirror. The harsh light picked out gray in the rumpled, black thatch of hair, and the heavy musculature of his jawline and neck appeared to have lost its tone.

He wanted the cold to numb the hot, wild thoughts that raced through his mind. Lee had never loved him. Lee waited for him to go to sea. Lee let someone in the back door when he went out the front . . . No: none of that was true! Lee was the best woman he would ever know. She had waited longer, endured more, given more love. . . .

Westholme plunged his head into the cold water and came up spluttering. His groping hand found the towel and he dried himself. As he was dressing in his cabin his preoccupation made him clumsy—but then *Haida Noble* rolled sharply to starboard, and his mind was torn from the woman and returned to the sea.

Stepping outside, he made for the companionway to the main deck. The wind was building all right, a good southwesterly—and they weren't out in the open yet. When they cleared the dubious shelter of Cape Flattery they'd be into the worst of it.

"Never got a straight forecast from a Met man in my life," he said audibly, and then realized that he was talking to himself. He shook his head in disgust and entered the galley-cafeteria.

Two deckhands were playing blackjack at one of the six bench-table arrangements. Ernie Bibaud he knew, a good seasoned man, but he didn't know the other deckhand—young, wearing glasses with wire rims, thick, blond hair.

Bibaud looked up briefly. "This here is George Tait. George, this is Mister Westholme, the skipper on this thing."

Tait nodded and picked up his cards.

"Too late to deal me in?" Westholme asked.

Bibaud grinned at him, his black eyes reflecting the mischief he was famous for. "You want to deal in before you check the cards?" His accent had the cadence of French-Canadian patois, though he could speak almost flawless English when he wanted to.

"Come on, Ernie," Westholme said. "If you've got it stacked I'll find out. What's the game?"

"Ten cents to get in. Ten cents to raise. You got that kind of money?"

From the galley, the cook, who was new to the *Haida Noble*, called across to Westholme. "What can I fix you, Captain? Got some real good steaks this trip."

"Something simple. Coffee, a couple of eggs, bacon." Westholme looked at his watch. "I'll need it in a hurry." To Tait he said: "Been with the company long?"

"Short of a year. I came over from Oceanic last October."

"Working on papers?"

Tait nodded. "I've got my deep-water mate's ticket."

"Good," Westholme said. He might have known the company would crew *Haida Noble* with the best. Tait was just a deckhand on this run but a year or two from now, with more experience, he'd probably sit for his deep-water master's and qualify for his own tug.

Tait rose and slid into his jacket and slicker. Then he lurched heavily against the bolted-down table as *Haida Noble* shrugged off a big sea. Behind them they heard the crash of crockery, and the cursing of the cook. "It's all here, Captain," he said, surveying the tray, "but you got a little coffee with your eggs."

Bibaud, in jacket and slicker, joined Tait. "You gonna need help checking that deck gear," he said. "That's a good sea piling up."

Westholme tried a forkful of bacon, drained his coffee cup and

414

headed for the bridge. "Maybe you can hustle me a sandwich in an hour or two," he called over his shoulder to the cook.

On the bridge, First Officer Lindstrom was making his final entry in the log before going off watch. Young Galbraith was taking a turn at the wheel, gripping it with a wide stance as the sea continued to attack from the southwest abeam. Westholme crossed to the barometer to check the calibrations.

"Twenty-nine eighty," Lindstrom said, turning away from the log. "She hasn't changed a degree all night."

"Just a dirty little squall," Westholme said. He glanced at the chronometer: seconds away from 0800. "I'll get the weather report." He switched the receiver to 1630 and almost instantly the voice of the Canadian Weather Bureau burst through the static: "West coast cloudy with sunny periods. Winds southwesterly at five to ten knots, seas moderate . . ." Westholme turned it off.

"Who makes up that patter," Lindstrom said indignantly, "a junior Boy Scout with a wet finger? I figure the wind at twenty to twenty-five."

Westholme nodded. "We'll keep an eye on it." He took the wheel from Galbraith. "Get some shut-eye, both of you, and see if you can round up Tait on your way. I'll need him on the wheel for an hour or so."

Alone, Westholme scanned the oceanscape. In the early-morning light he could see the dark outline of Cape Flattery slightly ahead of him and ten miles to port, and the unbroken white line of surf ribboning in the foreshore of San Juan Point directly to starboard. The sea was marching, dark and chunky, past the bow. The rain was abating, but the wind streaked it like diamond slashes across the glass of the navigation bridge. There were startling tunnels of brilliant blue sky in the tattered cloud cover moving overhead. "Cloudy with sunny periods," the man had said. Maybe so . . . Tait was standing at his shoulder, and Westholme turned to give him the wheel. "Can you take her for a while, George?"

"I've done a turn at the wheel before now," Tait reminded him. He positioned himself and almost immediately had to compensate for a larger than usual wave piling in on the port bow.

Westholme was satisfied with the youngster's cool assurance. He went over to the navigation desk and sized up chart 3001. Perhaps 60 miles to go. Eight hours to reach the drill rig. They'd have two hours of good light left to put the tow line on it. Better to wait and start the tow to Ucluelet Inlet tomorrow morning, he decided. At four knots, they could have the rig in the shelter of the inlet by early afternoon. He crossed over to the VHF radio set and switched to BUTCO's frequency. "*Haida Noble* calling BUTCO 17," he said, "*Haida Noble* calling BUTCO 17. Come in please."

"Hello, *Haida Noble*. What can we do for you?" inquired a cheerful voice.

"Captain Westholme here. Can I speak to the rig super?"

A new voice introduced itself in a relaxed Texas drawl: "Charlie Knight here, Captain. Whereabouts y'all located?"

"Mid-channel, Juan de Fuca Strait. We've got something like sixty miles to go. How are you riding?"

"Tolerable, Captain, but we got a wind building up out here."

"That's our problem, too," Westholme said. "Keep smiling. We'll have a line on you by four o'clock, all being well."

"We'll hold you to that, Captain. If this wind keeps on, we're going to put the legs down at 1600 hours on the button. There's no way I'm going to drift this rig onto the beach."

"Nothing to worry about," Westholme assured him. "Get yourself cleaned up for company in eight hours."

"Captain," the Texan said in a flat voice, "we got all the company we can handle right now. Thirty-seven Russkies sitting four or five miles west of us, like they're going to spend the winter."

"Sit tight," Westholme said. "We'll keep this frequency open."

Chapter 7

Volkoff tried first to get the helicopter to scout the fleet, but the repair to the rotor blade was more difficult than expected, and the pilot needed three or four more hours. Volkoff settled for a ride in the drill-tower elevator to the 100-foot level.

There, with the gusty southwesterly driving rain into his eyes, he tried to train his binoculars on the Russian flotilla. It was a frustrating exercise. The movement of the drill rig, 100 feet up, was magnified into a sickening, slow oscillation. The high-powered glasses brought the fishing boats close—when he was able to fix them—but the boats heaved one way and the drill tower swung another until Volkoff began to feel seasick.

The four-mile-long fleet, principally trawlers and seiners, showed igns of wear and tear from months at sea. On the far edge of the group, like a buttress between the smaller vessels and the open sea, at a rusty-hulled tanker. Closer in, two cannery ships were processing a catch. Volkoff couldn't identify the species, and regretted it. A preponderance of salmon would have been further evidence to support the claim of the Canadian fishermen that their salmon resources were being intercepted and depleted.

He tried desperately to focus his glasses. What was that? He found a vessel and lost it again. Fully half its hull was concealed by one of the cannery ships. He swallowed hard to keep his stomach down and tried again. There it was, and there was no doubt this time. He had seen its prototype in Baltic waters during the International Oceanographic Congress. It was one of the *Nikolai Zubov* class, designed and equipped for oceanographic research. There had been quite a stir at the conference when the Russians refused delegates a tour of the impressive vessel.

A strong gust of wind threw him off balance and the ship disappeared from his field of vision. The motion sickness got to him and he stumbled over to the elevator. Knight was waiting for him when he stepped onto the drill deck.

"What's the matter, Mike?" Knight grinned. "You don't like the view from the top?"

Volkoff was feeling better already. "The view is great. . . . Well worth the trip."

"Let's get out of this damn' wind." Knight led the way to the communications shack, scowling up at the moving pattern of cloud and blue sky. "The helicopter can't start ferrying the crew until two at the earliest. Fifty men and their gear to Ucluelet before dark! We don't stand a snowball's chance in hell."

Inside the hut Volkoff moved to the radar screen. "Look here, Charlie," he said. "We've got some interesting people in the neighborhood." He poked his finger at a cluster of blips. "This big one is a cannery ship, a ten-thousand-tonner. And this one here, tucked in, maybe two ship's lengths behind, is a *Nikolai Zubov* class oceanographic research vessel. Twenty-six hundred tons displacement, two hundred and ninety-five feet long. Tremendous lab facilities and accommodation for seventy scientists. The United States hasn't anything to compare with her."

"You sure? What's a ship like that doing, keeping company with a bunch of rusty trawlers?"

417

"Anybody's guess," Volkoff said. "We've got to send a signal t
the office right now, Charlie."

"What for? Those are international waters."

"Because she's carrying new equipment. I made out a fair-size
protector globe for electronic stuff mounted above the bridge. An
she's got some impressive-looking direction finders and troposca
tering sensors up on the foremast. We ought to let the office know."

"Go ahead, but my betting is they know all about it. You can
keep a ship like that a secret."

"The point is," Volkoff said patiently, "that a first-class, superla
tively equipped research vessel is sitting five miles west of BUTCO 1
It's not a coincidence, Charlie. This drill rig is a bit more than
tourist attraction. You and I know it. How long will it take for ther
to know it?"

"We're inside the Twelve Mile," Knight reminded him. "If the
come over for a look they'll find themselves in Canadian custody.
say live and let live, Mike. We'll be out of here in twelve hours."

The telephone rang. It was the lab reporting that the baromete
had dropped from twenty-nine eighty to twenty-nine sixty in a ha
hour. Outside, the wind pummeled the wall of the shack with nev
vigor. The light coming through the uncurtained window possesse
a startling clarity, as though it had filtered in from the distan
horizon.

Knight pulled up his coat collar and headed for the door. "I'n
going to light a fire under those mechanics. That helicopter shoul
be up and flying by now."

Chapter 8

Neither weather-station ship *Union* nor weather-station shi
Nectar could be faulted for having paid small attention to the mino
system that had passed them by two days before. Spawned north
west of the Hawaiian Islands, the hurricane infant had crawled pas
them in the night, its rage beginning to show only in fitful squall:
and patches of troubled water on a moderate sea. Thirty hours later
a United States Coast Guard weather plane found it grown to a ful
gale, but relatively localized and butting itself against a formidabl
cold front to the north. One thousand miles due west of Sacramento
the system was moving northeast at 15 to 20 knots. The time wa:

4:00 p.m. and the crew of the weather plane had little doubt that the marauding wind would beat itself to death against the cold front in the hours of darkness.

But hurricanes are unpredictable. This one, which would later be named Faith, grew to deadly maturity that night. The winds in her spiral attained 100 knots, and by dawn she was screaming ahead at 30 knots, pushing giant seas before her.

If any shipping lay in her path, it issued no warning and it was not until 10:00 a.m. the following day that the first signal was received and processed. A lonely NOMAD, a moored weather buoy, bobbing 300 miles west of Portland, Oregon, caught the right edge of Faith as she passed over. NOMAD's transmitter continued to function for twenty-two minutes after the hurricane struck. In that time she relayed information that caused the duty officer at the US Weather Bureau station to file a report with Weather Information within minutes.

Chapter 9

By 1100 hours Westholme had no doubt that they were heading into trouble. He tapped the barometer and turned to Tait: 'We've got ourselves some kind of a record. She's down to twenty-nine inches on the nose.''

On the port beam a gray mountain of water heaved itself up. It was as though the entire ocean had placed its shoulder below that wave and pushed upward. The wind chewed white fringes on its curling edge. *Haida Noble* dipped her bow momentarily and then climbed up on the gray-green mass, angling through it and plummeting down the other side to bury her foredeck under water.

"That sea is bigger than the wind," Westholme observed, "so the real stuff hasn't reached us yet. There's something big southwest of us, that's certain. I think we'd better have a talk with BUTCO." He reached for the switch on the VHF set: "BUTCO 17. *Haida Noble* here. Are you receiving? Over.''

The voice came through, brisk and cheerful as ever. "Nice to hear from you. Mr. Knight was about to call you.''

Knight's voice cut in abruptly. "We're getting strong winds up here, Captain. This rig'll turn into a sailboat real soon. How far away are y'all?''

419

"A good six hours," Westholme said. "Put the legs down now. Get her rock solid, and lower your wind resistance."

"If that's all you called about," Knight said, "we're wasting time. I was going to put the legs down anyhow."

"Good. We're both thinkers. We'll be with you in six hours and put a line on board. We'll ride this thing out together."

"That's real sociable."

"Russians still hanging around?"

The humorless chuckle came through clearly. "That's the one bit of joy. Those Russkies are tossing around out there like corks in a cauldron."

"So are we," Westholme told him. "And I'm not laughing."

Knight signed off and Westholme crossed over to tune in a frequency on the transmitter-receiver. The recorded voice boomed in halfway through a sentence: ". . . warning. Hurricane-force winds reported approaching west coast in northeasterly direction, position forty-five degrees north, one hundred and thirty degrees west . . . all shipping take warning."

Westholme turned the volume down and returned to the chart table. "That would put the trouble about three hundred miles from us at 0800." He looked at Tait. "Two more hours and we could be in the middle of it. So-o . . ." He scratched his head and stared out at the seas piling past *Haida Noble*'s bow. "We'd better give this beauty a better margin of safety. Bring her around to port, George. Two-ninety should do it. We'll hold her on that course as long as we can. I want to put more water between us and the rocks."

Tait looked dubious, but swung the wheel over, putting *Haida Noble* on a compass course of 290. The tug was taking the full brunt of the seas on her port side now, causing her to roll alarmingly.

"She can take it," Westholme said. "When the big stuff comes we can decide whether to go with the wind or turn and face it." He braced himself on the sharply tilting deck. "I'd like you to go below and raise Brad Fenton for me—the second officer." He took the wheel from Tait and squinted through the rain pattern on the glass, aiming *Haida Noble*'s sharp bow down the green trough of the troubled sea. Beside him the ship-to-shore buzzed sharply. He picked up the receiver. It was Jake Harmon, a VP at Oceanlink and a good administrator, though maybe a shade too pushy. By now the office would know about the weather situation. It was their option to call *Haida Noble* back.

"Chris. . . ? Christy, I suppose you've heard the weather report. What's it really look like? I mean. . . ."

Westholme felt Fenton's hand reach under his arm to take the wheel. He slid away and said into the ship-to-shore: "You call the shot, Jake. There's still time for me to turn round and take her back."

"I'm not sure there's any advantage," Harmon said. "That wind's got a three-hundred-mile spread. You'd be pounded all the way home. How much time do you think you have?"

"Hard to tell. An hour and a half maybe. I could duck into Port Renfrew. . . ."

"What I'm trying to say," Harmon cut in quickly, "is that we've got a good contract with BUTCO. If you think *Haida Noble* can take it, I think you should get up there and stand by. Show them we're trying. You know what I mean?"

"I'm with you, Jake," Westholme said. "I promised them I'd be in the vicinity around 1700 and they're counting on us."

"Good enough! Look, I'll give your wife a call. Tell her I've been talking to you and everything's fine. Can I give her a message for you, Chris?"

"The way you put it was pretty good," Westholme said. "Tell her everything's fine."

"We'll keep in touch. Good luck, Christy." Harmon hung up.

Without removing his eyes from the trough along which *Haida Noble* plunged, Fenton said, "The VP?"

Westholme nodded. "He's asking us to stand by BUTCO 17."

Fenton shrugged and thrust chest and belly against the wheel as *Haida Noble* plunged into a steep roll to starboard. Westholme wedged himself against one of the radar housings and watched a needle move on a dial on the instrument panel.

"Forty-seven degrees of roll that time," he said.

Tait and Fenton were silent: they both knew the tug's low center of gravity gave it a critical angle of roll approaching 55 degrees. No real danger yet. The waves were increasing in size, but they remained uniform in both interval and impact.

WHEN THE TUG rose on a crest, Westholme took a sharp look port and starboard, squinting through spray-fouled glass. The dangerous Pachena Point lay 15 miles to starboard, close enough with the pre-vailing current and the sea running at it together.

421

"The cook's having a hemorrhage," Tait reported drily. "The galley looks like elephants ran through it."

"He knows everything should be stowed for heavy weather," Westholme said sharply. He turned to Fenton. "That's what I called you for, Brad. I think you'd better look things over. Go along with him, Tait, and lend a hand. Start with the wire room and the salvage gear lockers. I don't want one of those spare anchors running wild and punching holes in us when the going gets rough. And Tait, I'll need you back here as soon as you've finished. Brad, you can cool your heels until your watch. But keep your shoes on."

After Brad and Tait had left, Westholme glanced at the chronometer and turned up the volume on the radio receiver for the weather report. The corner of his eye caught the approach of a new wave— a rogue, higher, broader, more aggressive than anything preceding it. He swung the wheel hard and rammed the throttles on the remote control, spinning the tug to starboard in the blue-green trough. The turn was almost completed when the rogue wave struck, mounting the stern and rising just short of bridge-deck level before it parted. He felt *Haida Noble*'s stern thrust down by tons of water. Then, as the foaming mountain passed, the vessel hung suspended on the trailing edge of the wave before it tobogganed stern first into the trough. From below, penetrating thinly through the sounds of the wind and sea, Westholme heard metal and wood colliding. Near his left ear the recorded voice continued with the weather report, ". . . hurricane-force winds . . . Estimated diameter of storm center three hundred plus miles. Warning to all shipping . . ."

"Nice to have plenty of warning," Tait shouted behind him. He was dragging himself toward the security of a stanchion, working hard against the tilting deck.

"What was all the commotion down below?"

"A rack of welding tanks broke loose in the machine shop. Galbraith and Bibaud are lashing it down."

There was no feeling of forward movement in the following sea, but wind and current were working with the tug's engines now.

"What does the barometer read?" Westholme demanded.

"Twenty-eight ninety . . . I've never seen a barometer drop like that—in three hours."

"The way I see it, we don't have much choice. The wind hasn't changed direction, which means the eye of this thing, if it has one, is going to pass close by. But we'll stay on this course and try to get as close to the drill rig as we can. It's the only breakwater on this whole stretch of coast."

It had been a tough day. It was going to get tougher.

Chapter 10

It rained all night in New York. It was still raining when the Sea Bed Committee reconvened at two o'clock the following afternoon. Three hours later, when tempers among the hotly debating committee members began to wear thin, the rain obligingly began to fall harder.

Charges and countercharges; protests, accusations, innuendoes. The chairman called sharply for order. "This meeting is in danger of deteriorating into something totally unconstructive. I recognize the representative from Canada."

The Canadian rose. "Mr. Chairman, I can only concur that we have not yet come to grips with the critical problem of the disarmament of the sea bed. While the USA and the USSR appear to agree in principle that the sea bed should not be used as a battleground or a base of attack, there is no clear evidence that it is being disarmed. I submit that tension could quite easily build over this issue. Presented with a crisis, I doubt seriously that we have established either the authority or the accord to provide a solution."

The Russian delegate stood. "My delegation interprets that statement as defeatist. We will not stand by and . . ."

The chairman rapped his gavel and pulled his papers together. The meeting was adjourned—to be reconvened the following day at the same time.

The tall glass windows streamed with water against the black sky. Far in its depths, a plane swam by, its navigation lights blinking like phosphor beads on a lost sea creature. Then the low clouds engulfed them and the illusion was very much as though the sea creature had drowned.

Chapter 11

Volkoff stood huddled in the entrance to the recreation room dining hall on the deck of BUTCO 17. Minutes before, the rig's massive pumps and hydraulic systems had completed the flooding and lowering of the legs. With the gigantic tripod firmly planted on the gently angled continental shelf in 20 fathoms of water, BUTCO 17 stood as steady as a piece of the mainland in the 70-mile-an-hour wind and mounting waves. Many of the waves were cresting at 25 and 30 feet now, but with the deck of the rig riding 50 feet above the surface, the margin of safety was ample.

Butting their heads against the slashing rain, the roughnecks struggled to secure fuel drums and other potentially dangerous objects, and completed the stringing of one-inch nylon rope between the various buildings and shelter areas on the deck. If the wind attained the predicted velocity of 100 knots it would be foolhardy to venture anywhere in the open without a safety line.

An empty grease bucket tumbled past Volkoff and disappeared beyond the far edge of the deck. The wind was louder now, more urgent, and the encircling roar of the ocean was made resonant by the rig's hollow underpinnings. He marveled at the enormity and the chaos of the sound contained in the unbroken cadence of the waves.

Ahead of him, Volkoff could see the helicopter tugging at its moorings. Though it had been repaired, the wind velocity was too great to risk a flight, so the entire crew remained on the rig—fifty-three roughnecks and technicians.

Having built up the expectation of a four-week leave and come within a few hours of achieving it, Volkoff felt something approaching a bitter personal grudge against the storm. The rig could be pinned down now for a week or more, trouble could develop. He would feel considerably better with BUTCO 17 in deeper water. He would feel better still if he was the hell off this rig, getting ready for a night out in San Francisco.

Volkoff turned and entered the recreation hall. Half the crew were inside, playing cards or watching a dated movie on the closed-circuit TV set. He looked for Knight and found him in a corner, crouched over a cup of coffee, talking to the rig's geologist. He carried a chair over and sat down, aware as he did so that the crazy sounds of the storm were filling the room. Knight was in a bad mood, dragging viciously on his cigarette.

"Where do we stand in relation to that wind?" the geologist asked. "Are we going to get the edge of it?"

"I've been watching it for the past half hour," Volkoff said. "If we were on one side of it there would be a wind deviation. There isn't, so we must be close to its central line of approach. If the thing has an eye, we could get a breather when the center reaches us; an hour or two to clean up before the tail end of it gets here."

"Great!" Knight said savagely. "You got me feeling better already." He pushed his chair back and stood up. "I'm going over to the radio shack and get the latest bad news. You coming?"

"Think I'll get some bunk time," Volkoff said. "Things could get interesting in the next hour or two."

Back in his room he stretched out on the comfortable bunk and pulled a blanket up over him. He didn't expect to sleep. Lying there he tried to distinguish one individual sound familiar to him—something he could befriend: the rattle of a loose aerial wire, the whipping of a tarpaulin—but the rage of the thing outside had drawn every sound together into one concerted roar. Volkoff thought he knew the sea at its worst, but this thing surpassed his experience. He listened intently, to detect a break in the unwavering metronome of the oncoming waves. No break . . . unchanging. He slept.

WHEN HE wakened it was to the sound of a splintering crash and a sudden gust of wind and wetness across his face. The room was in darkness and he groped frantically for the light switch and turned it on. Outside, all hell had broken loose. The exterior darkness was filled with a hoarse, falsetto scream, and impaled in his doorframe was the remains of an empty nail keg hurled at it like a cannonball. Rainwater rifled through the jagged hole.

He rolled out of his bunk and charged at the door, trailing his blanket behind him. He managed to pull the smashed keg clear but the blanket, even balled up, was useless for plugging the hole. He tossed it away and scrambled around the room getting his gear out of the path of the water beginning to move across the floor.

He looked at his watch—7:40! He had been asleep five hours in the middle of this. In his closet he located the rubberized pants and jacket he used for foul weather, climbed into them and joined a group of exhausted, drenched roughnecks who were trying to draw

some comfort from hot coffee and cigarettes in the dining area.
"Any idea where Charlie Knight is?" Volkoff asked.

"Somebody seen him at the radio shack," one man said.

Volkoff pulled the jacket hood over his head and laced it tightly
under his chin before he went to the door. Two of the roughnecks
followed him. "You're going to need help with that door," one said.
"There's a safety rope on the left-hand side as you go out. When we
open the door, grab it and don't let go."

Volkoff nodded and the three of them put their shoulders to the
heavy panel, easing it open. Half-blinded by the wind and the solid
sheet of rain, he groped for the rope with both hands, pulling himself clear of the door. Then the light was gone and he was alone in
the drenched and howling darkness. Even with the rope, he wasn't
sure of his bearings. He began to pull himself through the inches of
driven water on the steel deck as arrows of rain stabbed his eyeballs.

It took him ten minutes to get the 200 feet to the shack, backing
up the last 50 feet, jackknifed by the force of the hurricane, his
hood ballooning with wind and water. He pounded the door, and it
eased open a foot or two. Releasing his grip on the rope, he dove
for the yellow oblong of light. A hand steadied him as he came
through, and the door slammed shut as though it had been hit with
a pile driver. After the chaos of sound outside, the interior seemed
silent. He stood there dripping and speechless, his eyes burning.

"Don't just stand there, for God's sake," Knight said. "Get out of
that stuff and draw yourself a coffee."

Volkoff looked around as he slipped out of the wet gear. There
were Knight and the geologist, one of the drill bosses, and three
roughnecks. The radio operator was playing with knobs and
switches, a worried tension in his movements.

"Where've you been?" Knight demanded.

His manner irritated Volkoff. "I was building a kite," he said.
"Somebody told me there might be a breeze coming up."

Knight glared at him and turned back to the operator. "Well,
what do you think, Ron? Hell, you should have some idea where
the trouble is by now."

"It's got to be atmospherics, Charlie," the operator said
defensively. "Everything checks out here just fine. So far the
antennae are holding out."

"I want a weather report," Knight said.

"What for?" the geologist demanded. "We've got the weather

report all around us. We've got ourselves a hurricane. I saw the anemometer clock one gust of one hundred and twelve knots. Average wave height twenty-seven point four feet and it's not going to get any better."

Knight made a frustrated gesture. "All right, but one thing's for damn sure, the company's going to hear from me on this. Letting us sit here into the winter storms, grabbing for that last thousand feet of drilling. If we could make radio contact I'd tell them now. Ah-h!" He brushed the problem away with the flat of his hand. "Who's got a deck of cards?"

"Right under the radar panel," the operator obliged. "Middle drawer." He was eager to get Knight off his back.

Volkoff looked at the blank radar screens and was reminded of the Russians. "What's happening to the fishing fleet?"

"They started to scatter to hell-and-gone a couple of hours ago," Knight said. "Last time we looked there was one cannery ship still in position, the research ship and two trawlers. Turn on the set, Ron."

The operator manipulated dials and the first screen in the bank of four came alive in the semi-darkened room. They watched the scanning beam go around . . . and there were five ghostly lights on the screen. Of the five, three were scattered on the periphery while two—the cannery ship and one other—occupied a central position in the left-hand segment.

"My guess is the smaller of the two is the spy ship," Knight said.

"Research vessel," Volkoff corrected him.

"Come on," Knight scoffed. "Direction finders, sonar domes . . ."

"Spy ship's moving off," the operator cut in.

The gap between the two blips was widening. The research vessel was moving slowly astern until she was four ship's lengths from the cannery ship.

"She's coming about," Knight said excitedly.

The others crowded in to watch as the vessel made her slow, dangerous way in the trough of the sea toward them.

"She's pushing it!" Knight said, as though he were trying to warn her away. "She's pushing it!" He nudged the operator roughly. "She must be damn near on top of the Twelve Mile?"

"She's across it," the operator said. "That piece of tape on the edge of the screen marks the Twelve Mile."

"Hold it," Volkoff cautioned. "He's discovered his error. He's changing course."

428

The ship was making a 90-degree turn to port and running north with the hurricane riding her tail. But she did not go back across the Twelve-Mile boundary. Instead she rode the trough straight across to the vertical center line of the radar screen. There she appeared to halt for a moment before she turned hard starboard and came down the screen toward BUTCO 17.

"She's breaking the law, by God!" Knight exclaimed. "We've got her, cold turkey!"

No one spoke. The approach of the yellow-green blob of light mesmerized them. Out there in the dark, riding south toward them into the teeth of one of the worst West Coast hurricanes in years, was a foreign ship, a Russian ship trespassing in Canadian waters.

"She must be in trouble," Volkoff said. "She wouldn't try a thing like this otherwise."

"Then where are the rockets?" Knight demanded. "She'd be firing rockets. Try that bloody radio of yours again," he told the operator. "We're going to let the Defense Department know."

The operator returned to the radio panel and began riding the frequencies again, while the others watched the blip approach dead center and then fade from sight.

"She's arrived," Volkoff announced. "She's behind us in the lee of the wind, using us as a breakwater."

"They can't do that," Knight protested. "They're breaking every damn law in the book."

"They're doing it," Volkoff said, "And there's not a navy or a coast guard that can stop them tonight."

Chapter 12

At 2000 hours Westholme was too busy to listen to the weather report. There was a certain amount of damage throughout the vessel in spite of the fact that *Haida Noble* was secured for heavy weather. The galley was a shambles. The cook had failed to take any precautions whatever until he was lying on a deck tilted at a 45-degree angle, with pots and pans descending on him, and frozen food tumbling out of the freezer to mix with scalding coffee from the percolator he had moved from its bracket for his own convenience.

Lindstrom gave the cook no sympathy as he treated his badly scalded forearm. "It's the last time you ship on *Haida Noble*," he promised. "What the hell did you think this was going to be—a bloody Mediterranean cruise? Clean up this mess and start building sandwiches, baskets of sandwiches!"

The welding tanks, running amok in the machine shop, had broached a gallon can of drilling lubricant and smashed a cabinet full of cutting tools, leaving the razor-sharp instruments skidding in a slick of oil. In the wire room, gasoline spilling from a tipped auxiliary pump was ignited by a spark from metal striking metal. But Galbraith had the thing under control.

On the bridge, Westholme let Fenton have the wheel while he tried head office again. It was a tradition with the company to have the president stand by when the flagship was in a critical situation. When Westholme picked up the ship-to-shore and dialed, the dispatcher answered almost immediately.

"Christy? We've been waiting for you to ring through. Mr. Alward's right here."

"Hello, Chris. We've been waiting to hear from you." There was a veiled reprimand in Alward's hearty voice.

"We've been pretty busy, Andrew. This is a big wind."

"We know that, Chris. Worst in years. How's she standing it?"

"Fine, just fine. You're going to have a million-dollar cleaning bill."

"Don't you worry about that. You keeping in touch with BUTCO 17?"

"The VHF isn't making it for some reason, Andrew. They've tried to get through to us a half-dozen times, but it's mostly static. I don't think they're picking us up at all."

Alward's voice took on a boardroom persuasiveness. "This is an important one, Chris. The contract with BUTCO is just the beginning of larger things. I want you to do your best . . . don't endanger lives, mind you, but you're not to concern yourself if you have to run a little risk. There's a lot at stake."

Suddenly Alward's message was coming through. Westholme couldn't mistake it. Neither could he believe it. "I understand, Andrew. Look, I've got to go now. Things are beginning to hot up."

"Absolutely, Chris, I—uh—there's not another captain in the fleet who could manage this, Christy. Take care now."

Westholme didn't answer. Very carefully he hung up.

There wasn't a man on board *Haida Noble* who wasn't holding onto a stanchion or a bulkhead now. The high scream of the hurricane penetrated every corner of the ship. At intervals Fenton activated the port and starboard spotlights on the bridge roof and the forward mast, to signal the drill rig that they were approaching. The big arcs could be seen for miles under normal conditions, but all they did tonight was illuminate the agony of water surrounding *Haida Noble*.

Alward's message was that *Haida Noble* was expendable. What a sweet contract that must be when the company could write off four million dollars' worth of tugboat and still make a profit! Behind him, Westholme felt the next wave descend on the tug, slamming her deck with a thousand-ton impact. "To hell with it," he thought. *Haida Noble* deserved better.

Twenty miles ahead, the drill rig was sitting solid as a rock, its whole structure designed to take this kind of punishment. Alward had said, "Do your best." That meant: "Make the BUTCO people feel they're getting their money's worth." Put *Haida Noble* on the block—and the crew too, when it came right down to it!

Westholme reached for the wheel. "I'll spell you off, Brad," he said. Sliding in behind the wheel, he felt the surge of the passing wave and waited until *Haida Noble* was tipped skyward. Just as she began to slide back, he pushed the throttle levers to full speed and started the wheel swinging hard to starboard in a full 180-degree turn. By the time the next wave was in position the bow of *Haida Noble* was facing it, engines throttled back to one quarter speed.

Fenton stared at him incredulously.

"Nothing we can do tonight," Westholme said. "We're going to let this sweetheart fight back for a while."

Chapter 13

In the aftermath, they would say that all the signs and warnings were there, if only the seismologists had taken a little more time to pinpoint the activity.

The Aleutian Chain of dead, active and latent volcanic islands extends in an arc from the Russian peninsula of Kamchatka to the Alaskan mainland, precisely on the edge of one of the earth's great

431

rifts. Its south side plummets 25,000 feet into the depths of the Aleutian Trench, and its north edge contains the relatively shallow water of the Bering Sea. For centuries, the magma, the molten ooze from the earth's deep layers, has crept along this rift, seeking freedom to surface along this North Pacific arc.

The United States Coast and Geodetic Survey station at Adak was probably the first to pick up an insignificant tremor at about 11:00 p.m. It was duly triangulated and discovered to be Bogoslof Island clamoring for attention. Approximately forty minutes later Bogoslof demonstrated again, not much more dramatically—between three and four on the Richter scale. The seismographic stations were unimpressed, and it was observed only later that their triangulation did not fall precisely on Bogoslof Island, but on a small volcanic island some seven miles west and south of it.

Its few acres of spiky grass and rudimentary beach inhabited by sea lions were the focal point of the catastrophe. At roughly 1:30 a.m., 100 miles of rock structure along the Aleutian Trench collapsed. Gases and fluids raced through channels centuries old, reaching the island, straining at it, and then blowing out the side of its 7000-foot, semi-submerged volcano. Three hundred feet beneath the surface of the sea, the earth's guts spilled out, white-hot and explosive. Then a lava fountain reached the surface of the sea, turning the water into steam. The small island endured for seven hours until a gigantic explosion tore it open, and it tumbled to the bottom of the Pacific.

By that time, the aroused sea was attacking the coastlines of the Pacific. When the segment of the Aleutian Trench collapsed, the ocean had poured in to fill the sudden depression in the bottom. Then, underwater avalanches created by the shock started masses of clay-like sediment plunging 25,000 feet down the nearly perpendicular walls of the Trench at velocities of 60 miles an hour. The upheaval of waters was colossal, and a four-foot tidal wave—a tsunami—started its devastating journey across the Pacific at a speed of 435 miles an hour.

A SHIP AT SEA would scarcely have been aware of the wave's passage; because of its relatively low contour and its velocity it would pass a ship's length in a second or less. But in the shallower coastline waters the wave began to drag, reducing its speed but increasing its height, as though the ocean bottom were thrusting the

432

tsunami into view to reveal its awesome presence to the land it would engulf.

Long before the first wave report was received at Honolulu Observatory, the tsunami had claimed its first land victims among the small coastal settlements on Unalaska Island. At Dutch Harbor the wall of water was 45 feet high, its speed more than 100 miles an hour. It thundered into the town, carrying its upended burden of boats and floating debris, enfolding houses, schools, and office structures. When it pulled back, it took most of the town with it. Then it returned, cresting to almost 60 feet, and creating absolute destruction.

Yet Dutch Harbor was not directly in the wave's line of attack as were other points on the coasts of North America and Japan. Sitka and Prince Rupert suffered tremendous damage. Masset, on the northern tip of the Queen Charlottes, was gravely hit. Communities and logging camps on the mainland and on Vancouver Island were visited by the periphery of the wave. There was much property damage, but no deaths along Queen Charlotte Strait.

On the other side of the Island, however, hundreds of lives were lost. Nowhere had there been time to issue adequate warnings. In the hour and a half to two hours it took to alert even a fraction of the population, the tidal wave had traveled more than 800 miles. The true death toll would never be known because the retreating tsunami took with it vast quantities of debris intermingled with the dead and the dying.

Chapter 14

It was Lindstrom's watch again, but *Haida Noble*'s entire complement stood watch that night. No one could sleep.

At 0317 a particularly vicious wave reared high above the bow and broke halfway along the foredeck with an impact as solid as a 20-ton metal slab. It parted at the forward mast house and raced along the main deck to the ugly sound of metal ripping and abrading. The tug rose from the blow, seawater streaming from her scuppers in long white veils.

"I'd like to see the eye of this thing," Lindstrom shouted.

"Don't count on it," Westholme warned. "She may be solid wind all the way across." He tried once more to put a call through to

BUTCO 17, but without success. "I don't think we're going to hear from them until this thing slows down," he said. "They must have lost their antenna."

Westholme stared incredulously through the salt-crusted glass as a grotesque figure moved slowly through a bar of light on the boat deck. He had difficulty identifying Bibaud; the 100-mile-an-hour gusts were remolding the flesh on his face, parting his lips back from his teeth. The deckhand was working in a slow-motion nightmare, his body tilted at an impossible angle against the wind, water streaming from his rubber storm gear as he hitched a long coil of rope around a stanchion and disappeared into the blackness, paying out the coil as a safety line.

"Idiot!" Westholme muttered. "No one's passing out medals."

He pondered their last position, marked with a neat X on the chart. The seas were pushing them back, which was good. *Haida Noble* was now 20 miles west of Cape Beale with the drill rig in her line of drift, 32 miles northeast. BUTCO 17 would be in sight by sunrise if Hurricane Faith continued to close the gap.

Tait came into the wheelhouse, his storm gear dripping, his eyes dazed-looking. "Had a little trouble on the main deck. That last one tore a life-raft loose. We had to secure it. It was pounding hell out of things on the starboard side."

"What was Bibaud doing out there—trying to commit suicide?"

"He had a notion we might be losing the lifeboats."

Westholme kept his satisfaction concealed. This was a good crew. "We don't pay heroes extra," he said.

"Maybe that wasn't Bibaud's thinking," Tait suggested. "He wants to make sure he can get off if she sinks. He says Quebec needs him."

Westholme chuckled and crossed over to look at the barometer. It had risen a fraction but was still under twenty-nine. "Poor old Willie must be spitting diesel oil," he said with compassion. An engineer's position was less than comfortable in a heavy storm.

"Thomson would spit diesel oil on a calm day, with a movie queen for his second engineer," Lindstrom stated. "That damned Lowlander isn't happy unless he's miserable."

"Then tonight he should be out of his mind with happiness." Westholme braced against the navigation desk as another giant sea came over. Tait was thrown against him heavily.

Beside Lindstrom the ship-to-shore signal filtered through the

434

general din and Westholme struggled up the sloping deck toward it. It was Andrew Alward. He started to talk just as a burst of static issued from the other radio receiver, followed by a voice. "Hold it a minute, Andrew," Westholme said. "We've got something coming in on 1630." He motioned Tait to turn up the volume.

". . . severe earthquake has occurred . . . in the vicinity of Unalaska Island. . . . A tsunami has been generated and is spreading over the Pacific Ocean. It could cause great damage to all coasts and islands in the Pacific area . . ."

"The ETA," Westholme said quietly. "Give us the ETA."

". . . Preliminary earthquake force eight point nine revised Richter. Reported wave heights: sixty feet Dutch Harbor, sixty-two feet Sitka, ETA information as follows: Pacific Standard Time conversion, Prince Rupert 0400; Tofino 0425; Port Renfrew . . ."

Westholme spoke into the ship-to-shore. "I just heard it, Andrew."

"You've got to make for shelter," Alward said.

"We've got less than an hour, Andrew. Time to go five, maybe eight, miles in any direction. Our best bet is to find deep water."

"It's a new ball game, Chris. The drill rig can take this better than you can. . . . Get *Haida Noble* into a safe situation. Do you understand, Chris?" As a sudden afterthought he added: "We've got to think about the crew, their families . . ."

"I understand, Andrew. We'll find the deepest water we can in the time we've got left. You getting any wind in Vancouver?"

"Wind! My God, Christy, roofs are ripped off, fires all over the lower mainland. It's a bloody mess!"

"Did anyone contact Lee?" He had deliberately held the question back until now.

"Jake tried two or three times. There's no one answering at your place. I'd say she was holed up with friends."

"Probably," Westholme said. "When you reach her, tell her everything is fine."

"I wish that were the truth. Don't forget now, Chris."

"I've got to sign off," Westholme said curtly. "We're running out of time." He replaced the phone. Holed up with friends! The *old* Lee would have been sitting at home waiting for the phone to ring on a night like this.

Lindstrom was looking at him with a questioning expression. "You heard," Westholme said. "We've got one hell of a hurricane sea moving north-northeast and a seismic sea wave moving south. When those two babies meet—well, your guess is as good as mine."

"We've got seventy fathoms under us. What are the chances of the tidal wave building up on that kind of bottom?"

"Pretty good," Westholme said. "Sixty-two feet at Sitka! That's one helluva big wave." He glanced at the chronometer. 0353. "According to Honolulu, we've got thirty-four minutes to wait. Lindy, I want you to organize a complete stem-to-stern check on stowage and loose gear. And I want all lifejackets on. At 0420 I want everyone up on the boat deck, except for manning in the engine room."

He took the wheel as Lindstrom fought his way out through the doorway. Tait pulled himself up the tilting deck to take a position beside one of the engine-room telegraphs.

Westholme thought he had faced everything the sea and the weather could provide: icing and gale-force winds on the Murmansk run; tide and wind propelling an 11,000-ton barge at him faster than his tug could tow it; the night *Thrace* parted the line on the edge of a hurricane—two-inch steel cable threshing like a live thing on the afterdeck, killing two of the company's best men. But he knew there would never be another night like this.

Westholme braced himself for the onslaught of a 50-foot wave picked out by the beam of one of the arcs. No sign of a let-up; if anything, the seas were becoming higher, more powerful.

He wracked his brain to recall all he knew about tsunamis. The chance of experiencing one in a lifetime was rare. The odds of being caught in the confrontation of a tsunami and a hurricane had to be astronomical. What were *Haida Noble*'s chances?

There was no doubt that coming about in these seas was an invitation to disaster. The tug would have to continue to ride into the hurricane. So the tidal wave would take them in the stern. The mountainous hurricane waves were on the face of the ocean, but the tsunami involved the entire depth of water through which it moved. How big would it be, this bottom-raking curler?

THE CHRONOMETER showed 0402: dawn was two or three hours away. Then, if visibility permitted, the drill rig would be large on the horizon. At dawn, Westholme thought, perhaps Jake or Alward himself would telephone Lee again, find her at home and pass along an encouraging message. If she wasn't at home, where was she?

436

The house could be damaged and she injured for that matter. Those big poplars in the backyard . . . But he supposed every man in the crew was worrying about a wife or girl friend at this moment.

"You a married man?" he asked Tait abruptly.

"In a manner of speaking," Tait said.

"Kids?"

"Yeah."

The deckhand was making it plain it was none of Westholme's business . . . and Westholme was beginning to suspect that Tait had his own kind of misery.

Above the wind, he said: "I don't know how it is with your girl, but with Lee I would guess . . ."

"Mr. Westholme," Tait broke in, "are you trying to tell me something?"

"Shooting the breeze."

Tait held on tight as *Haida Noble* heaved herself against the sea. "My wife and me are breaking up . . . and it couldn't happen soon enough."

Both men ducked involuntarily as a 60-foot wave reared out of the darkness, struck the glass of the wheelhouse a solid, metallic blow, and then crashed thunderously on the deck before washing astern.

"This is as hairy as anything I've seen," Westholme said. "There's a grab bag of stuff in the left-hand drawer under the navigation desk. See if you can find some safety goggles. We could be traveling without glass before this is over."

Tait found them and delivered a pair to Westholme. He tucked them into his jacket pocket, checked the chronometer and punched a button on the intercom. "OK down there. You've got two minutes left to make yourselves comfortable on the boat deck. This isn't panic stations, it's action stations. There's just an outside chance we'll have to abandon this tug. If that happens, Eric Lindstrom will be in charge of the operation. Lindy, are you getting this? Over."

"We're reading you, Chris."

"OK. Have a couple of the boys bring up six sheets of half-inch plywood, a power drill and a half-inch bit, some quarter-inch nylon lashing material, and as big a sheet of plexiglass as you can scrounge."

"We'll be up there too de swee," Lindstrom said cheerfully.

Westholme turned his mind to the tidal wave again. Its approach should be from the northwest. He wanted to take the wave, and the next one which would be even bigger, dead center on the stern. "I'm going to alter course thirty degrees to port," he told Tait. "But we're not going to do it before we have to."

"We'll be taking a hell of a sea on the starboard quarter."

Westholme nodded agreement. "And there's the chance we could broach. There's also the chance that we'll be sliding into a trough when the tsunami hits us. If it's a half-decent wave we could be flipped right over. You've got your choice."

Standing in the entrance to the wheelhouse, Lindstrom shouted, "Christy, ready and waiting. Where do you want these panels?"

"I want them ready to board up this bridge if the glass goes on us. Who's in the engine room?"

"Willie. He wouldn't trust it to anyone else."

Westholme punched the intercom key to the engine room. "Willie, are you there?"

"Where else would I be?" the angry Scots voice came back at him. "D'you know what they've done to us this time around, Mr. Westholme? They've left off the boxes of wiping rags. The place will be a bloody mess in a day or two."

Westholme loved him for it. "Are you comfortable down there?"

"Aye, it's tolerable. But you'll talk to the proper authority about the rags?"

"You bet I will, Willie. Look, we may have to abandon . . ."

"Ah-h! I've heard all about it from Lindstrom. It's nothing compared to a good blow off the Hebrides. We'll manage fine."

"If I say 'jump', you jump, Willie."

"D'you think I'd stay down here in a bog of bilge water?" the voice demanded incredulously.

"Hold on tight, Willie." Westholme flicked up the button. The time was 0422. Five minutes to go. . . .

Lindstrom was beside him. "Want me to spell you on the wheel?"

Westholme shook his head. "Stick around, just in case. I'm going to swing her thirty degrees to port at 0426. That's a pretty slim margin of safety, but I don't want to hold that course any longer than we have to. We could be dumped before the tsunami hits us."

"We're ready," Lindstrom said. "The boys are wrapped around stanchions on the boat deck."

Together, with Tait standing behind them, they watched the

hands of the chronometer move toward 0426. "Here we go," Westholme said. He started the turn to port. The first wave hit the starboard side like a granite reef. Another, just as large, slammed against the side, and the tug swung several degrees farther into the trough.

"To hell with it!" Westholme decided. "One more of those and we'll be in the trough and rolling over." He eased the tug's bow back into the oncoming sea. The next wave was somewhat easier, and the following one split itself on the steeply rising bow.

By 0430, the combined rage of Hurricane Faith and the sea seemed to fill the wheelhouse, building up a pressure of sound and vibration that made thinking and speaking painful.

It was Lindstrom who finally made the attempt. "You know what I think? I think the tidal wave has passed us by. It's four minutes past the ETA. . . ."

He never finished. The next movement of the hull was so incredibly swift and violent that the breath was jerked from his lungs. *Haida Noble* was lifted by the stern and tilted into an approaching trough, her bow swinging sharply starboard into a broaching position from which there could be no recovery.

Westholme had a fleeting impression of white water high above him to port, the presence of something vast in the darkness to starboard. The tug was deep in the valley of two opposing waves, and then *Haida Noble* was picked up bodily, lifted toward the crest of the oncoming hurricane wave and tossed upward on the exploding elements of two giant waves in headlong attack against each other.

The tug spun in a pale phosphorescence of white foam and spindrift, and then began a stomach-wrenching descent into a bottomless trough. Inside the wheelhouse the lights flickered and failed.

Somewhere in the darkness Westholme thought he heard a man cry out in pain, and then he braced himself for the impact that was to come, one hand darting up in an unconscious reflex to adjust the safety goggles he had clamped on minutes before. It seemed to him the tug was plunging bow first, rolling to starboard all of 30 degrees, corkscrewing into the ocean. All he could do was secure the wheel and maintain steerage in the event that *Haida Noble* ever emerged from the dive.

The bow went in deep. In the roaring blackness Westholme had no way of knowing how far or fast, until the bridge glass shattered and the sea entered. It seemed that the whole tug had gone under, that a solid wall of water was pinning him to the wheel. For the first time in twenty-seven years at sea, Westholme stood outside himself and waited for his tug, his crew, and himself to die. There was no feeling attached to it.

Then something in *Haida Noble*'s motion jerked him back to reality. The bow was coming up, slowly, the deck leveling out as the tug fought to break clear. Hurricane Faith was blasting into the wheelhouse through the shattered glass, but the sea was gone. *Haida Noble* had climbed out and was bow into the waves again.

Standing knee-deep in cold seawater, Westholme shouted for a light. "Break out some storm lamps, Lindy, and check the situation on the boat deck."

Lindstrom didn't reply, but Westholme saw the yellow beam of a storm lamp approaching. It was Tait. "Lindstrom's out cold," he said. "Pretty badly cut around the face." He held the lamp up to Westholme. "So are you," he added.

Westholme felt no pain. "Get him out of this water and check him over. Send the second engineer down to help Willie, and tell Fenton I need him."

Tait stumbled away in the receding water, and Westholme pushed the engine-room intercom button. "Willie? Willie Thomson?"

The angry voice came through loud and clear. "I can't waste time talkin' now, dammit!"

"That's all I wanted to know, Willie. Stan Read's on his way down. We've lost the wheelhouse lights."

"If ye'd allow me, I'd give 'em back to ye!"

Minutes later the lights came on again. Fenton stepped in to take the wheel, recoiling from the blast of wind howling through the window. He accepted Westholme's goggles. "You'd better have someone look at your face, Christy," he shouted.

Westholme turned away from the wheel clumsily, feeling bone-weary and rubber-legged. In the cramped boat-deck shelter, little more than a partitioned extension between the radio room and the tug stack, he found most of the crew gathered. Lindstrom was propped against the wall, turning his head groggily from side to side as Bibaud poked an ammonia stick under his nose. His face was a bloody pattern of glass cuts.

Bibaud looked up. "My God, you're as bad as this guy!" He passed the ammonia stick to Galbraith and stood up, reaching to extract shards of glass from Westholme's face.

The captain backed away. "We'll patch ourselves up later. We've got about half an hour to get things back in shape. I want panels up over the navigation bridge windows for starters."

The men hesitated, a question in their eyes.

"That was the first wave," Westholme told them. "In a tsunami, the second one is always the biggest."

"I think you better take a look at Lindstrom," Galbraith interrupted sharply. "He's passed out again."

Chapter 15

At 0332 Volkoff finally lost patience with Knight as he poured out his anger on the radio operator. "Son," the Texan was saying, "you've been free-loading on this rig all summer, far as I can make out. I wouldn't trust you to fix a crystal set, and . . ."

"Lay off, Charlie," Volkoff called sharply from the other side of the room where he was trying to concentrate on a game of poker with the geologist and a roughneck. "The wind has taken out every antenna on the rig. It's that simple. Why don't you come over and help me lose some of my money?"

"Volkoff," Knight shouted above the hurricane, his face reddening, "you're a company man, a head-office watchdog. Everybody on this rig knows that!"

"Knock it off, Charlie."

"But until we leave this rig, Volkoff, I'm calling the shots. File any kind of report you want, but my report is going to lay all the cards on the table. British United doesn't give a damn for the boys on this rig. All they wanted was that extra thousand feet of drill hole. If they lose the rig it's just another book entry."

"The rig's doing fine, Charlie. You worry too much." Volkoff turned away, feeling the super's angry eyes burning into him. The drill rig *was* standing up to the seas remarkably well. He could sympathize with Knight, though. The man's strong awareness of responsibility was eating at him like acid.

Knight continued to pace restlessly back and forth behind the radio operator's chair, his eyes wandering over the maze of dials and lights, trying to dominate them into operation.

Then, "Look at that, would you!" Knight pointed suddenly to the radar screen. For the past two hours it had been clear of anything resembling shipping, its field marred with the ripples and distortions created by the hurricane. Now a distinct blip had appeared in the center, in the lee of BUTCO 17.

"The Russian," Volkoff said. "She's trying to move away from the rig. Afraid of a collision," he decided. The blip was moving painfully slowly. "None of it adds up though. She had shelter in our lee. Now she's facing a full sea again." He went back to playing cards.

The blip on the radar screen was still easing north, but everyone except Knight had lost interest in it. He sat astride a chair and glared balefully at the dot of light, his anger diverted from the radio operator to the Russians. The poker game went on in spite of him, but no one played well; attentions were divided by the immensity of the wind, by Knight's troubled state of mind, and by the feeling of utter isolation that the blacked-out communications imparted.

At 0430 Knight swung in the direction of the operator. "It's 4:30, son. See if you can get a broadcast out of that bunch of junk."

"I've been trying for anything I can get, Mr. Knight."

Knight directed an angry glance at the radar screen. "You can bet the Russians are getting radio signals. They . . . God!"

The others turned to see him pointing unbelievingly at the screen as the small line of light spun sideways and plummeted down the badly scrambled screen toward center. Before it disappeared Volkoff had shouted a warning: "Cut the power, Ronnie! Hit the deck and hang on!" All around him bodies were diving for the floor, clutching for handholds. He wrapped his arms around one of the legs of the console housing as the lights went out.

Only Volkoff had any inkling of what they waited for in the solid blackness. Knight yelled plaintively, "What the hell is this, Mike?"

And then the impact . . . massive, shocking. It was more than a crushing blow to BUTCO 17's northern perimeter: there was a huge lifting force coupled with it. One of the rig's tripod legs lifted from the sea bottom, tilting the steel island into the face of the hurricane. Beneath the deck, seismic sea wave and hurricane wave met in a gigantic explosion, buckling and tearing loose inch-thick steel plates. On the southern perimeter of the rig, Hurricane Faith's waves, rearing high against the attack of the tsunami, raced across BUTCO 17's tilted deck and washed away installations as though they were cardboard. But the very weight of the waves pressing down on the deck saved the rig from total destruction, for the displaced tripod leg was forced to the sea bottom again.

The cold water and the bite of the wind shocked Volkoff back to reality. He lay with the others in the ruins of the radio shack, his arms still locked around the metal leg of the console. Moments before, water had been mounting over him, roaring in his ears, pounding him, but so cold and water-laden was the wind that it was never clear when the rushing sea retreated from the shack.

Still lying flat he craned his head around. "Charlie," he called. Some distance away, he thought he heard a voice reply. Much closer, the radio operator shouted in panic.

"Hey! Mr. Knight? Mr. Volkoff? Gimme a hand, quick. I got something across my legs!"

"Coming, Ron!" Volkoff slithered over. The operator was lying on his back with a substantial portion of the heavy console collapsed across his lower legs. Someone else crawled in alongside Volkoff. It was the roughneck. He broke into a violent coughing spasm, trying to tear the salt water out of his lungs.

On the other side of the operator's body, Knight's voice cut in. "Isn't this beautiful! The whole damn rig falling apart! 'She can take anything!' they said. Any kind of a wind, any kind of a sea. I tell you, Volkoff—"

"Shut up, Charlie, and give us a hand." The roughneck followed Volkoff, and they eased ahead and knelt, their shoulders against the face of the console. "Are you over there, Charlie?" Volkoff shouted.

"Tell me when," Knight called back.

"Here we go," Volkoff shouted. "Heave!"

The console came up slowly, and the operator began to scream. The sound became animal in its pain and then faded abruptly.

The three men wrestled the heavy weight back onto the deck, and Volkoff inspected the injured man's legs. From just below the kneecaps to the feet he felt nothing he could recognize as solid bone. "He's a mess," Volkoff reported. "He needs major surgery."

"We'll take him to the infirmary," Knight said. "Get some morphine into him."

"No time," Volkoff told him. "If we're lucky we've got an hour before this rig breaks up. The next wave will be bigger. We've got to get off before that. What we need right now, Charlie, is a light."

"I got a light, by golly!" the roughneck said in a startled voice. Almost immediately a beam from a flashlight speared the blackness.

"Do you think you can find your way over to the infirmary?" Volkoff asked him. "Pick up an armful of blankets and some

443

morphine ampoules and splint material. If the first-aid man can be spared, bring him back with you. And tell anybody you see to get ready to abandon rig. They should start making their way to liferaft stations now."

The roughneck nodded, struggled to his feet and was gone.

Only then did Volkoff remember that there had been others in the radio shack when the wave hit: the geologist, another roughneck. "We'd better round up the others," he said in Knight's ear.

"What?" Knight said in a thick voice.

"The other two who were here. They're around somewhere."

"That's probably so," Knight slurred disinterestedly. He had lurched to a standing position. "Be right back."

"Where are you going, Charlie?"

From the distance Volkoff heard, ". . . send a telegram . . . company's going to hear about this . . ."

He scrambled in the direction of the sound. "Charlie! Wait! I'll help you send it, Charlie . . ." Only the wind, and the thundering sea, and the metallic death sounds of the rig came to his ears.

He couldn't see to follow Knight in the black tangle of destruction, so he returned to the torn square of the radio shack. He crawled around, looking for the radio operator, found him, and checked his pulse. He was still alive. Methodically, he began to look for the others. The geologist he found, glasses still intact on his dead face, his upper body projecting from under a fallen wall. The roughneck was gone—swept away or buried under the wreckage.

The lamp light brought him around to face the returning roughneck, still coughing. Totally exhausted, he lowered himself to the deck.

"How did you make out?" Volkoff asked. He knew the answer from the man's dejected attitude.

"We got to get off this thing," he said. "I didn't see no one. The infirmary is gone."

Although they would never know it, there were nineteen men alive at that moment. Knight was not among them. He had gone over the south edge of the rig minutes before, intent on his errand.

Of the nineteen survivors, seven were seriously injured. The other twelve were mobile but disoriented and panic-stricken. Four of them finally made it to one of the rig's special untippable life rafts, only to find it had been smashed when the remains of the helicopter were hurled upon it.

Volkoff shook the man roughly. "My name's Mike Volkoff . . ."

The roughneck nodded. "Me, I'm Nick Bianco. I seen you around."

Volkoff shone the light on his watch. 5:05. Better than half an hour had gone by: "Nick, we've got to get to the life raft fast, and we've got to take Ronnie with us. OK?"

"Sure."

Together, they got to their feet and lifted the operator, inexpertly trying to keep his crushed legs clear of the shambles as they stumbled toward the ladder leading down to the raft deck. The slashing wind bullied them savagely from behind, and the tangle of timber and steel was under their feet every step of the way. But once at the ladder, they were out of the direct blast of the wind as they lowered themselves to the deck.

The flashlight played over the streamlined life raft, a miracle of sea-survival design fashioned in reinforced fiberglass and resembling a mammoth curling-stone. Volkoff climbed the boarding ladder and scrambled in through the entrance port, turning to help the roughneck as he struggled up the ladder with the operator over his shoulder. As they fell into the safety capsule, Volkoff left them and scrambled down the ladder again, to throw off the mooring clamps. In the distance he heard a new sound, more ominous than the contralto scream of the wind. For the first time he felt fear, absolute, muscle-dissolving panic. He climbed back into the capsule, slid the hatch closed, slammed down the two hatch fastenings . . . and a moment later the entire dark world turned upside down.

Chapter 16

At 0617 the third great wave passed under and over *Haida Noble*. Compared with the second it was an anticlimax. But short of disabling the one remaining engine or breaching the leaking hull, not much more was needed to kill the crippled tug.

Westholme had had *Haida Noble* in a somewhat better position to receive the second wave; storm panels in position, both first and second engineers on station in the engine room, the crew deployed on the upper decks. Lindstrom, protesting violently, was strapped into a stretcher on the boat deck and lashed securely between two stanchions, with Galbraith detailed to keep an eye on him.

But there was no describing the tsunami's second blow. It didn't seem possible that a force so massive—a 400-foot submarine wave whose upper limits peaked 30 feet above the surface of the sea—could strike so suddenly. Westholme felt as though the sea's fist had slammed into his entire body, bruising the marrow of his bones.

Haida Noble was propelled ahead and up, emerging on the furious peak created by the two opposing sea forces. In the glare of the arc lights, Westholme caught an unbelievable glimpse of the entire sea beneath him for a thousand yards ahead like a dark range of mountains. Under him was the deep valley into which they must plunge.

None of them remembered too much about it afterward, least of all Westholme. *Haida Noble* herself was in command in those lost minutes. Crippled and leaking, with stunned and injured men aboard, she rose once more from the sea and Westholme's only feeling as he swung the wheel and reached tentatively for the remote controls, was gratitude to the tug for his life.

The damage was extensive. Some of it was serious, particularly where water poured in around the cracked stern gland on the port engine shaft. Willie Thomson called for help and Bibaud and Galbraith went below to rig auxiliary pumps in the event that the main engine pumps couldn't cope.

The forecastle deck was a shambles of mast lengths, broken booms and the remains of radar and wireless installations, all wrapped together by the sea and tied with the tangled remains of guy lines and stays. The side band radio and ship-to-shore communications systems were out, but the tug's intercom was still working. Tait was the first to use it, calling the bridge to report water entering the crew's quarters through fractured plates around the toppled forward mast. Life rafts and one lifeboat had been carried away, and sundry portholes stove in. In the wire room, a three-ton anchor had broken loose and punched a hole through a bulkhead.

Westholme let Fenton make the general damage survey and supervise the emergency repairs. Until the third and fourth wave passed by, his place was in the wheelhouse.

Tait joined him in time to help with the third wave, which was damaging enough but manageable. "Is this thing slowing down," Tait said, "or is it my imagination?"

Westholme had sensed a different feeling to the sea, a different

446

sound to the wind for some time now. "George," he said, "I think you're right. This thing *is* slowing down some."

Had *Haida Noble*'s radio been working, he would have had confirmation. The weather report was being revised. Right in their theory though wrong in their timing, the meteorologists now reported that the arctic cold front which was supposed to have subdued an upstart of a gale three days earlier had finally shouldered the hurricane off course. Faith was moving back out to sea, leaving unprecedented death and destruction along the Pacific northwest coast. There, emergency resources—land, sea, and air—would be taxed to the limit for days to come.

By 0800 hours, the sea and the wind had abated dramatically. The fourth giant wave created no real problems, and as Bibaud returned with Fenton to the wheelhouse, he said in his old clowning way: "After you get hit with a sledgehammer two, three times, a tap from a baseball bat feels real good."

It was now officially Westholme's watch and he took it unthinkingly, until Fenton persuaded him to get some rest. "Christy, things are under control," he said.

Westholme looked around the wheelhouse skeptically: the shattered glass, the battered storm panels, the unserviceable radar scopes. "Things look great," he said.

"The pumps are working fine," Fenton persisted, "and we'll be able to get at that stern gland in another hour. With any luck we'll be back in Vancouver this time tomorrow."

"No, we won't," Westholme said. "The instructions were to pick up the drill rig."

"There's no way we can handle her with half power," Fenton protested. "We've got trouble of our own."

"Not as much trouble as that rig. We should be in visual contact with her right now. We're ten, maybe fifteen miles off Barkley Sound, dead center, so somewhere ten miles astern there should be a drill rig. I'll take you up on that bunk time, but I want you to come about and start a search. Begin with the drill-rig coordinates and work shoreward from there following the line of drift. When you spot anything, I want to hear about it."

Fenton nodded and turned to the wheel.

Westholme didn't go to the master's stateroom immediately. First he made it down to the engine room and said a few words to Willie and the deckhands sloshing in ankle-deep water. Then he

447

prowled all the trouble spots on the vessel, from the hold to the main deck. *Haida Noble* had taken a terrible beating. For the first time since he had captained her, he saw the visible signs of the sea's massive punishment in buckled plates and battered bulkheads.

In the galley a table, tearing loose from its floor bolts, had ripped through benches and set them free to pound the area to splinters. There was literally no place to sit or to set a cup. In spite of this a large pot of coffee in a metal grid simmered on the stove. A cold roast of beef and a loaf of bread had been pinned to the galley's cutting board with knives. Westholme made himself four sandwiches dripping with mayonnaise. He filled a plastic carafe with hot coffee, topped it with an inverted mug and headed for his cabin.

Before his banquet, he went through the bathroom to Lindstrom's cabin and opened the door carefully. The first officer was asleep, but breathing strenuously.

In the bathroom again, Westholme stopped to examine his face. His skin was pocked with glass wounds, many still oozing blood. With a clean cloth he sponged away some of the mess.

Then, seated on the floor with his back against his bunk, he poured the coffee and spread out his sandwiches like a deck of cards. He chose the biggest and took a whole quarter of it in one bite. Great! He was damned hungry!

Tait found him asleep on the floor two hours later. "We thought you should come up on the bridge, Mr. Westholme."

"Sure . . . sure." Westholme hauled himself to his feet, the sleep still dark in his eyes. "What's the trouble?"

"Looks like the rig may be gone. The way Fenton figures it, we should be over the coordinates now."

"Have you been watching the echo sounder?" Westholme asked as they headed for the wheelhouse.

"We're picking up twenty fathoms. It looks clean down below."

When Westholme entered the wheelhouse, Fenton turned the steering back to Tait. "The rig could be drifting, Christy. There's always that possibility."

"Slim chance," Westholme said. "What's your procedure?"

"We're on the second leg of a one-mile-square search. If it's down there we're bound to pick it up."

Keeping his eyes on the echo sounder, Westholme asked, "The leak in the engine room under control?"

"Just about. We're shipping ten or fifteen gallons an hour."

448

Tait said quietly, but with a note of apprehension: "We're over something. . . ."

"Dead slow!" Westholme cautioned. He had seen it at the same time. The jittery line on the echo sounder, which had been tickling the mark at twenty fathoms, had suddenly jumped to ten; then eight; then abruptly back to fifteen fathoms.

"That's as far as we go," Westholme said. "Reverse engine, dead slow, George." To Fenton he said, "Get a sea marker out before we move off."

Fenton issued brief instructions into the intercom and a moment later Bibaud hustled out on the forecastle deck with a fluorescent red sea marker and its coil of anchor rope. He tossed them over the side, waved jauntily up at the bridge and disappeared.

"I think we'd better make a turn to starboard," Westholme decided, "circle around and then follow the line of drift toward Amphitrite Point."

"You think that was BUTCO 17?"

"I hope not, but if it wasn't then she's drifting toward Amphitrite. The job now is to find her—or her survivors."

"Man!" Fenton said in frustration. "What a little bit of radar could do for us now! Get back to the sack, Christy. You've got a few more hours coming to you."

On the way back to his quarters, he looked in on Lindstrom and found him half asleep and groggy. There was a large contused bump on the side of his skull just above the right ear. Westholme leaned over and studied it closely. "If you got it brass plated it would be a doorknob," he said. "Any idea what did it, Lindy?"

"Who knows!" Lindstrom said impatiently. "Christy, I'm going to climb into my pants and walk out of here."

"Stay put until 1200 hours," Westholme instructed. "We don't need you for anything right now and I'd like you to take your watch tonight."

"What about the rig, Chris? Are we in sight?"

"She's not where she's supposed to be," Westholme said. "There's a strong possibility she went down. The echo sounder picked up something near her coordinates. All we can do now is follow her probable line of drift in case she's still floating, and pick up survivors if she isn't."

"The rig gone down," Lindstrom said in disbelief. "Chris, how bad are things?"

"Chances are they couldn't be any worse. We'll finish the search and then duck into Ucluelet for information—if Ucluelet is in shape to tell us anything. Now lie back, you lead-swinger. We may need you sooner than you think."

He crossed to his own cabin, uneasy about the first officer's appearance. It took a lot to shake this man; but this time he was hurt. His eyes showed it.

In his bunk, Westholme thought about the drill rig. If it had gone down, then most of its crew were down there with it. The chances of anyone abandoning it successfully were slim.

And there would be death and destruction in every inlet along the west coast. Was Lee safe? Was she at home? It didn't matter where she was, he wanted her with him right now, bringing him her special kind of comfort, listening to him try to explain that she was the only reason he went to sea—and the only reason he came back.

FENTON DIDN'T send for Westholme until the life raft was almost alongside. Sighted at a distance, it could have been just a piece of flotsam. Its orange fiberglass lid was almost totally camouflaged with broad strips of kelp and, floating in the big swell, it resembled a giant lacquered bowl inverted on the surface of the sea.

Fenton edged *Haida Noble* toward it cautiously. Fifty yards away Tait, balancing in the debris on the ruined foredeck, employed a loud hailer.

"Hello, life raft. Can you hear us? Hello, life raft." As *Haida Noble* closed the gap to 25, then 15 yards, Tait continued to use the loud hailer. Finally he shrugged his shoulders and looked up to the bridge for further instructions.

"We'd better try and get it alongside," Fenton told Galbraith. "Put a hook on it. I'll come about and place it in our lee."

When the raft was almost within pike-pole distance they heard rappings, weak but persistent. Tait waved violently to the bridge to stand off and Fenton swung the tug to starboard, opening the gap to a safe distance.

Fenton summoned Westholme to the bridge then, and he stared at the bobbing capsule speculatively. "Brad," he said finally. "The people in that thing are either too weak to open the hatch, or the fastenings are jammed. I'd like to take the raft on board."

Westholme reached for the binoculars Fenton had been using and went out on the navigation deck for a better view of the raft.

450

He spotted lifting rings and, returning to the wheelhouse, told Fenton, "We'll have to take it aboard with one of the stern booms. Use a boat to fit the lifting hooks. Will you see to it, Brad?"

Fenton departed, and minutes later Westholme saw the boat pulling away toward the raft with Fenton at the tiller while Galbraith held the line from the tug's afterdeck boom.

Arriving alongside the pitching orange disc, Galbraith worked quickly and expertly, inserting the hooks into the three eyes around the raft's fender. When the third hook was in place, he attached a towing line and began to pay the line out as Fenton started back to the tug. In this manner they towed the raft back to within 30 feet of the tug, with Bibaud on the afterdeck taking in the slack of the boom cable.

Galbraith cast loose the towline, and the lifeboat returned to its retrieval position under its davits, leaving the raft secured to the boom cable. Westholme called for Tait to take the wheel while Fenton and Galbraith scrambled out of the lifeboat. They fell into step behind him as he made his way down to the afterdeck to size up the situation.

The raft was floating at a safe distance, several yards beyond the tip of the extended boom. Bibaud had the winch power on and was standing beside the control levers. Westholme turned to him: "Slow and easy, Ernie. Like a crate of eggs."

The slack bridle pulled taut, hesitated a moment and then drew the capsule clear of the ocean surface.

"Start her coming inboard," Westholme shouted.

Bibaud maneuvered the raft, mottled with seaweed and oil scum, dead center above the cleared stern portion of the afterdeck and lowered it gently onto the deck.

They circled the raft looking for the entry. At first glance there was no visible hatch opening, so streamlined and well-fitted was the capsule; but brushing away the strips of kelp, Westholme finally found the thin, oblong line marking the entrance. He slapped the smooth surface. "Hello, in there! Can you hear us?"

Immediately they heard a muffled voice.

"Can you open the hatch?" Westholme shouted.

This time words could be understood. "No . . . stuck."

"Galbraith," Westholme instructed. "See if you can hustle up the tools we need to break into this thing. Ask Stan Read to come up and give us a hand."

451

It took the better part of thirty minutes to drill sufficient holes into the entrance hatch to gain the leverage to pry it open. It yielded slowly at first and then sprang open, releasing a thick cloud of incredibly foul air.

Over his shoulder Westholme said: "Someone fetch a couple of stretchers and an armful of blankets."

Stan Read handed him a flashlight and Westholme shone it into the fetid interior. He could make out three men amongst a heap of water-soaked blankets, broken ration boxes and first-aid supplies.

"OK," Westholme assured them. "This is the end of the line. Can any of you get out under your own power?"

"I'm hurting too much, damn it!" a husky voice said.

"We'll get you out. What condition are the others in?"

"One is in very bad shape. He hasn't moved for hours. The other has breathing troubles. Pneumonia, maybe."

Westholme shone his light around the edge of the raft's dome and spotted the hand clamps at spaced intervals. "Does the top half come off this thing?"

"Supposed to. Although you'll probably have some trouble. Maybe I can loosen some of the clamps for you?"

"Don't move," Westholme instructed. He clambered inside, ankle-deep in seawater and sludge, his nostrils tightening against the stench. He released the spring-loaded clamps and then placed his hands against the raft top and pressed upward; the top popped suddenly like a pressure lid on a jar of preserves, spinning off to land on the deck.

In the full light of day Westholme stared at the three men who lay sprawled on plastic-covered foam-rubber mattresses in man-sized "bins" molded into the raft's perimeter.

Two of them looked dead, although the rapidly heaving chest of one indicated that he was still fighting for life. The other lay with his legs encased in two badly applied splints, his head tilted back in a frozen grimace of agony. Westholme checked for the pulse he knew he wouldn't find.

He eased himself out through the raft entrance and glanced at Fenton. "Do you think you can take care of things here? Move these two up to the infirmary. I'll go ahead and get things ready. The third one . . . wrap him up in something and put him on the floor of the freezer."

He thrust his head back into the capsule. "We'll talk later," he

452

told the haggard, youngish-looking man with the black thatch of hair. "Just one question. Are you from BUTCO 17?"

"We are. She's on the bottom. . . ."

"That's all we need to know for the moment. You're on the tug *Haida Noble*. My name's Christy Westholme, skipper. See you in the infirmary in a little while."

On the way there, Westholme stopped off at the cook's cabin. The cook was lying face to the wall in the semi-darkened room.

Westholme shook him roughly. "Come on, get up. We need you. We've got sick and dying men on board. On your feet."

"Captain, I can't. I'm not up to it. Ask the other fellows; they'll tell you . . ."

"What's your name?"

"Telford, sir. You ask any of the crew. They'll tell you I shouldn't be on this tug. I've never been on anything bigger than a two-hundred-tonner since I started with the company."

"You're on *Haida Noble* now, Telford. Get out of that bunk and start pulling your weight." He ripped the blankets away. The cook lay curled up in shock, his fat thighs and buttocks bulging the pale fabric of his thermal long underwear.

"I want you in the galley in five minutes. I want a good beef broth for the two men in the infirmary . . . and I want a square meal for the entire crew. And I don't care if you die in the process, Telford. The next time you lie down it'll be because I told you you could, or you're sick . . . or you're dead!"

Westholme left abruptly. The infirmary was as he had expected after the hurricane. The three fixed bunks on one side of the room were a shambles. He straightened out two of them, and then returned to Telford's cabin. The man was into his trousers and buttoning up his shirt.

"Telford, when you're finished in the galley, I want you in the infirmary. There'll be two sick men in there, and you're going to take care of them. If they need their teeth brushed, you brush them. If they need an enema, you do the job."

"Are they that bad?" the cook said, in an appalled voice.

"Worse," Westholme assured him, and turned to leave.

"Captain Westholme," the cook said behind him, his voice tight. "I am a ship's cook. I signed on as a cook. I pay my dues to the guild as a cook, and I don't have to nurse anybody."

Westholme turned back. "Telford, if you don't do what I tell you, the chances are that you won't return from this trip. Now hustle!"

"The guild is going to hear about this!"

"Not if you don't get back, they won't." Westholme departed for the bridge.

Chapter 17

Tait was doing all the right things on the bridge, but with a strange air of detachment. Westholme had seen other men like this: glaciers trying to cap active volcanoes.

"Where are we, George?" he asked.

"About six miles southwest of Amphitrite Point. How are we making out in the engine room? It would be nice to have the other engine turning over again."

"Not a chance," Westholme said. "That's a job for home base." He returned to the immediate concern. "With Lindstrom under the weather, and the two from BUTCO 17, I think we'd better approach as close to Amphitrite Point as we can get and then swing into Ucluelet for medical help and company instructions. It'll give us a chance to check with the home front—if the telephones are working."

Tait said nothing, and Westholme suspected that the man would not be telephoning anyone when they reached Ucluelet. But Westholme would be. He would telephone Lee and tell her how he felt about her. . . .

"Come home," she would say. "Please come home, Christy . . ."

"I've been watching this for a few minutes now," he heard Tait say in a new tone of voice. "With the size of the swell and this plexiglass abortion to look through, it's hard to tell which end is up."

Westholme returned to the reality of the tug with a feeling of guilt. He peered through the panel, and had a fleeting impression of an island with torn trees leaning across its spine.

Tait said: "I think it's a hulk."

Westholme went out on deck and with binoculars tried to home in on the spot where he had seen the island. Nothing but the huge, silken gray swell shouldering its way to the rocky beach of Amphitrite . . . and then he didn't even need the binoculars. In the gray overcast of midafternoon he read the plain language of an Aldis lamp.

"Distress!" Tait called. "There's a ship close in to Amphitrite."

The distant light continued to flash its call for help. Westholme lifted an Aldis lamp from its bracket and from the bridge rail acknowledged the message. He returned to Tait. "George, another hour and they'll be on the rocks. Go below and tell the boys to start gearing up for a towing job. And tell Brad Fenton I'd like to see him."

Westholme took the wheel and nudged the throttle ahead on the remote control. Running at three-quarter speed, he estimated the tug would be in line-firing range within half an hour. Squinting ahead he could see the low, cluttered silhouette appear again on a heaving dome of the sea and he adjusted his course to center on it.

When Fenton entered the wheelhouse, Westholme explained the situation briefly. "It's a routine salvage job, Brad. But if the first line misses or breaks, I doubt we'll have time to put on another."

"The boys are getting things set now," Fenton assured him. "The recovery chain is just about ready to go on deck."

"That's fine," Westholme said, "but we may have to use a wire bridle instead of a recovery chain. Better have one handy just in case. How are the BUTCO 17 people?"

"One of them appears to be all right. A few cracked ribs maybe; bruises on him like big tattoos." He shook his head doubtfully. "I don't know about the other one. His lungs are full of stuff. His friend is certain it's pneumonia."

"I'll go down and have a look," Westholme said. "But what we need right now is a good doctor. Hold her on this course until we're in line-firing position. I'll be back up before then."

Telford gave him an aggrieved look as he entered the infirmary. The cook was trying without success to get some hot broth into the mouth of the comatose roughneck.

"Forget it," Westholme told him. "He's too far gone for that right now." The man's breathing was alarmingly congested. Even Westholme's unpracticed hand could feel the fever in the dirt-streaked forehead. "Clean him up," he instructed.

"We've already put him in pyjamas," the cook protested.

"Get some hot water and soap and sponge off the worst of it."

The other patient was propped up in his bunk, his hands wrapped around a mugful of beef broth.

Westholme turned to him. "Feeling better?"

"Back from the grave? I couldn't feel better. My name's Mike Volkoff."

"What happened on the drill rig?"

Volkoff shrugged. "She was taking the hurricane without any trouble, but the first of the tsunami's waves started to break her up and . . . the second finished her. We were in the life raft by then. It was like being in the middle of a cement mixer."

"I'm sorry we didn't make it in time," Westholme said, "but we were having our own problems. At one point we were hoping to ride in the lee of the rig. That was before the tidal wave changed our minds."

Volkoff sat up suddenly. "It had gone right out of my mind! I suppose I'll be remembering details for the rest of my life. One of the Russian ships tried to ride in our lee. Charlie Knight was all for dropping sticks of dynamite on her—poor old Charlie."

"Was she in a bad position when the wave hit?"

"The worst, although she was moving back just before it happened. I'd say she was a thousand yards north of us. And then everything started to move. The last thing we saw on radar she was coming straight at us. If she weathered the first wave, the second would have brought her up against the rig."

"Probably," Westholme agreed.

"BUTCO 17 has got company down there." Volkoff's eyes had become distant, remembering the final moments of the giant rig— the men who had died.

"Now get some sleep," Westholme said. "If you feel up to it later, take care of your friend here."

"A couple of suggestions," Volkoff said. "If you prop Bianco up in more of a sitting position, it'll help his breathing. If you had some oxygen . . ."

"Better than that," Westholme said. "We've got a tent to go with it. Telford, give me a hand here."

Together they rigged up the heavy plastic tent over the unconscious man, and started the gas hissing softly into it. Westholme gave him an injection of penicillin.

"That's all we can do for him now," he said. "Shout if you want help." Westholme returned to the bridge to find that the crippled ship lay directly ahead of them, dead in the water, and listing to starboard.

It was no ordinary vessel. Even with the larger portion of its superstructure smashed, the ship had impressive lines. Its hull was black with a sharply raked bow. The remains of the superstructure

456

were a sandy color surmounted by a squat, yellow funnel which bore the USSR hammer and sickle emblem.

Both the ship's forward and afterdeck masts had been carried away Seventy feet back from the bow, something had dealt the starboard hull a crushing blow, tearing a ragged hole in the plates. An indentation reaching from the stack to the bridge had collapsed the decks into one another, and at some point fire must have broken out amidships and swept aft before being extinguished. Meantime, half a mile away, the Pacific swell was pounding the rock-studded shoals of Amphitrite Point. The swell and the incoming tide were pushing the crippled vessel inexorably toward destruction.

"We'll have to tow her by the stern," Westholme said. "She's down by the head and taking seas through that hole."

Fenton nodded. "What the hell did she run into, a battleship?"

"Just about as bad," Westholme said. "She collided with BUTCO 17. You'll have to go aboard her, Brad. Take Galbraith and Tait and organize some muscle from the Russian crew—you're going to have to hand-haul the bridle lengths into position. You'll manage fine. Before you go below, ask Lindstrom if he feels up to giving me a hand for an hour or two."

Westholme took over the wheel. Until now he had been barely aware of the Russian crew members scattered along the vessel's upper decks, some of them waving. At a hundred yards, their dark attire and the knitted toques worn by many made identification difficult; but it seemed to him that a good many of them were women.

Lindstrom's voice behind him was incredulous. "That's a *Russian!* Man, what's keeping her afloat?"

"God knows," Westholme said. "We'll have to hustle if we're going to hold her off the rocks." He made a swift appraisal of the mate's condition. Not good. Still the dullness in his pupils, a sagging in the lines of his face. "First, I'd like you to hold the wheel while I take a look at the boys in the infirmary. Then I want you to supervise the transfer of the bridles onboard that ship. Brad is taking Tait and Galbraith with him to handle things from that end."

Westholme went below where he found the condition of the roughneck unchanged, although his fever seemed to have dropped a degree or two. Volkoff appeared to be sleeping but he stirred and opened his eyes when Westholme turned to leave.

"Didn't want to wake you," Westholme said. "By the way, do you speak any Russian?"

"Some," Volkoff said. "Why?"

"We may need you in a little while. Meantime, get some sleep."

Back in the wheelhouse, Westholme slipped into his insulated jacket as he talked to Lindstrom. "I'll take over on the aft controls now. You'll have Bibaud to help you, Lindy, but you'll need more than that. Better give Stan Read a shout."

Westholme made his way aft to the remote-control station on the stern of the boat deck. The relation of the tug to the disabled Russian was going to be stern-to-stern, and he would have to hold her there as though she were at anchor.

Below him on the afterdeck, one of *Haida Noble*'s big inflatable life rafts was ready to go. He checked out the gear assembled on the deck—the two bridle legs, a bucket of heavy grease, rubber chafing tubes, two coils of floatable, polypropylene line and six gasoline-powered bilge pumps. From the look of the Russian's waterline, they were going to need all those pumps and more.

The small items were stowed in the rubber raft with a waterproof case of rations and two portable walkie-talkies. Bibaud, at the winch, swung the raft up and over the rail into the lee of *Haida Noble*. The others manhandled a cargo net over the side. Fenton, Galbraith and Tait, in waterproofs and lifejackets, followed one another into the raft. They picked up the oars and pushed away, putting a safe distance between the raft and the crushing weight of *Haida Noble*. The next great swell picked them up like a cork and Galbraith started the outboard.

Westholme swung the tug into a careful turn and cut across the swell toward the listing ship, waiting until Fenton and his crew had secured the raft to a cargo net let down by the Russians. They clambered up to the rail, walkie-talkies and other gear slung over their shoulders, and Westholme caught a glimpse of them as they were hauled on board by many reaching arms. One of them was roundly embraced as he was dragged onto the deck.

They would use the time-tested method of manhandling heavy cable aboard a dead ship—a light line hurled aboard to pull a heavier line which, in turn, could take the strain of a steel towing cable. Bibaud trotted to the stern with the light heaving line, the other end already attached to heavier polypropylene line. He waited, as Westholme brought the tug broadside to the stern of the Russian and made a sharp turn. *Haida Noble* was now stern to the broken ship's stern and slightly more than 100 feet away. He

458

reversed the engine to bring the tug close enough to transfer heavy gear without being lifted into the ship's overhanging stern by the heaving sea. When 50 feet separated the vessels, a gigantic ripple of sea slid under *Haida Noble*'s stern and she started to rise. Now Westholme was above the Russian ship, looking down. The moment was right. "Let her go!" he shouted to Bibaud.

The whirling heaving line arrowed toward the Russian's stern, its weighted end landing a good 10 feet inboard as *Haida Noble*'s stern began to drop well below the Russian ship's afterdeck. By the time the next swell raised the tug, the end of the heavy polypropylene line had been dragged aboard and was being passed down a double rank of Russian crew members, a number of whom were unmistakably female. Bibaud hammed a baritone version of "The Volga Boatmen" and waved wildly at the Russians before the swell passed and dropped the tug out of the line of sight.

Westholme could hear the surf clearly now, and see the breakers, white as chalk against the rocky coastline, approaching Amphitrite Point. Fifteen minutes left. No more.

The end of polypropylene line was now attached to an eye in the first leg of the steel wire bridle. *Haida Noble* rode high again and the first few feet of bridle began to move off the deck, as gravity helped the transfer of the 100-foot length of inch-and-a-half wire.

Now the other leg of the bridle was ready to go. A new length of polypropylene line had gone aboard and a second group of Russians began to move it down their ranks, pulling in the other section of the towing bridle. The entire operation was governed by a kind of desperate efficiency. "Those guys want to get out of here so bad they can taste it," Bibaud chuckled. "By God, this calls for a party!"

Lindstrom turned on him in an explosion of rage that shocked even Westholme. "Can't you keep your mind on the job, you bloody frog clown! We're not even started, and you're calling for a party."

"Sorry about that," Bibaud said in a low voice. There was black anger in his eyes as they flickered toward Westholme.

"Lindy," Westholme said. "We can manage fine here, if you'd like a breather. We'll have her on the line in a few minutes."

Lindstrom glared at him. His throat tightened convulsively and he ran to the rail to vomit. He returned, embarrassed, and glanced obliquely at Bibaud. "I don't know what came over me, Ernie," he said. "Whatever it was, it's gone over the side. I'm sorry."

460

"Back to the bunk, Lindy," Westholme commanded. "Nobody's blaming you."

"Let's get her on the line," Lindstrom said. "Then I'll go."

A particularly heavy swell carried the tug 15 feet ahead. Both bridle lengths began to pull away from the Russian. At the peak of the swell, Westholme saw a score of bodies sprawled on the deck, trying to recover the loose ends of moving steel. He increased power and the tug began to ease back to its former position. Westholme took a deep breath and glanced at the others. "All right," he said. "Brad should have those bridle legs secured before the next swell. We're just about ready to move off."

And not a minute too soon, he thought. The surf crashing on Amphitrite was loud now, but his anxiety made it deafening. They should have been towing the ship by the bow, using its own massive anchor chain as the point of connection for the towing line, but at least they now had a standard towing arrangement; two 100-foot lengths of heavy cable, fastened to mooring bollards on the Russian's afterdeck, and fed through fair-leads to the afterdeck of *Haida Noble* where they were shackled to the tug's big towing cable.

On the peak of a swell, Westholme looked down and judged that Fenton was ready. He had to be, for when the tug descended into the next gray-green trough, they all winced as they heard the Russian ship grate and shudder on the bottom.

"To hell with it!" Westholme shouted. "Give us some line, Ernie, we're going out." Bibaud worked the towing winch like an artist, matching the speed of the cable drum to *Haida Noble*'s smooth forward acceleration. They had to get at least 600 feet of cable out, or the acute angle between the ship's high stern and the tug's relatively low stern would break the bridle. Westholme covered the distance by angling out from the shore at three-quarter speed. Then he braked the tug with a full-speed astern maneuver that shook her battered length. "Put her on the line, Ernie!" he shouted.

Slowly *Haida Noble* eased forward in the first critical effort. As the next swell passed under the Russian's hull, Westholme pushed the power up to full speed. The ship moved! In the distance they heard the thin sound of the Russians cheering. *Haida Noble* was away, her cable tight as a fiddle string and the Russian following.

Lindstrom cheered loudly and ran up to slap Bibaud on the back. "We did it! Ernie, you were right—this calls for a party!" Then he lurched over to the rail and was sick again.

"Back to your bunk," Westholme called to Lindstrom.

He nodded. "But I'm going to stand my watch," he warned Westholme, and left the deck.

As Westholme had expected, the tow was now showing signs of becoming a nightmare. The Russian vessel, unbalanced by the tons of seawater in her forward compartments and rendered even more unstable by a jammed rudder, was beginning to yaw off the line of travel. The motion would become more pronounced when the line was lengthened to a safer 1500 feet, but there was no alternative. With a short line, it was only a matter of time before the bridle weakened and snapped. Westholme signaled Bibaud to pay out more line, and switched to "send" on the walkie-talkie.

"Fenton? Westholme here . . . are you receiving me? Over."

Tait's voice came back. "Fenton's talking to the captain over here. Things are bad. They've lost half their company. They've got no power, no heat. And we're going to need more pumps if we want to keep her head above water. . . . Here's Fenton."

"Christy?" Fenton was breathless. "Things are in a hell of a mess over here. People dead and injured. Men *and* women!"

"OK, Brad. What do you need?"

"The pumps, for starters. And, Chris, the captain asks permission to transfer five or six injured to *Haida Noble*, along with a doctor."

"Brad, you know we're not set up to take care of that many people. We haven't got enough medical supplies to . . . Hold it a moment, Brad." Below on the afterdeck, Telford had appeared, gesticulating to Stan Read and Bibaud.

"What's up, Telford?"

"Lindstrom, sir. He's on the deck outside his cabin. He's not in his right mind, and he can't seem to move his arm and leg."

"You and Stan take care of Lindstrom. Ease him onto a bed in the infirmary. No pillow and strap him in. Get a move on. I'll need Stan back up here as soon as possible."

Westholme went back to the walkie-talkie. "Tell the captain we'll take the injured aboard. We'll run for another fifteen minutes into deeper water, and then shorten up to transfer the pumps and take the injured on board. The doctor is essential. Tell them we've got a case of pneumonia, and something that looks like brain damage." Westholme signed off.

Haida Noble was making painfully slow progress; and her speed wasn't likely to improve with the yawing ship at the end of the line.

462

Still, the white line of surf on Amphitrite was receding and with luck they'd have the ship at Ucluelet in five or six hours—expert hospital care for the serious cases, sleep for everyone. Sleep . . . suddenly the word held a new meaning for Westholme. He felt leaden fatigue enveloping him, and thrust it away. The others were as tired as he and none had complained. They were a great crew. . . .

WESTHOLME had been hearing the sound in a corner of his consciousness for several moments. His gaze went south, searching the sky, and almost immediately he located the plane—an ancient PBY flying boat at a height of about 500 feet.

"The Air-Sea Rescue boys," Bibaud shouted enthusiastically.

Westholme put the tug on automatic pilot and ran into the wheelhouse to find the Aldis lamp. He wished the swell was lighter, to enable the flying boat to land and pick up Lindstrom and the roughneck; but the fact that the plane was in contact warmed his heart.

The PBY came in low between the two vessels, slowly circled and then returned with its Aldis lamp beginning to flicker. It was the International Code message: "Can we render assistance?"

He countered with the letters TA—"I can proceed." The plane had its work cut out. Scores of vessels and communities had worse problems than *Haida Noble*. He would be in Ucluelet with the Russian in five or six hours. He repeated the TA and waved cheerfully at the lumbering plane as it made a final low pass and continued north. In a few minutes Ucluelet would be prepared for them, and the company—and Lee—would know that *Haida Noble* was still afloat and earning her money.

Chapter 18

Ten minutes later, with nineteen fathoms under her, *Haida Noble* began to shorten her line, drawing in toward the Russian, and the difficult business of transfer began.

"We'll take the pumps first," Fenton's voice instructed.

As the tug started to drop below the swell, Galbraith hurled a heaving line onto *Haida Noble*'s stern, and the lifting of the pumps began. When all six pumps were safe on the Russian ship, Fenton made use of the vessel's one undamaged lifeboat to transfer her

463

injured crew members. Carefully, he put the injured into it, two stretchers at a time, lowering the boat to *Haida Noble*'s waiting life raft. Galbraith and Tait slid the stretchers aboard the raft for conveyance to *Haida Noble*.

There were six stretcher cases in all. On the third and last trip the doctor, a short figure bundled up in heavy jacket and oilskins, accompanied Tait and Galbraith. Bibaud, working the davit tackle, stared down, his expression half amazement, half reverence. "That doctor's a woman!" he said to Read.

She came aboard behind the stretchers. "You are the captain?" she asked Bibaud, who stared into her very tired, but attractive face.

"The captain's aft, ma'am, at the controls," Read said.

Tait eased past them and went to relieve Westholme. "The woman seems nice enough," he told him. "Speaks better English than Bibaud."

Westholme was convinced of this when the brief introduction was made.

"I would like to install these men in a warm place, Captain," she said. "I understand there is a treatment room."

"Not too adequate, I'm afraid," Westholme told her. "We've got three people in there now. Two of them can use your help."

"I will do what I can."

"The crew's quarters will be the next best thing," Westholme decided. "You'll have them all together where you can keep an eye on them." Telford was hovering in the background. "Mr. Telford here will see to the arrangements. Ask him for anything you need."

She smiled at Telford. "I will be grateful to you, sir." Her green-gray eyes had a straight, honest look.

"Show the doctor to my cabin, Telford . . . you may want to organize yourself, Dr. Davodov. Meantime we'll see to your injured." He looked at his watch. 3:45. "We should be in Ucluelet by no later than 9:00 p.m. There are hospital facilities there."

"Thank you, Captain Westholme," she said. "May I also say that Captain Kutskov wished me to convey his profound thanks to you and your crew for what you are doing. It has been a sad time for your people and ours." She reached to take up her medical bag, but Telford darted in and captured it.

"Would you like to come this way?" he inquired tentatively. She turned and followed him.

464

Galbraith drew his hand across his sweaty, exhausted face. "Amazing how much more I feel like working for her than I do for you," he told Westholme.

"Then grab the end of one of those stretchers," he instructed the deckhand. "Show her how much you like working for her."

Back beside Tait at the stern controls, Westholme heard a little more of the story.

"The ship really got clobbered," Tait said. "They figure the tidal wave carried them up against one of the rig's legs. The gouge aft of the navigation bridge happened when the top of the drill tower fell on them. Part of it is still there."

"How many hurt?"

"There were a hundred and eleven on board, and sixty-two are dead or injured. Eleven missing. They had a fire through the crew's quarters and out onto the afterdeck."

"All those women!" Westholme said. "I know some of the trawlers carry women, but . . ."

"It's quite usual to have women deckhands, technicians, scientists —even captains and ship's officers—on Russian oceanographic vessels." Volkoff spoke behind them and Westholme turned to see him, bundled in an over-large jacket and hood, squinting at the crippled ship now riding at the end of the 1500-foot line. "That is *Irkutsk*, an oceanographic research ship." The words emerged tightly. "That bastard sank BUTCO 17."

"Probably contributed. I wouldn't want to say either way."

"OK, Captain, I won't argue with you. Let's just say that ship is *Irkutsk*; it says so on the stern. I know her by reputation and my opinion is that you're towing a piece of very hot merchandise. She's rigged to gather special information. Call her a spy ship."

"She's a ship," Westholme said. "I've towed a lot of ships in trouble, all nationalities. This one has had more trouble than most. Now I suggest you find yourself a bunk somewhere and sleep it off until we get to Ucluelet." He turned his back on the American and stared hard through the gathering dusk at *Irkutsk* as she yawed at the end of the cable. It wasn't any of his damned business what she was. Let the Canadians figure that one out when he got to port.

"Look . . . I'm sorry," Volkoff said. "I'm taking this pretty damned personally."

"That's all right. I can understand how you feel, but let the experts sort it out later. OK?"

465

"That suits me."

The walkie-talkie crackled and Westholme turned it up. The voice emerging from the speaker was deep, precise. "Captain Westholme? Captain Mikhail Kutskov here. Are you receiving me?"

"Loud and clear," Westholme said. "What can I do for you, Captain?"

"I wish to thank you, Captain, for your assistance. The situation was very serious, as you can appreciate."

"I'm glad I was at this end, not yours," Westholme said. "How is that bridle riding?"

"Very well, I believe. Captain Westholme . . . may I ask what power you have?"

"We're running on one engine—five thousand horsepower. Why?"

"I would like to make a salvage contract with you."

"I don't think that will be necessary under the circumstances. You can make your own arrangements with my company when we arrive in port."

"That is something I must avoid, Captain."

"I don't understand. Do you mean you want to avoid a formal salvage contract because . . ."

"No, no, no!" The Russian captain was almost apologetic. "I mean I do not wish to enter a Canadian port. I would like to commission you to tow my ship back beyond your Twelve Mile boundary. For this I will pay you whatever reasonable amount you ask."

Westholme wasn't certain he had heard right. "You want us to tow you out to *sea?* No deal."

The voice at the other end was patient. "Captain . . . it will be no more difficult to tow us back to our fleet than to reach a Canadian port, and I am prepared to reimburse you."

"Don't listen to him!" Volkoff hissed in Westholme's ear. "That guy is in deep trouble and he knows it. He has enough electronic intelligence gear on top and under the hull to make the US spy ship *Pueblo* look like a ferryboat."

Tait added, "He doesn't mean it! You should see the condition of that ship. God, Kutskov himself is supposed to be injured!"

Westholme made up his mind. "Captain Kutskov, for the good of your ship and mine—and both our crews—I am taking you into Ucluelet. I understand you are injured, and I can guarantee . . ."

"There is no time left to argue." The voice was crisper. "You *must* tow my vessel as far as the Twelve Mile limit and leave me there. I would suggest a fee of ten thousand dollars. It is a very simple request."

"He'll have the whole fleet waiting for him," Volkoff said. "That's the last you'll see of any of them. You've got yourself a spy ship, Westholme, and he's wriggling to get off the hook."

"Get off my back," Westholme told him coldly. "This is none of your business." To the Russian captain he said: "I'm sorry. We're taking you in. I've got critically injured men in my own crew, and I've got six of yours. This is no time for politics, Captain."

"I am sure we will both try to live up to our responsibilities, Captain Westholme." The voice receded and broke into a brief staccato of Russian.

"You've got him buffaloed," Tait decided. "He's having a conference."

"Like hell he is!" Volkoff exclaimed. "He's issuing instructions on another wave length. Telling someone to put a plan into action."

Kutskov's deep, unruffled voice was back again. "Captain Westholme, you leave me with no alternative except to borrow your vessel to tow us to the Twelve Mile line. You will be paid, of course, but my crew will man the tug. They are excellent seamen."

Westholme turned away from the speaker, two red spots of anger on his cheekbones. "I don't believe this! The man is stark, raving crazy. . . ."

The Russian captain's voice interrupted. "I want you to understand, Captain, I will not willfully hurt either your vessel or any member of your crew. It is highly unsatisfactory negotiating with you over this intercommunication system. I would like you to join me aboard my ship."

"That does it," Westholme said tightly. "We're going to set you adrift, Captain. When you come to your senses, fire a flare."

Behind Westholme a thickly accented voice commanded, "You will turn around from there, please."

In a reflex motion Westholme switched to automatic pilot and swung around to stare at two husky, bandaged figures who, not twenty minutes before, had been brought aboard on stretchers, "critically injured". One still wore a bloody head bandage. Both held automatic pistols, and the one with the bandaged head had a compact walkie-talkie slung across his shoulder. Keeping his weapon steady, he spoke a few words into the set.

Volkoff began to say something, but Westholme stopped him. "Too bad none of us speak Russian," he said with deliberate emphasis. "Stick around, Mike."

Kutskov's voice began again. "You have been boarded, Captain. For a few hours you will not be responsible for your vessel, and then you may have it back, together with the salvage fee."

In Westholme's advanced state of fatigue, the entire scene became dreamlike. He took a long moment to collect his thoughts, then said, "You know this constitutes an act of piracy?"

"I would like to discuss it with you, Captain. You will come aboard, please. Your second officer may then return to your vessel and assist my crew if he is inclined to."

Westholme saw no way to refuse. He glanced at Volkoff and then said: "I have one of my top salvage people with me. I'd like to bring him along."

"That could prove useful, Captain. By all means."

The feeling of unreality was departing, replaced now by anger and the need to match the Russian captain's impressive control. "You're taking a lot on your shoulders. This is piracy in any court of law. You are deliberately endangering the life of my first officer and an American citizen on board my ship. Both must have expert medical attention."

"We will discuss this matter of responsibility shortly if you wish. By the way, Dr. Davodov has been sent aboard solely to treat your people. She is not a party to the game I am forced to play."

"You expect me to believe that?"

"It doesn't really matter whether you do or not. You and your colleague must join me at once. It is getting dark. My crew will help you to your lifeboat."

Westholme hunched his shoulders in profound frustration as one of the Russian crewmen beckoned impatiently with his pistol.

"I'm not going," Volkoff protested.

"You're my salvage specialist," Westholme told him in a low voice. "I'm going to need you to—interpret a few things for me. Come on, Mike."

Westholme handled the outboard motor, while Volkoff glared at the Russian crewman. Under the muzzle of his gun, they made their way across 1500 feet of pitching sea to the battered *Irkutsk*.

"You don't worry," the man assured them in his bad English. "We be friends. Soon everything be good again."

Fenton was waiting at the rail when Westholme clambered up and over the side. He looked stunned. "There was no way I could guess this, Christy. They were so glad to see us. Friendly."

"They're still friendly," Westholme said, "but with just a little twist. Better get back to the tug, Brad. Take care of our boys the best way you can. And, for God's sake, don't try to be a hero. The way things stand now, this ship is going back over the Twelve Mile and there's not a thing we can do about it."

Fenton went down to the waiting raft, cheered on his way by several crew members, his pockets bulging with gifts of Russian cigarettes and cans of caviar. He shook his head in disbelief as the raft began its journey back to *Haida Noble*.

Westholme heard the word "captain" being passed along the deck. Hands reached out to shake his, to thump him on the shoulders. A girl in her early twenties, dressed in crew dungarees and jacket, gave both men tins of chocolate as an officer led them toward the captain's quarters.

"I'd be willing to bet," Westholme said quietly to Volkoff, "this crowd thinks it's heading for port."

As they threaded their way through chunks of twisted steel and splintered timbers, Volkoff nudged Westholme. In a maze of girders and metal crossbeams, was a piece of half-inch plate with characters stenciled on it in black marine paint: TCO 17.

The guide turned right into the ship's main deck interior. It was cold and there was an all-pervading stench of scorched things: blistered paint, incinerated cloth, charred steel—and a smell Westholme had never forgotten from his navy days—the smell of burned flesh.

Up companionways and along corridors they went, with the stench following them and the cold striking into their bones. It was like walking through a gigantic tomb. The Russian officer parted a heavy tarpaulin, and beckoned with his flashlight. "You must watch your footing here," he warned them in quite good English.

They were outside again, on the edge of a jagged canyon slashed into the ship's superstructure. The drill-rig tower must have gone right through the ship's quarters, the galley, God knew what else! A gangplank had been jury-rigged to bridge the terrible gap and Westholme and Volkoff picked their way along it toward a tarpaulin wall on the far side.

Parting the heavy canvas, Westholme found himself in what must have been the forward portion of the radio room. The officer hustled

469

past them, shining his light on a heavily paneled wood door with impressive brass fittings. He knocked twice and said loudly:

"Captain Kutskov. They are here."

"Please come in," a deep, placid voice replied.

Westholme entered a handsome, elaborately appointed navigation bridge and felt a wave of comfortable heat surround him. Past a massive chart cabinet he turned hard right and came face to face with Captain Mikhail Kutskov.

The man sat, semi-reclining, in what looked like a heavily constructed deck chair on which some foam rubber and blankets had been arranged. He wore dark blue uniform trousers, well-polished black shoes. From the waist up he was naked except for a red smoking jacket draped over his shoulders. The reason for this was readily apparent: his left arm, side and face were swathed with wet, medicated gauze, covering the burns he had sustained in the fire.

Kutskov was the first to break the silence. "Well, Captain Westholme, it would appear we have both been through the wars." He was staring at Westholme's lacerated face.

"I'd say you got the worst of it," Westholme said, then, "I'd like you to meet Mr. Michaels," coining a new name for Volkoff.

"Ah-h!" Kutskov's expression was one of satisfaction. "The expert in the saving of ships. We can use you, Mr. Michaels."

Volkoff smiled humorlessly. Meanwhile, Westholme was trying to get some clue to the Russian's real state of mind. It wasn't possible. The good side of his face was strongly molded—he had gray eyes with a trace of a slant, and gray hair, wiry and curling. Possibly fifty years old, the man was relaxed and friendly—like a genial host welcoming friends.

"I'm having some food served in a moment," he said. "I hope sincerely that you gentlemen are hungry?"

Suddenly Westholme realized that he was ravenous.

Chapter 19

Fatigue and the mind-numbing events of the day were the enemies Westholme had to guard against . . . and they were almost too much for him. Fortunately, Volkoff succumbed rapidly to vodka, the surprisingly good food placed before them, and the warmth, for he was becoming quarrelsome, beginning to assert his rights as an

American citizen. He managed to get through the vodka aperitifs, the caviar and anchovy appetizers washed down with more vodka, and then the fine borsch. But when the ocean perch in egg batter was brought onto the bridge, Volkoff was asleep and Westholme and Kutskov had the conversation to themselves.

There was a knock at the door. It was the ship's doctor, once again a woman. She was somewhat older than Dr. Davodov, gray-haired and slightly plump. The captain introduced her while she placed items from her bag on a sterile cloth spread out on the desk beside him.

"Dr. Lebedovitch, I would like you to meet Captain Westholme, master of *Haida Noble*. Captain, my ship's doctor."

Westholme smiled. "I thought *we* had your ship's doctor."

Kutskov chuckled. "This is an unusual ship. I believe we have four medical doctors on board. Is that not so, Dr. Lebedovitch?"

"Two now, Captain," she said in an emotionless voice. "Dr. Davodov and myself remain." Deftly, she began to work on the captain's burned body, removing gauze, spraying the blistered skin with fluid from an atomizer, then covering the treated area with saturated gauze from a sterilizer.

During this procedure the captain talked, breathing deeply when the soiled gauze tore rather than slipped from his burns. It was an impressive display of stoicism, which Westholme chose to believe was being performed for his education.

As the doctor finished her dressings, she spoke to Kutskov in Russian.

"An excellent idea," he said. "The doctor suggests she examine your cuts. In her opinion some of them appear irritated."

"I'd appreciate that," Westholme said. The vodka was making each small wound pound individually.

She worked quickly with probes and cotton wads soaked in an aromatic, soothing fluid. "You are fortunate that stitches are not required," she said. She gave him a tablet with a glass of water, left him half a dozen more to be taken at specified intervals, and left.

471

"An impressive woman," Westholme observed.

"I agree. In the past thirty-six hours, she has seen as much of mass suffering and death as any military surgeon." The captain adjusted himself more comfortably on the tilted chair. "Now then, may I tell you what I believe our position to be, Captain Westholme? While matters have taken a somewhat unusual turn, basically what we have here is a salvage operation." He held up a hand to prevent Westholme from interrupting. "My ship's owner, the Academy of Sciences, represented by myself, has contracted with your company to tow *Irkutsk* to safety. Under standard salvage arrangements, the owner reserves the right to state how his ship will be disposed of. We have elected to be towed into international waters."

"OK, Captain Kutskov," Westholme said angrily, "if we have a salvage contract then I am in charge until your ship is delivered to a safe destination. I have the right to decide where that is—and it is *not* some Godforsaken point out in international waters!"

"I hope we will discuss, rather than argue."

Westholme lowered his voice. He wished Volkoff were not sprawled asleep in his chair. "My responsibility is first to my crew and ship, then to yours. This tow should be going into Ucluelet, but you have pirated my tug, without concern for the lives of either crew. The decision to tow into international waters is yours, and by every law of the sea, by every responsibility of your command, you are wrong . . . and you know it!"

"Captain Westholme, I admire and respect you. I do not expect you to reciprocate. But both of us command ships. Both of us have orders to follow. I respect you for the importance you place upon your responsibilities. Perhaps you may come to respect me for the same thing."

Westholme gestured in frustration. "Let's forget diplomacy, politics, or whatever the hell else you're trying to pull. What's this all about, Kutskov? What's driving you? Are there orders you are bound to follow?"

"There is no need for you to know why I have taken these actions. It is much safer for you if you do not."

Westholme sat with his head in his hands, feeling the tight bands of fatigue closing in.

"We have managed to build an impasse between us," the Russian captain said earnestly. "Quite possibly sleep will reduce it to nothing by morning." He picked up a makeshift microphone attached to the arm of his chair, pressed a button, spoke into it, then turned to Westholme. "The officer of the watch will escort you to your quarters. By the way, I inquired as to the power of your vessel earlier today. Five thousand horsepower, you said. Sufficient to tow this ship at considerably more than two knots."

Westholme stood up wearily. "Not with the towing gear we're using, and the yaw this ship is developing. Two knots is pushing it."

"I would like to be in international waters by dawn."

Westholme looked at his watch. "Eleven or twelve hundred hours will be more like it," he said. "Push it any faster and you're in trouble."

Kutskov laughed with genuine humor. "No matter how we look at it, we are in trouble. No?"

The officer of the watch knocked and entered. Captain Kutskov gestured toward the sleeping Volkoff. The officer marched over and helped Westholme pull the American to his feet. He came up grimacing as his sore muscles unwound. "God, I feel as though the drill rig landed on me when it went over," he groaned.

"What did he say?" Kutskov asked pleasantly.

Westholme grinned and shook Volkoff roughly. "He's back in the Caribbean somewhere, towing a drill rig. He's the only one I know who works in his sleep."

"Good night, gentlemen," Kutskov said.

Westholme said good night and nudged Volkoff to do the same. As he rounded the corner of the chart rack, he looked back. The Russian captain's eyes were closed, and in the light of the lanterns strung across the ceiling, his face had become very old.

THEIR CABIN was a damp, small one on the upper deck, with two bunks. A kerosene lamp hung from the ceiling, providing the only heat and light, and the door was locked from the outside.

"We're prisoners," Volkoff said tautly.

"I suppose so. Frankly, at this moment I don't give a damn. I'm bushed."

"Do you actually believe any of us will get out of this alive?"

"If we don't do anything foolish, I think we'll be back on *Haida Noble* by noon tomorrow, heading for Ucluelet."

Volkoff stared at him in disbelief. "I don't know how you can be so casual. This is a spy ship. Can't you get that through your head? Do you think they'll let any of us free to tell what we saw?"

Westholme started to undress. "Mike, we haven't seen anything except a Russian ship that was tossed inside the Twelve Mile in a hurricane."

"It came in under its own steam. It sank BUTCO 17!"

"There was a collision. The ship damn near sank herself."

Volkoff moved close, his eyes gleaming like a conspirator's, but circled with tiredness and pain. "We can't let them get away with this, Westholme. They've broken every rule, every law . . . ."

"They've also got us on their ship," Westholme reminded him, and got into the bunk. "Better keep the lantern on. It throws heat."

EXACTLY WHAT wakened Westholme was not certain. Volkoff was snoring lightly and Westholme himself should have continued to sleep, because he was warm under the blankets and fat quilt the Russians had provided. But something was wrong. He tried to analyze it: *Irkutsk* had stopped. She was rolling, not yawing. So either the tug had stopped towing—or the bridle had snapped. He studied his watch. 5:17. Not long before dawn.

Seconds later a key rattled in the door and it opened.

"Captain says, for you and your friend, coffee with him. In a minute, please. You dress. Yes? Outside I wait." The voice was friendly enough. Westholme dressed quickly, then woke Volkoff, who sat bolt upright.

"What's happened?"

"We'll find out on the bridge. The captain is pouring coffee. One thing is certain—this ship has stopped."

"Perhaps we're over the line. Now they've got to decide what to do with us."

"It's too early for that, and we've got enough trouble without you inventing more," Westholme said in disgust.

"Don't read me wrong," Volkoff said. "I'm not scared. I'm mad, I'm suspicious, but I'm definitely not frightened. We've got to second-guess these bastards. We've got to take a stronger stand."

"Fine. I'd like that. What do you suggest?"

"We've got countries behind us, man! I'm an American citizen. You're a Canadian. Your tug is Canadian property. But you seem to think we're fighting this thing all by ourselves."

Westholme zipped up his jacket. "The hard truth is, Mike, we *are* fighting this thing by ourselves. Yesterday, we signaled to an Air-Sea Rescue plane that everything was fine. You can bet we're

474

not even on the priority list right now. *Haida Noble* is proceeding, and every other ship on this coast is busy with its own trouble."

Volkoff was getting the message. "No way to communicate. We're on our own for a while, that's true."

"And true for Captain Kutskov too, don't forget that. He holds a lot of good cards, but he doesn't have his country telling him what to play. So far I trust him. Let's continue to play our little game. Keep your ears open whenever they talk Russian. Pick up clues. Try to find us an advantage."

"I'll do what I can," Volkoff said, "but I still think we can play a tougher game."

"OK, Mike," Westholme said as he opened the door. "You be the United States. I'll be Canada. Let's go up on the bridge and talk it over with Russia."

A YOUNG, broad-cheeked girl in a blue smock had just finished shaving the master of *Irkutsk*, the gauze bandages had been changed again, and his appearance was alert and efficient. On a low table beside him were tea and coffee pots, cups and saucers, and a plate of sweet biscuits. A walkie-talkie set lay at the end of the table, and *Haida Noble*'s own set hung from a hook above the navigation desk.

His second and third officers had joined Kutskov. They were middle-aged, well built, with uniformly rigid features. Both spoke English reasonably well but seemed preoccupied. In Westholme's opinion both were functioning under severe strain.

"Perhaps you would like to serve yourself," Kutskov invited. "There will be something more substantial later on."

"The ship has stopped," Westholme said abruptly.

"That is why we were obliged to call you. As you may have guessed, the towing bridle has broken."

"You increased the towing speed," Westholme accused him. "I warned you about that."

"The towing bridle has broken," Kutskov repeated patiently. "That is the immediate problem. I am afraid the cable has worked considerable destruction on your vessel and your crew is giving us some trouble. Their attitude is understandable, but we must have a new line put aboard us."

"How much damage to the tug?"

"I would suggest you talk to your second officer. We have not been able to reason with him." An officer handed the *Haida Noble* walkie-talkie set to Westholme. "The object of your conversation, of course, is to obtain his cooperation."

Westholme pushed the button to transmit. "Brad. Brad Fenton? Westholme here. Brad, what's going on over there?"

"It's bloody awful! Poor Bibaud . . . . Tait blew his stack and tried to fight all the bastards at once. He's out cold and locked in your cabin. It's a mess, Christy, just a . . ."

"OK, Brad. Slow down. Now what's the situation?"

"The Russians increased the towing speed. The cable kicked back and . . . Bibaud's dead, along with one of *them*. There's cable all over the afterdeck."

Westholme turned to Kutskov. "Safeguarding my tug and crew, are you!" His voice was dry with anger—and sorrow.

"I am as distressed as you are, Captain. Perhaps you will understand that later. I elected to take a risk—and a heavy price has been paid." His eyes closed momentarily. "Our personal feelings must not be allowed to surface now. My objective is to return my ship to international waters and I will proceed from risk to increasing risk until the objective is achieved." The words were not a threat, but a statement of absolute fact.

Westholme went back to Fenton: "Brad, I can't believe this has happened. It's a terrible thing. Bibaud was . . ." There was no way he could express how he felt about Bibaud. "Brad, I don't want any of you to put up any more resistance. It can only lead to trouble. Is the towing winch still operating?"

"How do I know, with a thousand feet of cable lying on top of it!" There was rebellion in Fenton's voice.

"Start Stan Read cutting away that cable. Drop the whole works overboard, and get the boys to pull a new bridle out of the wire room. Tell them I don't want any heroes. We need to put the new line aboard within the hour. Possible?"

"I don't know until I've talked to the others."

"Tell them we're dealing with a man who has wiped out more than thirty of his own people. Now Bibaud. He'll go the limit if he has to."

"I read you," Fenton said. "I'm on my way."

Westholme put down the walkie-talkie. "You heard my orders," he said. "That's the best I can do."

"I am grateful," the Russian said. "Your bluntness may have per-

476

suaded him—although I think you misjudge me. I am not inhuman, but I *am* in an extremely difficult position, Captain."

"So was Ernie Bibaud when that cable hit him," Westholme said harshly. "Your orders killed him! That's your trouble; you're hooked on orders."

"You have made your point, and I have told you I am deeply sorry. But you are in no position to pass judgment. You are under my command until I release you. Now I must ask you to help me with my ship."

"OK," Westholme said, "let us do a damage survey, stem to stern. Maybe we can do something about the leaks—or are there things down there you don't want us to see?"

Kutskov glanced at one of his officers, who shook his head. The ship's master turned back to Westholme. "Our own people have gone over the ship thoroughly. Apparently you can be of most use in transferring the new cable."

"OK, let's get started."

"There is time for you to have some coffee or tea."

"We don't have the appetite for it," Westholme said. They were escorted to the ship's afterdeck. *Haida Noble* lay 1000 yards astern and binoculars brought the scene up close. Westholme could see Read working with a cutting torch to free the tangled cable. A Russian crewman was helping him while two other Russians stood by.

Three members of the boarding party remained to be accounted for. One, he knew, was dead and lying somewhere in the bowels of the ship with poor Bibaud. Logically, the others would be in the engine room and on the navigation bridge. Dr. Davodov? Taking care of Lindstrom and the roughneck, Westholme hoped. He still believed that the doctor had been sent aboard *Haida Noble* as a gesture of goodwill. Strangely, he continued to trust Kutskov in many ways.

The booms on *Haida Noble* were beginning to swing as Galbraith worked the winches. Grapnels on the boom cables dug into the mass of tangled wire on the deck, lifted it clear and swung it over the side, returning for additional loads. When the deck was clear, the big tug made a turn across the diminishing swell and approached *Irkutsk*, swinging her stern around to meet that of the Russian ship. Galbraith heaved the two thin lines on board, and the Russian work parties began the task of hauling in.

Just then, Westholme felt Volkoff tug his jacket.

"The two in uniform on your left, up above," the American said. "I know one of them . . . and I think she knows me."

Scanning the group on the upper deck, Westholme saw a young woman pointing toward him and talking animatedly to her male companion. "Who are they?" he asked.

"She's an oceanographer, and a good one. I met her at the Oceanographic Congress in Moscow in 1966. We saw a lot of one another, if you know what I mean."

"I have a feeling the fat is in the fire." Westholme turned around slowly to survey the progress of the cable transfer.

"I shouldn't have come with you," Volkoff said harshly. "It's the worst thing you could have done."

"Cut it out," Westholme ordered him. "The worst thing either of us can do is lose our control."

The first of the bridle ends was on deck and being dragged toward a mooring bollard. "Come on, Mike," Westholme said. "It's time we went to work."

Volkoff fell in beside him unwillingly. Westholme could feel the tension in him. The work party was struggling to aim the bridle eye at the bollard and Westholme helped them guide it into position. Volkoff watched, hands in pockets, eyes smoldering. As *Haida Noble* began to move ahead, taking up the strain, Westholme felt *Irkutsk* swing around ponderously, aligning herself with *Haida Noble*'s towing cable, and she was under way again.

Taking the in-going tide and the prevailing current into account, Westholme estimated that the ship had lost three miles in the almost two hours it had taken to hook up the new cable. The Twelve Mile limit was about ten hours away, if all went well.

A crew member offered him a cigarette which he accepted gratefully. Volkoff refused. The Russian was young, out of breath from helping haul the cable, his forehead liberally beaded with sweat. "We go Vancouver, yes?" He answered his own question with a nod. "My brother, Vancouver . . ." But an officer interrupted and sent the boy away.

So the people on board the Russian ship did not know what Kutskov was doing. Beside him Westholme heard Volkoff say, "Brace yourself. Here it comes." Out of the corner of his eye he saw the first and second officers shouldering through the crowd.

"You will come to see the captain . . . and your friend too," one said, and reached out to take his arm.

478

"There's no need for that," Westholme said. "Let's keep it friendly." His hands deep in his pockets, he walked beside his escort, Volkoff following sullenly. As before, they passed through a gauntlet of well-wishers; tired, battered, smiling faces, trying to express gratitude to the men who had snatched them to safety. The irony of the situation was overpowering. Westholme was beginning to understand Volkoff's unreasoning frame of mind and what the death of BUTCO's crew, because of *Irkutsk*, had done to him. The nightmare was getting to Westholme as well.

Chapter 20

Captain Kutskov had a tribunal waiting for them, or so it appeared to Westholme. There was the oceanographer woman, an attractive brunette in her early thirties. Her smile when she saw Volkoff was tentative, nervous. The man with her was older, balding, a little heavy in the paunch but with bright, probing eyes. Only the woman's manner approached friendliness. The others—all ship's officers—were cold and wary. Two enormous crew members stood in the background.

Mikhail Kutskov, pain and tiredness showing in his eyes, still reclined in his chair. An effort had been made to fit the upper part of his body into a light, woolen pullover, but in spite of the stuffy warmth in the area, the chill of shock was beginning to tell on him.

"I believe introductions are unnecessary," Kutskov began abruptly. "Mr. Volkoff, you are apparently acquainted with Miss Baliuk, staff scientist, Institute of Oceanology, USSR?"

Volkoff looked at her. "Hello, Serafima."

She nodded uncertainly.

"This, of course, changes the nature of our relationship," Kutskov said to Westholme. "I have dealt with you honestly, but you have chosen to practice deceit. Two simple tugboat men, is it?" He pointed at Volkoff. "This man is an oceanographer of sufficient capability to have attended Moscow in 1966."

"I didn't know that."

"You knew he spoke Russian?"

"I brought him with me for that reason. It was one of the few advantages I thought I had."

"And it turns out to be a serious disadvantage, Captain. How long have you known him? Since the sinking of the British United drill rig number seventeen?"

Westholme nodded. "We picked him up. He was one of two survivors."

"Out of more than fifty," Volkoff cut in. "Two out of fifty. And you can hold yourself responsible for . . ."

"Quiet!" Kutskov roared in a surprising display of rage. He tried to raise himself from the chair and fell back in pain. The man was suffering from more than burns; a back injury, possibly. He addressed Westholme. "I presume you know these waters well?" Westholme nodded. "Knowing the condition of this ship and the technical difficulties of towing her, how much time do you think it will take to reach international waters?"

"A minimum of ten hours . . . Captain, can I make a couple of comments? They may not prove to be practical, but I'd like you to hear me out."

"What are they, Captain?"

"I'll speak like a tugboat skipper now. From where *you* sit, there may be larger issues here—orders from your academy, your navy, the state. But the only issue that really counts is that I have sick and injured on my tug and you have even more. If you don't want this ship to go into a Canadian port, let me take all of you aboard *Haida Noble*, and let this ship go to the bottom. That's where she's going to end in any event."

"It is a generous offer," Kutskov said wearily, "but it lacks understanding of the true situation. I think Mr. Volkoff could explain it to you."

Volkoff took up the challenge. "I'll try, Captain. This vessel could be classified as a spy ship. The USSR has scores of them; so has the United States. The orders are the same on both sides—if your vessel is in danger of seizure, you must destroy it. The *Pueblo* was a classic example of what can happen if you can't or don't follow the destruct order. Am I close?"

Kutskov was silent.

"All right. Suppose I'm partly correct. Your country has no equipment on its intelligence collection ships that the United States doesn't have. I speak from a fair knowledge. Oh, you may have a temporary advantage in one or two areas; but then we make up for it in others."

"That is not true!" For the first time, the male oceanographer entered the discussion. "The United States has lagged far behind us in oceanography—has been more concerned to rape the sea bottom than to perpetuate it for mankind."

"You're changing the subject, Professor," Volkoff said sharply. "I'm talking about intelligence collection ships like this one. Under the rules of the game it must be destroyed before it is captured. All right? Then accept Westholme's offer. Put your people on board his tug and destroy this goddam hulk!"

"Transparently clever," the oceanographer said. "Destroy it here on Canada's continental shelf, in twenty or thirty fathoms of water. How long do you think it would take to bring up the pieces and fit the story together?"

"So that is the situation," Captain Kutskov said to Volkoff. "The ship must be sunk . . . but in international waters deep enough to prevent the retrieval of any significant part of her."

"Why?" Volkoff insisted. "The chances of your having something on this vessel beyond the knowledge of the United States are pretty slim. Let me try guessing. Serafima . . ." He turned to the woman. "The paper you delivered in Moscow was on the feasibility of underwater storage depots. So . . . this ship is surveying for—or perhaps installing—such depots. Your partner here could be an expert in the establishment of submarine detector networks, or atomic submarine maintenance facilities—or simply the farming of kelp. The point is that anything you are doing, we are doing too— give or take a few twists on either side."

"I'm afraid," Kutskov said, with what seemed genuine regret, "you have expressed much better than I could the fact that our problem now encompasses more than the destruction of the ship. You, and by association Captain Westholme, have become too knowledgeable."

"You know," Westholme shook his head in disbelief, "here we are, throwing our weight around, and the people who stand to lose the most haven't a clue what we're deciding for them. How many of your ship's company know that *Irkutsk* is going to be blown to bits in international waters?"

"Before that, they will have been transferred to other vessels in the fleet," Kutskov said.

"What vessels? What fleet? I haven't seen anything shaping up on the horizon."

The two Russian crew members looked instinctively toward the

481

starboard bridge window; then the taller one craned to get a better view of something. He spoke rapidly, only to be interrupted by a voice emerging from Kutskov's walkie-talkie.

Volkoff turned to Westholme, his eyes excited. "There's a Canadian vessel approaching!" To Kutskov he said, "There was no way you could get away with this."

"At this moment nothing has changed," Kutskov said. "See if you can identify the vessel for us, Captain Westholme."

Westholme crossed to the starboard side. A medium-sized craft, some three miles distant, was approaching.

"It's *Blackfish*," he said, as he trained binoculars on the vessel. "Canadian Coast Guard." He returned to Kutskov. "Captain, no one could fault you for surrendering to one of our coast guard vessels. You and your ship's company would be better off . . . ."

"I am sorry, Captain," Kutskov said, "but nothing has changed. We will proceed on into international waters. The coast guard ship will approach the tug and communication will be by loud hailer. Is that not true, Captain?" Westholme nodded. "I would like you to instruct your second officer to conduct a normal exchange of information with the master of *Blackfish*. The line broke during the night. The tow is now proceeding without difficulty. *Blackfish* need not trouble herself with us further."

"I won't do that," Westholme told him flatly.

"I would have been disappointed in you, if you had agreed. However, it must be done." Kutskov picked up his walkie-talkie and issued some instructions. While he waited, he explained to Westholme: "I have asked to talk to your second officer . . . Mr. Fenton, is it? I should inform you that your first officer now appears to be in a more satisfactory condition, but he will require surgery at the earliest moment. Dr. Davodov gave me her report earlier."

Fenton's voice emerged belligerently from the speaker. "Is Westholme there? I want to speak to Captain Westholme."

"In a moment," Kutskov assured him. "Mr. Fenton, we would like you to tell the coast guard that the cable broke, that there was a delay in rejoining it, and that you are now prepared to proceed without difficulty. We will not require their help."

"You're joking!" Fenton said incredulously. "I want to talk to Captain Westholme!"

"Very well, but briefly."

An officer carried the walkie-talkie to Westholme. "I'm receiving you, Brad," Westholme said. "My orders are absolutely clear. Tell the boys on *Blackfish* we've been pirated. Tell them there are injured aboard both vessels, and that we need help."

The set was pulled away from him abruptly and returned to Kutskov, Fenton still talking: "They're giving us a pretty bad time over here, Christy. I'll put the message across if I don't get slugged first."

"I doubt you would be injured in full view of the Canadian Coast Guard, Mr. Fenton," Kutskov said sharply, "but we could no longer be responsible for the safety of your captain. Do you understand? Now please cooperate. Send the coast guard vessel on its way."

"Let me talk to Captain Westholme . . ."

Kutskov switched off and laid the set down. "I am afraid we have posed him a rather difficult problem," he said to Westholme apologetically, "but I had no alternative."

Westholme turned to the others: the officers, the two scientists. "He *did* have an alternative," he insisted. "He still has. Get off this ship, all of you. Blow it up! Destroy it! Do whatever the rule book calls for . . . but do it now while you've got a ship out there that can render aid and send for more."

The oceanographer looked at Captain Kutskov in exasperation. "I have already explained it is too shallow here. Regulations prohibit the scuttling of . . ."

". . . of an intelligence collection ship on any continental shelf where the possibility of the retrieval of classified materials remains," Volkoff recited. "We must buy our rules from the same guy. But the facts are that you were forced by natural causes beyond your control to come inside Canada's Twelve Mile limit, and forces beyond your control are keeping you here. Your ship's company would testify that you have done everything humanly possible to live by the rule book . . . but the game's over, Captain Kutskov. Quit! Relax! You deserve a medal."

Kutskov waved the argument away as an officer reported that *Haida Noble* and *Blackfish* were about to make contact.

Volkoff said to the woman in an undertone, "Serafima, I think we got to know one another very well in Moscow. The theme of the Oceanographic Congress brought a lot of people together: 'Ocean Research for the Good of Mankind', wasn't it?"

Her expression was more than reproach; mingled with it was regret and the shadow of fear.

"Then what are you doing here?" Volkoff persisted.

"Research!" she said, goaded out of her silence. "For the good of mankind!"

"For the good of the USSR!"

"What is good for the United States is seldom good for the rest of mankind," her fellow scientist said loudly and angrily.

Kutskov slammed the table angrily. "Stop it, Dr. Baliuk, both of you! We have no need for more scientific opinions. Go now!"

The Russian oceanographers left and complete silence settled over the navigation bridge. Outside was the muffled rush of the sea and thinly in the distance the sound of voices from the tug and *Blackfish* filtered through loud hailers.

Westholme watched *Haida Noble* and *Blackfish* running a parallel course 1500 feet ahead. He could make out figures standing at both rails. One of them would be Fenton—following whose orders, his or Kutskov's? On the *Blackfish*, Captain Lewis was probably doing the talking. He knew Jack Lewis from navy days, a hard-nosed, superlative seaman now in his fifties.

Blackfish began to accelerate, pulling ahead of the tug and swinging in a tight turn to starboard to approach the Russian ship. Kutskov's walkie-talkie came alive and the Russian captain nodded with satisfaction and looked up at Westholme.

"Your second officer is both sensible and loyal to you, Captain. We are being allowed to proceed."

Westholme said nothing. He watched the approach of *Blackfish*, saw the Russian crew members assembling at the rails to cheer, and realized that Lewis would be completely deceived by this display of goodwill.

Blackfish swung in close, her crew waving, catching the packages of cigarettes and chocolate thrown to them.

Above the general confusion a speaker-amplified voice broke through abruptly: "Captain Westholme? Is Captain Westholme aboard? Lewis here."

Kutskov's eyes narrowed for an instant. Then to his first and second officers he said: "Walk out on the bridge. Exchange greetings with them. Take a seaman with you and position yourselves at intervals along the rail. Take a loud hailer."

"Captain Westholme?" the speaker boomed again. "Are you there? Lewis."

"Now," Kutskov instructed Westholme, "you know this Lewis?"

Westholme nodded. "Very good. Go out and assure him that things go well here."

"I'll need the loud hailer."

"Not necessary, and a temptation. The fact that you are unharmed, smiling, will be reassurance enough. You are a married man, Captain Westholme?"

"Is that important?"

"At a time like this it is well for a man to think of his loved ones as well as himself."

Westholme walked out to the bridge. Kutskov had asked, "You are a married man?" It was a threat . . . but it was also a reminder. He was married to Lee, a woman who despaired of his ever coming home for good.

At the rail, Westholme looked across and down at Captain Lewis standing solidly on the bridge of the cutter. The look of impatience on his sea-hewn face altered to a broad grin when he spotted Westholme and Lewis held up his loud hailer. "Holed up with some of those nice-looking girls, were you?"

Westholme grinned and made a gesture of denial. "You know I'm an old married man," he shouted, above the noise from the two crews. The cutter was moving slowly past and he walked down the deck to keep abreast of her.

"What was that?" Lewis shouted through his speaker. "Ah, never mind. You sure you don't need some help into port?"

Westholme shook his head, still moving along the deck toward the officer with the loud hailer. "Everything's fine," he shouted. "We've got it under control." Three feet from him, *Irkutsk*'s first officer was smiling broadly and waving at the crew of *Blackfish*. Westholme stepped to the rail beside him, pivoted, and drove a left hook to the man's jaw, putting all the anger, frustration, and grief of the past days into the punch.

The Russian lurched back, and his loud hailer went skidding along the deck. Westholme dived for it but was tackled from behind by crewmen, and hit by the ship's second officer.

Inside the navigation bridge, Volkoff put his shoulder into the ship's third officer and made for the door. Along the deck, three men were struggling with Westholme. He could hear Lewis bellowing: "Hold on there . . . ! Release Captain Westholme. Take your hands off that man. This is an official order."

From his breast pocket Volkoff drew an oblong piece of plastic-

485

enclosed pasteboard, and flicked it with a strong forearm motion toward the cutter as a crewman charged on deck and hit him behind the ear, following it up with a blow to the left kidney. Volkoff dropped without a sound.

Westholme was dragged inside where Kutskov ordered: "Take them to their quarters. Place a guard outside."

As Westholme was hustled away he heard Kutskov issuing orders; precise, unwavering—as much in control as ever.

Chapter 21

The *Irkutsk* crisis put Canada's government to a test which was to last for the better part of a year. The immediate result of the encounter between *Blackfish* and *Irkutsk* was approximately this:

At 1217, the Coast Guard Rescue Officer in Vancouver received the following radio message from Captain Lewis: "We have made contact with salvage tug *Haida Noble* and tow, *Irkutsk*. The tug has been taken over by the Russians . . . I saw Captain Westholme of the *Haida Noble* being manhandled on the Russian's deck. An American on board tossed us his ID card—an employee of British United working on BUTCO 17. Name, Michael M. Volkoff . . . Les, I wish to hell I was kidding, but this couldn't be more serious . . . Sure I've talked to them. In plain terms, they want their ship returned to international waters and they're using Westholme and the others as hostages . . . It's hard to tell, Les. The ship has taken heavy damage; collision and fire by the look of it. There's not much doubt about it, she's rigged for intelligence collection. You must have some record of her movements. Right . . . right, I'll repeat . . ."

Coming right on the heels of a natural catastrophe, word of the hijacking was in danger of being lost in a flood of incoming emergency reports. But the Rescue Officer immediately phoned a report to the regional headquarters, Department of National Defense. Fortunately it went straight to a colonel with a taste for military rather than civilian crisis. He saw the far-reaching significance of the report and set numerous wheels in action within minutes.

A fully armed Canadian Forces Albatross was dispatched from Comox Air Base to fly low-level circuits over *Irkutsk* and a subchaser was sent at full speed to the scene of the tow. Neither, however, altered the Russian vessel's course or speed in any way. With the subchaser flanking her to port and the coast guard to starboard, *Irkutsk* moved inexorably ahead at the end of the towing line.

At dusk she was slightly less than six miles from the Canadian Twelve Mile limit. Undoubtedly Kutskov drew encouragement from the appearance in mid-afternoon of seven vessels from the scattered Russian fishing flotilla. Their dark silhouettes could be seen in line along the Twelve Mile limit and Aldis lamps began a steady exchange of messages between them and the crippled ship.

It was regrettable in a way that information on Volkoff was passed to the US authorities at the same time that notice of the incident went to Canada's Minister of National Defense. Before Canada had settled on a clear course of action, the US State Department issued its first note—a combination of inquiry and protest. Receiving no answer within the next hour, the US Department of Defense requested Canada's permission to allow a destroyer entry into Canadian waters for the purpose of lending assistance . . . and the permission was flatly refused in a brisk diplomatic note. Canada recognized her national responsibility and said as much.

Nevertheless, the American destroyer proceeded north along Canada's Twelve Mile limit. Shortly after 2100 hours, she took up a post one half-mile distant from the remnants of the Russian fleet, establishing her presence with a theatrical display of searchlights and the intermittent launching of parachute flares.

Meanwhile, when the Russian ambassador was summoned to a meeting with Canada's External Affairs Secretary in Ottawa, he professed total ignorance of the event and returned to his embassy promising that he would try to clarify the situation within the hour.

In less time than that, the Canadian External Affairs Secretary received an official note. The oceanographic vessel *Irkutsk* was indeed reported to be conducting scientific experiments off the Pacific coast of North America, but no messages had been received from her, nor had she acknowledged any since the storm and tsunami in that area.

At the same time, the ambassador let it be known that Russia could not tolerate any punitive action directed toward *Irkutsk* until Canadian charges of trespass, piracy, and kidnapping had been proven to the satisfaction of the Russian government.

After that, the official accusations would circle viciously, magnified by the international press. The next meeting of the Sea Bed

Committee dissolved in a barrage of questions, accusations and counter-accusations. Later Canada would accuse Russia of deliberately buying the time required to destroy effectively a quasi-military intelligence collection ship. Russia would accuse Canada of conspiring with the United States to escalate an unfortunate minor incident into an international crisis.

Thus, while the Pacific northwest still lay in the shock of natural disaster, the world learned of another storm developing, a storm involving nations.

Chapter 22

Volkoff was only half conscious when they dragged him back to the cabin. Westholme did what he could for him, applying a cold-water compress, trying to calm him, but Volkoff was outraged. The blow to his head, though not serious, climaxed the series of indignities he had suffered to his pride, his emotions, and his sense of justice. "The bastards!" he raged. "They can't do this!"

"Cool it, Mike," Westholme said quietly. "We stuck our necks out and they chopped us. I'm sorry you got hurt."

Volkoff's eyes were black with anger. "You haven't changed, have you? You'd lick their boots if they asked you."

"I may have it figured wrong," Westholme said carefully. "When this is over we may discover that we missed an opportunity, or that we should have played a stronger hand."

"When this is over! Where do you think we'll be then? Do you think Kutskov's going to consider us when the chips are down?"

"But he *has* considered us all along. He put a doctor aboard *Haida Noble* to take care of Lindstrom and your roughneck. He made an effort to treat us with what he calls 'goodwill'. The man's humanity may be his big weakness."

"God almighty!" Volkoff exclaimed disgustedly.

"That's what got him into trouble in the first place," Westholme insisted, "that plus—what would you call it—a flair for the dramatic? I'm guessing he took the ship into the lee of BUTCO 17 because he wanted to give his company a more comfortable time of it, and also because it would make a great story afterward—how *Irkutsk* rode out a hurricane behind a symbol of British and American capitalism. If it hadn't been for the tidal wave . . ."

Volkoff rejected Westholme's logic. "Kutskov's got his orders," he said, "and he's going to follow them over our dead bodies."

"Maybe so." Westholme decided to change the subject. "You said you had an idea what this ship was up to. What's your guess?"

"I'm willing to bet they were scouting underwater silo sites for the refueling and provisioning of subs and other military vessels, if and when the time comes. It burns me that we were within an inch of laying our hands on a vessel crammed with stuff that our people are itching to get a look at."

"I thought there was no difference between yours and theirs?"

"In the final analysis there isn't, but the psychological victory would have been great."

"Is it my imagination," Westholme said then, "or is the smell of smoke getting stronger in here?"

"I believe you're right." Volkoff crossed to the door. "There's something burning out there!" he said in alarm.

Westholme sat on the edge of the bunk, considering. "Maybe they've got a fire going somewhere to warm themselves up. It's getting damned cold in here."

"They could be getting ready to leave her," Volkoff said uneasily. "I think we'd better check on this."

He pounded on the door. "Hello! Hello out there!"

A heavy object thumped on the door panel, and a deep voice shouted a few Russian words.

"What did he say?" Westholme asked.

"Roughly translated he wants us to keep our bloody mouths shut. The fire hasn't frightened *him* off, that's for sure."

Volkoff sat down on the bunk beside Westholme. "Look, Chris, I know I've been behaving like an idiot, but I haven't intended to be personal. For the life of me I don't know what other action you could have taken."

Westholme took a deep breath. "This has been a hard one to figure." He shook his head. "I don't think I could have done anything differently. My first responsibility is to my ship and my crew, then to this ship's company and the ship itself. You understand the international political stuff better than I do."

"Not really. The oceanographic aspect, yes. I think I know the direction the world is heading there. That's one of the things that has really shaken me. That very attractive girl up on the bridge today. Serafima Baliuk. A good oceanographer and a great woman.

490

In 1966 we drank vodka together in Moscow, shared our ideas on oceanography and agreed that it was the hope of the world. We were bloody idealists. Today she was up there endorsing the kind of thing that can turn the sea bed into a battleground. . . . How do you figure it?" he ended dejectedly.

Both of them leaped violently as three bursts of a siren-like whistle pierced the cabin from beyond the sealed porthole.

"What in God's name was that?" Volkoff said.

"Hard to tell," Westholme said. "But without raising your hopes, it sounds like the navy." For the next fifteen minutes, the two men sat and listened, trying without success to gather information from the muffled exchange of loud-hailer information.

"It's not the navy," Volkoff decided abruptly. "If it was, we'd be out of here by now."

"I don't think so," Westholme said slowly. "As long as Kutskov has hostages, he calls all the shots . . . unless the Canadian government decides this ship is more important to the national cause than you, me, or the *Haida Noble* crew. . . ."

He stopped, and they listened to the sound of jet engines as a plane thundered overhead and was gone.

"That must be the twelfth pass he's made," Westholme observed. "With a plane up top, and the coast guard and navy riding herd, I think we're safe enough. We're just Kutskov's guarantee of delivery to the edge of the Twelve Mile—and then we can go home."

Volkoff shook his head stubbornly. "Alive, we're trouble. I can testify to the destruction of BUTCO 17, and make some educated guesses on this ship's equipment and assignment. You're a star witness, too. I think Kutskov will release your crew, but if he sinks this ship, he has to sink us with it."

"I hope you're wrong." Westholme rubbed the heavy stubble beginning to grow on his lacerated face. "I was thinking . . . Kutskov might be an interesting guy to know—if none of this had happened."

Volkoff was no longer angered by Westholme's attitude. His grin was sympathetic: "I'll bet you befriended rattlesnakes when you were a kid because no one else really understood them."

Outside, the loud hailers were shouting at one another again. The acrid stench of smoke was becoming more pronounced. Westholme brought out the chocolates given to him the previous day and offered Volkoff one.

491

Volkoff took two. "We haven't eaten since last night," he recalled. "The hospitality has dropped off around here." He climbed onto the upper bunk. "My mother used to buy us stuff like this. It was amazing what chocolates could do for the morale on a cold winter day in a Colorado mining town. . . . Are you a Canadian born and bred?"

Westholme nodded. "And my folks before me." He stretched himself out on the lower bunk and drew the blankets up. "My wife's Canadian, too—a Nova Scotia girl. She had the Atlantic in her blood and I had the Pacific in mine. Lee used to say it was the ocean that brought us together." And it was the ocean that had divided them. "You know," he went on, and it was a promise more than a statement, "when I get back to port I'm going to put in for a desk job. . . ."

He rolled over and pulled the blankets up around his ears, his eyes open while a confusion of thoughts raced in his mind: Lee and their chances of a future together; poor Bibaud lying under tons of twisted cable; and *Haida Noble*, battered, crippled—as much a captive as any of them. Woven through all these images was the voice and the face of the Russian captain. . . .

Suddenly he heard shots in the bowels of the ship: three or four single shots, and then the sustained rattle of an automatic weapon; more isolated shots—and then nothing.

"Did you hear that?" he called up to Volkoff softly.

Volkoff's deep, regular breathing was the only answer. Westholme settled back on the pillow to wait and listen.

HOW LONG HE LAY there in a torpor he did not know, but when a soft tapping began on the door, he was instantly alert. He was sitting with his feet on the deck when the door opened to admit Dr. Lebedovitch. Behind her he glimpsed the guard and the blue steel of a gun barrel. Then she closed the door and stood looking down at him, her eyes shadowed, her strong cheekbones and broadly chiseled nose gleaming in the guttering light of the lamp.

"I had intended to visit you sooner," she said, her voice steady and professional, as if explaining the lateness of a house call. "But many people have required my services."

"We're doing fine," Westholme told her.

"This light is very bad," she said disapprovingly.

"I'd put the cold ahead of that," he said.

492

"The entire vessel is cold," she told him. "The injured ones are suffering from it."

"What's that?" Volkoff exclaimed in a loud, slurred voice. He rolled on his side, his eyes coming level with the doctor's.

"The captain said you had taken a blow," she said.

He sat up and ran his fingers through his thick black hair. "I'm over that." He pulled up the collar of his jacket.

"Dr. Baliuk wishes me to tell you that she regrets what has happened." She searched for the appropriate words. "The entire— circumstance—is most unfortunate. Do you have local pain in the head?"

"I've had worse headaches."

"And you, Captain Westholme . . ." She took a small flashlight from her pocket and played its beam over Westholme's face. "Not too pretty—but you will have no serious scars." From her voluminous bag she took several bottles and deftly began to swab the cuts.

"I heard gunfire some time ago," Westholme said.

Seeming not to have heard him she leaned in close to examine what she had done. Finally she said: "This ship has endured great trouble, but no one wishes you any harm, Captain . . . Mr. Volkoff, though you are in grave danger."

"What were the shots? The smoke?" Westholme asked.

"The shots?" She placed her bag on the deck. "May I sit for a moment?"

Westholme eased himself along the bunk. She sat down beside him without ceremony, and extracted a package of cigarettes from her pocket, offered him one, and passed the package up to Volkoff.

"The shots," she said, "were an effort on the part of certain crew members to . . . mutiny." She shook her head violently. "Mutiny is not the right word. Protest?"

"Were they successful?" Westholme asked carefully.

"Two are dead, others wounded."

"You came here to tell us something," Volkoff said impatiently. "Can you help us?"

She ignored him, directing her words to Westholme. "I am a doctor, not a politician or a statesman," she said. "I am concerned to save lives if I can, and to relieve pain. It troubles me to see good lives destroyed for principles—even good principles. Perhaps that is why I came here." She groped in her bag, found what she was looking for, and passed it up to Volkoff. "Very shortly," she said, "you

493

may be given a single alternative—to die. This will make it almost painless. Break off the tip of the vial and swallow the contents."

There was fear in Volkoff's voice. "What the hell are you talking about?"

"We are all in a critical situation," she said. "As a physician, I have done what I can." She stood up. "To you, Captain Westholme, I offer the same release." She extended her hand to him and he received the cold, hard steel of an automatic pistol. He put it hastily under the blankets.

She went to the door and rapped on it before turning back to Westholme. "You should understand that Captain Kutskov is a strong and admirable person . . . in different times, a good person. Circumstances force him to do what he must do."

Volkoff swore loudly and hurled the vial at her. The glass shattered and the fluid trickled down the door panel as she opened it and let herself out. They saw the handle swing upward, sliding the bolt into place.

"What's she trying to tell us?" Volkoff said.

Westholme went to the door and swabbed off the pungent smear of liquid with a cloth. "I don't know what this stuff is, but I wouldn't want us to get it on our hands."

"Potassium cyanide," Volkoff guessed. "They sent her down here to set up a suicide! Where's your capsule?"

"She didn't give me one," Westholme said. He decided not to mention the revolver.

"How do you like that! They want me out of the way but not you . . . It figures," Volkoff said agitatedly. "I can hang them with a *firsthand* account of the drill rig's sinking, and the details of this ship."

"That's true," Westholme said, "but I don't think it's right. I'd say she's done this on her own—as a kind of a favor."

"A comfortable death," Volkoff muttered. "Some favor!"

Above them, through the layers of deck, they heard the low-flying jet approach and pass by. Volkoff slammed an ineffective fist against his bunk, pulled up the blankets and closed his eyes.

Westholme, sitting on the edge of his bunk, finished his cigarette in slow, deliberate puffs. He took the gun and examined it with detached curiosity. Then he put it in his pocket. Perhaps later on . . . He reached for the lantern and wrapped his hands around the glass, absorbing the small heat.

494

In the resulting darkness Volkoff's voice rose in alarm. "West-holme? You there?"

Westholme removed his hands. "Still here."

In the corridor, they heard the sound of feet approaching. Volkoff sat up as the door opened to reveal their guard with *Irkutsk's* first officer and the two giant crew members who had been on the navigation bridge earlier. Both wore belts and holstered sidearms.

The first officer wasted no words. "You will come with us to the bridge please." They fell in behind their armed guard; the first officer and the two crewmen brought up the rear. Smoke hung in the corridors—the smell of burning paper.

Through an open porthole, as they passed by, Westholme glimpsed the impressive bulk of a vessel, its deck and sides awash with light. "We were right about the navy," he said to Volkoff. "There's a Canadian subchaser to port."

Arriving at the jury-rigged catwalk, Westholme was greeted with another spectacle. Two to three miles ahead of the ship and to port were scores of ship's lights, representing at least half a dozen vessels. The Russian flotilla was assembling at the edge of the Twelve Mile, just as Kutskov had said it would. He was going to achieve his objective.

"The bastard's done it!" Volkoff exploded.

Abeam of them, a hundred yards to port, the low-contoured sub-chaser held its station, several batteries of searchlights painting the hull of *Irkutsk* with dazzling light; off the starboard beam, *Blackfish* held a similar position with fore and aft spotlights playing restlessly along the decks of the Russian ship. The scene was so arresting that Westholme stopped halfway across the catwalk, but the Russian officer's hand propelled him on through the heavy tarpaulin curtain into the shattered remains of the radio room.

The first officer pushed past them and advanced to the door of the bridge, knocked twice, and when the door opened, gestured Westholme and Volkoff into the familiar, sickeningly stuffy room.

Captain Kutskov's position and appearance were changed. Fully uniformed, he had walked or been lifted to the navigator's chair. Dr. Lebedovitch was attending to a black leather strap which passed across his waist and fastened to the arms of the chair to support him. Westholme did not know how he could tolerate the weight and friction of shirt and uniform jacket against his raw and blistered flesh.

The Russian's face was a yellow-gray in the lantern light, the lines of pain shockingly apparent. Only the eyes remained unaltered, and the voice with its level, unperturbed inflection.

"Your salvage assignment is nearing its end, Captain Westholme. All things considered, I am satisfied with our progress. In two more hours we should be out of your nation's territory."

Ahead of him, through the windows of the bridge, Westholme could see the lights of the Russian fleet. Somewhere in the center of the line an Aldis lamp blinked a staccato message.

"Your trawlers?" he asked Kutskov.

"They began to gather at mid-afternoon."

"I still say you won't get away with it!" Volkoff blurted. "It's piracy."

"Cut it, Mike," Westholme ordered sharply. He turned to the Russian: "There were shots this afternoon. My guess is that some of this ship's company don't agree with your decision to return to your fleet instead of the safety of a Canadian port."

"My officers and I anticipated a certain reaction from those who do not comprehend the essential nature of our orders. The incident was handled with as little violence as possible. Sit down, gentlemen." His eyes rolled inquiringly toward his first officer. "There is vodka here somewhere?" A crewman hurried over with a bottle and glasses.

"What happens next?" Westholme demanded.

"You will regain possession of your tug. Now the least we can do is make you comfortable in the short time we have left. Sit down!"

Westholme shrugged and settled into a chair. Volkoff didn't budge. Kutskov glanced at his first officer. "Sit down, all of you. Gregori, take off your greatcoat and relax a little."

The first officer hesitated and then obeyed.

"Drinks!" Kutskov insisted. "For all of us . . . please. Dr. Lebedovitch, drink with us."

The doctor spoke to him quietly in Russian, and he chuckled. "My doctor has advised me that alcohol is not good for my condition, but the occasion overcomes all medical logic. We are celebrating." He lifted his glass. "A toast . . . to all of us . . . and to better times than these." His gaze traveled the circle of faces. "Drink! Drink up!" He set an example by tossing back the substantial shot of vodka and holding his glass out for a refill.

All of them were seated now—even Volkoff, who was holding an

496

untasted glass of vodka. "I don't understand you," he said to Kutskov, then pointed at the doctor. "You send her to feed us a dose of potassium cyanide, and now you toast our health."

"You're out of your mind, Mike," Westholme said flatly.

Volkoff was livid. "Are you trying to tell me she didn't?"

"What is he talking about, Doctor?" Kutskov asked pleasantly.

"I visited their cabin this afternoon," she said. "Mr. Volkoff showed every sign of needing a sedative. I gave him one."

"That's right," Westholme said. "He needed slowing down."

Kutskov lifted his replenished glass. "Here is the only sedative any of us requires at this moment. To you, Mr. Volkoff, the ocean scientist—and may we make amends to you one day."

"Go to hell," Volkoff muttered, but he lifted his glass.

"Good!" Kutskov approved. "The best medicine." He glanced to the side as his second officer hurried in with a message. Kutskov read it without a change of expression, then handed it to his first officer. "In approximately thirty minutes we are going to have a visitor out there . . ." Kutskov inclined his head toward international waters. "It is approaching from the south at high speed according to the message from our flotilla." His eyes homed in on Volkoff. "I think we can safely suppose it is an American destroyer."

Volkoff leaned forward, then sat back, lifting his glass to his lips.

"The right attitude," Kutskov said. "The molehill has grown to a mountain . . . and we should drink to it. What began as a simple arrangement between a crippled ship and a tugboat has become a *cause célèbre*, complete with planes, submarine chasers and now—" he sipped his drink "—an American naval vessel of considerable size." He paused, then beckoned to the crewman with the bottle. "Fill your glasses, everyone. We must enjoy the spectacle."

Chapter 23

For a bizarre half hour, Captain Kutskov performed the role of genial host in an atmosphere of accumulating tension. He was by turn a raconteur, an encouraging listener, and a generous host, urging drinks on everyone. Westholme could not suppress the empathy he felt with him. Probably everything Kutskov said and did in these past minutes was significant, he decided. The Russian captain was celebrating—but it was more of a ritual.

"You talk about the hunting of animals," Kutskov said, taking a cue from a hesitant statement made by the first officer. "I do not understand the instinct to kill. I am thinking of the hardy sport of our old Cossacks in the dead of winter for instance—to find and pursue a wolf for miles in the bitter cold, running it and your horse to the point of exhaustion . . ." His pause, as he took another sip of vodka, was unintentionally dramatic. "And then—when the wolf is down in the snow, unconquered, but incapable of running further—to whip it to death. I do not understand this kind of killing."

"It was not so much a killing, perhaps," Dr. Lebedovitch suggested, "as an act of magic. The wolf was the enemy, and cruel death was a warning to all wolves."

"Perhaps, perhaps," said Kutskov cheerfully. "The subject is a morbid one, and there are some empty glasses. . . ." He shaded his eyes to a sudden flash outside the windows of the navigation bridge.

And Westholme's eyes throbbed in the harsh light—vibrating splashes of stark white flame, descending slowly through the dark. Parachute flares! Focusing at sea level, he saw the cluster of Russian trawlers spread out to port, and to the right of the flotilla made out the American destroyer.

Kutskov's voice announced genially: "Our company has arrived. Very impressive! Extremely impressive!"

Volkoff was on his feet, his depression gone. "It'll blow you out of the water," he said, "and your trawlers with you!"

Captain Kutskov shook his head. He looked at his drink and then surveyed the others. "One more small glass, and then we must bring this to an end." He nodded briskly to the crewman, who began to top up the glasses. "We are now abandoning ship, Mr. Volkoff, and I would like you to be among the first to go. My officer will see you to a boat."

"Like hell!" Volkoff told him. "What about Westholme?"

"You will not leave together," Kutskov said.

"No deal!" Volkoff said, and settled heavily into his chair.

Kutskov issued a short command to his crewmen. Without hesitation they descended on the American, pinned his arms and lifted him bodily out of the chair. Westholme gripped the hidden revolver and made an involuntary move toward him. He was stopped by the first officer who now held a gun.

"There is no cause for alarm," Captain Kutskov said calmly. "We are merely playing this game to the finish. Goodbye, Mr. Volkoff . . .

and I hope you will not judge us too harshly, when you have had time to think about it." He held out his hand and saw it rejected by the American as he was led from the bridge. The flares from the destroyer continued to rise and descend, carving the faces of Kutskov, the doctor and the first officer into weird masks. Kutskov turned to Westholme. "Captain, I will be honest with you. We need a final hostage, and you are the logical choice."

Westholme sat down and reached for the vodka bottle.

"Would you put a little in my glass?" Kutskov asked. Westholme poured. "Let us admit it," he went on sadly. "The evening has not been a good one." He squinted at his drink dejectedly. "So . . . This business is drawing to a close. I, for one, am glad of it. What is our position, Gregori? In English, so all of us can understand."

"We are within fifteen hundred meters," the officer said. "The tugboat will be in international waters shortly."

Captain Kutskov drained his glass. "The game is played out, Captain. It is a stalemate of sorts, but I am not entirely dissatisfied. We must stop your tug."

"Go ahead," Westholme said. "Stop it!"

"Some hours ago this incident began to escalate. If we are not very careful, Captain Westholme, we will be the pebble that starts the avalanche. The rumbling has begun."

Another brilliant, blue-white arc from the destroyer's deck reached toward *Irkutsk* and searched the battered hull.

"It might be better," Westholme said, "to sink your ship here. That destroyer would like to get you into international waters. The trawlers wouldn't be much help to you."

"None at all," Kutskov agreed. "Gregori, what depth of water do we have here?"

"It is difficult to say, Captain. Perhaps a hundred fathoms."

"It will have to do. I am going to turn your tug back over to you, Captain Westholme." He switched on his walkie-talkie and there was a brief conversation in Russian. Abruptly Kutskov reverted to English and beckoned to Westholme: "You are now in command of the tug. I would be grateful if you would accommodate my crew and Dr. Davodov. Your second officer has been sent for. I would like to stop your tug in Canadian waters, Captain."

Fenton's voice came through the speaker: "Chris? Christy, are you OK?"

"I'm fine, Brad. What's the situation?"

"They've put down their guns. It's all sweetness and light. You sure you're OK?"

"Nothing to worry about, Brad. The tug is ours again. You can start shortening the line. There may be a few of us coming aboard in a minute. We're abandoning."

"Is she sinking, Christy?"

Westholme glanced at Captain Kutskov. "That's about it, Brad. How's Lindstrom?"

"Not bad, not good. That Davodov woman is doing everything she can. What's the plan, Chris?"

"Haul in the line. We'll throw the bridle off right away. It looks as though we're going home."

"You too?" Fenton asked, his voice heavily suspicious. "What's happening over there?"

"Just start that cable coming in. The Russian boarding party won't give you any trouble."

"That's for sure! They're locked in the wire room."

"Yeah . . . well, go easy on them. The war is over. See you soon, Brad." He turned the set back to Kutskov. "What now?"

"Our people should be ready to disembark. The sick and injured are on deck, Doctor?"

Dr. Lebedovitch nodded. "They have been moving up for the past half hour. The stretcher cases will be difficult."

"No doubt . . . Gregori, go and see how things are proceeding. I would like to begin the disembarkation."

The first officer departed silently, leaving the three of them on the bridge. Captain Kutskov's glass was empty; he looked at Dr. Lebedovitch and she poured him another drink without a protest, and turned to Westholme with the bottle.

"Pass," Westholme said. "I've had plenty." The liquor was beginning to pound in his temples.

"If you please," Kutskov insisted. "This will be our last drink together for some time." He nodded imperatively to the doctor, and she poured a short drink into Westholme's glass.

"Yourself as well, Larissa," he said.

She took a glass and Kutskov lifted his to the light. "I think I have always been fortunate," he said, "fortunate in the people I have known, in the things I have done—and in the things that have been done for me. I would say my misfortunes have been mainly my own fault. This trouble we find ourselves in now, Captain Westholme.

500

Largely my own fault." He reached into his jacket pocket, stopping as pain overcame him. "There are envelopes in here for Captain Westholme."

Dr. Lebedovitch rose and felt inside the jacket, bringing out two long bulky envelopes which she passed to Westholme.

"This is merely a precaution," the Russian captain said. "Naturally I will insist on making my own statement to your authorities . . . but if that is not possible, for one reason or another, my account of this incident has been placed in writing. The responsibility is clearly mine, and I do not hesitate to say so."

Westholme shook his head. "The sea got both of us into trouble."

"The sea is impartial," Kutskov said. "I would never blame my mistakes on the sea, she has given me too much. You too, I suspect, Captain?"

Westholme thought of Lee. "It gives and it takes," he said.

Kutskov returned to business. "The other envelope contains a rather mixed collection of currency—I believe the equivalent of ten thousand dollars. The salvage fee."

Westholme stared into the man's exhausted, rigidly-controlled face. The eyes revealed no duplicity. He admired Kutskov more than he could say.

"Until this minute," he admitted, "I was convinced that, with you, the end justified the means—that anything and anybody was expendable in order to get the job done."

"You are a good judge of character," Kutskov told him, "and you are absolutely right." He shrugged his shoulders. "Now the job is done . . . and you have been paid the agreed amount."

"There is more to it than that." Westholme was almost angry. "A lot of people are involved in this. Some of them are lined up on your decks now; some are on the bottom."

"No price can be placed on that," Kutskov said. "No price can be placed on the fact that you and I never became friends—in spite of the many things we hold in common. If I regret anything in these later years, it is that I have been cheated out of so many friendships. It is a greed with me that has never been satisfied."

Another salvo of flares burst in the sky and began a slow descent. The Russian trawlers, caught in the circle of light, rode silently at anchor, their signal lamps darkened.

Impulsively Westholme held his glass up. "To your health . . . and good luck. . . ."

Kutskov waved a protesting hand. "Too soon, Captain West-holme. It could be an embarrassment. There are things we require you to do yet. If they go badly, we may still have to use you as our last line of defense."

Westholme studied him warily. "What's your problem?"

"None whatever, if your coast guard and naval escorts follow your instructions. You will now give the orders, Captain."

Behind them the door to the bridge opened to admit the first officer. "We can begin the disembarkation," he said.

"Good! What is the tide doing to us?"

"It is ebbing, Captain. We are drifting slowly toward the fleet."

"How far to go?"

"Perhaps a thousand meters . . . one hour."

"I want us to be off in an hour or less," Kutskov said. "Captain, we concede defeat and ask you to intercede on our behalf with the escorting vessels. We are abandoning ship."

"Fair enough," Westholme said. "I'll need a loud hailer."

Kutskov smiled. "This time I think you should have one."

Westholme walked out to the port rail and when *Blackfish*'s moving beams had passed him, sent the message across: "Captain Lewis? Christy Westholme here. Jack, can you hear me?"

"I hear you, Captain Westholme," Lewis said formally. "Are you all right?"

"Fine, Jack! Just fine! I've got a request for you. This ship is sinking. We've got to get the crew off in a hurry."

"Can you come aboard to assist?"

"I'm needed here, Jack. Can you start taking them aboard?"

"Are you a prisoner, Captain Westholme?"

"No, but I will be if you don't get cracking! Come on, Jack! These people are in the worst possible shape, and the ship is going, whether you like it or not."

"Hold off a minute, Christy. I'll check with the Canadian forces."

Westholme waited on the bridge with the cold wind numbing him, while *Irkutsk*'s crew assembled on the decks below him—a hushed cacophony of voices, male and female.

Presently the voice came from *Blackfish*. "We'll start moving the crew, Christy. All able-bodied and walking-wounded to *Blackfish*; all stretcher cases to the subchaser. Stand by to rig a bosun's chair, or some kind of breeches buoy. How much time have we got?"

502

"Forty-five minutes, no more."

"That's pretty rough," Lewis protested. "Let's get started."

"Send over your boats for the able. This ship can lower two or three of its own. Tell the navy we're standing by for the breeches buoy line."

He lowered the loud hailer and returned to Kutskov. "You can start discharging your people. Able-bodied to starboard by ship's boat. Stretcher cases to port. They'll be putting a line aboard any minute."

Kutskov gave his first officer brief instructions and dispatched him to the bridge rail with the loud hailer. "*Blackfish* is worried about our timetable. Do we have to have everyone off in forty-five minutes?" Westholme asked.

Captain Kutskov looked at his watch. "I am afraid so. Our rate of drift will take us too close to that—" he nodded toward the American destroyer "—rather formidable pyromaniac. I have no desire to create an international crisis."

Without thinking, Westholme picked up his half-finished drink and took a tentative sip. Kutskov shifted in his chair, grimacing with pain. The doctor poured two inches of vodka into his glass and he raised it to his lips gratefully.

"I can't think of anything that has not been done. Doctor, you are ready to leave?"

When she nodded, he addressed Westholme. "Obviously my authority goes when this ship does. I would like to think you would do whatever you can for Dr. Lebedovitch. She has performed as a doctor superbly. I will testify to that."

"I'll support it," Westholme promised. "I have a feeling we'll be seeing one another in court from time to time."

"Larissa," Kutskov said to the doctor, "I think you should go now. Some of the injured will need you during the transfer."

"Yes, Captain."

"It has been a good ship, Larissa; for the most part a happy ship. We should feel fortunate to have been associated with it."

"There will be other ships," she said.

"And I will see to it that you are signed as ship's doctor. It would not be the same without you. Go, now, and don't worry. There will be other good times."

She embraced him, kissing him gravely on either cheek. "I have never been associated with a finer captain—or a better man." She turned to Westholme. "I would like to know you better. Perhaps it will be possible."

"I hope so," Westholme said. "I'd put you in a class with my wife as a wonderful person. That's the best compliment I can pay."

"I am sure it is. Will you walk to the door with me?"

He went with her. Before she opened the door she said in a low voice: "I would like you to return the thing I gave you. It was a mistake—a lack of faith in the captain. I believed you were in danger."

"Chances are I was." Westholme took the gun from his pocket and extended it to her. "What will you do with it?"

"I will see that it goes to the bottom with this ship and all it represents. Goodbye, Captain Westholme." She reached out her hand, and he shook it firmly. The door closed behind her.

The captain's expression was inquiring. "She was troubled about something, perhaps?"

Westholme shook his head. "I admire her. I wanted to tell her."

Kutskov nodded slowly. "For one reason or another I never married; a certain restlessness that has never quite left me; the lack of opportunity; the impossibility of it in wartime . . . but if I did have a wife, she would be the one. And you compare her to yours, Captain —so, we have both been fortunate in our own ways." He paused, and shifted to a more comfortable position. "Perhaps I should tell you what will happen now?"

"I'd appreciate that."

"As soon as the last man is off, the ship will be ready for destruction. The final documents and logbooks were burned this afternoon. . . ."

"We smelled the smoke," Westholme admitted.

"I apologize for what I was obliged to do." Kutskov spoke earnestly. "'The war is over,' you said; and it describes perfectly what has happened between us. We have fought to save our own domains; my ship and its people; your tug and its crew. Mr. Volkoff's domain was destroyed very early in the battle."

"If there had been a clear winner," Westholme said slowly, "we could say that something good has come out of all this. . . ."

"We both win; we both lose. Of the two of us, you have undoubtedly won the greater victory." Kutskov extended his good hand. "Should we agree that our war is truly over, Captain?"

Westholme's big hand wrapped itself around Kutskov's fingers

504

and squeezed briefly. "What bothers me," he said, "is that something like this can happen again. The precedent has been set. . . ."

"Is not that the good thing that emerges from our little war? No doubt this will impress our respective countries with the fact that continental shelves and international waters can become formidable battlegrounds." Kutskov shrugged. "In any event, it is out of our hands." He looked at his watch. "Ten more minutes."

"You'll leave with me?" Westholme questioned.

"Directly after you." He smiled at Westholme. "In my position, *you* would insist on your right to leave your ship last."

Both turned as the door opened to admit the first and second officers and a crew member.

"The last boat is loading now," the first officer informed Kutskov. "I think we can begin making our way down."

"Very well." Once again, the Russian reached for Westholme's hand. "There will be better times," he said cheerfully. "I hope to know you then."

"See you ashore," Westholme promised. He pulled his collar up and departed with the second officer, picking his way carefully across the catwalk illuminated by the officer's flash lamp.

Chapter 24

The surrounding scene had not altered, except that the formidable lights and pyrotechnics of the American destroyer were considerably closer. The drift and the tide were going to take *Irkutsk* almost to the edge of the Twelve Mile.

"How are you going to get Captain Kutskov off?" he asked the second officer. "The navy's breeches buoy will be safest for him."

"He will leave by ship's boat in company with the first officer, Captain."

Stumbling through the cold, black bowels of the ship, Westholme felt new misgivings. Was Kutskov going to make a run for the Russian fleet and leave his ship's company to fend for themselves? Had it all been smooth talk after all?

They emerged onto the main deck in the full glare of *Blackfish*'s lights. The deck was empty, but Westholme saw a loaded boat making its way toward the cargo nets draped over *Blackfish*'s port side.

"We have one last request to make of you, Captain," the Russian officer said. "You will ask your coast guard vessel and the Canadian forces ship to stand off five hundred yards immediately upon taking the last person aboard. The demolition of *Irkutsk* will begin within minutes."

"Will Kutskov make it off in time?"

"Everything has been carefully planned. Will you go now, please."

Westholme peered over the rail and saw *Haida Noble*'s powered life raft, manned by three Russian crew members. He went over the side and down the net into the raft, followed by the second officer. The motor sputtered and caught and they left *Irkutsk*'s side.

Halfway between *Blackfish* and the Russian ship, the raft cut its power to idle and sat in the circle of the cutter's lights. The second officer handed a loud hailer across to Westholme.

"You must warn them," he said. "Tell them we will follow at a safe distance."

Westholme lifted the loud hailer: "*Blackfish* . . . *Blackfish* . . . Captain Westholme here."

"Come aboard, Chris." It was Lewis.

"Jack, the Russian ship is going to blow. Advise the subchaser and get a signal to *Haida Noble*. As soon as the last man is on board, stand off at least five hundred yards."

"Come aboard. We'll wait."

"That's not the deal. They'll deliver me when the ship goes."

"Do you believe that?"

"That's the deal we have to go with. Better hurry, Jack."

He lowered the loud hailer and glanced at the second officer for further directions. The Russian nodded approval.

There was a wait of several minutes while the tension built. A cold northwest wind buffeted the raft and its occupants. The flares of the destroyer continued to demonstrate no more than half a mile away while, at the same distance, the seven Russian trawlers huddled silent as death beneath the magnesium glare of the American's parachute flares.

The coldness in Westholme's marrow was as much apprehension as anything, and he was grateful for the cigarette that was handed to him.

Captain Lewis called again. "Tell those bastards to travel astern of us by a hundred yards, no tricks. The subchaser will follow."

"We agree to that," the Russian officer told Westholme.

506

"No argument," Westholme relayed through the loud hailer. "Let's get out of here."

"Is everyone off that hulk?"

"One more boat to come. The captain, first officer, and one of the crew."

Shadowy figures were moving about on *Irkutsk*'s boat deck, loading and lowering the sea boat. Finally it hit the water and the davit lines were cast away.

"That's it," Westholme called to *Blackfish*. "Let's move off."

The coast guard cutter began to move almost immediately, swinging away from the Russian ship in a slow turn, its searchlight holding on the life raft which followed in its wake. A hundred yards astern again came the Russian ship's launch. Behind *Irkutsk*, the subchaser positioned herself to port abeam of the strange procession of vessels, cutting off all possibility of an escape attempt to international waters. Westholme relaxed a little.

Three hundred yards away from *Irkutsk*, Westholme watched the pale lanterns burning on her fore and aft deck. The Russian ship was within minutes of her burial. *Irkutsk* had spelled grief for him and death for Ernie Bibaud, but that did not prevent him from feeling what every master feels for the death of a good ship. In spirit, Westholme was with Captain Kutskov when the first, barely audible explosion reached his ears, followed by a series of explosions in different parts of the ship's hull. Ugly bursts of flame appeared along the waterline and at the various deck levels. The efficiency of the demolition crew had to be admired.

Irkutsk's trim was level as she settled into the water, with great cauldrons of seawater boiling in the wounds along her sides. The second officer, watching intently through his night glasses, put them down suddenly and turned away. Westholme took the glasses, and focused them hastily. The ship was sinking fast with the entire hull under, and geysers of water and steam bursting on the main deck.

The glasses were good ones, bringing the superstructure in so close that it filled the field. On the navigation bridge the strings of lanterns burned steadily. Westholme could see the neat rolls of charts slotted in their cubbyholes and the oblong, brass plate on a stanchion which spelled out *Irkutsk*'s name. He could see Kutskov reclining in the navigation chair—and was grieved, but not shocked. He had sensed it.

507

Clearly he saw Kutskov lifting the glass to his lips . . . and just before the final series of explosions blotted out the bridge, he saw a second figure move past Kutskov to stand behind him, the features grave and tired, but glowing with a tenderness that the distance could not conceal. It was a glimpsed thing, but it could not be mistaken, nor would Westholme ever forget it. The captain and Larissa Lebedovitch had gone down with *Irkutsk*.

AND PARTLY because of that, Westholme elected not to return to *Haida Noble* that night, but to go aboard *Blackfish* where he could use a ship-to-shore telephone to talk with his wife. It didn't mean that he had turned his back on the great tug, or that he ever could . . . but in that final glimpse of the Russian couple in the light of the lamps and the outer flames, he had seen himself and Lee. He saw what they had almost lost—and he wanted to begin to restore it.

He heard the operator putting the call through and then the bell ringing a total of three times—cut off on the fourth as the receiver lifted.

"Hello," Lee said in a low, worried voice.

"Lee, honey. . . . It's all over, darling. I'm coming home."

The silence at the other end was as bad as anything he had endured those past five days. "Lee? Are you there?"

"Yes, darling . . . Christy, come home! Now! Please, darling, now—before I lose you again!"

510

E. G. Perrault

BILL ROOZEBOOM

E rnie G. Perrault, author of *The Twelfth Mile*, has published two other novels, *Kingdom Carver* and *Spoil!* He is at present researching a new novel and has been working on a number of film projects.

Born in Penticton, British Columbia, in 1922, Mr. Perrault was brought up in Vancouver. He graduated from the University of British Columbia with a BA in Sociology, English Literature and Economics. During World War II he served for nearly four years in the RCAF.

E. G. Perrault's short stories have appeared in British, US and Canadian publications and in translation in several European countries. He has written poetry, radio and television dramas and documentaries, and musicals for the CBC National Network.

For a number of years, he was associated with the Canadian feature-film industry and was involved in the construction of film studios near Vancouver. He has also written several feature-film scenarios.

Mr. Perrault works professionally as a communications and public relations specialist. His hobbies and interests relate to the out-of-doors: an avid photographer and fly fisherman, he is also a collector of unusual and off-beat material on the history of British Columbia and Canada's Northwest.